Pass in Review

COUNTRY

Brian Utermahlen

*"A man who is good enough to shed his blood
for the country is good enough to be given
a square deal afterwards."*

- Theodore Roosevelt

Cover art provide by Jeff Sanson
Sanson Illustrations, Houston, TX

www.pass-in-review.us

Brian Utermahlen

ISBN:149734011X
ISBN-13:978-1497340114

LCCN:

DEDICATION

To those incredible Sky Troopers of the 1st Cavalry Division (Airmobile)

To all the grunts of the 8th United States Cavalry – 1st and 2nd Battalions

To all the Ghostriders of C Co 227th Aviation Battalion

To my Classmates from the Class of '68
United States Military Academy, West Point NY
who didn't make it back

Donald F. Van Cook, Junior
William F. Ericson, II
Denny L. Johnson
Kenneth T. Cummings
David L. Sackett
Peter M. Connor
James A. Gaiser
William F. Little
Donald R. Colglaizer
Jeffery R. Riek
Harry E. Hayes
Richard A. Hawley, Jr.
John E. Darling, Jr.
Donald R. Workman
David T. Maddux
Douglas T. Wheless
William F. Reichert
David L. Alexander
Lewis J. Speidel
Harry M. Spengler, III

" NO TASK TOO GREAT FOR '68 "

ACKNOWLEDGMENTS

For Assistance in Research and Editing, and encouragement – MANY THANKS to:

The Ghostriders – Company C 227ᵗʰ Aviation Battalion, 1ˢᵗ Cav Division
Paul Bromley – Bruce James – Ned Schantz and many others

General John R. Galvin – former CINCEUR
Ginny Galvin

1/8 Cav Troopers

LTG (retired) Pete Taylor

Capt. Tom Bell

MSG Chris Manis

The men of A Co. 1/8 Cav

LTC (retired) Doug Johnson
for his assistance with Army War College oral histories

Susan Schmidt

Jim Campbell

John Fox

George Considine

'68 Classmates - Dick Steiner, John Hedley, Jim Bodenhamer, Scott Vickers, Dave Clemm,
Dave Gerard for story ideas, editorial help and encouragement in writing this episode

B.G. 'Jug' Burkett Author of ***STOLEN VALOR***
for his research help and his lifelong commitment to setting the record straight about
the heroes and history of the Vietnam generation of soldiers

Thanks to Jeff Sanson of Houston, TX for another incredible cover

A very special THANKS to my wife, Dianne
for her longsuffering, her critiques, her patience and her love

This is a work of fiction and all fictional characters are the product of the author's imagination, not any one person living or dead although some fictional characters are composites of several persons in addition to the author's invention.

Historical characters in this saga are portrayed as they have been presented or recorded in history and with rare exception in positions they held at times and places they held them. The military and political viewpoints of historical characters are accurately portrayed.

Dialogue between historical persons and fictional characters is the product of the author's imagination with attention however to the political and military views they are recorded to have held using the language and personal circumstance known to history.

Most of the characters in Pass in Review - COUNTRY are fictional – some are composites of multiple people who actually lived in history; many are not.

Much of the action in country is fictional as well, although military actions that include actual historical characters are historically accurate as to place and time.

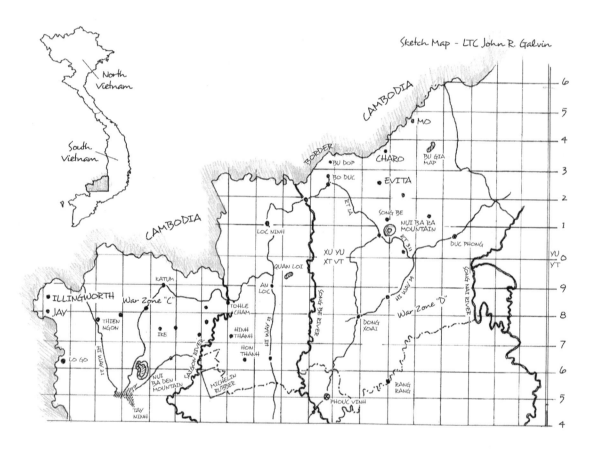

Sketch Map - LTC John R. Galvin

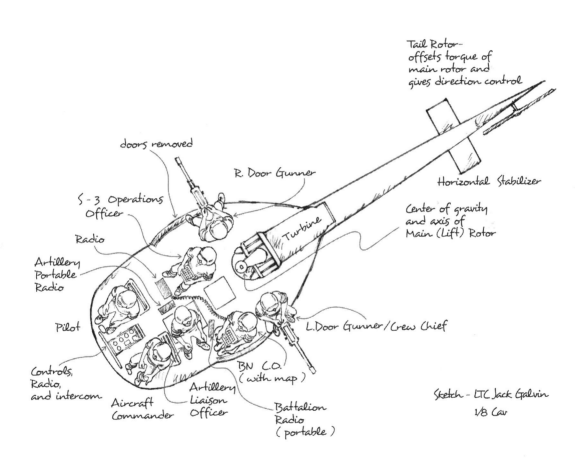

Tail Rotor-
offsets torque of
main rotor and
gives direction control

Horizontal Stabilizer

Center of gravity
and axis of
Main (Lift) Rotor

doors removed

R. Door Gunner

S - 3 Operations
Officer

Radio

Artillery
Portable
Radio

Turbine

Pilot

L. Door Gunner / Crew Chief

Controls,
Radio,
and intercom

Aircraft
Commander

Artillery
Liaison
Officer

BN C.O.
(with map)

Battalion
Radio
(portable)

Sketch - LTC Jack Galvin
1/8 Cav

NOLAN FAMILY TREE

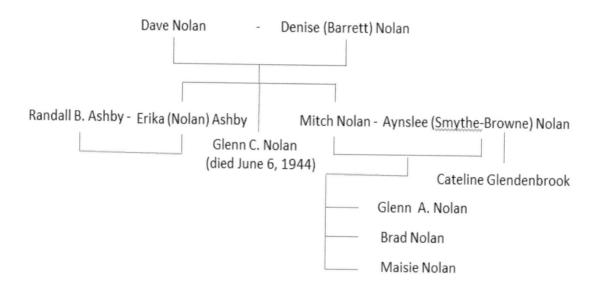

Dave Nolan   -   Denise (Barrett) Nolan

Randall B. Ashby - Erika (Nolan) Ashby

Glenn C. Nolan
(died June 6, 1944)

Mitch Nolan - Aynslee (Smythe-Browne) Nolan

Cateline Glendenbrook

Glenn A. Nolan

Brad Nolan

Maisie Nolan

GLOSSARY OF TERMS

The U.S. military in Vietnam had a language of acronyms / slang all its own. Troops communicated with one another in a shorthand specific to their times and situation.

A/C – aircraft commander – senior pilot on board the aircraft

ACL – allowable cargo load; maximum number of troops to be carried in a combat assault

ACR – Armored Cavalry Regiment (such as the 11th ACR)

ADF – automatic direction finder (NDB – non directional beacon); a navigation beacon

AIT – Advanced Individual Training; specialized training after completion of Basic Training

ALO – Artillery Liaison Officer; an artillery officer assigned to a battalion to coordinate all supporting artillery fire support available to the ground commander

AO – Area of Operations

API – Armored Piercing Incendiary (an armored piercing shell)

ARA – Aerial Rocket Artillery – helicopter gunships

ARVN – Army of the Republic of Vietnam; also, any soldier in the South Vietnam military

Blue Max – (Max) call sign of ARA gunships (AH-1 Cobra) of 2nd Battalion 20th Artillery

Bounce – to call in a request for aviation support; usually helicopter gunship support

C&C *(Chuck-Chuck; Charlie-Charlie)* – command and control helicopter

CA – combat assault; helicopter combat operation to land infantry soldiers

CG – the commanding general

CO (C.O.) – the commanding officer of a unit ("*six*" – a company commander)

Cobra – specifically the Bell AH-1 Cobra gunship (often called 'snakes')

Cosmoline – a generic class of rust preventives that are a brown colored wax-like mass and having a petroleum-like odor

CP – command post; the location of any infantry commander or headquarters element

DEROS – date of estimated return from overseas

DT – Defense Target- artillery targets fired and registered by a unit 'just in case needed'

FAC – Air Force Forward Air Controller (1 Cav Division callsign – *Rash*)

FARP – forward area refueling point

Fire box – a designated area on the ground (usually by a battalion) in which air resources were allowed free fire because it was devoid of friendly troops and civilians.

FDC – fire direction center (either artillery or mortar)

FSB – fire support base (a named LZ); the location of artillery supporting ground units

F.O. – Forward Observer; one who coordinates and adjusts supporting artillery fire

GCA – ground controlled approach – radar guidance during landings in instrument flying

GP – general purpose (such as: GP Medium tent)

Grunt – common designation for infantry combat soldiers; any infantryman

Guns (or **'snakes'**) slang for helicopter gunships; usually a section of two aircraft

HE – high explosive; a type of artillery or mortar round that detonates on contact

HUEY – a Slick - the UH-1 Iroquois aircraft (see C&C aircraft diagram); primary combat combat assault and workhorse helicopter during the Vietnam war

IFR – Instrument Flying Rules (flying solely by reference to cockpit instruments)

JCS – Joint Chiefs of Staff; the group of senior generals representing the Armed Forces

Klick – kilometer; military terrain maps use metric measurements; 1 klick = 0.62 miles

LBE – combat load bearing equipment; pistol belt with shoulder straps

Loach / LOH – 4 passenger light observation helicopter (OH-6); a scout helicopter

LRRP – Long Range Recon Patrol; 5-6 man operations; a type of dehydrated field ration

LZ – landing zone; an opening in the jungle for landing helicopters; when given a name refers to a fire support base (LZ Mo, LZ Evita, LZ Illingworth, etc.)

M-16 – a caliber 5.56 magazine-fed rifle; the primary U.S. individual infantry weapon

M-79 – 'chunker' – a short barreled individual weapon similar to a shotgun which fired a 40mm shell; an area weapon used like a hand grenade but with greater range

MACV – Military Assistance Command (Vietnam); US Military headquarters

Mad Minute – a sixty second burst of highest rate of fire from all weapons in a unit

MEDEVAC – medical evacuation by helicopter synonymous with 'dustoff')

MOS – military occupational specialty

Mule – small self-propelled flatbed vehicle used to move supplies short distances

NVA – North Vietnamese Army (Regulars, not guerrillas); an individual in the NVA

OCS – Officer Candidate School – training for qualified enlisted men to become officers

OJT – on the job training; knowledge gained by experience

OpCon – operational control; the command relationship when one unit is temporarily placed under the control of another, higher level unit for a specific purpose

OER – Officer Efficiency Report; the annual performance rating of an Army officer.

OP/LP – outpost / listening post; a 2-4 person group sent outside a perimeter for the purpose of providing early detection of the enemy to the main body.

Pax / Pack – passenger (plural / singular)

Peter Pilot – slang term for any new, low time pilot / co-pilot recently arrived in-country

Pink Team – two helicopter hunter/killer team; one LOH (low bird), 1 gunship (high bird)

POL – petroleum / oil / lubricants; generically, any helicopter refueling point

'Pop Smoke' – 'throw out a colored smoke grenade to mark your position'

PRC-77 – 'prick 77' - the standard infantry man-portable FM communications radio

PZ – pickup zone; a landing zone used to move troops *from* as opposed to combat assaulting troops *into*

R&R – Rest and Relaxation - one week vacation/leave at any of several locations in Asia; also be any short relief within Vietnam; generally any time away from combat

REMF – a derogatory slang term used by infantry troops for rear echelon personnel (anybody a grunt thinks has it easier than he does)

RTO – radio operator

'Shake and Bake' – slang for a soldier who attended a short course in the U.S. to become an enlisted sergeant/leader as opposed to being promoted through the ranks.

SKS – Korean War vintage Soviet bloc semi-automatic rifle used by the NVA

TO & E – table of organization and equipment

TOC – Tactical Operations Center

UCMJ – Uniform Code of Military Justice – the written code of laws governing behavior

USMA – United States Military Academy, West Point

VFR – Visual Flight Rules; weather conditions allowing for visual flight

VVAW – Vietnam Veterans Against the War – an anti-war group supposedly made up of military veterans who had served in Vietnam – John Kerry was one of their leaders

WIA – Wounded in Action (**KIA** – Killed in Action)

WP (willy pete) – a white phosphorus rocket, artillery shell, mortar shell used for marking

Military Organization / Staffing

Infantry line company in 1st Cav division (Vietnam) –

- approximately 100 soldiers (3 platoons, each 30-35 soldiers; CP – 8 to 10)

Infantry Battalion – 500-600 personnel

four line companies plus HQ company and services company

staff groups: S-1 – personnel; S-2 – intelligence; S-3 – operations ; S-4 – supply

Infantry Brigade - 3 to four battalions plus staff , administration and services

Infantry Division – 3 brigades plus aviation, artillery, services support; 15 -17,000 men

Brian Utermahlen

Prologue

Thursday - June 8, 1961

Wearing a light blue shirt, a loosened silk necktie fashioned into a careless half Windsor knot, and a dark suit jacket draped casually over one shoulder, Attorney General Robert Kennedy strode purposefully down the White House's west colonnade. He turned left, passed by the rose garden and a moment later entered the office of the President's personal secretary through the exterior door.

"How's he doing today, Evelyn?" Bobby Kennedy asked, looking worried.

"Better now after a good night's sleep and a dose of his meds from *Doctor Feelgood*."

Evelyn Maurine Norton Lincoln, a very protective and efficient woman now in her early fifties, had been John F. Kennedy's personal and private secretary since his election to the U.S. Senate in 1953. She had accompanied the new President everywhere, including his most recent trip abroad to meet for the first time with Nikita Khrushchev in Vienna.

"I've lightened his schedule for the next week to give him time to recover," Mrs. Lincoln said, looking at the President's younger brother over the top of her reading glasses. "I would appreciate your being brief as well."

The Attorney General smiled at her and was about to comment about the protectiveness of 'momma grizzlies' but thought better of it. "He'll kick me out when he's had enough."

Inside the Oval Office, Bobby Kennedy found his older brother seated in his specially padded rocking chair with a shawl over his shoulders, reading from a pile of correspondence on the coffee table in front of the fireplace. He looked frail and a good decade older than his forty-four years. His face was drawn and his forehead furrowed; a large box of Kleenex sat next to the correspondence, and his crutches were propped against the wall behind him.

"Bobby, thanks for coming." The President sighed. "It's good to see a friendly face."

"Wasn't MacMillan glad to see you the day before yesterday when you stopped in London?" Bobby asked, tossing his suit coat over the arm of the sofa and sitting down.

"I'm afraid I disappointed him, too. The British were none too happy about my hard line with the Soviets on Berlin. And I probably said too much about how I got run over in Vienna."

The younger Kennedy would have been surprised had he not already heard the same thing from the Russian Georgi Bolshakov with whom he'd had several conversations leading up to the Summit meeting between his brother and the Soviet Premier. The relationship had been instigated by the Soviets as an informal back-channel for the off-the-record exchange of ideas between the two leaders before the meeting, but it seemed now to have been mostly a one-way conversation with the Russians getting much but giving little if anything of value.

Bolshakov had let Bobby know that Khrushchev had wondered both during and after the meeting if the U.S. President was really as indecisive and immature as he appeared to be. The old Kremlin pol also questioned, in typically crude euphemisms, the new American President's courage in the wake of the Bay of Pigs debacle of mid-April. The Attorney General had been wondering during the drive over to the White House exactly how he'd break all that bad news to his older brother; he was relieved now that he didn't need to.

"How was it really?" the younger Kennedy brother asked.

"It was the worst thing in my life. He savaged me." Bobby Kennedy took a deep breath and nodded in reply; the look in his brother's eyes indicated he was telling the whole, awful truth. "Khrushchev attacked me personally and violently – on American imperialism and on Berlin. So, now I've got two more challenges."

"Figuring out why he did it in such a hostile way… and what to do about it," the President's younger brother offered.

"Exactly. Khrushchev's acrimony so far exceeded what I expected that I'm utterly pessimistic across the board on all the issues we discussed." The President absently stroked his chin and gazed out the window toward the rose garden. Finally, he said, "It's the Bay of Pigs fiasco. The Russians think anyone so young and inexperienced as to get into that mess, and then not see it through, has no guts and can be taken. So he just beat the hell out of me."

The Attorney General let the silence linger. He knew that a part of the reason for his brother's poor performance at the Vienna Summit was the combination of drugs he was taking for back pain and the flu. His personal physician was injecting him more and more frequently with a drug cocktail that included amphetamines, steroids, hormones, vitamins, enzymes and even animal organ cells. The younger Kennedy had recently become aware of the increase in his brother Jack's mood swings, his uncharacteristic nervousness and hyperactivity. Even his judgment was impaired from time to time.

"We can work through this, Jack."

"I know we can. Just wish I'd been more on top of my game in Vienna." The President turned from gazing out of the window. "Anything from General Taylor yet with the Cuba Study Group?"

"As a matter of fact…" Bobby Kennedy turned and retrieved two sheets from his suit coat and handed them over. "First draft of the executive summary from the committee. It puts the lion's share of the blame on the Joint Chiefs while appropriately acknowledging that the buck stops on the desk of the commander-in-chief. While you were gone, I had it unofficially run up the flagpole with a couple of the wire services and two of the dailies. They all seemed to go along, more or less."

"More or less?"

"The *Times* and the *Post* both pointed out that the Study Group was significantly overloaded with supporters of your administration. If called on it, they both said they'd have to admit it did give the impression perhaps of a white wash job. But we can fix that."

"Go on."

"Bob McNamara and General Taylor both agreed we need at least one somewhat well-known, pro-Eisenhower figure to sign off on the report. We think we've found someone who fits that bill and will stand up to press scrutiny. He's registered Republican, but fiercely independent. A longtime friend of the former president, but one who's spoken out before against Eisenhower's "New Look" defense policy. Still, they're fairly close friends. He once worked in the Roosevelt Administration and consulted with Eisenhower on non-military matters. At times during the war he worked directly for Eisenhower and also served with General Taylor. Max thinks he'd be a good name to add to the Study Group report, maybe as co-chair, to give its findings the appearance of balance it needs."

"All right. It sounds good to me." The President gave his brother an appreciative glance. "I'm glad I've got you, Bobby. I don't have many political or military advisors I can rely on." The President took a few minutes to read through the summary of General Taylor's report. "I like it – both the tone and the conclusion. Tell me, who's the man Robert and General Taylor are proposing?"

"A retired Army general named Nolan. Dave Nolan."

"I've heard the name before. Where?"

"He's the CEO of E.W. Barrett Enterprises headquartered in New York. He's the man who headed up the study group for Wilson when he was Secretary of Defense under Eisenhower. He came up with the base case and fine-tuned overall strategy for the Interstate Highway System. As we speak, he's testifying before Senator Reeves' Judicial subcommittee."

* *

"It grieves me to bring this up," Senator Harrison Reeves, Democrat of Maryland said, looking pained as he peered down from the raised dais at the business man being questioned. "But, for the sake of clarity in our deliberations, I must."

It was just past mid-morning; both the gallery and the well of the committee room were filled with reporters, cameramen, staff members and onlookers.

The Senate chamber was silent and acutely attentive to the committee chairman who had made it abundantly clear at the beginning of the scheduled three day hearing he brooked no distractions. It was known by those versed in the machinations of Congress that Senator Reeves was the harshest disciplinarian on Capitol Hill when conducting open inquiries. Already a reporter, two cameramen, and a handful of spectators in the gallery had been ushered out by Capitol Hill police at the direction of the Sergeant-at-Arms.

"Is it, or is it not true, Mr. Nolan," Senator Reeves said in his typically condescending tone, "that your corporation has been awarded a lucrative no-bid contract to build a second span of the Delaware Memorial Bridge commencing next year?"

"Harrison, you and I both know that's not true," Dave Nolan replied.

Reeves squinted angrily over the top of his reading glasses at the CEO of E.W. Barrett Enterprises. "The witness is reminded he is being questioned by a United States Senator and will address the interrogator appropriately."

"Interrogator? That sounds ominous," Nolan replied with exaggerated surprise registering in his voice. "I was informed by your office I was being asked here to help you clarify some facts about the Highway Appropriations in the latest Transportation Bill."

"That is precisely what we're doing. Now, once again: isn't it true your corporation –"

"It's not my corporation," Nolan interrupted. "It actually belongs to the shareholders of E.W. Barrett. If you'll check your own portfolio, you'll find you own over eight thousand shares and our records show you voted them by proxy last year."

A vein on the Senator's forehead grew prominent, the lifelong indicator of his irritation and one that Dave Nolan had seen on many occasions over the years, beginning with their time as roommates at West Point that first summer in 1912. Out of the corner of his eye, Dave saw the attractive young legal intern lean over and say something to his corporate counsel. The Barrett CEO smiled to himself.

"Another remark like that Mr. Nolan and you *will* be held in contempt of Congress. Now, once again, have you been awarded a somewhat questionable no-bid contract for construction of a second span of the Delaware Memorial Bridge?"

"Asked and answered, Senator," the young woman at Nolan's table said into the microphone. Her voice was crisp and her pronunciation carried a hint of an English accent.

"I beg your pardon, young lady," Reeves said, glaring at her. "And who might you be?"

"Cateline Glendenbrook, Senator. I am currently an intern at Blaine, Johnson, Armistad and Meyer PLLC, in New York. Our firm represents Barrett Enterprises."

Senator Reeves smiled paternally. "The committee is pleased to have someone so young and charming with us today. But I'm going to have to rule you out of order on two counts. First, you have no standing here as only Mr. Blaine is listed on our records as providing Mr. Nolan with legal counsel for our purposes today. And secondly, I'm quite sure this is the first time I've asked this question of Mr. Nolan."

"Actually, sir, you asked the question twice before and received the same answer on both occasions – once in a deposition dated 5 January 1961 and prior to that at a hearing in this very room on 11 November 1960. You'll find the question and Mr. Nolan's complete and thorough answer on page 207 of the committee's minutes. I can provide a copy if you like."

Senator Reeves looked around for his staff legal counsel and saw him in hushed conversation at the far end of the dais. The Senator caught the young lawyer's attention and signaled him over.

"The truth of the matter," Nolan interjected, "is that E.W. Barrett will see no more profit as a percentage of fixed cost on this construction project than it has on any other project on which we have bid successfully over the last decade. It's the government that'll benefit most since it won't have to undertake a long and costly bid process according to its own rules and processes."

"That's a point still under question and the primary reason for these investigative hearings," Reeves countered.

"If that were true, one would expect to see representatives from the state of Delaware on the witness list since they're the ones letting the bids and overseeing construction. It's their money and their process... and in the end, their bridge, Senator."

"It's Federal money –"

"Given to the state without strings attached," the young woman interrupted, "to do a small portion of the Interstate Highway System, Senator."

Senator Reeves turned away, covered the microphone directly in front of him with his hand and whispered to his committee legal counsel, Brandon Oakes, "Do you know anything about the bothersome young lady at Nolan's table? She's one outburst away from a Contempt of Congress citation."

Oakes glanced quickly at the girl. "Cateline Glendenbrook. Yale Law, ranked second in her class even though she's the youngest student. Very bright and quick on her feet. Her father was an ace in the RAF flying Spitfires during the Battle of Britain and was later killed in North Africa. Her grandfather was on the British Royal Staff throughout the Big War."

"She's a Brit?"

"Yes, sir – according to her passport."

"How do you know all this?"

"Had dinner with her last night. She was trolling for info about the hearing. According to her, she's in the U.S. because she wants to study law in the land of Justice Story and Simon Greenleaf. She's in the room today because she wants to learn how a representative republic really functions, or so she says." Oakes looked up and glanced at the girl again. "She'd be a hell of an addition on your staff, and we've been talking about letting Jenoff go. I bet she'd go for it."

Reeves frowned at his lawyer. "I don't know. But find out more about her, counselor."

"My pleasure, mister chairman." Oakes looked back at Dave Nolan and said, "On another note, we're going to have to recess this hearing until tomorrow morning. The White House wants to talk to our witness immediately."

"The subject?"

"Don't know, but the President and the Attorney General are insistent."

*   *   *

The door to the Oval Office opened and Dave Nolan entered.

President Kennedy rose deliberately from his rocking chair with the hunched back of an older man in pain, though his smile was warm and welcoming as he slowly straightened. Offering his hand the President said, "General Nolan, so good of you to come on such short notice. Thank you."

"I learned decades ago never to dawdle when the White House calls, Mr. President," Nolan replied as he looked first at the President, then at his younger brother.

"My brother, the Attorney General," the President said, and continued making introductions. "McGeorge Bundy, National Security Advisor; Secretary of Defense McNamara, and General Maxwell Taylor with whom I hear you have a long-standing friendship. I've just recalled Max to active duty to fill a position as my chief military advisor in the White House."

Nolan shook hands with each man. All except the general seemed to him to be tightly wound, in contrast to the young president.

Bobby Kennedy had many of the mannerisms of his father, Joseph. The elder Kennedy was the U.S. Ambassador to England when Nolan first met him; he'd instantly disliked and distrusted him, as had his traveling companion, Wild Bill Donovan. The elder Kennedy had sided with the defeatist liberal crowd in England in 1940 and urged President Roosevelt and others in the U.S. government to stay neutral in the European conflict which would have isolated Britain and ensured Nazi Germany's victory. It had left a bad taste in his mouth and created a wariness toward this arrogant rich man, untrained in diplomacy, unlearned in history and politics, and a publicity seeker. Nolan thought he saw a lot of Papa Joe in Bobby.

McGeorge Bundy was one of the president's "Wise Men", a reputed intellectual and he stared at Nolan with a ferocity as hot as his smile was cold. He was old Boston money and a Yale alum.

McNamara had the same look about him – like Bundy, his glasses were rimless, straight, imposing. People said when you looked into the eyes behind the lenses, you instantly understood the warning and kept your distance. Both men were known for their drive, for their certitude and for getting things done and, many said, for their highbrow arrogance. In addition, the Defense Secretary also had an $85 billion budget and the reputation for silencing rooms filled with generals. Since E.W. Barrett Enterprises manufactured parts for all the automobile companies, he'd studied up on the re-emergence of Ford Motor Company after the Big War. Apparently much of that was due to the group of ten "Whiz Kids", including Bob McNamara. Tex Thornton had brought the group of young statistical geniuses with him out of the Air Corps and into the executive offices of Ford after the war. They had breathed new life into the old company, and McNamara had eventually become CEO, to the benefit of the company and its stockholders before John Kennedy tapped him for government service. There was something he couldn't quite put his finger on that gave Nolan pause concerning the new Secretary of Defense.

At last Dave's glance fell on the familiar, welcoming face of General Taylor. "Good to see you again, Max. It's been a long, long while."

"Too long. You still owe me a rematch on the skeet field, Dave," General Taylor said. "I hope we can remedy that sometime soon."

"Your memory is still scary, General. That was more than ten years ago."

Maxwell Taylor served as superintendent of West Point for four years following World War II. In 1947, he drafted the first official written "Cadet Honor Code" at the Academy and had invited Dave Nolan to drive up from New York to attend the unveiling ceremony. Afterwards they had spent part of the afternoon together on the school's skeet range.

"Perhaps there'll be time for settling old scores later," the President said amiably, signaling for them all to have a seat and indicating the silver coffee service. "I'll get right to it, Mr. Nolan. Your country needs your expertise and experience once again. I've reviewed your record of service as far back as your appointment to West Point and graduation in 1916. Your service since then in two wars and scores of places around the world is most admirable."

"I was just a foot soldier doing the best I could, Mr. President – like millions of others."

"I admire your modesty but must humbly disagree. I was provided your personnel records, both military and civilian government service, and noticed not only the high rank you yourself achieved, but the letters of commendation from such people as William Donovan and President Roosevelt. My immediate predecessor also highly praised you for your contributions in both spheres."

Dave Nolan felt the back of his neck growing warm and sensed he was being manipulated. Out of the corner of his eye he could see both Bobby Kennedy and McNamara staring intently at him.

"The nation finds itself at a crucial crossroads vis-à-vis our allies as well as our adversaries in the Soviet bloc," President Kennedy continued. "We cannot falter in our resolve to resist communism, and we must not make unforced errors in that opposition. I'm sure you know I just returned from a summit with Premier Khrushchev in Vienna."

"Yes, sir. I'm very aware of that, Mr. President."

"What you don't know is that the Premier roundly berated the U.S. for our role in the failure of the Bay of Pigs operation. I've commissioned General Taylor, under the guidance and authority of the Department of Defense, to do an "autopsy" of that fiasco to see what we can learn from it so such high profile mistakes are not repeated."

Nolan remained silent, quietly troubled as he gazed at each of the men.

"I would like you to be part of the Bay of Pigs review effort," the President was saying, taking a sip of coffee.

"How much time is required of me for this review, sir, and more importantly to me, when does the effort begin?"

"Actually, Dave," Maxwell Taylor interjected when an awkward silence descended, "the study itself is underway already, so the time commitment will be minimal."

"How far along is it?"

"Nearly complete," the general replied. "But it's been done by people who spent most of their lives inside the Beltway in the rarified atmosphere of Washington, D.C. We need someone with a fresh set of eyes who hasn't been breathing his own air most of his life to give the thing a 'murder rehearsal' before it's finalized. I remember how you scorched the combined staff in the Med over the plans for Salerno, and the British staff in London over their initial plans for Overlord. As an outsider with no political dog in the fight we're hoping you'll do the same slash and burn job on this study."

Warning signals were going off loudly in Nolan's mind. *This is a political hot potato*, he thought. *This is why a wise man stays far away from Washington...* "How soon?"

"Immediately," Taylor replied.

"Then, sadly, I'm going to have to say no. I'm right in the middle of what's become my semi-annual grilling by Senator Reeves. This usually goes on for a week or more, followed a month to six weeks later by follow-up sessions to answer all the questions not in the initial interrogatory. In between I'm meeting with teams of lawyers while attempting to cover a lot of business bases. As much as I hate to turn you down, Mr. President..." Dave Nolan let the thought linger as he turned his head slightly and gazed at the President's brother.

"I think we may be able to help you, Mr. Nolan," the Attorney General said.

"Certainly my company and I could use some assistance in our dealings with Washington. Each one of these Senate committee testimonies costs my corporation nearly a million dollars just in attorney fees, not to mention the lost productivity of my financial and business staff."

"I'm sorry your government is costing you money and causing you difficulty in running your business. I'm sure we can give some assistance in the matter," the President said, looking at his brother and nodding slowly. "What can we do, Bobby?"

"I'm not certain at the moment, Mr. President, but I'll talk to the president of the Senate and to the Senate leader, both of whom are in our party. I'll prevail upon them to speak with Senator Reeves and work something out."

"I should point out, Mr. Attorney General," Dave Nolan added, "that since these semi-annual grillings started a decade ago, not a single instance of illegal or unethical practices has been uncovered, nor has anyone from Barrett Enterprises been convicted, arraigned or even accused of a crime. Frankly, it's time for this to stop once and for all. The government, at least one of its members in the Senate, is costing my company money and the government itself a lot of its precious tax dollars for no reason. If you could put an end to this harassment, I could likely find time to review and provide an editorial critique of General Taylor's study."

"Then I would say we have a deal. I thank you for stopping by, Mr. Nolan," President Kennedy said, smiling and rising to his feet to signal an end to the meeting. After the CEO of Barrett Enterprises left and closed the door behind him, the President again sat down and stretched his back. "I think we got what we needed."

"I hope you're right, Mr. President," McNamara said, glancing at Bundy with a look that said he didn't necessarily agree. "We'll now have to wait and see how he responds. General Taylor and I will keep you informed on how things go with him."

The general and Secretary of Defense excused themselves and left the Oval Office. Halfway down the hallway General Taylor turned to McNamara. "How do you think the meeting went?"

"I think Nolan got what he wanted – agreement from the President and the Attorney General to get Harrison Reeves off his back for good. We didn't get much in return – just a promise to provide an editorial critique to our already completed study – that's all. I didn't hear him agree to sign off on it when done, only to review it and give us his comments. He's not as politically naïve as what I was led to believe. You need to keep a very close eye on Nolan."

"I plan to."

"Good. I'll keep the Joint Chiefs at bay and you stay close to the President and his brother – they both hold you in high regard. Between the two of us we need to keep him from future mistakes and enhance his reputation for guts and savvy with Khrushchev.

"That's going to keep us both well occupied for a while after what happened in Vienna."

EXORSUS

Brian Utermahlen

Chapter 1

Baltimore – May 1964

I can't make any sense of it at all," Mary Anne MacEagan said, frowning and wrinkling her nose. "Sister Mary Catherine tried to explain in class and got so confused she finally gave up. Who cares what happens in some little jungle country on the far side of the world no one ever heard of? And what difference does it make anyway, Glenn?"

"One tiny spark can start a forest fire."

"Well, that certainly clears up *everything*!"

"Always glad to help," Glenn Nolan said as they sat undisturbed on the second floor balcony swing of her parents' sprawling old house. Kids in the community called it *MacEagan Mansion* because it sat on a huge double lot and was the biggest house in the neighborhood.

Mary Anne took a deep breath and swept a stray lock of long blond hair behind her ear as she turned her head and stared hard at him for a moment. She was a tall girl who'd grown to be a woman in the four short years since the Nolans moved in across the street in Guilford, a tony old Baltimore neighborhood of tree-lined streets and big Colonial houses not far from Johns Hopkins University. Her deep blue eyes looked at everything, and everyone, with piercing candor. "You're no help at all. I wonder some times what I ever saw in you."

Glenn Nolan gave her a roguish grin. "That's not what you said last night."

"That was different. We were watching the submarine races at Lake Roland."

"Oh yeah – we were, weren't we? What were we doing that for? I've forgotten."

She slapped his upper arm, then suddenly pulled his face toward her and gave him a deep and lingering kiss. "Remember now?"

"It's beginning to come back, I think," he said idly, giving her a distant gaze.

"You're so sure of yourself – and about us too, aren't you?" He didn't reply, which irritated her even more, and finally she said, "You're the slowest and most difficult boy I ever dated… and yes, for your information, I dated others besides you."

"But you still keep coming back to me."

He loved teasing her, but had learned over time not to take it too far – she had warned him early on she had both Scottish blood and Highland temper. They'd dated the last two years of high school and spent most of their scarce free time together.

She was co-captain of the field hockey team at the all-girls *Catholic High School of Baltimore* and chaired their senior class activities committee. Glenn looked at her now and felt a pleasant tug behind his heart. She rested her head on his shoulder and snuggled close to his chest while he gazed over the large back yard with its immaculate landscaping, tennis court, over-sized pool and small gardener's potting and tool shed, all now bathed in golden late afternoon rays.

She'd kissed him for the first time in that little shed…

He had just turned fourteen, in the early summer of 1960, when his father resigned his military commission to take a management/lobbyist position with Glenn L. Martin Corporation in Maryland that paid him appreciably better and allowed him to continue flying in the Maryland Air Guard.

He'd been hugely disappointed with his parents' decision – he loved the life of an Air Force brat. Every few years they'd be off to somewhere else – some exotic place like Kadena Air Base in Japan, or the Philippines or Germany; sometimes to a hole-in-the-wall, but not all that often and usually for not all that long. Baltimore, he knew with certainty, was going to be a *big* disappointment.

He had been in his room unpacking boxes the day after the moving van had come with their household goods, feeling sorry for himself, when his mother called upstairs for him to come down to meet the neighbors who had stopped by. The woman was medium height and pretty in a way he thought all rich middle-aged women probably were. She'd brought along her daughter, who was dressed in a Catholic school uniform of white blouse, blue plaid skirt, knee socks and saddle shoes. *Some stuck up little private school girl*, he'd thought upon first seeing her as she looked out the kitchen door window with her back to him. When she'd turned around, he had gasped and mumbled a mindless, unintelligible greeting. She was the cutest girl he'd ever seen and he was rendered speechless. He was so embarrassed he'd spent the next fifteen months avoiding her and her family's house as best he could. All that changed the summer after his sophomore year, in that tiny shed…

"The whole world is turning upside down," Mary Anne complained, looking up at him. She lay on her back with her head in his lap, had unbuttoned his shirt and was slowly running her fingers through the hair on his chest. "President Kennedy assassinated, then Oswald was killed – live, right on television! These race marches and riots… even in little Cambridge across the Bay last summer. All this business of thousands of American soldiers training in Viet Nam and those pictures on television of the Buddhist priests setting themselves on fire. Then the president of their country and his brother getting killed by their own generals in a military coup. This is all so crazy! Doesn't it scare you?"

"The world's a mess… a big mess. Like always."

"Corey says the Kennedy assassination is linked to the death of President Diem."

"Don't let your brother lead you into believing conspiracy theories. Nobody really knows anything yet. Let the Warren Commission sort it all out."

"And then there's you," she continued. "Why do you have to go to a school all the way across the country?"

"The Air Force Academy isn't all the way across the country. It's in Colorado Springs."

"It might as well be in Kathmandu," she complained, sighing theatrically and rolling her eyes. "I'll never see you for the next four years. Why couldn't you go to Hopkins? It's within walking distance – you walk further than that in the dead of winter carrying all your gear to play ice hockey at Memorial Stadium."

"I'm just not Hopkins material," he said absently.

"My father thinks you are. That's why he went to bat for you with the Admissions office."

"I never asked him to do that."

"I know. But he wanted to. And he didn't have to twist any arms to get them to offer you those scholarships. You could have gone to college for free! – at *the* Johns Hopkins University. I still for the life of me can't understand why you turned them down."

They had had this conversation before – numerous times. He appreciated her persistence as much as he loved everything else about her, but he had his mind set on something else.

"Where I'm going the tuition is free also. They even pay you half a second lieutenant's base pay every month. I don't want to be a doctor, or an economist, or involved in foreign affairs or a –"

"Of course not! You want to go Mach two with your hair on fire. I've heard it a *million* times." She sighed theatrically again, exaggerating desperation and hoping to change his mind. "Oh, Glenn, that sounds exciting now, but one of these days you're going to have to stop being a little kid and grow out of that old comic book mentality and… and what about us?" Her eyes grew moist and she blinked quickly. "Really. What about us? After next month, we'll never be the same, will we? You're more in love with this silly notion of being a fighter pilot than you are with me."

"You know that's not true." Their conversations the past few weeks seemed to always find their way to this moment and he was tiring of it. "All my life, since I was five or six years old I've wanted –"

" – to be a pilot like your father."

"Everything else is a hindrance, a stumbling block – even getting a free ride through Johns Hopkins."

She sighed deeply and asked, "Even me?"

"Not fair, Mary Anne. You know how I feel about you – you're the only girl I've ever been in love with."

"If you really loved me –"

"I wouldn't change who I am because that's the guy you said you fell for. If I don't go to Air Force, I'm not the same guy. Not at all. C'mon Mary Anne… gimme a break…"

Mrs. MacEagan's voice filtered up to them from downstairs. "Glenn!... Glenn! Your mother just called on the telephone. There's a visitor from the Air Force to see you, and you're to come home right away."

"Thank you, Mrs. M," he called back, suddenly nervous.

Abruptly, Mary Anne stood and walked over to the porch railing, looking toward the skyline of center city. Wrapping her arms around herself, she stood for a moment, breathing deeply. When he put his arms around her, she turned and looked into his eyes. "It's over, isn't it?" She put her teeth on her lower lip and shivered involuntarily. "This is the saddest moment of my entire life. We're finished, you and I, aren't we? You're going to school two thousand miles away, and that's the end… the end of the two of us, isn't it?"

"Mary Anne, please." He was lost for words. Without her, he was certain his life would be meaningless, but if he denied what he was confident was his destiny, his calling, he would be equally insignificant. Giving up on either was beyond his comprehension. But she sounded unmovable; and his destiny seemed to him etched in granite.

He felt hopeless.

"I'll call you later," he said, but when he tried to kiss her she turned away.

*   *

"Your dad was the best fighter pilot and worst sailor I ever knew," Colonel Crosley said.

"I remember you told me that for the first time at Hahn Air Base in Germany, sir, right after your squadron won the Hughes Trophy."

"Was that the time? It was 1955 – you would've been eight years old? Nine, maybe?"

"I just turned nine, sir."

Glenn remembered the colonel from several places around the globe over the years. He had sat for hours in their quarters or squadron outings on base listening to Crosley, Yeager and others, along with his father, swapping tales about the wars in Europe and Korea. They had flown together in many places around the world, and still unapologetically loved to tell their stories – Glenn had heard them all more than once, but never tired of them. But now, his father's old friend and classmate from West Point was nervous – he kept looking at both the front door and his watch, fidgeting.

"He should be here any minute, sir," Glenn said, when the silence grew awkward. "You know my dad – if he told you seventeen hundred, he'll walk through the door ten seconds either side of it. Can you tell me what this is all about, sir? I assume it has to do with my appointment."

"It does, but I want your mom and dad to be here as well when you open your letter."

Moments passed uncomfortably and the constant audible *tick-tick-tick* of the big mantle clock seemed to make time drag inexorably slower. His mind conjured up a host of scenarios for the reason why the Air Force Academy liaison officer for Maryland had driven all the way from Andrews Air Force Base in afternoon traffic to deliver a letter to him. None of his reflections were encouraging, and just when he thought he couldn't stand the wait any longer, his father opened the front door.

"Marv! Good to see you," Mitch Nolan said, smiling and shaking his old friend's hand before crossing the room to kiss his wife. "It's Happy Hour in an O-club somewhere – how about a drink?"

"No, thanks. I have to drive back through town."

"So soon?"

"I asked him to stay for dinner but he declined," Aynslee said in her British accent, still obvious after nearly two decades of marriage and constant Americanization. "I fear he still has memories of my mother's cooking."

Colonel Crosley looked even more uncomfortable. "Come on, Ayns. There's a statute of limitations on stupid comments."

"Not when you make them in a toast at my wedding," she replied.

"You're not going to let me forget this, are you?"

"Not bloody likely."

"Well, I'm going to have a drink, Marv. Final offer," Mitch said, throwing his suit coat over a dining room chair before disappearing into the kitchen. After a brief minute, he returned with a small glass of Irish whiskey and sat in the big wingback chair next to the fireplace.

"Obviously this is about Glenn's appointment. It's been a long time coming. I thought we'd have heard something the beginning of April instead of the end of May. It's good news, right?"

Crosley grew visibly more uncomfortable. Without replying, he opened his leather briefcase and retrieved a letter which he handed to Glenn. "This is for you. I requested the courtesy of being allowed to deliver it in person rather than having it sent through the mail."

Glenn took the sealed envelope and felt his pulse begin to pound. *This is it, finally – all the marbles. The Poly-City game, the NFL Championship, the World Series – all of it wrapped together. Bottom of the ninth, two out, bases loaded... three and two count.* He pulled out the small pocket knife his grandfather had given him with the stern warning to always carry a folding blade of some sort – Nolan's Rule #4, the old general called it. He slit the back of the envelope, removed the single sheet of Air Force Academy letterhead and read:

> *Mr. Glenn A. Nolan*
> *3918 Greenway*
> *Baltimore 18, Maryland*   *25 May 1964*
>
> *Dear Mr. Nolan,*
>
> *We regret to inform you that the United States Air Force Academy (USAFA) is unable to offer you an appointment to the Class of 1968.*
>
> *Should you have any questions concerning the details of this decision, you are directed to your state's USAFA liaison officer and/or the Congressional member to whom you initially applied at the...*

He had no idea how long he stared at the page, reading the words in its four short paragraphs comprehending nothing but the first sentence... *regret to inform you... unable to offer you an appointment...*

His first reaction was disbelief, followed quickly by self-pity and finally by a growing, seething outrage. All his parents' friends, the coaches and teachers at Baltimore Polytechnic, his teammates on various athletic teams had always marveled at his calm in the midst of difficulty. It was his great strength, and the reason for his being named the co-captain of the state champion football squad and the outright leader of the baseball team his senior year. *A fat lot of good it did me*, he thought. *A fat lot of good anything did for me... son-of-a-bitch...*

His father was saying something and then he saw his unflappable mother gazing at him aghast. He heard none of it, or his own coarse muttering until his father raised his voice and got his attention.

"What is it, son?!"

He looked down and realized he'd wadded the letter into a tight round ball. "Sorry. Guess it's not suitable for framing anymore." He stood and tossed it unceremoniously in his father's direction. "I'm going for a walk… or a ride. Maybe I'll just go find something to kill."

"Glenn!" his mother said. "You'll do no such thing, young man. Supper will be ready at six and you still have chores, even if you no longer have school work."

He started for the front door and said over his shoulder, "Not hungry. I'll be back…"

Standing on the front porch, he looked across the street at the MacEagan mansion. "Well, at least someone will be happy over that damned letter," he mumbled under his breath, and immediately regretted it. Still, his anger and disappointment grew, seeming to feed on itself. He stuffed his hands in his pockets and felt the car keys to the Morgan +4 he and his father had restored the previous summer in the detached garage behind the house. It was nominally his car as long as he was living at home, which now appeared to be a situation that would last a lot longer than any of them had anticipated. He walked to the street looking up and down for a while and finally stomped back to the garage, threw open the door, and started the British racing green sports car.

As he reached the end of the driveway, he turned left, going against the one-way direction on his street and roared a half block to the next intersection and turned right without slowing until he saw Mary Anne at the end of her driveway standing half out into the street trying to flag him down. He stomped on the brake, and squealed to a stop.

"What are you doing?" she said to him as she rested her hands on the passenger side door of the roadster. "Are you trying to kill yourself going the wrong way on your street and then screaming around the corner without slowing down? What *are* you doing?!" she repeated, with emphasis.

"Doesn't matter what I'm doing," he said angrily, glaring at her. "Life's a cheat and a fraud, and then you die."

"What?!"

"Get off my cotton-pickin' car."

"Does this have anything to do with that Air Force officer?"

"Yeah, it does. No big deal, though. The Air Force decided I wasn't good enough for them. Looks like I won't be going to Colorado Springs after all. That should make you happy."

She gasped and looked at him as if she'd been slapped. "That's not fair, Glenn."

"Fair or not, it's life. Now get off my car before you get hurt. I'm out for a little ride to clear the cobwebs and… whatever."

"I'm going with you!" she declared, reaching for the door handle.

"Like *hell* you are!" He popped the clutch and floored the accelerator leaving a long black streak on the road in front of her house. "How about that?!" he said aloud. "Didn't know this crate had that kind of acceleration." He looked at her in the tiny rear view mirror until he turned at the next corner headed north out of town. Hours later he sat in the dark on the secluded, mostly untraveled road near Lake Roland where he and Mary Anne usually ended up at the end of a date.

You're a real grade-A, pure-bred jerk, Nolan, he said to himself as he sat alone, his mind tumbling, listening to the ticking of the engine as it cooled. *She didn't deserve that . What happened wasn't her fault,* he thought guiltily. *She has a right to expect better – I hope she finds it in somebody someday.*

*   *

The light in the kitchen was still on when he got home, well after dark.

"Coffee, or a beer?" his father asked when he came in through the back door. "Get it all out of your system?"

"Some of it. Afraid it'll take more than a few days… or weeks." Glenn went to the kitchen counter, poured himself a mug of coffee from the percolator and sat down at the table.

"For your sake I hope it doesn't take much longer. Son, you've got the two most important women in your life confused, angry and not just a little frightened. Good luck with that."

"Luck? Guess I'll need some, won't I?" Glenn mused. He sat back, ran his fingers through his hair and asked, "Dad, what just happened? I was getting nervous when we didn't get word all through May, but Colonel Crosley kept saying it was a sure deal, that I was certain to get the appointment. He even said you should buy me a pair of boots to break in because I was going, that since the senator said he was awarding his appointment on a competitive basis…" Glenn shook his head dejectedly. "Then, this letter."

"I was really pissed at Marv – Colonel Crosley – when I read the letter, and I let him have it. He was embarrassed. And now I guess I am, too. I should have known better."

Glenn was confused and said as much.

"Senator Reeves might have said he was going to give his appointment based on competitive scores, but I'm certain now he never intended to select you from day one, regardless of your qualifications." His father took a sip of coffee and slowly set his mug on the table. "All along, Colonel Crosley was telling us the truth, as far as he knew it. What he didn't know – but something I did, or should have – was the character of Harrison Reeves. Our family has a long history with him, going back fifty years to when he and your grandfather were classmates at West Point. I used to work for him and his wife when I was your age, taking care of their stable of horses in the Philippines. I was hoping that would help in some way. It probably did the opposite."

"A U.S. Senator would lie like that?"

"At least one of them, obviously. Colonel Crosley showed me the worksheets he did on all six finalists. All of you passed the class A flight physical, but in every other area – high school grades, SAT scores, Civil Service exam, physical fitness test – you came out on top, usually by a significant margin. You were the only one who captained a state champion athletic team, and the only one who got all-state recognition for sports. Competitively, you were clearly number one."

"I don't know what to do now," Glenn said, disconsolately. "I'm tired and I need to sleep on this. Maybe it'll look different in the morning. I've got to get to work pretty quickly if I'm going to get into *any* college next fall. But…" He leaned back and rubbed his eyes. "I don't know."

"It's not the end of the world, Glenn. You could re-apply next year, through a different member of Congress."

"No. That's out. To hell with the damned Academy!" he said with conviction, realizing this was the first time he'd ever cursed in front of his father. "That's the one thing I did get out of my system tonight. I don't know what I'm going to do, but a military academy… nope, for sure that's not one of the options. I'm finished with the military. Now, it's one step at a time I guess. Sleep first."

"Step two is to mend fences with those two women I mentioned."

"I'll do that first thing in the morning. Mom first. I can probably work through that."

"And Mary Anne?"

"That'll be a lot tougher."

"After you left, she came by and spent a long time talking with your mother. If I were you, she's the one I'd worry most about."

"I know. She deserved better than the way I treated her. I acted like a petty dim-wit, and I'll apologize to her. She's been a fun high school girlfriend these past couple of years. But, I'm not so sure there's anything beyond that for either of us."

"You sleep on that too, Glenn. that'll look a lot different in the morning, too."

"Sure, Dad." But he wasn't so certain – about anything.

… we regret to inform you…

*　　*　　*　　*

The MacEagan's imposing front door opened slightly when he knocked the second time.

"I came to apologize," Glenn said, able to see only half of Mary Anne's face through the crack. "May I come in?"

"You can say you're sorry from right there, I'd think. It's been a whole week."

"Actually, it's only been five and a half days since I tried the first time."

"You gave up after just one try? You must not be very sorry."

He took a deep breath and bit his lip, trying to keep from making the bad situation worse. "You didn't want to see me the first time so I thought you…you and I needed a few days to cool off."

"I wasn't home."

"That's what Hailey said."

"You sound like you don't believe it."

He took another deep breath and let it out, contemplating. "You really shouldn't ask your baby sister to lie for you… I saw your car in the garage, so I knew you hadn't gone shopping for your mother."

Mary Anne was silent for a moment. "Did you come by to lecture me or to apologize?"

"I came to say I'm sorry for acting like I did… that, and to ask for your forgiveness."

"All right, go ahead," she said flippantly and opened the door all the way. She placed her hands on her hips and cocked her head in anticipation. "I'm waiting, Glenn Nolan."

Exasperated, and growing annoyed at her, he thought, *she's really making this hard, isn't she? All right, Mary Anne – I get it.* "I'm sorry. I'm very sorry. I was rude and I spoke harshly to you. I behaved like a complete idiot. I apologize for the way I acted, and I hope you'll forgive me."

She stood glaring at him for a long time until finally saying, "That's not enough, Glenn. That's not even close to good enough!" With surprising strength, she grabbed the front of his shirt below the collar with both hands and shook him. "You shut me out when I tried to help you! Don't you *ever* do that again! Do you hear me?! Don't you *dare* shut me out!"

"Yeah. I hear you," he stammered, surprised by the outburst. He looked at her angry face and the tear now trickling down her cheek.

"Say it!" She shook him again. "Tell me you'll never do that to me again!"

"I won't shut you out again."

"Promise?"

"Yes, I promise."

"You'd better mean that, Glenn Nolan. I'm dead serious. Now, go out and wait for me by the pool. I'll be there in a few minutes." She turned and ran quickly up the steps to the second floor. He closed the front door and then walked through the house to the patio beside the pool where he sat at a table and waited until she came out minutes later. Her eyes were red..

"I want you to know," she began earnestly, staring into his eyes after sitting down, "I *was not* and never will be happy you didn't get into that academy. I know how much it meant to you. And I really did want to help you deal with it that night. At first, I didn't know what had happened but I could tell you were upset about something when I saw you stomp out of your house. When you roared out of your driveway and up the street the way you did, I knew it was something serious. You really scared me the way you were acting." She blinked and wiped her eyes with a tissue. "I worried about you all night, even after I saw you drive the Morgan back into your garage."

"I'm sorry I did that to you. I was selfish. I was only thinking about myself."

She placed her hand on top of his and patted it gently. "I have a stake in what happens to you. I'm in this for the long haul, Glenn. If you think I'm going let you dump me after putting two whole years of my life into this relationship, then you have another think coming."

"But that afternoon?"

"I was being selfish myself. We have such a good thing going, and I hated the idea of your being so far away. I was afraid I'd lose something that's become so comfortable. That doesn't mean I want you to give up on your dreams."

"Well, I have. After the last few days, the world looks even darker. There's not a school in the country that would even consider admitting me at this late date."

"You couldn't possibly know that."

"I've got a good idea. I called the coaches at Maryland and Penn State. They already filled the scholarship slots they offered me long ago. The same with Hopkins."

"Delaware and U.Va.?"

"Same story. I even had an appointment yesterday morning with the Director of Admissions at Towson State Teachers College. He looked over my transcripts and stuff – said I was the kind of person he was trying to recruit, and would love to have me under different circumstances. But I was way too late for the coming academic year." He took in a deep breath and expelled it loudly. "I was an idiot – an absolute, purebred idiot. Put all my eggs in one basket."

"But the senator kept telling you –"

"He kept telling me a lie. I was too dumb, too thick to recognize it. Apparently Senator Reeves has a history of messing with our family dating back to long before I was born. I don't know the details, and don't care. All I know is I'm not going to the Air Force Academy, or anywhere else."

"But you will eventually. There are lots of schools that would love to have somebody like you. I'm certain of it."

"Maybe. But it turns out I just might be going into the military after all – different branch than I wanted." He grunted and shook his head. "I have a low enough draft number that I could be looking at being called up as an Army private."

"Oh, Glenn. Don't talk like that. They can't."

He chuckled mirthlessly. "They certainly can. With my luck, they probably will. That little fracas over in Southeast Asia is heating up. That means –"

"You're mad at things and feeling sorry for yourself. It doesn't have to mean that!"

"I'm afraid it can." He sighed deeply and gazed over the back lawn of her parents' house. "Always enjoyed seeing the world. Never been to *Southeast* Asia. But I speak a little Japanese…"

"That's not the least bit funny, Glenn."

"No, but it's reality. And it's *my* reality. Yup. Private Glenn Nolan – carrying a rifle in the jungles of Vietnam… killin' gooks and making the world safe for democracy. What a great deal."

"You can't know any of that for sure," Mary Anne said, suddenly filled with a horde of conflicting thoughts as she looked at his determined face. "It's so far away… and they say it's just those Green Beret people they're sending."

"Yeah. Right… you can trust every word from the mouth a politician. Politics and politicians," he said scornfully, and gave her a fearsome sideways look. "They spend half their lives telling people things they don't believe themselves or know to be completely false. A pox on the whole damned lot of them."

She suddenly reached up and locked her arms around his neck and gave him a quick kiss, and then another – more passionate, wondering if he felt the same delicious, mystical tension that tightened and released her again and again each time they kissed. He murmured something but she couldn't make it out.

"Oh, Glenn," she whispered, as he pulled her tight to his chest. "It's going to be fine, I just know it is. You'll see. Things always work out for you. They do, you know they do."

But looking at his troubled face now, she wasn't so sure.

*　　*

The small light over the kitchen table was on when he got home and his mother was sitting by the back window snapping beans into a large bowl. As she turned toward him, he thought again she was still very pretty and he smiled at the memories of the stories his English grandfather had told him about his parents' volatile courtship during the Big War. He was sure he'd gotten the edited version from Grandfather Henry that summer trip to England between his freshman and sophomore years in high school, but what he'd heard was interesting enough.

"Hello, mother," he said, and on impulse he went over and kissed her on the forehead.

She gave him a wily smile. "Rather formal, aren't we?"

"I was just thinking about some stories your father told me a couple of summers ago and was reminded I'm half English. Descended from royalty, aren't I? It seems appropriate to get used to acting like it for when we go over." He gave her a rueful grin. Their trip back to England had been a graduation present for him and reason for a holiday for the family. "Your father's letter to me said I have *responsibilities*… and I've only got a week to practice."

"I shan't let it go to your head. The title isn't what it used to be when my great-grandfather said grace over the last vestiges of the Cistercian Abbey and grounds from the estate house where your grandfather now lives. Looking at him with hooded eyes, she said, "I see the apology to Mary Anne came off well. Come here and let me wipe the lipstick off your face and mouth before Bradyn sees it and gives you the hairy eye and a hard time over it."

Brad would be giving you the 'hairy eye' if he heard you call him that, Glenn thought.

His younger brother, by four years, had been given a name from his English grandmother's side of the family and it had apparently been, and remained, a point of some bright and breezy contention between his parents. It was also a source of a great deal of amusement to General Henry Smythe-Browne, his grandfather. While the English side of the family called him Bradyn, the American side called him the more masculine-sounding, Brad.

"Your father called not long ago," Aynslee Nolan said as she rubbed his cheek and the corner of his mouth with a tissue. "He'll be home shortly and we'll be eating soon after. It appears you and he have an appointment this evening with a Colonel Webb. He's the liaison officer for the Military Academy. He wants to talk to you and your father about an appointment to the school."

"Colonel Webb? Never heard of him. I thought Colonel Crosley was the liaison officer for the Air Force Academy."

"He is. It all seems rather confusing." Aynslee looked away, puzzled, her forehead creased as if she was deep in thought. "Your father says this Colonel Webb is an Army officer.

"He wants to talk to you and your father about West Point."

Chapter 2

"Things are really getting heated between State and Defense over the hands-on operational control and support our advisors are giving the South Vietnamese," Randall Ashby told his wife as he took the menu from the waiter and ordered a Scotch and soda.

"I thought that was the whole idea behind sending advisors over," Erika replied.

"Not at all – in fact, quite the opposite. That's what McNamara and his generals told us when the first Green Berets went in under Kennedy. Something's changed over there. If we don't watch out we could suddenly find ourselves in a damned shooting war in China's back yard. And for what?!"

KAVANAGH'S boasted an elegant dining room, a favorite luncheon and dinner destination of senior Capitol Hill and Cabinet staffers since the days when she and her husband worked for Senator William Howard Payne during World War II. The first time she'd dined in the place was when she introduced her mother to the senator's legal advisor, a young lawyer named Randall Ashby. His drink came and she placed her hand over his and patted.

"I'm not letting you go back until you settle down, get your attention off that little jungle country and back on important matters – like celebrating us. You did remember, didn't you?" she asked, giving him a sultry sideways glance.

"You mean did I miss the 'all caps' note in red ink on the calendar?" he asked squeezing her hand. "The reminder this was the day I proposed? You can be so subtle, Erika Nolan."

"Ashby –"

"There's still a bunch of your dad in you, and I'm glad to say, your mom as well. They say a guy marries a whole family on his wedding day, not just the girl."

She exaggerated a look of innocence and fluttered her eyelashes at him. "But you got the best part, didn't you?"

"The very best," he replied.

They had both done well in Washington since Senator Payne's death weeks before VE Day. They had helped his daughter Michelle close the office and sort through the memorabilia of his four decades in Congress. Randall had gone on to work in the State Department, rising to the position of Political-Military Assistant Secretary reporting to the Under Secretary for International Security. He routinely briefed the Secretary of State Rusk. Erika had eventually finished college, graduated from Georgetown law school and after a short stint as a public defender was now a Federal prosecutor in Washington, DC.

Randall caught his wife again glancing at the entrance to the dining room.

"Looking for someone in particular?"

"I asked Michelle to join us. She was here when you popped the question."

"She was the only one in the dining room, beside you who knew what was going on. You two had it all figured out, didn't you? You talked behind my back?"

"And with the senator."

He saw the laughter in her eyes, and felt himself drawn to this lovely woman as he had been the first time they'd met. "Don't think I'm clueless about what you're doing now. You're trying to get my mind off what's going on in 'McNamara's Band'… and its working. I'm glad I didn't walk past this place and keep on going that day, like I thought of doing."

"Liar."

"Is that the prosecutor or the wife talking?"

"Both," she replied, opening the menu. "Something must have kept Michelle. When I invited her, she mentioned a morning meeting in Gaithersburg to sign a deal with a developer. Order me the Jumbo Lump Maryland Crab Cake with Mustard Crème Fraiche."

They lingered longer than usual over their lunch, reminiscing about special moments during their marriage. After nearly an hour, he leaned close to her and whispered, "I have to get back. I'm meeting with guys from Defense in a little while over some issues about South Vietnamese operations."

"That's why you were so distracted earlier?"

Randall nodded, "I'm worried about mission creep that recklessly raises the stakes. That's all I can tell you." He leaned over and kissed her. "Lunch was a first-rate idea."

Erika watched him navigate the crowded room before finishing her glass of champagne. It was just after 1 PM when the waiter placed the check on the table; as she looked over the bill, Erika saw Michelle Payne crossing the room toward her.

"So sorry to be late," the older woman said as she took a seat across the table, "but it couldn't be helped. It was nice of you to ask, but I'm sure you two really didn't need or want a 'fifth wheel'. Randall was always one of my favorites. You're a lucky woman, Erika."

Michelle Payne looked years – some said at least a decade – younger than her age, and she still wore the same dress size as the day she graduated from Vassar. She walked five miles each day, rarely ate red meat, and breakfasted on whole grains. Hers was a classical beauty aged well.

Her father had served in the U.S. Senate for almost forty-five years and had given Erika's father and her older brother Mitch their appointments to the Military Academy at West Point. She'd married Harrison Reeves, the son of another senator, a few months immediately after the Great War, a decision she now called the most epic mistake made by any woman in the twentieth century. Michelle had partially remedied that by divorcing Reeves during the 2nd World War and leaving him much less wealthy than he'd been when he first came into his inheritance from his paternal grandfather. Since escaping from the abusive Reeves, she had gone on to make her mark in the post-war real estate boom in the northeast – first in New York and Long Island, and more recently in the mid-Atlantic in the ocean resorts along the New Jersey, Delaware, Maryland and Virginia shorelines.

Michelle motioned to the waiter requesting a champagne flute, poured herself a glass from what remained of the bottle, leaned toward Erika and spoke in a low but animated voice. "I spent the last two hours with three men I'm convinced will give your federal prosecutorial career a huge boost. How would you like to be the one who finally puts Senator Harrison Reeves behind bars where he belongs?"

*   *   *   *

Glenn parked the Morgan next to the old neglected train station, got out and looked around at the small town square thirty yards down the shallow hill to the west, then at the baseball diamond to the south that sat huddled, unkempt, at the foot of the railroad right of way embankment. A half mile beyond, where the Susquehanna made a sharp bend, a tall hill he knew as Cove Mountain loomed over the little village.

This was an old, old town that had seen better days.

He crossed the tracks at the bend a couple of hundred yards down the rail bed near a trestle beneath which ran a creek that emptied into the river. There he found the old man he'd come to see sitting on a flat rock smoking a pipe and looking out to where the red and white float attached to his fishing line rested motionless on the water. Next to him sat a large Labrador retriever, whose coat was amber bordering on fox red. He ambled over to nuzzle Glenn's hand, looking for a handout.

"How are you and Ol' Yeller doing today, Grandpa?" Glenn asked, quickly adding, "When did you take up smoking?"

Dave Nolan slowly removed the stem of the corncob pipe from his mouth and turned to look at his grandson. "I don't smoke, at least where your Grammy-D is concerned. I may get up the nerve to break it to her someday, but probably not any time soon."

"I expect she knows already," Glenn offered, sitting down on the gravelly shoreline. "I don't think much gets past my grandmother, sir, and from what I can see, she seems to have you pretty well figured out."

"You're probably right." The older man puffed contently on his pipe for a while before saying, "You'll learn that a man needs a vice or two in his life. This is mine. Has been since the day after I retired."

"From Barrett Enterprises?"

"From the world, son."

"Smells good from here. Always liked the smell of pipe tobacco."

"Tastes like hell," Dave Nolan said, sucking hard on the pipe stem.

"You come here often?"

"Every day when your grandmother and I aren't up in Long Island at the summer home. My best friend growing up – Dewey Martin – meets me here and we talk and smoke and every now and then catch some fish." The old man took the pipe from his mouth and gazed across the broad expanse of the river. "This was my grandfather's favorite spot and we came here after dinner most evenings during the summer. He told me about seeing Confederate cavalry watering their horses right over there beyond the trestle just two days before the Battle of Gettysburg – that's only forty miles from here."

"Not far from President Eisenhower's farm. Do you stay in touch with him?"

"Not often enough."

Grandpa Nolan, he knew, had rubbed shoulders with many high-ranking people over the years. He'd been close to "Wild Bill" Donovan most of his adult life and had been a general in the War reporting directly to Patton. But he never spoke of it unless prodded – and then only in vague terms. But Glenn's father, by comparison, loved regaling him, and pilots in the Guard with stories about flying with Dixie Sloan in North Africa, Chuck Yeager in northern Europe and at Edwards after the war, and with Boots Blesse in F-86s over Korea.

"Why did you move back here?" Glenn asked, after a long silence. "There's not much going on in this little town."

"The fishing's good early in the morning and at last light. Deer and pheasant and dove hunting have never been better in these parts." He blew a cloud of sweet aromatic smoke that hung over where they sat. "I can grow most of what we need to survive. Your father's in

Baltimore, your aunt Erika lives in Silver Spring. The grandkids except for Cateline are within easy driving distance. The pace here is easy – which is what an old man like me needs."

"You're not that old, grandpa."

"I'll be seventy in a year and feel every day of it. Now, I get up every morning and plan to do absolutely nothing – by the end of the day I'm only half done. Duncannon suits me fine these days. But you didn't drive two hours from Baltimore to ask me why I moved back here," Dave Nolan said, striking a match and re-lighting his pipe. "This is about that letter from the Air Force, isn't it?"

"It is," Glenn began, taking a deep breath, "Dad and I had a meeting two nights ago with a Colonel Webb. He's retired Army, the West Point liaison officer for Maryland. His son is an All-American lacrosse goalie at Army and he lives five or six miles from us. When he learned that I'd been turned down at Air Force, he called his counterpart – a friend of my dad's from the Big War – and got my file. I need some advice – that's why I'm here."

"So, why did the Air Force say they turned you down?"

Glenn suspected his grandfather already knew the details but wanted to hear his version. "That's a long, sad tale. My senator told us he was going to make his appointments to the academies solely on competitive qualifications. In the end, according to Colonel Crosley, he didn't. Instead, Senator Reeves parceled them out to the sons of his friends based on quid pro quo. Political payoffs."

"You're certain of this?"

"As certain as I can be. Dad said that after looking back on it, he's convinced. He says that Senator Reeves has a long history with the family."

"So what happened when you met with Colonel Webb?"

"He convinced dad right off I should go to Army. Said he could arrange an appointment to West Point for me if I wanted one. Both Air Force and Navy have student bodies a lot larger and this year's incoming class at Army is the first of the so-called 'expansion' classes."

Dave knew the story, how John Kennedy had gone to his first Army-Navy football game as Commander-in-Chief and watched the Corps of Cadets march onto the field following the Naval Academy. George Decker, a man he'd crossed paths with in the late thirties at Command and General Staff had been the Army's Chief of Staff back then. The formation of Midshipmen had filled the entire playing field from end zone to end zone while the Corps of Cadets had filled little more than half that. The President had asked General Decker where the rest of the cadets were and learned that's all there was. The next week, he'd ordered the Army to increase the size of the Corps at West Point with some sense of urgency.

"They haven't filled all the openings yet for some reason," Glenn said, "and the liaison officers have been notified there are seventy more slots for 'qualified alternates' to be filled competitively nationwide. He said I'd be a shoe-in; all I have to do is say 'yes' and I'm in."

Dave looked enquiringly at his grandson and said, "So, what do you want from me?"

"I want to know what you think – what you'd do in my place."

Glenn's grandfather exhaled a thick white cloud of smoke that hung in the still air like talcum sifted through gauze. "I don't know what to tell you… because I don't see a problem or a question here. The scholarship offers you had are long dried up and you don't have a way of going to school this fall. This seems like a godsend. What am I missing?"

Glenn took a deep breath. "I don't know if I want to go to West Point. Or if I should. Getting turned down by Air Force really soured me on the idea of an academy – maybe on the whole idea of even going to college. I think I might just stay out of college for a year, get a job somewhere and see what the real world is like outside the damned military."

The older man grunted and stared silently across the river without replying.

"I can always apply to college for next year," Glenn said when the silence grew awkward. "So, what would you do?"

The elder Nolan looked sideways at his grandson for a long moment. "First, I'm not you. I'm not in your place now, never have been and won't ever be. So, I'm not going to tell you what you should do. I will tell you this, though – you sound like a man having himself a pity party." There was a long silence as Dave Nolan looked unwavering into his grandson's eyes. At last he said, "You didn't like that did you?"

"Not much, actually," Glenn said.

"Good! Life won't ever be as fair as you'd like it to be and the sooner you get over any idea that it is, the better off you'll be. Stop feeling sorry for yourself, son."

"You think that's what I'm doing?" Glenn asked, feeling his face flush hot.

"Yup, I do. I hear it in your voice and see it in your eyes. You've had a major setback after pretty easy sailing through a high school career. Your grades and SAT scores – excellent. You graduated something like sixty out of over four hundred in your class, played on two state champion football teams, and played varsity baseball team. Lettered three years in each and made all-state in football. You did pretty darned good, right?"

"All right, I guess."

"After your high school career and what you'd been told by your senator, you had every reason to believe you were going to the Air Academy. So, you got your heart set on Colorado Springs. There it is, right in your grasp and suddenly…"

"I lost it."

"Somebody took it from you. It's not a lot of fun having your heart set on something and having it suddenly snatched away, is it? Now you're being tried in the fire. Listen close. There's absolutely nothing wrong with not going to college. But you're gifted with more abilities than most. To whom much is given, much is required. When you get knocked down, get up and keep moving forward. Always forward. It may not be down the path you expected, but don't stop and don't go backward. Nobody ever got anywhere in life moving rearward. Leaders always move forward."

Glenn watched the older man silently check his fishing line and put another worm on his hook. After a long silence, he said, "You're right – I've been blessed with a lot of good luck."

"Nolan's rule number 1: never believe in luck – there is no such thing. Rule number 2: look for the real reason behind everything – nothing happens by chance." Dave held his grandson's gaze for a long while before saying, "I know you always wanted to be a fighter pilot like your dad, had your heart set on those sharp blue uniforms at that school in Colorado. But that's all superficial. The whole reason West Point exists is to develop officers in the combat arms for high level responsibility in times of national distress. People who can think on their feet and respond well under the pressure of combat. You have that. I've seen it."

"So you're saying I should take the appointment."

"I'm saying you should think it through before you make a final decision not to. I'm also saying young men don't always get to pick and choose their duties… or their obligations."

Dave Nolan took a deep breath and for a brief moment was lost in a memory.

It was July of 1918, the afternoon before the attack at the Ourcq River. He was sitting with his back to a tree writing a letter to Michelle Payne, the woman he was engaged to and would have married if the Army hadn't shipped him to the War in Europe – *Over There* – on such short notice. He'd been interrupted by one of his company commanders in the old Rainbow Division who requested to be relieved from his duty. *What was his name?... Mulcahy. Good man. Fine commander. Just a little overwhelmed. I told him 'life would be a lot easier for all of us if we got to choose our duties and obligations'. Same thing I'm telling my grandson now. Am I like MacArthur? – giving the same tired old speech over and over.*

"You don't have a lot of time to make up your mind. But there's a reason the one door closed and another one opened. I can't tell you what the reason is or what you should do about it. But I can tell you how you should make the decision. The first thing to do is crawl out from under the broom tree. The final decision is yours and whatever you decide will be supported by your family. Me included. But you're the one who has to make it and live with it." The elder Nolan went through the ceremony of relighting his pipe before continuing. "If you go to West Point and decide you really want to fly one of those jets, you can. Your dad retired from the Air Force so you can opt into the blue-suiters when you graduate – if that's what you really have your heart set on. That's an option most other fellas there won't have, but like I said, your hay to bale, not mine."

Glenn continued to look at his grandfather and then turned to look across the river. "Tell me, if you could live your life over, what would you change?"

"Not a single second or one choice I ever made," the elder Nolan said without hesitation.

"You'd still make the Army your life? After all the things the Army did to you?"

"Did to me, but also did for me. The finest people I ever met or worked beside were soldiers – of all ranks. Even the things that looked bad to others or even to me at the moment mostly turned out positive. My experience said that was common in the Army."

He remembered being relieved of command from his very first platoon by MacArthur – it had been devastating. But it had provided him a week alone with Senator Payne's daughter he'd never forget. He'd been brought up on court-martial charges in Germany during the Great War, and that too had ultimately worked to his advantage. Even the demotion back to major following the Lindbergh fiasco in '38 had forced him to change career courses, and from that had come financial security and civilian business experience leading to working for and with President Roosevelt, Bill Donovan, and others high up in the political and military leadership of the country before and during the War.

"There are a lot of things I wish hadn't happened – wars I wish hadn't come about, friends of mine who died young. The death of the son your dad and mom named you after. But I wouldn't change any of my own decisions. If I had changed one second, you and I may never have had this conversion." The older man paused with a distant look in his eyes, reflecting as he tapped the ash out of his pipe's bowl. "You think about that. But for now, stop by the house to see your grandmother. She was throwing together a farmer's casserole for your lunch when I left. I'll be along shortly after I make a phone call and stop at the hardware store for some copper pipe and solder flux."

Dave watched his grandson walk up the incline to the railroad tracks, and then he reeled in his line. He grabbed his small tackle box and walked slowly into town. At the entrance to the Hotel Doyle's bar, he set his fishing gear down and waggled a finger at his dark yellow Lab before going inside and making a call from the pay phone; when the call was answered, he said, "Earl, this is Dave Nolan up in Duncannon."

"Yes, sir, general. What can I do for you?"

"First thing you can do is to call me Dave, like I told you more than once."

"No, sir, can't do that. You'll always be The General to me."

"We'll have to work on that, but for now, I need for you to do me a favor."

"Anything you want, sir. I'll do my best."

"You told me you were going back to Normandy a couple of weeks from now for the twentieth year D-Day reunion of your old buddies from the 82nd Airborne. That still on?"

"Yes, sir. Ruth and I are already packed and ready. What can I do for you?"

"My son is taking his family to England to visit his wife's folks that same couple of weeks and I'd like to have you show them around Sainte-Mère-Église – tell them about Glenn the way you did for me and Denise when you stopped by the farm. I'll work it out with my son, Mitch, if you can do it. His oldest boy is named Glenn, after his brother. Neither my son nor my grandson know the story you know. I'd appreciate your telling them."

"Sir, I can do it. Tell me where and when to meet 'em, and I'll do my level best."

"You always have, Earl... Thanks."

*   *   *

Denise Nolan waved at the little green sports car as it turned out of the circular drive in front of the farm house, pulling a long plume of dust the color of woodstove ash as it headed down the gravel drive that ran alongside the new stock pond. When it turned onto the farm road leading south toward Harrisburg, she walked over to the porch swing and sat down next to her husband.

"I'm glad he came by. Every time I see that boy he's two inches taller." She wrapped her arm under Dave's and placed her head on his shoulder. "And he eats like a horse. Our Glenn was always a finicky eater."

"That boy's just a typical teenager."

"So was *our* Glenn."

It had been two decades since the two bereavement representatives – an Army captain and a senior sergeant – had shown up at the door of her Washington town house with the sad news about Glenn, her paratrooper son who had enlisted against her will and without her knowledge. He'd left for Europe just after Christmas 1943 and been killed in a little French town she'd never heard of until then; and, like her grandson, he wasn't yet eighteen years old. The Army's bearers of the bad news had brought with them a form letter, a citation and a medal, none of which comforted her. It was two and a half years later when a skinny young man showed up at her door to give meaning to the three keepsakes.

His name was Earl Wright, and he had parachuted into Sainte-Mère-Église with their son. He told them about his last hours and filled in all the details about the meaning behind the Distinguished Service Cross and the citation accompanying it. Until that day, she was certain her remaining time would be spent wondering what had *really* happened, but the visit had given her a peace she had until then thought certain would always evade her. She'd not seen or spoken to Wright again, and hadn't had the chance to thank him properly for the comfort he'd given her.

"I've always been glad Mitch named his first son after his little brother," Dave said, patting her hand and leaning his head toward her. "They're a lot alike. I can see this boy ending up a hunting or fishing guide."

"Not a soldier? Aynslee says he's been offered a qualified alternate appointment to West Point. Isn't that how you got in?"

"Not exactly, but similar. I received a Presidential appointment engineered by Michelle Payne's father way back when he was running for re-election at the end of his second term in our Keystone State. There are still some given each year. Qualified alternates are something new with this year's entering class. It's a bunch of extra appointments above and beyond the normal congressional allocation. About seventy nationwide, from what I've heard."

She looked at him sideways with hooded eyes. "Nolan, you continue to surprise me after all these years with your kitbag-full of odd knowledge."

"Keep 'em guessing… the secret to a long marriage." She poked him softly in the ribs and asked him to explain. "Well, to make a long story practically endless…" They rocked slowly for a while, and finally he said, "I called Cateline back while I was in town. She's compiling a dossier on Harrison Reeves and wants access to my personal papers, especially my journal."

Denise sat up and looked across the cornfield south of the house and beyond that, Cove Mountain. "I'm glad somebody is doing something about holding that man to account."

He knew what she was thinking. Reeves had been instrumental in covering up their underage son's enlistment during the War and then got him assigned to the 82nd Airborne as a paratrooper just in time for D-Day. Denise had never forgiven his classmate for the duplicity, and had pressed him for years to do something – *anything*. But he knew that their son would have found some way to get into the war, as difficult as that was to reconcile with the quiet, introspective boy they'd thought they had raised. Pearl Harbor had changed him as much as it had changed the country. What she didn't know was Reeves' part in getting their other son, Mitch, assigned to a mission even before the war began that Hap Arnold had deemed "suicide". Lord Beaverbrook had hatched a scheme to ferry planes from America to Britain in the winter of 1940, a feat never before considered much less attempted. Somehow it worked and it was one of Mitch's favorite episodes in a brilliant aviation career spanning two wars and now found him in senior management with Martin Aircraft in Baltimore.

"I never understood how you could forgive him for everything he did you – to our family," Denise said, looking at him as puzzled as she was angry.

"I didn't at first, but that changed. It wasn't easy but I had to. If I had continued to harbor that bitterness, he would have gotten exactly what he wanted – I would have be a slave to resentment... in essence a slave to him. That's what he wanted all along. In the end, Harrison lost everything of any value and I gained peace of mind. I'm not sorry for that."

Reeves' ex-wife, Michelle Payne, had told him everything after he'd come back at the end of the Second war. It was, she'd said that day on the porch of her house at Eton's Neck Point, a time for the two of them to finally have some sense of closure. And so, she'd told him everything she'd wanted to say all those years since the time in 1917 when they had been together at that little beach house on Long Island Sound the week before he'd gone off to France during the first war.

"He didn't lose everything," Denise was saying. "He's still a U.S. Senator with all the publicity and power he ever wanted."

"Harrison doesn't have a thing worth having. We do – family, friends. A clear conscience. I'm a very happy man with the way things turned out."

"But there's something still troubling you."

He took a deep breath. "I'm worried about what's going on in Washington."

"What brought that up?"

"This conversation with our grandson today. I wanted to stay neutral with him about his going to the academy, but I probably tipped him toward going there. Not sure that I'd advise anyone in that direction just now. That surprises you, I know. But I don't trust Johnson. Not sure that I trusted his predecessor all that much after I was asked by Max Taylor to sit in on a study about the Bay of Pigs. I think Kennedy may have set us up to do something ill-advised in Southeast Asia. And I'm worried Johnson is going to get us even further committed."

"Vietnam?"

Dave nodded slowly. "Ike sent about seven hundred advisors there in the late '50s and Kennedy upped the ante. We now have five times that many so-called advisors. What I hear is that Johnson is leaning toward more. Worst case scenario is that we get involved directly. Guys like our grandson – especially guys from the Academy are going to be in a shooting war soon. I'm worried for him, for all of them. I'd hate to see them go off to something like that."

Denise rested her head on his chest, looking into his eyes. "You're a good man, Nolan."

"And you're still the loveliest nurse this doughboy ever had." He pulled her close and kissed her, then whispered in her ear. "Every soldier should be lucky enough to fall in love with a pretty nurse like I did."

Chapter 3

Lyndon Johnson was a man of restless ambition who possessed spectacular drive. His appetite for achievement and recognition had never been tempered by humility. Many said he was the most masterful legislator ever seen in Congress and his skill in crafting deals was legendary, even among his opposition, but he was equally haunted by incredible insecurity.

There was something fascinating about the Texan: it seemed the more he tried to hide his flaws – and they were many – the more he revealed them. Johnson had always been a living, breathing contradiction. Bigger than life and confidant he could talk his way out of anything, but he could also be petty. By the time he assumed the presidency following Kennedy's assassination, the country had become so large and powerful, and so diffuse and discordant that only a man of his towering strengths and energies could harness America's potential.

Or so he'd convinced himself.

His energies, when properly channeled, were marvelous to behold. But given his drives, his ambitious instincts, it was disastrous when he harnessed himself to the wrong policies. He was not a man given to much, if any, reflection and surrounded himself with few contemplative men. He preferred advisors who said 'yes! it can be done', and who would do it, whether it was passing a budget, building a dam, negotiating a bill, writing the speech or winning a war.

Johnson was uncomfortable with abstract loyalty. Loyalty to a concept or a cause or an issue might, he thought, lead one to casual rebellion, and might mean a man was caught between loyalty to *original intent Constitutionalism,* for example, and *devotion to Lyndon Johnson.* Loyalty was absolutely essential, and that was one of the many reasons he was never at ease with the American military, like his young Massachusetts predecessor but for different reasons. Career military loyalty was very distinctive – first to uniform, followed close quarter to branch of service, and only then to civilians, in a subordinate way it seemed to him. But to Lyndon Johnson loyalty was crucial because Washington was, after all, a city with enemies everywhere. Thus his inner circle had to be secure. Lyndon Johnson demanded men around him he could trust. Robert McNamara, former Ford Motor Company CEO and Secretary of Defense, was thus the perfect underling and confidant.

And so was Walter Jenkins – a fellow Texan and Johnson's political advisor.

Jenkins was more Johnson's friend than employee; he was very close to Lady Bird and involved in the Johnson family finances as well. The Johnsons had celebrated the First Lady's fifty-first birthday at a party at Jenkins' home and the President was not shy about telling people that nobody other than his wife was more responsible for his success than Walt Jenkins.

"Mr. President, the latest set of polls show a shift away from Goldwater and toward you on national defense. Our strategy of painting him as something of a fanatic, a loose cannon with an unstable finger on the nuclear button is beginning to take hold." Johnson had never put much stock in political polls, at least not for determining what path or position he should take. It was like trying to find out where the parade of public opinion was going and getting in front of it. He preferred to bend public opinion to follow him instead of the other way around. "But rhetoric alone won't entirely do the job. We need a clear demonstration that you and our administration are just as committed to national defense and opposing Communist expansion as the senator from Arizona, only without the bombast and recklessness."

LBJ leaned back in his chair and read the summary. This was the best news yet. *If the party ever canonizes political aides*, the president thought, *Walt will be the first one. This son-of-a-bitch really knows how to navigate the shark-infested waters of the Potomac.*

"A demonstration, Walt?"

"Yes, Mr. President," Jenkins replied, watching the president's craggy face as the wheels turned inside his mind. "It wouldn't have to be something big – a small incident involving your standing up to the communists somewhere. Anywhere would do. We don't need a Berlin Airlift; in fact, the smaller the better I would think. We don't want to take away the spotlight from your domestic priorities, just give the public confidence in your decisiveness in foreign affairs without a wholesale shift in our successful strategy thus far."

The President thought for a few more seconds, reminded of a small scrap of information about a Vietnamese navy operation that was actually being funded, and operationally directed by U.S. military personnel in Saigon. A-34 it was called. That might be the ticket. He'd get Bundy and Bob McNamara on it. Bob was a man of both guile and force, pushing, moving, getting things done; he was a 'can-do' man in a 'can-do' Democratic administration.

Now he'd be useful in a 'can-do' campaign to give Lyndon Johnson his own elected term as president.

"All right, Walt, let me think on that," the President said, already knowing what he was going to do. "Got anything else for me?"

"Just one other thing, Mr. President. We've got to start thinking about your running mate for the November election and quietly begin the vetting process so we don't run up against a stone wall at the convention. We want it to be an afterthought. All peace and harmony."

Johnson nodded. "Work with the boys over at the national committee and give me some recommendations, and I'll think on that, too."

Jenkins cleared his throat nervously. "Bobby Kennedy has already begun lobbying the DNC for the VP slot on the ticket."

"That little peckerwood?!" Johnson roared, but his eyes lit up with execrable amusement. "After spending the last four years treatin' me like a red-headed stepchild with his whole damned Ivy League crowd?! That boy's nuttier than a squirrel turd if he thinks he's gonna be *my* vice president. Walt, you tryin' to make me laugh or ruin my day?"

"Just informing you of a situation, sir."

"Then let me inform you of this. That boy may think he's slicker than snot on a doorknob but one of these days I'm gonna make him kiss my ass on New Year's Eve in Times Square and tell the world it smells like roses. Now you figger how to say that in a way it gets my point across to him and the national committee and makes 'em like it. That's your job, Walt. Don't let me down."

*　　*　　*　　*

"It's horrible… and it's utterly magnificent," Aynslee Nolan said, looking over the vast field of white crosses and stars of David in perfect symmetry that dotted the massive emerald green lawn of the American graveyard on a bluff overlooking Omaha Beach and the English Channel. "I'm glad we came. I hadn't wanted to, but now I'm grateful we did."

Mitch nodded agreement, close-lipped and without taking his eyes off the white cross.

GLENN C. NOLAN
505 PRCHT INF 82 ABN DIV
MARYLAND JUNE 6 1944

"Shoulda had a Medal of Honor citation carved on there, too," a soft voice behind them said. The family turned and gazed at the short, wiry man and the woman clutching his arm. Long seconds of silence ensued until at last the man said, "He was a buddy of mine. We were in the same squad and jumped out of the same plane that night. I was probably the last person he saw this side of Glory when he was killed late that first afternoon… I'm Earl Wright and this is my wife, Ruth."

Glenn had noticed the middle aged couple standing not far away when they entered the American cemetery at the Normandy graveyard and found his uncle's grave marker.

Mitch Nolan searched his memory and said, "I remember you. We met briefly at the airfield, on the runway, an hour or so before my brother's flight took off."

"Yes, sir, that's right. At Cottsmore. I remember you, too. But I think that was the second time we met, sir. I seem to recall you visited Glenn twice up there. The second time was the evening before we jumped in. Your father was there that night, too."

Mitch thought about it briefly. "You're right. On both counts. Years ago my dad told me you stopped by his farm to see him and my mother. Both of them appreciated it greatly."

Earl looked at Aynslee, furrowed his brow and finally said, "You were the general's driver, weren't you?"

"I was, Mr. Wright. It was my privilege to do so on two occasions separated by four years." She smiled and stuck out her hand first to Ruth and then her husband. "Aynslee Nolan, the general's daughter-in-law and these are our children – Cateline, Glenn, Bradyn and Maisie. We're pleased to meet you both."

"Dad's going to be sorry he missed you, Earl. I wish he'd come with us."

"Well, colonel, he's the reason I came by to meet up with you. We talked a week back. He gave me your schedule and asked me to look you up. The general wanted me to walk you through Sainte-Mère-Église and tell you exactly what happened that day with your brother. If you like, I'm sure I can although some of the town must have changed. This is my first time back." Wright looked at the Nolan kids and fixed his gaze on Glenn. "Wish you'd known your uncle. He was real special."

It was mid-morning when they arrived on the outskirts of the small French town in the large, chauffeur-driven van. They entered the town from the south road and Earl grew silent as he took in the sites and remembered the sounds now two decades old. In the middle of town they turned west and stopped a half mile later.

"This is the field where we landed in the dark that morning; it was a little before three a.m. We rallied up in the southeast corner there and moved out as soon as we had better than fifty percent accounted for. Our platoon led out and Glenn was the point man – point man for the battalion. So you could say he was the first man into the first town liberated on D-Day. That's what Colonel Cannonball said anyway."

"Colonel Cannonball?" Glenn asked.

"He was our battalion commander. Cocky s.o.b. Had a bad temper and was always runnin' his mouth over something. He busted me back to private E-2 three times while he commanded the battalion. One time down in Salerno, he busted me and put me in the stockade as the guard. It was just a corral, that's all. Told me that if anybody escaped I'd have to serve out the fella's time, and there were a dozen of 'em. I told those boys I was an expert shot with the M-1, which I was, and had no intention of serving their time, so if anyone tried to escape I'd shoot to kill."

"Did anyone try to escape?" Brad asked eagerly.

"Let's say I never served any time over it. Anyhow, we moved into the town here and we cleaned it of Germans right quick. They were concentrating on a big fire that broke out, and then on the guys from F Company that got dropped right into the middle of the town about the same time. Your uncle Glenn and me and a buddy of ours named Kenny Cook ran off the machine gun crew and a bunch of others and the rest of 'em took off not long after." Wright paused and looked up at the sky and then around the field. From where they stood they could see the spire of the church. "This is where our day began, and I remember that dirt road between those two hedgerows. That's where Glenn led us down into the town. I'll show you the town square and then where our day ended. It's close to the road where we came in. What say we walk down that little trail? It's not terrible far."

On the edge of the town square they saw the church, adorned with a dummy dressed in jumper fatigues hung up by his parachute on the steeple. Earl explained that wasn't exactly how it happened but was close enough. They walked around the town square, went inside the church and then bought some souvenirs and picture postcards at one of the stores. Earl showed them the old flagpole where Colonel Krause had raised his tattered American flag that morning. "Glenn was on a detail to pick up ammo resupply at first light and the colonel shanghaied him to help raise it. Then he gave him the Nazi flag that had been flying there for four years since he was the first man into the town. Wish I had that flag to give to you now, but don't know whatever came of it."

A half hour later they stood beside the N13 road on the south side of Sainte-Mère-Église.

"This is where we set up just before sunup that morning. That little ridge is two hundred yards away and once it got light enough to see, Glenn decided to go tell the company commander he'd put us in a bad place – that we needed to move back or better still, go forward to the rise so we had a better field of fire. I don't think the captain liked that much, coming from a buck private but he told Glenn if he wanted he could go scout it out on his own and report back. And darned if he didn't do it.

"He was gone about an hour and the next thing we hear a lot of shooting from just over the ridge. Soon enough, Glenn comes runnin' down the road pursued by half the damn German Army. We learned later he'd slowed down and just about stopped a battalion of German infantry supported by a panzer company. That gave us time to get a 57 mm anti-tank gun set up and ready for a fight, but a German machine gun – or maybe it was a tank shell – killed the AT gun crew. Glenn ran over and got the gun working on his own and knocked out the lead tank before another tank finally got our gun. Somehow he survived and the Germans turned back."

"My little brother did all that?" Mitch asked. "He was always the quietest, most easy-going of all us kids. Growing up, I don't think I ever saw him get into a fist fight, or even a shouting match."

"Oh, he was a hell of a fighter, colonel. He became the regimental middleweight boxing champ after knocking out a guy who wouldn't let up on him when he first got to the division in Ireland. I wouldn't mess with him. Don't know anybody who did after that. But you know what? – he was just a kid, like the rest of us – doing what he had to do. None of us were really soldiers… and yet, all of us were."

They walked the two hundred yards up the small rise and stopped at the top, looking out over a mostly open landscape of trees and fences and several houses.

"Twenty years ago, there weren't any of these houses here. It was all open fields. This is where we set up after Glenn did his recon. To the north, the east and south we found dead Germans. That was what he was doing on his patrol. I told the captain later that afternoon I was glad this Nolan kid was on our side, and the CO agreed." Wright looked around, walked a few paces down the road and stopped. "He should have gotten the Medal, the big one. We all thought that, and I still do. And he might have if the captain hadn't been killed a week later, and if the citation hadn't been written up by some clerk in England who hadn't even made the jump with us. But, you know, that's the way life is sometimes. But he stepped up when he needed to, and he did what had to be done, because, by damn, somebody had to." Wright wiped his eyes, then took out his handkerchief and blew his nose.

After looking around from the small rise, Mitch asked, "So, how did he die?"

Earl looked down and slowly shook his head. "Colonel, don't think I care to dwell on that. I had a lot of friends, including your brother, that I watched die. I care more about remembering how they lived. I think you should, too. We pass, some sooner than others, and I come to realize it's more important how a person lives than how he dies. Your brother lived less than eighteen years and he lived a full life and he saved the lives of a lot of men; some of them and their kin realize that and some don't. The important thing is that when he was called on he did his duty. That's the most important thing a man can do… Sad to say, there's lots of people who will never understand that and because of it, never have the privilege of living it. Your brother Glenn did. I think that's the most important thing to remember about him." Wright took a deep breath and let it out, then shook his head and slowly walked down the small rise toward the town with his arm around his wife.

Glenn watched the middle aged man and thought about everything he'd seen and heard. Looking around from the small knob he sensed this was somehow sacred ground. It all seemed to make sense now – his father bringing the family to Normandy after two decades; his grandfather not telling him what decision to make but how to make it; this old man showing up precisely twenty years after perhaps the pivotal moment in the American century, and as well his own desires for the Air Force getting unexpectedly shot down in flames.

"Dad," he said to Mitch, "we need to get back to the hotel. I have to call Colonel Webb."

*　　*　　*

"Brandon! What the hell is this?!" Senator Reeves stood in the doorway of his Chief of Staff's office waving a sheet of paper, his face crimson.

Oakes was caught by surprise at the outburst and quickly covered the phone's mouthpiece and mouthed: *give me one second*, then returned to his caller. "Sure Walt, I'll run that by the senator and I'll get back to you in an hour, two at the most. Fine. That'll work out just fine. Call you back soon."

Reeves was still fuming when his Chief of Staff hung up the phone.

"Senator, before we do anything else, let me tell you who that was and what he wanted. This should go right to the top of your list... That was Walt Jenkins at the White House. He's working with the re-election committee and DNC on the short list names for the President's running mate in November. Yours is one of four names on the list, and the President wants to know if you're interested enough to stop by the Oval Office this afternoon and begin the vetting process."

For the first time in his life, Harrison Reeves was at a loss for words. *Vice President,* he thought, quickly warming to the idea... *of the United States of America. I wish the old man was still alive so I could rub his nose in this.* Quickly, his mind began to process the possibilities – national attention, president of the Senate, point man for an aggressive domestic agenda the Texan had in mind, a running start for his own Oval Office bid down the road. Some might say he was too old to be thinking of occupying the White House himself, but he was in excellent physical shape even for a man half his age, had several journalists on a short leash – one at ABC, another at NBC, and a few in print media on both coasts. He'd be sure to let that slip with Johnson in their conversations so that the crusty old warhorse knew how valuable he would be in shaping media coverage during the election and afterward.

"I told Walt I'd get back to him in an hour," Oakes said, intruding on his thoughts.

"I heard. Tell him I'd be glad to talk with the President. We'll see where that leads."

"Sir, nobody in his right mind turns down the President of the United States for something like that. It would be the capstone to a brilliant career."

"Capstone, my ass, Brandon. More like a stepping stone." Reeves smiled again, his thoughts running on and spilling over one another like mountain stream water rushing and roiling around smooth rocks. At last he looked at the crumpled sheet in his hand and held it up. "What about this thing that just hit my desk. It says here that I appointed that damned Nolan kid to West Point. I already disqualified that little son-of-a-bitch for the Air Force Academy, and now I'm supposed to sign off appointing him to that school on the Hudson? How in hell did this happen?!"

"It's just a formality, sir. The academy up there gave out five or six dozen appointments they call 'qualified alternates' nationwide and their director of admissions just assigned them to one of the Congressmen in the individual's home state. That's all. It was a random choice by some clerk, I guess. I thought you'd welcome getting another appointment – it'll look good in a press release."

"No press release, damn it," Reeves fumed. "No pictures. Nothing. You get West Point to rescind this. Oakes, you're going to need to step up your game when you're working for the Vice President of these United States."

Chapter 4

Wednesday - July 1, 1964

It sounded – and looked – like unbridled chaos.

Glenn's first notion as he peered through the shade of the granite sally port into the open rectangle of West Point's Central Area was that someone had unlocked the gates of an insane asylum and let the inmates loose. On further reflection, he grimaced and thought: *oh damn, this is going to be a bigger pain in the ass than you expected...*

He'd just completed an hour-long process in which he had received a battery of shots, been divested of all the civilian gear in his possession except for a small hand-carried bag containing his shaving kit, wallet, tooth brush and a couple of candy bars sneaked in when the young Army captain wasn't looking. They clothed him in a pair of gray gym shorts, a white T-shirt, black plain-toe dress shoes, and encumbered him with a heavy duffel bag stuffed with an assortment of military equipment and uniforms necessary to get him through the first few days of Beast Barracks. After interminable standing in line in the big, open gymnasium and being warned more than once not to talk or look around, a cadet with a clipboard called out about a dozen names, put them in single file and walked them through an area ringed with four-story granite barracks.

Now, he stood looking at pandemonium only a few yards away, watching guys dressed as he was running here and there, or standing at attention being loudly yelled at by other young men in gray trousers, white shirts with gray epaulets and white hats sporting highly polished black patent leather visors pulled low over their noses. The sound was like the roar of the ocean crashing ashore, only louder.

Glenn guessed his dad and his grandfather were at this moment at home, chuckling.

"DROP THOSE BAGS, MISTER, YOU DROP 'EM, YOU HEAR ME, MISTER? DROP 'EM WHEN I TELL YOU TO!"

The voice had a coarse, artificial edge to it, but not so fake that it wasn't just a little unnerving, though his father and Colonel Webb had prepared him for this moment.

He had jogged across the concrete expanse of the Central Area of barracks beneath the harsh summer sun, reported to 'the man in the red sash' as the cadet in charge of his group had told him, and now was being indoctrinated with a ritual he guessed as old as the school itself.

"PICK 'EM UP! PICK UP THOSE BAGS!" The words were not yelled so much as angrily chewed off and spit out. "DROP 'EM!... PICK 'EM UP... DROP 'EM... PICK 'EM UP! DROP 'EM... DID I TELL YOU TO PICK 'EM UP, DUMBGUARD? Glenn looked into the eyes of the cadet leaning forward only inches from his face.

This really is going to be a monumental pain in the ass.

This guy was yelling at the top of his lungs, and he was taking this silliness of dropping bags and picking them up seriously! Glenn involuntarily leaned back as the cadet pressed forward until with elbows locked, pelvis shoved forward, and chin back trying to avoid the cadet's face, he was contorted into some crazy-looking human question mark.

"WHAT'S YOUR NAME?"

"My name's Glenn."

"YOU HAVE A LOT TO LEARN MR. GLENN AND YOUR FIRST LESSON IS RIGHT NOW!" the cadet yelled at the top of his voice, his face only an inch away,

"That's my first name, not my last –"

"DID I SAY YOU COULD TALK?... I HAVE HALF A MIND TO RUN YOUR SORRY ASS RIGHT OFF THIS POST RIGHT NOW! YOU UNDERSTAND?!"

"Yes, sir."

"LOUDER!"

"YESSIR!"

"That's better, Mr. Glenn... I'm here to teach you two things. Two simple things. The position of attention for New Cadets, which you will adopt as your very own way of life. And your three answers."

The cadet looked at his clipboard and then up again. "I don't see any New Cadet Glenn on my roster. What's your real name."

"Sir, my name is Nolan. Glenn Nolan."

"Why didn't you say that when I asked you your name?!"

Glenn got the idea of what was going on and replied, "No excuse, sir,"

"Damn right, there's not!" The cadet again looked at the list on his clipboard and said, "Room 312, New Cadet Nolan. Drop your bags in there and report back here in twenty seconds. YOU GOT THAT, MISTER?... POST!"

On the way up the three flights of stairs, he was accosted and yelled at by a half dozen more cadets, braced against the wall, threatened with all manner of punishment for looking around, smirking, slouching and a score of other imagined infractions. Finally he located the room, saw his name tag and that of another new arrival in the slots on the door frame, and at last found refuge in a small room with two utilitarian beds and a small sink. When he entered, another new arrival in tee shirt and gray shorts gave him a 'deer in the headlights' look.

Glenn quickly closed the door and took a deep breath. Offering his hand, he said, "I'm Glenn Nolan. I guess we're roommates."

"Benny Barnes. From South Carolina. Beaufort."

"Baltimore. The last four years or so."

Barnes was inches shorter than Glenn, but stockier; a good looking guy with a square jaw and broad shoulders and now a look of bewilderment on his face. "What the hell's goin' on out there?" he asked in a nasal southern twang.

"Typical military BS." Glenn replied dropping his bags on the empty, unmade bed. "They're trying to weed out guys who can't take a little bit of harassment. That jerk in the red sash already threatened to run me down the road. That's just part of the drill. Hopefully they'll get tired of it in a couple of days. Don't let it bother you. Your nametag on the door says: *Barnes, B.S.* so you probably know all about bullshit," Glenn offered off-handedly, smiling. "B.S. Barnes – your momma must not have liked you very much when you were born."

Barnes yelled an epithet and threw a punch that connected with Glenn's jaw, knocking him backward onto the bed; immediately Barnes was on top of him throwing another roundhouse right hand. Glenn pushed the smaller man back, hit him with a glancing blow and then grabbed him in a head lock. Barnes was surprisingly strong and they stumbled across the room and into the closet doors, grappling briefly.

Suddenly the door was violently flung open. "What's going on in here?!" An upperclassman in a white shirt with light blue crests on both his epaulets stood in the doorway with his hands on his hips, glaring at them. Nolan and Barnes quickly came to attention. "I asked you two a question! What the hell's going on here?"

"Getting acquainted with my new roommate, sir," Glenn said quickly.

The upperclassman continued to glare at them. "Just getting acquainted? Looks like more than that. What's your name?"

"Nolan, sir."

"That's New Cadet Nolan, mister. And don't your forget it. I'm Mister Gundry, your squad leader for First Beast, and you're already on my excremental list, New Cadet Nolan. This is gonna be the longest four weeks in your sorry life, mister. You two dump that gear on your bunks and get back outside and report to the man in the red sash!" The door slammed shut behind him.

"We'll finish this later, Nolan," Barnes said, as they each dumped out the contents of their barracks bags.

The next hour became a jumbled kaleidoscope of sights and sounds and orders and counter orders sending them to one place after another to pick up additional personal gear, sign various documents, be issued the M-14 rifle, be measured and fitted with various pieces of apparel. Halfway through the frenzied, turbulent morning, Glenn caught Benny Barnes entering the barracks as he was leaving. Grabbing him by the arm, he nodded toward the stairway leading to the basement where the latrines and showers were located.

Inside the bathroom, Barnes turned to confront him. "You want to deal with this now?"

"Bad news doesn't get better with age…" Even in the stillness of the basement they could hear the dull roar of shouting from outside. "Listen Barnes, I didn't mean anything by that comment earlier. I apologize. But that wasn't why I steered you down here. I wanted to tell you to slow down and cool it. You're running around like a chicken with your head cut off. Those upperclassmen on the detail will run your ass ragged if you let them. But here's the deal…. they don't know who you are or where they sent you or when to expect you back from the last time they sent you off somewhere. Soon enough they'll begin to recognize us and take control, but right now they're just trying to scare the hell out of us. Take my advice, just relax a little and cool it."

Barnes stared at him for several seconds, until a voice came from inside the last stall.

"You'd be wise to take his advice, friend." A lanky young man with a long, thin nose, sun-bleached hair and a reddish tan that made his freckles stand out opened the stall door and beckoned them inside. He sat with his back to the wall and leisurely took a drag on a cigarette. Blowing a smoke ring and looking at Glenn he asked, "Your daddy in the Army?"

"Air Force," Glenn replied.

"Yup. Had to be something like that. My dad's a two star in the Army and I've seen this kind of crap my whole life. My ol' man used to wake me up every morning at six sharp by ripping the covers off me and yelling 'up and at 'em soldier'. That sorry son-of-a-bitch. The only reason I'm here is to get as far away from him as I can." He looked at Barnes. "You need to learn how to slip and slide like your friend here is telling you."

"I know how to handle myself. I can deal with this."

"Well, that's just bitchin' my man," the cigarette smoker said with a smile. He reached under his tee shirt and produced a pack of cigarettes. "You guys want one? I'm guessing these will have to last me three weeks, but I don't mind sharing. I'm Hughie Wharton. You in 7th Company, too?"

Glenn nodded.

"Didn't I see you last night in that bar just outside the gate?"

"I was there for a couple of hours with some friends from back home I went through high school with. Four of us rode up with one of the guys' dads and tried to enjoy our last few hours of freedom over several pitchers of beer. You too?"

"Yup. Got the headache to prove it. Right now I'd rather be on the beach at Santa Barbara catchin' a wave and chasin' surf bunnies. But my old man is at the Presidio and I need to be on the opposite coast." Wharton blew another smoke ring. "Where you boys from?"

"Beaufort, South Carolina," Barnes replied, looking worried.

"Baltimore."

"Fort Meade?"

"No. The city itself. My dad retired from the Air Force after twenty years and went to work at Martin Marietta as some kind of manager. He's leaving there at the end of the summer and moving to St. Louis with McDonnell to head up flight testing of a new fighter and sales to the Air Force. In the next few months I guess I'll have to claim Missouri."

"Yup. The life of a brat. Well, friends, be cool – this is gonna be one long, unhappy summer," Wharton mused. "I got to go get a haircut. That red sash guy sent me to the barber shop twenty minutes ago so I guess I need to get goin'. You two want to come along? You can kill time over there as easy as here and the chairs are comfortable. Just keep letting these other guys go ahead of you and you might be able to hide out until lunch time." Standing and casually tossing his cigarette butt into the commode, he looked at his watch and said, "See you boys in the funny papers... *he-hee*."

*   *   *

Erika Ashby made a final note and looked up at the distinguished, perfectly coiffed older man across the table from her in the District of Washington Prosecutors' conference room. He looked stern and disgruntled as he examined her with his slate gray eyes in a way that made her acutely uncomfortable. Rupert Whitcomb had been around the District Prosecutor's office since before Truman became president and was now, as the head prosecutor, its most powerful man. He was also Erika's boss's boss.

She took a deep breath, and said, "I know you have some reservations about this investigation, but I believe it has merit."

"I see," Whitcomb responded. "Let's take a look at what you've got. I understand from Hartman it centers around Trevor Callahan. Tell me why, and lay out your theory of the case."

"Let's begin with Callahan. Basically, he's corrupted the legislative process and is perhaps the most effective vote buyer in the lobbying ranks – and has been for a decade. He's one of the most well-known men on Capitol Hill. He served three consecutive terms as U.S. Representative from Maryland's 4th Congressional District in the forties and early fifties beginning during the Second World War and culminating just prior to the cessation of hostilities in Korea. It has long been rumored that he coveted one of the two senatorial seats from Maryland, but instead left government service and branched out into lobbying Congress just as that enterprise was becoming enormously profitable in the economic post war boom of the fifties. The perversion of the practice in the following decade, and Callahan's participation in the corruption of it is at the center of the case. Everything about him looks and smells like bribery. He and his ilk are a cancer on our government."

Whitcomb smiled paternally and withdrew a cigarette from a silver case and lit it. "I know his background well. And I agree lobbyists are growing bolder and more destructive. This office has taken more than one run at him with, unfortunately, little to show for its efforts. What makes your investigation more likely to succeed?"

"The number of Congressmen co-opted and the trail of evidence leading from Callahan to many of them."

"Give me your best shot, Erika. Your most damning evidence against Mr. Callahan."

"The *Rochade Elegante*."

Whitcomb frowned. "And that is what?"

"A lovely, expensive boat. Market value about three million four hundred thousand when it was built three years ago. Crew of seven; sleeps ten in five cabins. It's registered in Connecticut but tied up in Washington."

"A yacht."

"Yes, sir. A very expensive yacht put at the beck and call of Congressmen in return for voting along the lines favorable to Callahan's clients."

Whitcomb frowned – a look bordering on disapproval. "That's a very strong and far-reaching accusation, counselor. I hope you can back that up."

"I believe the facts will confirm what I just said," Erika replied looking directly into the senior prosecutor's eyes. "And it's not simply my interpretation of the facts, but also that of a previous prosecutor whose case notes also support my conclusion."

"Ah, Anderson's files," Whitcomb replied, squinting and looking off into the distance. "I remember he went down the same, or a very similar trail, until the evidence ran out."

"Yes, sir. But some further evidence has come to light and I think it's worth reopening the line of investigation once again." Erika watched the elder prosecutor's face closely. *I wonder if it was the case that the evidence ran out or that someone got him promoted out of the office so that he couldn't follow it any longer.*

"This yacht," Whitcomb was saying, "it's the first I've heard of it. Tell me more."

"Well, sir, from what I've been able to find out so far, it's a very thinly veiled 'business venture' of one of the corporations Callahan represents." Erika pushed a sheet of paper across the table. "A very exclusive and limited clientele – a half dozen U.S. Representatives and four Senators. Callahan's yacht broker charges them a pittance, claiming its part of the corporation's marketing plan to attract a broader following and expand operations."

"How much?"

"A hundred dollars a day, fully found including fuel and crew. That's certainly a pittance for a vessel with an approximate thirty-eight hundred a day operating expense when underway. They claim to charge each 'customer' a maintenance fee, but it only amounts to twenty-five dollars a trip, regardless of duration."

Whitcomb cleared his throat. "They could say that's aggressive marketing."

"I don't think that passes the 'ha-ha' test, sir."

"Perhaps. Perhaps not. I would guess that neither of us has much experience brokering yachts. Before we hang too much on that peg, you'll need to do some further investigating."

"Certainly, sir."

"Go on."

"In addition to Anderson's documentation about congressional trips Callahan has provided to Caribbean hotspots for no discernible business purpose, he was also following several leads about violation of both the Tillman and the Taft-Hartley Acts."

Whitcomb frowned again, appearing deep in thought. "My memory of where Anderson was on his investigation at the time of his promotion to the Columbus office, tells me that he had some, but not many, conclusive findings on any of the Tillman or Taft-Hartley violations. More accurately, I should I say alleged violations. And I think he had been working on them for some time. Anderson was an excellent prosecutor and I remember the management of the DC office coming to the conclusion that if Anderson was unable to finalize any formal charges that there probably wasn't anything there."

"Sir, is it possible that Anderson just didn't have enough time to pull everything together?" she asked hesitantly.

"What exactly are you suggesting, Erika? I'd be careful implying that political pressures might have influenced this office."

"No, sir, I'm not inferring that at all. It's just that workloads don't usually coincide well with available time in a Prosecutor's office. There's never enough time, and we all leave loose ends when we move on; I left several important investigations half-done when I departed my office in Baltimore to come here. I hope they were picked up and kept alive by the person who filled my slot, but I'm sure some of them never got touched."

"We like to think that doesn't happen here, but the truth is that it does from time to time." Whitcomb stubbed out his cigarette and immediately lit another. "You said there were a half-dozen U.S. Representatives and about an equal number of senators connected with Callahan's yacht brokering? Do you have the list there?" Erika slid another piece of paper across the conference table and watched the senior prosecutor as he read the names. At last he said, "Some heavy hitters here. If we do follow this line of inquiry you're suggesting, we'll have to be absolutely sure of our case before making any moves. No fishing expeditions, Erika. No Perry Mason theatrics. That only works on television. I would expect to be kept informed all along the way."

"Of course, sir. I understand, and I agree completely. I've prepared an overview and I'd like to lay out for you the overall scope of the investigation to put everything in context."

The chief prosecutor cleared his throat and said, "Let me do this, Erika – I'll review your files this evening to refresh my memory of Anderson's investigation so I can get up to speed and not waste your time proctoring me on your work and his." Whitcomb thumbed through the file and as Erika looked on silently, he again read the list of names listed as passengers on the *Rochade Elegante*. "What exactly brought Callahan's activities to your attention? I understand from Hartman that you, like everyone else in this office, have a caseload that is a cup that runneth over."

"Some new information was brought to me recently by Senator Reeves' former wife."

Rupert Whitcomb drew his brow down in a look of disapproval. "In this town, ex-wives are notoriously bad sources of credible information about former spouses. I've crossed paths with Michelle from time to time over the years and she's still an angry, vindictive woman two decades after their divorce. You need to tread carefully if hers is the only new information you have to add to this case. What did she give you?"

"A lead on three witnesses."

"All having some kind of dirt on her former husband, I'm sure. Have you interviewed any or all of them?"

"I made an initial contact with two of them. One is a former superior in the Army during the first war and the other a subordinate from World War Two."

Whitcomb clucked reproachfully. "That's reaching way back into history."

"They confirm a pattern of behavior and character traits supporting Senator Reeves' propensity for unethical and illegal behavior. It's a small piece of the puzzle, but clearly corroborating. Both men are credible witnesses."

"But, by itself, this kind of testimony has no probative value."

"Except to impeach any character testimony that would paint the Senator as morally upright and beyond reproach as surely he would attempt to do when this goes to trial."

"*If* it goes to trial, Erika – something yet to be determined by the evidence you're still gathering on behalf of this office."

"I take it that I have your approval to forge ahead."

"For the moment, of course. Malfeasance in this town is our *raison d'être* and we don't lack for work. But we have to choose our battles and husband our resources to do the best and the most with what we have. For the time being, charge on. From what I know of your work in Baltimore, you produce results and that's precisely what we need in this office." Whitcomb rose and picked up the file. "Have the evidence boxes sent around to my office before the end of the day so I can sift through them after reading this. Good job, Erika. I knew we made a smart move when we convinced you to come join us. Keep up the good work."

The smell of cigarette smoke and the fragrance of Old Spice lingered in the conference room long after Whitcomb had gone. So did the nagging disappointment at the brief conversation for which she had planned an hour long presentation complete with charge sheets and supporting evidence. The overhead transparencies she'd carefully prepared still sat inside her briefcase, untouched and she had the definite sense of having been brushed aside, despite the laudatory comments of the chief prosecutor.

Erika was still nursing frustration and a bruised ego along with her vodka martini four hours later as she waited at the small corner table in the Round Robin and Scotch Bar.

The old pub was one of her favorites, or rather it was one of Randall's – *a real nostalgic experience: grand and sophisticated, a bar in a class of its own*, he'd told her the first time they met here after work. He'd found it with some friends when they were still both working for Senator Payne during the war and added it to *KAVANAGH'S* restaurant as one their 'special' places. It was rumored Walt Whitman and Mark Twain had frequently imbibed here, and it was in this plush-carpeted room with its subdued lighting that Kentucky statesman Henry Clay supposedly mixed the first mint julep tasted in D.C., which was now the bar's signature drink. She wasn't convinced any of it was true; so much in this town was contrived falsehood masquerading as gospel that she'd become a staunch skeptic even before the disappointing session with Rupert Whitcomb earlier that afternoon.

She was about to finish her drink when she spotted her niece and waved her over.

"Auntie Erika, so good to see you once again."

"Cateline, you need to drop the 'Auntie Erika'. It was cute when you were little, but now it just makes me feel old. I'd be much happier if you simply called me Erika. "

"Really?! So sorry." Looking quickly around the bar she said, "I hear one of your frontiersmen created a drink called the mint 'something or other' in this rather rustic place. I shall have one of those."

Cateline Glendenbrook was one of the most interesting, independent and intelligent young women Erika had ever met..

Mitch had married Aynslee in England soon after VE Day. According to her brother, Cateline had been the catalyst for the marriage, insisting by a little girl's irresistible logic that her widowed mother needed a husband, she needed a father and he, being single and unencumbered with a mate, needed a wife. Mitch proposed adopting her but left it up to her in the end, and accepted her decision to keep the Glendenbrook name.

At age 12, she entered Benenden, the English boarding school for girls attended by her mother, an hour's drive from her British grandparents. Soon after her sixteenth birthday she graduated a year ahead of schedule, with a résumé that included academic honors, letters in varsity field hockey and numerous other awards. The following fall, she entered Brown University at Providence, Rhode Island as the youngest member of the Class of 1958. Graduating in the top five percent of her class, she was also the mainstay of the university's Debating Union for two years. Three years after completing Brown, she graduated from Harvard Law and was hired by Blaine, Johnson, Armistad and Meyer PLLC, in New York.

"I spent the day with Michelle Payne," Cateline replied in her crisp British accent. "We went for a long ride, and talked. She said she'd often spent similar time with you in years past and has rather fond memories of it."

"She stabled horses in Manila and my mother and I often rode with her when I was a teenager. What prompted you to come down from New York to see her?"

"Fact finding. Frankly, I was appalled when I learned of Glenn's treatment at the hands of Michelle's ex-husband."

"The flap over his appointment to the Air Force Academy."

"Precisely. But I learned this day it goes far beyond that."

"So now you know Senator Reeves is not a very likeable character."

"He's an abomination. The man is bang out of order the way he treated my brother and I shan't let him get away with it. Things have been allowed to go on far too long. I've come to speak with you concerning what should be done with this uncircumcised Philistine, Harrison Reeves, who seems to take great pleasure in mucking things up for people in our family."

"I'm not sure there is anything the two of us can do about any of that just this minute."

"Michelle tells me she provided you with three witnesses to the nefarious acts of this Reeves. Let's have a round with them. You are looking into this, I presume."

"Yes, I'm looking into it, Cateline."

"I shall help, then."

Chapter 5

USS Maddox (DD – 731)
DESOTO Patrol – Gulf of Tonkin
Off the coast of North Vietnam
2 August 1964–1548 hours (local)
[03:48 a.m. – Washington, D.C.]

Chief Petty Officer Art Jordon entered the sonar room located just aft of the bridge, glanced at the round yellow screen of the AN/SQS-23 Sonar stack and then said to the sonar operator, "Steady hand there, Vic."

"Roger that, chief." The sonar technician continued looking at his large screen, tracking the North Vietnamese PT boats.

"Bridge, sonar, we have three at range fifteen thousand seven hundred. No fish in the water," the third man at the sonar station said into the microphone hung from a loop around his neck. Jake Bennett was a sonar technician 1st class and was now linked into the gun circuit as the sonar 'phone talker'. All the action on board the Maddox came together in one constant conversation that included almost everybody on the ship involved in responding to the operations threat that had brought them to General Quarters twenty minutes earlier.

"Roger that, Sonar. Say bearing." The calm response on the line carried a moderate hum of side tone like white noise.

Bennett watched Mace fine tune the Sum/Diff switch and looked at the stern cursor on the screen that marked the dead zone at the aft end of the ship where the sonar couldn't traverse. Vic Mace was a damned fine operator. He'd set the equipment for shallow echo ranging knowing the Tonkin Gulf wasn't deep enough for subs. *Do the North Vietnamese even have subs?* he wondered. *Don't know, but their friends do.* "Targets bearing one-three seven."

"Roger, Sonar...Guns, Bridge, range fifteen thousand seven hundred, bearing one three seven. Spooks three... and closing. Confirm."

"Roger, Bridge."

"Fifty rounds. Engage at twelve thousand five hundred on my mark."

"Standby for computer check."

"Roger that."

Bennett could hear the business-like chatter in the Combat Info Center in the background over the open connection. A knot formed in his stomach. *Somebody's gonna die tonight if those North Vietnamese PT boats don't back off.* He'd not been in a shooting contest with anything that could shoot back, and suddenly the banter about the DESOTO radar patrols off the coast of North Vietnam being a pleasure cruise seemed foolish. He looked at the little round logo someone had painted beneath the *DANGER – HIGH VOLTAGE* decal on the SQS-23 Sonar – it was yellow with three red horizontal stripes with a sampan under a scalloped oriental sail. Superimposed around the periphery was black lettering: "Gulf of Tonkin Yacht Club'. *Right. Not so much this afternoon,* he thought.

"Bridge, Radar. Range now thirteen thousand two hundred. Bearing now one two eight."

"Roger that.... Sonar?"

"Confirm no fish in the water," Bennett said into the mic. He knew that the Vietnamese torpedoes were essentially worthless if launched outside ten thousand yards – the reason for the CIC deciding to engage the targets well outside that range if they were stupid enough to challenge the *Maddox's* five inch guns. He hoped this was just another drill.

"Bridge, this is Radar... Range twelve thousand eight hundred and closing. Bearing still one two eight degrees."

"Roger Radar. Guns, fifty rounds. Five-zero for these North Vietnamese, folks. Target height four yards. Stand by for computer check. One two eight, twelve thousand five hundred. On my mark the guns will bear. Standby... Mark... Fire on my mark... three... two... one...

MARK!"

"Rounds on the way."

A long series of shots from the forward gun turret began that sounded like extraordinarily loud pops inside the sonar room.

"Torpedoes in the water!" Mace called out, pressing his right earphone hard against his head. "... bearing one two seven. I count three, now four..."

"Oh, damn," Petty Officer Jordan thought, *"this is going to get ugly."*

"Two more fish in the water," Mace reported. "These bearing one two zero."

Jordon hoped they were getting a false return and was about to ask Mace if maybe they weren't just getting a bogus echo off the bottom of the shallow Gulf. But Mace was too good to be fooled and the commo on the gun circuit required all his concentration.

*   *   *

The White House
2 August 1964–11:30 a.m. - local
Washington, D.C.
[2330 hours – Gulf of Tonkin]

"So all you fellas agree, then," the President said, looking around the Oval Office at his senior advisors. "You're telling me that even though our boat was shot at by the damn North Vietnamese that you don't think their government was behind it. Is that what you're saying?"

"Yes sir, it's our considered opinion, certainly at Defense, that a local North Vietnamese commander took the initiative rather than a senior official. It looks like, from all the evidence we have, that it was not at the direction of any ranking official from Hanoi."

Lyndon Johnson looked displeased. At best disappointed.

"What you're saying then is that we should just send a protest note to Hanoi and go about business as usual. Cy, you and your folks at Defense say that we ought to add another boat or two and continue to patrol."

"Yes, sir, that's our best course of action for the moment," Cyrus Vance replied. "We'll add another destroyer to the *Maddox* patrol – the *C. Turner Joy* – and continue the mission of listening in on their radio traffic and keeping a close eye on their military movements."

"Your boss agrees, I take it."

"Yes, sir. Secretary McNamara wanted me to assure you that's his considered opinion."

"I see," the president said. "General Taylor doesn't hold to that view and I regard him highly now that he's my ambassador to South Vietnam. He sent a cable to the State Department sayin' we should retaliate because a failure to respond to an unprovoked attack on a U.S. destroyer in international waters would be construed as an indication that the U.S. flinches from direct confrontation with those North Vietnamese fellas. Ain't that what he said, Dean?" Johnson asked Secretary of State Dean Rusk, who looked uncomfortable being put on the spot.

Randall Ashby glanced quickly out of the corner of his eye at his boss.

Ashby was certain he'd been dragged along to the meeting because Rusk wanted someone there he could later blame for anything untoward that might come of this particular 'hot potato' attack by the North Vietnamese. Ashby had been in the State Department for a half dozen years when Rusk was brought in by Kennedy. The Georgian was intelligent enough, and everyone spoke well of him. But he appeared to the professional staff like a man who cast no shadow. He seemed to have no real history behind him, wrote little and over the past four years it became clear that no one at State really knew anything about him – even his closest direct reports like Randall Ashby.

One thing was clear about him, however. He loved being Secretary of State with the title and trappings that went along with that position. Rusk was a controlled and patient man. He had never been burned – or even slightly singed in the Washington sense of the word – for any of his decisions, advice or positions held. That told Randall Ashby everything he needed to know about Secretary of State Dean Rusk.

"I would add, Mr. President," Rusk was saying, "that Max is well-grounded in his geopolitics and a product of an outstanding military career. Although he might have some misgivings concerning this one incident, I believe it likely he would concur with the consensus of your senior advisors. Based on the bigger picture in view of their perspective a little further away from the incident in question, the consensus of the advisors seems prudent."

Johnson frowned. "What the hell does that mean in English, Dean?"

"It means, sir, that it's a minor incident, likely as astonishing to the government in Hanoi as it is to us here in Washington. It's not the worth military retaliation that could escalate and have unintended consequences beyond our imagination."

"What if it happens again?"

"That's a horse of a different color, Mr. President."

The president looked at Cyrus Vance and his assistant, Paul Loory. "What if it does happen again, boys?"

"Then the option for even more severe action is still on the table," Vance replied.

"More severe? Hell, we haven't done a thing."

"Sir, the Navy was not at all passive in this incident. The *Maddox* expended over two hundred and eighty 3-inch and 5-inch shells. Four F-8 Crusader fighter bombers strafed the torpedo boats. There were no U.S. casualties. Only one U.S. aircraft was damaged and one 14.5 mm round hit the destroyer, three North Vietnamese torpedo boats were badly damaged – as good as lost – and four North Vietnamese sailors were killed. Six were wounded."

Johnson stroked his jaw and contemplated. "All right… for now. But I'm not sittin' by if those little slant-eyed rice gobblers try anything like this again. Now Dean, you and Bob McNamara go talk to the Congress tomorrow afternoon – they got questions – and you fill 'em in on what happened and what's gonna happen if our boats get attacked again, you hear me?"

"Yes, sir, Mr. President."

"Good enough for now. Cy, you make sure to tell the Navy I'm damned proud of 'em."

"I'll do that, sir."

The meeting broke up and Ashby found himself sharing a ride with Paul Loory. As the car entered traffic just outside the White House guard gate, the assistant to the SecDef turned to him and said, "How about I buy you a drink?"

Ashby glanced at his watch. "A little early for me."

"Drink club soda then. But I need a half hour of your time. Driver, drop us off at *The Wisdom* on Pennsylvania Avenue, Southeast." Fifteen minutes later they were in an isolated back booth of a tony bar sharing some snacks and drinking draft beer.

"I needed to talk to somebody I trust about what the hell's going on," Loory said.

"And you chose me?"

"You're not the enemy, even if you are in the State Department. You have some standing with a number of the guys in Defense and elsewhere. Your name is associated with Senator Payne from back in the day. It gives you some street cred in this town. Even the guys you butt heads with in my department speak well of you."

"Are you dipping me in honey, Paul?"

Loory grinned crookedly. "Greasing the skids for something that might be heading down the road at us. Something evil this way comes. You saw what happened in the meeting."

"I saw a consensus reached on some reasonable advice to the Commander-in-Chief." Ashby shrugged. "From where I sit, what happened made a lot of sense."

"On the surface. Suppose I told you my side lied. The North Vietnamese didn't fire on us. We started it – fired on them and that's why they launched torpedoes. Sure, they were provoking us directly, but the *Maddox* fired first. They shot the torpedo boats before they got within ten thousand yards. That's why the torpedoes never reached the *Maddox*."

"You know this for a fact?"

"I do."

"Maybe the skipper thought it better to be questioned for taking an action to save his ship and his men rather than losing a Navy destroyer and being fish food on the bottom of the Tonkin Gulf. It looks like the captain made a good military decision that folks a literal half world away shouldn't be second guessing."

"My question is: why didn't my department tell that to the President."

"I don't know. If you're so concerned, why didn't you tell him?"

Loory took a deep breath. "I was told not to bring it up because it was irrelevant."

Ashby remained briefly silent but finally asked, "What would be the purpose in that?"

"I don't know for sure. This is a political town and everything – and I do mean everything – has a political purpose. But somebody, or a group of somebodies, is shielding the president from the truth. And that's not good, for either your department or mine or both."

"Paul, I don't know what the President does and doesn't know. Are you sure your side lied? Maybe they withheld some information they're still checking out."

"A half-truth has the same effect as a whole lie. Look, I'm not trying to stir things up just for the hell of it. I've been around Washington longer than you have so… Look, I've got kids in college and a couple more going soon, so I'm not looking for trouble where there is none."

Ashby didn't like the way this was going. He knew little about Loory, though they had worked cooperatively on a few issues over the years. "All right, Paul. I'll take this under advisement. I don't know that I see all that much out of whack here."

"How much do you know about the DESOTO patrols, like the one the *Maddox* was on?"

"Not much," Ashby admitted.

"They're part of the system of worldwide electronic reconnaissance carried out by specially equipped Navy vessels. From what I know, they operate in international waters collecting radio and radar signals that come from shore-based stations run by communist countries like the Soviet Union, China, North Korea. And I guess I can say now, North Vietnam. We're doing the same thing as those Soviet trawlers off our coasts do to us."

"The way the world is, Paul."

"Right. So what do you know about the 34A operations?"

"Never heard of it."

"A lot of people haven't. Basically, they're operations run out of South Vietnam, ostensibly by the South Vietnamese, but under the watchful eyes and with the assistance of MACV in Saigon. Basically they're incursions into North Vietnam. Sometimes those operations are supported by U.S. Navy ships providing covering fire from offshore. Almost always, we provide the matériel and the communications used by those operations"

"I didn't know anything like that was going on," Ashby replied.

"Most people in our government don't. Even fewer know of *both* the 34A and the DESOTO operations. The approval process for each is compartmentalized so that the funding and operational activities of both is known to very few people. Here's something that's interesting. During the same timeframe that the *Maddox* was patrolling along the coast of North Vietnam, 34A operations were underway in the same area. To the North, it probably looked like the *Maddox* was providing cover for the 34A operations even though they - the *Maddox* - had no idea of what the South Vietnamese were doing. That's probably why the North Vietnamese attacked like they did."

"I wasn't aware of that."

"Very few people are. I think we just started a shooting war because one hand didn't know what the other was doing – in the military or in Washington... or both."

*　　*　　*　　*　　*

"I'm sore as a whipped dog, Nolan," Benny Barnes said in his Southern twang while they lay on their bunks in the darkness, trying to ignore the sweltering heat of early August filtering through the wide open windows. It was fifteen minutes after Taps, and their squad leader had checked their room just after lights out.

"You're always '*something* as a whipped dog' Ben-bo – tired as a whipped dog; hungry as a whipped dog; ugly as a whipped dog…"

"I'll ugly you, yankee-boy," Benny replied.

"Sure you will."

They had spent the day at the rifle range learning how to zero the M-14 rifle.

The 'First Beast' detail was gone on leave, replaced by another well-rested and eager crew of upperclassmen – juniors, or *Cows*, as squad leaders and assistants, and first classmen as company commanders, platoon leaders and platoon sergeants. As far as Glenn could tell, the first four weeks except for the evening of the 4th of July had been spent in pure harassment as the new cadets learned to polish brass, spit-shine shoes, march in squad, platoon and finally company formations. They had been measured for and drawn essentially all the uniforms they'd need year round. They'd done calisthenics *ad nauseum* including hours of bayonet drill and memorized a seemingly endless litany of "plebe poop" such as the Alma Mater, all the football fight songs and cheers, the number of lights in Cullum Hall, gallons of water in Lusk Reservoir, and the definition of leather. A small hard bound book chock full of that and similar arcane information was issued and became their "Bible" to be memorized and regurgitated at the inexplicable whims of any and all upperclassmen whose favorite time for spouting off was during meals. Thus, at the end of the first month, Glenn had lost twelve pounds he couldn't afford to lose, and expected he might drop even more in the second.

But now, after the first week of the second detail, the emphasis seemed to have shifted to what he thought was something useful. *Finally*. That something centered on the M-14 – disassembling, assembling, cleaning, and now (*at last*) learning how to shoot the Army's primary individual infantry weapon. He was cautiously delighted after spending the final hour before lights out cleaning the weapon well enough it passed his squad leader's white glove inspection on the first round.

"Anything good on the radio tonight?" Barnes asked.

"A little."

"If you can find some western music, I'd like a listen or two."

"So far, just a couple of Rock and Roll stations, and news." The idea of smuggling in the radio had turned out to be a good one Glenn thought. Before traveling to West Point he had looked up a friend and former team mate from high school who'd just finished his first year at the academy and was home on leave in Baltimore after June Week.

Don Winslow had been the starting quarterback at Baltimore Poly and, had made first team All-State his senior year in both football and lacrosse. He'd gone to West Point the year before and Glenn had looked him up for some inside information as soon as he returned home. One conversation had given him the idea of bringing a small crystal radio he'd made years earlier in a false bottom he'd created in his one piece of personal luggage allowed when signing in. He'd found a hiding place for it under one of the lockers in the basement the first morning and retrieved it on the weekend the third week. Then he'd hidden it, along with twenty feet of tightly coiled thin copper wire and a single small plastic earphone, on top of an air duct accessible through one of the tiles in the suspended ceiling of their room. So, for a week and a half he and Benny, unlike all the rest of their classmates, had access to the outside world.

"Maybe we could get better reception if we re-oriented the antenna."

"I'll run the knob across the coil again, and then maybe we'll try it." Glenn moved the metal selector slowly across the coiled wire and this time picked up an additional station from New York City. He stopped and listened for more than a minute to the surprisingly clear reception. When the news report began to repeat, he said, "Benny, listen to this. Right now."

Barnes rolled out of bed and took the small earphone. A minute later, he handed it back to Glenn and asked, "Where in the world is the Gulf of Tonkin?"

"It's a body of water in Southeast Asia just off the coast of North Vietnam and southern China. It's actually the northern part of the South China Sea."

"How do you know that kind of crap?!"

"I used to live in that part of the world when my dad was stationed at Kadena Air Force Base on Okinawa. Did you hear the report say there's been some kind of incident there between our Navy and the North Vietnamese. It's the second one in as many days."

"And they also said the President met with his top advisors today at the White House. What do you think it means?"

"Don't know, Benji," Glenn replied. "Could mean something big just happened. Could mean nothing. The only thing I'm worried about is qualifying expert this week with the M-14."

"You don't think we're at war, do you? There's a lot of that talk among the upperclass."

"I don't know what to think. But it's probably nothing. This kind of stuff happens all the time," Glenn said with a nonchalance he didn't feel. "Why would we want to get into a big war in Asia? Everybody knows that'd be stupid."

*　　*

"Your brother called and said he's going to be in town on business the last week of the month," Randall told his wife as she came into the kitchen and dumped her briefcase on the built-in desk. "I promised oysters for dinner one night that week, so he's stopping by."

"Then you'll be doing the cooking when Mitch gets here," Erika said, irritably.

"Bad day?"

"Haven't had a good one since I took this job in Washington." She looked around the room, clearly agitated.

"I'll mix us Old Fashioneds and we can share sad tales – you first – while I play chef. How about something Italian – say, Parmesan Chicken Cassiato a la Ashby?" He moved close and gave his wife a quick kiss.

"Go easy on the garlic this time, please."

"Why? You got a date tonight?"

"I don't know… Do I?"

"You need to go change, and I can see I need to make your drink extra strong."

When Erika returned, her husband already had a tomato base going in a large pan over a low fire and was fine grating a large wedge of fresh parmesan. Their drinks sat side by side on the island in the middle of the kitchen. She picked up one and took a sip.

"Perfect," she declared wistfully "Not only did you turn out to be a reasonably decent chef, but also an accomplished mixologist."

"I studied at the feet of the very best – your mother. So, why the dark cloud over your head today?"

"The lack of progress on a case. Actually, roadblocks the lead prosecutor is throwing in my way. It's been two months and he's still finding reasons to keep me from going forward."

"This is the case concerning Callahan and Reeves?"

She shot him a sideways glance. "I don't discuss specific cases outside the office."

"You talk in your sleep."

"I do *not*!"

"All right, you win. I know you don't talk about your cases outside work, but you mentioned it in passing back when you first started looking into it. I still have my law license

75

even if I don't practice any more. You know I'm a good listener, and if you want to talk… I can keep a secret. I've got all kinds of secrets."

Erika sipped her drink and contemplated briefly. "I'm being stonewalled. I've got good circumstantial and direct evidence on Trevor Callahan, and much of it has to do with his relationship to Reeves since before World War II. But my boss keeps loading me up with minor cases and asking for more evidence before letting me run with it."

"Is it possible you're too emotionally involved to be impartial?"

She stared back at him for long seconds and finally said, "You know I can't say that I'm a hundred percent impartial. But a good, seasoned prosecutor never is. The best prosecutors are passionate about the law and justice being served. I think that's where I am."

"But it's also very personal."

Ashby knew about many of the acts both Senator Reeves and then U.S. Representative Callahan had perpetrated against his wife's family. And from what he'd learned slowly, fragment by fragment over the last twenty years since becoming part of that family, he'd been surprised if anyone in their place could be impartial on the subject of either man. He knew that Callahan had tried to seduce his mother-in-law when Dave Nolan was in Europe for three years during the war. Even now, the Senator seemed intent on making life hard on a third generation of the family with his treatment of his nephew Glenn.

"I don't blame you for not being impartial where these two men are concerned," Ashby told his wife. "But if any prosecutor allows impartiality to be replaced by prejudice…"

"I haven't let that happen. And I won't."

"I believe you," Ashby said as he carved two chicken breasts into thin slices and placed them into the sauce in the large frying pan "So why is the head prosecutor delaying you?"

"I don't know."

"But you have suspicions."

"I can speculate. I'm good at it because I married a man who does that for a living."

"Touché. You think the boss is either afraid of one or both of the targets of your investigation, or that he's part of the crime; he's somehow involved." When his wife didn't respond, he continued. "Senator Reeves is in a position of power right now. He always has been with the money he inherited from his father that bankrolls a number of Democratic Party high fliers. And now he's being talked about as Johnson's running mate against Goldwater. The President picked him out, along with his old long-standing friend Bill Fulbright, to shepherd the Gulf of Tonkin Resolution through Congress six weeks ago. A prosecution of Senator Reeves at the moment would draw a lot of fire and make a lot of enemies."

"I'm aware of all that, and it doesn't frighten me."

Ashby smiled. "That's my gutsy girl. You get that from your dad."

"And my mom. I think in a lot of ways, she's tougher than the ol' man."

"Maybe so. I can tell you she's the person on the planet I'm most afraid of."

"Come on! She adores you, Randall."

"I know. But she carries a brick inside her velvet glove." He tasted the sauce in the pan with his chicken and added a dash of salt. "I know how frustrated you feel, but there are always a lot of really disturbing things happening in this town. You're aware of that."

"I am. Doesn't mean I like it. I wish things were like they were back when I was working for Senator Payne and you were the counsel on his Senate Committee. Things were so much simpler just twenty years ago. Before television; before Sputnik."

"Before Korea."

"And before this nasty little business in Southeast Asia."

"It could get a lot nastier."

"Is that why you had such a bad day?"

"Bad day?... Bad month is more like it."

The President had made it so.

It appeared to Ashby that things for the President could not have gone better had he planned them in microscopic precision. As long as he moved slowly and publicly toward escalation in South Vietnam, he had the Right politically handcuffed and the Left wing of his own party, while still bothersome, was rendered quiet and not very dangerous. He had locked up both sides. With his saber rattling, he would kill the Right in the fall presidential campaign, and along with them his political opponent, Senator Barry Goldwater. With the Left in the Senate, he had quickly wrapped himself in the flag and moved forward under its cover. He had decided to push immediately for the congressional resolution because the timing could not have been better – it was too good an opportunity to miss. He had brought on board his old friend William Fulbright, an odd combination of public man and private man, who still held to some lingering reluctance about the president's motives and the political process LBJ had used. And in that process, the President had also co-opted a man he didn't trust as far as he could throw the ten year old Chevy pickup truck on his ranch in Texas.

That man was Senator Harrison Reeves of Maryland, who had supported Jack Kennedy over the Texan in 1960 at the Democratic convention. Reeves was also increasingly vocal about his dislike for the American military. Ashby expected the President would soon distance himself from the self-aggrandizing Senator. So, the way the President had played Reeves was the only bright spot Ashby could find in Johnson's handling of the situation in Southeast Asia.

But the rest of it…

Though he couldn't prove it, he was convinced the Secretary of Defense on more than one occasion had misled the Congress on a number of points – most important of all, the role of the covert 34A operations in initiating the entirety of the Gulf Tonkin episode. It looked very much like McNamara had lied to the president... and that LBJ had wanted to be lied to. Paul Loory had hinted strongly to it at their second discussion over a beer at *The Wisdom* the week following the passage of the resolution. Within days, Loory had been moved out of the inner circle at Defense and calls to him went unanswered. Ashby knew that wasn't a good sign.

"I shouldn't complain, though," Randall said as he ladled tomato sauce over the chicken again. "I could be going through what our nephew is up at the trade school in New York. When your brother called, we talked for a little while. He said he's gotten a half dozen calls from Glenn and none of them contained any happy-talk."

"Poor Glenn. I feel sorry for him, but he was warned."

"That may be, but he's still not liking it. He even talked about leaving – twice. Mitch said he told him he wasn't old enough yet, that he needed his parents' signature to do that."

"So is Mitch going to sign his papers?"

Ashby laughed. "Not any time soon. He says he likes the idea of knowing where at least one of his boys is at ten o'clock each night. Apparently Brad is giving them some problems now that he's in high school. No, I think your brother is glad to pay for long distance phone calls and willing to listen to Glenn's rants as long as the tuition is free and he's under close supervision. Mitch sounded like he finds the whole deal kind of amusing.

"That nephew of ours has a long four years ahead of him."

CAUCHEMAR

Chapter 6

Fall, 1968

Light streamed through the window of the small two bed university dorm room on the ground floor of Harrington Hall E; the Westminster chimes of Memorial Hall near the campus library tolled the noon hour, and although the sound was almost inaudible, it caused the hung over undergrad to cover his head with a pillow in hopes of going back to sleep.

"Hey! Brad! Get up, man. You have an appointment with Dean Comings in less than an hour. You don't want to screw this up – especially now!" The Resident Assistant, a senior who most of the undergrads in Harrington E viewed as a sniveling wimp and a royal pain, shook him roughly when he rolled over. "Come on Nolan, out of bed. You look like hell."

"I feel worse," Brad replied, pulling the covers over his head.

"No damn wonder. Your buddies poured your drunk ass into bed at four in the morning two days ago. You've been out for over thirty hours this time."

"What day is it?"

"December 17th."

"No, I mean what day of the week?"

"Wednesday."

"You sure?"

"I'm not the one still hung over, Nolan. Of course I'm sure; I actually attend classes. What's the problem, anyhow?"

"I had a big engineering test in Mr. DeJoseph's class on Tuesday," he mumbled from under the cover. "This is not good."

"Don't compound it by missing the appointment with your dean," the RA said, as he shook him again and then opened the door to leave. "I'm going for some lunch. You're on your own now. If I were you I wouldn't keep Doctor Comings waiting. But if you do, that's on you, man. Not me."

Can't believe I missed that test, Brad Nolan thought to himself as he struggled out of bed and down the hallway to shave and shower. ... *damn you, Nolan, this binge drinking is getting out of hand* – just how far out of hand he found out an hour later in Assistant Dean Brockenbrough's office in Evans Hall, the main facility for the College of Engineering.

"I don't relish this conversation Mr. Nolan. I want you to know that," the austere fiftyish man said, looking up from a folder after Brad was ushered in by his secretary. "Frankly, Doctor Comings and I are utterly astounded that a meeting such as this is necessary."

"Sir, I'm really sorry I missed that test yesterday, and I promise it won't happen again. If you can just see your way clear to allow me to make up the exam, I can assure you and the dean there won't be a repeat episode like that."

Brockenbrough cleared his throat. "I believe you've made similar promises to two of your professors in past weeks." Brad took a deep breath and remained silent. "I'm correct, aren't I?"

"Yes, sir, you are. But I…"

"But what? You want me to overlook your record and now take your word. Frankly, I'm not inclined to. You're not in high school any longer. You're at the University of Delaware, and this is an entirely different atmosphere, with much higher expectations." The Assistant Dean of Engineering looked back at the folder in front of him, scanned one of the sheets and looked back up. "We had very high hopes for you, Mr. Nolan even though you just squeaked by getting in here. Each of your professors commented positively on your participation in class discussion and some went so far as to label you an engineering prodigy. Sadly, it appears we – all of us – erred."

"Sir, I got a little off track for a while, but I can make the necessary corrections."

"You didn't get just a little off the track, Nolan; you completely derailed. Your record shows in the last seven weeks, you've cut three quarters of your classes. Yesterday's examination is not the first you've missed in that time, but the third. Your professors now describe your participation – when you're present, that is – as listless, distracted, and fundamentally unprepared."

"I've had some problems, but I'm getting a handle on them."

"Mr. Nolan, you certainly have had some problems. But they're your problems, not ours. The campus police record you've badly behaved in the last six weeks – two instances of public intoxication. Quite a record at this early stage of your education. This university cannot and will not allow such recalcitrant behavior from students."

"I'm not proud of that, sir." Brad realized he'd let the partying on and off campus get way out of control. He'd fallen in with the Sigma Nu crowd, and while he couldn't rush any of the fraternities until spring semester, he'd still been included in their social life. He knew Delaware had the reputation of being straight-laced but it seemed they were taking themselves a little too seriously. "I know my conduct isn't faultless, but it doesn't rise to the level of setting fire to university property, raising hell on campus, or recruiting for SDS."

The assistant dean shifted uncomfortably. "Excusing oneself by pointing out bad behavior in others is not a sign of maturity, Nolan."

Brad's neck grew hot and he bristled at the rebuke.

Unrest on the Newark campus, like colleges everywhere was growing. Three months earlier a Molotov cocktail had exploded in the ROTC uniform storage room in the old Mechanical Hall. Soon after, campus life was disrupted on the anniversary of the previous year's interference of an ROTC drill by students and three faculty members. One professor had left in the summer of '68 but the two who remained received notice in October their contracts would not be renewed. Students reacted by petitioning, writing scathing editorials in the college newspaper, holding "teach-ins," rallies, and even brief campus strikes. Two weeks earlier, five hundred undergrads had staged a sit-in at the Student Center and then marched to the president's house and demonstrated outside it until 2:30 A.M.

The assistant dean closed the folder and looked up at him. "It grieves me to inform you, we've decided to remove you from the rolls."

"Sir, I'd like you to reconsider."

"There is a process, and you can follow it if so inclined. However, it's unlikely to result in overturning the decision." Brockenbrough handed him a form letter indicating his dismissal. "Perhaps you're just not ready for university yet. Take some time, deal with your personal issues and then try higher education again. With more maturity, you'll possibly do well. It is expected you'll settle all accounts and depart by the end of Christmas Break."

Without a student deferment, I'm going to be drafted into the Army with my draft number, he thought, looking at the sheet he'd been given. He left the office, walked back across campus to the dorm, and when in his room sat looking at the letter, wondering how he was going to tell his parents. They were expecting him home for Christmas, but not permanently. *Brad, you have screwed the pooch good this time. The old man is not going to take this well.*

But even more troubling than having to tell his parents was what was going to happen when the Draft Board learned his status. Officially, he was still a resident of Maryland by listing his Aunt Erika's address in Rockville as his home while completing high school when the family moved a few years earlier. Now without his student status, he'd be prime meat to be drafted and sent off to Vietnam as a rifle-toting target for the Viet Cong in the Southeast Asia war games. He reasoned he had to do something quickly to somehow get ahead of the Draft.

It took a pizza and a couple of beers for him to figure out how best to do it.

*   *   *

"I'm Sergeant Katzenbach," the hard-looking soldier with short flattop and tailored green dress uniform said from behind the desk as he stood and offered his hand. His eyes were the color of blue agate; his upper sleeves were adorned with gold chevrons – three up and one rocker down – and three rows of ribbons festooned the uniform jacket above his left breast pocket. He was tall and trim, and carried himself with an air of no-nonsense competency. "I see you saved the best for last."

Brad had driven down to the large Joint Services Recruiting Station in Havre de Grace, Maryland in early morning traffic; it was a short ride from the school on I-95 and he was the first in line when the Navy Petty Officer opened the doors at nine.

"The Air Force and the Navy recruiters said I shouldn't even bother with the Army."

"The junior services suffer from terminal envy," the sergeant said as if he'd heard the remark before. "And, rightfully so. Tell me your name and how I can make your day. Coffee? It's prime Columbian, dark-roasted yesterday and ground this morning."

"The name is Brad Nolan, and I think I will have some. It smells good."

The sergeant poured them each a cup and sat back to watch the expression on Brad's face. "Outstanding isn't it? Only the best for the best. So now tell me what I can do for you."

"I'm thinking of signing up."

"You're in a Recruiting Station, so that's pretty obvious. The question is: Why?"

"Does it make a difference why?"

"Motivation is to all other attributes as ten is to one in things military. I'm not going to sell you or anyone else a bill of goods based on what I or the Army think fits you if that conflicts with your reason for being here. Nobody in the Army wants an unhappy recruit turning into a disgruntled soldier. When I became a recruiter, I swore that I'd never send anybody out to the Army in the field I wouldn't want in my own unit. To hell with quotas."

"I don't want to go to the field," Brad said, sipping at the steaming cup.

"When I say the field I mean anywhere the Army is. Germany, Hawaii, Alaska, South America, CONUS… Sorry, what I meant to say was the continental United States."

"I know what CONUS means. I'm an Air Force brat."

This obviously caught Sergeant Katzenbach's interest and he said, "That's good to know. I won't have to hold your hand like I do with all these civilians who drop in. I can skip a lot of the really basic information and get to the nitty gritty. Certainly you've spent time overseas."

"I've lived and traveled internationally, yes – Europe, Okinawa, Panama."

"Ah, Panama," the sergeant said wistfully, smiling and half closing his eyes as if reliving a pleasant memory. "I suppose you were at Howard Air Force Base?"

"Yes, I was."

"I loved it there. Temps never got below seventy or above ninety. Howard had the best PX in the world, bar none. And Balboa was only a short ride away. Great place. Where else?"

"You mentioned Alaska. We were stationed at Elmendorf once."

"Another of the really outstanding places in the world to call home. I was there at Fort Richardson. The weather wasn't as good as the Canal Zone, but they had fishing and hunting like nobody's business. The best salmon fishing in the world and it lasted all through the summer with a different species swimming up those streams along the coast every couple of weeks. The Silver salmon run in August was the best, in my opinion. Did you dip a line?"

"Yeah. My dad loved the outdoors, and all us kids caught the same gene."

"So I take it you hunted there, too."

"I did. Once. My Dad flew my brother and I over to Kodiak Island and we hunted deer."

"I envy you," Sergeant Katzenbach said, slowly shaking his head. "Never got to Kodiak myself, but I heard it was out of this world. The limit on deer when I was there was ten."

"And the limit on moose was just one a season," Nolan added.

"As big as they are, one is plenty," the sergeant said, then leaned toward him and said in a low tone, "Is it true what they say about moose having just about no nutritional value?"

"I think so," Brad replied, warming to the Army non-com. "One of the locals told me and my brother that a man could eat a whole moose and die of starvation. I don't know how true that is; he may have been yanking my chain because I was from the lower forty-eight."

"I'll be damned," Katzenbach said, as if he'd received an epiphany. The sergeant topped off Brad's cup, and lit up a cigarette after offering one to Brad. "Smart move not getting hooked on these. I did when I went to Basic. Anyhow, what exactly brings you here and what have you talked about with the Air Force and the Navy?"

"I'm here because I have a low draft number and I just lost my student deferment. I figure the best way to keep from getting drafted and assigned to the infantry in Vietnam by this summer is to sign on voluntarily and get a job that keeps me from that."

"I see," the sergeant said, interlocking the fingers of both hands and looking concerned. "You're not the first, and you won't be the last in that predicament. Tell me something – just between me and you. Why not go to Canada and skip the whole damned thing?"

"That's not an option," Brad replied emphatically. "Not part of my equation."

"Really? Why not?"

"Because it's just plain wrong." He waited, and watched the Army sergeant lean back in his chair and look him over. At last he said, "Plus, the family would disown me. My grandfather is a retired Army three-star. My dad is a retired Air Force colonel, and my older brother is an Army lieutenant in Germany. I don't want to get out of serving, but I want a choice of jobs."

"All right, Brad, I get that. So how does your family feel about you wanting to volunteer for one of the services?"

"Don't know. Haven't talked to them yet."

Sergeant Katzenbach leaned further back in his chair. "Brad, that raises a warning flag on my screen here. It makes me very uncomfortable. Why haven't you discussed this with the family – especially your dad?"

"Because I'm here and he's in St. Louis with McDonnell-Douglas; and, this all came up very suddenly. I'm just looking at options right now."

"All right. That's definitely a wise thing to do. How old are you?"

"Eighteen."

The recruiter opened a drawer and retrieved a five by eight index card. "I need to get some basic information from you. These cards help me keep track of the guys I talk to and what we discussed. You don't mind giving me some info like that, do you?"

"The other recruiters I talked to had me fill out something similar. This isn't a commitment, or a contract is it?"

"No, not at all – just a way to keep things straight for me." Katzenbach waited until Brad completed the form and then asked, "What do you think you'd like to do, and what is the Air Force or the Navy offering?"

"I was studying engineering," Brad said, "and I've always been mechanical – I get that from my father. I was hoping for something technical, in the mechanical field. The Navy had a few jobs – machinist mate positions operating and maintaining steam turbines, ship propulsion and auxiliary machinery like refrigeration plants, air conditioning systems. They also had openings for sonar operators aboard destroyers."

Sergeant Katzenbach frowned. "Somehow you don't strike me as a mechanic bending wrenches. One thing is for certain in the Navy – you *will* be a painter if you're on one of their boats. All those jobs you mentioned are aboard ship, so you'll be at sea a lot. And when you're at sea, every enlisted man spends a fair share of his time putting another coat of gray exterior enamel on everything made of steel, which is essentially everything, period." Katzenbach blew a smoke ring. "How about the Air Force?"

"They have openings in facilities maintenance."

"What does that mean?"

"It's like, well, taking care of just about everything on an Air Force base in their facilities."

"You mean like plumbing and heating and air conditioning and electrical?" When the sergeant spoke, it made the jobs sound something less than meaningful.

"Sure, but they also have positions that work on aircraft avionics and guidance systems, on engine repair and general maintenance," Brad said defensively. "There are a lot of things I could find worth my while."

"Are you thinking of a career in the Air Force?"

"No, not really," he admitted. "I'm looking at three and out."

"Then maybe in civilian airline maintenance?"

"Not that either."

"All right, Brad, so what are you really looking for?"

"I'm looking for three years of time in military service where I can do my duty and then go back to college afterward."

"Do you want to enjoy that time?"

"I don't want to hate it. That's for sure."

The sergeant paused and tapped the tips of his fingers together. "You said your dad spent a career in the Air Force and he's still in the aerospace industry. What did he do while on active duty?"

"He was a pilot, flying just about everything in the inventory – not everything, just fighters. He flew p-38s and P-51s during WW Two and just about everything else since."

Katzenbach's face registered surprise. "Wow! He flew Lightning's and Mustangs?"

"And F-86s in Korea, followed by F-100s, 102 Delta Daggers, 104s. He was about to check out in the F-4 Phantom when he retired and went into the aviation business with Martins in Baltimore."

The recruiter gave him a wholly perplexed look. "You have that in your background and you're thinking of settling for maintenance on refrigeration systems on a Navy boat, or being a plumber or electrician at some Air Force base? That absolutely floors me. Have you ever thought about flying?"

"I'm a pilot already."

"What?! You're already a pilot?"

"I've had my civilian pilot's license since I turned sixteen. My dad taught me how to fly and I got my single engine certificate from the FAA as soon as I was old enough. I have an instrument rating and I'm halfway to getting my commercial pilot's license. I love flying. But I can't do that in the military. I'd need a college degree."

Sergeant Katzenbach's face lit up. "Are you kidding me?! Nolan, listen. You don't need a degree in the Army to be a rated pilot. You do need a degree to fly in the Air Force and the Navy, but you don't in the Army. Those other services have only commissioned officers as pilots, but most Army pilots are Warrant Officers. You could easily be a pilot – like your father – only in the Army."

"But they're all helicopter drivers. And all of them go to Vietnam."

"Who in the world fed you that line of bull, Brad? Must have been the Navy or that Marine Gunny over there. Truth is, the Army has a lot of Warrant Officers flying fixed wing." Katzenbach looked around the office and finally caught the eye of another recruiter and waved him over. The tall, trim man wore the wings of a Master Army Aviator.

"Brad, this is CWO-3 Clifford. He's a twenty-two year Army vet who's a rated helicopter *and* fixed wing pilot. Tell him what fixed wing birds you're qualified in."

The older Warrant Officer looked uncomfortable as he frowned at the recruiting sergeant and said, "I've flown Beavers, and Otters, and Mohawks, and the de Havilland C-7 Caribou. I'm enroute to the Beech factory to get checked out in the Super King Air that the Army is planning on buying in the next couple of years for embassy support, medical evacuation, and passenger transport."

Sergeant Katzenbach quickly added, "When he says passenger transport, he's talking about doing the job of a civilian commercial pilot, executive pilot stuff. Any interest in that?"

"Maybe a little," Brad admitted, trying not to sound too excited or appear overly eager. He had quickly warmed to the idea – it was both interesting and likely something that might go down easier with his father when he finally had to break the news about the U. of D. to him. That would come, sooner rather than later – it was just a week away from Christmas and he was flying to St. Louis on Tuesday afternoon. "I'd still have to go to military flight training, wouldn't I?"

"Of course. About nine months at Fort Rucker, Alabama. That's where they have the fixed wing training. For the next two years after that, who knows?" The recruiter turned to the Warrant Officer pilot. "Chief, where have you flown fixed wing around the world?"

"Mostly CONUS, but also in Thailand, North Africa, some of the NATO countries and South America," Clifford replied hesitantly.

"Ever been shot down… or even shot at, while flying fixed wing?" the sergeant asked.

"Can't say that I have," the CWO-3 replied.

Things that are too good to be true usually are, he thought. "You're sure I'd be eligible for that?" Brad asked, cautiously.

"I'd have to do a little investigation to make absolutely certain," the sergeant was saying. "And of course you'd have to first pass a Class-A flight physical and also the Army's Flight Aptitude Test, but if you're already a pilot… That should be a piece of cake. Fortunately, those are both easily scheduled at Aberdeen Proving Grounds, which is like right next door."

"How soon?"

"Any time you're ready," the sergeant said casually, picking up the coffee pot and offering some to Brad. "I'm sure I could schedule them both in the next few days."

"This week?"

"Not positive, but I could check if you're interested."

"How about doing that? Can I get your business card? I'd like to think about it a little more, but it might work. Do I have to sign paperwork if I decide on flight school?"

"There's a standard form – not much to it," Katzenbach said nonchalantly. "If I'm not mistaken, there's a flight school class in early February you could get into."

"I don't have to go to boot camp or anything?" Brad asked.

"Boot camp is for Marines," the recruiter offered with a big smile. "You don't strike me as being crazy enough to be a jarhead. But yeah, there's Basic Training in the Warrant Officer program. There's a couple or three weeks tacked onto the front end of flight school that sorta makes do for officer training. Being a Warrant is the best damned job in the Army – especially if you're an aviator. They don't have any of the responsibilities of commissioned officers, and none of the crap NCOs have to deal with. I wish they'd told me about that when I signed on."

Brad didn't have to hear any more. This was almost too good to be true, and he would have signed the papers and told the recruiter set up the physical and the aptitude test but he didn't want to seem overly eager.

"Sergeant, I'll call you tomorrow morning after I have time to sleep on it. But I have to admit this is interesting."

"More interesting than being a plumber in the Air Force or a refrigeration mechanic in the Navy?" Sergeant Katzenbach forced himself to shut up. *When you've made the sale, just shut up, Katz*, he told himself. "I'll wait for your call, Brad."

They shook hands and Nolan left the recruiting station.

CWO-3 Clifford stood next to the desk and watched Brad pull away. Without looking at the recruiter he said, "You know you're going to burn in Hell for this staff sergeant."

"I think he'll make a great pilot. He'll be satisfied and the Army will be the better for it."

"You know he's not going to get into fixed wing. All our requirements are for rotary wing aviators for Vietnam."

"And I'm on the Captain's shit list for not making my quota on them in the last two quarters. I won't give him the satisfaction of chewing my butt again this quarter. Nolan will put me over the top and I don't feel the least bit guilty about doing my job for Uncle Sam."

"You're still gonna burn for lying to that boy," the older man said. He'll finish Rotary Wing at Rucker and go straight to Nam… or he'll be one of the fifty percent in his class who washes out of flight school and ends up exactly where he doesn't want to be – in the bush carrying an M-16 and an eighty pound pack."

"Life sucks and then you die. He wants to fly like his old man did."

"He's not going to be a jet jockey."

"Well, he could have been if he hadn't screwed up and lost his deferment. We see kids like him every day almost – partied too hard in college and flunked out. Frankly, their screw-up ain't my problem."

"You don't know that's what happened."

"Chances are pretty good, but like I said – not my frickin' problem." Staff Sergeant 'Cats' Katzenbach picked up the phone and dialed. "Yo, Fitz, this is Katzenbach at the recruiting office, I need you to set up a Class A flight physical and a FAST test. Yup, Friday… the kid's name is Nolan, Bradyn H., 218-67-8129. Go ahead and start a file and get him in the queue. He'll be slated for Rotary Wing class 69-13. I'll get you the rest of the details when he calls me back tonight or tomorrow… Yeah, right – like an early Christmas present…"

*   *   *   *

Brandon Oakes entered the hotel bar and hesitated while his eyes grew accustomed to the subdued light cast by chandeliers hung from the antique sculpted ceiling.

Soon he recognized his crowd of fellow Congressional committee legal counsels holding down their usual table across the room, situated in a shallow alcove against the plush, tufted wall and matching bench seat across from a semi-circle of high wingback library chairs. Throughout, the furniture was upholstered in a muted persimmon giving the appropriately named bar – *The Off the Record* – an old world charm, with islands of privacy provided by the generous chairs. Although it was not yet five, the place was growing busy with the usual thirty-something crowd of upwardly mobile Washington movers and shakers to be.

Oakes took his seat in the chair facing the entry to the bar and ordered a Jameson on the rocks. The lawyer knew that more Congressional business was being conducted at this moment at similar places around the capitol than was transacted in any given week in committee rooms on the Hill. Five hundred thirty-five men and women were elected *by* the people to *do* the people's business, but the real nuts and bolts of government was decided by people like him – the vast army of bureaucrats and unelected decision makers. Oakes and his friends around the table liked their power and unaccountability. The perks were damned nice, too.

On top of that, the pay was pretty good, and getting better every year.

As he and his friends talked about the results of various meetings that day, decisions made or contemplated, and compromises being offered to keep the machinery of government greased, Oakes' saw a group of four young women in business attire enter the bar. They found a small round pedestal table by the wall where professionally drawn caricatures were hung in black frames featuring famous guests of the historic Hay-Adams Hotel. The lawyer was certain he knew one of the women, but couldn't for the life of him remember her name or where he'd met her. After staring at her, and searching his usually reliable memory, the name at last came to him.

Cateline Glendenbrook.

It had been seven, maybe eight, years earlier. She was working for a firm out of New York that represented Barrett Enterprises and she'd spoken up out of turn during a committee hearing and earned herself a dressing down by his boss, Senator Harrison Reeves, in the process. Oakes smiled to himself. The night before the hearing, she'd taken him to dinner – at her expense – to troll for information about the next day. *Cute girl then,* he thought, *and she's turned into a beautiful woman.* Back then, he'd half-heartedly tried to recruit her for the senator after the hearing, but she'd not been interested and blew him off, but nicely. Now, he wondered about several things: what was she doing here; was she still with that same law firm; was she still single; and, could he charm her onto a date and into his bed?

"So, the offer on the table is that Carlton will change his vote on Reeves' amendment to the Transportation Bill if Reeves supports his amendment to the Defense appropriation," Harry Elliott was saying. "Brandon, where are you? Have you heard anything I said in the last five minutes?"

"Of course," Oakes replied, but his mind was on the girl, and as he turned his head to gaze at her again she caught him and glared fierce disapproval. *Caught. No better time to go talk to her than the present.* "Guys, you're going to have to excuse me."

"Wait a minute, Brand, we've got to settle this for my Senator," Elliott insisted, looking upset and leaning forward in his chair. "I can't go back to him without something in hand."

"I'll think on it and get back to you in a couple of days."

"No, dammit! I won't go into him tomorrow morning with nothing resolved."

"I said I'd think about it, Elliott. Now, you're just going to have to excuse me because there's a woman over there giving me the 'come hither' stare, and a gentleman doesn't keep a lady waiting." He rose and walked across the room, stopping next to the table where the four women sat. "Ladies, I'm Brandon Oakes, senatorial legal counsel and it would be my privilege to buy you a round of drinks if I might be allowed a private minute with Miss Glendenbrook."

Cateline gave him a look laced with suspicion, and the other women registered surprise.

"I was hoping you'd remember me, Cateline," Oakes continued. "It was –"

"Why should I?"

"I tried to recruit you for Senator Reeves' staff eight years ago. You were interning with Blaine, Johnson, Armistad and Meyer as I recall, and your conduct at one of the Senator's hearings caught our attention. We thought we could use a mind like yours on staff; however, you declined – very graciously, I might add."

She furrowed her brow and looked skeptical.

"We had dinner the evening before the hearing and you grilled me for information. Surely you remember. I made a bad joke about your being from Yale Law instead of Harvard."

"You're from Harvard, I take it. Unfortunately, someone has to play second team."

Her British accent was pleasing to his ear and brought back memories. "You *do* remember."

"Vaguely. Perhaps some of it is coming back. Your senator was quite the bore during the hearing. And I recall now that I paid for dinner, didn't I?"

"You did. But, if your friends are agreeable, I'd like to return the favor if I can pry you away from their company tomorrow evening for a couple of hours and take another run at recruiting you for my Senator's team."

"I'm sorry, Mr. Oakes, but –"

"Please, call me Brandon."

"As I was saying, Mr. Oakes, that won't be possible. I shall return to New York tomorrow by train at eight in the morning."

"Go ahead, Cate," one of the women said. "Let him buy you an expensive dinner. We'll catch up down in the lobby around nine for a stroll around the White House and drinks back here. Marge and I have phone calls home to make; Phyllis has been complaining all day about needing a nap."

"I can't do that to you," Cateline said, looking at each of them in turn. "We only get to do this once each year."

"It's a couple hours in the week. We'll survive it. And I could use some down time," the one called Phyllis said, and then looked at Oakes. "I want your driver's license and a major credit card, mister. If you don't treat my friend right in every way, the four of us are going to max out your card and ruin your credit rating first thing in the morning."

"This is a tough crowd," Oakes said with an utterly charming smile. "Are you all Republicans? I promise not to leave the premises and to act the perfect gentleman toward your friend."

"We're going to hold you to it," Phyllis declared and with that, the women rose and left.

When they were gone, Oakes sat in a chair across the table and said, "You're lucky to have friends like that."

"A good crew, they are. I'm fortunate to have buds that are ace." Cateline sipped her drink and continued. "You weren't serious about trying to recruit me, were you?"

"I might have been."

"That's not an answer a-tall. We've not gone a step and we're already off on the wrong foot. I've let you chat me up, and I'll let you buy me dinner, but I shan't be played with by the likes of you, Mr. Oakes."

"Brandon. Brand would be better. No more 'Mr. Oakes', please. I'm not *that* much older than you and I'd like you to look on me as your friend."

"All right, Brandon it is."

"There you go. Let me make a quick phone call and get us a table in the upstairs dining room. I'll do that, order us another drink, and be right back." Oakes made a call using the bar phone and returned a minute later as the waitress was placing two drinks on the table. "All set. The table will be ready in fifteen or twenty minutes. Let's take the elevator up now. I've got something I want to show you about our fair city."

They got off the elevator and walked through the restaurant called the *Top of the Hay*, through the tall glass doors to a balcony that wrapped around the top floor. A few hundred yards away, was the north portico of the White House with its remarkable columns; further south was the towering spire of the Washington Monument. To the east was the tall round dome of the Capitol building. The early evening radiance of a setting sun washed the white structures in an amber glow and the city around them glistened as if cast in purest gold.

"This is magnificent," Cateline remarked, leaning against the railing. "I've never in all my life seen a city more beautiful. This is stunning."

"It really does take one's breath away, doesn't it?" Oakes agreed, leaning against the railing next to her, holding his glass in both hands. "This is what the founders and the original architects had in mind when they envisioned this city. Maybe this is truly the shining city on the hill alluded to in the Bible."

"Perhaps," Cateline agreed. "The Church of England doesn't seem to put much stock in that Good Book these days, except in Africa, so I'm not much of a Bible scholar."

"Nor am I. But I do believe this is a special place. That's why I'm here. That's why I think you should be here, too." Oakes turned, looked directly at her and seemed to grow melancholy. "I hope you see what I see here, in this city. We in government have the privilege and duty to make our country, and the world, a better place – for everyone."

"Through government action? You really believe that?"

"I do. President Johnson made the most far-reaching and important legislative proposal to that end since the Roosevelt's New Deal. From civil rights to education, to health in the form of universal medical care, education, the environment, arts and culture. The range and scope of what government can and will do is breath-taking. Cateline, you can be part of that. You *should* be part of that."

"You're again trying to recruit me."

"I am. I remember from our last encounter you have a sharp and inquisitive mind. You were the youngest law school grad ever recruited by one of the most prestigious firms in New York. You're still there, I presume."

"You presume correctly."

"That tells me more than I need to know about your qualifications."

"It tells you nothing about my interest or lack thereof in your position."

Oakes smiled at her. "It's an important position working alongside Senator Reeves and the rest of us on his team. He's a great man with a very clear vision for our country. Not everyone can see the benefit of enlightened government action in the areas I just mentioned – and others. Yet it's clear this is absolutely essential. Do you see the potential, Cateline?"

She shook her head slowly. "Honestly, I'm not so sure. In my country, we seem to be eroding individual liberties with that kind of thinking. That worries me."

"Perhaps it should," Oakes replied quietly, then brightened and said with conviction, "But I'm sure that will never happen here. We love and admire the old country, but we're different. With people like Senator Reeves and me… and you – that's not going to happen."

"You're glib, but you haven't sold me…"

"Before the night's over, I will."

"Perhaps. Perhaps not."

They were silent for a long while, looking across the city.

"Would you stay the weekend?" Oakes asked at last.

"I can't. You know I have a train to catch in the morning. Early."

"I want you to see more of this city – my city. The hotel has a tour on the weekends they call *Monuments by Night*. It's a private affair in a personal limo of all the sites after dark. It's beautiful. I can extend your room reservation through Sunday night and get your ticket changed at no cost."

"How?"

"I know the concierge here. He owes me favors. I can't say more."

"That's the way things are done here in your city?"

"Sometimes."

"I'm not sure I'm comfortable with that."

"Perhaps over dinner I can make you so."

"I'm not so sure you can." She saw his face fall, and continued, "But I am willing to let you try your best to change my mind. You *are* the one paying, *n'est pas?*"

"I'm a man of my word." The *maître d'hôtel* signaled then from inside with a casual nod and a simple gesture with an open hand indicating a table by the ceiling length window looking out over the White House. "It appears our table is ready."

"My, that was quick," Cateline said, smiling up at him and taking his arm. "You must be a man of considerable influence."

"Hopefully. We'll know how much or how little depending on my convincing you to consider my proposal."

"To stay over and take your little monuments excursion?"

"That and becoming part of Senator Reeves' staff."

"As I said, you haven't persuaded me yet. Not quite."

"We'll have to see where we stand after the best dinner on the East Coast."

She gave him an impish look of incredulity. "You set your expectations very high."

"That's why I set my sights on you years ago. You're right, I do have high standards and equally high expectations – of myself and the people I work with. From what I know, so do you. You and I are together going to do great and important things in this town. I guarantee it."

"It was the most marvelous dinner," Cateline said, taking a sip of the wine.

"And…"

"If you can arrange to extend my room to Sunday morning –"

"It's as good as done," Oakes said nonchalantly.

" – and reschedule my ticket on the Amtrak to New York, I would be happy to sightsee your Capitol city."

"Cateline, thank you. I only wish I could convince you to stay over for a week instead of just two days. There's so much to see and experience here. The cherry blossoms are out, the Congress is in session. I'd love to show you both, plus the Smithsonian and the Museum of Natural History. The National Archives."

"Is that where you house your Declaration and the like?" she asked. Her expression was aloof, distant. "At least it isn't the Fourth of July. In my country, we don't celebrate your colonists breaking with our long-suffering and benevolent sovereign."

The Congressional counsel smiled. "We may have to work on your phraseology of certain issues before you meet with the Senator. Could we do that tomorrow perhaps?"

"The witness coaching session or meeting with the senator?"

Oakes chuckled softly. "Both, I'd say. Coaching in the morning and perhaps a late lunch in the Senate Dining Room."

"My goodness! You can get me into the most exclusive dining room in Washington with nary a day's advance notice? It would certainly be smashing, but I don't know I'm quite ready for such power-drenched ambience just yet. You really are putting the rush on me, counselor."

"I am. I'm trying to give you an experience and make you an offer you can't turn down."

"I don't know I'm worth all that, Brandon."

"Trust me, you are. I spent a lot of time years ago going over your school records and internship at Blaine-Johnson. I expect your last few years at the firm will confirm my suspicion that your professional accomplishments are consistent with the promise you showed academically."

"Methinks you're schmoosing me a bit too much."

Oakes sat up straight and puffed out his chest theatrically. "I've not yet begun to schmoose. Let's have another drink down at the *Off the Record* and let me continue my direct examination of why you are the perfect person at the optimum time in your career to take us up on this offer."

Cateline looked at her watch, then folded her linen napkin and placed it beside her plate. "That, I will have to pass on. It's almost time for me to meet up with my friends; it's our last night for another year. And I'm going to pass on the morning's activities as well. If I'm not going back to New York tomorrow, I'll have to conduct the business I'd planned by phone from my room. We could meet for drinks at the bar, say five-ish, and you can show me what a Friday night pub crawl looks like in your fair city, if your wife doesn't mind. I assume she'll be joining us Saturday night also."

"Actually, I am matrimonially unencumbered at the moment."

"My! What an awkward turn of phrase."

"I'm a lawyer – awkward phrases are a barrister's stock in trade. You know that," Oakes said, looking into her eyes and covering her hand with his. "I'll speak with the concierge about extending your reservation and leave a message on your room phone."

"Thank you, Brandon – for the dinner, and for your interest in my career… I mean that."

"Thank you for making memorable what would otherwise have been a very boring evening with my peers from 'the office.' I'm so glad we ran into each other like this." He raised his wineglass toward her and said, "*Salud*. To us, and a future of working together."

Cateline raised her glass to gently touch his. "To the future, whatever it holds. But no promises. I'm not in the least interested in leaving New York for Washington, at the moment."

A half hour later, after changing into casual clothes and comfortable shoes, Cateline left the hotel and walked three blocks to a telephone booth. She dialed a phone number in Maryland that was picked up on the third ring.

"Randall B. Ashby," the voice on the other end of the line said.

"Uncle Randall, this is Cateline."

"Cateline! So good to hear from you again. I suppose you want to talk with Erika."

"Yes, I would, thank you."

"I'll get her for you. But before I do, I understand congratulations are in order. Did I hear right that *The American Lawyer* recently named you one of the *Most Promising Lawyers in America Under the Age of Forty*? That's quite an honor. You were the youngest on the list. We're both very proud of you."

"Thank you. It was quite the surprise."

"Not to us it wasn't. Anyhow, let me get Erika for you."

A minute later, Cateline's aunt Erika came on the line. "So, my dear, how are you?"

"I'm in."

"He offered, and you accepted the job already?"

"Not exactly. Oakes was at the hotel bar tonight and I made sure he saw me. As we expected, he approached and over dinner he dangled the bait of a job in Reeves' office."

"But you didn't accept."

"No. Over the course of the evening, I expressed the vaguest curiosity, making it sound like a courtesy instead of actual interest. I'm going to let it simmer for a few weeks. As for now, Oakes is taking me on a private, personal tour of the city monuments Saturday night and after that I expect he'll do a cursory check of my background again when I show a slight bit more interest in his offer."

"Cateline, be careful. Be very careful. He's a very dangerous man. Almost as much as his boss. I need to be sure you're aware of how risky this business is for you."

"I'm well aware. After hearing Michelle's story, I had to be a part of this investigation. And when Reeves' again did damage to someone in the family the way he treated Glenn, it was absolutely clear that the senator had to be taken down as you Yanks say. If Michelle is right, this man is the worst kind of public figure. He's a liar, a fraud, and much worse."

"That will make him extremely dangerous, especially if and when he's cornered. Are you absolutely certain you want to do this?"

"There's no way I'd back out," Cateline replied. "Justice is long, long overdue. "I can help you set the balance right, Erika. And I will… believe me I will."

Chapter 7

"These new OCS butter bars will never fill our shoes," Benny Barnes said to Glenn and tipped up the white regimental mug, finishing the last of his beer. "You and I were the best bar tenders, the hottest band, and the most outstanding Hohenfels rifle range officers that the old 'Rock of Chickamauga' ever saw." Benny handed his personalized 19th Infantry Regiment beer mug to one of the 2nd lieutenants behind the bar and looked back at his friend. "Hell of a thing you goin' off and leavin' me here with this sorry ass outfit to carry on by myself."

"You're the lucky one, Ben-bo. You get two Christmases in Germany; we only got one."

Although almost midnight with snow falling for the last few hours, the 3rd Battalion officers' call showed no signs of winding down.

The officers and their wives had gathered in a room off the main bar in *The Schloss* – a small, ancient Bavarian castle converted to an Officers Club. It stood about a half mile outside the former German barracks complex on the outskirts of Augsburg, built in the early thirties and commandeered by the American Army in '45. Now it was home to the Third Brigade, 24th Infantry Division (Forward) to which Nolan and Barnes' battalion was assigned. The infantry battalion's officers and their wives gathered at the club once a month on a Friday evening to socialize, but tonight they'd gathered for a farewell party for Glenn and Mary Anne.

"Yup, this is one sorry outfit now that Vickers and Connell and VanDermark went home last June," Benny said, retrieving his mug and taking a drink.

"That crew of company commanders here when we showed up was something special," Glenn agreed. "I'm glad I got to command Charlie company for five months, but I hated to see Vickers go. He was one great guy. I couldn't have had a better C.O. for my first assignment. He worked hard, and played even harder. Connell, too. They gave the battalion some class."

"Now we got Sasquatch and Avery in their places. From class to ass in one fell swoop."

Sasquatch was the nickname Benny had given Captain Nolting, a wrestler from Boston who graduated West Point a year ahead of them and returned from Vietnam to Germany at the end of September. He was a gruff, stocky officer with a dark beard that made him always look unshaven, and thick dark hair that covered his body. He had taken over the company Benny had been assigned to command a month earlier. Both he and Glenn had known Nolting in

97

passing while at the academy and thought him long on war stories and short on diplomacy. Within a few days of his arrival, he gathered them and another classmate in 3rd Battalion – Johnny Ball – together and chewed them out for failing to live up to his idea of the West Point standards of decorum and military bearing.

"You want us to be typical assholes like you?" Benny had asked when the captain was finished lecturing them. Things got more tense after that.

The band in the main bar of the club shifted into a slow Tom Jones number, and Benny's wife Deanna sidled up to them and announced. "I'm dancing with the guest of honor now."

"Don't forget who's takin' you home, girl."

"You... and him, and Mary Anne. We all came in the TR-4, remember?" She smiled prettily and took Glenn's arm. "I would have words with you. Dance with me."

She led him to the parquet dance floor and let him take her in his arms; they began to sway with the music and she smiled up at him saying, "I have some kind words and some harsh words for you tonight. Which would you like first?"

Deanna was, like him, a military brat. He had liked Benny's girl instantly upon meeting her in the fall of their plebe year at the academy.

Her father was a Marine colonel at Camp Pendleton back then, a decorated soldier who was one of the few living Marines who had survived both Iwo Jima in the big war and the Chosen Reservoir during Korea. She had come to West Point to visit Benny the same weekend Mary Anne visited for the first time and the two became close friends, more like sisters, in the years that followed. When Deanna decided two years later to move to the town of Cornwall-on-Hudson to be closer to Benny, Mary Anne transferred to Maris College and the two girls roomed together for Benny and Glenn's senior year. They did everything that year as a foursome, and the girls coordinated their weddings so that they could all honeymoon and spend their graduation leaves together. It seemed only natural they would choose their first assignments in Germany at Augsburg.

"Have I ever told you how much you look like Natalie Wood?" Glenn whispered in Deanna's ear.

"More times than I can count – but you're dodging and weaving again, Nolan."

"I'd call what we're doing more like dancing."

"Not even close. You're an awful dancer – Mary Anne thinks so too."

"It's hereditary according to my grandmother."

"Well, isn't that interesting? But back to my question. Good or bad news first?"

"Bad news doesn't –"

" – doesn't get better with age. Glenn, you are the most predictable of men."

"You think?!"

"All except for one thing; only one thing in five years – until this craziness we're celebrating tonight." She stopped dancing, looked up at him clearly puzzled and furrowed her brow. "Tell me –why in the world are you even in the Army? – and in the infantry of all places? Benny always said you were Air Force blue through and through, in all kinds of crazy ways – your West Point bathrobe was decorated like a zoomie flight suit, you wore an Air Force Academy parka all the time as an upperclassmen, and he swears you rooted for the Falcons over Army in football."

"Benny exaggerates. You of all people should know that. It's complicated."

"I bet it is," Deanna replied.

Glenn had tried, and mostly failed, to explain it to Mary Anne a few months before graduation when the class had gone through selecting branches and initial assignments. It had all started in the summer between his plebe and yearling years.

He had loved that summer at Camp Buckner, living in the old, airy barracks and spending long days learning how to be a soldier – not a spit and polish parade ground martinet, but an actual functioning combat arms trooper. There was something about the early morning platoon formation runs in the dark, and the day-in day-out training that intrigued him. It was hard, and challenging – both physically and mentally. He'd learned to operate and shoot a variety of arms from small individual weapons to large crew served artillery. They taught him how to adjust artillery and mortar fire, how to rappel down cliffs and conduct patrols in the mountain forests west of Main Post. And, there was free time to enjoy canoeing and swimming in Popolopen Lake and the hops Saturday evenings each weekend. He saw close up active-duty soldiers from the 101st Airborne Division who served as their cadre instructors, and he liked what he saw of their officer ranks. It changed him.

The next summer he spent a month at Fort Bragg with the 82nd Airborne, in his uncle's old unit from World War II – the 505th Parachute Infantry Regiment. That same summer he and Benny completed the three week parachute training at Fort Benning.

So, the fall he entered his final year at the Academy, he had been transformed and his perspective on a future career in the military substantially altered. He'd not completely given up on the idea of going into the Air Force as a fighter pilot, but now imagined that he might have more than just one military career path. He saw himself finishing the assignment in the Army his uncle had begun in World War II. He concluded that was now as important as it had briefly seemed the June day at Normandy when he'd met that old soldier, Earl Wright. He decided he would get his jumper's wings and Ranger tab, serve his time in the infantry, finish a tour in Vietnam on the ground, and then transfer to the Air Force to follow in his father's footsteps. After much consideration before branch selections, he decided that made perfect sense. But he'd decided without Mary Anne.

She'd neither understood or much cared for his decision.

It had been a tense time that final spring at West Point as the evening news reports from southeast Asia grew darker and the country turned harshly against the war, led by college campuses and the media. Her family sharply disagreed with the war and despised the idea of his involvement in it. There were moments when he was sure she was reconsidering the wedding they'd planned for two weeks after his graduation.

"All right, lieutenant, I agree with you that bad news should be dealt with right away," Deanna was saying. She raised her eyebrows and declared, "I'm upset with you for taking away my best friend. Really upset."

"It's the life. You're a brat – you know how that works."

"But you didn't have to volunteer for Vietnam."

"It's kind of a long story," he said uneasily.

"If it goes past the end of this song, I'll ask them to play it again, or we can go out to the foyer. But you *are* going to explain it to me. And then you need to talk with your wife and do a better job than you have of explaining it to her. She was upset – I mean really upset, especially having to learn it from Colonel Parker instead of you."

Glenn bit his lip. "Yeah. I really screwed this up. Didn't I? You're mad at me, too."

"Well, *yeah* – of course! I'm on her side in this." She gave him a stern look through narrowed eyes, wrinkling her nose; quickly she relaxed and poked his ribs with a finger. "But I can't stay mad at you for long. Not after what you did for me."

In the last quarter of their senior year at the academy, he'd talked Benny out of putting in for a tour in Vietnam as his first assignment upon graduation. His friend had always been more 'gung-ho' than he let on and had convinced himself that the earliest possible tour in Southeast Asia would be the best for his career and be a more favorable mark in his file. Glenn, over that span of two months convinced him otherwise.

"I've never said anything, but I know you talked him into coming to Germany first so we could spend at least a little time together."

"And he made me promise to do the same if he did it. We picked the same division and the minions of the assignment gods in Washington put us in the same battalion. Things worked out better than expected. We got to spend our first assignment together with our wives."

"Not that much better, it turns out. Mary Anne and I were adding it up a while ago. It's depressing how much you guys were gone between three month-long trips to Hohenfels and Grafenwohr, plus another month on that NATO training exercise in January. Almost every week when you weren't at a major training arear, you spent three or four days in the field locally, or a week or so out somewhere on a move out alert. When we counted it all out, you two spent over six months away, somewhere."

"Well, you know – it was the Rooskies and their galloping Communism. Remember they invaded Czechoslovakia when we were in Infantry Officer Basic at Benning," he offered. "But we did have some really good times over here, didn't we?"

That summer, the four of them had traveled to the Bavarian Alps one weekend for a quick tour of Garmisch-Partenkirchen and both the Hohenschwangau and Neu Schweinstein castles. Months later, they had spent two weeks together at the town of Murnau in the foothills of the Alps while Glenn and Benny attended a military wheeled vehicle maintenance course. But it was true he and Benny had been away from their apartments in the military housing complex more than they'd been home.

"And you two are accomplished *touristas,*" Glenn was saying.

"Paris and Marseille and Brussels and Amsterdam were interesting."

"Thank goodness for *Eurorail* Passes. I assume Innsbruck and Vienna were too."

"So was Nürnberg. It would have been better if we hadn't had to do it by ourselves."

"Next time we'll do it differently."

"I hope there is a next time… for all of us," Deanna said softly. Her eyes grew moist; she looked away momentarily and then back at him "I want you to promise me you won't do anything stupid. Listen to me – bravery is only a short half-step away from stupidity, so don't you go playing the hero over there. I told Benny the same thing when I first heard you got orders. I still don't understand why you had to go and volunteer. Benny and Johnny Ball and your three classmates in the other battalion will all be going over in another two, maybe three months. I don't get it. And neither does Mary Anne."

"I wanted to get my unit of choice by volunteering, by getting ahead of the cattle call. You're a brat – you know what I'm saying."

"Maybe. Maybe not."

The band on the raised platform broke into a fast number played loudly and he said, "Not here. Too much noise. Out in the entrance hallway." They found high back chairs in a small alcove and sat facing one another.

"The guy on the first floor in our stairwell in the apartment complex was a helicopter pilot who'd done two tours in Vietnam. We got to know them, played bridge with he and his wife now and then. He loaned me a book called 'The Year of the Horse' about the 1st Air Cavalry Division in 1965. I asked him about the unit and he said it was the best over there – they lived like pigs but they took care of their people better than any unit in Vietnam. He hadn't flown for them but knew their reputation. I was impressed by what I read and what I had heard of them at the academy and from this guy downstairs. That's the unit I want to get into. So I volunteered rather than waiting for the desk jockeys in Washington to arbitrarily put my name into the next wheelbarrow-load of guys going overseas."

"How do you know you're going to get your wish?" she asked.

"I'm not sure I am. But I might. I think my chances are better by doing it this way. I also wrote a letter to a battalion commander volunteering for his unit and asking him to request me by name with the replacement headquarters over there."

"You think that'll work?"

"I'm hoping so. It's worth a try. I chose this battalion based on what I read in that book. None of those guys named in it are there now, but the unit is."

"You volunteered for this division because you think it improves your survival odds?"

"That and they have a really cool patch that'll look good on my greens down the road."

She slapped him hard on the arm. "Can't you be serious just this once?"

"I am serious."

"Then why are you smiling? You know Mary Anne thinks you've done this because your little brother is over there now and you don't want him getting all the glory."

"She told me that, too. And she's wrong. You and I both know that because we know there's no glory in any war, this one especially."

Deanna shifted uncomfortably in the chair. " Didn't mean to set you off. Shouldn't have said it that way. It's just that – well, you're special to me."

"And you're special to me, too."

"She's special to you?! How so?" Mary Anne asked, standing in the gray stone doorway with her arms folded across her chest. "I come looking to tell you Benny wants to get going before the snow drifts get above the roof, and here I find you hiding away in a castle alcove holding hands with my best friend. What gives?"

"We were just talking."

"I'm not even going to ask about what." She walked over and took Deanna's hand. "I hope this isn't a problem in the making. Husbands these days are a dime a dozen, but it's really hard to find a good friend." Mary Anne looked at Glenn. "You go help Benny shovel out the car and warm it up for us. And don't expect us to walk through snow, either. Drive it up to the front door when you're done. Now go."

After he'd gone, Deanna turned and said, "I talked to him and got the same story you told me. Don't be too hard on him."

"He should have talked to me about it before he made a decision."

"Probably so. But he had your best interests at heart. He'll be coming back earlier."

"Hopefully they won't have to go at all," Mary Anne replied wishfully. "President Nixon just announced he plans a second withdrawal to pull out what? – thirty-five thousand troops? Maybe none of them will have to go over there."

"Wouldn't that be great," Deanna said, sounding hopeful. But she knew the fighting in South Vietnam was far from over, and that even the president's most optimistic predictions wouldn't keep Benny and Glenn and their classmates from having to spend some time in that place at best. Glenn at least had a plan, and she thought it would have been nice if Benny had given the situation as much thought. "I'm not going to worry about it. Right now our biggest problem is fitting all four of us into a two-seater. We have *no* room at all. I told him not to buy a sports car, but he wouldn't listen."

"Listening is something neither of them do well," Mary Anne agreed.

"Truer words were never spoken."

"Agreed. Let's get our coats and say our 'goodnights' to the brass. I'm going to miss this place – and you."

"I've been thinking, and I have some ideas how we might work something out for the next year – you know, make the time go faster while they're gone. We've got three days to work out the details."

*   *   *   *   *

The sweet voice sifted into his subconscious and intruded on his dream. When he slowly, reluctantly opened his eyes she came into view – hazy at first but gradually more distinct – and his vision of the young girl he'd been sitting with on the Ocean City beach slowly dissolved, replaced by a woman in her late thirties. He rotated his head working out kinks in his neck.

"We'll be landing at Tan Son Nhut airport in about fifteen minutes, soldier," the stewardess said, smiling at him. "Please stow your tray, fasten your seat belt and bring your seat back to the full upright position."

"What's the weather on the ground in Saigon?" Brad asked.

"Ninety-six degrees, and clear. Not much wind. Now stow your service tray, please."

Nolan looked around at the packed cabin of the Seaboard World stretch DC-8. *Sardines*, he thought. *Wall to wall olive drab sardines. Damn! What a long, uncomfortable flight. Ten and a half hours with a cabin filled with a hundred and thirty-five other hapless souls wearing OD green fatigues.*

It had been miserably cold and rainy in Washington state at SeaTac airport when they took off on the first leg of his flight – but not as cold as it had been in St. Louis a week earlier on the day after Thanksgiving when he said goodbye to his mother and father. His brief stay at Fort Lewis had been a real pain in the butt, not at all like the fond memories his father had from when he was a boy while his family had been stationed there in the mid '30s. *Times do change*, Brad thought and leaned forward to get a glimpse of the countryside out of the small window.

Grinding flap gears and the hard thump of landing gear locking into place announced their final approach into the South Vietnamese capitol. The land outside their windows was lush and green and, in his mind, filled with wiry little Viet Cong guerillas intent on shooting them down with their RPGs and AK-47s. After the long, bumpy approach they were down and lazily taxiing until they stopped at a terminal that could have been located anywhere in the lower 48 of the good ol' USA.

Fifteen minutes later he was walking through the relative comfort and – he assumed – security of an airport that came fairly close to rivaling some smaller terminals in America.

"Yo! Nolan!"

Brad looked around and saw a familiar, friendly face belonging to a tall, sandy-haired Texan. "Lee Haskell?! What in the hell are you doing here, man?"

"Come to rescue your sorry ass from the 90th Replacement Battalion."

"I have no idea what you're talking about."

"Suffice it to say, I'm goin' to pull your chestnuts out of the fire once again, as I have been for the whole of this year. Ol' Lee-O the Legendary Longhorn is here to be your guide since you lack not only a sense of direction, but a sense of purpose. Rest easy. You're in good hands now, pard."

Lee Haskell could trace his family back to the Goliad Massacre, an event as infamous in Texas as the treatment of the Alamo defenders just two weeks earlier. He was tall, skinny and when out of uniform, was always found wearing cowboy boots and a cattleman's crown western hat. He and Haskell had been assigned to the same instructor pilot after the initial training phase at Fort Wolters near Mineral Wells, an hour west of Dallas-Ft. Worth. Both had done well enough in flight school by the end of their Advanced time at Fort Rucker to be offered a transition into Cobra gunships.

"So you came straight over?" Brad asked as they made their way to the baggage area.

"Yup."

"I thought you were going to marry that girl from just outside San Antonio, the one whose picture you carried around all the time. She was absolutely gorgeous. I can't believe you passed that up."

Haskell got a pained look on his face. "You know, Nolan, I got to thinkin' about it there at the end of our time at Rucker and I came to the conclusion that a woman that good lookin' was probably just after my money."

Brad scoffed at the idea. "You're a Wobbly–one. A junior, junior warrant officer."

"I made a lot of TDY money in flight school."

"Which you spent nearly as fast as they gave it to you. And then you bought that Vette when we left Rucker."

"When you're a legend you need an outstanding set of wheels."

"You know Lee, I'm not so sure I want to be rescued from anything by you. Actually, I don't have a clue why I need rescuing."

Haskell breathed deeply and sighed. "Here's the drill. If you go through the 90th in Long Binh, they'll send you to the first slot they have on the top of the list. Hell, son, you could end up flying ash and trash for the Vietnamese Arvins for a year. Those pencil whippers at the 90th don't care what you want or what may or may not be good for you or your career."

"I'm not a career man, Lee-O. You know that. I'm a guy who screwed up a really good deal in college and got hoodwinked by a recruiter. You know that, too."

"I do. And I know you had your heart set on flying King Airs in Europe, living the high life. Well, friend – life is full of big disappointments, and then you die."

"I don't plan on dying any time soon."

"You might," Lee said, raising his eyebrows emphatically, "if you get assigned to the wrong unit. And that can damn sure happen goin' through the Replacement Battalion. But your old stick buddy is here to keep all that nasty from happenin' to you."

"And how do you plan to do that?" Brad asked suspiciously, very much aware of some really hair-brained schemes the Texan had been the progenitor of during their many months together at Wolters, then Rucker.

"Here's the deal. My C.O. has in the past worked some arrangements with the C.O. of the 90th Replacement in Long Binh. He's traded him some souvenirs and equipment for just such a moment as this. We're gettin' a little low on pilots and crew chiefs, and kinda close for a goodly number rotatin' back home. Seems like all this talk back in the world about pullin' out slowed down the pipeline some. Now, my commander got hold to a list of names on this and a bunch of other arriving troop planes coming in. I got a look from one of the company clerks and saw your name. Told the major and he sent me down to lasso and carry you back to the

Ghostriders. Then they'll do somethin' back there with orders and such to make it all legal, sorta. The whole Army over here runs on shenanigans and monkey business like that."

Brad thought about it for a while. Strange as it sounded, he knew the Texan was probably right about how things really got done in a war zone where the rulebooks got tossed out the window. "I don't know, Lee. I've heard the Cav gets in a lot of scrapes – that they go looking for trouble all the time. What if I just take my chances with the replacement battalion?"

"Bad move, Brad. Real bad move. For lots of reasons. Lots and lots of 'em."

"People who say it like that usually don't have reason one on their sheet of paper."

"Okay – listen up. First, the Ghostriders are probably the premier Huey outfit in the Cav; and the Cav is the best unit you could get assigned to coming through III Corps. Point two – the 1st Air Cav will take better care of you because they know how to treat pilots; they wrote the book on it from the beginning back a half dozen years ago. Point three – there is no division over here that has a better working relationship between air assets and ground troops; we take care of the grunts and they take good care of us. Point four – Charlie Company, 227th is located at Phouc Vinh, a generally pacified area now. Point five – I'm in the company and since you lack common sense and a sense of direction and purpose, I'll be on hand close by to keep you out of trouble like I did in flight school."

"You almost had me convinced until that last comment. Is that all, Lee?"

"I'm just getting' warmed up, but I'm tellin' you –"

"You're telling me a story, but not the whole truth. I know you too well, Haskell. What's the rest of the story? You're sounding just a bit too eager to get me to your unit. What's the rest of it."

The Texan cleared his throat. "I was getting' to it. Just hear me out, all right? The worst thing you can be over here is an FNG – you know what I'm sayin'?"

"Sure – the new guy."

"Well, turns out right now I'm the FNG in the Ghostriders, and –"

"When I get there, I'll be the new rookie and that'll take the heat off of you. I knew there had to be something."

"Now look, that's not as bad as it sounds. I'll be there to read you in and watch your back. I got it all pretty well scouted out. I can tell you who to watch out for and all – like there's a guy named Conrad Goff. He's called *ConMan*. You need to be real careful with him. But I'm tellin' you, it ain't all that bad. We're flying from before sunup to after sundown most every day so there isn't all that much time for grab-ass."

Brad was still thinking about it when a truck pulling a trailer loaded with their baggage showed up. He found his duffle bag and hoisted it over his shoulder.

"Whatta you say, ol' stick buddy?" Haskell asked, "You with me or not?"

Finally he said, "Okay, Lee-O, I'm in. But if this turns out less than wonderful, for any reason, I'm going to be all over you."

Haskell nodded giving him a big grin. "You can thank me now, because I *gare-on-tee* you're gonna be happy as a pup with two tails. Welcome to the Ghostriders."

* *

Mortar rounds exploded nearby, splitting the heavy evening air with that distinctive, hollow double *wha–hump*. Brad cringed, ducked his head and looked around quickly for the closest cover. *Damn that Lee Haskell*, he thought.

"They're not after us," offered Conrad Goff, a CW-2 and one of the old hands in the company. "This happens about once a week. Sometimes more. The gooks hate the 1st of the 9th because they're so damned gung-ho in the local AO. So, they mortar the shit out of them all the time. We'll grab a few beers and watch the fireworks. This is what passes for entertainment in this place when there's no Filipino band at the Red Hawk, Nolan – which it turns out we also have tonight. Your timing is perfect showin' up for both in one night. This is like an early Christmas present. Enjoy it," he said and disappeared inside the first platoon hooch.

It was the end of his second day in country for Brad Nolan, now officially assigned to Charlie company, 227th Aviation Battalion. He was still a little disoriented.

ConMan reappeared from inside the hooch with his red cooler and two lawn chairs. They climbed to the top of the sandbagged company clubhouse and joined a half dozen other bare-chested pilots lounging on top the bunker drinking beer and watching the fireworks across the runway. For the next ten minutes mortar rounds sporadically landed among the revetments and bunkers a couple of hundred yards away on the other side of the northeast/southwest runway. To the north, two gunships took turns making runs on the suspected NVA mortar position; the firing of rockets from American Cobras and the explosion of enemy mortars close to the Ghost Rider spectators met with occasional whoops and hollering from C Company pilots.

"This wouldn't be any fun at all if they were shooting at us," Goff said, opening another Miller. "But since it's those Black Stetson assholes in the 1/9, it's a hoot."

Brad frowned, wondering. "They're Americans."

"Those guys over there have this 'they can't kill me attitude.' Besides, it's only 82 mike-mike mortars. Those bunkers – and ours – can take a direct hit... almost. It's only their birds that are in real danger, but it sure rattles those glory hounds over there. They could stand a little humility." After a while, it got quiet and *ConMan* passed him another beer, looked around the group on top of the bunker and said, "Anybody know whose turn it is to steal the CO's jeep?"

Furtive looks were exchanged.

"Bailey's, I think," Nick Sheppard quickly replied. Sheppard, an aircraft commander, was on the schedule to give Brad his area orientation the following day. "But he's got the Nighthawk mission so he'll be gone this evening. Why?"

"I thought maybe I'd introduce Nolan to a Charlie company tradition. He's gotta start earning his patch sometime," *ConMan* said. "Nolan, let's go purloin the CO's jeep and take it for a spin. Stealing a commanding officer's ride is great sport – happens all the time."

Brad's antennae went on alert. "Really?" he said, suspiciously.

"Sure. Pilots take and hide it somewhere on Phouc Vinh and the old man has to go find it in the morning. Filching the CO's jeep is a requirement for a new guy to get his Ghost Rider patch. It's one of those little things to keep up the morale of pilots. There's a free case of beer for the guy who does it the most in any given month. I think Bailey holds the company record with eleven, but he's one of the old timers in the unit now. It'll be dark in less than a half hour. We'll do this and then meet everyone in the *Red Hawk* for a celebratory beer."

Brad caught Lee Haskell's eye; his friend glanced back at him, slowly lowered his hat over his eyes and looked away. *All right, I see what's going on here,* Brad thought. It was the same everywhere in the military – each new arrival had to be tested, and humiliated, before becoming one of the group. It was a time honored service tradition.

His first night they had baited his bunk with sausages tied at the corners of his mosquito net to attract rats. He'd awakened at some point to the sense of something heavy sitting on his chest. He reached out and touched a hairy object, let out a shout when it ran down his stomach and a leg, and then realized there were three or four others inside the netting with him. He was thrashing around ripping at the poncho liner and finally escaped from the bunk, landing hard on the floor. He could hear laughter coming through the thin plywood walls up and down the hallway. *Welcome to the Ghostriders,* he had thought, and began plotting payback.

"I'm game," Brad said finally, catching amused glances being traded back and forth. "I've got to tighten up my mosquito netting so those visitors don't get in again tonight. I'll meet you down by the latrine as soon as it gets dark and we'll go for a little ride."

"You're on, new guy," Goff said, looking satisfied. "The first one doesn't count. I'll get the credit so I can keep up with Bailey."

"No problem," Nolan replied easily. "I'll make sure you get all the credit."

They met outside down the road from the first platoon hooch in total darkness an hour later and scoured the area until finding the commander's vehicle sitting alongside several others in the darkness outside the *Red Hawk*. The spare tire's plywood insert on the back of the Jeep read *Ghost Rider 6* beneath the company emblem –a Huey flying head-on with a ghostly apparition surrounding it. Brad got into the driver's seat and immediately found the lock on the chain looped through the steering wheel and welded onto the floorboard.

"What are you going to do now, Nolan?" *ConMan* asked.

Brad took a key ring out of his pocket, shined his flashlight on the lock and inserted one after the other until, on the fifth try, the hasp sprung open.

"How'd you do that?" Goff asked, incredulous, as he jumped into the passenger seat.

"I went out to the motor pool and found the spare keys to all the vehicle locks. Let's get out of here before the major comes out of the club."

They took off down the road paralleling the runway until they came to the fence at the northeast side of the compound. Brad switched off the lights and the ignition; they sat in the darkness listening to the faraway sounds of Led Zeppelin and Janis Joplin coming from somebody's radio. From overhead came the sound of helicopter blades beating the air. *ConMan* pulled a flask from his hip pocket, took a swig and handed it over to Nolan.

"Didn't think you could pull it off," Goff said. "I'm impressed."

"I thought you would be." Brad replied, taking a sip of bourbon, and then another before passing the flask back. "You've never done this before, have you, *ConMan*?"

"Sure I have. Lots of times."

Nolan knew Goff was lying to him and decided to have a little fun.

"Have you ever seen a Jeep fly, *ConMan*?"

"What do you mean?"

Without replying, Brad turned around, flipped on the FM radio, and tuned it to the Phouc Vinh tower frequency. He started the jeep, pulled onto the runway and keyed the radio mic. "Phouc Vinh tower, this is Army six-niner-one, ready for south departure."

"*Roger, Army six-niner-one. Phouc Vinh tower. Winds two-five-zero at ten... altimeter two-niner-niner-four... I have negative visual contact, six-niner-one. Do you have lights?*"

"Roger, tower. Lights coming on." Brad flipped on the Jeep's headlights and popped the clutch, quickly accelerating down the runway.

"What the hell are you doing, Nolan?!"

"Seeing if this crate can fly, *ConMan*. Watch my airspeed – tell me when I hit ninety."

"You crazy son-of-a –"

"Army six-niner-one. This is Phouc Vinh tower. Identify yourself! Identify... immediately!" the tower operator yelled into the mic, his voice tense and shrill. They were halfway down the runway when a deep, calmer voice came over the frequency.

"All right, you crazy bastard, get off my runway... NOW! The MPs are on the way."

Brad switched off the lights and slowed the Jeep, pulling off to the side of the airstrip. He spotted an empty revetment in the 1/9 Cav area, turned into it and turned off the engine. Within seconds, an MP Jeep appeared from beside the tower with its lights flashing and siren wailing in the still night.

"Damn you Nolan! We've got nowhere to run," Goff yelled at him. "There's no place we can go that they can't see us... and they're getting close!"

"No problem," Brad said easily. "You stay in the shadows here, and I'll take care of everything... trust me."

The MPs were driving down the middle the runway, a searchlight probing both sides. Brad stepped out of the shadows, directly in front of the MP Jeep and started waving his arms and yelling to get their attention. One of them got out of the vehicle, walked toward him and shined his flashlight in Brad's face and then up and down his uniform, stopping at the nametag above his right pocket.

"What's going on Mr. Goff?" the youngish MP asked him.

"I was looking around our revetment area and out here on the flight line for my sunglasses," Brad replied. "I'm sure they fell out of my helmet bag when we got in earlier this evening... then these two drunk nutcases in a blacked out Jeep almost ran me over on the edge of the runway."

"Are you all right, sir?"

"I will be.." He turned around and pointed down the runway beyond where they stood. "They went that way and turned left at the end of the runway.

"Don't worry, we'll catch 'em, Mr. Goff. Thanks for your help, sir." The MP jumped back in the Jeep and roared down the runway in the direction Brad had pointed. When they were gone, *ConMan* joined him and they ran across the runway, disappearing into the darkness.

They stopped in shadows and watched the MP's headlights move through the 1/9 area.

"What did that MP call you back there?" *ConMan* asked.

"He called me Mr. Goff," Brad said. "I guess I should have asked if you minded me borrowing your nomex shirt, but mine is still covered with rat droppings and sausage grease from last night."

"Damn you, Nolan!"

"What's the big deal? You said you wanted credit for this one, right? Now you've got it."

Brad handed over the flight suit shirt and jogged in the dark toward the Red Hawk.

Chapter 8

It was nearly dinner time, and the Fort Lewis Officers' Club was crowded.

Glenn sipped his drink at the end of the long bar where he had a view of the lounge. Some kind of special event for nurses was scheduled according to the free-hand sign just inside the front door and a small, noisy cluster of Air Force and Army nurses in class A uniforms occupied the far side of the dark lounge. They chattered loudly among themselves, drawing as much attention as a crowd of drunken second lieutenants in the *Infantry Bar* at Benning.

He looked at each of the women and graded their looks on the scale he'd used while a cadet on the First Class Trip the summer before his senior year at the Academy. Most of them passed muster and there were even a few who were off his chart; one of them, a stunning Air Force 1st lieutenant with blond hair, reminded him of Mary Anne.

His gaze fell on an Army nurse lieutenant – a petite, moderately attractive girl sitting at the fringe of the female gathering, looking weary and out of sorts. She seemed strangely distant and detached from the rest of her crowd and he idly wondered why. *Little Orphan Annie*, he thought; *now there's one unhappy camper*. He watched her briefly, finished his drink and checked his watch. It was still fifteen minutes until the dining room opened.

It had been a miserable day.

The chill had seeped into his marrow out on the rifle range where he had spent a damp, drizzly day shooting the M-16, not for qualification but familiarization. It had been an utter waste, as had the day before on another range being taught patrolling and ambush techniques by a cadre of old sergeants he doubted had ever been on a mission in Vietnam. If Fort Lewis was typical of the level of training given to troops en route to Nam, the war really was lost – as the nightly news commentators were saying more and more frequently.

Glenn looked back at the group of nurses and noticed *Orphan Annie* still looking lonely and detached. He understood. Leaving home this time was one of the most difficult things he'd ever had to do and guessed that, like the nurse lieutenant, he too probably looked decidedly miserable. As he sat there thinking about Mary Anne, his mental arithmetic told him they had been married eighteen months but had spent only half that time together as a married couple.

By the end of this tour we'll be married two and a half years and spent less than nine months together. This is no way to live your life, son.

His young bride – and her parents – had already told him that in so many words.

They had spent a long and awkward two weeks with her parents before he caught the flight to St. Louis to see his family. She had elected to stay in Baltimore with her folks while he was overseas – that bothered him because her father and her older brother, Corey, were openly hostile to what the country was doing in Vietnam. For the first time, he sensed he wasn't welcome in the MacEagan's big colonial home.

He glanced around at the group of noisy women and once again his attention was drawn to the solitary, melancholic nurse. Something about her piqued his interest. Her dirty blond hair was pulled back into a French roll and he continued watching her as she gazed toward the foyer as if looking for someone.

Abruptly she stood and walked slowly over to bar and took a seat on one of the few unoccupied stools near where he was sitting. As the bartender moved past him toward the girl, Glenn caught his eye and slid a twenty forward. "Whatever she's drinking, it's on me."

He watched the girl order a drink, and when it came she placed a bill on the bar; the bartender whispered something and then motioned toward Glenn who nodded when she raised her glass in his direction. She took a short sip, set the glass on the bar and immediately turned her back to him. *Well, Nolan, that didn't make much of an impression did it?*

"You look lonely," Glenn said, and the girl turned, looking him up and down as Sergeant Gerber had when he'd taken over his first platoon that December day in Germany a year ago.

"You think you saw that as dark as it is in here? I'm not lonely, and can I tell you something else? – that's the worst pickup line I ever heard. But, thanks again for the drink."

He smiled at this. "I'm not trying to pick you up."

"Sure. If you say so." She took another sip of the drink and again turned away from him.

"I'm trying to be neighborly, that's all. My guess is you're like me – a long way from home and just a few days away from an overseas assignment, stuck in a crowd of people you don't know and maybe don't even like. You're feeling alone and just trying to cope. I get that. I've been there… in fact, that's where I am right now."

The girl looked back at him, frowning. "You buy me one drink and you think that allows you to psychoanalyze me?"

"Tell me I'm wrong."

"You're… you're annoying."

"If you say so. But I'm not wrong."

She rolled her eyes. "All right, Mr. –"

"Lieutenant. Glenn Nolan."

"All right, lieutenant. But I'm not lonely, and I'm definitely not interested in doing anything with you. I'm not *that* desperate."

He chuckled softly. "I'm just a guy who hates to eat alone. I'm not looking for anything, except dinner conversation. They teach you that bedside manner in nursing school?"

"Absolutely. In my clinicals at the Methodist Hospital in Houston."

"Texas girl, eh?"

"Not all my life. But I got there as soon as I could." She sipped the drink without taking her eyes off him and said, "I suppose you're going to Vietnam on your first tour?"

"It is. You're going there, too, I take it."

"For the second time, and hopefully the last. With *Vietnamization,* the shooting war is just about over." She looked him up and down again and asked, "You're not a lifer or a helicopter pilot, are you? I won't even drink with you if you are – there's no future in that. "

"A lifer? I haven't decided yet. But certainly not a helicopter pilot." He stood and moved to the stool next to her. "You don't look old enough to be going on your second tour."

The girl gave him a withering glance. "You think I'm just a child? Lieutenant, that's socially clumsy. One more strike and you're out."

"Let me buy dinner and make it up to you. They have a great surf and turf here. I had it last night and plan on it for dinner every day until the big bird takes me out of here. It's filet mignon and a lobster tail, both done perfectly. This is going to be your last chance for a while to enjoy a –"

"Thanks, but no," she said emphatically, lowering her eyebrows in a frown. "I have this reception to attend for all us girls headed over to the jungle tomorrow; command performance."

"All the more reason –"

"Are you deaf? Can't you take *no* for an answer?!" she said, turning and fixing him with a suddenly fierce gaze. "Why are you men always so hardheaded and… and unthinking. A tear rolled slowly down her face, streaking one of her cheeks with mascara. She took a tissue from inside her purse and blotted her eyes and then looked at herself in a small compact mirror. "Now look what you've done!" she said loudly, attracting the attention of people nearby.

Glenn felt suddenly guilty and reached out to touch her arm. "I'm sorry – really I am. I was only trying to make conversation."

"Damn you!" she said shrilly, looking away and tossing her head. "Damn all you silly, noble, mulish sons-of-bitches!"

"All right," he said softly, surprised at the sudden outburst from this girl who seemed to be precipitously close to melting before his eyes. "Who was he?"

The girl looked at him through her tears. "Who was he?! None of your business and –" She took a deep breath and sighed, then said softly, "His name was Bobby – a medevac pilot who flew out of Lai Khe. Everybody called him *Short Stack* because he could barely reach the tail rotor pedals. The last time I saw him alive was three weeks ago, late one afternoon at the helipad outside our hospital. He brought in three patients from a Special Forces camp that was under attack, and he was wounded himself. But he wouldn't let me treat him – there were still others he had to save before the sun went down. They allowed me to accompany his body back home. I won't ever have anything to do with a helicopter jock. You're sure you're not a pilot?"

"Honest, I'm not. This guy meant a lot to you. I'm sorry," he said softly.

"How could you be?" she replied in a quiet, grief-filled voice. "You don't know a thing about him… or me."

"Tell me about it over dinner. I'm a good listener. My wife says I am, anyhow."

She took a deep breath. "You're married?"

"To my high school sweetheart. We've been a couple for six and a half years; married eighteen going on nineteen months."

"What would she say if she knew you were asking some strange woman out for dinner."

"She'd understand. And, you don't *seem* all that strange."

"You know what I meant," she said caustically, looking at him with a look as cold and hard as Damascus steel. "You're buying?"

"That's what I said."

She held his stare for a while, contemplating, and at last stuck out her hand and said, "I'm Jennifer Kolarik and I'm an operating room nurse at the 45th Surgical Hospital."

"Glenn Nolan. Duties unassigned at the moment, but I hope to get sent to the 1st Cav sometime in the next week."

"What branch are you?"

"Infantry."

"Then we do have a lot to talk about," she replied, pursing her lips and shaking her head sadly from side to side. "I accept your invitation, you poor unlucky schmuck – for dinner and conversation only. I won't play 'the *other* woman'… not even for one night."

"We're on the same wave length." She took his arm when he offered it and let him lead her to the small, and plainly decorated dining room. "I've seen nicer dining rooms in lots of clubs but the Surf and Turf made up for the atmosphere and better than that, I don't have to eat alone." Soon the waiter returned with drinks, took their orders and then Glenn raised his glass in a toast. "To a good trip out and a safe return home."

"I'll drink to that," the girl replied, nodding at him as they touched glasses. "And to an injury free and quiet tour. May I never see you again after tonight."

"Am I that bad a conversationalist?" Glenn smiled to himself.

"Well, Lieutenant Nolan, trust me you don't want to see me again because if you do it'll be under the worst of circumstances. I told you I'm an operating room nurse."

"You did. So, why did you go into nursing, and why are you going back to Vietnam?" he asked, leaning forward and looking into her eyes.

"My mother was a teacher, and I knew I didn't want to do that. I'm not really all that good with kids, and I wanted a job that paid more than fifty bucks a week; at least close to a living wage. As far as why I'm going to Vietnam… To finish my tour, but now that I've seen the elephant and had time to think it over, I'm not so sure anymore that my reasons for going in the first place were really all that good." She smiled at him and tilted her head. "And please don't call me Jennifer. That's how my mother and the Sisters at school addressed me just before punishment was administered. Call me Jenny."

"So you're a Catholic girl? So's my wife."

"I'd rather think of myself as Polish. You think that's funny?" she asked when he smiled. "I'm really offended by Polock jokes and... You're laughing at me."

"Not really," he said, and chuckled.

"You're not a very good liar. You *are* laughing at me, aren't you?"

"Have you ever been to Baltimore?"

"No fair answering a question with a question. But, no, and I have no desire to. I grew up in Springfield Township, New Jersey. Is that close enough?"

"Not quite. Because, you see, there's a little walk-in restaurant in Baltimore that makes the best hotdogs and Polish sausages anywhere on the East Coast. They've been there for probably three or four decades and it's a local landmark – *everybody* in Baltimore goes there. It's called *Polock Johnny's*. So, when you said to call you Jenny and that you were Polish, it was the first thing that popped into my mind. Polock Johnny – Polock Jenny; you see why…"

"So now I'm Polock Jenny." She gave him a look of incredulity. "You think I enjoy being made fun of, lieutenant?"

"I'm not trying to make fun."

"Then you're trying to insult me?"

Glenn laughed loud enough to draw the attention of those at nearby tables. He leaned forward and whispered, "I'm digging myself a pretty deep hole here, aren't I?"

"You've got a good start on one," she replied. "Polock Jenny, eh? You think you're pretty clever, don't you?"

"I'm not real sure I want to answer that," he replied, sensing her demeanor had changed, brightened, and that she wasn't as upset with him as she wanted him to believe.

"This is going to cost you a very expensive bottle of wine, lieutenant. Maybe two."

"As long as you drink them instead of throwing the bottles at me."

"Deal." She waved the waiter over and ordered a bottle of wine from the list. "I took it easy on you. It's only the second most expensive on the list. No more Polock Jenny."

"Not from my lips." He took another sip of the drink and said, "You're not so sure why you went to Vietnam? It sounds like you volunteered."

"I did. To follow in my father's footsteps, so to speak. He was a tanker in the big war, serving under General Patton. Of course, I couldn't do that but I could do my duty with the skills I have. In my neighborhood, growing up, most of the men were returning veterans from the war. And I remember thinking, just like all the other kids, that they were all heroes – people of great courage, champions of democracy. I wanted to be like that, somebody who went and did something important for the country and came back a hero. It's not working out the way I thought it would. This thing in Vietnam… A lot of people are saying it's not a good war."

"But it's the only war we've got."

Her eyes narrowed. "I hate that expression. It's the kind of thing those Saigon warriors and ticket punchers in headquarters somewhere would say. I hope for your sake, and the sake of your troops, you're better than that."

Before he could reply, the waiter interrupted with their salads and Glenn decided to let her comment slide for the moment.

They ate in silence for a while until she said, "I can be pretty hard on people. You wanted light dinner conversation and ended up seeing my worst side. You didn't deserve that."

"You seem to be wound a little tight."

"You're right. I am." She took a deep breath and sighed. "The world isn't the way I thought it would be just a few short months ago, and here I am having dinner on your dime and thanking you by being a harping bitch."

"I think you're being a little too tough on yourself."

"Actually, I'm not. I've changed since before I went over there, and I don't like what I've become. It's because of the war. I hate it, and I don't want to go back. I dread the thought."

"Tell me why – I'm a good listener."

"You keep saying that."

"Try me."

"I'm not sure I should." She took a sip of wine while looking at him over the rim of her glass, contemplating for a long time. "All right, Nolan. Remember, you asked for it."

"Fire away."

"I worked in the emergency room in our hospital at Lai Khe. An Army surgical hospital is essentially one big emergency room – or multiple ERs with attached recovery wards. More often than not, I was assigned in the triage area. I picked up wounded off the helicopters or the ambulances, and brought them into an emergency room – surgery prep, and stabilized them as best I could. Triage is where you prioritize and do life-saving procedures before sending them into the operating room, but the worst part is making the decisions. The 'expectant' category, that's the hardest." Jenny looked away momentarily, blinking back tears. "Nurses are trained and socially groomed to see every life is important; my job is to save every one of those boys. But I learned that was impossible. So when casualties come into triage fast and furious, and many of them with extensive injuries, what I'd end up doing was sacrificing one life for another. I was playing God – deciding which life was most valuable."

"You wanted to save everybody – like your medevac pilot. It sounds like you were determining which ones had the best chance of survival."

"I like to rationalize it that way. But there are times when…" She paused and tears formed in her eyes. "That was hard. Our hospital covered a pretty large area, and it would happen routinely – often a half dozen times in a week we'd get a flood of wounded from one of the units and we'd be overwhelmed."

"That's real pressure."

"It cauterized my soul – deadened my conscience. I feel like I'm one big scab all over, and when I let people get too close, they rub against that and knock it off. It's painful. So, anymore I keep my distance. I don't know how I'm going to manage when I get back there."

"I wish I could help, but that's far outside my experience. Sorry."

Jenny looked at him and nodded slowly. "But you *are* helping – just by listening. You may not believe this, but I've never really told this to anyone. You're the first. And just vocalizing it, hearing it out loud, helps me to make more sense of it." She reached across the table and rested her hand on top of his. "Thank you. You really are a good listener."

But it wasn't a matter of his listening, she thought while gazing at his face. It was more likely the indefinable freedom of talking about her troubled feelings with an anonymous stranger who knew virtually nothing about her or her circumstances, and whose path she would never cross again after this evening. It was, in a way, liberating and she felt better for it.

Dessert came, and she changed the subject, razzing him about the way her New York teams had overwhelmed their counterparts from his hometown of Baltimore.

"I seem to remember," she said, looking at the ceiling as if scanning her memory, "the Jets beat the Colts in the Super Bowl just about a year ago. And then right after that the New York Knicks swept the Baltimore Bullets four straight in one of the NBA semi-final series."

"Please don't tell me you're one of those insufferable New York sports fans. They're sore losers and even worse winners. You're too nice to be one of them."

"I grew up in the metropolitan area, and my dad was a big fan. Let's see, what else? And then the Mets beat the Orioles in the World Series this fall. '69 has not been a very good year for your guys."

"Then again I could be wrong about you," Glenn said, with resignation in his voice. He pulled a pack of cigarettes from inside his jacket. "Do you mind?"

"Nice of you to ask, but no, go ahead."

"Would you like one?"

"I tried it once. Couldn't stand it. Why do you? It's not good for you, you know. As a medical professional I should warn you – and you might ought to read the warning on the side of the box. Really, what made you pick it up? – not that it's any of my business."

"It was a little over a year ago; I was in Ranger school. It was a defense against hunger."

He and Benny had teamed up as 'Ranger buddies' in the Airborne platoon at the beginning of the nine week course. Early in the jungle phase at Eglin, their platoon had made a night parachute jump and Benny's gear malfunctioned dropping his rucksack with all his food, water and gear from a height of a thousand feet, destroying everything. They had subsisted on Glenn's food – one C-ration a day between them for over a week. In the process they learned the cigarettes in the C-rations cut their hunger; and while they were issued only one C-Ration of food for each day, they could get all the cigarettes they wanted. They both became smokers.

Glenn looked at his watch. "I think I've probably delayed you beyond the time of your nurse's shindig. I hope I haven't gotten you into trouble, Jenny. If I did, I'm sorry"

"I'm not. It was most likely a rubber chicken dinner followed by a long, boring speech. What are they going to do, Glenn? Send me to Vietnam?"

He gave her a crooked smile. "That's some attitude, Nurse Kolarik."

"I've had too much to drink. That's on you."

"Do you need me to walk you home?" he asked.

"For three good reasons the answer is no. I haven't had *that much* to drink. Fort Lewis is a very safe place for a female officer to walk around at night. And, I already told you about where I stand on playing the other woman."

Glenn nodded slowly. "I get it."

He left a tip, took the bill to the register and paid it, then walked with her outside after they retrieved their coats.

"Thank you for dinner," Jenny said as they stood beneath the covering over the main entrance. "Tonight was a pleasant surprise and I'm glad I let you talk me into it, Glenn. I enjoyed the surf, the turf, and the conversation."

"So did I. Well, good luck, Nurse Jenny." They shook hands and he walked toward the visiting officers barracks a quarter mile down the road. She watched him until he passed through the parking lot, and then she went the opposite direction toward where the transient nurses were housed.

She stopped and looked back in the direction he'd gone, but he was out of sight.

* * * *

Even now – almost an hour before sunrise – it was warm and muggy on the flight line.

Brad walked in darkness beside Don Machein, carrying a helmet bag and lighting their way between and around the revetments with his issue flashlight. The early morning missions consisted of a Log Bird and a C&C ship for each of the four infantry battalions in 2nd Brigade – eight aircraft. Crew chiefs were already pre-flighting and he could see their flashlights shining back and forth. An aircraft on the other side of the narrow taxiway was beginning to crank with the high pitched turbine whine and smell of burning kerosene drifting toward them.

"VIP mission," Machein shouted over the noise, pointing at the Huey starting up. "A big wig in Saigon wants to visit some firebases on New Year's Eve. Him and some hot babe and three or four photogs. We ought to strap his butt into a gunners well and let him come along on the lift this morn."

Donny 'Yank' Machein was one of the most respected of the old timers and a senior instructor pilot. He was on his second tour with the 1st Cav, and had flown every model helicopter in the division. Brad had learned he was on the mission back in April '68 on the day when the 5th Battalion 7th Cav broke through and relieved the Marines at Khe Sanh.

Nolan had seen the lift mission with his and Machein's names next to aircraft 67-16255 posted on the board in Operations when the duty NCO awakened him at O430. the plan was for first platoon to conduct the lift of 1st Bn. 6th Cav's Recon Platoon from Firebase Evita to a landing zone twenty-five kilometers to the west. Mike Nicholson, callsign Yellow One, was flight leader running the mission scheduled for 1045. Three of the log/resupply birds, including Machein's crew, would join him. Simple plan – the Ghost Riders had done it hundreds of times. Nicholson would do the recon, coordinate with the ground commander and the lift ships would brief on the company UHF radio frequency. No big deal, Machein told him.

But for Brad it was his first live combat assault and he was nervous enough it had kept him awake a good part of the night.

After completing their pre-flight inspection and starting their aircraft, 'Yank' hovered back out of the revetment and onto the northeast-southwest runway. He called the tower, received clearance for take-off and told Nolan to take the controls. "Depart southwest and make a climbing right turn to heading zero-one-zero when clear of the end of the runway. I understand you have experience taking off from the Phouc Vinh runway," Machein said as they accelerated through translational lift. "That's what I heard from the *ConMan*. That true?"

"I'm not sure I know what you're talking about," Nolan replied.

"Oh, I bet' you do, Nolan." Machein keyed the mic and called the tower announcing they were departing the area "What *is* the minimum controllable airspeed of the CO's jeep?"

"Does the commander's jeep have *any* airspeed?" Brad asked over the intercom. He glanced to his left and though it was still dark he could see in the reflected glow of the instrument panel lights that his aircraft commander was smiling.

"Sergeant Syzmanski, what do you think?"

The crew chief keyed his mic. "Mr. Machein, I don't like to get drawn into the officer's grab ass. You and Mr. Nolan and Mr. Goff need to work that out on your own. As far as I'm concerned I know nothing, and that's the way it's gonna stay."

Machein threw his head back and laughed. He tuned in the NDB and twenty minutes later pointed out LZ Buttons off to the east where 2nd Brigade Headquarters was located. Fifteen minutes after that, Machein was indicating the location of LZ Evita, nestled in the rolling, fog-shrouded jungle hills and barely visible as darkness receded. He dialed a frequency into the FM radio and made a call to the infantry battalion operations.

"VIP pad is on the east and the log pad is to the southwest side of the firebase. We'll land at the log pad and see what the S-4 folks have going for us. Hopefully some hot coffee to start with. Tell me how you'll set up your approach and landing."

Brad guessed his being paired with Machien was another test. He had flown two days before with Tuttle, another instructor pilot, and they had done landings and takeoffs and simulated engine failures from altitude, and hovering autorotations. Tuttle had quizzed him on emergency procedures in the UH-1 before and after the two hour flight which had also been a quasi-orientation of the Phouc Vinh area. He was vaguely disappointed in his performance and wondered if the pairing with Machein was some kind of remedial instruction.

The first two hours went by quickly as they began to carry a mountain of supplies out to a unit north of Evita. Brad spent the entire time on the controls as 'Yank' watched him, smoked cigarettes, and bantered with Syzmanski. They went to a refueling point and returned to LZ Evita as the other company aircraft were assembling on the southeast side where there was a space big enough for six or eight Hueys.

*"Yellow flight, this Yellow One. Yank, you're number two, "Pull' you're three, "Fitz"
number four. Guns are Max one-four. LZ is a one ship hover down... maybe 80 feet. No prep.
Yellow Two, set up holding, left turns two West.* On the UHF radio frequency Brad heard a
quick succession of acknowledgements and a call from the gunship escort.

"Yellow one, Max one-four is with you, two minutes out."

"Here's the drill, Nolan," Machein said over the intercom as he looked out his window
toward where the overburdened grunts were moving toward their UH-1, "We have an SOP for
this kind of mission when we've got six or fewer ships, which is most of the time."

Brad felt like he should be writing this down but he'd been doing most of the flying all
morning and now had his hands on the controls as the ground troops were loading.

"Yank' seemed to be reading his thoughts. "You'll have time to write this down when we
get back tonight. In a couple of weeks, it'll be old hat. We're inserting a platoon into a single
ship LZ. ACL is always five troops per aircraft – that's for all missions, not just this one. I
know that back in the 'world' they tell you to load eight. That's bull over here with the high
density altitude we deal with in the dry season. I'll fly the first sortie in and out. You fly the
second. If anything feels or looks like it's going south to you, sing out. I will, you can be
assured. In the cockpit, the crew talks – all the time. Crew Chief, door gunner, you me, all of
us. Their job in a hover down is to make sure the main and tail rotors are clear and that the area
below us is suitable to set this thing on the ground. Right Syzmanski?"

"Roger that Mr. Machein."

"Nolan, you've got the controls. You fly us out there. I'll take it when we make the first
approach in and out of the LZ. I always want my co-pilot to follow me through on the controls
during final approach and takeoff during a lift mission – the final half mile in and the first half
mile out. I'll do the same for you – not fighting over the controls, but always ready to take over
if one of us gets hit. Things happen real damn fast close to the ground."

"Roger that."

They took off in formation continued west for six minutes, then turned north for another
four. Their airspeed slowed slightly and the radio came alive.

"Yellow one, two mile final."

"I've got the controls, Nolan," Machein said over the radio as he looked out his window
and began a slow turn toward the west.

From Brad's vantage point in the right seat he could see Yellow One descending toward
a small opening in the mountain jungle canopy. Machein rolled out headed south, watching out
his window as the flight lead stopped and then began to descend into the trees.

"One is down," came the radio call.

"Two is in." Machein called, and then made a left tight turn, keeping his eye on the hover down hole in the green canopy, Brad looked back into the cabin, and saw the infantry troops sitting on the helicopter's deck with their feet hanging out the side in the ninety knot slipstream. It seemed they were looking almost straight down toward the ground. *I'd never ride like that, he thought."* Brad watched as the lead aircraft cleared the trees and stabilized briefly before nosing over and beginning to climb.

"Half mile final," Machien said calmly. He gradually slowed the Huey, stopped over the opening and stabilized. Brad was amazed at Machien's control touch as the trees whipped in the wind just feet from the main rotor disc. It seemed the nose never moved left or right and they descended quickly to a five foot hover and then slowed.

"Clear down left."

"Clear down right," the door gunner repeated.

The aircraft barely touched the ground, the infantry was gone and they were rising in the tall narrow column of space. "Yellow two coming out," Machien announced over the radio. A few seconds later, they cleared the top of the hover hole with their skids; Machien stabilized the Huey, pulled in more power and began to lower the nose into take-off.

"Pretty tight little hole," the instructor pilot said. "But you're smooth enough that –"

Suddenly a loud noise erupted inside the helicopter sounding large and heavy – like a bowling ball being rolled around inside the cabin.

"What the hell is –" Machein began and then the plexiglass chin bubble at his feet exploded over him as his head was violently thrown back in a shower of blood. The aircraft shuddered, then skewed violently right and the cockpit tilted left wresting the cyclic stick from Nolan's hands. He grabbed and centered it quickly and pulled in more power to keep the Huey from descending into the trees.

"I'm hit, I'm hit, I'm hit!!" the door gunner screamed.

"Get us out of here, Mr. Machein!" Syzmanski yelled.

Brad couldn't say or do anything. He kept pulling in power and when he glimpsed the torque meter it looked like he'd pulled in more than the fifty pound redline limit. He looked back outside and they were climbing quickly at low airspeed. He lowered the nose, turned left, and as he did so he saw the blood all over the seat and door next to Machein and the shattered lower side of his flight helmet. His stomach convulsed.

"Yellow flight, this is Yellow two," Brad said over the UHF. "Taking fire! The LZ is hot! LZ is hot!" He looked at Machein again – the whole side of his face and the front of his nomex flight suit was covered in blood. "Syzmanski, are you hit?"

"No!"

"Frankel?"

"My leg! Took a bullet that I think went all the way through. Damn it hurts!... there it is! Went through the ceiling, too! I'm bleedin' like a stuck pig."

"How's Machein?" Syzmanski asked. "There's blood running down the back of his seat."

Brad looked over at the pilot again. It looked bad – really bad. He wondered if Machein was still alive. "There's a med facility at Sông Bé , isn't there? We gotta get him a doctor." He looked at the ADF needle and saw it pointed almost in the same direction he was now headed.

"*Yellow two, this is lead. Your situation?*"

"Three miles south southwest of the LZ. Two wounded. En route Sông Bé."

"*Return to Evita immediately. There's a battalion surgeon there.*"

Brad weighed his options. He guessed the Battalion aid station wouldn't help Machein any at all. He decided going to Evita would do nothing except add unaffordable delay in getting his crew to the medical facilities that could do some good.

"Negative," Brad replied. "I'm direct to Sông Bé , Yellow One. That's the best option."

"*Yellow two. I'm telling you to go back to Evita. It's closer. I say again, return to Evita.*"

"Yellow One, you need to replace me as Red Duke log bird," he said instead of replying, "and also get someone to pick up my second sortie of pax for the lift. Yellow two, out." He looked at his pilot in the left seat again. "Syzmanski, any idea of damage to the ship?"

"Not yet, other than the chin bubble being blown out."

The helicopter was vibrating more than it should. *It's the airspeed*, he thought, and looked at Machein – his chin was on his chest and his head was bobbing up and down. *Gotta stop that vibration, Nolan. He's bleeding more.* He slowed to just below 115 knots, then dialed in the tower frequency on the radio and made the call. "Sông Bé tower, Sông Bé tower, this is Army One-Six-Two-Five-Five twenty-five north declaring an emergency and requesting straight in landing to the tower with wounded on board requiring immediate attention."

"*Roger Army two-five-five, say nature of emergency.*"

"Two wounded. Both life threatening. Request medical personal, equipment, and transportation. One casualty with head wound and extensive bleeding. Second casualty is a leg wound also with a lot of blood loss."

"*Roger Army two-five-five, we'll see what we can do.*"

"Screw that, Tower!" Brad yelled into the boom mic on his helmet. "I don't want you to try, for cryin' out loud! You DO something for these guys! I'm landing at the base of your tower and there better be transport and doctors and nurses who are all elbows and assholes ready to work on these guys! Just do it!" Immediately he felt foolish at his outburst. *Must have sounded like some scared crazy kid... maybe I am.*

"*Roger that, two-five-five. We're on it.*"

He could clearly see Nui Ba Ra – one of the twin sisters mountains - located just south of the huge American base. He started to roll the ship over to increase airspeed and immediately the severe vibrations started again. Machein's head lolled on his chest and a feeling of absolute helplessness invaded Brad's thoughts. The American base and the east-west runway inside the wire came into focus; and everything seemed to slow down giving him the sense they would never get there.

They were on the outskirts of the little town just outside the wire of the base before he knew it. He keyed the mic; "Sông Bé tower this is Army two-five-five, four north for landing with the active in site."

"Roger two-five-five. In sight. Cleared to land at the tower east of the med ambulances."

"Mr. Nolan," he heard Syzmanski say over the intercom the instant they touched down, "you need to shut this bird down right now! Emergency shut down."

Brad rolled the throttle to idle, depressed the detent switch, fully rolled off the throttle and turned off the battery. He felt wasted, totally exhausted and worthless now as he watched the medics lift Machein from his seat, place him on a gurney and quickly push him to the OD green ambulance that whisked him away.

Syzmanski looked over the damage to the aircraft. "You all right, Mr. Nolan?"

"I'm fine. Never seen anything like that before. How's the bird."

"Busted up, and some of it looks pretty bad. Blood everywhere inside the cabin. The round that got Frankel rattled around and went through the engine deck and nicked a transmission line. There might be more, but we'll wait until I get it back to Papa Vic. They're sending a Chinook out to sling load it back. You done good, Mr. Nolan, getting Yank here like you did. You gave him the best chance you could."

"He looked awful."

"But you made the right choice coming direct here. Thought you should know that. First time is rough on all of us."

"You mean...?"

"Talking about everything here –first lift mission, first time you get shot at." The crew chief took a long drag and blew a cloud of smoke upward into the breeze. "I'm thinking that my ol' two-five-five bird is headed to depot maintenance for an overhaul. I'll probably be gettin' another bird to replace her. If that happens, well…

"Just want you to know, Mr. Nolan – I wouldn't object to flyin' with you again."

Chapter 9

The cargo plane dipped a wing, shuddered, and a hollow cracking sound rumbled through the ship's frame like expanding pond ice on a cold winter morning; but it was stifling hot inside the C-7 Caribou as it hit a thermal, roughly jolting Glenn and the other passengers.

The aircraft leveled and began descending as he peered through the opposite windows at the mountain rising like a tall thin cone from the surrounding flat plain of III Corps. Nui Ba Dien, was one of the two Black Virgin mountains and it bordered on the outskirts of Tay Ninh, referred to as *Rocket City* by the old sergeant at Bien Hoa who'd handed Glenn his orders sending him to the 1st Brigade. As he peered out at the neat, quiet picture three thousand feet below, he felt for the first time a tight little knot of apprehension in his stomach. At least he was escaping from the surreal, disillusioning 'in-processing' area of the 1st Cav Division. It had been ten days since he'd reported in to Fort Lewis on the first leg of his journey.

"It don't look all that bad," Lieutenant Colquitt said leaning over Glenn to look out the window at the tranquil scene below. "Kinda reminds me of back home in Decatur."

"From this altitude, probably the way it looks to the Greek gods on Olympus... or the Pentagon brass back in Foggy Bottom," Glenn replied irreverently.

Colquitt laughed. "Ain't that the truth."

The engines quieted and the Caribou slowed, followed by a whining of electric motors as the flaps lowered. Then the wheels came down, locking and causing the airplane to lurch awkwardly as if constantly stumbling and having to catch its balance. The first time he'd seen one of these ungainly high-tailed deHavilland ships had been his senior year at West Point, on Target Field down by the Hudson. He was certain it would never take off and get out of the little field on its own power, but it had completely surprised him. It was another lesson in not judging books by their covers. He wondered if Colquitt wasn't another of those lessons.

They were down and the Caribou was clumsily bumping along. The plane swung around and came to an abrupt stop; the engines raced for a few seconds, stopped and then the crew chief came back to the rear from his seat near the cockpit. He turned a switch lowering the ramp and foul, heavy air hit them – a wave of decay and the smell of burned fuel instantly overpowering in the sticky, damp heat. Glenn felt sweat break out immediately on his forehead and neck, trickling down his back and under his arms.

"When the wind's out of the south like this, the smell of burning latrines gets pretty bad," the crew chief said. "You'll get used to it."

Somehow Glenn didn't think so.

They finally got a ride to Brigade headquarters where the Personnel Officer, a captain named Fowler, welcomed them and apologized half-heartedly that they hadn't been picked up by the staff duty driver. He took their records, looked quickly at the contents, then checked a large personnel chart on the wall covered with thick plastic and marked with grease pencil.

"Lieutenant Colquitt," Fowler began, making a note on the wall chart, "you'll be going out to 2nd Battalion, 8th Cav. Lieutenant Colonel Conrad is the battalion commander and he's short of platoon leaders. We'll get you a ride down to 2/8 Cav headquarters and by this time tomorrow you'll be on your way out to Firebase Ike. Lieutenant Nolan, I think we'll keep you here at Brigade for the time being. I'm sure we've got something you'll find both interesting and rewarding. I need an assistant brigade S-1. You're a senior first lieutenant and a West Point grad – this seems like a perfect fit."

Glenn's face and neck went prickly hot. "Sir, I hoped to be assigned an infantry platoon."

"That's not going to happen. We need a good, solid staff and your background makes you an ideal fit."

"But, sir –"

"Look, Nolan, I know what you're worried about. Trust me, there's ample opportunity for you to do what you need to do to punch your ticket. The war's not going to end in the next few weeks so there's plenty of time to get you out to the field. Do a good job here, keep your nose clean, and in six months, you just might get a company to command," the captain said off-handedly, sounding annoyed. "For now, I'll have someone show you the hooch where you'll be living and take you to headquarters company supply to draw your equipment. You also need to stop by the Med detachment – it's co-located with the Surgical Hospital. Drop off your medical records and have them check that your shots are up to date. Then come back here and we'll get some lunch at the Brigade mess."

It was not the beginning Glenn had hoped for. He was still unhappy a quarter hour later when the driver took him by the brigade staff hooch and he dropped off his gear in one of the unoccupied rooms.

"Sir, I'll run by the Officers' quarters and then down to supply and you can draw your field gear and rifle," the young buck sergeant said when they returned to the jeep. "Then we can go by the Med detachment and get you back in plenty of time for lunch with Major Fowler. Chow here at Brigade HQ is mighty fine, sir."

"Take me right to the hospital," Glenn said, sitting down heavily on the canvas passenger seat. "No need to go by supply. I don't need any field gear, and certainly not a rifle."

A damned assistant S-1, Glenn thought, muttering to himself as the sergeant gunned the jeep and took off down the macadam road. *This place looks safer and in better condition than downtown Columbus. Ranger school, airborne, four years of B.S. at the Trade School on the Hudson, company command – all that prep to be a pencil pusher, fighting the war in triplicate copies - one of which has to be readable... and the captain said, what? – that if I kept my nose clean I might get a shot at commanding an infantry company in six months... son-of-a-bitch...*

He was still feeling surly a half hour later, while waiting impatiently in an empty operating room of the Surgical Hospital.

The hospital clerk was surprised that he'd gotten through Ft. Lewis without being inoculated with gamma globulin, and made him wait for a nurse to give him the shot. After twenty minutes he got up and paced, growing more impatient and irritated; he stopped and looked outside through the small, yellowed window near the back of the inflatable building.

This is why you don't go to military hospitals, Nolan. They always manage to cram a one minute event like getting a simple damned shot into an hour-long saga... walking around with clipboards in their hands, moving like the world is coming to an end... like that damn class A flight physical for the Air Force Academy, down in Washington at Bolling Field... six hours to run fifteen of us through... should have taken an hour at most...

A nurse came in at the far end of the room, and he turned, catching a brief glimpse. She was wearing a blood-stained surgical gown, a square cotton mask over her nose and mouth, along with gloves which she was busy removing and dumping into a large plastic drum. Her head was covered with a cotton cap that she removed while turning her back to him to pick up his medical records.

"All right, soldier. Let's get this over with quick. Roll up your left sleeve... Hepatitis C shot?! For crying out loud, you should have gotten this before arriving in-country. How did this happen?!" she asked with an accusing edge in her voice, her back still toward him as she removed the surgical mask and tossed it into the waste drum.

"I guess some stupid nurse at Fort Lewis screwed up when I processed through," he replied crossly. He was close enough to hear her gasp. "I'm sorry. I've had a bad morning."

The girl turned quickly and for long seconds they stared wordlessly at one another. "If you call me Polock Jenny, this is going to be one painful shot, lieutenant."

*　　*

Jenny Kolarik took another sip of coffee, looked at her watch and said, "You're going to miss that lunch date with your new boss if you don't get a move on."

"What's he going to do – send me to Vietnam?"

She frowned and gave him a disapproving look. "You didn't use to be this surly."

"How can you possibly know that? We only spent a couple of hours together over dinner one time, and as I recall, you'd had an awful lot to drink."

"You kept yourself busy refilling my wine glass."

"You noticed?"

"I've been to the rodeo before, cowboy."

He sipped his coffee, and gave her a doleful smile. "Give me a break. You've never been to a rodeo in your life. You're from Jersey."

"Lieutenant, I might surprise you," she said, her fine blue eyes daring him and lighting up her face. "There's a rodeo in Pilesgrove Township at a place called Cowtown and it's been up and running since '29. My dad used to take me there when I was a kid."

"I'm going to check it out."

"You do that."

She drained the rest of her cup, went to the coffee maker and poured another cup for them both. Her eyes kept coming back to his and he had the feeling the nurses and doctors and orderlies in the hospital mess hall were moving around and passing by out of focus in some curious hazy twilight even though it was a few minutes past noon. She spooned some sugar into her cup; when she turned her eyes fell on him with a kind of peaceful wonder, and her mouth parted slightly in a smile. He took a deep breath and felt a tightness in his chest. *Careful. You might get the idea this staff job isn't a half bad deal after all.*

"I never dreamed I'd run across you again," he said when she sat down across from him. "You said your hospital was in Lai Khe. That's a long way from here."

"Fifty miles east, on Thunder Road. Big Red One territory. When I got back, they were in the midst of packing up and getting ready to go home with the division. I didn't have enough points to go back with them, so they shipped me here." Jenny shrugged. "The docs are competent; the girls here seem fine. Most of them have more time in country than I do and several are on their second tour. Coming here to the 45th is really a step up. It's like getting traded to the Yankees after playing for the Orioles."

"I hate the Yankees."

"Oh?" Jenny said, looking at him over the rim of her coffee cup with a stagey look of surprise. "So, you're one of *them*."

"We had this conversation not long ago at Fort Lewis. I'm upset enough already without you rubbing my nose in the New York sports scene. What's so special about this place?" he asked to change the subject.

"The 45th was the first of a new kind of hospital when they put it together a few years ago. Semi-permanent, but self-contained. All the bells and whistles – radiology, labs, pharmacy, dental facilities and, as you can see, a nice little kitchen area. This place is doing some really leading edge kind of work on burns and wound care and stuff most hospitals back in the world haven't even thought about." She looked into his eyes and tears danced along her lower lids. "We're doing a lot of good, saving a lot of lives of boys who would never have had a chance to survive before. The staff here does procedures even the best emergency wards in the largest hospitals in the big cities back home never imagined dealing with."

"You see a lot of wounded."

She took a deep breath and nodded. "We get more traffic here than I ever saw in the 2nd Surg; more serious casualties. It's because of the 1st Brigade of the Cav, especially the 2/8 Cav Battalion. They have the highest casualty rates." A shadow of doubt, or fear, crossed her face and she looked at him with a sudden intensity. "Don't ever let them send you to the 2/8. The life expectancy of second lieutenants in that battalion is measured in days, not months."

"Good thing I'm a first lieutenant, isn't it?" he said airily.

"I didn't say that to be funny, Glenn," she said with anxious intensity. "Platoon leaders don't last out there. I've only been here a week and already patched up two. One is still here in a recovery ward and the other got evac'd to Japan. I don't think he's going to make it." She bit her lip and looked away, appearing distraught and suddenly weary. "He was a good kid. When they brought him out of the helicopter and put his stretcher down in Triage, he looked at two of us nurses there and said, 'I must've died and gone to heaven . . . roundeye girls – wow, you look so beautiful!' He was so concerned about the way he looked because of us standing there. He said, 'Gee, I must look a mess."

"He obviously had an eye for beauty."

"Probably delirious. I've been called 'perky', and even 'cute' once, but never beautiful. These boys are great. I could be the ugliest thing in the world, but they'd still call me special."

"You need to learn to take a compliment."

"I need to learn lots of things. But this is such a hard way to do it." A solitary tear rolled down her cheek. "My first real lesson about this war came five days after I got to Lai Khe when a Huey brought in five body bags. I'll always have flashbacks about – unzipping those bags. I don't want to unzip a bag some day and find you."

"How do you get along with the other nurses?" he asked, quickly changing the subject. "My grandmother was a nurse in France during the Great War. Did I tell you that at Lewis?"

"I'm not sure." She looked away, trying to remember. "Maybe you did. We don't have anyone here from that far back, but there's one or two from Korea. That must have been really bad. They had mobile Army surgical hospitals back then – MASH units – and they had to pick up and move to stay close to the front or get out of the way of Chinese offensives." She looked around slowly. "I can't imagine packing and moving this place with just a few hours' notice."

"I thought all Army hospitals are mobile."

"A little. Given a week, we could move all this to the other side of Tay Ninh city, or in two weeks to Phouc Vinh or Sông Bé by helicopter. But it would be a big, big job. And there's not a need to right now. Not with the Cav here, operating along the border twenty miles north."

They fell silent momentarily, looking into each other's eyes until he took a deep breath and looked away. "I can't believe we ran into one another here in this place. But I guess it's not really *that* strange when I think about it. All my life while growing up as an Air Force brat I was always crossing paths with people I'd known in other places and other times."

"You've seen so much of the world, haven't you?" she said softly.

"I guess. It was pretty exciting before. But this time, it's probably going to be a pretty gruesome way to do it."

"It doesn't have to be."

"Because of the assignment at brigade?" He shook his head slowly and looked away. "I feel like a slacker."

"Because you're in a headquarters and not out there getting wounded or killed?"

"Because I'm trained for this way better than your average grunt who was in high school six months ago and is now over here after Basic and AIT and some pretty damned awful in-country training. I'm older, more grounded, and over the last five years I've come to grips with the what, why and how this war has to be fought."

"So one way or the other you're going to get yourself shipped to the bush and go win the war for the rest of us."

"That's not what I said."

"So, why then do you feel like a slacker?" she asked. "Haven't you gotten the word? People in Washington have thrown in the towel. A month ago Nixon announced we're pulling out another fifteen thousand troops by mid-April. Everybody with an ounce of common sense has figured out what's going on. We're bagging it, Nolan. There's no winning this war, or police action or whatever the politicians who got us into this mess want to call it. And nobody wants to be the last one to die. The change in the attitude of most of the troops is noticeable from when I went back to the states over Christmas. So, what possible good do you think you're going to do at this moment in history?"

It was not the first time he'd been confronted with the question.

Mary Anne and her parents, and especially her older brother had asked the same thing in so many words. Each had been incredulous that he didn't see the folly in what he was about to do. One day he'd gone to lunch at the Lexington Street Market with a half dozen of his classmates from high school. It had been a great time of reliving events from their football and baseball days, telling stories about teachers and coaches and some of the more colorful guys in their circle – until Billy Chambliss asked why he was still planning on going to Vietnam. The humor and goodwill of the moment disappeared like vapor and the atmosphere around the table went cold as ice. Chambliss had said he no longer believed in *my country right or wrong*, and everyone else but Glenn agreed. He was suddenly an outsider in the group. Shifty Randall said he hoped Glenn didn't go over the edge and become one of those 'baby killers' like all the rest of them over there. Though he'd said it in jest, the spell of bonhomie had been shattered. He'd returned to the MacEagan's house sad, and utterly disenchanted with the event.

"Whatever I do over here," Glenn said, "I'm not doing it for me, or for the politicians, or for *anybody* back in the world. The North Vietnamese aren't ever going to be marching down main street in Ottumwa, or down H Street in D.C. I get it. I also get that we can't force democracy on any country or win their freedom for them – North or South Vietnam, Cambodia, Poland, Surinam… anybody. I'm not fighting for them. I'm not fighting for the politicians in those countries or mine."

"Then who are you doing it for?"

"I'll do it for the same people as you do – the poor old underfed, mistreated, tough luck grunt," he said quietly. He held her gaze and thought he saw recognition seep into her eyes. "And I'd do it for the same reasons, given the chance."

That chance came sooner than expected.

*   *   *

"There are only two reasons to change anything," Major Fowler said, pouring ketchup on his meatloaf and cutting a bite-sized piece with his fork, "and that's to make it easier or better."

He'd been counseled by Fowler the previous afternoon for missing their lunch meeting, and for not drawing an M-16 or field gear from supply. Now, sitting across from his new boss, he tried to look attentive if not interested and tuned out the field grade officer's rambling sermon about the importance of staff work and the need to put the very best of the best in those positions. Anyone, he said, could carry a rucksack and a rifle and bathe in a steel pot, but brigade and division staffs did all the thinking and planning and he'd soon appreciate the absolute necessity of both in the Cav.

"That's the brigade commander," Fowler said, breaking into his thoughts, nodding at a small square table in the corner separated from the rest of the dining room. "That's Lieutenant Colonel Conrad with him, the battalion commander of the 2nd Battalion, 8th Cavalry."

Glenn turned his head to get a glimpse.

"He's in here to review ops plans with the '3' shop."

"I hear his battalion has seen a lot of action recently."

"Oh, yeah. He's come up with an ops plan where he moves his battalion every three or four days in a series of 'Jump LZs' to keep from getting targeted and fixed by the NVA. Intel says his AO is home to the 95th NVA Division, and his companies see a lot of action. In the past two months, the 2/8 Cav has been the number one battalion in the brigade, and usually the division, in terms of number of contacts and enemy killed. Number one in casualties, too."

Glenn turned his head again to look at the two officers deep in conversation; instantly he made a decision.

He went to the food line, got another drink and returned to a table closer to Conrad and the brigade commander. When he and the brigade commander got up to leave, Glenn walked over to the table and introduced himself to Colonel Conrad.

"Sir, I'm Lieutenant Nolan. I just arrived in the brigade yesterday morning and I'd like to talk to you about getting assigned to your battalion."

"New in country, or just transferred in from another division?" Conrad asked looking over his new jungle fatigues.

"Brand new, sir."

Conrad looked at him briefly and finally said, "Officer assignments to the battalions are handled by the brigade S-1. You ought to talk with him and make your desires known."

"I already have sir, and –"

"Good, that's your best course. I'm sure things will work out," the colonel replied, turning to leave. "If you'll excuse me."

"I know you're nine lieutenants short in the battalion and you'll be losing another to DEROS inside a week. That's not counting potential operational losses."

Conrad stopped and looked at Nolan. "Well, lieutenant, we don't expect this officer shortage will be the case for long... How do know about my junior officer status?"

"Because, sir, despite requesting your battalion, I've been placed on brigade staff in the S-1 shop. I'd prefer an operational assignment in a line battalion."

"Like I said, lieutenant, I don't make officer assignments for the brigade."

"But you can express your desires. You have a shortage of platoon leaders and I can fill one of those slots and help you. I'd hoped to be the recon platoon leader, sir."

The colonel grinned. "I'm pretty happy with the one I have. That's a slot that goes to my most experienced and able lieutenant. Unlike you, he's got a good seven months in the field."

"Sir, I'm a Ranger School grad, and I served as both a platoon leader and company commander in the 24th Division in Germany. I'm asking for a chance. I won't let you down."

"I've been informed the pipeline is full of lieutenants."

"I'm not all that sure, sir. Even if it was the case, most would be brand new OCS butter bars at this time of year – the most recent Academy and ROTC grads are pretty much unavailable until later this Spring, a good forty-five to sixty days off."

The battalion commander's face grew somber and he gave Glenn a hard stare. "Are you saying OCS officers don't pass muster?"

"I'm not saying that at all, sir. It's just that Academy grads will have Ranger school and a four month tour before arriving in country. That's not the case with OCS lieutenants."

"So, you're a ring knocker?"

"I graduated from the Academy, yes sir. But what I am is an infantry officer with ranger training and experience as a platoon leader and company commander in Europe who wants to serve in your battalion. I've had five years since the Tonkin Gulf to get prepared, and I'm hoping to use what I've learned."

Conrad cleared his throat and looked closely at him for long seconds. "You've done your homework, lieutenant. All right, tell me why I should stick my neck out with my boss and request you be assigned to me instead of his staff."

"Because I'll do an excellent job wherever you put me. I'll take care of your troops, and I'll do you and them more good in your battalion than I can on brigade staff."

The colonel furrowed his brow and said, "Tell me again what your job is, lieutenant."

"I'm told I'll be an assistant to the Assistant S-1, where I'll spend most of my time in the 1st Brigade TOC during the graveyard shift just trying to stay awake."

"All right, lieutenant. I'll give it some consideration. No promises, though."

"Consideration would be greatly appreciated, sir." He wanted to keep the conversation going, but the battalion commander was looking around for someone or something and appeared eager to be on his way. "Thanks for your time, sir."

Glenn watched Conrad walk away and his heart sank.

Chapter 10

"Wow man, ain't this insane?!" Lee Haskell took off his big white Stetson and yelled in Brad's ear to be heard above the noise in the *Red Hawk*. "Ah'm lovin' this!"

The Filipino band on the raised stage of the 227th Club was belting out American music from the '50s and 60s; the band's amps were turned up so loud that nobody could think much less understand the words being sung by the thin little mini-skirted lead singer. She smiled and writhed and puckered her lips at the Americans who cat-called and tried to stick money in the form of war zone Military Payment Certificates, into her garter.

"I'm goin' to take that little thing back to my hooch tonight when this is all over, boy!"

"Haskell, you wouldn't know what to do with that if you could get her there."

"I understand there's somethin' real special about slant-eye girls." The overly made-up girl blew Haskell a kiss with her full, ruby-red lips. "Man-o-man, I tell you Brad, ah'm in *LOVE*!... L-O-V-E type love."

"You're drunk."

"That, too, mi amigo siempre. I'm of a mind to get up and sing with her to teach these boys a few things from the life of Lee-O the Legendary Longhorn."

Brad could only laugh at his friend from flight school. Haskell was larger than life, like most of the Texans he'd met in his nineteen years.

The lights suddenly went on and the band stopped playing. Major Shurtleff, the battalion operations officer, ascended the few steps to the stage and took the microphone. There was a loud screech of feedback that was met with hoots and howls. The major held the mic close to his mouth and said, "I have some news tonight for you guys in Charlie Company. Shut up! – all of you – and listen. We all knew '*Yank*' Machein, and how he was med-evac'd to Japan."

Brad was surprised at how quickly the Red Hawk became deathly silent. He watched *ConMan* Goff walk slowly up the three steps to the platform and stand next to Shurtleff; everyone in the 227th knew that Goff and Machein had been close friends for years, dating back to '65 at Benning when the Air Cav was formed out of the 11th Air Assault.

"We just received a message from the hospital in Tokyo where they took the 'Yank'." The major looked at *ConMan*. "You want to tell them the news, Mister Goff?"

The *ConMan* nodded solemnly and took the microphone and hesitated, blinking his eyes. At last, he said, "That sorry son-of-a-bitch Machein is goin' home with a 'million dollar wound'. The bastard is skippin' out on us and going back to the Land of the Round Doorknob."

The hand clapping and whistling quickly became raucous.

"And because of this –" Goff began, but stopped due to the noise. "– because of this we have a ceremony we need to do tonight. Brad Nolan, get up here and take what's comin'. And take it like a man instead of the sorry-ass Wobbily-One with no time in-country that you are."

He was being pushed and shoved toward the stage, surprised and ecstatic over the news about Machein doing well. He'd worried and second-guessed himself dozens of times since that day when they had been hit coming out of the hover down on his first 'real' mission.

"With this happy piece of news from Tokyo, we in Charlie company have decided to 'honor' the guy who was Machein's 'Peter Pilot' on his last mission."

There were hoots and hollering and people whistling – *drunk people*, Brad thought.

"Despite being a worthless right-seater with less than fifty hours in-country" Goff was saying, "and because you did make one decision on your own that turned out right – we, your betters, are going to make you an official 'Ghostrider' with all rights and privileges. Of course, according to our tradition, that requires you successfully wear the silly hat and sing the hallowed song."

Suddenly Brad found himself standing on the stage, looking out on a raucous crowd of pilots with the Filipino band nervously moving around behind him. Goff was putting a service cap on his head with aviator wings and a Ghost Rider patch both sewn on upside down, and he draped a large medallion of the backside of a horse around his neck.

"Now," *ConMan* said, "you have to sing '*Ghost Riders in the Sky*' well enough to get a majority thumbs up from Company C before you get your Ghostrider patch from our C.O."

Brad knew he couldn't carry this off by himself. "I gotta have Tex Haskell here with me to do this song justice. He can't sing and he only knows the chorus, but he plays a mean bass." When Tex came onto the platform wearing his white Western hat and picked up a guitar, Brad grabbed a guitar from a band member and began to pick the notes of the song. The crowd clapped and the noise inside the *Red Hawk* rose toward the threshold of pain.

An old cowpoke went ridin' out, one dark and windy day,
Upon a ridge he rested as he went along his way,
When all at once a mighty herd of red-eyed cows he saw,
A-plowing through the ragged skies, and up a cloudy draw....

The crowd sang along with Brad at the top of their voices as he picked the notes and the Filipino band tried to play along with the song. Haskell stepped up to his microphone and crooned off tune:

Yippee-yi-ay, Yippee-yi-o-o
Ghost Riders in the sky…

The sound inside the club grew louder through two more stanzas and several more choruses while the Filipino band got into the song and the pilots yelled and threw peanut shells at him. At the final chorus the crowd erupted into applause as Brad raised the guitar over his head and handed the goofy-looking hat and medallion back to *ConMan* Goff. Major Garber jumped up on the platform and buttoned a Ghostrider patch onto the left breast pockets of Brad and Tex Haskell.

The episode, like the entire evening, seemed chaotic and wholly muddled to Nolan as he made his way off the platform toward the area near the bar where the Charlie company pilots had rallied. Haskell was still onstage taking bows with a sweeping gesture of his cowboy hat, his arm around the Filipino girl and a big smile on his face.

"Helluva job, Nolan! Helluva job," *ConMan* said to him as he pushed another can of Budweiser into his hand. "You sound like a guy with a cold bawling inside an echo chamber."

"What are you talkin' about? That's my best Vaughn Monroe impersonation."

"Do the old boy a favor and make that the last time you try it," Goff said, almost yelling to be heard. After a two more songs, the band took a break and Haskell joined him.

"That little Filipini gal don't understand a word I say," Haskell complained.

"Maybe because neither of you speak English," Brad offered, aware he was slurring his words. "Try Navajo sign language."

"Think you're hot shit, don't you, Nolan?" Brad glanced over his right shoulder and looked into the eyes of Mike Nicholson who had been flight lead the day Machein was wounded. "I don't think so. Not me."

"Mike, cool it," *ConMan* said quickly.

"Cool it, my ass. This FNG should have been put up in front of a flight eval board as far as I'm concerned. Now he thinks he's a hero for disobeying an order from his flight lead."

"Hey, Mike. That's enough. This isn't the time or place," Goff said sternly, putting his hand on the pilot's chest.

"This isn't your business, *ConMan*. This is between me and the new guy, so you back off." Nicholson glared at Goff for a few seconds and then turned his attention to Nolan. "You need to learn your place, newbie."

Brad was instantly sober, his senses alert. There were a few of the older pilots in the company who liked to play hard-ass with the new guys. It was stuff like this that had soured him on the military as an option, until all the options had been cancelled by his own foolishness in the second half of his first semester at Delaware.

The tension grew in the air surrounding the small group at the back of the Red Hawk.

"I'm telling you again, Mike," *ConMan* Goff was saying, "this *is not* the time or place."

Nicholson shifted his gaze from Goff to Nolan. "Then we can take this outside."

"Don't be a jerk," Goff said. "Go back to your hooch and sleep on this."

"Slept on it too long already. Let's step outside you and me, Nolan."

"Mike, I'm telling you –"

"No, *ConMan*, it's okay," Brad interrupted. "I'm fine with that – whatever he wants, I'm for it. It'll clear the air."

Goff looked at him, frowning. "You realize what he's saying, don't you?"

"Of course I do," Brad replied, breaking into a broad smile. "And to tell you the truth, I'm glad he's finally saying it to my face instead of behind my back – even if it took him getting drunk to dredge up the courage to do it."

"You got a smart mouth on you, Nolan."

Brad took a step toward Nicholson. "If you want to go outside, just you and me, so you can get something off your chest, I'm cool with that. You do what you have to do... and I'll do what I have to do. Remember, you're the one who wants this, not me. But in all fairness," Brad said casually, "I have to tell you something first. Actually, it's two or three things. You need to be aware of some of the baggage I drag around with me."

He saw confusion creep into Nicholson's face and Brad gave him another big smile.

"You see, my dad was a fighter pilot in War Two, and he was the middleweight boxing champ of the 15th Air Force in the Med. He taught me and my older brother, who was the light heavyweight champ at West Point two years running. Now, I never was able to whip my brother in the ring, but he never whipped me either." Brad started toward the door leading outside, but stopped and turned back to face Nicholson. "One other thing... If I get you down, not saying I will but I just might... if I do, I'm not going to stop beating on you even if you're out cold. That's the way we Scots are. Fights are serious business to us. Just thought you should know. Now, I'm leaving and I'll be waiting for you down by the 1st platoon hooch. Come alone and we'll talk... or whatever you want to do ."

A half hour later Goff approached the sandbagged bunker next to the 1st platoon hooch and saw a lone figure in a lawn chair sitting on top of it smoking a cigarette and drinking beer.

"Hey, Nolan. It's me, Goff."

"Come on up. Want a beer?"

Goff climbed to the top, sat down and took the can Nolan handed to him. "So?"

"Nicholson never showed. I knew he wouldn't. I could see it in his eyes. He was drunk and the liquor was talking, not him. But he wasn't too drunk to think he wanted to fight me. Would you want to fight somebody you really don't know who promises to keep stomping you even after you're down and unconscious?"

"Yeah, I thought that was out of bounds. You wouldn't have done that, would you?"

"Nicholson thought I would."

"He probably did." Goff took a long pull on his beer. "None of us knew you came from a family of boxers."

"I might have embellished that just a little." Brad cleared his throat. "My dad wasn't really the 15th Air Force champ. I don't know there was one. My brother did box at West Point – in gym class, like everybody else. That's about it."

Goff chuckled. "Yeah, the story you told Nicholson at the Red Hawk was better. I guess you aren't much of a boxer either."

"Haven't been in a fight since third grade… and I think I lost that one."

"That was a hell of a chance you took, Nolan. What if he hadn't bought it and showed up looking for a piece of you?"

"I knew he wouldn't show up. If a guy really wants to fight, he doesn't go flapping his gums like Nicholson did, he just gets it on. He was trying to intimidate me in front of everyone and thought he could because he has a reputation and I'm just a new guy. When I realized that, I just upped the ante and he had to fold."

"But you couldn't know that for sure. Nicholson is a pretty tough guy."

Brad reached down and picked up a two foot length of steel pipe. "I had an equalizer. I know – that isn't fair, is it? Well, a street fight isn't about being fair. It's about winning. That *is* something my dad taught me. He shot down seventeen planes in World War Two plus six in Korea, and told me not one of them was a fair fight as far as he was concerned."

Goff lit a cigarette and shook his head. "Nolan, you're beginning to impress me." They drank quietly in the dark until Goff said, "I appreciate how you stood up for me with the MPs when they came around after we hijacked the CO's jeep."

"You mean when I lied for you."

"You told them a tale that created enough 'probable deniability' for us both."

"It's in the family genes. My little sister got all the looks; my older brother got all the athletic ability and the sense of responsibility. But I got all the brains." They sat in silence for a while longer. Brad finished his beer and got another, then lit a cigarette. "That was good news tonight about Yank. Wish I'd gotten to know him better."

"He's something special. You did good that day – that's part of Nicholson's problem with you. I'm going to watch your back, Nolan. I'll talk to the platoon leader and Captain Hill in Operations – you'll be my co-pilot for as long as I'm here."

"I appreciate that. And I also appreciated that little induction ceremony tonight. Despite all the humiliating comments and the guys throwing stuff at me while I was up there, it was really an important event for me as a new guy."

"You didn't see the things that girl was doing behind you while you were singing the song in that terrible voice you have."

"What things?"

"You don't want to know."

"It was all good grins. I can't wait until I get my chance to do it to the next newbie."

Goff smiled devilishly and said, "There won't be a next time. You see, we don't really have an induction ceremony – that was payback for what you did to me that night on the runway. And those guys were laughing at you, not *with* you, pal. You were had. And I have dozens of pictures of you in that hat and the Filipino girl behind you to prove it. They were all in on it, even your buddy, Tex.

"Maybe you weren't born with all the brains after all, Nolan."

*   *   *   *

The big, twin-bladed Chinook came to a hover thirty feet over the a bare spot butting up to the three foot high berm defining the perimeter of LZ Ike.

From inside the helicopter, looking out the rear over the Ch-47's ramp, Glenn could see the primitive facilities of the small firebase now being blown about and covered in dust by the helicopter's rotorwash. There were six round artillery pits housing 105mm howitzers, three or four GP medium tents, a low mound of sandbags in the middle of the base that on closer inspection defined the Tactical Operations Center with several two-niner-two radio antennas clustered close by. The troops on the ground nearest the log pad had turned their backs away from the dust storm of the Chinook as it lowered the sling load of artillery ammunition to the ground and released it, then slipped forward to land and let off the seven passengers inside.

As Glenn went down the ramp he was assaulted by the heat of the aircraft turbines and the shimmering waves of ambient heat from the jungle clearing now baking in the midday sun.

It took his breath away. He was carrying a ruck sack full of gear over his left shoulder and an M-16 under his right arm when his foot slipped at the bottom of the metal ramp and hit the ground hard. His helmet went askew and he lurched to one side before catching his balance. A handful of nearby bare-chested troops gave him a weary look and turned away.

That was graceful, Nolan. You only get one chance to make a first impression. Way to go. He went through the break in the earthen berm and headed for the TOC at the center of the LZ, glancing around surreptitiously to keep from appearing to be a brand new arrival in-country. *That should work – your fatigues are dark green and look like they're straight off the shelf. Everybody else is wearing rumpled faded stuff the color of the dirt around here. Well, everybody's a new guy once.*

He went down the crude steps into the large, dark sandbagged bunker that was the operations center. Nobody challenged or said anything to him; when his eyes adjusted to the minimal light, he found a captain seated in front of an easel, marking an acetate overlay spread over a large map. The officer glanced up and then looked him over from top to bottom.

"Whatta ya need, lieutenant?"

"I'm looking for the C.O., sir. I was told back in Tay Ninh to report to him out here."

"For what?"

"Honestly don't know. I got assigned to the battalion this morning and told to get a flight out here – that I'd get my instructions from him."

"He's not here right now – he and Major Moore are up in the C&C. Should be back in an hour or so. They didn't tell you back in the rear what the assignment was?"

"No, sir."

"If I were you, I'd go down to the log pad and get Higgie to spot you a couple hundred rounds of ammo and a dozen mags and six or eight C-Rations. You might need that soon."

"Who's Higgie?" Glenn asked.

"He's the assistant S-4. Tall, freckled guy with curly brown hair. Talks like he's from *Minnesoooota* 'cause he is. International Falls." The captain gave him a sly grin. "You be sure to ask him how he likes the cold spell we're having this week."

"Is there something I should know, captain?" Glenn asked suspiciously.

The captain smiled again, shook his head and went back to his map.

Back outside, Glenn shielded his eyes, looked around and then headed across the firebase toward the helicopter landing area as two of the 105 artillery pieces began firing somewhere off to the north. He watched as they fired three more rounds each and then all six guns fired, repeated twice and then someone was calling "end of mission." When he glanced around he found he was the only one paying any attention to the artillery action.

"Hey you! New guy." Glenn looked around quickly and saw a soldier in his mid-thirties only a few yards away walking toward him. "Your first time on a firebase?"

"How'd you know?"

"It's not hard to tell." The soldier had a ruddy complexion and a very short-cropped flattop of reddish hair. His face was round, his body thick; he might have played linebacker for a Big Ten school. Captain's bars and a cross, both camouflaged black, were on his collar. His uniform looked worn and he was carrying a small mongrel dog under his left arm. "Father Patrick Donohoe," he said offering his hand. "Father Pat to everyone in my parish – that's all of First Brigade…And this is No-Nuts."

"You had your dog neutered in the middle of a war?"

"No, but I did catechize him. The little guy wandered into our chapel one day at Tay Ninh without his equipment. Felt sorry for him, so I took him in. You had the same sorta hang-dog look about you when you stumbled off that Chinook."

"I was really hoping nobody saw that." Glenn felt his face and the back of his neck growing warm. He held out his hand and introduced himself. "The captain inside said I should go down to the log pad and look up somebody named Higgie, the assistant S-4, and scrounge up some ammunition and C-rations."

"You planning to go out to the field for a few days?"

"Not sure. Just this morning I got assigned to the 2nd of the 8th and I caught the first bird out here. They said that Colonel Conrad would tell me what my assignment is."

The chaplain squinted at him, looked like he was deep in thought and finally said, "I have an idea why you're here."

"And that would be –?"

"Not my prerogative to tell you, lieutenant. That belongs to the battalion commander, but after you talk to him you come spend a little time with me. I *will* tell you this, Colonel Conrad is one of the finest officers you'll have the privilege of serving under no matter how long your Army career may last. Not only is he tactically brilliant, he's a man of character."

"That's quite an endorsement, padre."

"I meant it to be." The chaplain looked closer at Glenn's equipment and said, "Got enough weapons, lieutenant? I see an M-16, two knives and a holstered .45 automatic. You're a walking arsenal, aren't you?"

"I also have a C-ration can opener on my dog tags chain."

The chaplain smiled. "Okay, well of course; that always a good move. But the pistol…? Only medics get issued pistols. Why are you carrying a .45?"

"Because they don't make a handgun in .50 caliber yet."

Father Pat grunted again. "Smarting off to a priest is a sin according to the Council of Trent – that's why the church condemned Martin Luther, you know. Be careful. You could wind up getting yourself anathematized."

"I was only responding to your question, Father. And I should correct something. I've actually got three knives – the Ka-Bar attached to the web harness, the Swiss Army knife linked to the holster, and a Buck folding hunter in my pocket. All gifts." His grandfather had given him the old Ka-Bar; as it turned out, it was a decades-old family heirloom...

"Earl Wright thought you should have this," his grandfather had told him as they sat at the kitchen table drinking coffee. He'd then handed over the knife, still in its original leather sheath. "When I told him a few days ago you were headed to Vietnam and that you'd be stopping by here today, he drove up from Avondale and dropped this off for me to give to you. There's a story behind it."

Glenn had looked it over carefully, handling it like a fragile artifact unearthed at an archeological dig. Other than the sheath discoloration, it looked brand new.

"This knife belonged to your uncle Glenn. He received it a month before the 82nd Airborne jumped into Normandy, but he never got to use it. It's a Ka-bar fighting knife, one that was originally designed for the Marines early in the war and later issued to the Army and the underwater demolition teams of the Navy. It's stout enough to do most anything down to and including opening ration cans. All these years Earl kept it on a shelf next to a picture of your uncle and a guy named Kenny Cook. Earl thought you should have it."

"...you *really are* well armed," he heard the chaplain saying.

"My grandfather told me an officer should always carry a pistol *and* a rifle. He commanded a company and a battalion in the Irish 69th during the First War."

"The 69th? That's the regiment of Francis Duffy. Every Catholic chaplain in the Army since then has heard of Father Duffy. You'll have to ask your grandfather if they ever crossed paths and let me know, Nolan."

"He's mentioned that they did cross paths many times. I'll write and ask him."

"You do that. Look me up between now and lunchtime tomorrow. I make it a point to get to know all the new people in my parish as soon as I can after they arrive."

"I'm not really in your parish, Padre."

"Don't tell me a nice boy like you isn't a Catholic."

"Not now, and never have been. But I am married to a Catholic girl."

The priest scratched his cheek, nodding. "This is something I'm dying to hear. You're lucky my specialty is counseling. You can find me there beyond the artillery mess tent," he said pointing to the far side of the base. "You go see Lieutenant Higgins and I'm sure he'll fix you up with what you need if he's got it. Make sure to get one of those new five-quart bladders and two two-quart canteens. As a minimum. That may sound like a lot right now, and it *will be* heavy, but after you've spent your first three or four days in the bush you'll thank me. You can pay me back by coming to Mass this evening after dinner," the priest said quickly with a smile working at the corners of his mouth. "Tell your wife about it. I'm sure she'll be pleased."

"I just might stop by – assuming I'm still here this evening."

"My guess is… Well, I hope you are. I'll see you then. Welcome to the *Mustangs*."

Glenn watched the chaplain disappear into the TOC, noticing that he had a 1st Cav patch on both his right and left sleeves – he'd had at least one previous tour with the division.

Now that's interesting, Glenn thought. *A priest who's a Cav sandwich. I doubt there's many of those around.*

*　　*

"Your sales pitch yesterday sold me, Nolan," Mike Conrad said as he sat on top of the sandbagged Operations bunker and looked across LZ Ike in the early evening heat. It was nautical twilight – that ethereal in-between time separating dusk and night. The ambiguity of the evening light mirrored his own feelings as he looked at Conrad who sat with a leg pulled up under his chin with both hands.

"You had less than a day in the brigade but you'd done your homework. That made the sale. Brief, to the point, and accurate. The summary of your experience told me everything I needed to hear in two sentences and I liked what you said about taking care of the troops. You got your foot in the door. So now I have a job for you. It may not be what you wanted, but it's what I need done. This is important to me… to the battalion."

As Conrad spoke, Glenn got that same sinking feeling he'd had in the mess hall watching the colonel walk away. It suddenly crossed his mind that the commander had in mind some sort of dirty extra duty, or a battalion staff position that nobody wanted – the dregs old timers wouldn't stand for.

"Whatever you need done, sir, I'll do it." Glenn held his breath until he couldn't stand it anymore. "What do you want me to do, sir?"

"Echo company. The battalion mortar platoon. You probably saw them earlier when you landed at the log pad. They're set up over there. Major Moore and I discussed our problem several times over the last two or three weeks, and we can't solve it. I'm hoping you can."

Conrad's answer was somehow anticlimactic.

"I don't understand, sir. What problem? And why do you think I can solve it?"

Conrad took a deep breath. "With our shortage of junior officers, we haven't filled the mortar platoon leader position for almost a month. During that time the platoon's performance has suffered. We've had several incidents of short rounds that wounded our own troops, and the companies coming onto firebase security refuse to use the mortars when they go on daily patrols. They don't have confidence in them anymore and so our overall defense suffers. You need to turn that around. The 81mm mortars are a key element of our firebase defense plans."

Glenn hadn't done any hands-on mortar work since his Yearling year at West Point when he'd been trained on everything from Fire Direction Center plotting, to actually firing rounds, to adjusting fire as a forward observer. In Germany, he'd had the best mortar crew in the 24th Division (Forward) with Dorrance and Marshall in the FDC, and sergeant Emerson running the platoon. They'd gotten an outstanding rating at Grafenwohr from the evaluation team from the States without any help – or better stated, without any interference from him.

"I don't know exactly what the problem is, lieutenant," the battalion commander was saying as he swung his leg. "I don't have the time to figure it out and fix it. That's a lieutenant's job, and until you came along, I couldn't find anyone I had confidence in to solve it. Just fix the problem, Nolan – quickly. It'll be evident to me when you do."

Glenn spent the next half hour off to the side of the briefing area inside the narrow subterranean ditch that had been dug to house the operations center. He listened to a brief litany by the S-2, the captain he'd met earlier – weather, enemy situation relayed from Brigade Intelligence that included an intel summary of all the battalion reports from the day before, reports from B Company of a trail with recent signs of usage, a small abandoned bunker network D Company had come across. Just before noon, a Pink Team had sighted three NVA on a trail, engaged with their Cobra and the Loach had claimed two kills. The S-3, Major Moore, summed up the day's movements of each company, the brief firefight reported by Company C before they called in the Pink Team. Moore announced the battalion's move from IKE three days hence to a yet-to-be-determined location to the west.

The rest of the briefing washed over him in a cascade of information about C-rations and water resupply, ammunition expended, personnel status of each company in the field. The Sergeant Major gave a little talk about morale and what he'd observed in the field while Company B was being logged.

Glenn didn't know whether to be disappointed or relieved that his arrival as the new mortar platoon leader went unannounced. When the briefing was over, he found his way over to the tent that served as the artillery battery's mess hall.

"Welcome, proselyte," Father Pat said, drinking coffee from a well-worn canteen cup as he sat on a chair outside the artillery mess tent. "I've found that, without exception, the cannon-cockers on firebases have the best food. I hear you're the new mortar platoon leader."

"You knew, didn't you?"

"I guessed. There aren't many secrets on a tiny, tiny piece of terra firma like this."

"What else do you know about my new assignment?"

"Not a whole lot. I know the troopers in the mortar platoon are aware they're under the gun, so to speak. They think they're wrongfully maligned."

"Are they?"

"Maybe, maybe not. That's your job to figure out and remedy, not mine."

"You seem to have your finger pretty much on the pulse of everything that's going on around here. What do you think, Padre?"

"What I think doesn't matter, lieutenant," the chaplain said, sipping noisily from his cup. "But what's really going on does. So, Nolan, have you decided how you're going to find out what's really going on in your new command?"

"I'm workin' on it, padre."

Donohoe sipped at his coffee again, and then said, "That might satisfy the commander this evening, but I doubt it will this time tomorrow. If I were you, I'd have a plan pretty well in mind before I rested my head this evening."

He did already, and he began to work it even before falling asleep on the ground with his helmet for a pillow.

* * * *

"Cateline, the Senator is impressed and appreciative… and he wishes to show it to you."

Oakes looked at the pretty dark-haired girl in front of him and knew he wasn't getting through. He moved from behind his desk and came around to sit next to her hoping he could dial down the tension and take the chill out of the room.

"Our boss wants you to know he's going to raise your salary thirty-five percent and –"

"I should be happy with this, Brandon?! If what you say is true, then I shall now at last be on the level of his secretary, and for that I'm supposed to be not only happy but accepting of this latest indignity from him?" Her nostrils flared and her look became more piercing. "This latest intrusion into my privacy – and that of my dear grandparents – has been most egregious. You shall have my letter by mid-afternoon and I shall have cleaned my desk and departed before the cock crows tomorrow morning."

She stood suddenly and turned to leave; he grasped her forearm gently. "Please."

"Please, you say? Yet you accost my grandparents at their estate in Essex, not once but twice and without so much civility as *'By your leave'* to me from either you or his lordship, the senator from Maryland. Your manners are boorish and I say as much for your Senator Reeves."

"Cateline, please sit down and let me explain."

Oakes finally prevailed and she sat on the edge of the large high-backed chair but would not look at him. He was amazed at how quickly things had gotten out of hand with her.

She had suddenly stormed into his office that morning with the righteous indignation of an Old Testament prophet of doom and demanded an apology from him over someone from the London embassy stopping by the estate of General Sir Henry Smythe-Browne to ask about his granddaughter's middle school attendance. Indignation swelled into accusations and she stomped out threatening resignation and demanding an audience with the Senator immediately.

Harrison Reeves had at first been amused – as he usually was with the antics of his 'fiery Irish lass masquerading as a genteel Brit'. He dismissed Oakes with the admonition to 'double her salary if necessary, but keep that girl on my payroll whatever the cost.' Reeves had quickly realized the value of the young lawyer to his own standing and power in the Senate.

In recent weeks, she had provided priceless information on various bills pending and prepared him for the insider horse-trading that inevitably ensued before final votes. He'd been able to garner support for his own legislation while positioning himself as power broker inside his own party. He was savvy enough to realize it all came from the work done in the trenches behind the scene by his pretty little legislative assistant. No one on his payroll had ever adapted as quickly and effectively as Cateline Glendenbrook. And he knew she was being paid peanuts compared to her real worth.

"I doubt very much there is anything you can say, Mr. Oakes, that would –"

"Cateline, please call me Brand. We don't have to be so formal, you and I."

"Oh, but we do, Mr. Oakes. The man who wined and dined me and lied to me about the wonderful opportunities associated with my coming to work for Senator Reeves appears now in hindsight to be chimera – an illusion."

"I never lied to you, Cateline."

She scoffed at the idea and said, "Of course you did. That night you shepherded me around this town you made the U.S. Senate out to be a fraternity akin to the Knights of the Bath, but they are not much more than a rogues gallery of petty little men, and now a few women... as is the government at large, sir."

"I think you're being a little extreme here, Cateline."

"Not a-tall, Mr. Oakes. Didn't our own Senator Reeves get shafted – as you Americans are so fond of saying – by the former president himself? Wasn't he promised a place as Vice-President only to have that bauble snatched from his grasp at the last minute?"

"There weren't any promises. Only possibilities."

"If that is what you care to believe, sir. I daresay our employer believes otherwise."

She's right, Oakes said to himself. *Reeves was apoplectic when he heard the news at the convention that Hubert Humphrey was to be the VP nominee. The senator is right about this girl – she seems to be clairvoyant at times.*

"Whatever the truth of that is," Oakes said, "you and I will never know. But I can tell you this with absolute certainty – Senator Reeves desperately wants you to remain on his Washington team."

"I believe you. But I also say he has an abhorrent way of showing it. I shan't be the subject of his – and I suppose your – incessant invasions of my privacy and that of my grandpa-pa and my grandmother back home in England."

"I can assure you we had nothing to do with that."

"I don't believe you, Mr. Oakes. Should you swear on a stack of the King James Version, I would still not believe it. I shall deliver my letter of resignation as promised."

Oakes grew more nervous as he thought about the senator's directions earlier. "What can I do to change your mind, Cateline? I'll do anything within reason."

She turned toward him and said. "My first inclination is to not believe you; however, I am willing to take one further step."

"And that is...?"

"That from the Senator himself, I receive his promise to treat me and my grandparents with the respect we are due by not further harassing us."

"Cateline, you have it. I promise I'll do everything in my power to persuade him."

"I'll not settle for less than his word from his very own lips," she said, drawing back and looking down her nose at him.

"All right. Do we have a deal?"

"Not quite. You said the senator would increase my salary. But thirty-five percent is not enough. I've been contacted by the firm I left in order to come here. They have made me an offer. A substantial offer. The senator should at least meet it."

"So tell me what the offer is."

"It amounts to a salary twice what I now make, with the clear intention of adding bonuses to that for performance and living expenses in New York."

Oakes shook his head. "I doubt he'd consider doubling your salary. That's a big jump."

"Then you may tell him the glad news tomorrow afternoon that I have moved back to New York City. He will certainly be pleased to be rid of me."

She rose and walked briskly from the room. An hour later she received an overseas call.

"Cateline, my dear, you asked in your message that we call on this number at precisely nineteen hundred thirty our time," her grandfather said. "What are you up to, young lady?"

"Oh, just this and that and the other. You know grandpa-pa, it's always difficult for a Brit among the colonists. You remember how it was dealing with them during the war."

"Good lord, don't remind me. What are you trying to do, give me a second heart attack? The old man stammered, coughed and then noisily cleared his throat. "Shame on you."

She smiled and would have laughed out loud but was afraid someone in the office next door might hear and ruin her scheme with Senator Reeves and Oakes. "I was wondering if you'd received any more visits lately from the Americans."

"If I had you'd quite likely have seen it on your CNN. Pity the person from London who comes about again looking into your life or mine. I have the double barreled fowling piece stashed behind the front door and it's loaded with more than just bird shot."

"You really wouldn't shoot someone."

"Perhaps not to kill, but I would most assuredly give him good reason to visit his doctor."

"And I shan't argue with you for it."

"Wise you are young lady. But you still haven't told me what you're up to and why this secrecy about the reasons for visits from the American embassy and arranged phone calls for unstipulated reasons. Are you in some sort of trouble?"

"Not terribly. Certainly not as much as the time I dyed all of grandma-ma's chickens blue when I was six."

She heard the old man laugh heartily. "Ah, yes. I remember that episode well. Strangely it does still come up in conversation."

"And this conversation might well also – not at the estate, but here in America. I have a favor to ask, and shant tell you why, but if I could you would agree I am doing what is right."

"Good heavens! Prince Machiavelli himself would be hard-pressed to concoct anything more convoluted. Now you have me interested. But Cateline..." The old man hesitated.

"Yes?"

"One day I should like you to tell me what all this is about."

"I shall. I promise. But for now it must remain our secret. I ask you this one last favor and then I must ring off. Should anyone ask – by that I mean anyone – should they ask about this phone call I wish you to tell them that you called me, on this number, and advised me that representatives from the American government came by the house asking further questions about my early education."

"You're asking me to lie."

"I'm asking your help in a ruse, an innocent subterfuge."

"Dress it in any cloak you like my dear and it's still a lie."

"Perhaps you're right. But it is important you do so. That is all I can say at the moment."

Silence lingered on the other end of the trans-Atlantic call, until at last her grandfather spoke. "As you wish, my dear. But remember, you owe me an explanation at some point."

"And you shall have it at the appropriate time. My best to grandma-ma." She hung up the phone, unlocked her bottom right desk drawer and removed a set of earphones. She placed them on her head, and listened. A nervous tightness grew in her stomach and her mind raced. *This could be catastrophic*, she told herself. *Be calm, compose yourself; think your way out of this.* She forced herself to relax by breathing slowly and finally a stillness came over her. She slowly removed the earphones, replaced them in the drawer and locked it. Then she stood and looked at herself in the tall mirror on the back of her door. Finally she picked up the single sheet of paper on top of her blotter and left the office.

Two doors down the hall was the main entrance to Senator Reeves' office and she entered, nodded to Helene, the senator's secretary, and walked quickly to the closed door marked *PRIVATE – Senator Harrison Gibson Reeves.*

"I'm sorry Cateline," the secretary said, "he's in conference with Brandon at the moment. I'll be glad to call you when he's free."

"That won't be necessary!" Cateline opened the door and walked in. Reeves and Oakes looked up at her, surprise etched on their faces.

"I'm so sorry, Senator," Helene was saying, standing in the open doorway. "I told her you were in conference and –"

"That's quite all right. In fact we're just wrapping up," Reeves said, while standing and looking charming. "We were just talking about you, Cateline."

"Nothing complimentary, I'm sure," she said nastily, glaring at Oakes. She slammed the sheet of paper down in the middle of the senator's desk. "My resignation!"

"Cateline –" Reeves began, looking shocked at her outburst.

"You lied to me!" she said, turning viciously on Oakes. "And so did you, senator. I *will not* work any longer for people I cannot trust."

"My dear, before you say anything you might regret –," Reeves said calmly.

"I just received a phone call from my grandfather. Do you know what he told me?!" She looked quickly back and forth between them. "The American embassy has again visited them at their home and asked about my early education! Both of you…" She waved an accusing finger at Reeves and then at Oakes. "Both of you lied to me. Not a half hour ago, you promised no such thing would happen again – that you knew nothing about such an inquiry. My grandfather's call puts the lie to that, I should say. You obviously don't trust me and I can assure you the feeling is mutual!"

"Let's all take a deep breath," Reeves was saying. "Cateline, calm down. Helene please close the door."

"No!" Cateline shouted. "I will not sit down; certainly not with Mr. Oakes."

The senator glanced at his chief-of-staff. "Perhaps just you and I could talk, then. I assure you this latest incident with your grandparents is something I know nothing about."

"Nor do I," Oakes said quickly.

"You seem to be saying you did know about the previous visits."

"Every government employee has to go through a background check," Reeves said. "We deal with highly secret and very delicate information in the Congress."

"I am not a government employee! We have had this conversation already, Senator. It was a condition of my agreeing to come to work for you. I am a private contractor working directly for you, sir, not a GS-something or other. If that changed, I knew nothing of it."

"No, Cateline. That hasn't changed."

"Well, as a matter of fact it has, senator. You have my letter. I shall return to New York and my previous employer tomorrow. I have grown greatly displeased with my treatment here in this office and no longer wish to continue in your employ."

"Let's talk about it." Reeves produced a paternal look and motioned to the chair beside Oakes. "Please, this is the first I've heard of any of this. Had I known, I would have talked to you. I swear."

Cateline looked him in the eye, knowing for certain he was lying to her now. She'd heard him talking about this just minutes earlier while sitting in her office. Not only had she heard, but she'd also recorded it.

"Please, sit down and the three of us can talk through this like adults."

"No," Cateline said. "I will talk to you, and you alone, senator."

"I hide nothing from my chief-of-staff."

"He hides much from me, and now I will hide my conversation from him. This is a private matter for you only, Senator Reeves, and I will not be the object of intimidation from Mr. Oakes. If you find that unacceptable, I shall take my leave immediately."

Reeves looked uncomfortably at Brandon Oakes and then back at Cateline. A thick, ugly vein grew prominent on his forehead as he tried to remain calm. "Brandon, if you will excuse us please."

"Certainly, senator. I understand."

"Thank you for your consideration," Reeves said while looking at the young woman. The chief-of-staff left and quietly closed the door behind him. "May we continue?"

"As you wish," she said, taking a seat across the desk from him. "I must tell you, Mr. Oakes has made my time here a living hell from the first moment until this very day."

Reeves looked genuinely surprised. "He's always had only the most complimentary things to say about you, and I observed the two of you always got along famously."

"First, I find it hard to believe he never had an off-putting comment about me. I'm not saying I disbelieve you, only that his invective against me was frequent, the more so as time passed. Perhaps he was careful in the ways he couched his negativism toward me around you."

"That's possible, but I like to think I'm more observant than that."

"I've found Mr. Oakes to be quite the slicker, able to deceive the best of us. It took me a long while to catch on to it myself. I'm certain he was more careful around you than he was with an underling such as I."

"You're being a little harsh, Cateline."

"I think not, sir." She looked away and took a deep breath before looking at him and continuing. "I do apologize for my comment earlier linking you and he to the falsehoods perpetrated against me by Mr. Oakes. I assumed you must know of them, and that was wrong of me. But my observation of him remains my position. I must leave because I cannot conceive of working as closely with him in the future as I have thus far."

"I really wish you'd reconsider," the senator said, resting his elbows on his desk. and looking benignly at her. "You've brought so much to this office and made our lives much more profitable for our constituents. And, I must admit, for me personally. You bring an expertise and competence I've not seen from any staff on Capitol Hill during my twenty-six years in Congress." He stopped and looked around. "Even my office. The redecorating of this old mausoleum of mine has made me the envy of every senator in the Democratic caucus."

"That's kind of you to say, sir."

"But, I also have many good things to say about my chief-of-staff. Brandon has been with me for a dozen years. I value his counsel. You've been with me only months yet you've made yourself virtually indispensable. I can't begin to tell you how much I appreciate all you do for this office."

And for you personally, Cateline thought. "I appreciate that, sir. Which makes the events of this morning all the more confusing to me."

"In what way?"

"Mr. Oakes advised you wished to show your gratitude by increasing my compensation."

"I know. I asked him to do that since he's your direct supervisor. I had hoped you'd be pleased with the offer."

She looked down at her hands as if deeply troubled by her contemplation. Finally she said, "Sir, I was shocked and frankly embarrassed by the offer. When I came here, it was at a salary significantly less than I was making at the law firm in New York. I did so assuming I could in short order show you my worth and earn an increased salary commensurate with what I was then receiving."

"I'm aware of that, Cateline."

"Then why did you offer me a paltry 35%? I thought I was contributing more to your agenda than your secretary."

Reeve's face underwent a quick metamorphosis. "That can't be."

"I assure you it was. He offered me that – take it or leave it. I'm not a mercenary, but I believe my contribution is greater than that, and my former employers in New York assure me my earning potential far exceeds that of the secretary in your office. I must confess something else to you. Mr. Oakes' treatment of me in the office and his advances to me – if you know what I mean – have made my working here a nightmare."

"I was unaware of that. Totally unaware. Believe me. My policy now and always has been that such actions are wholly inappropriate."

"I thought you would understand. What I must confess is that I have in the past week contacted the federal prosecutor's office and am in the process of filing a complaint."

The senator looked as if someone had slapped him – color drained from his face and his jaw dropped. "I don't know why you would do such a thing."

"To stop him from harassing me, senator."

Reeves was visibly nervous, and the tell-tale vein was throbbing again. "Who have you talked to at the prosecutor's office, and how far along are you with this complaint?"

"I met with a Mr. Adams, and he brought in a female prosecutor who said she was attracted to the case for its precedent-setting value." Reeves' look grew more concerned. "I wasn't interested in making case law, but this other prosecutor seemed to be."

"And her name was...?"

"Ashley, or Appleby maybe. Something like that. I'm not sure she even gave me a card."

"Could it have been Ashby?" Reeves asked. "Erika Ashby?"

"Quite possibly. I remember he called her Erika once or twice."

"That bitch!" Reeves mumbled into his hands.

"Excuse me, senator?"

"Just mumbling to myself." His eyes darted around the room quickly and he said, "Cateline, I'm sorry it's come to this. I apologize for what my chief-of-staff has done, and I assure you it will be corrected."

"I'm sorry sir, but I cannot work for him."

"You don't have to. You'll report directly to me, bypassing him. On everything. I'll put it in writing to both of you. In time I *will* move him out, but that can't be done immediately. You have my word."

"I can't have him continuing to spy on me and harassing my family."

"I don't know that he is, but I'll be very direct with him. The harassment stops now. Take the rest of the day off and think about it. We'll talk first thing in the morning."

"Thank you, sir."

She could tell Reeves was uneasy by the nervous drumming of his fingers on the desk. "I have only one thing to ask of you." He gave her a most charming smile. "I ask that you drop the idea of filing any complaints against Mr. Oakes. Let me deal with him. I'll be harder on him than any court."

"Why would you do that for me, sir?"

"Because – and I'm sure you can figure this out on your own if you already haven't – if this case with Oakes goes public, I'll get some of the backwash on me. Frankly, I just don't want to have to deal with that."

They looked at one another, and at last Cateline said, "I will see you in the morning, sir. And thank you for your consideration."

"Thank you for yours."

She got up and went to the door, paused and turned toward him. "I believe what you just said. Thank you for your candor."

She went through the outer office and walked down the hall to her own small workplace. Once inside she locked the door and sat down behind her desk. Only then did she allow herself to relax; her hands shook and she bit her lip.

Much to do, tonight, she thought. *First, a drink and then talk to Aunt Erika so she can be prepared if anyone comes asking about the story I just made up. Reeves... stupid bugger thinks I had his office redecorated to please him.*

Have to get more tape for the recorder.

Chapter 11

"Look, Nolan, I don't want or need you on this patrol."

The Bravo company platoon leader looked him over as he inserted a full magazine into his M-16 and released the bolt. "This is a simple little first light sweep a hundred yards inside the tree line. Even if we run into gooks, I'm not calling in mortars. Your guys almost wiped us out the last time we were on the firebase. I gotta protect my men."

Glenn bit his lower lip. *What was it Thomas Jefferson said? – if you're angry, count to ten; if really angry, a hundred.* He got to thirty-four.

"Your C.O. wants me to go along."

"No, you badgered him until he finally gave in." Lieutenant Worrell looked and sounded exhausted. All of the line company troops were.

Including LZ Ike, the battalion had opened and closed five firebases in as many weeks – Jamie, Mary Gwen, Heather, Victor and now, Flashner. This would be their first full day on Fire Support Base Flashner and everyone guessed they would be moving out again in a matter of two or three days. Moving a battalion firebase was a monumental task, and while the artillery battery and battalion headquarters, like his mortar platoon, had to put up with the choking black dust of Tay Ninh province and airless hundred degree temperatures, the grunts in the field had to hump eighty pound rucksacks day in day out. It wasn't hard to understand the lieutenant's attitude. Glenn was worn out himself and had hoped for a better reception from the Company B platoon leader.

"Worrell, I'm not going to argue with you. You're putting me in a bad spot here – your company commander told Colonel Conrad his platoons would employ the mortars and that he wanted me along with all his first and last light patrols until I finished training you guys on F.O. procedures. The battalion commander told me straight up to be in harness every time a Bravo company patrol goes out. How about giving me a damned break?"

The lieutenant glared at him while lighting a cigarette. "You follow my RTO. Don't get in the way and remember I'm the one who makes all the decisions from the time we walk over the berm until we get back inside."

"No problem."

"And there won't be as long as you follow orders." Worrell looked around and then called out to his platoon sergeant, "Hobbsey! Let's get everyone saddled up and ready to go. Second squad leading, followed by third, then first. Move out in five minutes."

"I'm going to have the mortars fire two registration targets before we leave. Put a couple rounds on the ground in each spot so I can adjust from there if I need to," Glenn said, taking the map out of the side cargo pocket and grabbing the handset of the radio strapped to his back. "This won't take long. Targets are already plotted and one crew is laid in on each. Let me show you on the map where targets *Alpha* and *Bravo* are located."

"Don't give damn where they are, Nolan. Like I told you, I'm not using 'em." Worrell looked around at his platoon. "Listen up, third platoon! Everybody! Heads up because the mortars are going to fire a couple rounds into the jungle before we go. Keep an eye out – I don't want anybody gettin' WIA before we get off the firebase." Worrell shot him a withering glance and walked away.

"Pisses you off, don't it, Nolan?" someone behind him said in a lilting Southern accent.

Glenn turned his head and looked at the 2nd lieutenant standing behind him with his arms crossed over his chest and a smirk on his face.

"Combat Al Colquitt – how goes the war?"

"Better for me than you, Nolan. You need to get out of mortars and into the real Cav."

"So, why are you here? C Company's still in the field and you're not out with 'em?"

"Had to go to the rear last log day. They're gettin' resupplied this mornin' and I'll be takin' the first bird back out. Can't let my boys down, Glenn. No, sir, don't want to miss any chances to kill me a bunch of gooks, you know what ah'm sayin'?"

Running into Colquitt made worse a day that had already begun badly.

He now had nearly six weeks under his belt leading the battalion mortars. It had been a rocky start – with his own troops and with the line companies, especially the platoon leaders. Only one of them in the battalion during the first month had so much as tried to work with him.

He had recognized within his first couple of days, there were problems in his new platoon. They lacked training, and leadership. Slackness in operational discipline had crept in and two incidents came close to being catastrophic. The worst involved Worrell's platoon.

Weeks earlier, during a fire mission for another of B Company's platoons, a short charge had somehow been mistakenly affixed to a high explosive round fired by one of the mortar crews. They were shooting a mission, across the breadth of the firebase, over the log pad and impacting four hundred meters beyond the tree line; Glenn was inside the Fire Direction Center plotting the mission alongside Margrave and Jones. The round from Tube #2 sounded strangely hollow and muted, and when he looked outside he saw the projectile arching away from him and knew instantly the round was going to impact well short. He tried but failed to get the attention of the dozen men from third platoon and the battalion logistics section to warn them off the log pad as the round topped out and begin to arc downward toward the crowd.

The round barely made it to the wood line. Fortunately, there were no injuries, except to the already diminished credibility of his platoon. Gaining the confidence of the line companies after that had been a long uphill battle. But he'd improved procedures, spent every minute he could find on the LZs and out on patrols with each platoon, and had managed to build their faith in the battalion mortars over the following weeks.

"You need to get off this gravy train on the firebase, Nolan," Colquitt told him. "Three hot meals a day, all the beer you can drink, clean clothes and showers – hell, you might as well be back in the world, friend. Get your butt out to the field where the action is."

Seeing the Virginian again bothered him. But he shook it off and got on the radio to the FDC. Two quick missions later, he pulled the PRC-77 onto his back, clipped the handset to his web gear and set off toward where Worrell's platoon was forming up.

The heat was already thick and oppressive as the platoon moved in single file from the firebase and entered the jungle less than a hundred yards away. By the time they'd moved fifty yards his fatigue jacket was soaked and sweat ran off his forehead and into his eyes.

Another fifty yards further on, Worrell halted his twenty-four man platoon.

Glenn saw the lieutenant turn around and quietly say something to his RTO who whispered into his handset, "Asher three, Asher one, this is Asher Oscar, close up and tie in."

Troops were milling around and slowly forming into a perimeter around Worrell, his platoon sergeant and RTO; in a matter of minutes they were all sitting down, propped against trees and lighting up cigarettes.

Glenn approached the platoon leader with a whispered question. "What's going on?"

"Taking a break," was the platoon leader's answer, as he lit up his own cigarette.

"We haven't even gone a hundred meters according to my pace count."

Worrell gave him a hard look. "Remember the rules, Nolan. I give the orders, and you follow them with your mouth shut."

Glenn nodded and sat down a few feet away, drinking from his canteen.

Everybody around him looked relaxed – some appeared to have fallen asleep. *I know it's a time-honored tradition, and a common infantryman's rule of thumb to sleep whenever the opportunity presents itself. But this doesn't feel right. Didn't see any OP/LPs go out, and these guys don't seem very alert. I wonder when - or if - we're going to do the sweep of this side of the firebase.* He remembered seeing what he thought was a narrow game trail off to their right just before reaching the tree line. *Wish we had checked that out,* he thought.

A half hour and two cigarettes later, he approached Worrell.

"What's the plan?" Glenn asked him in a low whisper.

"We'll move around to the east in a little while and check that out, then head back."

"That's it?"

"Just about, Nolan." The platoon leader got up slowly and moved toward the north side of the small perimeter.

Glenn watched him and then looked at the RTO who shrugged. "What gives?"

The Spec-4 radio operator shrugged again and said in a barely audible whisper, "LT's DEROS is in three weeks. He wants to be around when *it* comes around. Ol' *Luke the Gook* gives us plenty enough trouble without goin' lookin' for it on a puny ass patrol like this. The lieutenant ain't spoilin' for a fight these days the way he was when he first got here." Glenn was still thinking about what the soldier said when he heard someone yell out.

"Get DOWN!"

The warning carried through the silent jungle and he felt his neck tingle and his heart race. Looking around he could only see one soldier other than the RTO, giving him the sensation of being exposed and unprotected.

Worrell was suddenly in front of him, taking the radio handset and speaking urgently.

"Lantern one-four, this is Asher. We have movement to the west and southwest of checkpoint one, over." He listened for several seconds. "No estimate yet. Negative on that. I'm holding here until we can ID what we have, if anything. Roger that. Asher out."

He looked at Nolan briefly and then moved off. He was back in less than a minute.

"What do you think it is?" Glenn asked, hoping his voice didn't betray his anxiety.

"Don't know," Worrell spat at him. "If I had, I'd have told the C.O. Second squad leader thought he saw a gook. Maybe two. Could be a whole damned NVA division for all I know."

Worrell's nervousness didn't help Nolan's state of mind. *We can't just sit here. Got to do something, sometime.* "How about a little recon by fire with the mortars." When the platoon leader gave him a sour look and shook his head, Glenn said, "Too close to the firebase for 105s. My registered target Alpha is southwest of where we are about six hundred meters, and it's already fired in. I'll bring it in to about a hundred yards from us and see what it scares up."

"No. Hilldebrandt, call the company and tell them to send a Pink Team."

"Unless they're already on station," Glenn said, "it'll take twenty minutes to launch and get here from Tay Ninh. I can have rounds on the ground in thirty seconds." He could see Worrell struggling with idea. "I've done this dozens of times in the last month."

"Pink Team is on the way. ETA fifteen minutes."

"You may not have fifteen minutes."

The platoon leader looked anguished. "All right, Nolan. But I'll have your ass if –"

The first shot came from an M-16 and was answered by two AK-47s, then several more.

"Bangor FDC this is Bangor one-four, fire mission, over," Glenn yelled into the radio handset over the increasing volume of rifle fire.

The response was instantaneous. *"Bangor one-four, fire mission, send it."*

"Fire target Alpha, two rounds HE, and lay all tubes to that target. Will adjust, over."

"Bangor FDC, roger. Fire Mission, two rounds HE, Target Alpha, will adjust, out." Only seconds later he heard the hollow echoed *THUNK... THUNK* and the radio call. *"Bangor one-four, rounds on the way, over."*

"On the way, wait." Glenn nervously lit a cigarette.

The two rounds exploded a few hundred yards away, where he expected. He looked at the map, shot an azimuth to the sound of the tubes firing and the sound of the rounds impacting. *Slow down, don't rush this,* he told himself as the firefight around him grew louder.

"Bangor FDC, this is one-four. Will adjust on your gun-target line. Do you copy?"

"Roger one-four, adjustments on the gun target line."

"This is one-four, two rounds - left two hundred, drop one hundred. Fire when ready."

He could visualize Jones and Margrave running the calculations. *Be accurate, guys. This is me out here, and this one's for real-real.* Except for that time, over a month ago, when he'd caught them in an error, they'd proven to be excellent plotters, and he knew they could do this.

"Bangor one-four, this is FDC. Rounds on the way, over."

"On the way, out."

He made two more adjustments and then said, "FDC, this is Bangor one four. Next adjustment is *DANGER CLOSE*. Left five-zero add five zero, over."

"Bangor one-four, this is FDC, understand Danger Close... left five zero, add five zero."

The six rounds went off almost simultaneously, and the incoming rifle fire diminished. In another minute it ended altogether and the jungle grew strangely silent.

"FDC, this is Bangor one-four. Mark that last target as Target Charlie, and keep all guns laid. End of mission... for now. Good job. I'll be back to you."

Glenn was strangely elated. Nervous but delighted by how well his guys had done. *Didn't Churchill once say that the greatest thrill in life was to be shot at and missed?*

He lit another cigarette while sitting on the ground with his back to a tree when the team of one OH-6 low bird plus a Cobra gunship came on station. After identifying their smoke the low bird scouted around them, barely above the trees, in ever widening circles.

"Low bird reports sighting three gooks heading down a trail toward us," the RTO said, offering the radio handset to Worrell. "High bird is going to roll hot on them. He wants another smoke to verify our location."

The sound of the gunship firing rockets that impacted less than a football field away startled Glenn as he sat near the platoon leader. The sound was initially a hollow echo and turned into a sharp crack just as the rockets impacted the ground. The low bird moved back in after the gun run and buzzed around, this time reporting two kills. Suddenly the jungle erupted in a fierce barrage of automatic gunfire, followed by the sound of a straining turbine engine. Glenn turned in time to see a vague outline of the little OH-6 tossed about as it descended into the jungle canopy and proceeded to beat itself into pieces.

Hildebrandt yelled something, his eyes wide as he turned and ducked behind a tree.

The rotor blades disintegrated and the fuselage of the little helicopter crashed to the ground, halfway rolling over.

Nobody could have survived that, Glenn thought, as he grabbed his rifle and took a few steps toward the crash site. Firing erupted from in front of him again. He looked at Worrell, whose face was frozen in shock. He yelled above the sound of gunfire, "We gotta get those guys out of there!"

The platoon leader still hadn't moved, his dazed eyes fixed on the horrendous crash.

"Worrell!" He shook the lieutenant hard. The firefight had started up again and now he could see movement on the far side of the crash site. "We gotta get to that Loach."

"Can't! Too many of them."

Glenn picked up the handset to his radio. "Bangor FDC – Fire mission! Registered target Charlie – six rounds per gun – fire when ready!" He thought he heard the acknowledgement from FDC but wasn't sure. He grabbed Worrell and shook him again; the lieutenant blinked, and seemed to rouse like a man awakening from a nightmare. The first mortar rounds impacted on the far side of the shattered OH-6.

Worrell was yelling instructions to his squad leaders over the sound of the firefight, gesturing wildly and pointing toward the downed aircraft. Half the platoon finally formed in a ragged line and moved cautiously from tree to tree while the rest laid down a base of fire. Glenn followed behind the RTO until they finally got to the downed OH-6; he helped drag the pilot and observer from the wreckage. Both were unconscious but still breathing. The platoon medic, a kid with red hair and freckles and a short-timer's calendar drawn on his helmet's camouflage cover, went to work bandaging cuts while the rest of the platoon moved forward and set up a perimeter. Off to their left front he could make out a small clearing.

Suddenly a machine gun opened up with a long burst from the far side of the open area. The automatic fire was frightening, so close he thought he could reach out and touch the gunner; and then several AKs joined in. A B-40 rocket exploded like a great clap of thunder off to Glenn's right; he ducked and cringed, hugging the ground.

"Medic!... Medic!" someone was yelling from that direction.

"Lieutenant!" Someone had grabbed his web gear strap and shook it. It was Worrell's RTO, his eyes as round as saucers, holding out the handset to his radio. "It's the gunship – he wants to know if we got the crew, and he's waiting to make a gun run."

"Where's Worrell?"

"Don't know! He took off that way!" the radio operator yelled back over the sound of gunfire, pointing in the direction where the B-40 had hit."

"Medic!...Medic!!"

Nolan grabbed the handset. "What's their callsign?"

"Sierra Hotel one-one!"

"Hotel one-one, this is Bangor one-four, fire mission."

"Who are you Bangor?" came the quick return call.

"I'm the FO on the ground. We got a perimeter around the downed Loach. We're on the east side of the clearing near where your ship went down. Taking fire from a few dozen NVA on the west side." Glenn rolled over and pulled a smoke grenade from the radio operator's back pack, then pulled the pin and threw it into the clearing. "Smoke is out."

Seconds later he heard, *"One-one has the Goofy Grape smoke."*

"Roger that." *Where the hell is Worrell?* he thought. *I've never done this before. Not live.* "Hotel one-one, make your runs north to south. Target is west from the smoke, heading two-eight-zero, distance seven-five, over."

The pilot's calm voice came back with the quiet turbine hum as background. *"Roger Bangor. Hotel one-one rolling hot."*

Glenn gave the handset back. "Tell the squads to keep their heads down."

The gunship made a run firing two rockets and Glenn told him to 'add five-zero, repeat'. On the next run the Cobra salvoed his remaining rockets and swooped low, firing his 40 mm gun. The enemy firing stopped.

"Bangor one-four, got another team five minutes out, callsign Sierra Hotel one-seven. One-one is off station to rearm, refuel. We'll keep a team over you until we get our guys out."

A half hour later another platoon of Bravo company found their way to the downed aircraft, and shortly after that a medevac helicopter lifted out the injured aircrew and two wounded from Worrell's platoon. B Company did a sweep and found an ammo cache with a series of fighting positions dug in around it. By sundown the engineers had rigged and blown up the ammo after the brigade commander and the Assistant Division Commander had their pictures taken by an official 1st Cav photographer standing next to the haul.

*   *   *

"Jenny!" Lynda Thornton yelled, sticking her head inside operating room #2. "Ops just got word that the inbound has four wounded, not two. They're from the 8th Cav, 2nd Battalion. We've got to get OR-1 ready pronto. I've got Judy and Dot started on prepping the room along with Atterbury and another orderly. Can you take charge?"

Jenny felt a sweeping dread pass through her. 2/8 Cav. *Oh, no!* She instantly saw Glenn's face and heard the cavalier tone of his voice telling her nothing was ever going to happen to him. "You're covered, Lyn," Jenny replied, nervous now. "Who's the first call surgeon?"

"Giovanni!" the head nurse said, and ducked out of the room.

That's great... no it's better than that, Jenny Kolarik said to herself.

Gino – Captain Lisandro Giovanni – was the easiest going and probably the best surgeon in the whole hospital staff; the nurses fought over working with him. Jenny learned early on why all the girls called him 'sweet' and polite. He was the doc she'd want working on someone she considered special. But weren't they all?

By the time the dustoff helicopter arrived, Jenny along with the two other nurses and the orderlies were three quarters the way along toward finishing the preparations for surgery. Three of the patients had been transported using ponchos; the hospital personnel on the helipad placed each patient on a military gurney. The three unconscious patients were moved immediately inside to operating tables while the one who was still conscious waited outside for Jenny's crew to finalize prepping the last operating room.

"It says here that you're from Wyoming," Jenny said to him, looking at the paperwork that the infantry field medic had stuck in the right breast pocket of his jungle fatigues. She saw that he was squinting up into that awful, bright midday sun and stepped close to him to shield his eyes. "In short order we'll have you back busting broncs or whatever it is you cowboys do out there. I don't think I know anybody from Wyoming."

"Well, I do," the young soldier said weakly with the tiniest indication of a smile.

"Girl back home?"

"Yes, ma'am," he replied. He didn't seem to be in any pain as he said it.

"I'll tell the doc to be real careful when he sews you up so he doesn't leave any scars."

"She'd like that," he said appreciatively, and then he closed his eyes and dozed off.

Jenny opened the boy's fatigue jacket and saw the tiny bullet hole just above his left nipple. *That doesn't look too awful*, she thought and was just about to check his vitals signs when Atterbury came outside and yelled at her.

"OR-1 is cleaned and all the counts are done. I'll give you a hand moving the gurney."

"Thanks I appreciate that," she said, but the black orderly only glared at her.

Jenny didn't know Atterbury very well except by reputation. He was a tall muscular black man who supposedly had been in a street gang in south Los Angeles. She'd often wondered how an LA gang-banger had gotten a name that sounded like British high society. It was said that he was part of the Black Panther movement, and now wore a black beret most of the time to prove it. Jenny had tried to make friends with him because he was new and she was also, but the man kept to himself and wanted nothing to do with anyone who was white, or even any of the black brothers who cooperated with the mostly white staff.

Inside the operating room, the nurses along with the two orderlies carefully lifted the soldier onto the operating table. He was a good-looking kid, Jenny thought, even with all that mud and what looked like a two-week old beard; he was blue-eyed, blonde, and looked like the kind of youngster who ought to be taking his high school sweetheart to a drive-in on Friday night instead of tromping around in the jungle carrying an M-16.

The anesthetist came in and started his IV of sodium pentothal as Jenny soaped up the soldier's chest and started to shave him, following precisely the nurse's operating room textbook. A few minutes later, Gino came into the room, walked up to the table and took a quick look at the patient. Immediately he shoved Jenny aside with an elbow and yelled, "No time for prep! Nurse, get me some gloves! NOW, nurse!... NOW!"

Jenny was shocked into action. Gino never pushed people around, never demanded anything – only asked, and never raised his voice. She dropped her razor and immediately ripped open a pack of gloves for the doctor who was throwing a gown over himself and dumping sterile instruments onto the side table. Another surgeon, Thad Stevens, rushed into the room; Gino gave him a scalpel and dropped a handful of clamps on a mayo stand next to the operating table. Jenny gloved up Stevens just as Gino cracked the kid's chest.

Except for Atterbury, who stood in the corner watching wide-eyed as Gino and Thad worked feverishly on the Wyoming cowboy's chest while the nurses hung extra bags of blood and inserted IVs into both his arms and legs,

Black Panthers be damned! Jenny said to herself. "Atterbury, get over here! We need every hand on board to save this kid." She grabbed his arm, yanked him away from the wall and placed his hand on one of the plastic bags of blood. "You pump this bag like the rest of us are doing until I tell you to stop!"

"But, I'm... I'm..." the big black man stammered, pulling back from the operating table.

"You do what I tell you! If you lay down on me and this patient I'll take you into the street outside and beat you up one side and down the other in front of all your bruthas! We need you... HE needs you!"

They continued on in a mind-numbing haze squeezing pint after pint of the universal donor O-negative blood. Dot Sciuto was running around taking down empty bags and replacing them with new ones. Jenny realized that as hard as they were working to keep the blond cowboy filled with blood, he was just as quickly bleeding it back out. She thought about her cavalier attitude about the little hole in his chest. *I am such an idiot! Damn it! Why didn't I check his back instead of chit-chatting about... I would have seen where the exit wound caused all the damage... IDIOT!*

Gino was working on the kid's heart that looked to her like a mangled lump of meat oozing blood and resisting every effort of the doctors to stitch it. Every time Gino put a stitch in to close a hole, the thread would tear out and he'd start over. Thad worked to keep the heart pumping but every time he'd squeeze it the blood would bubble out of the myriad holes cut by NVA bullet fragments. Everything was covered in blood – Thad, Gino, the kid's chest and all the surgical drapes over his body – all running down the table and onto the floor, pooling.

They worked on, unaware of the amount of time that passed, hardly breathing; saying nothing – except for Gino who was begging out loud for the heart to beat and encouraging the kid to stay with him and not to die. Giovanni began cursing under his breath, and then out loud, until he was almost yelling. Jenny found herself praying for the kid and for the doctors.

Atterbury was like a machine now, pumping with a strong, constant rhythm, the sweat pouring down his forehead and dripping into his eyes. His big muscular arms bulged and the veins stuck out prominently. His eyes never left the scene of the two doctors, both covered in blood trying feverishly to keep the boy's heart beating while trying to repair the organ.

Another of Gino's sutures pulled out and a spurt of blood arched out from the cowboy's heart and covered the doctor's face.

"I think it's time to call it, Gino," Thad said softly. "He's been gone for a while,"

Giovanni took a deep breath and then expelled it loudly, all the time keeping his eyes on the boy's heart. His last suture slipped out of the bloody mass like every other one had over the last thirty or forty minutes. He threw down his needle holder and stood up straight. "Damn!"

Gino and Thad slowly took a step back, looking first at the boy's face and then at one another. Thad shook his head sadly; they both removed their gloves and wordlessly left the operating room. The clock on the far wall indicated 1317 hours.

Dot and Atterbury wheeled the boy's body out of the room and Jenny began the cleanup.

It took them more than six hours to clean the operating room and ready it for the next time. Jenny, tired beyond exhaustion, sat outside the tent watching the evening Retreat ritual across the street where a detail of troops lowered and folded the flag. She was too tired and discouraged to stand for the ceremony as military custom required.

Dot Sciuto came out and sat down on the flat board bench next to her and lit a cigarette, then offered the pack to Jenny. "Sorry, forgot you don't smoke."

"No, I think I'll try one this time, Dot. It's either a coffin nail or the world's most outrageous alcoholic binge." Jenny took the cigarette and lit it off of Dot's. "I killed that boy."

"No you didn't." The NVA did – you tried to save him. We all did. It wasn't your fault."

"I wish that were true. Dear Lord, I wish it were." Jenny looked at the older nurse with tears streaming down her face. "But I know it's my fault."

"You didn't pull the trigger that sent the bullet."

"I could have saved him."

"Don't go saying that. You're not the cause and you *are not* necessarily the solution."

Jenny shook her head slowly from side to side. "I killed him with kindness. Instead of being professional and checking him out the way I was trained, I thought I'd try to cheer him up. We chatted about his girl back home and about how I'd get the doctor to sew him up so it didn't leave a scar and…" She started to sob. "Why l didn't I just do my job?"

"Comforting patients is part of the job."

"I dropped the ball, Dot – big time – and it cost that boy his life. I killed him."

"Look, Jenny, we do all that we can and the rest is up to the Almighty."

She looked across the street to where the detail of soldiers who had lowered the flag were forming up to march off. "I'm soft. But I'll promise you this – I will never again allow that kind of weakness, in me or anyone else, kill an American boy.

"As God is my witness, I swear it."

*   *

"Our count stands at a little over forty thousand rounds of AK ammo, twenty-three thousand rounds of belted .30 cal. machine gun ammo and five thousand .51 Caliber."

Captain Martelino slapped the chart with his pointer, and looked around the small underground wing of the TOC where the nightly briefing was held. He liked being the battalion intelligence officer because he was always right in the middle of all the information there was to be had in the 2nd Battalion, 8th Cav. He spoke almost nightly with the G-2, a lieutenant colonel named Galvin, and this evening he was really looking forward to the conversation with the affable Division Intelligence officer. Jack Galvin had a well-oiled sense of humor which Martelino appreciated almost as much as the man's appreciation for the intel business and the work done by people like himself, especially on days like this.

"We also found a mortar with a hundred HE 82 mm rounds, and the real coup was the dozen 122 mm rockets," the battalion S-2 was saying.

"When you say 'we' there captain, you really mean those wonderful bastards in the damn third platoon of Bravo company, right?" Captain Bramlett interjected. The Company B commander was a big, well-muscled man with unusually long arms and a shaved head that made him look like Mr. Clean without the ear ring. He talked loud, swaggered like John Wayne when he walked and his favorite word was *damn,* followed by *bastard* and both were usually found in the same sentence. He considered himself the best damn commander in the Cav, its toughest damn soldier and promised to whip the ass of any bastard who thought otherwise.

"Of course, Mike," Martelino responded with a lighthearted grin, looking at the captain and then Colonel Conrad. "Lieutenant Worrell and his men did an outstanding job rescuing the pilots and locating the cache site. We also found two Chi-com telephone switchboards and three bodies were recovered – an unusual event as we all know. Two in olive drab fatigues and one in khaki; all three decked out with new web gear, backpacks and carrying B-40 rocket grenade launchers. They are identified as belonging to the 95C NVA Regiment. It seems we happened to set up our firebase right next to one of their supply caches."

"These NVA rice eaters are tough little bastards and damn well know how to fight," the B company commander said.

Mike Conrad sat quietly, listening to Martelino's recitation. Now and then he looked at Glenn who was standing off to the left rear of the line of folding chairs facing the charts set up on a wooden tripod. At last he asked, "Anything to add, Lieutenant Nolan?"

Glenn wondered why the colonel would put him on the spot like this. He was never invited to the nightly briefings – this was the first time he'd come to one, and Worrell had already given a brief summary of the operation. The platoon leader hadn't mentioned the mortar platoon's role, but he let that go by.

"No, sir, nothing to add. Second platoon did an outstanding job. Everything about the morning's mission went real smooth. "

Conrad gave him a weary look. "I doubt the OH-6 crew would agree with you. All right, S-3, what's on the docket for tomorrow?"

The briefing continued for another twenty minutes; Major Moore covered operational plans and afterward there was a discussion about the lack of replacements in the last three weeks. When it was over, Glenn left quickly and went to the mess hall for some lukewarm coffee and came back to the TOC after almost everyone had gone. He saw Conrad and Major Moore sitting in front of the briefing map that was propped against the earthen wall, deep in conversation while making marks on the acetate overlay.

The commander glanced his way a few times, and finally said, "You've been hovering over there for a while, Nolan. Something important on your mind?"

"Yes, sir. When you have a moment."

"Sure. How about now? Let's get out of here; it's hot and stuffy." The colonel led the way up the steps. It was almost dark as the battalion commander sat on the sandbagged roof of the operations center pulling a leg against his chest. "You've done a good piece of work with the mortar platoon in the few weeks you've been here. Sorry I haven't spent much time with you, and them. But their work – and yours – doesn't go unnoticed. You've pretty much turned things around with the line companies. After today, that even includes Bravo company."

"The platoon's been doing a fine job all along. Today especially. I'm proud of them."

"So am I," Conrad said.

"As you should be, sir. I'd like to ask you to stop by soon if you have the chance, and tell them that. A pat on the back from the boss goes a long way."

"I'll do it," the colonel said. "But that's not what you have on your mind."

"No, sir, it's not."

"All right, it's your dime, lieutenant. Go ahead."

Glenn took a deep breath. "Sir, I'd like to be transferred to one of the line companies." He bit his lip and took a deep breath. *Be careful how you say this, Nolan*, he said to himself. "Sir, I've seen a number of lieutenants come in and go out since coming to the 2/8. I have a classmate who came in the Big Red One with only two months left on his tour and he'd been in the field for over six months when he came to us. He was immediately sent to the field."

"Your point, Nolan?"

"Sir, I expressed a desire to be transferred to Charlie company prior to his arrival because they were short of officers."

The battalion commander rubbed his chin with a knuckle. "You think you got passed over, or that you're being held back."

"I don't know, sir. What I do know is that six lieutenants came into the battalion after I was assigned here and all were sent to line companies ahead of me."

"You're unhappy with the way I make assignments in my battalion?"

Glenn took a deep breath. "Sir, I can't possibly appreciate all the variables involved in decisions made at battalion level. But I do believe that nobody in the Army can or will do himself, or the service, any good by keeping his career desires a closely guarded secret. I chose infantry because I want to command – it's what infantry officers do. And I'm good at it. I wouldn't have been given an infantry company in Germany if I wasn't. I still have a lot to learn, and I would like the opportunity both to learn and to serve as a rifle platoon leader."

The battalion commander looked at him as if measuring.

"Anything else?"

"Not at the moment, sir."

"All right, I'll take that under consideration. You do know what you're asking for?"

"After today, I'm as informed as I'm ever likely to be. So, yes sir, I know what I'm asking for."

"I'm not sure you do. And I don't need any glory hounds or ticket punchers commanding troops in my battalion."

"I want to do what I was called to do, sir."

Conrad gave him a long, sideways glance. "I'll think on it, lieutenant. No promises."

"I appreciate the consideration, sir. I just want to do my duty… it's a personal as well as a family thing."

The colonel nodded. "I understand… and Nolan. Keep up the good work with the mortars." He watched Glenn walk away toward the far side of the firebase as the S-3 came out of the operations center and sat on the sandbags next to the commander.

"What's with Nolan?" the major asked, looking at the lieutenant as he walked away.

"He thinks the war is passing him by. Not in those words. But he wants a rifle platoon."

The major thought briefly and asked, "He's been around for what? – five weeks now?"

"He showed up at LZ Ike on 23 January, so it's a couple days more than that. How do you think he's done so far."

"You know I was one of the most vocal about the mortar platoon's performance going back a few months. But, now? No complaints, and none from any of the companies since he got here. We used to hear a lot of grumbling from all of them about the mortars – not any more. Haven't had a short round incident, or a complaint about long response times in over a month. I know he plots every mission along with his FDC crew, and he's also spent time on patrol. Most of the companies have gotten to know and trust him."

"I gave him the chance to toot his horn at the briefing and he didn't bite."

"I wondered what you were doing when you did that. I was just kibitzing with Martelino and he tells me from his debriefing of Bravo company troops that Nolan did more out there than just call in fire missions from the mortars."

Conrad was quiet for a moment, and then said, "At the end of our little chat, I got the strong feeling there was something else he wanted to get off his chest. I didn't press him on it but he has something stuck in his craw. What do you think about sending him out to the field?"

"I wouldn't hesitate. But we don't want to upset the applecart with the mortar platoon, either. I'd do it, but I'd make sure to have a backup on hand first, and give Nolan time enough time to bring him up to speed."

Conrad nodded. "Agree. Maybe the next time we get a lieutenant in from the Big Red One or one of the other divisions going back home, we'll pack Nolan off to the field."

"Stief's company? They're short two officers right now. Third platoon has been without a lieutenant for two, maybe two and a half weeks."

"Yeah, probably Stief's company." The colonel rubbed the side of his face. "I don't know if they're just a hard luck outfit, or if there's something more than that going on."

Moore cleared his throat nervously. "Their last log day, I went in and talked with Stief and he told me his third platoon didn't want an officer as platoon leader. They'd just as soon leave the slot vacant."

Conrad frowned at this. "I should get the Sergeant Major out to talk with the senior NCOs. You think there's something serious going on there?"

"Maybe. But I don't think it's a discipline problem – like refusing orders or anything like that. It appears to be more of a morale issue with the platoon sergeant specifically, and likely it's impacting most of the platoon. The sergeant is a *Shake and Bake* with about seven months in the field."

"So, what's his problem?"

"From what Steif was telling me, the platoon is tired of losing lieutenants. They think they're jinxed," Moore said and shrugged his shoulders.

"That's worrisome."

"I think Nolan could handle that."

A hollow '*thunk*' sounded in one of the mortar positions and an illumination round arced upward from one of the mortar pits exploding in the dark sky overhead and bathing the small open area amid the jungle called LZ Flashner in an eerie yellowish glow.

"He may have to," the colonel said.

Chapter 12

The Huey settled quickly into the small jungle opening and was instantly swarmed by sweat-soaked infantry grunts hauling off the crates of ammo that Higgie pushed out the door. Glenn dodged the onslaught and saw Captain Stief standing off to the north side of the LZ, bareheaded, nervously rubbing the side of his face with an open palm. He ran bent over toward the company commander with his heavy rucksack bouncing off his back.

"Lieutenant Nolan reporting in, sir. Where do you want me?" he said over the noise of the helicopter as it lifted quickly, did a climbing pedal turn and departed.

Stief looked at him thunderstruck, and let out a string of profanities. "I ask for a platoon leader and they send me out the damned mortar guy?! Are we completely out of officers in the friggin' Cav?"

Glenn bit back the smart answer that instantly formed on his lips. *Let it go, Nolan. Stief's in deep trouble and has a lot on his mind. Even on his best day, he's not wound all that tight if the LZ scuttlebutt is anywhere close.* "Where do you need me, captain?"

"Third platoon."

Glenn waited for more direction. It wasn't forthcoming.

"Okay, sir, where's third platoon?" he finally asked. Stief turned and looked at him, surprised, as if he'd suddenly materialized out of thin air. "Where's third platoon, sir?"

Without responding, the captain said to his RTO who was just inside the tree line, "Cookson, get Sergeant Meyer up here. Tell him he's got a new platoon leader."

"He won't like that, six," the RTO said.

"Like I give a shit. Tell him to get his ass up here." Stief gave Nolan a worried look. "I'm giving you your first assignment. Don't screw this up – if you do you're probably dead, and a bunch of my guys with you. Here's the deal. When 2nd platoon led us out this morning we ran into beaucoup gooks and lost four wounded. We had to pull back to this clearing. But the colonel is on my ass to get moving. I was going to have 1st platoon take point, but when I called their platoon leader up to the CP, we got hit here. I turned around and my lone lieutenant had jumped on a bird with our wounded and medevac'd his sorry ass out. I'm trying to get him back out here but nobody on the firebase seems able to locate him."

"Lieutenant Colquitt, sir?"

"Yeah. That's him."

"He's not on the firebase. I saw him leave on a dustoff bird headed for Tay Ninh."

"Sorry little bastard. Never seen anybody so scared of his own shadow. "

"So exactly what *is* the mission?"

The captain looked at him, incredulously, and laid his map on the ground. "Your mission, lieutenant, is to lead us out of here and make it to this point," he said, tapping a dot he'd circled on the map. "I told the colonel we'd be there by noon today and I aim to honor that promise."

Glenn looked at the map, his watch and then up at the captain, thinking, *He can't be serious – that's over five kilometers in two hours... in this jungle? That's a brisk walk – and after they got hit this morning?! I must not be hearing it right. He can't mean that.*

"Sir, I need to know why my platoon sergeant is going to be pissed that I showed up." It wasn't the most pressing issue, but it was important and he had to deal with it sooner rather than later. The day had started bad and was quickly becoming worse.

Sergeant Meyer looked and carried himself like a man who'd checked into the old folks home some years ago. He knelt in a semi-circle with the squad leaders facing the platoon sergeant and squad leaders. They were all looking at him expectantly.

"I'm Lieutenant Nolan, your new platoon leader. I need to know who I'm working with and so do you. My name's Nolan, but call me Knocker – that's what they called me when I played rugby."

"Lieutenant, we'll call you Shotgun, or Shotgun 6," Meyer said flatly. "That's the company's internal callsign for third platoon. That's what we always call our platoon leaders."

"Alright," Glenn said, "that works. Who am I dealing with; how long have you been with Charlie company? Platoon sergeant, you first."

"Staff Sergeant Meyer. Platoon sergeant. 8 months."

"Sergeant Storck. Third squad. In-country seven months; squad leader two."

"Spec-4 Halley. First squad. Six months in-country and squad leader for a week."

"Sergeant Kimsey. Five months in-country as squad leader."

"You're wondering about me. I've been in-country five weeks, most of that in Echo Company as the mortar platoon leader. I average eight or ten patrols a week. None of that means shit to you unless it translates into getting you home, and it doesn't matter to the colonel unless it translates into the same... *and...* into accomplishing his mission. I aim to do both."

They were silent until Sergeant Meyer spoke up.

"Nice speech, lieutenant," he said sardonically and spit on the ground.

"Not a speech," Glenn said, looking at each squad leader and his platoon sergeant. "It was the answer to the question – *who the hell is this guy?* Now, tell me about the platoon. How many troops do we have and how many DEROS in the next month, Sergeant Meyer?"

"With you, we're now twenty-three, lieutenant. Medevac'd one out this morning. We've got a half dozen who are so short their 'short timer's sticks' are the size of toothpicks. Two of them go back to process out next log day. Replacements have been few and far between since we were on Ike."

Glenn glanced around at the worn faces of these young boy-men he had for leaders.

"We'll be leading the company out when we move. That'll be pretty soon, so tell your people they have a new platoon leader. I'll try to get around to see them before we move out, but the C.O. told me he wanted to get going right away. Everybody got ammo, food and water?" They each stared at him and nodded wordlessly. "Which squad last walked point when the platoon led out the company?"

"Shotgun 2, and Shotgun 1 before that," Sergeant Meyer said.

"Alright, third squad has the honors. Followed by 2nd and then 1st squad." Glenn pointed out the check point marked simply as *CP 1* on the map that the company commander had showed him. "We'll be heading generally north on a heading of zero-one-zero."

"Any particular mission, lieutenant?" Sergeant Kimsey asked.

"None that I heard," Nolan admitted. "The way I see it, the mission is to get to Check Point 1 with all hands alive and accounted for, and all enemy we run into either dead or captured." He sent the squad leaders back to their troops with the order to tell their troops what little he'd been able to tell them. The platoon sergeant caught his attention.

"There's a lot of gooks out there, lieutenant," Sergeant Meyer said. "This is their personal playground. They've been kicking our ass. We hump and they watch everything we do and hit us when they choose. We used to be over three dozen guys – now it's less than two dozen."

"Guess we'll have to be alert… and smarter and tougher than they are."

"Yeah. Right. You keep your head down, lieutenant."

It struck Glenn as a strange thing to say. "My grandfather fought in both the first and second wars. He told me that in the field a troop leader had to keep short accounts, meaning that bad news never got better with age. If a problem showed up it had to be dealt with right away. We're not going to have a problem here, you and I, are we?"

"Nope."

"You're not unhappy that I'm taking command of a platoon that you've been leading for a while on your own?"

"That's a different question. Since you asked, I'll tell you. We didn't ask for a lieutenant, and we don't want one."

"That's blunt enough, I guess."

"Got no time for bullshit. We've lost four lieutenants in the last three months. One was killed, two were wounded – one bad enough to be evac'd all the way to Japan. The jury is still out on whether or not he's going to make it. We're jinxed. And frankly, I'm tired of breaking in new platoon leaders and watchin' 'em do stupid shit that gets themselves and my men killed."

"I'm not your average lieutenant."

"Yeah, I see that Ranger tab and those jump wings. I'm impressed by that – Luke the Gook won't be, and neither one of them doo-dads will stop an AK round or a B-40."

The platoon RTO held out the radio handset. "Blazer 6 on the horn, lieutenant. He says saddle up and get your ass movin'."

*　　*　　*

They moved through the thick jungle with an acquired indifference common to infantry soldiers from all wars who have seen their share of combat. They had, and more.

Except for their leader.

Glenn had been with 3rd Platoon for a week and had been through one brief clash lasting two or three minutes which he guessed was a chance encounter with a handful of NVA. There had also been two prolonged firefights with small NVA units – a couple of squads or maybe a platoon. The last skirmish had produced the first death in the platoon on his watch, and he endured the first attack of uncertainty about his own leadership.

But more than doubts about himself, he now had serious reservations about Captain Stief.

The company commander had either a strange or perhaps non-existent grasp of infantry tactics in the jungle and so far, Glenn hadn't seen any evidence of small unit patrolling. Every morning, the company would saddle up in their eighty to ninety pound rucksacks and start humping through the jungle. There was no attempt at clearing the area around them before or after they had something for breakfast. The mission every day seemed to be simply to go as far as was possible; so, they would move out in single file and walk until noon, stop for something to eat, and continue on to their night location and set up. By Glenn's calculation, that meant that the company was strung out in a line nearly five hundred yards long, and one shoulder-width wide. An attack at any point would split the company, render control of the battle hugely difficult; and that would get people killed. This, Glenn decided was unacceptable.

On the fourth day, when it was 3rd Platoon's turn to walk point again, he took a squad out early to clear the area through which his platoon would be leading the company. They happened on some black-clad NVA moving into an ambush position and fired on them, driving the enemy patrol off. The next day, first platoon followed the normal practice and got caught in an ambush soon after departing the night location, setting off an hour long firefight in which the other two platoons didn't participate because they were still in the previous night's location. He talked to the captain about his observations and suggestions, to no avail.

Now, as they moved through the jungle as the lead platoon, he'd formed them into three parallel columns instead of one which gave him a form of flank security for the first time and shortened the length of his column by two-thirds. It wasn't as perfect as the platoon formation they taught him in the last phase of Ranger School at Eglin, but it was better than before. In this patch of Tay Ninh Province the visibility was a little better – he could see ten or fifteen yards, sometimes even a little more. The heat was as bad as always – already in the nineties – and the humidity was close to a hundred. Word came back from the point to hold up; Glenn dropped his pack and went forward.

"Point man spotted some bunkers," Sergeant Kimsey whispered to him.

"I can check that out and report it back to you, *Shotgun*," Sergeant Meyer said.

Glenn looked at him, and frowned. "No, platoon sergeant, you stay here with Froggy and the radio. I'll check this out." He went forward with the squad leader several yards and knelt next to the point man, a private whose name he couldn't recall. *I don't really know half these guys*, Glenn thought. *What the hell kind of platoon leader are you, Nolan?*

"Whatta you got, Perlow?" Kimsey whispered.

"There's a trail just up ahead running east-west. Six inches wide, used in the last day or two. Light to medium traffic. Maybe ten to twelve NVA."

How can he tell that? Glenn wondered.

"Off to the northwest a couple of small bunkers. Fighting positions with overhead cover."

"Show me," Glenn whispered, his pulse quickening. *Bunkers? That doesn't sound good. What does it tell me?* He crept forward with the point man and his squad leader until Perlow knelt and pointed at the trail. At first he didn't see it; then gradually, as the soldier traced it with a sweeping gesture of his hand, it came into focus. *I'll be damned*, he thought. *This guy is good – I'd have walked right past it.* Perlow was pointing to the northwest and holding up two fingers, then pointing at each of the positions with a finger and repeating it until Glenn nodded.

They crept back to the rest of the platoon. Glenn took the handset from his RTO – a kid everyone called Froggy – and called the company commander to report the situation.

"All right. You go check it and report back," Captain Stief said over the radio. *"Be quick about it. We're behind schedule already so you need to pick up the pace."*

"Shotgun, roger." *Can't let the damned schedule slip, can we?* he grumbled to himself. He turned to Sergeant Meyer. "C.O. wants us to check out those bunkers. Get me the squad leaders up here."

A minute later Storck, Halley and Kimsey were kneeling in front of him. "We have an east-west trail just in front of 2nd squad – moderate recent use and looks to be running into at least a couple of bunkers just to our left front. Here's how we're going to do that." He cleared a spot on the jungle floor and drew a line on it with a stick and sketched out a plan.

"Here's the trail… the bunkers we can see are here and here. 2nd squad to set up on line like this facing the bunkers with our machine gun. 1st squad on the right facing down the trail toward the northeast. 3rd squad, Sergeant Storck with me on the left. We'll be the search element, and swing around on line flanking the bunkers we can see and sweep over them from left to right. Two man teams search each bunker. We keep searching until we find and clear them all. If we make contact, Sergeant Storck, keep your eye on me. If it's light contact, we'll press forward, if it's heavy... well, just follow me. Any questions?"

The squad leaders got up and left quietly as Glenn lit a cigarette.

"Lieutenant, you should stay with the largest part of the platoon and let me go with the maneuver element," Sergeant Meyer said in a low voice.

"No, I need you to keep an eye on our machine gun and make sure the base of fire doesn't hit any friendlies. If we do get into a fight, I also need you making sure ammo gets distributed, and helping the other platoons to tie in with us when they move up to support."

Meyer bit his lip. "I still think your place is with the majority of the platoon. You really ought to let me take the maneuver element."

Glenn took a deep drag on his Marlboro and slowly let out the lungful of smoke. "Sergeant, I'm going to have to lead these guys for the next few months at least. I can't be their leader if I don't go with them on the tough missions. We'll just let things ride the way they are."

Minutes later he stepped off next to Sergeant Storck with the seven men of third squad spaced three to four yards apart in a ragged line. They had gone only fifteen meters when they saw the movement and caught a glimpse of a figure in black fatigues just as the first AK shot rang out and a Russian .30 caliber RPD machine gun opened up on them.

The platoon's M-60 answered immediately with a sustained burst, along with a score of M-16's. A sporadic hollow *thunk* of an M-79 grenade launcher added to the roaring firefight.

Glenn low crawled forward to a tree, got to his knee and surveyed the area. He looked around and saw that every eye in Storck's squad was on him. *Okay, so what are you going to do now lieutenant?* He fired three rounds into the observation slits on both the bunkers he could see, flipped the selector to full auto, and fired quick bursts until the magazine was empty and then replaced it with a full mag.

"Storck! Get some M-79 rounds into that bunker on the right!" he yelled to be heard above the noise even though the squad leader was only a yard away. After the second 40mm round exploded, Glenn ran forward to the nearest tree, fired several times and then ran forward again. Twenty yards away, a black clad NVA jumped from behind a bush and started to run. He got only a few steps before he was cut down.

The enemy's RPD machine gun chattered loudly. Glenn could now see the end of the barrel with its strange looking front sight and rounded flanges sticking part way out of the slit of a firing position. The dirt was being kicked up all around the front of the slit and 3rd Squad's M-79 gunner was targeting it now. A khaki clothed soldier wearing a pith helmet rose up ten feet in front of him from under a large palm frond; before he could bring his M-16 around, someone to his left rear from Storck's squad opened up and felled him.

The level of firing ebbed and then suddenly roared back to life.

He caught the attention of the soldier to his left, pointed to himself and the soldier, then to the NVA machine gun. He slithered forward on his stomach to a position where he could get a shot, and along with the other soldier in his platoon, unloaded a magazine into the slit. The gun went silent. While he was changing magazines, an NVA soldier burst out of the back of the bunker and limped hurriedly into the jungle before he could get a shot. There was movement ahead of him and to the right which the M-60 targeted.

"Cease fire! Glenn yelled several times when he realized the incoming fire had ceased. The call echoed and soon the jungle was silent. "Third squad… check these bunkers!"

"Medic! Medic!"

The dreaded call deflated him.

Along with Sergeant Storck, he checked the fighting position where the NVA machine gun had been. The gun was still there but the gunner and his assistant were gone, leaving only a heavy blood trail behind. As they swept the area they found an additional seven fighting positions surrounding a large dugout trench covered by recently cut tree limbs and foliage. The trench held fourteen bags of rice, some black pajama uniforms, a wooden crate containing a dozen Model 99 Ariska sniper rifles and several thousand rounds of 7.62 ammo for AK-47s. It looked like a small supply depot.

Glenn had the platoon move up around the area and then advised the company commander. He stood at the edge of the covered trench smoking as he watched the platoon form a perimeter around the haul. *You were lucky, son, Good thing you had a smart guy on point who had his shit together or you would have blundered into beaucoup bad news. Am I ever going to figure out this damned job?!*

Sweat poured down his face from underneath his steel pot as he lit another Marlboro.

Sergeant Meyer came through the brush and looked at the captured supplies. "That was a nice piece of soldierin', sir."

Glenn was momentarily astonished. It was the first time anyone in the platoon had addressed him with a 'sir' tacked on. Did that mean anything? He wasn't sure.

"I think the men saw something they liked, sir. The squad leaders think you're settling in. Thought you should know."

*   *   *   *

Mary Anne opened the front door and her face lit up. "Deanna!"

"The very troublemaker!" They hugged and then brought in Deanna's single piece of luggage. "Good grief. Just look at you! Why do you always have to look like you just stepped out of a cover shoot for *Cosmopolitan?*"

"You *are* a troublemaker."

"Fresh from Bavaria with a tote sack of gossip and two bottles of Zeller Schwartz Katz." Deanna held her friend at arm's length. "It's so good to see you again. Do you realize the last three months is the longest you and I have been apart since we shared that tiny apartment outside West Point while the guys finished their last year at the academy?"

Mary Anne thought for a second. "You're right. Give me the wine and I'll put it in the chiller and then we'll get you situated. You're in the guest room at the back corner of the house. Let's get you upstairs and settled and then we can catch up. How long can you stay?"

"A week?"

"Make it two and you're on."

"What say we do a week here and a week at my parents' place at Parris Island. Dad's quarters were upgraded and there's a communications link there where phone calls can be sent to and from Vietnam. Benny promised to call me there when he gets to Vietnam."

"He can do that?"

"We're talking about the guy who had a full size pool table delivered and installed in his room when he was a cadet."

"But that was only for a week, wasn't it?

"He said he didn't like the color of the felt and had them take it back. But if anybody can pull off a call home from over there, it's my Ben. I can't miss the opportunity. Who knows, maybe he can find Glenn and get him conferenced in, too."

"That sounds too wild and wooly even for him. But why not? We'll do it. I'm game." They went upstairs and deposited Deanna's suitcase and carry-on, then went to the big family room that looked out over the back yard. "What's happened in Augsburg since we left?" Mary Anne asked as they relaxed after making tea and putting the wine in the chiller.

"I hope I can remember it all... Alice Compton had a baby boy on January seventeenth – six pounds twelve ounces. They named him William Matthew after George's grandfather. Jeannie Gresham and Joan Spearman are pregnant. They're both kind of mystified since Jeannie was using Endometrin and Joan used Advantage-S to keep that from happening."

"Oh, my. I'm shocked... and happy for them both really."

"Of course, neither of them wanted to start a family yet, but Joan is tickled to death, as it turns out. Jeannie is... well, coping would be a good word to use. Colonel Wadsworth's son got accepted to West Point. That word filtered out mid-January. What else?... That second lieutenant in Glenn's company who arrived in August – Jack Blanchard. He got engaged to a girlfriend back home and they're planning a wedding sometime this June. And of course the saga of Jim and Mary Cat continues."

"I can't even imagine. What's with those two now?"

Jim and Mary Catherine Witherspoon lived one flight down from Glenn and Mary Anne in the same stairwell of the American housing complex in Augsburg. Jim was a captain – a helicopter pilot recently back from Vietnam who had married Mary Catherine, his high school sweetheart, the year before he went to Southeast Asia. They had actually gone steady starting in the seventh grade. They fought constantly. And publicly. The MPs had never been called out to referee a domestic disturbance situation, but no one in the stairwell could figure out why not.

"The latest blowup started when they got into a screaming argument at the bowling alley during league night. They had been picking at each other throughout the first two games. So, apparently at some point Jim made the off-hand comment that his tour in Vietnam was the happiest year of his marriage, and that's when things really got out of hand."

Mary Anne covered her mouth with a hand and laughed. "I can see him saying that, too."

"You can imagine Mary Cat's reaction. She stormed out of the bowling alley and Jim followed her to the car and drove home. Poor Benny – he just happened to be outside walking the dog when they pulled up and he said a friendly hello. He told me both of them looked like they wanted to kill him. They stomped into their apartment; there was a lot of yelling and screaming and then it all went silent. Everybody was afraid the worst had happened, but were too scared to knock on the door. A half hour later they were outside taking a walk, hand in hand like nothing ever happened."

"That was them. Glenn and I played bridge with them from time to time and they were always at each other's throats about one another's lousy bidding when they were partners. I shouldn't say this, but I hope they never have children."

"Now that you mention it," Deanna said, raising her eyebrows.

"She's pregnant?! Poor child. You pray for the kid and I'll light a candle."

They laughed together and Deanna said, "So what have you been doing with yourself these past few months?"

"Not a whole lot of anything to tell the truth. I'm kind of at loose ends. I did get involved with a local group called the Officers Wives Club of Baltimore. They meet once a month, mostly to chat or share stories or talk about little presents their husbands send home from wherever they're stationed."

"Just Army?"

"All branches, really, but mostly Army and mostly the guys are in Vietnam."

"How do you like it?"

"Not sure. I've only been twice. It started out very positive, upbeat but it became like a pity party toward the end. That wasn't very uplifting. I'll try it one more time and if it goes the same way I probably won't go back. I hope that doesn't happen... How about some wine? The Schwartz Katz isn't chilled yet but we have something equally good that is."

"Let's do it!"

They talked the afternoon away and then had dinner with Mary Anne's parents and her two youngest siblings – Hailey and young Bob who were still living at home.

"That was a wonderful dinner, Mrs. MacEagan," Deanna said, when they had cleared the table in the large formal dining room and sat drinking coffee. "I hope you didn't go to all that trouble on my account."

"I've cooked for ten for so long it's hard to break the habit," Charlene MacEagan said. "I have to admit I look forward to the day all the kids are grown and gone."

"Not me," Mary Anne's father said. "I don't like the thought of reliving the days when dinner meant opening a can and heating it over a propane burner. Charlene's cooking has come a long way since then and I don't relish the idea of returning there."

"We've all come a long way," Charlene MacEagan replied. "I don't want to relive the days when my husband was a penniless resident working thirty hour days and sleeping in a hospital dayroom three nights a week while I cared for an infant in a small apartment."

"I think I'll have another cup of coffee to stay out of the middle of this conversation," Deanna said, pouring herself another cupful from a silver coffee server.

"My dear, I'm afraid you're a bit late," Dr. MacEagan said. "You've been the topic of talk around this table since your letter arrived advising you'd be stopping by for a visit."

Mary Anne's father had a tone and a stolid, ironic manner when he addressed her that was unnerving. He watched her closely when she spoke, not so much to hear and understand what was said, she thought, but to assess her against his own prejudices and presuppositions. The old, tired witticism about the man who had never made a mistake except once when he thought he had, could well have been less a punch line to a joke than an observation of Dr. MacEagan. He was a man unaccustomed to having his ideas challenged whether in medicine, or administration, or politics. Mary Anne had warned her about her father's idiosyncrasies and hot buttons – especially his liberal political views.

The front door slammed and a male voice called out, "I'm home. Any dinner left?"

"Corey, come meet your sister's friend," Mrs. MacEagan said.

"I was the topic of conversation?" Deanna said, looking at Mary Anne.

"I told them you were a Marine and that they should lock up the silver."

"That's not all she said," the young man offered as he came into the room, and sat down across the table from Deanna. "You're a lot cuter than she led me to believe."

"Corey, please stop embarrassing me and my friend," Mary Anne said.

Mary Anne had warned her about her older brother. She knew that he had graduated from Johns Hopkins University and was now attending a Catholic seminary to avoid the draft.

Corey smiled. "Believe nothing my little sister tells you about me."

"Come with me, Deanna" Mary Anne said, rising and dropping her napkin on the table next to her wineglass. "We'll have an after dinner drink in the library."

Deanna followed her friend down the hall into her father's reading room, a masculine enclave of books and sailing pictures and dark leather-upholstered furniture. Mary Anne poured them both a liqueur and sat down, propping her feet on a leather ottoman.

"I apologize for my brother. He's such an idiot and overgrown adolescent. He's the oldest one of us kids and he's sometimes less mature than little Bob."

Deanna laughed softly. "Don't let it bother you. I can handle it."

"I'm still embarrassed."

"Don't be. Nothing can upset me on this little trip."

"So, you saw Benny off this morning?" Mary Anne asked after they fell briefly silent. She remembered her ambivalent feelings about Glenn's departure – part dread, part disappointment that he didn't seem as upset about the looming year-long separation as she was. "How are you doing?"

"It's only been a day, so not too bad." She looked up at the mantle clock above the small bar. "He should be walking through the gate at Fort Lewis right about now. Pacific Time is three hours off. You know that, I'm sure. Did you know that Vietnam is exactly twelve hours different than it is here?"

Mary Anne realized she hadn't known, and a glance at the clock told her Glenn was probably just now eating breakfast. They were as far apart as they could possibly be – she'd never thought of it that way. She was about to ask Deanna how her mother had dealt with all the separation over the years when Corey walked in, went to the bar and poured some liquor into a rocks glass before plopping down on the sofa.

"You girls mind if I park here a while and have a drink? I wasn't that hungry after all."

"Corey…" his sister said, looking and sounding noticeably perturbed. Mary Anne rolled her eyes and looked at her friend apologetically.

"So, you're married to a guy who's a friend of my sister's husband," Corey was saying.

"His name is Glenn," Deanna offered, smiling at him.

"Well, I call him the little general. He was one of those bratty military kids. That's what he called himself."

"I'm sure he said he was a military brat. I am, too. Marine Corps. *Brat* is a term of endearment and we're proud of it."

"I hope *my* kids won't be called brats."

"Why? Afraid you might be called up for duty and sire a child while in the Army?"

Corey raised his head and stared at her with cold, implacable reproach. There was absolute silence in the room except for the martial ticking of the mantel clock.

"I'm not afraid of that," Corey said, flashing a pretentious, hollow smile.

"It's comforting to know there are still American men willing to do their duty."

"It all depends on what you mean by 'duty', I think. Your husband and my sister's husband are under the illusion that doing one's duty means participating in this immoral war in Southeast Asia. I, on the other hand, believe there's a higher duty. What is that, you ask? It's to stop the war and all the carnage associated with it. Why would anyone want to kill innocents and commit atrocity in the name of *duty*?"

"That's not what we're doing over there." Deanna replied.

"Are you sure they're not?"

"Are you sure they are?" Deanna sipped on her liqueur while watching Corey over the rim of her glass. *This pompous, silly ass and his holier than thou bullshit…*

"I'm sure enough to try stopping it."

"I hope it stops, too. And soon. I don't like wars either, and neither do the guys who have to fight in them. You obviously don't understand the military or the men in it."

"I understand enough to know that our government needs to bring this unholy, unnecessary crusade to an end immediately. I'm willing to do anything to stop the fighting… and so is she." Corey said, pointing a finger at Mary Anne. "We're both active members of

Hawkish Dove, and we *will* stop this dishonest war in Southeast Asia by whatever means it takes. You can take that to the bank."

Deanna looked back and forth between Mary Anne and her brother. "Both of you?! You're both members of the group headed by someone calling himself Tripp Karter?"

Mary Anne quickly said, "I went with Corey to one of their parties in Washington a few weeks ago. That's all. We're not really members per se."

"Well, I'm a member," Corey declared. "And I'm proud to say it. And our father is too. He's just written them a sizeable check."

"Do you have any idea who this person is and what he's done?!" Deanna asked, stunned. "This guy who now goes by the name of Tripp Karter is a professional agitator and registered felon. His real name is Tanner Wallace. He's also a known communist sympathizer."

"I don't believe you," Corey said, in a stark rage barely under control. "You're making this up. How could you possibly know such a thing?"

"I learned it from my father. He's a Marine colonel who dislikes this guy very much. He helped Naval intelligence investigate Wallace, or Karter, when he showed up in the early '60s organizing an effort to relocate the Marine Corps War Memorial from Arlington Cemetery to some out of the way place on the outskirts of Washington. My dad survived both Iwo Jima and the Chosen Reservoir and he took it very personally. Are you familiar with SLID and SDS? Or the Port Huron Statement?"

"I heard of SDS when I was at Hopkins," Corey replied. "There was some quiet recruiting going on. No big deal. Never heard of this SLID."

"The Student League for Industrial Democracy – it's the parent organization of SDS. The person who led the SDS charge in support of the USSR was Wallace who now prefers the Tripp Karter alias, for whatever reason."

"I don't believe you."

"You don't want to believe me. But facts are facts." She looked back and forth between Mary Anne and her brother. The steady ticking of the mantel clock held the room in Bellini stillness. It was obvious they were both hearing the truth about this modern day messiah for the first time and silence confirmed their naïve incredulity. She turned her attention to Mary Anne. "I can't believe you'd get involved with such people."

"And I can't believe you'd come into our house as a guest and malign a person that our family is emotionally and financially supporting," Corey said. "He simply wants America to mend its evil ways and return to what it should be. You're in the wrong house if you want to peddle hateful lies about a dedicated patriot like Tripp Karter."

"Mary Anne?" Deanna said, looking directly at her friend. Silence answered. "You're right, Corey. I'm obviously some place I shouldn't be." She looked at her watch and stood. "I'll be gone in a half hour. I'll need to make a couple of phone calls."

"Deanna, please don't," Mary Anne begged.

"I'm afraid I have to." She went up the stairs to the guest room, and was in the process of repacking her small carry-on when Mary Anne entered.

"This can't be happening. You're my best friend and I don't want you to go."

"I don't want to go, but I have to," Deanna said. "This guy you're supporting *is not* about stopping the war in Vietnam; he's a Saul Alinsky acolyte whose goal is to destroy America. He hates this country and he despises the military." She stared hard at Mary Anne. "And you're helping him encourage the North Vietnamese while Glenn and Benny are in Vietnam?! Mary Anne, what in the world are you thinking? If I stay here it's like I'm agreeing with what you and your family are doing... and I don't! I have to go."

"No, you have to stay. Corey doesn't speak for me or for anyone in this house but himself. I'm not involved with Tripp Karter or his organization and I don't believe my father is either. I have to hear more. You have to teach me so I can stand up to my brother."

"This person and his organization – this Tripp Karter and Hawkish Dove – they've been implicated in several fire bombings of ROTC facilities and this Karter was convicted of masterminding the firebombing at the University of Michigan. He was and still is an avowed anarchist. Girl, you need to wake up and smell the coffee!"

"I believe you," Mary Anne said. "Please don't go. Please."

Chapter 13

From the moment he stepped off the helicopter, Glenn was worried – LZ Illingworth looked like trouble waiting to happen.

The outpost appeared both permanent and incomplete. It sat three miles from the Cambodian border just off a major twenty foot wide road running east-west and was way too big for a single half-strength infantry company to adequately defend. The berm surrounding the firebase was only two feet high in most places and in others less than a foot.

Other than the major fortified cities of Tay Ninh and Bien Hoi, it was the largest firebase he had seen. It sat on the south side of a large, dry lake bed – surrounded on three sides by thick jungle not more than a hundred yards away; to the north, the area widened and ran out for three quarters of a mile. As Charlie company troops walked toward the perimeter they kicked up clouds of dust like fine black talcum that hovered knee high in the still air.

The C&C ship approached and landed in the open field to the west of the firebase. Colonel Conrad and Major Moore got out, said something to the pilot and then walked toward him. Two of the 105mm howitzers fired a round apiece and the concussion raised a cloud of fine dust a foot high across the entire firebase.

"That was good work out there yesterday, Nolan," the battalion commander said as he removed his helmet. "But you're not done yet."

Glenn was the last remaining officer in the company and was by default its commander. For the last two days the unit had fought a non-stop running battle with the NVA until an armored Cav troop had linked up with them. The massed .50 caliber firepower of the armored Cav had convinced the enemy to disengage. Captain Stief had been wounded early on the first day and medevac'd out leaving him in command.

What's your current company strength?"

"Forty-seven, sir, and that includes a half dozen walking wounded." He looked around the large fire support base and said, "What's left of Charlie company is going to be spread pretty damned thin for this big a perimeter. Any possibility of getting Echo Recon in to help secure this place?"

"Way ahead of you Nolan," Major Moore said. "They'll be here before sundown. You figure out where you want them in the perimeter defensive plan."

Recon had been briefly attached to Charlie company when Glenn first got there and had remained about ten days so he knew the platoon and its leader. He was a tall muscular redhead named Peters whose troops called him Rooster, or Roo, apparently as much because of his rowdy personality and loud voice as it was because of his red hair. He'd played football in college and his size as well as the way he ran the platoon earned him the respect of his men. Glenn had witnessed that he was damn good in the field, as was his platoon sergeant, a tall thin black staff sergeant named Taylor.

Glenn looked around and quickly said, "I'm going to put Recon over there in that bulging part of the perimeter on the southeast side. I need to walk the rest of the perimeter with my platoon sergeants and set up boundaries. Any chance of getting more machine guns? One per platoon and a .50 Cal on a tripod would almost do the trick, sir."

"Do you know anybody who can operate a 50 Cal.?" Conrad asked.

"I can. And I can train half the company between now and nightfall. If you can get me an extra M-60 and one .50 Cal. per platoon I'll guarantee we'll hold this oversized perimeter against the whole 95C Regiment, sir."

Moore gave a quick glance to the battalion commander. "You may get the chance to prove that to us, Nolan."

"I hope not, sir. I was really hoping we could give the company a rest for a while. It's been a pretty hard month."

"It has," Colonel Conrad agreed. Glenn looked around at the artillery and all the ammunition stacked around the firebase, wondering why after two weeks there wasn't any barbed wire and why they still occupied this piece of War Zone C. The battalion had stayed in one place for too long, and staying put for more than a few days this close to the Cambodian border invited NVA attacks in large numbers. He saw the worry on his battalion commander's face; they both seemed to be thinking the same thing. "You've got about three hours to set your defense. Evening briefing at 1900. I expect you to walk us all through your plan. Make sure you have a ready reaction force."

"I'm going to have to use cooks, clerks, headquarters staff NCOs and every other able-bodied man, but I'm going to need you to run interference for me when they push back." The colonel looked displeased at his comment, and Glenn quickly said, "If you'll excuse me, sir. Got a lot to do before the briefing."

Conrad and Moore watched him walk toward the TOC.

"What do you think, S-3? Can he command Charlie company and hold it together?"

Moore shrugged. "He did it the last two days – probably better than Stief could have. He handled the Air Force FAC, the F-4s and A-37s along with the gunships like he'd been running the company for months, not hours. I think he deserves some consideration."

"He's too darned new. I'm not so sure he can command a company for the long haul. Going to have to work on getting replacements. Those platoons need officers and that company needs an experienced captain, not a new lieutenant. And, they need a strong 1st Sergeant. I don't know where they're coming from, but we need to find them pretty quick."

It was a half hour before evening briefing as the two lieutenants walked the perimeter.

"Those cigarettes are going to kill you, Nolan," Rooster Peters told him when he lit another from the one he was smoking.

"I hope so."

"Death wish?"

"Nope. I'm an optimist." Someone in the company rear had set up a clean set of fatigues for his use on the firebase, complete with nametag, rank, crossed rifle branch insignia along with his airborne wings, CIB and Ranger tab. The supply sergeant had also provided a small shaving kit with a toothbrush and Gillette double edge razor. "After a shave and a cold shower under a canvas bucket for the first time in a month, I feel like a new person. So, sure, I'm an optimist – that's a lieutenant in a Cav battalion who thinks he's going to die of lung cancer."

"I knew there was something really wrong with you the moment you showed up. You're not right in the head, pal."

"Guess that means I'm qualified to take your job when you're gone, Roo."

"Hell, you got C Company. All you Pointers want to command a company, right?"

Nolan pondered. "Not gonna have it for long. Conrad's looking to get a captain in here as soon as he can. Name one lieutenant in the division who has a company command."

"You!"

"I just happened to be the last lieutenant standing in Charlie company. Right now we're just a glorified platoon of mostly draftees."

"And after the Division re-enlistment NCO gets through with Charlie, you guys won't even be a real live platoon."

The comment surprised him. "What do you mean?"

"You haven't heard the new Division policy – anyone who re-enlists for a burst of three years gets to go to a rear area job. Taylor told me he talked with some of your NCOs and even some of them are thinking hard about it after this last month. I bet you lose a good half your guys tomorrow when that Re-Up NCO from division shows. This time tomorrow or the day after it'll be you, me, Sergeant Taylor and my twenty-nine guys defending the firebase. None of these draftees wants to be the last one to die in this war now that the president has decided to throw in the towel. And you know what? – I don't blame 'em."

Damn! Nolan thought. *What the heck are they thinking at Division? Have they really called it quits? Does the Division commander now get his OER rating based on his re-enlistment stats rather than the number of enemy killed and equipment captured?!*

Glenn went in search of the artillery battery fire direction center, a large underground bunker surrounded by a forest of tall antennas. A husky, shirtless guy about his own age lounged outside the entrance, sitting on the sandbagged roof. He drank from a Budweiser can as the final slant rays of sun before evening twilight cast a yellow glow on the firebase.

"Looking for the battery commander," Glenn said when the soldier turned to look at him. "I'm from C Company and I wanted to thank him for the support – especially yesterday. I wouldn't have a company left if it weren't for you guys."

"You're the company commander?" the soldier asked, looking at the nametag on Glenn's jungle fatigues and then up at his face.

"I have been for twenty-four hours, since Captain Stief caught a medevac out."

"The battery commander is over with Colonel Conrad. I run the FDC," he said, offering his hand. "Todd Lundberg... lieutenant."

"Glenn Nolan."

Lundberg shook his hand. "Nolan? You ever play rugby up in New England?"

"Do I owe you an apology?" Glenn asked guardedly after a pregnant silence.

"You *are* that Nolan, aren't you? You played for Army a few years back. Fullback, wasn't it?"

"Guilty as charged. And you?"

"Princeton. We played you guys both spring and fall. You had a short son-of-a-bitch on your team who played scrum half – quick little guy, who could really kick the ball, long and high. Real high. You two had a play where he'd kick it way up in the air, just short of the 'try' line and you would get there just as the other team's player caught it. You had pretty good speed yourself. And you hit like a damned Mack truck."

Glenn cleared his throat. "I do owe you an apology, don't I?"

"Only if you meant to put me out of the game both times you did."

"I've changed. I've mellowed out."

Lundberg glared at him for a while and then laughed. "To tell the truth, I'm sorry to hear it since we're now on the same team. What was that little scrum half's name. Baines? Burns?"

"Barnes. Benny Barnes."

"Yeah, yeah. That was him. Little bastard. I broke his nose once."

Glenn smiled. "You're one of several who did. That's the price of playing scrum half."

"I'd have done it to you too, but you were too damned fast. I could never run you down. And you covered the wing so our fast guys couldn't get loose along the sidelines." Lundberg reached into his small cooler and took out a cold, dripping can. "Here. For old times' sake; my congratulations for you guys winning the Notre Dame Challenge Cup Tourney in '67."

Glenn opened the beer and took a long sip. "We always liked you Princeton guys. Of all the sides we played, you were the most gracious hosts and threw the best parties."

"We worked hard at carousing." He finished his beer and crushed the can. "I can't believe it. Had to come halfway around the world to this stinking little war to finally run down Knocker Nolan. That's what they called you, wasn't it?"

"It was... back then. Like I said, I've changed."

"If you say so. You know, we always wondered why you didn't play football at that school. You had size and speed. The truth? You were the toughest damned guy we ever played against. None of us were religious, but we prayed they'd call you up to play football and leave us to hell alone."

Glenn had to chuckle. "I'm going to take that as a compliment and leave it there. But... well, it's a long, sad story and I haven't had enough to drink to tell it. And I won't as long as I'm on this firebase." He took another drink from the beer can. "How did you get here?"

"Long story short – ROTC, then artillery basic course at Sill, five months at Carson and then 'Hello Vietnam' and the Cav. Got here May of last year. Artillery forward observer for nine frickin' months in the field and now here I am finally on a safe firebase. I've got forty-three days and a wake-up until I get out of this hell-hole and go home to my wife and the daughter I've never seen. Want to see a picture of the two prettiest girls in the entire world?"

Lundberg pulled out his plastic 1st Cav wallet they'd all been issued upon arrival in the division. The pictures of the little infant girl strangely touched him. *Why?* he wondered. He and Mary Anne hadn't talked about starting a family since that first day of counseling with the old Catholic priest a few months before their marriage. How strange that is, he thought now.

"She's really cute," Glenn said. "Your daughter's a doll. And you really outkicked your coverage when you married that girl. Me too, so I know whereof I speak."

Lundberg took the pictures and for a long time was motionless as he stared at them.

"A guy really doesn't know the whys and wherefores of this life until he has a little kid of his own. Got any kids, Nolan?"

"Not yet."

"How long you been here?"

"About two and a half months. Got to the Cav in the middle of January. Had the mortar platoon for a while and then a rifle platoon in Charlie company for the last month."

Lundberg gave him a crooked smile. "Poor bastard. You got a long haul ahead. Here's some advice I won't even charge you for – wait until the last couple of months before going on R&R. I wish somebody had told me how time slows to a damned near dead stop after you get back from seein' your gal. It feels like I've done two tours back to back rather than one."

"I'll lock that one away."

They sipped at the beer and talked idly, watching the sun slip lower on the horizon and then completely beneath the horizon leaving a bright orange penumbra above the western jungle. Lundberg was from North Trenton, New Jersey and gone to college just up the road at Princeton to stay close to the girl he eventually married. He'd played football in high school but, like Glenn, hadn't made the team at the college level.

"I'm not just saying this Nolan, but I'm glad I didn't play football in college. In spite of the fact it's a Brit game –"

"Careful Lundberg, my mom's British."

"My point is – I got to like rugby a lot better than I ever liked playin' football."

"I know just what you're saying," Glenn agreed. "The same thing happened to me, and to my roommate, Benny Barnes. Rugby was faster, and you had to be in better shape."

"And tougher. No equipment." The artillery lieutenant gave him a cheery grin. "Yeah, I used to tell the guys on the football squad that football was the game the boys played while the men were playing rugby. Didn't make any friends that way but I had fun doin' it."

Glenn decided he liked Lundberg.

"Come back after the battalion briefing tonight and I'll have a case of Bud cooled," Lundberg said when Glenn looked at his watch and stood to go. "Yup, cold beer. I'm Artillery pal, not a damned gravel agitator like you. I'll tell you why we let you guys beat us back in the day, and why you need to get you one of these," he said, holding up the picture of his little girl and slowly shaking it in his direction.

*   *

"You did an outstanding job keeping the company together, Nolan," Captain Hobson said as they sat facing each other on the berm in the third platoon sector of Illingworth. It was just past noon and the sun beat down turning the lake bed into a frying pan. "Colonel Conrad,

Major Moore, and the platoon sergeants all say the same thing. You put together a good defensive plan for the firebase, and we're not going to change it much. Now, I need you to refocus on third platoon, and on the replacements we've gotten in. Lieutenant Bassett is brand new – this is his first assignment out of OCS. Lieutenant Meeker is a seasoned soldier. I hear he's a classmate of yours from the Academy."

Glenn and Alex Meeker had been in the same platoon Yearling summer at Camp Buckner, the best eight weeks of the entire four years he'd spent at the school. Finally out from under the year long hazing and fresh from a thirty day leave spent mostly in Ocean City, Maryland with an eight day trip to Bermuda on the side, he'd found his reason for being at the school. After that summer, he'd only occasionally crossed paths with Meeker. Running into him now, halfway around the world in a dusty hell-hole, seemed to both of them ironic; he shared Glenn's worries about Illingworth.

"Even with the Chinook-load of green replacements that came out with First Sergeant Beauchamp, we're still short of bodies," the captain was saying.

Glenn nodded agreement. *That's an understatement*, he thought.

He'd liked Hobson immediately, even though disappointed that Conrad had not had enough confidence in him to let him remain in command of the company. The new commander seemed a sturdy officer and well up to the task of rebuilding Charlie company.

A surprising number of the company's soldiers had re-upped when the Division recruiting NCO had arrived the day before on the same aircraft as the new company commander. The following day First Sergeant Beauchamp had arrived on the Chinook carrying thirty brand new replacements who looked awkward and scared. When Glenn took a count, they had less than eighty infantrymen to secure Illingworth's huge perimeter. Equally worrisome was the huge stack of eight inch howitzer ammunition which still sat above ground instead of below ground level underneath PSP and sandbags as division safety rules required.

Glenn's heart sank when he saw this because it meant that higher HQ had no intention of moving the firebase; and, the big guns would make Illingworth an even more tempting target. He thought he saw the same realization in Colonel Conrad's eyes.

"Third platoon is more intact than the others," Hobson was saying, "so I'm going to lean on you the next few days. I'm giving you responsibility for all first light patrols. First and second platoons will share last light responsibility for the time being."

"What about wire, sir? Is this place ever going to get some concertina set up? Triple strand would be great, but even a single strand would be better than nothing. And the berm. One or two feet is way too low – especially since we've been here for over two weeks. If we get hit, our people won't be able to shoot and move behind cover."

"We're working on it."

They told me that at the first night's briefing, and nothing's happened. Glenn looked around at his soldiers filling sandbags for overhead cover of the few pathetic culvert bunkers, and shoveling dirt into empty wooden ammo boxes as protection to their rear if they got mortared. He was working them hard and worried it was too little too late – a premonition that became more real early the next morning, shortly after 4:00 A.M.

He was awakened by the continuous loud reports from the 105mm guns firing directly over where he slept next to the M-60 position. His ears were ringing and dust choked him. He got up and looked south, where the sky had a red glow, roiling and pulsing as if on fire. It was the most malevolent sight he'd ever seen.

"LZ Jay," the man standing next to him said. Glenn recognized the brigade chaplain, Father Pat, his stocky body and severe flattop visible now in the dim yellowish glow of the illumination round drifting toward the west tree line of LZ Illingworth.

"Looks like how I imagine Dante's Inferno."

"Hell itself," the priest said soberly. "No radio contact with them. I should be there," he said, disheartened. "I chose to come here instead of to the 2/7 Cav. Both battalions, from all I could see at brigade, are sitting dead center on infiltration routes leading directly to the most important target in the province – Tay Ninh. I read the tea leaves wrong. Maybe I can still get there tonight."

Pat Donohoe was the strangest priest Nolan had ever run across. He routinely went on platoon patrols from the firebase, and spent extended time in the field with line companies. Glenn had heard the stories and had himself seen the chaplain on two occasions perform acts of bravery and escape harm in ways he could only ascribe to providential intervention.

"They won't let you go there until it's secured."

"Nolan, I work for someone who outranks everyone up to and including the president."

They stood watching for many minutes until the priest left and headed toward the TOC. Shortly after, an Air Force gunship and a flare ship showed up near LZ Jay with the large, powerful illumination rounds that burned much brighter and lasted a lot longer than the mortars. He and Sergeant Meyer continued observing the action. By the light of another illumination round fired by his old mortar platoon, Glenn saw that essentially the entire cadre of Illingworth was standing around watching the southern sky.

"What do you think is goin' on out there, LT?"

"Nothin' good. If we don't have commo with them, that means at best they got their antenna farm knocked out by mortars or rockets. But the way that sky looks, it's a lot worse than that. We dodged a bullet tonight – that could have been us. This place is a sitting duck. "At first light, I want you to have a cleaning party – everybody scrubs his weapon guard mount clean at first light and last light as long as we're here. Every time I work the action on my M-16, it sounds like somebody filled the thing with beach sand."

"Will do. We need more ammo, especially M-60, and M-16 magazines. I'll work on it."

"Good call. You think the chaplain will get there any time soon?"

"If anybody can, he will."

But Donahoe didn't make it to Jay that day, and when he did get there the day after, the battalion's wounded and dead had been airlifted out. He returned to Illingworth late on April Fool's Day eve – a Protestant holiday he told Nolan over a beer after the evening briefing.

By then, a PP-55 Ground Surveillance Radar unit, a quad .50 and two more artillery pieces had arrived on the firebase, along with another mountain of 8 inch howitzer ammo. This was supposed to harden the firebase defenses. To Glenn, it seemed to make it an even more enticing target. The worst thing about Illingworth was not the heat but the dust cloud that rose to a height of several feet and reduced visibility to near zero for long minutes each time one of the big 8 inch howitzers fired a round. Undermanned, and blinded by their own artillery, it was the worst of battle conditions.

Except for the NVA 95C Regiment that looked on War Zone C as their own back yard.

*   *   *

Artillery was exploding in a rolling thunder through the wood line on three sides of Illingworth in the darkness two hours before midnight.

The crew of the firebase's ground surveillance radar had detected movement to the south and west. The Fire Direction Center at Tay Ninh initiated a prearranged fire support plan and artillery began thudding around the base, silhouetting the nearby wood lines in macabre flashes of light. A quarter hour later a section of gunships rolled in, strafing the wood lines with machine guns, 40mm grenades and rockets. The woods remained silent and the radar crew no longer detected movement.

At two A.M. the firebase went on a four hour full alert, a precaution instituted the night LZ Jay was overrun. Charlie company radiomen passed the word and platoon sergeants roused their men, most of whom – like Glenn – had wrapped themselves in ponchos and slept alongside the berm line reclining against rucksacks with boots laced, M-16s cradled in their arms and a box of hand grenades within arm's reach.

Glenn was looking into the dark night sharpening the Ka-Bar when he heard the first hollow *'thunk'* of a mortar firing from his front. Instantly the crackling automatic firing of AK-47s and the *whooshes* from a phalanx of rocket propelled grenades launched in his direction; the wood line south of Illingworth erupted in winking muzzle flashes.

"Incoming!" he yelled, and heard it repeated throughout the platoon.

He scrambled into one of the improvised, sandbagged half-culvert bunkers and looked out just as the first mortar rounds began impacting inside Illingworth's perimeter. From behind him, a mortar flare went up, bathing the open field in front of him in dim light, and then two large explosions erupted nearby. His heart leapt into his throat. The bombardment continued on, growing in intensity.

His mind raced and when he looked behind him he saw the battalion antennas still standing but one of the positions of his old mortar platoon had taken a direct hit; he could see two bodies draped over the side of the pit, and the tube and baseplate had separated. Across the whole of Illingworth, smoke rose like fog over a cold lake. Shrapnel and huge clods of dirt pelted the culvert he was in like a colossal hail storm. The noise was horrendous, horrifying; the sound and constant overpressure pounding his head kept up for what seemed an eternity.

But in time they let up.

Glenn was out of the culvert as soon as the shelling began to ease off. He knew what was coming – he hoped they all did, but he was worried. Half his platoon were brand new replacements who'd never been shot at. He hadn't had time to get to know their names much less train them for something like this. *Hell, I've never been trained for anything like this!*

An artillery illum round went off overhead and then another. He could see American helmets across his area of the berm popping up. *That's good! That's good!* He knelt with his RTO behind the bunker with their M16s pointed toward the wood line to their south. The NVA bombardment had created a thick dust fog, and now the tree line facing them across a hundred meters of clearing was essentially invisible. Two more illumination rounds exploded overhead.

And then they came, materializing out of the dark cloud of dust like screaming demons.

The NVA were making a full frontal assault. There were multitudes of them wearing round pith helmets, coming at him as if the whole army of North Vietnam seemed bent on running right through him. They kept appearing suddenly, like ghosts through a dirty mist, with their AK-47s and attached bayonets glimmering in the light from the flares. A thought flittered through his mind; *what was the most dreaded command to an infantryman? – Fix Bayonets!*

The Americans were firing now all along his platoon front. Glenn methodically lined up NVA targets in the iron sights of his M16 and squeezed the trigger. Somehow he'd flipped the safety/selector switch to 'rock & roll' so his first trigger pull resulted in a ten round burst.

Idiot! Aimed shots! – or you'll be out of ammo before they even get here. No shortage of targets, Nolan. Be cool. Be calm. BE CALM!!! You don't have the luxury to be scared.

The whole bunker line was erupting against what appeared to be at least two battalions deployed in the jungle that faced Illingworth on three sides; the enemy poured out automatic weapons fire and rocket-propelled grenades that crackled across the firebase. From the southwest, two reinforced companies of NVA infantrymen swarmed out the trees toward Echo Recon, running across a clearing flat as a pool table with no defensive wire or obstacles until they reached the shallow berm.

Still the NVA indirect fire rained down as the enemy infantry advanced toward Illingworth under the covering barrage of 120mm and 240 mm rockets, 82mm and 120mm mortars; recoilless rifles. NVA incoming and U.S. outgoing artillery continued to fog the firebase.

Glenn saw off to his left the machine gun crew of Echo Recon spraying the field in front of them with withering enfilade fire, the tracers like a thin red rope whipsawing back and forth in the darkness. An RPG exploded into the berm near them and the barrel of the M-60 tilted up as the gunner and his assistant toppled backward. Loss of the gun would leave his platoon's flank open and the NVA would pour through unopposed.

He yelled at his RTO, a new man, one of the replacements, a kid who'd taken the radio the day before when Glenn's radio man had re-enlisted to get out of the field. He couldn't remember the kid's name. *What the hell kind of platoon leader are you, Nolan?* "Follow me! Stay low!"

Glenn could hear the rounds snapping inches over his head; he crabbed to his left, stopping every half dozen yards to raise his head up and fire off aimed shots with his M16. Each time he looked over the berm he saw more NVA, and they were closer. When he finally got to the Recon platoon to tie in his flank, he saw a strapping buck sergeant on a knee shaking his head to clear it, his helmet gone. Nolan helped him reposition the M-60; then, he opened the feed cover, inserted a long link of ammo and shut it. The sergeant charged the gun and pulled the trigger. Twenty feet in front of them, a line of a dozen black clad NVA wearing shorts and pith helmets went down.

The last illumination round went out and the firebase was plunged into darkness except for the red American tracers and the telltale incoming green tracers of NVA .51 caliber guns. Glenn worked his way back toward his platoon, again stopping and firing every few yards. Finally two more illum rounds exploded overhead. When he got back to the culvert bunker, he looked inside using the red filter flashlight clipped to the harness of the LBE he always wore, even when sleeping. Two of his troops were inside – Hanson, one of the old hands and a replacement whose name he couldn't remember. Both of them were badly wounded.

The replacement had been blinded by something – probably a mortar round landing nearby or an RPG; Hanson could see, but his hands were mangled and bleeding. They were working as a team to keep up steady fire on the advancing NVA. Hanson could see but not hold his rifle so he was giving left-right-up-down directions to the replacement. Somehow they were holding their own on this stretch of the perimeter though the enemy line advanced relentlessly.

"Where's your Claymore clacker?!" Glenn yelled. An illum round blossomed overhead.

"Right there!" Hanson yelled back above the noise, pointing with a bleeding stump at the thick plastic detonating device in the dirt. Nolan picked it up, glanced over the berm and his breath caught in his throat. Dozens and dozens of black and olive drab uniformed troops were only a few yards away, coming right for them.

"Heads down! FIRE IN THE HOLE!!"

Glenn squeezed the detonator handle, praying that the incoming hadn't severed the cables to the banks of Claymore mines they had received and set up that very evening.

The loud detonation crushed down on them and parts of the berm were blown away by the force of pounds of C-4 exploding and sending thousands of $\frac{1}{8}$-inch-diameter steel balls rocketing downrange waist high, cutting a wide swath in the attackers' ranks out to a hundred yards. When he looked over the berm he saw nothing except thick dust. His eyes felt as if they were filled with sandpaper grit and his ears rang; still, he could hear moans and cries coming from somewhere inside the dust cloud. He looked back at the Recon platoon machine gun position and it looked to be holding.

"Get me Shotgun 5!" Glenn yelled at his radio operator. They were close, face to face, looking at one another from inches away as the RTO made the call and gave him the handset. Suddenly the young soldier's face registered astonishment, disbelief and his eyes opened wide in surprise before he toppled sideways into the raised berm. Glenn yelled at him and there was no movement; then he saw half the soldier's neck had been blown away and was now gushing a large pool of blood. He checked for a pulse, found none.

"I can't remember his name or where he's from!" Nolan yelled at himself, infuriated.

A sudden rage engulfed him and he raised up over the berm to be faced with a half dozen NVA only a few yards away. He shot two of them with his M-16 before the magazine went empty. He pulled the .45 pistol from its holster and shot a third before the others disappeared into the dark cloud. He slapped a fresh magazine into his rifle and moved toward the right flank of his platoon. He took one quick look back at his RTO.

Dunfee! Marc Dunfee. That's your name!!

He ran bent over to keep below the berm's lip as another illum round popped overhead.

Chapter 14

Someone was calling her name in the distant, fuzzy catacombs of her sub-conscience.

"Come on there, girlfriend. No rest for the wicked."

She tried to open her eyes as she drifted closer toward consciousness but quickly gave up. But her tormentor was persistent, and roughly shook her.

"Jenny! Jenny! Got to get up. Not much time. There's a firebase being overrun."

She took a deep breath, blinked rapidly several times, trying to keep her eyes open and focused on the feminine face above her. "No, that was before. Two… three nights ago."

"Different firebase this time. That was Jay. Tonight, it's Illingworth."

Jenny Kolarik gasped and sat bolt upright, wide awake. "Second battalion, eighth Cav?"

"That's right. It's been going on for an hour. We just got the call. Medevacs can't get in yet but they're going to try as soon as they think they've got a corridor."

Jenny swung her legs over the side of the bed and cast around for her boots. It dawned on her that she had fallen asleep in the same fatigues she'd been wearing for three straight days now. They had all been working around the clock since the first casualties from LZ Jay started arriving. "What time is it, Nan?"

"A few minutes before three."

"In the morning?... of course it's in the morning, isn't it? How long have I been out?"

"This time, almost three hours. You've got to get more sleep, Jen. I hated to have to wake you but the colonel said all hands without exception and he emphasized the *all* part of it. I told him it wasn't fair… after all you've been through these past four days."

"No, he's right. We've got to get all the rooms and triage set up and functioning right away. And beds… are there any available?

"Very few. We're moving the least seriously wounded to other hooches to free up some beds. Brigade supply is setting up additional GP Medium tents and scrounging cots."

"What do you need me to do?" she asked as she laced up her boots.

The head nurse's face grew somber. "I hate to tell you this, Jen, but you're the best we've got at triage. I wouldn't ask if there was any other way."

"All right then, I'll do triage."

The head nurse took a deep breath. "When this is over, you're taking a three day leave to Saigon, or Vung Tau or some other place that has a decent beach. You have to take some down time. That's an order. Hear me?"

"We can talk about it," Jenny replied, standing and looking around her room.

"No, we *will not* talk about it this time. I won't have one of my nurses being section eighted out of here because she refuses to take time off."

Jenny acquiesced with a shrug and followed Nancy Tripler down the hallway. Now fully awake, her heart pounded and her mind raced, creating worse case scenarios and taking her places she knew she shouldn't go.

She had spoken to a captain from the 2/8 Cav earlier in the evening who had come in a few days before the attack on LZ Jay. His name was Stief, and he had turned over his company five days earlier to the only lieutenant left in the unit which was now at Illingworth for some much needed rest.

Damn you, Glenn Nolan. You fool! she thought, her stomach knotted. *I told you, didn't I, to stay away from that battalion.*

"I'll get an orderly to help you with the litters and gurneys," the head nurse told her, and then took hold of her arm just above the elbow. "I'm going to be checking on you, so hold it together. You hear me, Jen?"

With a last long look into her nurse's eyes, Nan Tripler turned and went inside the facility to check on the progress in the operating rooms where the atmosphere was tense but business-like. She went down the side corridor and entered the commander's small office.

"Sir, I need to talk to you about Jenny Kolarik," the nurse corps major said.

"Not now," Lieutenant Colonel Moretti replied, frowning over the top of his glasses. He had to admit Tripler was the best head nurse of the three he'd had on this, his second tour in Vietnam. He trusted her administrative skills implicitly. That said, he still didn't like her. She stomped around the hospital like a female Attila the Hun and he spent as much time smoothing the ruffled feathers of doctors and orderlies as he did cutting on patients. "We just got word the first medevac ship made it into that firebase. We'll be flooded with patients inside a half hour."

"I see where there's a new hospital being set up in Phouc Vinh that's going to be operational in a couple of weeks," the head nurse said, ignoring the commander's warning. "Jenny's a talented and dedicated nurse, but she's been through more in the last four months than any other girl on my staff – and many of them have more than twice her time in country. Papa Vic is a much quieter place than War Zone C and I want her transferred there."

"I don't see how we –"

"For the good of the service, sir, as well as for her state of mind. Kolarik's a good nurse, but right now she's fragile and I think she's close to breaking."

"We can't afford to –"

"We can't afford not to, colonel," Nan Tripler interrupted again. As head nurse, she was used to getting her way with the hospital commander. "We *will* send her there, sir. We must. And that's my final word… Now, we have a lot to do before the first bird arrives."

Glenn carted the unconscious soldier over his shoulder in a fireman's carry and let the surgical orderly and Father Pat at the aid station help him gently lower the man to a litter.

"He's one of mine. Cathcart. He's got a dog tag in his boot laces. I'll give you a hand putting him on the chopper!" Nolan yelled to be heard over the sound of gunfire and the noise of the Huey's blades. Somebody had been thinking – or was just plain lucky – when they decided to put the Battalion Aid Station on the north side of the LZ. The NVA had attacked on three sides only and left open the broad expanse of the northern dry lake bed; the medevac bird had flown nap of the earth after clearing the distant wood line and had been able to make it in without major damage. As Glenn approached the Huey, the pilot stared out the window at him with a look of vague indifference. Even before the aircraft was loaded Nolan picked up his rifle and started back to his platoon's sector on the run.

He ran past the TOC and encountered three NVA sappers headed for the 105 artillery guns, each carrying a canvas bag over his shoulder. He pulled the M16 up and locked it into his shoulder, sighting in on the lead NVA. *No! – not the leader!* he thought instantly – Grandpa Nolan's duck hunting rule: *shoot the last one in the flight first.*

He put two rounds into the third soldier, and another into the middle one. The leader ducked around the edge of a tent and disappeared into the dust fog. Glenn followed the way he'd gone. Several yards farther on he encountered two other NVA sappers inside an artillery pit strapping explosives onto the breach of the gun. Glenn fired two rounds at each and saw the second man go down while the first man got up and hobbled to the edge of the pit, disappearing over the side. Looking around quickly, he saw no more enemy soldiers and headed back to his own platoon line.

"Our last bank of Claymores pushed them back for now," Sergeant Meyer told him, breathing heavily as they hunkered down below the berm. "We've still got two arrays on this side of the platoon, lieutenant."

"How many wounded?"

"Three – Barton, Matthews, Gutiérrez. Matthews can still fight. I sent the other two back to the aid station on their own. Hope they make it – can't afford to send someone with them."

"Ammo?"

"Trooped the line a couple of minutes ago. Not bad, not good. If it slacks up a little more, I'll send a couple of men for resupply."

Nolan nodded and was about to reply when the shooting roared back to life on the platoon left flank. He got to his feet and ran to the position tied in to Echo Recon. There he saw one man fighting off a horde of NVA in black pajama uniforms. It was the sergeant in Recon who had manned the machine gun earlier and was now standing in front of the berm spraying the ranks of the enemy with his M60. Glenn wondered how the man survived.

"Cover me!" Glenn yelled at Cassidy. He shot an enemy soldier just yards from the sergeant, then two more in quick succession as the light dimmed. Another 105mm illumination round bathed the southern perimeter in light and he could see to shoot at four more targets.

His M16 jammed.

He frantically worked the charging handle and pressed the assist with his thumb and finally got it working again. When he looked up, the Recon sergeant was being pressed on two sides. Glenn found himself running toward the lone American who had dropped the machine gun and picked up his M16 to fight off a dozen North Vietnamese. On the run, Nolan fired on three of the attackers and saw one go down. By the time he reached the Recon soldier, he'd felled another. His M16 jammed again and he slung it over his shoulder, drew the pistol from its holster and waded into the NVA surrounding the American. A moment later the attacking North Vietnamese pulled back into the concealment of the dust fog as Glenn and the sergeant retreated behind the berm.

"Who the hell are you?" Glenn asked, wheezing and hacking.

"Lockhart," the sergeant replied, also coughing and spitting out dust and grit.

"Sergeant, you are one crazy son-of-a-bitch!" Nolan rasped. "What were you doing out there all by yourself?"

"I'm the only one left here." The sergeant's eyes were wide and wild, and he looked like he was on some kind of serious drug overdose. *Adrenaline?* His hands shook and he breathed rapidly. "I took one man to the Aid Station and when I got back, this position was abandoned or overrun or something. I had to stop them from pouring through here. Nobody goes through Recon. Nobody."

"No reason to expose yourself like that?"

"Best defense is a good offense."

"Bullshit, Lockhart."

The sergeant was racked with a coughing fit. "Worked didn't it?"

"Only because me and one of my troops covered you."

Lockhart, still looking like a wild man, glanced at him and then at his shirt collar. "Oh, man! You're a damned RLO lifer? I don't take no shit off no lieutenant except Roo."

Glenn ignored the soldier. "Get that gun up and running, Lockhart. How's your ammo?"

"Three cases left – six hundred rounds. Got a case of frags, too."

"Dammit. Next time use 'em. Claymores?"

"One bank of eight left. Clacker's around somewhere."

"Find it. And use them, too!"

The next time came a few minutes later as Glenn was frantically working on cleaning his M16 to get it operating again.

AK-47 fire from the tree line started up again and rose to a crescendo, followed immediately by a screaming horde like an evil animate tsunami of black-clad NVA whipped into a frenzy. Explosions erupted behind him near the 155mm howitzer position and a fire was glowing near the 8-inch guns. Mortars exploded in the middle of the firebase and Glenn guessed this was the big push by the NVA to completely overrun the fire support base. American artillery from somewhere was erupting to his left and right in the tree lines and two sections of gunships were making run after run along the western side of Illingworth.

I'm not going to make it through this, Glenn realized in a moment of sober clarity. A peace came over him, followed by a burst of rage as Lockhart let loose with the M60.

He threw frag grenades as fast as he could pull their pins, each time letting the metal handle flip off and counting two beats before throwing it high in the air to get an air burst to kill more of the little slant-eyed bastards. Green tracers flew a foot over his head; he cringed and ducked. NVA were dying by the dozens only feet from the berm in front of him and Lockhart's M-60. Claymores exploded and the assault seemed to waiver and peter out.

But then it roared back – renewed, unsatiated.

An RPG exploded into the berm with a flash and horrendous roar. Nolan and Lockhart were bowled over backwards and Glenn was stunned, unable to move. Lockhart grabbed him by the collar and dragged him back to the machine gun, yelling at him but Glenn was unable to hear above the rushing sound in his ears. The world slowed and the boundaries of vision closed in around him.

A helmetless NVA wearing shorts and carrying his AK high over his head crested the berm in front of him, screaming at the top of his lungs as he swept the long silver bayonet of his rifle at him in a wide arc. In an instant the soldier was down in the dirt, looking at him with terrified eyes, screaming louder even than before as he clutched at his leg now almost completely severed at the knee. Glenn felt a sharp pain in his forearm and looked down realizing he was holding the machete that had been strapped to the rucksack lying next to

Lockhart's machine gun; it now dripped blood. Another NVA loomed up in front of him and Glenn swung his machete but it was blocked by the AK's barrel. Glenn swung again, this time backhand, hitting the soldier in the upper arm and then at the base of his neck.

Lockhart was grappling with an NVA several yards away and Glenn ran to help.

Without warning he was face down in the black dirt, his mouth full of grit and a weight on his back that had a strangle hold around his neck. He tried to get up on all fours but the body on top of him was strong and had wrapped itself around one of his legs, forcing him face down and keeping him there. Glenn was gasping, having trouble breathing and rapidly grew light-headed. *Do SOMETHING!* he yelled at himself.

His hand went to the leather hilt of the Ka-Bar he'd tied to the left strap of his LBE suspenders. He flipped the leather sheath snap open with his thumb and pulled the long knife out; reaching behind him, he stabbed it into the North Vietnamese soldier riding his back. Once, twice. The man screamed in pain but wouldn't let loose the choke hold. Glenn's vision dimmed and spots danced in front of his eyes. Stab again. Again. Again.

Suddenly he could breathe.

He got up on all fours, coughing and gagging. The NVA soldier looked at him with vacant eyes as Glenn struggled to catch his breath. Three NVA soldiers carrying canvas bags over their shoulders ran past him without stopping, headed toward the 155mm artillery section. He searched around for his M16 but by the time he found it they had disappeared into the dust fog. He felt drawn to look at the NVA he'd stabbed and saw the man was wearing shoes made from pieces of tire treads held on by thongs of the same material – Ho Chi Minh racing slicks, the Americans troops called them. *They're kicking our ass like this wearing shower clogs?!* He couldn't believe it.

When he turned around, he was face to face with another NVA soldier who'd just crested the berm. *A straggler.* They simply stood there, looking fearfully at one another for a long, asinine moment. Glenn was the first to move.

He leapt at the short Oriental with savage brutality, driving his forehead into the enemy soldier's mouth, knocking him backwards against the berm and pinning the AK he was carrying against his chest. Glenn heard himself gasping and whimpering in fear. He kneed the soldier in the groin, wrapping his left hand fingers around the soldier's neck with all his strength; the knife's blade went into the NVA's stomach to the hilt.

He stabbed the soldier again. When the NVA stopped twitching, he rolled off the body and wiped blood from the blade on his jungle fatigues. A salty trickle from the crown of his head where he'd head-butted the man ran down into the corner of his mouth. He looked at the two NVA soldiers. Soldiers? They looked like kids. But they were soldiers. *Damn good ones*, he thought. Glenn replaced the knife back in its upside down sheath on his LBE, and threw up, groveling on his knees and gasping for air. Looking around he saw that the fire near the large stockpile of artillery ammo sitting on top of the ground was now a raging inferno.

Overhead, flares were igniting and falling all around the tree line surrounding Illingworth – *Air Force flare ships*, he thought instantly. Suddenly a thin red line of tracers rained down from high above, working its way along the south and east trees lines. Now artillery was pounding a football field away from where he was, screaming high-pitched echoes tearing the fabric of the night sky, the constant explosions reverberating through him and seeming to toss and shake the very earth.

Lockhart, back on his M60, was yelling above the cacophony for Nolan to break out more ammo. NVA were emerging from the concealment of the heavy dust cloud and Glenn threw the rest of the frag grenades at them. He loaded another long link of M60 ammunition for the recon sergeant – their last – and got off two shots from his M16 before the thick, gritty dust clogged it again. Behind them, NVA mortar rounds rained down.

"You're gonna have to fall back, Lockhart. I need to shore up the left flank of my platoon. Cover me while –"

The explosion was like the end of the world by overpressure.

It felt like some giant had clapped its hands over both his ears simultaneously while a great weight had been swung and struck him squarely in the middle of his back. He was floating in the dense black cloud with his arms spread wide and his head back; there was no up or down, left or right. No day. No night. Time was held in implacable stasis. He hit something tough, unyielding, and his head crashed violently against hard ground.

His universe went crimson and he slipped over the edge into nothingness.

The medevac Huey touched down and unloaded another load of casualties, this time including a field expedient stretcher bearing a 1st Cav trooper whose head was wrapped in a blood soaked O.D. towel; an emergency field tracheostomy trickled blood down his neck.

"Jenny! I need you to spell Doris in Op Room three," Nan Tripler called from across the triage area as her nurse moved quickly toward the badly injured soldier. Jenny Kolarik removed the towel from the trooper's head and her stomach convulsed. The boy had no face.

But he did have a pulse and there was no indication of cerebral spinal fluid leak; she couldn't tell if there was brain damage but willed there was none and decided to put him at the head of the line for the next available surgical table. *That porky new doctor – Ambrose – has some experience with maxillofacial surgery; maybe he can save this kid.*

"Give me a few minutes and then I'll scrub." She glanced again at the ugly mass that was now the boy's face and moved on to the next litter patient. She looked at her watch and saw it was just after four-thirty in the morning. "Who's going to do triage if I'm not here?"

"I'll cover it somehow. You've got one minute, Jen."

Her tour in Op Room Three lasted two hours, during which she could hear the medevac ships coming and going in all too much regularity. By the time she was relieved for a fifteen minute break, she had been working four hours in a blur of surgical trauma. Jenny sat down heavily on the bench outside the operating room; she stretched and massaged her neck while taking deep breaths and looking east toward the first hint of sunrise.

Her gaze fell on the pile of torn and bloodied jungle fatigues and boots and web gear, trash now that would be taken out and burned by one of the orderlies at the end of the day. Part of a collar caught her attention. It was bloodied like the most of the others, but it looked newer, darker green. It had the black bar of a lieutenant.

She reached down and pulled it from the pile and gasped. The nametag said NOLAN and the branch insignia was Infantry. *So much blood.* She was suddenly frantic to find him.

Jenny checked each of the operating rooms, then went back to the triage area, walked around the recovery rooms and checked the morgue. *You're losing it, Kolarik. What would you do if you found him?* She stood silently outside under the dim light, in a quandary until an agitated voice forced itself into her thoughts.

"Dammit, I could use some help here!... I could really use some help!"

Jenny turned and saw a shirtless trooper; the sight of the soldier was unsettling.

His chest was bare and streaked with blood from a cursory washing but there were no visible wounds except a long gash high on his left arm. His trousers were caked with blood and a dark substance like ash from a fire. His face was blackened, streaked from sweat.

"I could really use some help here," he repeated, sounding terribly upset and maybe unhinged. The tone frightened her.

"How can I help you?"

"I need to find my knife," he rasped, his voice weak and cracking. He ran his fingers through his wildly disheveled hair. "I lost my damn knife. It's a family *treasure,* damn it! Why won't you help me find it?" The soldier patted down his bare chest and the cargo pockets of his jungle fatigue trousers. "And my gun. Where the hell is my gun?! I can't lose my damn gun, too. What if the bastards take another run at us?!" he said, fitfully. The soldier was walking spasmodically, lurching as his head swiveled in fretful, erratic movements.

"Glenn?! Is that you?... Sit down. Here on the bench."

"Can't sit down. Can't sit down," he said, sounding confused; he slurred some of his words and lurched again, fighting to keep his balance.

"Please. Just sit with me for a moment."

"Got to keep moving. Can't sit down or I'll never get up. Got to keep moving."

"Look at me," she said, gazing into his eyes and grasping his hand. He looked awful and she hoped her face didn't give away her anxiety. "What's your name?"

The question seemed to momentarily confuse him, but at last he replied, "Glenn. Nolan. Lieutenant Glenn Nolan."

He'd lost a lot of weight since she'd seen him three months earlier. His eyes rested on her now with curious intensity, the look of someone adrift, grasping for answers, working hard to make sense of what was going on around him.

Smiling indulgently to mask her worry she asked "Do you know *where* you are?"

He thought for a long while. At last he said, "Vietnam?"

"Where in Vietnam?"

He frowned, closed his eyes tightly and then opened them. "Bien Hoa?... Tay Ninh?"

"Do you know who I am?"

Again he frowned. "You look like Claudia Cardinale... but you're not, are you? Should I know you?" He hesitated, chafed his jaw with a knuckle. "Should I know you?" he asked again, and then recognition crept into his eyes. "You're Ginny. Right? No. Jenny. Jenny the Polish girl. Right?"

She smiled and teared up. "If this is some kind of playact for sympathy, Glenn Nolan, I find it not one single bit funny."

"I'm not trying to be funny, damn it!" he said, irritated, breathing heavily. "I'm trying to find my knife... and my rifle. They court-martial you for losing your rifle."

"You're in the hospital located in Tay Ninh. Does that ring a bell. They brought you here from LZ Illingworth."

Confusion spread across his face. "Illingworth. We were in a firefight... at a firebase...Illingworth. Yeah. Illingworth. It went on and on and on forever. There was a guy there – Locker, Lockerby... Lockhart. Chris Lockhart. Recon platoon. He was their right flank position. They came at us four, five, six times. Finally got past us – some of them." He was breathing rapidly now, and in the dim light of a single bulb hanging from a pole nearby she could see he was sweating and anguish was etched on his face. "I told him to fall back and cover me when I moved back to my platoon. And then, the explosion. Huge explosion. Felt like I was picked up and... floating... that's all I remember... no, not all... hit something hard and I was on the ground. My head hurt like hell... remember saying – or maybe thinking 'man, that *really* hurt' and then... then nothing. I don't know how I got here. Did you ever tell me if I'm at Tay Ninh or Bien Hoa? Next thing I remember is realizing that I'd lost my uncle's knife and

I had to find it and… I'm rambling, aren't I? Is this making any sense? And then I saw you. I think it was you… and you wouldn't help me find that damned knife… why wouldn't you help?… and I knew my grandfather would never talk to me again if I lost it, and –"

"Glenn, look at me. You're at the American hospital in Tay Ninh."

He looked adrift. "Don't know how I got here," he said again. "You're the Polish girl."

"Yes, I'm Polock Jenny."

"You don't like to be called that," he said as if it was an epiphany.

"It is what it is." She looked into his eyes, then held up her index finger and told him to concentrate on it while she moved it left and right. "Your pupils are a little dilated and you're having some trouble following my finger. Do you have a headache? Feel pressure like from inside your head? Do feel dizzy or off balance?"

He nodded affirmatively to each question like a dumbstruck little kid.

"You've got a concussion. There's a scrape down the right side of your face and that would seem to confirm hitting your head on the ground. Have you been examined yet? Think. It would have been a nurse in her mid-thirties. Dark hair. Straight bangs. Wears glasses."

"I don't know."

"It appears someone swabbed you down to check for wounds. Do you remember that?" When he shook his head negatively, she said, "All right, then I'll clean you up. I'm going to take you inside to a pre-op room and check you over."

"Can we look for my knife first? I gotta find that knife."

"When we're done, all right?"

"You're the boss."

"Follow me," Jenny said, and led him inside. For the next ten minutes she wiped his face clean, sponged off his chest and back with deft, light strokes using a wash cloth, soap and water while checking him for wounds; she found several minor cuts, bruises and abrasions, small shrapnel punctures, but no bullet wounds. All the while she kept a constant dialogue of questions and answers going. By the end of the examination, he was beginning to act and sound more normal though he was still hoarse. "So far so good, except for that gash on your left arm. That's nasty. Do you know how you got it?"

"You and I met at Fort Lewis. We had dinner together and you ordered a real expensive bottle of wine."

She smiled at him. "You're gradually getting your memory back. That's a good sign."

"We talked about how you went to the rodeo with your father."

"Yes we did."

"*I* gave you that name – Polock Jenny. That's why you stuck me with the expensive wine, isn't it? You're not a cheap date."

"We weren't on a date."

"We weren't?!... Really? Well, I was."

Jenny ducked her head and looked away, not trusting herself to answer. His remark was delivered in such innocence it made her uncomfortable; her heart skipped a beat and reminded her of that initial rush of anticipation when he'd looked at her from the far end of the bar at the Fort Lewis Officers Club. She took his hand.

" Let me try this again. How did you get this gash on your arm?"

"From a bayonet. Maybe. There was a lot going on – a lot of confusion. The light wasn't the best. That artillery battery kept pumping out the illum rounds..."

"It's going to require stitches, and cleaning it out is going to be... well, unpleasant."

"That sounds like a euphemism... like the dentist saying this is going to hurt a little bit."

She laughed and winked at him. "Euphemism? Big word for a guy with a bump on his head. You're coming out of it. Take off your trousers so I can check you out below the waist."

He hesitated. "Have we done this before, you and I?"

She gasped and the color rose in her throat. "I'm a nurse. I do this several times a day."

"I'm not your first?"

"My first?! Not like that... not the way you're thinking."

"How do you know what I'm thinking?"

"Maybe I'm clairvoyant," Jenny said absently, unbuttoning his trousers.

"Claire? I thought your name was Jenny... why are you in my pants?"

She saw the quick little uptick at the corner of his mouth and allowed herself the guilty pleasure of imagining taking care of him in the recovery ward – plumping up his pillows, putting fresh water beside his cot, prolonging the ritual of checking his vitals while holding his hand and looking into his eyes; long, casual conversations. "You're incorrigible, lieutenant. Yeah, and you're thinking of something else stupid to say. You used to have a lot more mature sense of humor. Now turn around and take off your trousers." She threw a towel at him. "Cover yourself if you're modest."

"Should I be?... around you? Have I been hit in the... well, you know, in my...?"

"That's the first thing all you guys want to know. For what it's worth, probably not. The Nolan family lineage is likely safe. If you were hit there, you'd know it, concussion or not, unless someone gave you morphine. Have they?"

"Not that I know."

"All right, let's take a look at you. I'm going to clean the blood off your legs, your feet, your rear end and see what we have. Are you having any pain anywhere?"

She washed him down and examined him completely, keeping up a running commentary on what she was finding which, as it turned out was little compared to what she'd expected. She cleaned and covered his cuts and then had him sit on an examining table as she took a closer look at the gash in his arm.

"I'm going to clean this out with an antiseptic solution, and then I'll close it," Jenny said, positioning a surgical light over the examining table. She had him lie on his stomach, turned on the light and retrieved a small, C-shaped needle and a spool of thread from a cabinet. "Can't be certain, but it doesn't look deep enough to require anything beyond surface stitches. I've got to clean it out and take a closer look. This is going to take a few dozen stitches, and it'll hurt."

"You put this many stitches in people while they're awake?"

"Not usually – but don't think you're getting anesthesia just for a few stitches like this, Nolan. I thought you were one of those big tough Rangers." She doused the wound several times, first with water and then a fluid that smelled like distilled petroleum, felt like liquid fire and made his eyes water. After the first two stitches were inserted and knotted, he asked her if it was possible to simply amputate and be done with it.

She smiled and jabbed him with the needle again.

Jenny chatted amiably with him, asking about his family, his time at West Point, the weather – anything to keep his attention off of what she was doing. And before he realized it, she had put twenty-six stitches in his arm. She put a large gauze pad over the wound and taped it tightly.

"Anyone ever told you how pretty you are?" he asked, sitting up and turning toward her.

"Just when I think you're coming out of that concussion, you go and prove me wrong." She fussed over the bandage and said, "You have to keep that dry. So, I'm going to keep you here for a while just to make sure it doesn't get infected. Wouldn't want that, would we?"

"I can't stay here!" he said. "As much as I want to be with you..." He raised his eyebrows as he sat up on the table, turning toward her and losing the towel covering his loins. She turned her back and let him recover it. When she did, she noticed Nan Tripler watching them from the doorway.

"Jenny, I've been looking all over for you. I need you to assist Kaizerski in Op Two."

"Can't you find anyone else? I'm working on a patient myself."

The head nurse frowned at her and shook her head. "No, I need *you*, Jen. Stat! You seem to be pretty well done with this soldier. What's your name, trooper?"

"Nolan. Lieutenant Glenn Nolan. I'm with the 1st Battalion, 8th US Cavalry."

"Well, lieutenant, I'm going to get you some clothes from supply and I'll be back in two shakes. Jenny, your duty station is Op Two and I'll finish up with the lieutenant."

"But, Nan –"

"Op Two, Jen. Last time I'm going to say it. This night isn't over yet. Now, go!" The older nurse watched Jenny turn and leave after giving Glenn a sad smile and saying she'd check in on him later. When she was gone, the woman turned to him and took a deep breath.

"You won't be seeing her again, lieutenant. We don't have the beds to accommodate everyone, and you're ambulatory, so you're going back to your unit."

"I'm fine with that, major."

The woman gave him a long, callous look. "I overheard most of that chit-chat between you two and so I have to tell you something. You're not welcome here in my hospital. When I discharge you, I never want to see again."

Glenn gave her a crooked smile. "That'd be my choice. I understand perfectly."

The nurse took a deep breath. "No, I don't think you do, so listen up good, lieutenant. Let me be real clear. I'm telling you to stay away from Jenny. I saw the way you looked at her. I'm responsible for that nurse; she's a good one and I *will* protect her from these doctors and from any other soldier who thinks he wants to take advantage of her. She's a good kid, a fine nurse, but right now for a lot of reasons she's vulnerable. She's overworked and overwhelmed, and an easy target for somebody with a smooth line – like you. She had her heart broken once, and I won't let it happen again."

"I don't have any intentions –"

"That's what all of you say. I'm going to tell you this just one more time. In the future, stay away from this hospital and stay away from her."

"I'm a married man."

"Yeah, so are all these doctors. I don't know how long you've been married or how many months you have in-country, but this I know... all you men suffer from satyriasis," the head nurse said forming the word extravagantly with her lips and pronouncing it slowly.

Glenn frowned and gave her a confused look.

"What I'm saying, lieutenant, is that the male of the species doesn't usually think with his noggin but with that part of his anatomy you've got covered with that operating room towel. And because of it, I have to spend an inordinate amount of time protecting nurses from people like you."

"I'm a happily married man and have no interest in or intention to –"

"Good, then staying away from Jenny should be easy for you. I could have you transferred to the Evac hospital in Japan and then on to Walter Reed. Most soldiers over here would do most anything to be diagnosed with a million-dollar wound and go stateside."

"That's not me."

"Didn't think so. That's why when I get you a clean set of jungle fatigues, you're going to get dressed and get on the first bird out of Tay Ninh headed to LZ Illingworth. You will not pass "GO" nor will you collect two hundred dollars. And you won't see Lieutenant Kolarik, and I mean ever."

"That would be real inconsiderate of me, don't you think?"

"Your bad manners and lack of consideration will make it that much easier for her to wipe the slate clean of your name."

Nan Tripler watched Glenn's reaction closely. She wished she could get him sent out of country, but doubted she could really make that happen – at best it was a longshot. She would have the company clerks scrub Jenny's incoming mail for letters from him, but most important, she would do everything in her considerable power as head nurse to get Kolarik transferred out of War Zone C to that new three table surgical hospital far away in Phouc Vinh. She was certain she could convince Colonel Moretti to sign off on it. After retrieving a clean set of jungle fatigues for Nolan, Nan Tripler walked him out to the pad and waited until the next medevac came in and unloaded its wounded.

As the sun was coming up, she put Glenn on a Huey and waved goodbye as the ship lifted off and headed north toward what was left of Illingworth.

Chapter 15

"I realized I wasn't ever going to be a decent cop. I just wasn't cut out for it," the right seat pilot said to Brad Nolan over the intercom in response to his question. "So I turned in my badge and went down to the recruiter's office. Two weeks later I put Redcliff in the rear view mirror, hopefully for good. Now here I am, flying a million dollar machine instead of driving a beat up four year old police cruiser. Best swap I ever made."

The sun was barely above the horizon and they had just taken off from the large 2nd Brigade headquarters complex outside Sông Bé enroute to Phouc Vinh after what had promised to be a busy Nighthawk mission. They had departed their home base around ten o'clock the previous evening to be refueled and on-station by midnight. Firebase Jay had been overrun three days earlier and intel reports hinted the possibility of widespread attacks throughout III Corps and so they had been deployed forward, closer to the Cambodian border. At 0200 they had been scrambled and set up an orbit around LZ Snuffy because a firebase in War Zone C came under attack. They monitored calls on Guard but hadn't been dispatched to help. Two hours later, they refueled and went back on strip alert until being released. It had been as boring for them as it was exciting – apparently – for the firebase north of Tay Ninh City.

Brad enjoyed flying Nighthawk missions with their challenges of nighttime flying and gunnery, but Ed Norton was a brand new arrival. He passed his in-country check ride the day before and had been volunteered for the mission; that concerned Nolan. He didn't know what to make of Captain Shannaghan's decision and worried his platoon leader was sending him, as the newest Aircraft Commander in the unit, a message.

"Where did you say you were from, Mr. Norton?" Syzmanski asked from his position in the left gunner's well where the mini-gun was mounted.

"Colorado. An old silver mining town called Redcliff in Eagle County. Sixty to eighty miles southwest of Denver – way back in the mountains. Not too awful far west from Vail. But I was a township cop in Minturn, a slightly bigger town just north of us."

"What decided you to give up being a cop?"

"Divine intervention," the co-pilot said exaggerating both words.

"God told you not to be a policeman?"

"Something like that."

The intercom went silent for a long while until Brad said, "All right, Norton. Spit it out. What's the rest of the story?"

"Rather not say. It's not much of a tale – a real yawner."

"We're past the point of no return with you and that story. Go ahead and finish."

"It's not all the interesting."

"Norton... finish the damned story!"

The co-pilot glanced quickly at Brad across the console that separated them.

"I graduated high school with less than stellar grades but a job opened up mid-summer in Minturn's constable office. I applied and got it. There's not a lot going on around Minturn except people speeding on Highway 24, some long hairs from California pot smokin' down in Hippie Hollow near Redcliff. So, it's about four months later and the Constable decides he's going to ride with me.

"We set up on Highway 24 just south of Minturn. I'm pretty sure he's in the car because I still haven't written a speeding ticket, and traffic fines are a big chunk of the town budget. Just not my nature to write tickets. First car that comes through is the wife of the town council chairman, and she's speeding like always. We both recognize the car and I talk to her but let her go with a verbal warning. Three more cars come by speeding and each of them, as it turns out, has a real good excuse, and I let them off with warnings, too. Well, the Constable finally says, 'Ed, are you *EVER* going to write a speeding ticket?' And he gives me a look that says my job is on the line. So I told him I definitely would; that the next car that comes by even a mile over the speed limit is going to get a ticket even if it's the governor or his wife. I told him that nothing and nobody on planet Earth could stop me. Not five minutes later a big old white van comes barreling through twenty miles over the speed limit. I pull it over, get out of the cruiser and walk up to the window."

Norton paused for several seconds, took a deep breath and cocked his head as he gave a dead-pan look to Nolan. "There were seven sweet old nuns in that van."

Brad turned and looked into the back of the Huey. Syzmanski had a big grin on his face and the armorer in the right well behind Norton was doubled over.

"And you heard the voice – right, Mr. Norton?" The crew chief asked.

"As clear as I hear you now."

"What did you do?" Brad inquired, smiling, wondering if this was really true..

"I looked at the nun behind the wheel, made the sign of the cross as best a Methodist could and said, 'Bless you, sister; go and sin no more.' I went back to the patrol car, handed the Constable my badge and walked home. That's why I'm a Ghostrider instead of a deputy."

Syzmanski said something witty but Brad's attention was elsewhere as a call on Guard filtered through the background noise. "Did you guys hear that?"

"Hear what?" Norton asked, suddenly alert.

"Amber Spar calling for help. That's the callsign of the Air Force FACs who support the Vietnamese Airborne in III Corps." He turned his radio selector switch to VHF and made a call. "Amber Spar, this is Ghostrider one-four on Guard."

"Ghostrider 14, Amber Spar three-seven. I've got a convoy of ARVN with American advisors under attack. I need ordnance for close support of ground troops. Can you help?"

"This is Ghostrider 14, I'm a UH-1 configured with a mini-gun, a searchlight and a .50 cal. loaded with Armor Piercing Incendiary. We're a Nighthawk bird off Sông Bé five minutes ago enroute Phouc Vinh with full fuel. If that works for you, tell me where you need us."

"Perfect, Ghostrider, come on. The ambush is on Highway 13 about halfway between An Loc to the south, Loc Ninh on the North. I'll guide you in once you cross the Sông Bé River."

Brad pulled out his map after turning due west and having Norton take the controls. He did a quick calculation and made a radio call. "Amber Spar 37, Ghostrider 14 on Guard, we're fifteen, maybe twenty minutes out climbing to twenty-five hundred heading two-seven-five. Give me a freq."

"Amber Spar here. I'm on FM three-eight point two with the ground commander. I'll meet you there. Out." A few seconds later Brad contacted the Air Force controller. *"Here's the situation, Ghostrider... friendly convoy of ARVN airborne under attack in a pass eight miles northwest of Quon Loi on highway 13. A dozen vehicles all told – main vehicle is a 5,000 gallon gasoline tanker. Friendlies abandoned the vehicles and cleared the area to the west to set up a defensive perimeter leaving everything behind. The lead and trail vehicles are Jeeps mounting a .50 cal. The enemy has full control of the convoy. I need you to blow up the tanker and take out as many NVA as you can. I'll give you more instructions when you get closer. "*

"That sounds like beaucoup bad news, Mr. Nolan," Syzmanski said over the intercom. "They got .50 cals, too and who knows what else." Brad turned and looked at the crew chief whose eyes seemed to be saying: *You sure we really want to do this?*

Almost as if he was listening in, the Forward Air Controller called on the FM frequency.

"Ghostrider, we have NVA swarming over the vehicles. I'll cover you all the way through your runs. Request your first pass with the mini-gun to take out troops and then concentrate on the tanker with your .50 cal API on second run."

"Roger that, Amber Spar. Give us all the cover you can." Brad switched to intercom. "Those Amber Spar FACs fly out of Sông Bé, Phouc Vinh, Saigon – all over III Corps. Their birds are fitted with rockets. The O-2s and OV-10s have machine guns as well. This guy can

211

keep the NVAs' heads down when we go in. I'll fly the runs. We'll go in at a hundred feet or less at a hundred twenty knots, if this thing can handle it, so you door gunners are gonna have to be on your toes. Hopefully those gooks have never shot skeet. I got the controls, Norton."

They crossed the Sông Bé River; immediately Amber Spar spotted them and gave directions to intersect Highway 13 a mile north of the village of An Loc. A mile later they were skimming fifty feet above the trees at over a hundred miles per hour with the Air Force controller calling out the distance to the first vehicle in the convoy. Everything around them was a blur of greens and browns; and then suddenly the vehicles and swarms of black clad troops appeared, so close their faces could be seen. The doors guns began blasting away –

Suddenly both guns went silent at the same instant and Brad's first thought was that his gunners had both been hit. Dread fell through him like a heavy stone; he turned hard left and a second later they were clear. "What the hell happened back there?!"

"The guns jammed!" Syzmanski yelled.

"Both of them?! At the same time?!

"Yeah. Both of them!" the crew chief yelled, pulling and yanking on the weapon's charging handle. "Son-of-a-bitch!"

Glenn continued a climbing turn and rolled out heading south toward An Loc.

"Ghostrider, Amber Spar 37. Everything all right down there?"

"Weapon malfunction," Brad replied. "We'll sort it out and try that again. Afraid we lost the element of surprise. You got us in sight?"

It took another three or four minutes to clear the jams in both guns and test fire. Five minutes after their first aborted run, they passed over An Loc, headed north up the road into what Brad was sure was an alert and ready NVA ambush. *This is really crazy*, he thought as he leveled off at fifty feet above the trees and rolled the nose of the Huey over.

As the first vehicle came into view he saw the tracers from Syzmanski's mini-gun flashing by his window, impacting among the NVA troops and chewing up ARVN vehicles. It was bedlam on the ground and bodies were being flung in the air and dashed like rag dolls. The enemy troops were shooting back and he couldn't tell if the Nighthawk was taking any hits; before he could think about it, they were clear of the convoy.

"Everybody all right back there?!" he asked, making a shallow, climbing left turn. Both door gunners responded. "Norton. How about you?" The new pilot stared straight ahead, wordlessly. "Norton! Are you all right?" Silence answered. "Norton!?"

"I am *so* glad that's over. That's the scariest damned thing I ever lived through." He was silent momentarily and then looked at Brad. "We're not going to do that again, are we?"

"There's still the tanker. Are we clear right? We'll go north to south this time and put the tanker on the side of the .50 with its API" ... ." He keyed the mike. "Amber Spar, we're going back for the gas tanker – north to south. Ghostrider's in hot. Where are you, Amber Spar?"

The return fire from the NVA on the ground was more intense this time and Glenn knew they were being hit. The tanker was suddenly off to their right front and then –

Five thousand gallons of gasoline made for one very impressive fireball and an explosion that threw the Nighthawk almost out of control; the ground tilted crazily. Brad righted the Huey and pulled in all the power he could.

Seconds later they climbed through a thousand feet and he turned to see the mushroom shaped dark red and black cloud of explosion behind them. Brad keyed the intercom button and asked, "Does anyone see that Air Force FAC?" No one did and finally Brad contacted him on the FM frequency. "Marker 37 where are you?"

"I'm directly above you at five thousand. Been here the whole time, Ghostrider!"

Brad looked through the plexiglass directly over his head and saw a dot above that could have been an airplane.

"Marker 37, I see *where* you are. But tell me *what* you are!"

"Marker 37 is an O-1. Bird Dog."

"A Bird Dog? *Really!?* What weapons are you covering us with from way up there."

There was a long pause and finally the Air Force pilot replied. *"I've got my personal weapons in the cockpit. I was out of rockets when I called for help, but I had you covered with an M-16 and the Smith & Wesson .38 in my shoulder holster."*

"That son-of-a- bitch is covering us with an M-16 from five thousand feet up while we're on the deck getting' shredded by an NVA regiment?!" Syzmanski shouted through the intercom. "I say we follow him back to his home base and castrate him on the runway with my survival knife. Can you believe that guy?!"

"No!" shouted the door gunner from the other gunner's well, a Spec-4 that Glenn knew only as Gimp. "I took a round in and through my left leg. It burns like the fires of Hades. You got to get me to a medic."

"Anybody else hit?" Brad asked as he turned southeast toward Phouc Vinh.

Norton was looking at blood on his nomex flying glove and squirmed uncomfortably in his seat. "I got hit, too."

"Is it bad?"

"Is any wound ever good?" He gave Brad an exasperated look. "I've been shot before. You know I was a cop."

"So you told us. Where were you hit, Norton?"

"It was on a range in Glenwood the day I first qualified with my personal sidearm. I was a little late getting there and it was –"

"No, I mean where are you wounded *now*, so I can call ahead and get a med detachment to be ready for you and Gimp."

"Oh... it's really nothing."

"You're bleeding. It's not nothing. Where are you hit?"

Norton gazed at him forlornly, like a whipped pup. "... in my butt-tocks."

Brad tried hard to keep from smiling.

"Mr. Nolan," Syzmanski said over the intercom, "I believe we're in the company of the latest winner of the *Magnet Ass* Award."

*   *   *

The medevac chopper did a high overhead approach to what had once been the VIP pad on the north side of LZ Illingworth.

From his position on the floor behind the pilot, Glenn could see the panorama of the firebase. The flat, open field around the perimeter was littered with black pajama-clad North Vietnamese dead; inside the berm, smoke still billowed from scattered locations, most densely from a twenty foot deep crater where the 8 inch howitzer ammo had once been. Only a few Americans moved around; those who did moved like begrimed zombies from some low budget horror movie. The ground was littered with debris and blackened as if someone had haphazardly dumped truckloads of coal ash on a garbage dump. Tattered ponchos and tarps lay strewn about, covering American bodies.

Two UH-1s sat on the pad side by side in the early morning light. The red single star placard on one of them indicated General Casey, the Assistant Division Commander was on the scene. Casey had a reputation as an 'up and comer' destined for more stars, a general who knew how to fight the war and take care of the troops at the same time. Still, Glenn wondered if the presence of a general officer right now didn't create more problems than it solved. Wherever a general went the command post cowboys on his staff went as well, and that rarely spelled anything but trouble... *with a capital T.*

As he exited the medevac ship he saw Father Donohoe, bare chested and covered in black soot, helping a soldier to the ship on which he'd flown in.

The priest saw him and gave a tired smiled. "Did you forget to get off in Tay Ninh, Nolan?" Donahoe asked, shouting above the noise of rotor blades and grabbing his hand.

"Seems like I forgot a lot of things, but no, I got off and stayed a while."

The priest looked at his bandaged arm and nodded. "Do you remember taking a swing at me?... more than once before we got you on the medevac a few hours ago."

"I'd never hit a man of the cloth."

"You tried. But I never told you, did I, that I was a Golden Glove finalist in Boston back when I was in my prime. The Sergeant Major and I found you wandering around in the field in front of your platoon, and I took your pistol and knife. You were pretty much out of it when we finally got you out of here."

Glenn sighed. There was a long, dark period about which he remembered nothing and he found that unsettling. "If I owe you and the Sergeant Major an apology... what happened?"

"After the 8 inch ammo exploded, it took us all about fifteen or twenty minutes to come to our senses – us and the NVA. It turned the whole firebase upside down and inside out. Everyone was knocked over and just worthless... even the gooks. Sergeant Major and I, along with one of the battalion medics got our wits about us and started looking around for survivors. Honestly didn't think there'd be many. We found you out in front of the recon platoon position, wandering around like a drunk Irishman late on Saint Patty's Day. You were standing over one of the recon platoon soldiers, yelling and screaming, firing an AK-47 at a crowd of North Vietnamese stumbling back toward the tree line."

"I don't remember any of that."

"Not surprised," the priest said, running his fingers through his close-cropped flat top.

"I do remember some of the firefight, and a little bit about the explosion, but not much else until I was sitting in a hospital in Tay Ninh with a nurse asking me questions and sponging me down. You put me on the medevac? What happened to Lockhart in Recon?"

"We got him out not long after you left."

"How was he?"

"Alive. But barely."

In his memory, Glenn saw instants and snippets of Lockhart in the flash-shot darkness. "Lockhart was more Audie Murphy than Audie was. I hope he makes it. What about my platoon?... I got to get back to them."

Donahoe grabbed his arm. "We had to evac about half of them. Sergeant Meyer didn't make it, along with four others. All but maybe a half dozen of your men were wounded. Only recon platoon fared worse. And there's still one of their men unaccounted for."

A brief flicker of memory passed before his eyes. There had been a young, bareheaded soldier from Recon who had brought them a can of M-60 ammo some time during the fight. He had moved a few yards away and stood up to engage a line of NVA off to their left. Glenn thought now he'd probably taken a direct hit from B-40. He was there one second, and the next instant he wasn't – the trooper had simply vanished, right before his eyes.

"I'm afraid there's not much left of Charlie company," Father Donohoe was saying. "Let me walk with you down there."

Illingworth was deathly quiet and eerie in the light of the barely risen sun – the firebase was an utter disaster. Scraps of sandbags, ammo boxes and artillery canisters were scattered everywhere; all of the vehicles, except the D-6 bulldozer had been bowled over. The water trailer had been blown in half; pieces of culvert stuck up through the earth. Bodies lay partially or mostly buried in the debris littering what was left of the LZ; he could see small groups of soldiers placing dead Americans into body bags and he felt sick to his stomach. Craters, small and large, pockmarked the whole of the firebase. The artillery Fire Direction Center had taken a direct hit at the main entrance to the below ground bunker and the roof had collapsed, killing everyone inside. Three of the 105 mm artillery pieces were out of action; both self-propelled 8 inch howitzers had been knocked out and now lay on their sides. One of the mortars in his old platoon had been destroyed, and four ponchos covered bodies on the ground next to the demolished pit. Everywhere, soldiers sat on the ground with their heads in their hands, their bodies blackened; some wandered aimlessly or simply stared off into the distance.

Glenn felt piercing guilt for abandoning them to enjoy stolen time with a round-eyed nurse in Tay Ninh's safety. The chaplain stopped at the location of what had been his platoon headquarters and Glenn looked at the faces that remained of his command. One of his squad leaders, Sergeant Tannahill, a shake and bake buck sergeant who had arrived a month ago, the log day after Nolan, stood up slowly.

"LT, we were told you were dead," the NCO said.

"Guess they were wrong, Tanner," Glenn replied, looking around at the gaunt, haggard faces of his platoon. "I know about Sergeant Meyer. Are you my platoon sergeant now?" When Tannahill nodded, Glenn asked quietly, "Who's left?"

The sergeant pulled a scrap of paper from one of his breast pockets and read, "Johnson, Harlingen, Miller, Bartel... and the platoon sergeant – KIA. Cathcart, Walker, Bailey, Heintzelman, Price, Brierty, all medevac'd to Tay Ninh along with you." The sergeant handed over the list and another scrap with the names of the walking wounded. "Most of them are guys from the Chinook load of replacements we got in a couple of days ago. Now that you're back, we've got eleven men available for duty, counting Dodd and Umbaugh who are still up at the Battalion Aid Station."

"A squad instead of a platoon," Glenn mumbled, looking at the names of those left. He looked around and saw Captain Hobson and the first sergeant thirty yards away, sitting on top of a bunker, deep in conversation. Just beyond them another Huey descended and landed on the

VIP pad. Glenn saw the red placard with two white stars on the bulkhead behind the pilot's seat. *The invasion of the stars has begun*, he thought. "Tanner, there was an untouched case of Budweiser next to the platoon CP bunker last I knew. I know it'll be warm, but if it somehow survived, make sure these guys each get a can of beer. I'm gonna go see the CO and First Sergeant to find out what's up."

Hobson and Beauchamp looked wearily at him when he approached. They were both stained with gunpowder and covered with dark, oily dust. Their faces were black.

"Damn, Nolan, you look like you already got your shower and shave." Captain Hobson said, looking him over. "Rooster told me you were dead."

"Wishful thinking, captain."

"Your platoon thought so, too."

"Doc Boyle really didn't need to medevac me. They sewed me up back in Tay Ninh, then a head nurse meaner than First Sergeant Beauchamp kicked me out and said not to come back."

"Boyle expected you'd be halfway to Tokyo by now. So did the chaplain."

"I may still try to work that deal, but for the time being I'm back. So, what's up?"

"The relief column of the 11th ACR got here an hour ago and they're rootin' around in the bush mopping up NVA stragglers," the captain said, taking a long pull on his warm beer.

"We been told they're flying in more ammo, new bunker material, a few more 105 tubes, concertina wire – and that means work details for us," Beauchamp said loudly. Glenn noticed he had a large gauze patch taped over his left ear and it was stained with blood. Nolan guessed he'd probably had an eardrum shattered in the explosion; his own ears were still ringing and he wondered if he hadn't suffered some serious loss of hearing himself. That suddenly worried him, because he hoped to eventually transfer into the Air Force and fly Phantoms.

"Leave it to the Army," Glenn muttered. "We needed that damned wire two days ago."

Beauchamp shrugged and looked back to the yellowed sheet of legal paper that served as the company roster.

General Roberts and an entourage made a beeline for the Charlie company CP; Glenn started to turn and move away but Hobson told him to stand fast, then the commander and the first sergeant got off the culvert and gave the Division commander a salute.

"Captain Hobson," the two-star general said, "your company did a magnificent job here today. Fine job, yes sir, fine job." He looked past what remained of the berm line at the field littered now with NVA dead. There were a few filthy, still dazed Charlie company troops standing nearby and the division commander walked over to them and said with authentic sincerity, "You men performed an amazing feat here today; fantastic job, all of you."

"I'm proud of all you men," the division sergeant major added.

Turning back to Hobson the general said, "While everyone here is a hero in his own right, point out for me those in your command who deserve immediate special recognition."

Hobson looked a little uncomfortable at the idea and glanced at Glenn. "Sir, Lieutenant Nolan here is –"

"Willing to provide names from my platoon and Echo Recon, sir," Glenn interrupted. "One of the attacks came through the point where my platoon and Lieutenant Peters' platoon were tied in. One of my squad leaders – a sergeant Tannahill and one of Recon's sergeants named Lockhart are especially deserving."

"Splendid!" the general said. He spoke quietly to his division sergeant major, who quickly headed back toward the command helicopter. He turned to the battalion commander and said, "perhaps you could provide the names of some of your staff and men from the artillery batteries."

Glenn excused himself, went back to the platoon and sent Sergeant Tannahill back up to the company and stood drinking a warm beer an hour later as a half dozen soldiers stood at awkward attention and had medals affixed to their filthy jungle fatigues. When his platoon sergeant returned, confounded and full of questions as he unpinned the medal, Glenn patted him on the back and gave him another beer. They were talking in low tones when a voice from behind cut him short.

"Lieutenant Nolan. We would like a minute of your time."

He turned and faced two lieutenant colonels in clean, pressed jungle fatigues. Each had camouflaged 1st Cav patches on both their left and right sleeves. One of the officers was a couple inches taller than Glenn, had fair skin, blond hair, piercing blue eyes – his name tag said: **van Noort**. *A Swede, or maybe a Viking*, Nolan thought. The other was a few inches shorter with dark hair and wore wire-rimmed aviator framed glasses.

"I'm the division G-2," the shorter of the two officers said amiably. He spoke with a distinctive New England accent and his appearance reminded Glenn of an English teacher he'd had in high school. The Viking reminded him of Elmer Bright, the varsity football line coach and the only person on any football field or hockey rink that had ever actually scared him. "Colonel van Noort is assistant G-3 and we have some questions for you about the action here, lieutenant. Do you have a few minutes?"

As if a colonel has to ask.... Don't play games with me, colonel... You're not thinking straight at all, Nolan.

He was at the end of his rope – he'd had maybe an hour of sleep in the last twenty-four, had run on an overload of pure adrenaline for several of those hours. He was having a terrible time now staying awake much less thinking. It was like the time in the Florida swamps during Ranger School when he'd wildly hallucinated from lack of food and sleep.

"Sir, most of the last day and night is a jumbled mess in my mind. Some of it's a blank."

"We'll help you sort through that," Galvin said, with a small, friendly smile. "But first thing we want to know is why you didn't want to be decorated by the division commander."

"I never said that, sir."

Galvin and van Noort exchanged quick looks. "It was obvious to General Casey and to General Roberts. The only person who may have thought it wasn't is you."

Glenn took a deep breath. "Sir, to tell the truth, I think our enlisted men don't always get the recognition they deserve. This is a day to balance that out a little. If you're looking for one person to single out in this fight, I suggest you and the generals fly down to the 25th Surgical Hospital in Tay Ninh; look up Sergeant Lockhart from the recon platoon. He earned a medal."

"Still, we'd like to hear your account of the battle, beginning at around midnight."

Glenn sighed, and took a deep breath while gazing down at his blood-spattered boots.

"Colonel, the real story of this fight begins long before that... before LZ Jay got overrun three nights ago. Like Jay, this fight was inevitable. Both firebases were sitting on primary avenues of approach and logistics for the NVA who were camped less than five miles down that road – safely inside Cambodia.

"True," van Noort agreed.

"But that wasn't Colonel Conrad's plan. He didn't want to stay here for two weeks." Glenn nervously lit a cigarette and looked at the two colonels. "Look around this firebase and out toward the tree lines. What do you see?"

"I see a lot of dead NVA," van Noort said.

"What don't you see?" The colonel remained silent, looking puzzled. "What you don't see is any defensive structures. No wire. No decent bunkered defensive positions. I think we whipped them. But at what cost? Why was I defending the perimeter with a half-strength platoon of which half of *them* were new kids who had never fired their M16s? Why did we have so many artillery pieces and so much ammo that we couldn't properly store it? – much of which came here yesterday. We're still counting our dead... and theirs. After action reports are still some time away in the future. I think we'll find that the NVA marched right down that road over there with all that artillery, mortars and men. I wonder why there wasn't anyone or anything there to keep that from happening. Why don't we go across that border? – just once for crying out loud! – and kick their asses good... take away all their toys? Why don't we do that *just once, dammit* before we all go home? I know you have questions... so do I," Glenn said wearily. "I'm tired. For the past month I've been in contact most every day... Maybe only every other day. I've lost count. I'm not complaining – just asking the question.

"Asking – that's the one thing I think I *have* earned from this fight."

Chapter 16

The lone passenger in the Huey, looked out over the sprawling American complex known as Fire Support Base Buttons from his seat in front of the right side door gunner and wondered what he'd done. Glenn's head was still spinning as he gazed at the late afternoon shadows.

What have I gotten into now? The question had dogged him the entire forty minute flight.

That morning, he'd been on patrol with his platoon several miles north of the 1ˢᵗ Cav Division – *Forward* headquarters in a quiet little area of operations north of Phouc Vinh when he'd received a radio call to find a clearing big enough for a UH-1 and turn the platoon over to his sergeant. He was coming out of the field – that's all they would tell him.

The helicopter dropped him off in front of a building with a big sign out front that read:

Welcome to Sông Bé Airfield
REPUBLIC OF VIETNAM
HOME OF THE 2ᴺᴰ BRIGADE
1ˢᵗ CAVALRY DIVISION
BLACK HORSE

He hefted the rucksack over his shoulder and looked at the 1ˢᵗ Brigade order relieving him of duty in C Company, 2ⁿᵈ Battalion 8ᵗʰ Cavalry. and assigning him to 2ⁿᵈ Brigade. He got a ride to brigade headquarters, cooled his heels outside the S-1 office until a major finally talked briefly with him and handed over a two page set of orders with sundry abbreviations and lists of regulations assigning him to 1ˢᵗ Battalion, 6ᵗʰ Cavalry.

"First of the 6ᵗʰ is north of here, down the road a quarter mile," the officer said. "You'll see the signs for battalion headquarters. Report to the XO, Major Cameron."

Glenn scoured the orders. "What exactly is this assignment, Major?"

"They didn't tell you?! Those damned guys in 1st Brigade," the officer said, smirking and shaking his head. "You're the new commander of Alpha company. I can't believe they didn't tell you. Cameron will fill you in on the details. You're the only lieutenant in the brigade commanding a company. Maybe the whole division. Good luck. You're going to need it."

The walk to the battalion went by quickly as his mind filled with thoughts of what he'd tell his father and grandfather in a letter that he wrote and rewrote in his head.

Major Cameron wasn't back from the battalion firebase yet according to a clerk outside his office. Glenn found the unit mess hall and had an early dinner and lingered over several cups of coffee almost until dark. He composed a very brief address to his new command for the change of command ceremony. The ceremony in Germany, when he took over Charlie company from Barry Vickers, had been disappointing in its informality. The fact that he'd been a platoon leader, XO, motor officer, payroll officer, sole instructor... pretty much 'everything' including all the extra duties officer meant the soldiers knew him too well. And, if familiarity didn't always breed contempt it had at least bred indifference when he became the C.O. He hoped for a better launch this time, in this command.

It was close to seven o'clock when Major Cameron returned and sent for him.

"I got a feeling you don't know much about what you're getting into here, lieutenant," the major said as leaned back in his swivel chair and watched Nolan carefully across his desk. They were sitting in Cameron's office and sleeping quarters, thirteen steps below ground level in a nicely appointed underground bunker with that damp musty smell reminiscent of his grandmother's root cellar in the little farmhouse outside Duncannon. "I'm going to be harshly honest with you, Nolan, because I want you to succeed."

"Harsh honesty is appreciated, sir."

"Hope you still think that when I'm done. Smoke?" He offered Glenn a Marlboro and lit one for himself with an old, scarred Zippo. "Tomorrow, you're going to walk into a company that just lost a popular commander and first sergeant two days ago. It would have been bad enough if they had been killed in action, but they weren't. They were relieved by the battalion commander, who is – to be cruelly frank – much disliked by the soldiers of Alpha company."

Glenn felt a knot start to grow in his stomach.

"That's not the whole of it, Nolan. It gets better."

"Better or tougher, sir?" He smiled and tried to sound upbeat, but didn't feel that way.

"The troops in the company are convinced their C.O. was fired so that the battalion commander could bring in a hand-picked replacement in his own mold. That would be you."

"I don't even know the battalion commander's name, sir. I'm sure he doesn't know me."

"It gets better still. You see, the battalion commander doesn't want you in command of Alpha, either. He had someone else in mind."

"Then why am I here, sir?"

"Because someone, somewhere wanted you here. Who and for what reason, I don't have the foggiest idea."

Glenn thought about it. *I'm here because someone has confidence in me and thinks I can handle this... or... because somebody really has it in for me.*

"McInnes was informed of your selection yesterday and immediately flew back here to lodge a complaint with the brigade commander about the process and the selectee, which once again would be you." Cameron blew a smoke ring and watched it dissipate. "You should also know that since taking command of the battalion four months ago, McInnes has relieved every company commander except one – the man who preceded Captain Eaton, the officer you're replacing. Eaton's predecessor had only three weeks left in his tour and escaped being fired."

"You're not painting a very happy picture, Major," Glenn offered, again trying to sound light and cheery but feeling a sweeping anxiety in his gut.

"I don't do 'happy talk', lieutenant. It's not in my kitbag. Brutally honest, remember. There's more. McInnes runs each of the companies."

"Runs the companies? What do you mean, sir?"

"I mean, a company commander in this battalion doesn't command, he asks permission and follows orders to the letter. You'll understand better after talking with him tomorrow, and after you've talked with the staff at the firebase. I suggest you have a long, frank conversation with the S-2, Captain Kimball, assistant S-4, Lieutenant Webb, and the new S-3 Air who's been here about three weeks."

Cameron, Glenn decided, wasn't a fan of this Lieutenant Colonel McInnes. He referred to him by last name only and didn't append the commander's rank. Cameron looked and sounded like a career officer – he talked like a general, not the bottom rung of the field grade ranks. And, most notably, he had provided information that was vital to survival for a brand new company commander. Although the XO had scared the daylights out of him, he'd also provided information that a wise company commander could use to survive. The major was something of a martinet, but he was an ally and Glenn decided he liked Major Cameron. More important, he trusted him – so far. He'd have to wait for his interview with the battalion commander to see if his initial impression was accurate.

That night, he wrote a long letter to his father and another to his grandfather.

* * *

The Huey touched down on the log pad amidst a cloud of reddish clay dust; a lone passenger with a bulging rucksack jumped out, stood on the step of the skid and shouted something to the pilot before stepping back and giving a thumbs-up sign to the crew.

The passenger ducked his head when the UH-1 lifted off. Seconds later the dust cloud dissipated and Glenn Nolan walked through the gate onto LZ Evita.

The firebase had a more entrenched, improved look and feel about it compared to the firebases he'd been on with the 2/8 Cav; but in the end, it was still a primitive patch of dirt claimed from the jungle. The triple strand of concertina wire looked old and rusted but at least it existed, unlike the 'jump LZs' he'd been on with Colonel Conrad. There was even barbed wire around the TOC sitting at the center of the perimeter at the base's highest elevation.

Glenn dropped his rucksack outside the entrance of the Tactical Ops Center, placed his helmet and M16 on top of it and went down the wooden steps into the dark dampness of the operations center. He was surprised at the spaciousness, and the finishing touches of the command bunker.

In the place of dirt floors, someone had put down a level, raised floor made from wooden ammo pallet slats. Rather than a long single pass the width of a Caterpillar blade, the inside was wide; alcoves like small offices with wood slat walls had been created for the staff. The place had seven foot ceilings and seemed like the Pentagon when compared to Illingworth or Ike or any one of the eight forward firebases he'd been on in the last eleven weeks.

A black sergeant E-7 named Overton was standing behind the bank of four large RT-524 radios manned by Spec4 radio operators. He saw Glenn and walked over.

"Can I help you, lieutenant...?"

"Lieutenant Nolan. I'm to see Colonel McInnes or Major Jackson, the S-3."

"They're up in the Charlie-Charlie. Captain Kimball is usually in charge when they're gone but he's out with Bravo company that's bein' logged today. I expect he'll be back in an hour. Only officer is the assistant S-4, Lieutenant Webb down at the log pad probably. Uh, the S-3 Air, Lieutenant Barnes is sleepin' right now. He was up all night."

"Barnes? Benjamin Semmes Barnes? About this tall," Glenn said, holding his hand out flat. "Southern boy, with kind of a twangy voice and a nose that's been broken more than once? Kinda pushed up and off to the side a little. Dark hair and kind of a square shape to his face."

The sergeant's eyes grew a little wider with each additional piece of description. "You sound like you know him, sir."

"If that's the guy, oh yeah. I know him. When did he get here?"

"'Bout three weeks ago, sir."

"That fits. Sergeant, how about you go wake him up for me. Tell him the World's Greatest rugby player, Civil War historian and beer drinker is here to see his sorry carcass."

The sergeant's face grew worried and he looked down, clearing his throat. "Sir, Lieutenant Barnes got off duty this mornin' 'round zero eight hundred after a fourteen hour shift here in the TOC. Respectfully, sir, I don't believe he should be disturbed right now."

Glenn found him in the S-3's little quarters on the south side of the TOC. It too had wooden steps leading down into a small rectangular underground cavern in which there was an Army cot, a camp stool and a wooden table made from mortar ammo boxes. He sat on the stool listening to Benny's steady breathing until finally Barnes rolled over and squinted at him.

"I heard you through the wall, talking with Overton and telling him all that BS." He sat up on the edge of the cot, rubbing his eyes and working the kinks out of his neck. "Man, you talk as loud as Boomer."

"Boomer?"

"Cameron. The XO. Always sounds like he's giving commands at a Regimental parade. I'm sure you met him on your way out here. I wish I could say it's good to see you, but there's an Honor Code I swore to once upon a time. Why are you here?"

"I'm taking command of Alpha company."

Benny looked at him for several long seconds. "Who'd you piss off so bad?"

"So, at Cam Ranh Bay I ran into that sergeant from your company in Augsburg and he worked it out somehow for me to get assigned to the Cav," Benny told him. "At Bien Hoa, they sent me to 2nd Brigade and that's how I ended up here in this sorry ass battalion." It was high noon and they were sitting just inside the perimeter on a stack of C-ration cases, smoking and drinking warm beer from cans. "One of the few things I learned at the 'Trade School on the Hudson' was that a unit mirrors its leader, and that's true here in spades. This *is not* a happy command. And Alpha company is the unhappiest of the bunch."

"Because their C.O. and 1st Sergeant were relieved?"

"It goes back further than that." Barnes looked sideways at him and shielded his eyes from the harsh dry-season sun. "A couple weeks ago, they got into a firefight and one of their guys got hit pretty bad. They called in a medevac but just as it arrived on station, McInnes showed up in his C&C bird and waved them off. He picked up the Alpha company trooper, but the kid died on the way to Sông Bé. The guys in Alpha thought he would have made it if he'd been on the medevac bird with its medic and life-saving equipment. What poured salt in the wound was that McInnes got a second Distinguished Flying Cross for his efforts."

Glenn was astounded.

"Don't know how that happens," Benny said, shrugging. "The guy pressures people under his command to write him up. Sometimes he puts himself in for medals. The word I hear is that he's the most decorated soldier – officer or enlisted – in the whole damned division. Must have somebody in Awards & Decorations at division that's lookin' out for him."

"That stinks."

"And the whole battalion smells of it. I hate being around the man, and I'm not alone. We don't talk about it, but every officer in the battalion is looking for a way to get transferred."

Glenn took a long drag on his cigarette and looked around the busy logistics pad where a detail of shirtless soldiers was stacking supplies headed out to the company being resupplied that day. "Where's A company now?"

"They're holed up on an abandoned firebase called LZ Sally about ten miles northwest of here waitin' for the poor, sorry S.O.B. who's their new commander. Ain't ya glad you came to the party?" Barnes asked sarcastically. "Remember... No Task too Great for '68."

Glenn dropped his cigarette and stepped on it. A lot of things were coming together – like the wary reception he'd received at the company rear area in Sông Bé that morning. He'd had a long talk over coffee with Fitzgerald, the XO, who came across as forced and uncomfortable.

"I know you love a challenge, Knocker. You keep smilin'," Benny told him. "But don't you be the one to befoul the class motto. I'm countin' on you, son."

They had lunch at the battalion mess tent and caught one another up about events since they'd last crossed paths. Benny went back to his nap when the S-2, a plump, nervous infantry captain named John Kimball, returned from his visit to the field shortly after and gave him a ninety minute extemporaneous briefing. It was easily the most comprehensive intelligence summary he'd ever encountered.

"I'm sorry, Nolan, but I'm going to have to cut our little conversation short," Kimball finally said. "I've been gone all day and the evening briefing is only a few hours away. If you have any questions, maybe we can get to them after the briefing."

A few hours later the battalion commander and the S-3 came back to the firebase, but the colonel put off talking to him until after the evening briefing.

"Tomorrow morning, first thing, you'll proceed to LZ Sally and take command of Alpha," Colonel McInnes said, giving him a furtive, unfriendly glance and looking away. He was a small, nervous man with dark, closely set eyes and sharp facial features.

Glenn could hear the generators running outside and the frequent radio traffic through the wall separating the commander's quarters from the TOC. The battalion commander seemed uneasy, as he had been earlier in the afternoon and then again at the evening briefing. His new boss had avoided talking to him or even acknowledging his presence until a half hour after the nightly briefing when Glenn had pressed the issue by asking if it was protocol in the battalion for a newly arrived company commander to officially report in.

This has been a very strange twenty-four hours, Glenn thought.

He had made a quick trip around the firebase after talking with Kimball, had introduced himself to the artillery battery commander and his FDC personnel. Then he'd found the C.O. of Charlie company which was on the firebase providing security. Jeff Wagoner, a stocky captain on his second tour, was friendly enough but steered away from any discussion of command relationships in the battalion, even when Glenn asked jokingly what he needed to do as a brand new company commander to stay on the good side of their boss. Bringing up the name 'McInnes' seemed a sure-fire way to induce silence. Except with one officer – the battalion surgeon, Captain Norm Hadorn.

Glenn had gone to see him in late afternoon to have the stitches in his arm checked. The bandage was seeping a little and had bled through his jungle fatigue sleeve...

"That's gonna leave a nice little souvenir scar when *and if* it heals. You didn't do those stitches yourself, did you Nolan?" Hadorn guffawed loudly. He had a deep bass voice that made his laughter come across like the sound track for a haunted house.

"A nurse at the 25th hospital in Tay Ninh did it for me."

"She clearly wanted you to remember her. And you will. Too bad for your sake that I'm not a plastic surgeon, Nolan. What did you do to make her so angry?" He laughed again as he examined the rest of Glenn's arm. "You've got some jungle rot here, too, in a few spots. Both arms and a couple places on your face. You allergic to soap and water?"

"Not when I can find them. Spent the last month pretty much in the bush. You sure that's jungle rot? I didn't think you could get it until the rainy season."

"Why don't we let me do the diagnosing, lieutenant?"

"You're the doctor."

"That I am. And you're the new company commander replacing Captain Eaton. I think you'll find that an all-consuming occupation."

"Meaning...?"

"Oh, you'll find out soon enough. Have you met the battalion commander yet?" Hadorn asked as he applied a salve to the wound on his upper arm and taped on a new bandage.

"Just in passing. He was preoccupied this afternoon. I expect we'll talk later this evening after the nightly briefing."

"I suppose you will... He's a very difficult man. If you receive any further wounds from your encounter with him, feel free to come see me..."

You need to understand how things work around here, Nolan," Colonel McInnes was saying. "I'm committed to proper command etiquette in this battalion."

"I'm not sure I understand, sir."

"The proper exercise of the chain of command, lieutenant. What I mean is that you report to me and not the XO, S-3 or anyone else. Your orders come from me, directly and solely. The XO handles administrative matters in the battalion rear; the S-3 often transmits tactical information and plans I approve, but I *am* the final authority on all matters."

"I think I understand that, sir."

"Just *thinking* will not suffice. Knowing and complying is my expectation." McInnes glared at him and again looked away. "Your company is not an independent operator in this battalion. You're part of a team and you'll function as such. You *will* ensure any action you take has been either directed or cleared by me. Your company is an asset I use as necessary to accomplish my mission, so each platoon in it belongs to me. Do I make myself clear?"

Glenn had a bad feeling about this and wished he could see the colonel's eyes to try to read his intent. "Perhaps you can give me some examples, sir."

"All right. Each morning you contact me and obtain clearance to move the company. You will be sent an initial objective and report when you've reached it for further instructions. If for some reason, I cannot be reached, you will halt and await further instructions."

"What if the company makes contact, sir?"

"You're permitted to engage the use of artillery through your Forward Observer, but all requests – gunships and Air Force strikes –are managed through me, or the S-3 in my absence."

"What about Pink Teams, sir?"

"Pink Teams have gunships, right? That goes through me. I decide if and where to use assets. If you want or think you need an asset, ask for permission and I'll most likely approve."

"Most likely?!... Sir, if I ask battalion for something it's because I need it."

McInnes turned and stared hard at him through narrowed eyes. "Lieutenant, I'm on my second tour. I've commanded platoons, companies, and now a battalion in combat. I know how this is done far better than a new lieutenant with only two and a half months in-country. If you think you know your job better than me, then we have a problem... Do you and I have a problem, Lieutenant Nolan?"

"You're right, sir. You have more experience than I do," Glenn admitted, not wanting to say they had a problem, but he knew they did – a major one. "Will you be accompanying me to the firebase in the morning for the change-of-command ceremony?"

McInnes was suddenly flustered; his face turned red and he sputtered, "No, no... of course not. Ceremonies like that are for the garrison... there's a war, going on, Nolan!"

"Yes, sir, I realize that. I just thought that since it was a firebase that –"

"Out of the question, I'm afraid. It's an abandoned firebase, after all, and I have a lot to do in the morning. I can't possibly go to Sally with you."

"I understand, sir." He sighed, deeply disappointed in their conversation. "There is one other thing, colonel. I need to bring it up... about my first sergeant position. I understand that's vacant now, or has it been filled?"

This question, too, seemed to catch McInnes by surprise and his face flushed once again. "I, uh, Major Cameron is addressing that. He'll have an answer soon. I'll tell you who your new first sergeant is when I'm ready."

"The enlisted men should be informed as soon as –"

"Damn you, Nolan! I said I would let you know. But... it reminds me that I should point out that *all* personnel matters must be approved at battalion level."

"All, sir?"

"All is a universal affirmative, lieutenant. All means all. You will not move or promote or do any other personnel action with the soldiers in Alpha company without my approval."

Well that really does it! Nolan thought. *I'm left with no authority, no prerogatives, nothing I can do without this guy's approval. This isn't commanding a company.* He was blown away by the sheer absurdity of what this colonel was telling him. It seemed impossible! It *had* to be. *What he's demanding won't work. When people require the clearly impossible – and this is, isn't it Nolan? – then folks find a way to work around it. Maybe Cameron and the S-3 already have. Don't do anything right now. Sleep on it. Things will be different in the morning.*

Discouraged, he left the commander's quarters moments later. He found Benny inside the TOC and asked him to take a break and step outside for a smoke. They walked down the hill in the dark, past the Aid Station twenty-five or thirty yards from the TOC where they had a little privacy. He told Benny about his conversation with McInnes and asked what he thought of it.

"You're in deep mushroom soil, my man."

"I know that. I'm looking for some advice. You owe me that."

"I do?!"

"Let me count the ways, starting with the jungle phase of Ranger School down at Eglin. You remember that?"

"You're just S.O.L., friend," Benny said, as he crouched down and lit a cigarette. "There's only one thing you can do – probably the same thing Eaton did. Do what's right by the troops. Be the company commander, not the company water boy, or the company go-fer. Yeah, you're gonna get in hot water. Hell, you'll probably get relieved. There's worse things. You weren't all that high on a military career anyhow, right?"

The quiet, hollow echo from outside the berm instantly caught his attention. It was followed immediately by another.

"Incoming!" Glenn yelled at the top of his lungs. "Incoming!"

The call was echoed across the firebase and seconds later the sounds of the first sharp explosions rippled across LZ Evita. Two more explosions erupted as an illumination round burst overhead. For the next ten minutes, Evita was bathed in light; he'd counted four rounds total from the nearby woods, lasting at most thirty seconds. Five minutes later he'd sat down with his back against his rucksack and lit a Marlboro. The battalion commander emerged from his quarters and looked around. "All clear?" he called out. "Is it all clear?!"

"All clear, colonel," he heard someone respond.

Must be nice to have overhead cover, Glenn thought. There was a yelp nearby and then some cursing and thrashing around in the barbed wire surrounding the TOC. Glenn got up and went over toward the noise. He found Colonel McInnes snagged in wire.

"Let me give you a hand," Glenn said. The illumination round went out before the colonel turned to look at him. McInnes then wandered down the hill toward the Aid Station. Several minutes later, Glenn heard angry voices in an argument.

"I'm not going to do it!"

"I'm ordering you to, Doctor." The first voice belonged to the battalion surgeon and the second was the battalion commander. The argument went back and forth. Then a figure came back up the hill in the darkness and disappeared inside McInnes' quarters.

Glenn decided to wander down to the aid station and found Doc Hadorn inside drinking.

"You okay, Doc?" he asked, sitting across the table from the surgeon.

"That son-of-a-bitch!" Hadorn took a big gulp from the bottle. "He wants me to write him up for another Purple Heart. That clumsy bastard cut himself on some barbed wire and tried to convince me he was wounded while directing counter-battery fire against the attack. I bet there wasn't any more than a half dozen mortars fired at us. Got half a mind to prefer charges against that son-of-a-bitch. You see anything, Nolan?"

"Didn't see much... You ought to take it easy on that bottle, Doc."

Chapter 17

"So, Mr. Nolan, did you and this Donut Dollie find you had a lot in common back there on Firebase Buttons?" Sergeant Syzmanski asked over the intercom as they climbed away from the 2nd Brigade headquarters headed for LZ Evita.

Brad looked over his shoulder and saw the crew chief grinning at him from his position in the right side gunner's well. "What are you doing on that side, chief?"

"You seem to be flying with a heavy right foot today, Mr. Nolan, and it was awful windy on the left side today. I decided to exercised my rights as senior enlisted man to switch places in my own ship."

Brad took the controls from Norton and put the Huey out of trim so the crew chief got the full brunt of the ninety knot airflow. "Sorry, chief, what was that? Too much wind noise coming through your mic to get what you said."

"I said I wish you'd let Mr. Norton fly. At least he knows how to keep my bird in trim."

"Little chilly for you back there, Syzmanski?" Brad said over the intercom and then tuned in the artillery advisory frequency on the FM radio.

This was the type mission Brad hated most – all day taxi service. And this was the worst of the worst: a pre-dawn departure and only one passenger. He knew they had a day of absolute boredom ahead of them – short hops and long stretches of sitting around waiting for their passenger to show back up. She was a nurse with the newly established hospital at Phouc Vinh on a tour of the 2nd Brigade and each battalion's medical facilities. At least this would give Norton a look at all the firebases and hopefully that would end these daily orientations for him.

"What does a fella find to talk about with a round eyed girl while he's sittin' on an open air crapper for ten minutes of uninterrupted chit-chat?" Syzmanski asked.

"Give it a rest, chief. And I'd better not hear anything about this back in the company."

An advisory came over the FM frequency.

"...one-oh-five artillery firing now out of LZ Lolita, azimuth 258 – impacting grid Yankee Uniform two-one-two-four – max ord three-five hundred..."

Nolan pulled the map out the bottom pocket of his nomex trousers and located the coordinates of the grid square then passed it to his co-pilot. "Lolita is over there about ten miles, and the rounds are impacting over there," he said, pointing toward where he could make out tiny brown puffs of smoke two thousand feet below and to their right front. "First few days out this sounds confusing, I know, but in a couple of weeks it'll be like you've been doing it all your life."

"Max ord? What's that?" the new pilot asked.

"Highest point the rounds reach in flight. Stay above that or away from the gun-target line. You've got the controls. We'll skirt the area to the west. Stay about five miles out from the artillery strikes. Everybody keep your eyes peeled for Max and fast movers."

"Huey, nine o'clock low," the left side door gunner said on intercom, "five miles."

Brad saw the helicopter below them, which soon passed close enough for him to recognize the art on the battery cover – it was Tuttle and Schoepf who had drawn the C&C mission with the 1/8. He switched to the UHF radio and pressed the floor switch. "Ghostrider one-two this is Ghostrider one-four on company at your twelve o'clock high. Got the advisory of arty out of Lolita… Sitrep?"

"Ghostrider one-four, we've got a Blue Duke element – Coral Lighter - in contact with estimated NVA company plus. We're en route with Blue Duke 6 and ALO aboard. Section of guns and medevac off Buttons, five minutes out."

'Roger. We'll stay well clear to the west. Call if you need help."

"One-two, out."

Brad pulled the small booklet of 1st Cav signal instructions out of his pocket and leafed through the pages until he located the callsigns and frequencies for the 1/8 Cav battalion; he dialed in the *Coral Lighter* company frequency and said to Norton, "We're up the freq of the infantry company that's in contact. There are always three frequencies that get busy when a grunt company gets in a firefight – the internal company freq, the battalion freq and the artillery." Their headphones were filled with the noises of rifle and machine gun fire, and frantic chatter back and forth between troops on the ground; some voices were calm but most were high pitched and laced with fear. Someone was reporting movement and then the voice was drowned out by a long burst from a machine gun.

In the midst of it came the measured tones and whine of turbines from a Cobra gunship.

"Coral Lighter four-one, this is Blue Max two-five…"

"Guns and Air Force FACs work the infantry company frequency," Brad said, and then added, "usually, that is. Depends a lot on the experience of the grunt CO on the ground, I guess – or the battalion CO. The battalion C.O. running the 1/8 Cav, Lieutenant Colonel Musgrove, likes to do it all by himself – kind of a glory hog. A real jerk. None of us like flying C&C for him. Tarzan drew the short straw today and got stuck with it. You probably heard him bitching this morning; don't blame him. Even this 'ash and trash' mission we pulled is better than being stuck as C&C with an asshole like that."

"Ash and trash, did you say?" a female voice said over the intercom. "I've been called worse by better pilots."

Brad turned quickly and looked directly behind his seat and saw the nurse smiling at him, tilting her head with the innocent look of somebody's kid sister. Two short pigtails of dirty blond hair trailed out from behind the earphones she had on over her cap; a small mic on a thin wire boom was positioned close to her lips. She appeared to be enjoying the look on his face.

"I always carry a headset and a Y-cord when I fly so I know what the hired help is talking about," the young girl said. "This isn't my first rodeo."

"I didn't mean –"

"Of course you did."

Brad threw a withering glance at the door gunner on his side who simply shrugged and raised his hands in a futile gesture. "It's just a saying, part of the lingo."

"I know *exactly* what it is, Mr. Nolan. Don't let me distract you from your duties."

"That wasn't meant personally, Miss, ah…"

"Captain… Captain Jennifer Kolarik. And for your information, I'm a surgical nurse, not a Donut Dollie." She continued to smile and give him an expectant look.

"All right, you got me. Point made."

"*Coral Lighter four-one, this is Medevac three-three on your push – we're five minutes out but have to turn around and head back with a chip detector light. We'll call Buttons and get them to bounce another bird… Sorry.*"

Immediately, a loud, panicked voice of the ground commander came through the FM radio over the sounds of gunfire. "*Medevac three-three, this is Lighter four-one, you can't go back man! I got three wounded – two serious and one critical! Damn you, don't you leave me!*"

"*Three-three here. Got to put the ship on the ground as soon as I can with this chip light. Another bird will be here in about two-five mikes.*"

"*Damn it, medevac, my men aren't going to last that long!*"

"Mister Nolan! Get me down there!" the nurse's voice intruded over the intercom.

"Sorry, " Brad said. "I can't take a passenger down into that."

"You can and you will!"

"No I won't. You hear that firefight and see the artillery impacting? There's no place to land except out in the open, right between the friendlies and the gooks who are firing at them."

"That's a piss poor excuse, Nolan."

Brad turned and glared at the girl. "Listen up... captain. I'm the Aircraft Commander and I'm responsible for the safety of my crew and this bird... and, I might remind you, all the passengers as well. That includes you."

"Then I relieve you of the responsibility for my safety."

"It doesn't work that way, lady."

"I'm the senior officer on board this aircraft and I'm ordering you to –"

"It doesn't work that way, either. Inside this bird, nobody – not a four star general and certainly not some nurse – can override my decisions. I'm responsible for getting you and my crew back home alive."

She looked furious and stared harshly at him. "Those boys down there are going to die because of you."

"Neither of us knows exactly what's going to happen to the wounded."

"Am I the only one on board wearing pants?!" the nurse asked insistently, looking around at all four of the crew. "A grunt is the only reason for a helicopter's existence... and you guys have only one real purpose: to help him. It's too damned bad some birds never get to fulfill their true mission in life, simply because someone forgot that fact... *Mr.* Nolan. Three lives down there and we're the *only* ones who can help! Now's the time to man up."

Brad continued to stare back, and finally said, "If anything happens to you –"

"Nothing's going to happen – trust me."

"Yeah, that's what they always say just before the excrement hits the rotating air ventilator. When we land, you *will* stay inside the bird and let them bring the wounded to us – that is non-negotiable, *captain.* I've got it, Norton."

*This is **not** a good idea, son,* Brad said to himself as he took the controls, selected the UHF frequency then bottomed the collective; he turned hard left and began a tight downward spiral. "Ghostrider one-two this is one-four, I've got medical personnel on board and we'll go in for the wounded. Get your ALO to shut down that arty until we're clear. We'll contact the ground commander and coordinate with Max to cover us." Brad had Norton put him up on the infantry company's frequency. "Coral Lighter four-one, this is Ghostrider one-four a few miles north of you with medical personnel on board. We'll be there in a couple of minutes to pick up your wounded. Understand you have three to be lifted out. Be ready – we won't be on the ground long. Pop smoke now closest to the wounded where we need to land."

"*Smoke is out,*" came the call scant seconds later.

"One-four identifies goofy grape smoke. Understand the bad guys are to your south at the other side of the open field along the tree line."

"*Roger, Ghostrider... and some along that other line of trees to the east, about fifty yards. But the main attack is on our west flank.*"

"Max two-five, Ghostrider one-four on *Lighter* fox-mike, we're the slick five, six miles north of the purple smoke turning final for landing north to south to pick up wounded. Can you suppress the wood line a hundred yards south of the smoke, and also to the east?"

"*Ghostrider one-four, this is Blue Max two-five, have you in sight. Will make our run from east to west. Call one minute out.*"

"Roger, we're now ninety seconds... Coral Lighter, you get that?"

"*Got it Ghostrider. Which direction are you landing?*"

"One-four... We'll be approaching directly over you, north to south and then landing facing east right on top of your smoke. Make sure you have your troops cease fire when we get there. In fact, do that now." He heard Norton say, 'pre-landing check is good' and then he keyed the intercom. "We'll come in over the trees and do a left pedal turn. Clynch, the friendlies will be on your side when we land. *Do not* unstrap and get out... Ski, the gooks'll be out your side when we get over the tree line. Once I turn ninety degrees, you're cleared to fire on the far wood line. When we depart, there'll be gooks both to our right and to the front."

Both door gunners acknowledged, and Brad keyed the FM radio. "Blue Max this is Ghostrider, one minute from touchdown." He heard the acknowledgement and began to slow the Huey as they reached tree top level. The open field in front of the infantry company disappeared from view as Brad picked his way forward, slowing his airspeed with the skids of the aircraft almost in the trees. He felt naked and exposed going this low and slow.

"*Ghostrider, this is Lighter four-one we are cease fire and you're directly overhead.*"

The open field suddenly appeared and he saw the last of the purple smoke from the grenade. He slipped the Huey over the tree line with a hard left pedal turn, swinging the nose of the aircraft around. Descending straight down while leveling the Huey, he heard Syzmanski yell 'clear down' as he searched through the chin bubble for obstructions below. Suddenly, with a jolt, they were on the ground. His heart was racing as the smell of burnt kerosene and pale wisps of purple smoke invaded the aircraft cabin. When he looked out his side window, he saw the nurse running toward the troops emerging from the trees.

"Damn that girl!" he yelled, but the noise from Syzmanski's machine gun in the right gunner's well overrode the sound of his voice.

She took the IV bottle from the medic whose uniform was covered in blood and held it up as the four men carrying the soldier between them on a poncho struggled toward the aircraft. Brad leaned forward to get a better view and heard an explosion just behind his head. Quickly he looked around but saw no damage inside; Norton's face was white as a sheet and he'd scrunched down as far as he could go below the seat's armor side plate. Through Norton's window Brad could see the far tree line erupt when the second Cobra salvoed his rockets. As the gunship pulled up and started a climbing left turn, the nurse reached Nolan's ship, got inside and helped place the wounded soldier on the deck. She raised the bench seat to make room for the other two and as soon as they were on board, Brad keyed the intercom. "Pitch pull in three, two... Ski, keep an eye out!"

"... taking beaucoup fire from two o'clock, Mr. Nolan!"

The Huey shuddered as he cleared the trees in front of him by inches and tucked the nose of the Huey, climbing and turning hard left away from the enemy guns. "Everybody all right back there?" he asked as they passed through a hundred feet and continued to turn.

"I think we took some rounds through the tail," the crew chief told him. "I don't know where else... that first aid kit next to you got it good."

Brad turned his head and saw the shattered remains of the canvas kit attached on the bulkhead at eye level next to his helmet. *That was the explosion*, he thought, and then realized the round must have come through the aircraft from that far tree line and struck just at the instant he moved his head to get a better look at that nurse while she was outside the ship – against his orders. If he hadn't moved... *That was way too close*, he told himself, and then forced the thought from his mind.

They leveled off at fifteen hundred feet headed toward Sông Bé; Brad felt his pulse dropping to something more normal and his breathing beginning to slow. *Stupid to let that girl talk me into that*, he thought. *Only one of these guys looks like he's got a chance to make it.*

"We have to get these guys to the operating rooms at Phuoc Vinh," he heard the nurse say over the intercom. Brad turned his head to look; her face and the front of her fatigues were splattered with blood. She had put her headset back on and reconnected, and now was putting pressure on the gauze bandage slathered with Vaseline placed on the bloody chest of one of the soldiers. "The med detachment at Buttons can't handle this. ETA to Phuoc Vinh?"

"Twenty, twenty-five minutes," he replied.

"Can't you go any faster?"

"We're red-lined now. This is all she'll do. It's already bumpy as hell."

She gazed at the faces of the young soldiers – they looked nineteen, twenty at the most. she removed a stethoscope and blood pressure cuff from her medical bag, fumbled with them and gave up the idea of taking anything but their pulses. "I need to talk to my hospital. Put me on FM 39.80," she said, looking at each of the soldiers' dog tags. Norton gave her a thumbs up when he set the radio and she made a call. "Papa Vic Surge Five Ops, this is Polock Jenny."

"*Jenny, this is operations. Go ahead*," came the almost immediate reply.

"I'm inbound with three wounded. ETA twenty minutes. Most critical is a sucking chest wound – pulse one forty-five and weak. He's type A-negative and has lost a lot of blood. We'll need at least three units, maybe more. I know we're short of A-neg but I can be a donor; check around to see who else is. Have our best surgical team scrubbed and ready when we get there. Patient number two has a leg wound with a lot of bleeding. Tourniquet is applied at the top of his thigh. Blood type O-positive. Pulse one-thirty. Patient three has a shoulder wound. Blood type A-positive. Pulse one zero four. None are ambulatory. Will advise five minutes out."

"Jenny, this is ops, we'll have triage set up when you get here."

"No time for that – I've already done it," the nurse said as she marked each of the patients with a number from one to three in blood on their foreheads. "You tell my nurses to prep all three surgical rooms, and hang four units of O-neg in each if we don't have the blood types I gave you. When I get there, I expect to see three waiting gurneys, surgeries prepped and all the sponge counts, laps counts, sharps counts and instrument counts done and already signed off! You got that?"

"Yes, ma-am!"

"Jenny, out."

The radio call sapped all of her strength; she spent the remainder of the flight knelt over the soldier with the chest wound, applying pressure to his dressing and listening to his breathing with her ear pressed against his chest. When Brad turned to look at the scene in the cabin behind him the girl looked up with weary eyes, then went back to talking to the soldier with the chest wound over the sound of the rotor blades and the noise of wind whipping through the helicopter's cabin.

When Brad landed at the 5th Surgical Hospital helipad, there were a dozen medical personnel there waiting; the patients were off-loaded onto gurneys and whisked inside the Quonset huts. The nurse waited until they were all on the way to surgery and then walked over to the helicopter's left door and stood on the skid step. She looked at Brad through watery eyes and mouthed the words: "Thank you" before giving him a quick kiss on the cheek.

And then she was gone.

"I think I'm in love, Norton, even if she is Polock," Brad said over the intercom after getting clearance from the tower to reposition from the hospital pad to POL for refueling before shutting down in the Ghostrider area. "Syzmanski, you know what's dumber than one polock?"

"I don't know, Mr. Nolan," the crew chief said. "Two warrant officers, maybe?"

"That's real clever. I was going to offer Norton to help clean all that blood off the deck of your bird, but probably not now." Brad thought about the nurse – *one gutsy little gal.*

"That girl made the flight interesting, didn't she, Norton? For a minute there I thought you might just win the Magnet Ass Award again… something you *will* avoid at all costs when flying with me. Now you've only got three hundred fifty-one days and a wake-up until you get back to the 'land of indoor plumbing'. You're almost on the back side of the curve."

Brad glanced at his watch. *Wow... Mission complete and it's only nine o'clock. Nap this afternoon. Hot shower before dinner and catch the Filipino band at the Red Hawk. Easy day in the Nam. I could get used to this. Maybe I should stop back by the hospital and check on those patients... look up that cute little nurse...*

*   *   *

From his seat on the left side of the helicopter, Glenn looked down on LZ Sally as the Huey made a circling approach over the firebase and landed. The place was a mess.

What do you expect from an abandoned firebase? he asked himself. Illingworth had looked worse when he'd returned from Tay Ninh early in the morning of the attack – and that firebase had been occupied at the time. And for four days afterward. He remembered the cleaned, pressed and spit-shined captain who had approached Sergeant Tannahill and demanded he pull together a detail to police the firebase. It was all Glenn could do to keep from strangling the officer. The captain had backed off and was never seen again.

But now, LZ Sally and Alpha company were his assignment.

He climbed out of the helicopter with his rucksack slung over a shoulder and looked around. *Not real promising, Nolan.* His uniform was new, except for the jungle boots he'd had since arriving in country. His patches were sewn on his jungle fatigues according to regulation. He wondered if he looked like a REMF to the soldiers of his new command. *Probably.*

After loading a solitary soldier onboard, the helicopter lifted off, blasting him with dust. He walked up the hill, through an opening in the rusted barbed wire, and headed for a shallow trench which sat under a poncho spread between four rusted engineer stakes. Three bare-chested soldiers lounged in the shade next to PRC-77 radios with long whip antennas. One of the troops looked up indifferently and drawled:

"Can I hep ya, looo-tenant?"

"Maybe," Glenn said slowly. He dropped his rucksack and placed his M16 on it. "I'm Lieutenant Nolan, your new commander. Is this the company CP?"

The large black soldier blinked his eyes and sat bolt upright; another soldier, a thin, dark-haired boy with a scraggly beard looked at him apprehensively.

"Yep. This is HQ. Welcome aboard, LT."

"I appreciate it," Glenn replied easily. "Who's in charge here on the firebase?"

"Well, lieutenant, since you're the C.O., seems that'd be you now, dontcha reckon?"

Glenn looked back on him with a tight-lipped grin. "What's your name?"

"Gordon, lieutenant. Ewell Brown Gordon. That's *EB*. I'm the company CP RTO."

"Ewell Brown? You're not named after Stonewall Jackson's senior commander by chance? And Brown? Not *the* John *Brown* Gordon of the 6th Alabama? You tough enough to carry that kind of weight?

"I am, in fact."

Where you from?"

"Vicksburg."

"You folks down there still refusing to celebrate the 4th of July?"

EB gave him a crooked smile. "Since 1864, LT... seems you know a mite about southern history, but you talk like a yankee."

"I'm from all over." Glenn turned to a skinny kid with a ghostly pale complexion and a Guy Fawkes goatee. He looked very nervous. "What's your name and where are you from?"

"Specialist 4 Holmes, sir. I'm the RTO for the Battalion net. From Maine. Caribou."

"That's close enough to walk to Canada and bypass all this silly damned foolishness over here," EB said. "He might be a Holmes but he ain't no *Sherlock* Holmes."

Glenn ignored the comment asked the hulking black soldier, "And you?"

"I'm the Five-mike, lieutenant. Folks call me 'Heavy."

"Folks also call him Fatty – Blob – dumplin' – lead bottom, and brisket, too," EB offered. "The thing nobody calls him is late for chow. The boy, he looks like a damned pack mule in the bush carrying three cases of C's on top of his ruck each log day."

The hulking black man smiled blithely. "Them is what you calls me, EB."

"What do call yourself?" Glenn asked.

"I like 'em all, but 'Heavy' is good, lieutenant. Folks back home always called me that."

"And where's home?"

"Chicago."

"Not much like this is it?" Glenn observed looking around the firebase and the surrounding jungle. "You're a long way from home."

"Ain't we all, lieutenant?... ain't we all?"

"You got that right," EB said sarcastically, pulling out a pack of cigarettes and lighting one. "Smoke lieutenant? Ah always like to be on the right side of the military brass. What do folks call you, LT?"

"It all depends." EB's question gave him an idea. *One thing this outfit needs is a new identity – one they choose for themselves.* "Ewell Brown, call up all the platoon leaders and have them stop by here right now so we can get to know one another. Before you do that... tell me where we have OPs out around LZ Sally." They all looked at him with blank expressions. "We don't have any or you don't know?"

"A little of both," EB replied.

"You'll know that from now on. I expect my two RTOs to know everything that's going on in the company. I mean everything. Now, call the platoon leaders."

Over the next few minutes, they wandered down the shallow hill toward the CP, and Glenn saw his first indications of problems.

Of his three company officers, only one was on the firebase – one had gone to Evita on the ship that brought him in while another had gone to Sông Bé the day before – his platoon sergeant didn't know why. Only the 1st platoon leader, Lieutenant Pete Rankin, was on hand. Even the artillery forward observer had taken off to visit with his battery headquarters on LZ Evita. Staff Sergeant Hansen, an older looking NCO with a thick full mustache represented 2nd platoon while a tall thin black Sergeant named Connie Pratt stood in for 3rd platoon; according to Benny, Pratt was one of the best platoon sergeants in the battalion.

His first meeting with the officers in his command was a bust. He'd have to wait until they all came back and do this all over again. It told him something, and it didn't sit well. He led them over to the berm and introduced himself.

"Lieutenant Nolan. Until two days ago, I was in 1st Brigade – Charlie company, 2nd battalion 8th Cav along the border near Tay Ninh. I was a platoon leader in that battalion for the past couple of months until they pulled me out of the field and sent me here. This is a new outfit for me and I don't know anybody here in the 1/6 Cav except the S-3 Air, Lieutenant Barnes. But I look forward to getting to know you and doing the job here. You have any questions for me?"

He watched them for a moment as they shifted uncomfortably and glanced furtively at one another. The silence grew awkward.

"Well, I've got some questions for you, but first I'll address the elephant in the china shop. Here's what I've been told about the company. I was told Colonel McInnes relieved the previous company commander and the first sergeant four days ago – the reason told me was that they had a drinking problem. I was also told that Captain Eaton was popular and the men in the company weren't happy about his being relieved. Since I don't know either Colonel McInnes or Captain Eaton, or the first sergeant, I can't pass judgment, and I don't care to. In a few days we're going back into Indian country and my total attention will be on the two most important jobs of a company commander in the Cav – killing gooks and keeping American troopers alive in the process. I expect that to be your priorities, too." He couldn't tell how they had received this by the looks on their faces. "Now to my questions. First - what's going on in the jungle around this firebase from the berm out to a kilometer from where we are?"

Again they were silent.

"Alpha came onto Sally four days ago. How many patrols have been run to clear the area around the perimeter... Lieutenant Rankin?"

"We ran a last light patrol the first day... haven't run any since."

"No squad or platoon patrols? Aerial reconnaissance?" Rankin shifted uncomfortably, and the sergeants looked down or away. "You can't stay in one place for long and not do active patrolling without setting yourself up for an ass-kicking from the NVA. We're fixing that today. " He turned toward the CP and got Holmes' attention. "Call battalion and get a Pink Team out here right away. And while you've got 'em on the horn, tell them to send our artillery F.O. back out here right now. I've got some missions for him to fire."

"Sir," Sergeant Pratt began, "A couple days ago, Lieutenant Thorgier asked the battalion C.O. about operatin' around the LZ, but got told to sit tight and not do anything until he received orders."

"I'll take that up with the colonel when I see him. Until then, we patrol each morning and afternoon, starting today." Glancing around at their faces, he continued, "How would you rate the morale in the unit right now?"

"It's been better," Sergeant Hansen said evenly to break the silence.

"That doesn't tell me much, sergeant. On a scale of one to ten with ten being the best possible, what is it?"

"Maybe a three or a four."

"Lieutenant Rankin?"

"I'd give it about the same – a three."

Glenn turned to Pratt who looked like he was in a good mood – he'd had a smile on his dark face the whole time. "Depends on what's happenin'... and when you're askin'... and who you askin'. In third platoon, it's about a five or six right now. Three weeks ago, it was a seven or eight, but hit about zero when we lost Hawley two weeks ago." Glenn knew Hawley was the soldier who'd died in McInnes' C&C ship on the way to Sông Bé. "Folks in third platoon is kinda in the middle, waitin' to see how the new 'six' works out."

Glenn nodded and looked around the firebase and saw that almost every eye in the company was on the group of leaders – maybe just on him. "You're saying the morale of the company depends pretty much on whether or not I've got my shit together."

Pratt gave him a broad, toothy smile. "That'd be about right, Six."

"The rest of you agree with Sergeant Pratt?" Glenn asked, looking at each face. They nodded solemn agreement. "Frankly, I'm startled at your optimism about the company's morale. Knowing what little I do about the situation here, I'll be pleasantly surprised if the morale is as high as you told me. I hope you're right. But one thing I know you're *not* right about is that morale will be high if I have my act together.

"I do have my shit together, but the people most directly affecting the morale of the individual soldier in Alpha is his squad leader; next to that his platoon sergeant, then platoon leader and finally me. We all have to have our acts together – day in, day out, twenty-four seven. I'm gonna do my part. You need to do yours, too. Not for me," Glenn said slowly, and then swept his hand around the firebase, "but for them. *Do not* cut me any slack when it comes to doing my job, because I damn sure won't cut you any in doing yours. Are we clear on that? You got a problem with that or anything else about the way I do my job, you come to me – don't talk behind my back, especially to *our* troops. In the midst of the fight is not the time to bow up your back. But afterwards... I love to talk to soldiers – about tactics, strategies, their girlfriends back home, Joe Namath... whatever. Are we clear? We'd better be, because that's what I'm about to tell your squad leaders... Which is our best platoon?"

Instantly Connie Pratt said, "Third platoon, sir."

"Sergeant Pratt. Send a squad to the CP at 1300 for a patrol. I want to take a tour of the AO all the way around Sally. I want the patrol leader to brief me on his plan thirty minutes before we go out. I want to talk to all the platoon sergeants and squad leaders as a group in fifteen minutes and after that, I'll be walking around the firebase talking with the troops." He saw Specialist Holmes waving at him, trying to get his attention. "What is it, Holmes?"

"Battalion wants to know why we need a Pink Team."

"Tell them we have NVA observing our activities." Glenn looked back to the group of his leaders. "That's not a lie, it's an educated guess. With us being here out in the open for four days, they're watching. If not, they should be."

*   *

The patrol filtered out of the jungle into the cleared area around LZ Sally. They were soaked with sweat and shuffled along like the tired soldiers they were after three hours in the blistering heat at the end of the dry season.

"Sergeant Parolini, debrief at the company CP in a half hour," Glenn said, wiping his face. He walked up the hill to where EB and Holmes sat smoking, removed his soaked boonie hat and wiped his forehead with a sleeve. The company XO, and two sergeants awaited him.

"Here's the info you wanted summarized," Fitzgerald said, handing over a folder, "and this is our supply sergeant. Sergeant Kaiser was out on a run yesterday morning when you came by and I thought he should hear direct from you what your expectations are in his area."

Glenn looked at the supply sergeant who gave him a cocky smile; behind him, standing quietly was a heavyset black E-7. "And you, sergeant – what can I do for you? Didn't I run into you yesterday morning in the TOC at Evita?"

"We did meet, sir," Sergeant Overton said. "I just been assigned to your company as the First Sergeant. We need to talk, sir."

"You're right. And we have a lot to talk about. Welcome to Alpha company, Top. Grab an ammo box and sit in on this." Glenn quickly perused the pages in the file folder and then looked at his supply sergeant. "Got a few challenges for you, Sergeant Kaiser. When it comes to company supply, here's what I *don't* want – I don't want a soldier in this company to ever have to pay for a beer or a cigarette or a soda or a candy bar or writing paper. We all know that an Army travels on its stomach, so I need you to supplement the usual C-Rations with a case of LRRP rations per squad every log day. That's supplement, not a replacement."

"Sir, those things are impossible to get," Sergeant Kaiser replied quickly.

"I've heard. But I've had 'em and I like 'em, and so will the troops in Alpha company. You might want to check with a Sergeant Bagstad in Charlie company, 2/8 Cav to see where he gets them. Right now he's in Phouc Vinh while his battalion is on Palace Guard... I also need more firepower. We're only allotted four M60s by T.O.&E – one per platoon with a spare in the rear. I require one per squad, so that's nine in the field and two spares for Specialist Agnew to work on in the rear. Up the ammo draw for log days, too. I also need three more PRC77s."

"That's a lot to ask, lieutenant," Kaiser said.

"Not really. That's just for starters. Here's the upside: I'm offering you the chance to travel and see this beautiful country from top to bottom as you trade your way from I Corps through the Delta. I won't be surprised if this is not only the first but the last time you and I see one another face to face until you DEROS."

Kaiser frowned, thinking. "I'll need some good trading material."

"I don't have any to give you right now, Sergeant Kaiser. We'll work on it from this end as best we can but you're going to have to be a little creative. That's not a license to steal; but bending the rules is the mark of a good supply sergeant." The initial surprise had worn off and he could see on Kaiser's face he was turning things over in his mind. "As far as the machine guns go, I don't need all of them at one time. As soon as you find one and Agnew gets it ready, send it out to the field." Glenn looked at his XO and supply sergeant. "Any questions?"

"Who's going to carry all that machine gun ammo?" Kaiser asked.

"We are – every one of us. Except for the RTOs and medics, each man including me and the first sergeant will carry M60 ammo." Glenn ran his eyes over Fitzgerald who stared back at him apprehensively. "All right, you two get on with it. Let me talk to my new topkick."

Glenn led the black NCO to the side of the firebase where they sat down on wooden artillery ammo boxes. He saw Overton had Cav patches sewn on both sleeves. That, along with the three chevrons up and two rockers down, told him important things about the man's life.

"Sergeant Overton, we have some interesting times ahead of us, you and I. The Cav we're in now is probably very different than the one you served in on your last tour." The sergeant nodded his head in agreement. "When were you here?"

"May '67 through April 68, sir."

"That puts you here during the Tet '68 Offensive and the relief of Khe Sanh."

"That's right, sir. I been back this time since early October."

"Seven months almost. All that time with this battalion?" Overton nodded affirmatively. "Did you volunteer for this job or draw the short straw?"

"I asked for it. Been wantin' a first sergeant slot for a while, and then 1st Sergeant Reed got sent down the road. After you showed up, I talked with Lieutenant Barnes."

"I have a rule about Barnes," Glenn said. "Believe only half of what he tells you, and check that closely. So, even after talking with my old pal you volunteered."

"I liked what I heard, sir."

"Let me tell you some things you may not like. You probably already know this. It's about the company – my first impressions." Glenn lit a cigarette. "The 1st Cav you were in a couple of years back was mainly volunteers – professional soldiers, old school. That's changed. Almost all of the troopers in this company are draftees, including most of the NCOs. That doesn't mean they're inferior – in fact, I learned this morning that one of them was drafted out of a successful business he'd started himself. What it does mean is that they're not dedicated to the Army, and certainly not to this war since the president declared we're calling it quits and going home. Right now, in Alpha, I don't know how much that affects their ability to soldier. I had a lot of draftees in my platoon before I came here, and they performed magnificently. But we were pretty much in daily contact, so everybody was on edge and in survival mode. That makes a difference. I went out on patrol with a squad from third platoon and it went okay. They were a little cavalier, but you never really know how good a unit is until the first round goes off. I read the S-2 Journal and the Communications Log yesterday in the TOC. Seems like contact has fallen off in the last month, so that may account for some of what I saw."

"Sir, there's some hard feelings in Alpha toward the battalion commander."

"Yeah, I know all about that. As I walked the perimeter for the first time and talked with the troops, I saw two hand-lettered signs on scraps of C-ration cases. They both said: '*Red Spectre 6 not welcome here*'. You know who that is..."

"That's the old, old call sign of Colonel McInnes."

"Yup. They don't like our commander, and they think I'm his hand-picked replacement for Captain Eaton, who they apparently liked a lot. They're not happy I'm here."

"What you gonna do about that, sir?"

"I'm going to do my job, first sergeant. I'm going to be the best company commander in the Cav, prosecute the war to its fullest, and take care of the troops... with your help."

"Old School, sir."

"Guess it is.

"Sir, what do you need me to do for you and the company?"

"Honestly hadn't thought about it a whole lot since they pulled me out of the field and sent me here two days ago."

The truth was that he really didn't know how to deal with a first sergeant in combat – or in peace time for that matter. He'd not worked well with First Sergeant Ortiz in Augsburg who came to the company at the time Glenn took command. History seemed to be repeating itself.

"What I really need from you as first sergeant," Glenn told him, "is to be eyes and ears and champion of the enlisted men in the company. Know what they're thinking and keep me apprised. The way I see it, lieutenants are charged with tactically fighting their platoon and with taking care of the men through their platoon sergeant. I'm charged with fighting the company tactically and taking care of all the men through the first sergeant. You're my eyes and ears concerning enlisted soldiers. But here's the tricky part for you and me. You have to counsel me – keep me informed – about how well my officers are taking care of their people. A good platoon sergeant guides and counsels his lieutenant about his men. A good first sergeant does the same for his company commander. Am I making any sense?"

"Yes, sir, you are."

"The men need to see you as their champion, so you need to be visible. I don't want you in the field all the time. Several days a month in the bush, humping along with them I think, but more time in the rear taking care of the enlisted men there and the administrative matters of the men in the field so they can concentrate on the tactical mission. That's what I expect my XO to do for me and the officers, along with overseeing company admin and supply. We'll need to work out the kinks, but that's pretty much how I see it. "

Overton nodded agreement. His first impression of the new commander had been correct, he decided now. There had been something about him in those first few hours on Evita that said here, finally, was someone he could work with.

Nolan looked at his watch and saw he still had time before the debrief. "I've got to check my RTOs and see if anything needs my attention after being gone so long. We can talk later after dinner. I'm sure we can scare up a box of C-rations for you from somewhere."

"Sir, Before leavin' Evita, I took the liberty of layin' on hot chow for supper. The log bird will deliver it in marmite cans on their way home."

"I like the way you think, first sergeant," he said, and caught a glimpse of three soldiers standing a little way off, furtively glancing at him.

Glenn got EB's attention and asked him who they were.

"The little Jewish guy with thick glasses is Edelstein. He's from New York city – I call him Lone Wolf, and the real big guy is from Canada. WE call him TiJean. That's French for Little John," EB drawled. "The other guy I call 'Chief RunAmok' but his real name is Daniel Two Hatchets. They been shillyshallyin' around here all afternoon waitin' for you to come back. They got a request of the new commander. That'd be you."

"You know what the request is?"

"Of course. You said us RTOs had to know ever-thang goin' on in the company. Those boys want to know if you're gonna let 'em continue to walk permanent point for the company like Cap'n Eaton always did."

"Permanent point?"

"Don't ask me to pass judgment on what's lodged between their ears, loo-tenant. They're in the 'Lost Boys' but they walk point for all the platoons."

"And who are the 'Lost Boys' EB?"

"That'd be the mob of Lieutenant Peter Rankin, sir. Peter *Pan* Rankin," the RTO offered. "He's got a little trouble with map readin'. Well, maybe more'n a little. Ya see, Cap'n Eaton sent him out on a little scoutin' patrol once and it took us most of three days to find 'em agin. Had to call out a Pink Team finally. The captain wanted me to go be Peter Pan's RTO because I *can* read a map. I told him I'd rather be tied hand and foot to a fig bush, smothered in honey and have a nest full of bald-faced hornets crawlin' over my sorry ass..."

"EB, I appreciate the commentary. Go tell them I'll think on it."

"Did I hear right about our new first sergeant layin' on hot chow for us this evening?"

"That's right.

"Ain't that somethin'?" EB smiled. "Looks like we got us a real Topkick."

Well, at least one of us made a favorable impression, Glenn thought.

Chapter 18

"It is better for a woman to compete impersonally in society, as men do, than to compete for dominance in her own home with her husband, compete with her neighbors for empty status, and so smother her son that he cannot compete at all!"

The large hotel ballroom exploded in the applause of over five hundred women - mostly young, predominately married. They rose, clapped and screamed approval of what some were calling the 2nd Wave of Feminism and its leader – Betty Friedan, who stood behind the large lectern on a raised stage. This was the rock solid majority of women, not the fringe movement of the bra-burners, as Friedan liked to call the extremists in the feminist movement. Behind her was a huge poster, a picture of her recent bestselling book *The Feminine Mystique*.

"We can no longer ignore that voice within women that says: 'I want something more than my husband and my children and my home'. Housewives like you and me are unhappy despite living in material comfort and being married with children. And this is not an aberrant minority. We *will* be heard! I swear to you we are now, and we will be increasingly."

Mary Anne strained to catch every word the woman spoke. *Why have I not heard this or realized it before?* She thought of her mother, an intelligent and educated woman who had given up a promising career in marketing for a Baltimore clothing chain to raise a typically large Catholic family. In retrospect she saw her mother as unfulfilled and disappointed.

"I recall my own decision to conform to society's expectations by giving up a promising career in psychology to raise children," Friedan continued, her voice growing quiet and tinged with remorse. "Many of us have struggled with the same kind of decision. *Too many* of us dropped out of school early to marry, afraid that if we waited too long or became too educated, we wouldn't be able to attract a husband. How insidious was and is the lack of self-respect or self-worth bred into us by patriarchy. You and I will change that. We will!"

Mary Anne looked around. Three of the women were her classmates at the all-girl *Catholic High School of Baltimore*. Stephanie Alt and Felicia Ratcliffe had played on the field hockey team and graduated a year ahead of her. Both were married and had small children. Felicia had two year old twins and was pregnant again. Steph had a three and a one year old.

Neither had finished college although both had started and dropped out to raise a family. Melanie Winston, her closest friend throughout high school, had graduated from Maryland and begun a career which had been cut short when she asked for maternity leave.

Only Mary Anne had remained childless – Glenn had wanted to delay starting a family, making a case for waiting until he returned from Vietnam. She was certain he was simply kicking the can down the road, not wanting to confront her family's and her church's demand that their children be raised Catholic. His intransience had at first distressed her but now seemed providential in light of reading Friedan's book and discovering Bella Abzug, Simone de Beauvoir and Helen Gurley Brown in addition to Betty Friedan.

Their drive back to Baltimore from the hotel in D.C. was a blur of chatter about what they'd heard that night and by the time she got home, Mary Anne's emotions were running at a fever pitch. Dinner with her friends and the rousing diatribe by Friedan had set her nerves on edge and she was certain that sleep would be long in coming.

As she quietly opened the front door to her parent's house and entered, she saw a letter sitting on the small end table next to the deacon's bench in the hallway. Seeing Glenn's handwriting caused her to gasp, as if he'd caught her in a compromising act.

Guilty conscience, Mary Anne? she asked herself. Glenn had written her letters twice, and often three times a week. She tried to think of the last time she'd written. It left her feeling guilty. She opened the letter and walked into the kitchen to read it at the little alcove table where they'd often sat, from that summer of her sophomore year until they were married. On their last night together, just before Christmas the previous year, they'd spent time together there. They had quarreled that night, she remembered.

This letter was so typical of him.

He was upbeat and started right in talking about places with odd names, his unit, his hopes to live up to the expectations of superiors and subordinates. She knew he'd live up to it. It was so like him – a little self-deprecation to make himself sound humbled, frightened, worried. *He's loving this*, she thought, disenchanted.

He had a new address – a new unit he's been assigned to where he'd been excited to discover he and Benny were in the same battalion. They had talked, shared a beer and gotten mortared together. *Such fun.* As always, he talked about the people in his unit – a new company – each person described in great detail with all their odd quirks.

As she read on, she found it disappointing, irritating that he was taking this twelve month separation so cavalierly; his letter was more jovial than the ones from West Point years earlier. He related more stories about soldiers in this new company of his. It sounded like a cast of a Broadway comedy, and she wondered if it was for her benefit. He made the whole thing sound like a romp through the woods and he was some kind of adventurer in a Saturday morning serial at the cinema.

"I see you got another letter from the 'baby killer'."

She was startled and looked up into her older brother's eyes.

"Couldn't sleep and I toyed with the idea of raiding the fridge, and then I heard you come in. That settled it." He opened the refrigerator door and rummaged about, finally pulling out a package of sliced cheese individually wrapped. He sat down in a chair across from her. "What's going on with your knight errant, Ramar of the Jungle?"

"It's late, Corey. I don't need this right now, okay?"

He smiled benevolently at her. "I'm sorry, dear one. If I had thought that I –"

"Don't patronize me."

"I'm not. I just thought that I might be of some comfort. You've seemed rather off your stride of late, and I can understand why. What with your Galahad running off to muck around in his little Southeast Asian escapade, and our father less than happy with your recent interest in bra-burning and reproductive freedom. Very un-Catholic of you, Mary Anne."

"You're going to make a lousy priest, Corey."

"Actually, I won't be a priest – not starting out, and maybe never. I'll be on probation for some time after seminary."

"Doesn't draft dodging by going into the priesthood bother your conscience at all?"

He smiled paternally at his sister as he folded a slice of cheese in half and took a large bite. "No it doesn't – this immoral conflict in Vietnam isn't justifiable according to Augustine and church dogma on the 'justifiable war.' I see it as religious duty to oppose it, and where better than in the church? I see it as my civic duty, and so should you – our father still contributes to the *Hawkish Dove* cause. I also hope to provide spiritual counsel to the people who are actively propagating the war – like your absentee husband."

She tossed her head to shake out her hair and scoffed at him. "You never liked Glenn."

"One doesn't have to like somebody to help them. From a religious perspective, one *is required* however to love them. And truth be told, I have a problem with that when it comes to your husband. Immersing myself in the teachings of the church will help me, I'm sure."

She knew Corey's story was an invention. She'd once heard him tell someone over the phone that he didn't want to go to Canada and because he couldn't get into a school anywhere he needed an iron-clad deferment. Lots of guys in all the denominations were going into the ministry. Why not him, especially with his father's influence?

"Tripp has been asking about you."

Her face went hot and a shiver shot its way down her spine. "Why would he?"

"I've told him all about you. He's dying to meet you. I told him I'd bring you along the next time I come to Washington. He was delighted."

"I don't think that's such a good idea.

"*Hawkish Dove* is sponsoring a rally on the Mall – May 1. We're hoping for a million, but honestly we'd all be happy with half that. It's one of those nice, friendly kumbaya events. You like Phil Ochs' music, right? He's gonna be there, and somebody close to the Seekers is trying to get them to come out of retirement for it. You should talk to Tripp. You can do it on the steps of the Lincoln Memorial in front of all those people. There's nothing to be afraid of – nothing untoward is going to happen."

"My answer is still no."

"Think about it." Corey stood, went to the refrigerator and poured himself a glass of milk as Mary Anne went back to her letter.

*   *   *   *

The jungle opened unexpectedly into a quiet peaceful glade that looked like a scene from an old Frank Capra movie, *The Lost Horizons of Shangri La*. Beneath towering triple canopy it was cool, quiet; the only sound was the faint rippling of water tumbling over smooth stones.

It was mid-morning.

A wandering path they had been paralleling for the last hour had turned north away from them fifty meters back, went uphill and disappeared around a small hillock. When they'd discovered it earlier that morning, there were no fresh signs of usage, but on a hunch he'd pointed the company on a due west heading that kept the trail off their right flank. Now, he stopped Alpha on the edge of the tranquil, surprisingly open dell where sunlight couldn't penetrate to the jungle floor; it seemed almost like the sun had already set. There was an abundance of short ferns that dripped moisture from humidity trapped under the layers of jungle canopy, soaking their jungle fatigues.

He went forward to survey the scene with the point team –a Brooklyn Jew, a big-city Canadian giant, and a full-blooded Kiowa Indian named Daniel Two Hatchets from an Oklahoma Indian reservation. He had to smile thinking about this crew.

Alpha company had pulled out of LZ Sally early the previous morning; by then Glenn had been with them for three days and after going out with five squad-sized patrols was beginning to think he had a good grip on his new command. The first day out showed him just how naïve he'd been. After scouting the area around the firebase out to almost a mile, he felt comfortable letting them operate while he observed. Colonel McInnes had given him nothing in the way of a mission, only to move from the LZ to a map coordinate by noon, and then to another spot to set up a night location. He was grateful they'd not made any contact that morning and even more grateful the first night. Noise discipline and flank security had been non-existent, and last light patrols had been an accident that should have happened but luckily didn't. He had a long talk with the platoon leaders before dark, so day two started out better.

"What do we have here, Lone Wolf?" Glenn whispered to Edelstein, the team leader.

"A stream running from high ground to our north to lower ground south. Forty meters across to the other bank," Edelstein said in a hushed voice, pointing with an open hand. "Terrain rises three hundred feet on the far side to a long ridge line. Good fields of fire over there – fifty meters up - and downstream. We'll be exposed all the way, as open as it is here."

Glenn surveyed the scene warily. He wanted to get to that high ground on the other side.

"You hear that, Six?" Two Hatchets whispered. "There's a waterfall upstream." Glenn closed his eyes and strained to hear the sound. "A hundred meters, no more," the Indian said.

He was torn between continuing west and closing on the night location McInnes had given him or checking out this unusual terrain. They were in mountain jungle not more than a dozen miles from the Cambodian border; he remembered the S-2's map showing they were near one branch of the Jolly Trail system.

"The plan is this – you three are going to cross the stream while third platoon covers you. Assuming that goes well, then first platoon and second platoon join you on the other side. Third platoon stays on this side. Then we all move upstream toward the waterfall and see what we have when we get there."

Minutes later Glenn was kneeling over his map with the three platoon leaders and the artillery forward observer, Lieutenant Swedock. He traced the plan for them. Fifteen minutes later, his three scouts crossed the stream without incident, followed by second platoon – *The Gamecocks* – and then first platoon, *Rankin's Riffraff.*

The climb on both sides of the stream grew steeper and the sound of falling water became louder; a hundred yards from where they'd crossed, the terrain leveled off. Water cascaded from the top of a nearly sheer cliff face thirty-five to forty feet into a shallow pool that overflowed into the stream below. Glenn called a halt and radioed Thorgier and the other platoon leaders.

"I want the *Vikings* to cover the east side of the falls and *Gamecocks* cover the west side. *Riffraff* protect our back trail and keep a lookout toward the high ground to the west. I'm going to take the scouts for a closer lok at the falls."

"This is Viking. We have a trail coming from the east toward the base of the fall. About six inches wide and moderate use in the last three or four days."

"Roger that." Glenn put on his boonie hat, dropped his rucksack and helmet, went forward to his scout team and told them to lead out to the base of the falls. "That water is like a solid sheet," he whispered. "There might be something behind it. Let's take a look-see."

The four of them crept forward until they came to the nearly vertical wall, covered in thick vines and vegetation. As they inched along the wall, Glenn saw foliage moving just inside his peripheral vision; something black and light blue. He slowly removed his Kabar from its sheath and prodded the foliage with the tip. More movement. A rounded protrusion; smooth, glossy scales in bold, striped patterns of alternating black and light-colored areas.

Snake.

He froze. He'd not seen one snake since arriving in Vietnam, and had no idea what to do – run? attack with the knife?

A blur erupted at the edge of his vision. Something large and black imbedded itself in the middle of the vegetation inches from his face. He gasped and threw his head back as the severed body of snake fell writhing at his feet.

"Malayan krait, Six," Two Hatchets whispered, removing what he called his Hawk Axe from the tangled underbrush. It was a completely black weapon – a fifteen inch handle with a wide, upswept axe blade for chopping, slashing and cutting. The Indian had shown it to him on Sally as he was sharpening the cutting edges. "You need to be careful, commander. The Krait is a very poisonous snake. No pokey-pokey in the brush with your hands or a short knife. I'll carve you long pokey-pokey stick for that."

Up ahead, Lone Wolf and TiJean were desperately waving at him.

"There's a cave in there, behind the waterfall," Edelstein whispered. "I'm going inside."

"No!" Glenn said. "We go in at the same time. Lone Wolfe first – go in low and cover the right side. TiJean immediately behind goes in high and covers left. I'm right behind him, covering center. Two Hatchets right behind me – engage targets in your own area. Got that?" They all nodded at him. "On three... One... two... three –" They burst through the gray sheet of water into an open and surprisingly large cavern. Inside the light was dim; the atmosphere was heavy – damp and clammy.

It was an NVA hospital... and maybe something more.

There were five rooms carved out of the rock, one of which was a surgical suite. A couple of wards with bamboo beds flanked the surgery room, and both had fresh bloody bandages piled in the corners. There was also a good supply of medical gear as well as assorted cooking pans in a kitchen area that had a vent that went up to the surface above them. Glenn tied some of the bandages onto the end of a piece of bamboo, doused it in the fuel of one of the camp stoves and lit it with his lighter.

One room was an armory holding bolt action SKS rifles, AK-47s, and B-40 RPGs. Ammunition crates were stacked along one wall. A box the size of a GI footlocker contained gun cleaning supplies and magazines for the AKs. Another box yielded NVA black pajama uniforms, pistol belts and Ho Chi Minh racing slicks.

Sergeant Kaiser, here's your trading material. This should be worth a few M60s.

They discovered a couple of footlocker-type boxes in a storage alcove. When TiJean opened them, he turned to Glenn with a sheepish, embarrassed grin on his face and held up several lacy black bras and matching panties. They looked at one another and shrugged.

Two Hatchets examined the kitchen closely. "Used in the past two days, commander. Beaucoup soldiers here. Not long ago." TiJean and Lone Wolf nodded agreement.

Glenn tried to quickly pull together and make sense of everything he'd seen in the past two hours and what it meant for him and Alpha company. One thing was clear – they had stumbled onto an important way station on the long logistics trail between Hanoi and Saigon. Essentially none of the soldiers who left North Vietnam ever returned home and Glenn surmised they would readily die fighting for this position.

He was certain they had little time to prepare for a big fight over this NVA hideaway.

A half hour later, third platoon was repositioned above the falls, out of site and shielded from any firefight below. Nightfall came early, but by dark Thorgier had his platoon set up in an L-shaped ambush along a trail that followed the watershed; *Gamecock* and *Riffraff* were together in a perimeter below the falls, and three night defensive artillery targets had been fired in by Lieutenant Swedock. Glenn called in a report and Holmes encoded the locations and numbers before transmitting it to the battalion. The company settled down for a long night, and Glenn went to sleep satisfied that the company had done a good day's work.

Unfortunately, Colonel McInnes disagreed and made it known two hours after dark.

"You're a whole kilometer from where you're supposed to be set up!" the colonel yelled through the radio. *"You never violate operational orders! Do I make myself clear? Orders are given for a reason – to be obeyed... We will talk about this tomorrow! OUT!"*

Nolan handed the radio handset back to EB. "I think he was a little unhappy."

"A little? Hell, Six, everybody in the company and half the gooks between here and Saigon could hear he was. Even Cap'n Eaton didn't used ta piss him off that bad."

This is not going well, Nolan, he thought.

*   *

He was jolted out of a troubled sleep by the explosion of a Claymore and the immediate roar of automatic weapons. His heart pounded.

It took him only a few seconds to orient himself and figure out that Thorgier had sprung his ambush. He forced himself to be patient, knowing the platoon had their hands full and badgering them for information seconds after initiating contact at night was pointless. He'd had that experience with his own C.O. during nearly every contact he'd been in with C Company in Conrad's battalion. He hated it then and refused to visit that on his own troops.

Firing on the plateau above him continued on for long seconds, rose to a crescendo in the middle of which another Claymore exploded. The exchange of gunfire diminished then fell silent. He could hear shouts and then the company radio net came alive.

'Loki, this is the Viking... put Odin on.'

"This is Odin," Glenn said, forcing himself calm.

"This is Viking. Small party wandered into our site and tripped the automatic ambush. Firefight followed. Blew the second Claymore and the fight went out of them. They took off the way they came. Estimate an NVA platoon. Will check out the kill zone and get back to you."

"Roger that. Be careful." *No shit... be careful. What a dumbass thing to say*, Glenn told himself and shook his head, *especially to Rollie Thorgier.* The lieutenant had impressed him from the very instant he'd stepped off the Huey at LZ Sally three days earlier.

He was tall and blond with penetrating blue eyes and a bright white gauze pad taped to his cheek where jungle rot had formed. He'd gone to the Aid Station on Evita to get it lanced and doused with alcohol and slathered with ointment in hopes of making it heal before seeing his fiancée on R&R in Hawaii. He radiated confidence. Over the next day, Glenn observed and liked what he saw in the Swede and the way his soldiers responded to him.

Several minutes later, the platoon leader was back. *"Counted seven dead NVA... Will set up a perimeter with trips and flares and Claymores in case they come back and try to drag off the bodies. Request artillery fire DT one-alpha and will adjust closer, just in case."*

"Roger that. Loki will call you back this push. Relay adjustments through him."

"Roger, out."

He turned to where Heavy was sitting next to the company and battalion radios. "EB?"

"Yeah, Six?"

"Viking will be relaying artillery adjustments to you. Get Lieutenant Swedock and his RTO up here and then contact Thorgier on company."

"They get any gooks, Six?"

"Seven of them."

"How 'bout dat?"

"Yeah, how about it?" Glenn took the handset to the battalion frequency and made a quick report to the radio operator. Ten minutes went by and the S-3 came on the radio.

"This is zero-niner. Sounds like you've have a busy... and profitable day."

"Roger. The outfit did real well."

"Zero-niner, roger. Don't think it's gone unnoticed, two-one. It hasn't. We'll talk more on the next log day. Zero-niner out."

Nolan glanced at his watch and passed the handset to Holmes. It would be another four hours before the sun came up. He called *The Gamecocks* and *Riffraff* and told them to go back to fifty percent security until further notice, then told the rest of the CP to get some sleep while he stood radio watch, knowing there was too much on his mind to think about sleep. He was certain from McInnes' tone of voice earlier that he was probably in for a dressing down. Still, he hoped their finding the NVA way station and supplies might mitigate that.

Six days later he found out just how far off he was.

*   *   *

They were four hours into log day when EB advised him *Red Spectre 6* was inbound.

"Ya know, we could just up an' move out, and tell him we got tired o' waitin'," his RTO offered and gave him a sly grin. "Or that we're off chasin' Luke the Gook back to Cambodia."

"And what would that accomplish, other than getting me in more hot water?"

The far off slap of rotor blades echoed through the jungle and he looked up, dreading what might come of the battalion commander's visit. He'd decided before leaving LZ Sally four days earlier that he was going to command the company, not be its water boy or its hod carrier or the battalion commander's marionette.

The morning after finding the cave and third platoon's ambush, he'd updated his original reports to battalion. A sweep of the area above the waterfall had yielded two more NVA bodies, several blood trails and a half dozen boxes of medical supplies with Chinese markings. A small camouflaged hooch was located nearby containing more medical supplies and rolls of black plastic. The final tally on weapons captured stood at forty-two B40 rockets, seventeen AK47s, and eleven SKS rifles; he divided the SKS's among the three platoons after letting his scout team each have one.

When the battalion C&C ship landed, Glenn saw Colonel McInnes yelling on the radio and pounding the canvas seat next to him. Finally, he jumped off and walked over to Nolan, grabbed his arm and led him several yards into the tree line to get away from the helicopter's noise. The colonel carried a truncated version of the M16, with a short barrel and a round fore stock instead of the triangular shaped one. It was a neat little carbine, Glenn thought.

"Nolan, these are your orders... I expect you to follow them precisely. You seem to have a problem following even simple directives, so listen very closely.

"This is a classic hammer and anvil operation. I've been working hard with brigade to make sure this goes perfectly." His small, dark eyes bored into Nolan. "Copy this on your map as I walk you through it. Here is your present location," McInnes said, tapping the map with a finger. "Mark that down. Tomorrow morning move Alpha company to the location marked – Alpha 1, an eight ship LZ where two platoons will be extracted beginning at exactly 1200 hours and inserted into this LZ marked Bravo 2, to set up a blocking position. At 1400 hours, third platoon under Lieutenant Thorgier will be extracted and inserted into Charlie 3, here."

"I understand,, sir, but I should tell you that –"

"Damn you, Nolan!" McInnes shouted, jutting out his jaw and glowering at him. "I'm giving you the details of this operation and you're not listening to me. Don't you dare interrupt me again! Now, third platoon goes into LZ Charlie 3. It's crucial that Lieutenant Thorgier is the hammer in this operation. I don't trust any of the other platoon leaders to do this part."

Glenn debated. *Before this goes any further, He really needs to know that I just let Thorgier get on the bird four hours ago to go on R&R in Hawaii.*

"Sir, I really have to tell you Lieutenant Thorgier is not –"

"Damn your hide, Nolan! You're one word away from being relieved!" McInnes grasped his arm in a surprisingly strong grip and shook it. "If you say another thing, I'll place you on that helicopter and take you directly to Sông Bé. Am I clear enough, lieutenant? Am I?!"

"Yes, sir."

"No more interruptions, or you're finished in this division."

McInnes droned on for another ten minutes explaining the operation in minute detail, describing the mission of the 'hammer' element under Thorgier – his route of march and checkpoints. He also went into detail concerning the 'anvil' element under the command of Rankin as the senior officer between himself and Cleburne. Coordination between the hammer and anvil would be handled by battalion. Glenn wanted to ask about his own responsibilities as the commander of Alpha, but decided against it.

Ten minutes later, McInnes completed his briefing and looked up at Glenn.

"Now, lieutenant, what was so damned important you had to constantly interrupt me?"

"Sir, I have to tell you Lieutenant Thorgier can't do this mission the way you outlined."

"What?!" McInnes shouted at him. "You don't think this plan will work?"

"Sir, I do have some questions, but you need to know that Lieutenant Thorgier isn't available to lead his platoon and if you're counting on him to –"

"What do you mean he's unavailable?"

Glenn took a deep breath. "Sir, he's on R&R in Hawaii with his fiancé."

Color rose in the colonel's face. "How the hell did that happen?! You let him go on R&R without clearing it with me?! Damn you, Nolan, I specifically told you that ALL decisions concerning Alpha company have to be approved through me."

"Sir, he and his fiancé have been working on this for months. It was approved before I arrived. Even so, if it had been up to me –"

"Well, it's not up to you, Nolan!" The colonel stood and ran his fingers through his hair. "Do you realize what you've done?! All my planning. All my work with the brigade staff. You've ruined it, Nolan!"

"Sir, I can run the operation. I'll lead the maneuver element and make it work, sir."

"No! You're not Thorgier. I don't trust you. I didn't even want you!" The colonel threw his helmet to the ground. "You're finished, Nolan! If it's the last damned thing I do –"

McInnes grabbed his map and crumpled it into a ball, glared at Nolan and then the others in his command post. He picked up his helmet, stomped through the jungle and climbed into the passenger compartment of the Huey. He yelled something at the pilot and seconds later the helicopter lifted off.

"He seemed to be in a hurry," EB said wistfully, standing next to Glenn, watching the ship depart. "He even left his nice little carbine behind. Think we should keep it?"

Glenn took a deep breath. "I think we will. Let him deal with the headquarters property officer over his lost weapon. I need to talk with Sergeant Pratt. Be back shortly."

EB watched him move through the undergrowth and turned to Holmes. "I was jest gettin' comfy with all Nolan's little quirks 'n' stuff. Gonna miss all his little homespun homilies. That boy's a walkin' talkin' Josh Billings." The radio operator shook his head sadly. "I am afraid that our own Loo-tenant No-Lann ain't long for Alpha company... an' just when the boy was showin' some promise. Even Cap'n Eaton lasted a few months."

Chapter 19

The high-winged Air Force OV-10 crossed the fence at Sông Bé steep and slow, directly over a perimeter defense position where Glenn Nolan, naked from the waist up, was shaving using his steel helmet for a basin. He turned and watched the Air Force Forward Air Controller plane touch down, then went back to his morning shave.

That's what I should be doing now, Nolan mumbled to himself, looking into the small mirror – *flying Broncos as a FAC or Phantoms out of Udorn instead of mucking around in the damned bush getting jungle rot and ass chewings.*

It had been a week since his latest – and he suspected, last – skirmish with McInnes. Waiting for the guillotine to fall brought about both a sense of calm inevitability and a festering resentment made worse by the proliferation of jungle rot sores on his arms and face. He looked into the small mirror sitting atop the wooden ammo crate. The left side of his face was swollen and a large pus-filled abscess along his jaw line protruded like an angry boil. He decided to lance the thing just to see what happened.

After the run-in with his battalion commander, Glenn had been surprised at the silence from the battalion about his situation. Neither McInnes, nor the S-3 – Major Jackson, nor the XO – Boomer Cameron had contacted him about his future in the battalion. Army machinery always did grind exceedingly slow. Two log days had come and gone since that day, and instructions received from battalion had all come from the S-3.

Then, a couple of days ago, the company had been flown to LZ Buttons at Sông Bé for perimeter guard duty. The troops were happy to be out of the field and on a facility with bunks, hot chow three times a day, and access to music from *The World* on AFVN radio. He, on the other hand, felt alone and adrift.

Glenn nicked the end of the boil with his razor, squeezed out a surprisingly large volume of yellowish pus mixed with blood and was blotting the weeping sore with a gauze pad soaked in peroxide when a voice from behind called his name.

"Lieutenant Nolan. Do you have a few minutes to talk?"

Glenn turned, saw the black oak leaf on the officer's collar and immediately recognized Lieutenant Colonel van Noort.

"Of course, sir. If you'll give me a few seconds to apply this bandage..."

"Don't let me interrupt. I want to say you were most helpful in providing information about the attack on Illingworth. Both Colonel Galvin and I appreciated your detailed commentary. I believe Colonel Galvin may want to interview you again prior to finalizing his report before he takes command of the 1st Battalion, 8th Cavalry a few days from now."

"I'll do whatever I can, sir."

Colonel van Noort continued to look at him, and finally said, "Sergeant Lockhart was awarded the Distinguished Service Cross for his actions that night."

"Very much deserved, sir." Glenn looked down and nodded. "He's the most incredible soldier I've ever witnessed. I hope he's okay."

"His recuperation is coming along just fine. He's being considered for the big one – the Congressional Medal of Honor."

Glenn was pleasantly amazed. "He's certainly deserving. I hope he gets it."

"I know you do. The recommendation you wrote up and gave to General Roberts that morning before he left was typed and sent up the chain; one day soon you'll be asked to officially sign it."

"I'll do it in a heartbeat, sir." Glenn was ecstatic, and suddenly his morose, self-pitying grumblings seemed stupid and trifling. Something worthwhile was going to come out of what he'd been through. The idea that Lockhart might one day be presented with *The Medal* brought tears to his eyes and he looked away from the colonel to hide them. "Thank you, sir, for coming here to tell me."

"That's not my only reason for stopping by to see you. As of this time two days ago, I've been your battalion commander. Alpha company is here now for some rest and re-fitting because I have a special assignment for your unit. You've had Alpha company for a good long two and a half weeks – tell me everything about the unit."

*   *   *

"It came up like a summer thunderstorm," Benny said, finishing his beer and reaching for another. "General Roberts flew in at mid-morning, talked to McInnes down at the VIP pad; flew out with him five minutes later without a word to anyone. Spectre 6 cleaned out his personal effects and before anybody knew it, he was gone. History. By noon there wasn't a beer left on the firebase and the celebration was just gettin' started."

"Any idea what happened?"

258

They were sitting outside the company command post bunker smoking and drinking a beer. Barnes had shown up shortly after Colonel van Noort left, having come to the brigade TOC at Sông Bé for maps and a briefing.

"Boomer was there," Barnes said. "CG brought him out and left him on Evita. He gathered everyone in the TOC together and told us McInnes was being replaced by Colonel van Noort, effective immediately and that the new CO would arrive in a couple of hours. That was it. No reason given. Then he advised the artillery battery commander. He spent the next hour with Doc Hadorn."

Glenn looked in Benny's direction and asked, "Why so much time with the Doc?"

"Remember that night you spent on the firebase?" Barnes asked, popping the top on his beer. "The mortar attack... all that yelling and screaming between McInnes and Hadorn? Doc threatening to prefer charges against the Weasel."

"I also recall Hadorn was doing some serious damage to a bottle of bourbon in the Aid Station when I caught up to him."

"Doc had enough of McInnes and his false reporting to pick up decorations. He never did get over the loss of that trooper in Alpha when the battalion CO waived off the medevac bird and the kid died on the way here to Sông Bé. That night of the mortar attack was the proverbial straw that broke the camel's back."

"So Doc reported him up the chain of command?"

"Not exactly. He went to see the Division JAG two days later and officially preferred charges citing Articles 107 and 131 through 134 of the UCMJ."

Glenn frowned at his old roommate. "Benny, as much as I liked Military Law at the school, and as good as I was, I didn't memorize the whole Uniform Code of Military Justice."

"Those are the articles relating to making false official statements, perjury, fraud, conduct unbecoming an officer and a gentleman, and some similar general catch-all crimes."

"Doc did all that?"

"Oh, yeah. And more. He named names of people who'd written him up for bronze and silver stars, ARCOMS with and without "V", a Distinguished Flying Cross or two. They all did it under duress from McInnes, but..." Barnes raised his eyebrows and shrugged.

"In the eyes of the law –"

"Just as guilty," Benny said sadly. "That little weasel damaged some good people, like Action Jackson – a damn good person and a superior S-3 who's now in the JAG's crosshairs, too. Glad I wasn't important enough for McInnes to notice me. "

"You wouldn't have forfeited your honor for him."

"I'm not so sure, Knocker."

"I am!" They were silent for a while. Glenn asked, "Who's going to be the S-3?"

"Boomer. I guess he worked for the new C.O. on Division staff for a few months. They seem to get along pretty well, but my guess is van Noort gets along with most people. He spent one night on the firebase and this morning, most of the troops in Delta company, who's guarding Evita, have met and talked with him. After dark, he made the rounds of the positions on the berm at least twice and talked with essentially all the troops. Apparently that's the first time in anybody's memory that something like that happened. The guy's generated more good will in one night than McInnes did in five months."

"Military leadership is basically real simple."

"Well, I try not to think too much or too long on anything. Makes my head hurt." Benny lit another cigarette, looked around the outside of the bunker, and asked, "You ever think about why we're over here doing this?"

"You mean why we're fighting this war?"

"Yeah. Are we doing the right thing here? Is this a good war?"

Glenn shook his head. "Ben-bo, I haven't spent one second wondering about it. I don't have the time or the inclination. Got too much else on my plate day in and day out – especially now, with the company and with a new mission we're going out on the day after tomorrow."

Colonel van Noort had given him a warning order and a brief concept of the operation.

There was an old French fortress and a hard red clay runway twenty-five miles north of Sông Bé at a place called Bù Gia Mập. Like all the old French forts, it was now an overgrown ruins, but the Americans had gone in, refurbished and re-graded the runway and cleared the encroaching jungle back a hundred yards all around. There had been an American firebase named LZ Snuffy on the south end of the runway a few years earlier, but it now sat vacant. Glenn's mission was to secure the airfield for future operations.

The runway was capable of handling C-130s, which would be bringing in equipment, supplies, and possibly troops. Engineers would be setting up a water gathering and purification station on the north-south creek a quarter mile inside the wood line which paralleled the main axis of the runway. At the same time, a helicopter hot refueling point and rearmament station would be established near the north end of the airfield.

Alpha company's job was to clear the area around the airstrip and provide security.

"I know all about A company's mission."

"Wish I did, Benji. This afternoon I'm getting an intel brief from Kimball and first thing the day after tomorrow, we CA in and get started. For the next week, I don't plan on spending a lot of time worrying about the morality of the war. Actually, I don't plan to spend any."

"Smart ass," Benny said and flipped his cigarette butt at Nolan. It hit him in the chest with a shower of red ashes. "I was just asking."

Nolan grew silent for a while and Benny finally said, "Deanna stopped in to see Mary Anne at her folks' house in Baltimore. Grunts like you and me aren't supposed to marry rich girls, you know that, right? You hear anything from her lately?"

"Now and then. I think maybe the move to a new battalion caught the postmaster flatfooted." Glenn pursed his lips and got a faraway look in his eyes. "But I'm sure her letters will catch up to me pretty soon."

It was an awkward moment. His most recent letters from Deanna about her stay in Baltimore weren't encouraging. He wondered if his old roommate knew what was going on back home. He was debating what to say when the tall Swede from Alpha strode up to them.

Glenn looked up at him and said, "Thorgier, you smell like a French whore. I'm getting strong fragrances of clove, bay rum, rose water, and a heady scent of English Leather. Take a shower, three laps around LZ Buttons and repeat until you smell like a soldier. I assume you know Benny Barnes."

"Sure. The S-3 Air," Thorgier replied, still beaming at them. He reached into his pocket and pulled out a half dozen photographs. They showed the Swede with his fiancé, a statuesque blond girl, in front of various tropical scenes. "I highly recommend R&R."

Benny gave a low whistle while leafing through the pictures. "Why'd you come back?"

"I'm asking myself the same question." The platoon leader retrieved the pictures and slowly looked through them. "I'm going to put in for my seven day leave as soon as Annika-Ingrid sends me the dates for our next trip to Honolulu."

"That's her name?"

"Scandinavian tradition. The first-born girl is named after both grandmothers. It keeps peace in the family. We're not Scots, for crying out loud!"

They chatted for a while as Glenn gave him a 'heads-up' on the new mission, and then Thorgier went to his platoon in search of Sergeant Pratt.

"He's a really good platoon leader," Glenn told his old friend after Thorgier left. "I'm lucky to have him. I wish I'd have been half as good. He knows what to do and how to get his men to do it. He's a natural. I could use two more just like him."

"You have problems?" Benny asked.

"Not really," Glenn said nonchalantly. But even as he said it, he knew he was quibbling. Braxton Bragg Cleburne, his 2nd platoon leader, like a lot of the southerners in the Army, had roots going back to before the Civil War and a heritage of family military service.

"I've got this one platoon leader," Glenn said, "a butter bar with a Ranger tab and ancestors from the deep South who struts and talks like a general."

Benny smiled and took a sip of his Budweiser. "Nothing wrong with that. Hell, son, you could be describing me."

"Hope not. There's something going on with this guy. My gut tells me..."

"You and your damn gut, Nolan."

"Saved your butt more than once."

"We've had our moments, haven't we?"

Glenn stood, stretched and looked at his watch. "I need to walk our part of the perimeter. Nothing happens except the company commander checks and makes sure it does."

"Tactics one-oh-one, Knocker. You take care. Remember – No task too great..."

It took an hour for him to check the positions Alpha company had inherited and the word had filtered through the company about a new battalion commander. He sensed the troops were guarded in their conversations with him, despite the action at the NVA hospital where they had clearly come out well with only two Americans wounded and the destruction of a key enemy facility along with a dozen of their soldiers KIA. The first sergeant joined him halfway through the inspection tour.

"Sir, when I joined the company, you told me be... well, sir, you said we needed to be real honest," Sergeant Overton began as they sat down on ammo boxes after the walking inspection. "I need to talk to you about one of your officers, sir."

Even before Overton began, Nolan knew what he would say.

"Sir, second platoon leader, Lieutenant Cleburne, is causing you trouble with the black soldiers in his platoon. I seen it in the field, and I seen it here. Some of them have come to me."

"What have you been told and what have you observed, first sergeant?"

Overton took a deep breath and cleared his throat. "It's mainly the way he talks to them, sir. He calls 'em all 'boy' or 'boys', and you should know, lieutenant, that's kinda the hot button these days with black folk. They're men, not boys. Young men, sometimes not real grown up, but bein' called boy reminds them of the massuh in the big house and the boss man with a whip in the field."

The first sergeant paused and looked into Glenn's eyes with a steady unrelenting gaze.

"Go ahead, Sergeant Overton."

"Yessir. In the past two months, three men in the platoon have been promoted to buck sergeant and made squad leaders. None of them were black. I was told that the black Spec-4s weren't even considered for promotion."

Nolan nodded slowly. "Just to make sure, I understand... Second platoon has twenty-nine men and five of them are black, am I right?" Overton agreed. "How many of them are eligible for promotion to sergeant E-5?"

The first sergeant replied: "Only one of them."

"How did the one black soldier compare with the three men who were promoted? Time in grade, performance, that sort of thing."

"Right up there with them, sir. I think so, anyhow. That's what I was told?"

"By whom?"

"The soldiers who told me."

"What about the platoon sergeant. Sergeant Hansen. He strikes me as squared away, a straight shooter."

"Well, sir, he tells me, Spec-4 Phelan was right up there with the others."

"I want you to check it out for me, because I don't know. I haven't seen it myself, but I haven't been specifically looking for it either. One thing I do know – we need to have a roster, a list of promotables to sergeant from Spec-4, by order of qualification, *and also* a list for promotion to Staff Sergeant E-6. How about you and the XO working that up for me? That's something the three of us need to review at least every time we come on the firebase... If there is a problem, we need to stay on top of it and head it off. And we do it even-handed, and with facts, not emotions."

Glenn leaned back and tapped his fingertips across the edge of the makeshift table.

So it was here in his own company now, this subsurface racial tension he'd seen in Europe, only there he'd heard it had bubbled up in places and caused real problems. One thing he didn't need was division in the ranks rooted in race. He'd never encountered the kind of divide he'd seen on television and read about during that long hot summer of '67 when it seemed a different city each day was ablaze, literally. He'd been shielded from that type of tension as an Air Force brat, and later at the public school he'd gone to in center city Baltimore which was the melting pot of all melting pots, where the only things that mattered were getting passing grades and being an above average athlete. Race was a tinder box he'd never had to deal with... but that apparently was going to change.

"I understand what you're telling me and I appreciate that you did. Is there anything else you need to tell me?"

Sergeant Overton sighed deeply, chewed absently on his lower lip and briefly glanced away, sorely uncomfortable.

"There is something, isn't there? Bad news doesn't get better with age. Tell me."

"Sir, the men in his platoon... they... he doesn't lead the platoon when they go on patrol. He has Sergeant Hansen take the men out and he stays behind."

Glenn's heart leapt into his throat. *He's calling Cleburne a coward.*

"You're sure of this?"

Tightlipped and clearly stressed, Overton nodded his head slowly up and down.

Glenn had immediately changed some of the operating procedures in the brief time he'd been there. Noise and light discipline got his immediate attention as did the way the company moved and conducted operations. Platoon and squad-sized patrols from the company patrol base were the norm now; he wanted the company to operate with the stealth of a Ranger patrol, instead of the incautious headlong rush through the jungle that characterized a few companies He knew of in the division. Platoon patrols always operated within reasonable range of company reinforcement, and their silent clearing of the area through which the company would move provided security for the main body.

"You're absolutely certain of this?" Glenn asked not wanting to believe it.

"I saw it the first week out, sir. We weren't out that long and his platoon only went on one patrol. Last night, after we got here to Sông Bé, I asked some of the soldiers and the platoon sergeant. They confirmed my suspicions. You have a big problem in the company, sir. You need to act."

"Act how, first sergeant?"

"Remove him from command, sir."

"It'll ruin his career. He's only a second lieutenant, and his family has a long history of service that's now his responsibility to carry on. That's pretty drastic, don't you think?"

Overton cleared his throat. "He's not the kind of officer who should be leading your men, sir – or any other troops."

"And you think I'm the one who should end his career."

"Yes, sir, before he does more damage to Alpha, and bad damage to others down the road." First Sergeant Overton took a deep breath and stared without wavering into Nolan's eyes. "Situations like this don't get taken care of a lot of the time. The time to root out problem officers and NCOs is early on, before they can hurt more people, more units.

"If you don't do it now, sir, while you have the chance, who will?"

Chapter 20

"It's getting a little better, Six," Timmy Horner said, winding the bandage around Glenn's upper left arm. "But you need this changed twice a day, morning and evening, to keep it from getting infected again." They were sitting in the shade, just inside the wood line on the south of Bù Gia Mập airstrip, a bustling little oasis of American activity in the middle of the heavily wooded mountain jungle near the Cambodian border.

Six days earlier the company flew from Sông Bé to a field a mile east of the old French runway and from there had sent out platoon-sized patrols to recon the airfield. A day later, engineers flew in by Chinook and in short order had a potable water facility up and running on the small creek east of the runway. A six point hot refueling area sprang to life and quickly went into service. Providing security for both facilities was tedious and by the end of day two his troops showed signs of sloppiness, so he set up a rotating schedule of squad- and platoon-sized patrols that fortunately chanced upon enough enemy action to keep everyone on edge.

"This should have healed a lot better than it has," the medic said, wrapping tape around the large gauze pad.

Horner was the only conscientious objector Glenn Nolan had ever met, and the only soldier in Vietnam who flatly refused to take a rear area job or carry a weapon. He was the company CP medic, in charge of all other company medics assigned to the platoons; it quickly became clear that the skinny young kid was somebody special to the troops of Alpha company.

His father had been a Baptist missionary to the Philippines for twenty years until ill health had forced him to leave for the drier climate of Arizona. Young Timothy had been twelve when his family moved to the Hualapai tribe reservation on the west side of the Grand Canyon. He'd planned to attend Bible College in Springfield after high school but was drafted and declared his conscientious objector status. To the surprise of the Army, he didn't persist in resisting the draft but requested medic training with the intent of going to Vietnam.

"That'll do for now," Horner said, taping the bandage tight. "But first thing in the morning, we'll clean and rewrap it with fresh gauze. Taking your malaria pills, lieutenant?"

"When I can remember to."

"Not good enough.... sir."

"I can't swallow the horse pill. That thing is the size of a sewer lid."

"Break it into pieces. But one way or another you have to get it down. It's only one day a week for the Cloroquine-primiequine-phospate. You can manage it. How about the small one – the little white daily tablet?"

"Sometimes I forget, Parson. You don't mind me calling you that, do you?"

Horner got a little smile on his face. "It's better than some of the names EB has come up with. And a bunch of the Hualapai call me the equivalent in their language. I like it. It fits me."

Glenn put his fatigue shirt back on. "You like living among the Indians?"

"Yeah, I do. They're wise in a lot of ways and have some interesting proverbs. Like – 'Treat the Earth well; it was not given to you by your parents. It was loaned to you by your children.' That's sage advice for looking at our stewardship of God's creation. They look at the Earth *not* as a possession to be exploited but an inheritance we borrow temporarily. I shared that with Two Hatchets a couple of months back." Horner's face lit up and he smiled broadly at some private little joke. "He just grinned and said, 'Little Beaver, you wise in way of Indian' like he was Tonto and I was the Lone Ranger. You know that's all an act with him, don't you? – that *me talkem likem Indian* stuff. He learned how to talk like that watching TV."

"I'm not sure I do know that."

"It's true. Two Hatchets has a degree from the University of Oklahoma in geology with a major in petrology. He's probably the most educated guy in the company except for Howse, second squad leader in Rankin's *Riffraff*. And he speaks better English than EB or Heavy... by a long shot."

"You got any more of those proverbs?"

Timmy reached into his medic kit and brought out a small black leather Bible. "Got a whole chapter in here and the book has all the wisdom any man could ever need."

Glenn thought for a few seconds about his quandary and decided to take a chance. "Suppose I had a thorny problem to deal with and was on the horns of a dilemma. I had the ability and authority to take action to rectify the problem, but doing so would cause some hardship, maybe ruin the life of someone. What would your book advise me to do?"

Horner shrugged. "That's not much to go on, sir. I'm assuming there's a clear right and a clear wrong in the situation. One principle would be that it's never right to do wrong to do right. But I think there's something else that applies." The medic thumbed through the books pages and finally said, "It's here in the Book of James, four and seventeen. It says, *Therefore to him that knoweth to do good, and doeth it not, to him it is sin.* I'd say that's pretty clear. If a person knows that what he has to do is right and it's good, then not doing it would be sin because it wouldn't be either good or right. God is all about good and right."

"Even if it's hard?"

"Especially if it's hard. God's not about what's easy... He's about what's right. You're a West Pointer. Isn't there something in that Cadet Prayer about *"... help us to do the harder right instead of the easier wrong and to know no fear when truth and right are in jeopardy...?"*

"How'd you know that?"

"Read it somewhere in somebody's sermon," Horner replied, looking pensive, "A fellow in a big church somewhere out in California, I think. Always thought it had a good ring to it."

Glenn agreed and was about to ask Horner another question when a Huey landed nearby interrupting his train of thought. A sergeant and two soldiers, each carrying an M-60 machine gun, piled out of the cargo compartment and started unloading a dozen ammo cans and several cardboard boxes. Glenn motioned to Heavy and they went to meet the helicopter.

"You said you wanted more machine guns," Sergeant Kaiser yelled to be heard over the sound of the helicopter.

"No, I said I wanted *seven* more machine guns," Nolan yelled back into his supply sergeant's ear above the slapping of rotor blades. "Where are the rest of them?"

"You said six!"

"You're hearing needs to be checked, Kaiser. And we need a lot more ammo than this."

"I'm going to need more NVA ammo belts or other trading material. What you gave me last time was only enough for two guns, these Sundry Packs and six cases of beer." The supply sergeant looked crestfallen. "I thought you'd be at least a little happy with this."

"A little. I'll be happier with five more guns, more Sundry packs and cigarettes for all my smokers. Do I need to bring you out to the field and find another scrounger?!"

"NO SIR!" Kaiser yelled back. "You already got the best one in the whole damn Cav."

"I'll give you another two weeks to prove it to me. Don't let me down, Sergeant."

Kaiser shrugged with an opened handed gesture. "I ran into Lieutenant Cleburne back in Sông Bé this morning on the way out. He got off this bird as I was getting on. Said he was there to get some party fixins. You throwing a barbecue or something out here?"

"Maybe. Maybe not." Glenn didn't know what that was about, and was instantly angry. "When you get back to Sông Bé, if Cleburne is there, you tell him to get his ass back out here and report to me before the sun goes down." Glenn watched the sergeant climb back aboard the Huey, and wondered what he was going to have to do with his second platoon leader.

After the ship departed, Nolan and Heavy toted the machine guns back to the CP. Glenn told EB, "Call second platoon and have Sergeant Hansen send his best soldier up here. I've got an important job for him. And call the platoons to come pick up M-60 ammo."

A brief moment later EB looked up from his radio conversation. "Hansen wants to know who you want him to send."

"Tell him what I told you. I want his best soldier because I've got an important job."

A few seconds later, EB gave him a worn out look and said, "Six, he wants to know what the job is so he can pick the right guy,"

"Tell him I'm looking for his best soldier, period... if he doesn't have one, just say so."

"Listen here, Gamecock five," EB drawled into the handset. "Odin says he wants your best man. And he said, if'n you ain't got nobody down there that's worth a shit, he'll just hafta go find one elsewhere in Viking or the Riffraff 'cause he's sure they got one or two. Now stop screwin' with us before I have to send Heavy down there to take you out to the lick log... OUT!" The RTO rolled his eyes and threw his arms up in bewilderment. "Six, sometimes that boy is thicker'n a salt block. The Shake 'n Bakes we're getting' in here lately is dense as a marble and not near as smart."

"I think you explained well enough that he'll understand."

Minutes later Tyrell Hannam showed up at the CP; Nolan was pleased.

Hannam was a tall, well-muscled black enlisted soldier from St. Louis – a Spec-4. Nolan had observed him and decided that below the surface of his slow, measured ways lurked an intelligent and highly capable soldier. He'd exhibited savvy and coolness under fire more than once. Despite wearing his helmet backwards, his shirt open and a large ebony fist dangling by a leather thong around his neck, Hannam carried himself and behaved like a seasoned soldier. He was respected by the other black soldiers as their leader – Glenn had overheard one of them refer to him as "head brutha" his first day with Alpha company.

"Platoon sergeant said to come up here for a detail," Hannam said to EB and looked around. "What's shakin' little Jeb the Reb. Where's the Top Sergeant?"

"Hannam, this is my job, not a detail from Top. Come talk with me," Glenn said, motioning him over and moving out of earshot of the others. He sat down with his back to a tree and indicated for the Spec-4 to take a seat. "I just got two new M-60s today. I'm expecting the supply sergeant to come up with another half dozen in the next couple of weeks, so I can equip each squad with one, and carry a spare in the CP. Instead of infantry squads, I want us to have nine big machine gun teams with the firepower of a battalion instead of a company; that's where I need your help. I want you to check out those two new guns, and the others as they come in, and train the two-man crews and backups how to operate and maintain them."

The soldier looked at him with dulled eyes. "I don't carry a machine gun no more, Six."

"I heard. I don't expect you to carry one – all the time – except those times when you're training crews so you can show them on patrol how to handle one. I don't want a cherry gunner out there learning for the first time on his own under fire. I want you to be the unit trainer for the M-60."

Hannam leaned back and looked at him with hooded eyes. "Why'd you ask for me?"

Glenn smiled easily. "I didn't."

"Hansen said you wanted me."

"Not exactly. Didn't ask for you by name. I asked him to send his best soldier; it was a test – for me, and for him. I wanted to see if my perception was accurate. I was almost certain he'd choose you. Actually I wanted you and was not surprised that Sergeant Hansen and I share the same opinion about your soldiering." Hannam looked skeptical and a little unhappy. "I'm not blowing smoke up your butt, if that's what you're thinking. I've been over here long enough and seen enough to be able to pick out the good soldiers from the average or worthless. Your platoon sergeant's choice confirmed I've still got it."

"Don't know that I want to do it."

"I think you should. This isn't coming from anybody but me."

"You telling me to do it?"

"Do I need to? I could. But something tells me I don't need to put this in the form of an order. I'd rather you do it willingly."

"What you want me to do is to train more people to do a better job of killing these Vietnamese."

"Correction. The enemy."

"I don't have nothin' against *the little man*." Glenn had heard Hannam and some of the other black soldiers use the phrase in referring to the NVA. "He's just fightin' to see his people live free. I could see me doin' the same thing back in the world for my own people."

"Some day we might have time to talk about that. Actually, I'd like to. We'll do it. But look at it this way – having three times the firepower we have now is also a way of keeping more of us alive in a fight. Don't you want to see more of your brothers go home – and I'm talking about *all* your brothers in the company. I include me and you in that." He continued to look into Hannam's eyes which never changed or wavered.

Am I getting through to this guy? He couldn't tell.

"You say we got two new guns?" Hannam asked at last.

"That's right. And hopefully another half dozen."

"Who do you want me to train?"

"Start out with one soldier from second platoon, and me."

For the first time, Hannam's emotionless face looked surprised. "You?!"

"It's been five years since I trained on an M-60 and I'm really rusty. Don't look at me that way. I'm not as stupid as I come across. Not asking you to do *Mission Impossible*, Tyrell!" The corner of Hannam's mouth turned up a little. "You pick the other gunner."

"Pineapple," Hannam said immediately. "Lareto Mabins. He's from Samoa and we call him Pineapple because he looks Hawaiian and he calls Oahu home now."

"He's small," Glenn observed.

"But he's strong, like a bodybuilder. Good soldier, and smart. Most likes him, and everybody trusts him."

"All right, you and Pineapple give those guns a good going over to make sure they're ready to go. First thing tomorrow, after first light patrol, give me a refresher and I'll carry a gun along with Pineapple on the afternoon platoon patrol. Then in a couple of days, you train somebody from 1st or 3rd platoon. Fair enough? After that, we'll see what happens."

Hannam was silent for some time, his eyes darting around as he contemplated. "All right, Six. I'll do it. But I'm doing this for you, not nobody else."

"Actually, you're doing this for the guys in the company. And for their girlfriends and family. Any questions?" Hannam shook his head, and Nolan said, "I've got one. That name you've got written in big block letters on your helmet – what does it mean?"

"Masika... born in the monsoon. It's my African name."

"I believe Loo-tenant Bluster is fixin' to learn how the cow eats the cabbage," EB proclaimed to Heavy, Holmes, and Timmy Horner as they relaxed in the shade, just inside the wood line. "Jest like one o' them hang town draw-fighter showdowns from *Tales of the Texas Rangers*," the RTO offered, lighting a Marlboro. "Damn it's hot."

The Huey made a tight circling approach to what had been the log pad of the old U.S. firebase, kicking up a dust cloud. Lieutenant Cleburne climbed out of the UH-1, slung his rucksack over his back and strutted toward the wood line south and west of the abandoned LZ where Glenn Nolan stood casually, with his M-16 in his right hand.

"Lieutenant Cleburne," Glenn said loudly as the 2nd platoon leader walked by him several yards away. He motioned the southerner over toward the crumbling berm of the old firebase. "I need to talk with you. I got a problem and you're the one who can help me with it."

The platoon leader stopped and looked at him. "Can we do this later? Got something I need to do with my troops."

"As it turns out, this can't wait. We need to talk now." Cleburne looked perturbed but finally sighed deeply, reluctantly followed Nolan and sat down facing his commander. "Let me tell you the problem I've got. You see, I've got a leader in the company stirring up hard feelings between himself and his black soldiers. Know anything about this?"

Cleburne pursed his lips and looked like he was thinking hard but finally shrugged. "Nope. Why are you asking me? Are you sayin' this is goin' on in the Gamecocks? Nobody's brought anything like that to me. Is it one of my squad leaders, or the platoon sergeant?"

"No," Glenn looked directly into the lieutenant's eyes and held his gaze. "Actually, it's you. It's come to me that your manner of dealing with the black troops is viewed by them as demeaning. Any idea why they'd think that?"

"Who told you that?" Cleburne asked quietly, lowering his voice as his eyes darted away; the veneer of arrogance suddenly dissipated.

Glenn looked at the platoon leader and thought, *that's not how an innocent man reacts.* "There's a problem in your platoon. Tell me why black soldiers, including my first sergeant, feel they have to come to me with this complaint? I want to hear what you think is going on."

"I don't know what you're talkin' about, Lieutenant," Cleburne said, still refusing to look at him. He'd regained some of his composure but his neck and ears had turned red. There's nothin' out of the ordinary goin' on. I treat the black boys in my platoon just as good as the whites. They got nothin' to complain about. Why are you just now bringin' this up to me?"

"Because, Cleburne, it was just brought up to me a few days ago and I'm checking it out. I'm not talking behind your back. I'm sitting here a foot away telling you what I'm hearing and asking you what your response is. I haven't decided anything yet. I'm seeking to find the facts and understand what they mean. I don't sweep things under the rug."

"Well, there ain't none to be swept under. Nobody treats the Nigras in his platoon better than me. Not Rankin. Not Thorgier. Some of my best friends are black. Don't preach to me, Nolan." Cleburne started to rise to his feet.

"Sit down, lieutenant," Glenn said in his calmest tone. "We're not done here yet."

"Well, maybe you're not."

"That was a direct order. You know the penalty for disobeying a direct order from your commander in a combat zone?" *You should,* Glenn thought. *Your father retired from active duty as a one-star and is now the Adjutant General of the South Carolina National Guard.*

Cleburne scoffed and gave him a disgusted look, but he sat down.

"Today you absented yourself from the company without permission," Glenn continued looking at the platoon leader quizzically. "Where'd you go?"

"I caught a helicopter down at the POL point that was headed to Sông Bé. I'da asked you, but you weren't around. I guess you were out on one of your patrols."

"I was. Tell me why you spent the day in Sông Bé while the company was out here." He forced himself calm, but was angry beyond words at the platoon leader's disrespectful tone and contemptuous attitude.

The lieutenant relaxed and gave him a frosty smile devoid of mirth. "Tomorrow's my birthday, and I promised the fellas in my platoon a little celebration. Had to go get some party fixins." He reached into the rucksack and pulled out two bottles – a fifth of Jack Daniels and a quart of Beefeater gin. "Got two more in there."

"So you thought you had to go back so you could break rule number one."

Upon assuming command, he'd instituted his first of what would become many rules for operating in the field. Boomer Cameron had told him his predecessor and the former first sergeant were relieved for drunkenness on a forward firebase. Not only were they intoxicated, but apparently it extended to several of the troops. He laid out in plain, simple words what he'd been told about the incident and how it would never be repeated. Hard liquor – was strictly forbidden in the company. It was Nolan's Rule #1.

"Look Nolan, it's not that much. Besides, it's my birthday!"

Glenn smiled at him. "I don't give a damn if it's the president's birthday and he okayed it. You violated my first and most sacred rule. Pour it out on the ground. Right now."

Cleburne looked stunned. "Wait a minute. I spent a lot of money on this. You don't know how much those black market sergeants are asking for this stuff."

"You didn't spend a lot of money... you wasted a lot of money. Pour that liquor out on the ground, now. That's an order." Glenn pulled the .45 pistol from its holster and casually inspected it. The color rose higher on the lieutenant's face but finally he reluctantly poured out the contents and angrily tossed the bottles inside the abandoned firebase.

"Satisfied?" Cleburne asked lifting his head and jutting out his jaw.

Glenn ignored the question. "Here's my point, don't you ever again break Rule One. And don't ever absent yourself from this company for any reason without first getting my personal approval. If you ever do that again, you might as well keep on going. Is that clear enough for you?"

Cleburne glared at him but remained silent.

"One last thing," Glenn said, standing and looking down at the lieutenant. "I'm aware you've gotten in the habit of staying behind when your platoon is sent out on patrol. I hear that goes back some months, but it ends today. You *will* go on every patrol your platoon is sent out on. No exceptions. I won't tolerate that kind of behavior from the lowest private much less an officer, Lieutenant Cleburne... Now, you're free to go. Briefing at the company CP at eighteen hundred about missions for tomorrow. Do not be late."

Chapter 21

He felt the bed floating, bobbing, whirling like a cork in a storm-tossed sea.

"Wake up, Brad. We gotta fly the Nighthawk. Syzmanski is out pre-flighting already. Come on, man. We gotta get a move on."

"What time is it?"

"Twenty-two hundred, give or take."

"I can't fly, Ed. I'm sick as a dog."

"You're not sick. You're drunk as a skunk."

"An even better reason not to fly. Eight hours bottle to throttle. Remember?" He opened an eye, saw Norton hovering over him and rolled over. "I'm not scheduled tonight or tomorrow. Both of us are on crew rest... finally. I'm too drunk to fly. Haven't been this wasted since I flunked out of Delaware."

"The C.O. says we're going. There's a big push on bright and early tomorrow. Four o'clock wake-up, five-thirty crank for everybody. Something really big is happening in six hours. We're tasked for eighteen birds for lift missions alone. No log birds until further notice."

"In the whole 2nd Brigade?"

"I don't have any details but it sounds like the whole damned division. The way they were talking in Ops, it's like we're moving every grunt in the Cav at the same time. But that's not our worry. Getting airborne with the Nighthawk bird is. I just got the mission sheet and a real blunt order from the major to get cranked and out of here."

"I'm telling you I can't fly. Man, my head is spinning like crazy."

His memory was sketchy, but he had a vague recollection of drinking beer at the sandbagged bunker next door that served as the platoon clubhouse. He remembered being helped into his bed and the room swirling like a merry-go-round on afterburner. It was dark when that happened. He turned on his flashlight and checked the time. *Oh, yeah, that's right. Norton said it was twenty-two hundred. I've been asleep less than two hours. It feels like somebody imbedded an entrenching tool in my forehead. There's no way I can fly tonight. This is crazy. Plain crazy.* "Where's my flight suit?"

"You're wearing it. The C.O. says we're both on report if we're not on station in twenty minutes," Norton told him as he laced up Brad's boots."

"Are you sober enough to fly?"

"Sure. I had one beer tonight. That's all. But you're the A/C, and you *are* going."

"Wake me when we get back." The walk down to the flight line, the quick pre-flight inspection and starting the aircraft was a blur. At one point he thought he heard Syzmanski ask Norton if he wanted to put Nolan in the back to sleep it off while he sat in the right seat. 'I can probably fly this better than he can right now,' the crew chief observed. Brad dozed off; when he awoke they were hovering over the runway and Norton was talking to the tower.

"Six-six-five, southwest departure straight out with a right turn when able. Wind is calm. Ceiling five hundred overcast; one mile visibility. Cleared for special VFR departure."

"Six-six-five, roger."

Nolan was instantly awake as Norton lowered the nose of the Huey.

"Did he say Special VFR?" Brad asked, sitting straight up at the same time the helicopter shuddered and entered translational lift. "Five hundred feet and a mile?!"

"He did say that."

"We can't do this mission with that kind of ceiling." He was suddenly panicked; both he and Norton had a tactical instrument ticket and neither of them had any actual instrument flying time. This was suddenly very serious. Life-threatening. "I've got the controls!"

Brad turned hard left back toward the field just as the intermittent wisps of cloud visible in the glow of the landing light turned into a solid white sheet. His altimeter had just passed three hundred feet and he was disoriented.

This was no longer a tactical mission but a life and death situation - survival.

Fly the plane, Nolan! Stop the turn. Wings level; positive rate of climb. Don't worry about the radio yet. He looked quickly at Norton, and when he looked back, he was certain he was in a diving left turn. *Check the instruments! Needle, ball and airspeed. They look normal, but...* Sweat begin to drip down the back of his neck and he clung to the cyclic with a death grip. *Not a good thought to have right now, Nolan. Relax. .Don't hold on so tight!* He sensed the diving turn was tightening despite what the instruments said. *Oh no. I've got vertigo!*

"Norton, we're on actual IFR. This'll be good practice. You take the controls. Just keep your head inside the cockpit and your eyes on the instruments. Keep it straight and level, with the artificial horizon. Eighty to ninety knots, and a shallow rate of climb – three to five hundred feet per minute. It'll fly itself. You have the controls."

"I've got it," Norton said.

Brad closed his eyes and took a few deep breaths. *This is not good. But you've done a couple of GCAs into Phouc Vinh for practice. And we're only a few miles off the airfield. We'll be back on the ground in fifteen minutes with a funny tale to tell.*

"Shouldn't we call somebody?" Norton asked, glancing in his direction.

"Don't look at me, Ed. Keep your eyes on the needle, ball, airspeed and artificial horizon. I'll take care of the radio and navigation. The best instrument pilots are a little lazy, so relax and keep it right where you have it now. I'll get us a GCA from the Air Force and we'll call it a night," Brad said easily, but his heart was beating rapidly and his palms were sweating.

A call to the tower, revealed the GCA was down for end of the month maintenance and scheduled to be back up in three hours, four at the outside; they'd be out of fuel long before then. He cussed the Air Force while locating charts in his helmet bag for Tan Son Nhut Air Base outside Saigon, fifty miles from Phouc Vinh. Just before midnight, they landed, refueled after hovering around most of the perimeter fence to locate POL. They shut down outside Air Force operations where they made a call back to Ghostrider operations. The Ops officer chewed them out and ordered them to return to Phouc Vinh by zero five-thirty, or preferably sooner. They needed the Nighthawk bird for mission the next morning.

"Screw him," Brad said. "I'm not going back there until the sun comes up."

But a phone call at four-thirty a.m. from their platoon leader advised them the weather was lifting and the GCA was up and functional. They were ordered to crank and return immediately. Forty minutes later they landed back at home base and the company commander ordered them to offload the big search light and catch up to them at Bù Gia Mập airstrip as soon as they re-configured for carrying troops. He told them the 1st Cav Division had been called on to do what nobody in the U.S. or South Vietnam had ever expected.

It was going to be a long day for everyone.

*　　*　　*

Colonel van Noort and 'Boomer' Cameron climbed down from the Huey; it was ten minutes after official sunup.

"Something big just came up, Nolan," the battalion commander said to Glenn. "We need to talk. Bring your map." They stopped at the end of the dirt runway. "Remember bitching to me on Illingworth a month ago about having to stop at the border and not being allowed to chase the 95C Regiment back into Cambodia? Seems somebody in Washington heard you."

A flight of eighteen Hueys in staggered trail formation came over the trees directly above their heads and settled onto the grassy area to the east of the runway near the Engineer's water gathering facility. The racket was deafening as they slowed and landed; once down three or four dozen troops got off and moved quickly to the edge of the wood line.

"Replacements for Alpha, sir?" Glenn asked, thinking there must be a whole platoon; he'd be up to a hundred and twenty, maybe more.

"No, they're a polyglot of cooks and clerks and hangers-on from brigade, here to secure the FARP and the potable water operation. The 227th picked them up at oh-dark-thirty at Sông Bé." Van Noort looked at his watch. "In two hours the president will be making a speech to the nation. So you don't have much time. Boomer will brief you and your platoon leaders as soon as you can get them up here. You're getting your wish, Nolan. We're going to Cambodia for a few months to kill NVA and take away all their toys. "

Nolan's heart leapt into his throat. *Cambodia.*

The word created images of a deep, dark and deadly pit.

*   *   *

"Alpha company is to secure LZ Sabre located here on the map, fifteen miles inside Cambodia. Aerial photos taken by a Mohawk three days ago makes it look like a ten or twelve shipper," Boomer Cameron said, indicating with a wooden pointer a small rectangle drawn on the acetate overlay of the battalion map. "Sabre is, like I said, fifteen miles inside Cambodia but more important, it's also three to five miles from where some intel analysts in Saigon say that COSVN is located... here in the Kratié province. MACV says it moved there in late March after the 2nd Battalion 8th Cav threatened its existence in the Dog's Head. It's believed Illingworth and Jay were attacked to cover that movement out of Tay Ninh province into this part of Cambodia. We might get to finish that job."

"What's this COSVN, major?" Sergeant Renfroe asked. Glenn had all the squad leaders attend the briefing under the trees along with the officers, and he'd insisted battalion provide each of them a map covering the battalion AO inside Cambodia.

"It's the NVA headquarters – Central Office for South Vietnam. They're the field headquarters that controls all the regular and irregular forces of North Vietnam operating in the south. Where we're going they'll contest because its got lots of supplies and a lot of their command and control."

"You mean there'll be a lot of contact," Renfroe said.

"That's exactly what I mean," Boomer responded. "We're going to be using the same LZ to insert Charlie company right behind you, and the Recon platoon behind them. In the next day or two we'll be setting up a new battalion firebase called 'Charo' inside Vietnam about two klicks from the border. That'll be Bravo company's job. They'll be pulled out of the field and CA'd into there this afternoon if they can make it to the PZ we chose for them... Nolan."

Glenn got up and moved next to the map.

"Our mission is initially to secure LZ Sabre for Charlie company and Recon. Once they're on the ground, we move out east while Recon heads north and Charlie goes west. Our PZ time is zero nine hundred. Platoon leaders have their aircraft assignments. Company CP will be in chalks two and three. SOP on the LZ is that twelve o'clock is the direction of landing and initial location of the CP. First platoon outposts with one squad each at 12, 4, and 8 initially. When second platoon comes in they fill from two o'clock to six; when third platoon shows up they take from ten to six. First platoon covers from ten to twelve to two.

"The lift ships will go in two elements of eight ships each. If the LZ goes hot before the second flight of eight can get in, everyone then on the ground moves to twelve o'clock and we set up a perimeter there until we can sort things out and secure the LZ for follow on flights. Make sure everyone in your squad knows that. It's our standard procedure for all CAs from now on. Questions?" Thankfully there were none. "Time is now zero eight three eight. Platoon leaders move your troops to the ships as soon as you can. Load up when lead aircraft starts to crank. I'll see you in Cambodia."

Another large formation of Hueys loaded with Delta company approached and landed on the opposite side of the runway from the first lift. The troops unloaded and filtered into the jungle west of the runway and the lift departed.

"They're going back to Evita to pick up Charlie company and stage there," van Noort said to Nolan, looking at his watch. "In a half hour, give or take, the president will be finished with his speech and by then you'll be the first infantry company in the Cav on Cambodian soil. We'll have three companies on the ground on the other side of the river well before noon. Pretty heady stuff."

"Seems like it, sir."

The colonel turned toward his C&C ship then stopped and looked at Nolan. "Good luck."

Ten minutes later, the Alpha company CP group was sitting on the ground near chalks two and three. It was strangely quiet when Cleburne approached.

"I've got a problem with one of the black boys in my platoon. Cox says he's not going."

Glenn bridled at the message and the tone; he wished he had at least one more day to deal with the lieutenant before this operation got underway. "Tell him that's not an option."

"I have. But he insists on talkin' to you."

Glenn rolled his eyes. "You've got to be kidding. I don't have the time or... where is he?"

"Chalk ten."

"All right. Let's go talk to him."

They walked quickly back to the tenth aircraft in the rising heat of the morning. He was sweating and insects buzzed around his head; he grew more exasperated as they neared the aircraft. A short black soldier paced frantically while talking to himself and wildly thrashing his arms up and down. *This is not good*, Glenn thought.

Glenn walked up to the soldier who was wandering in circles and flailing his arms while talking loudly to himself. "Cox, what's your problem?"

The soldier suddenly stopped pacing. "Can't be goin' to no Cambodia."

"Well, we are. All of us – including you."

"I can't be goin'. I said to myself – self, you gone get yourself kilt in that Cambodia if'n you go over there, so don't do it. You gotta put me on a helicopter back to Sông Bé."

"No I don't. And I damned sure won't. You see, if you go to Cambodia you might possibly die. But if you don't go, I guarantee you'll die – that's for sure." Glenn pointed to the south where a narrow dirt road cut through the wood line. "You see that road? Thirty-five miles down that road is Sông Be. Between here and there is where Luke the Gook lives with all his buddies. In ten minutes, we're all gonna leave on these helicopters. Right after that, all those guys over there in the woods are gonna leave in their helicopters... and we're all going to Cambodia. You can go to Cambodia with the guys in your platoon, or you can go to Cambodia with those guys over there that you don't know. Or, you can walk down that road over there and try to make it to Sông Bé on your own, hoping that Luke the Gook doesn't catch you."

The soldier's eyes grew wide and troubled. "You can't do that. They'll court-martial you for leaving me out here."

"I doubt it... the only person getting court-martialed is you, if you survive."

"That ain't right, you doin' me that way."

"Maybe; maybe not. But I don't have time to mess with you and this phony crazy thing you're doing. I'll damn sure leave you here. Count on it. Like I said, your choice." Glenn leaned close to him and whispered, "I know you're not crazy. Get on the damned helicopter and stop fartin' around."

Cox drew back and blinked rapidly. He shot quick glances at the few soldiers from his squad standing nearby, and finally he put on his helmet before sitting on the floor of the helicopter. Glenn looked at Cleburne and said, "You make sure he stays on that ship. I expect you to handle the discipline in 2nd platoon. The next time something like this happens, you bring the soldier to me after filling me in on exactly what the problem is and why nothing in your power solved it. Understood?"

His troops were climbing into helicopters up and down the line as Glenn ran toward the front of the formation. The whine of turbines and shimmering exhaust heat along with the smell of burning kerosene invaded the still air around Bù Gia Mập. Nolan threw on his gear and sat on the floor with his legs dangling out, leaning back into his eighty pound rucksack. The troops he could see gazed straight ahead, cradling their M16s, muzzles down. He looked back over his shoulder and saw Masika staring at him; he looked remarkably serene.

The Huey felt squirrely beneath him, then suddenly broke ground and nosed over as it gained airspeed, shuddering momentarily and then seemed to float. A few hundred feet up, the formation went into a shallow left bank which from Glenn's seat, with nothing to hold on to, felt like a horribly steep turn. In a few minutes they leveled off; ten minutes later they crossed a winding river cutting through mountain jungle... and entered Cambodia.

"Eight minutes," Brad said over the intercom to the crew. "Slow it down very gradually to eighty knots, Norton. That'll give us sixty seconds separation from Yellow flight at the LZ."

A Cobra gunship moved slowly by him on the left like a malevolent shark, then another on the right. Up ahead two more, one on either side of Yellow flight, cruised near the rear of that formation waiting for the Hueys to begin their approach. Time seemed to stand still.

"Two minutes, Yellow flight."

The rate of artillery explosions on the landing zone increased noticeably.

"One minute to LZ." The gray-black explosions in the clearing ahead ceased and immediately a single white phosphorus shell exploded on the LZ. The first two gunships began firing pairs of rockets along the tree lines left and right on Sabre, then pummeled the LZ with 40mm grenades and machine guns. The second flight of Cobras fired rockets as their first section broke off.

Leaning out and looking ahead from fifty feet up, Glenn saw the end of the LZ rushing at them. Thirty yards left and right of the flight, trees were shattering to splinters as exploding rockets from the Cobras tore through them with horrendous thunderclaps, one on top of another. Both door gunners were spraying the wood lines with high volume M60 machine gun fire adding to the loud racket and throwing hot shell casings into the cargo compartment.

Suddenly, the Huey hit the ground hard and seemed to bounce and go airborne almost immediately. In that instant, the troops of Alpha company jumped from the Hueys and began moving toward the jungle. He saw Masika and Heavy heading for twelve o'clock on the LZ as the skids of the third ship in the formation passed by him at head height. When he turned to look at the rest of his company, his heart jumped into his throat as he saw a crew chief in a Huey half way back in the formation throw a grenade that instantly emitted red smoke.

Glenn knelt in the tall grass, thumbed the selector switch to AUTO and emptied a magazine into the wood line forty yards away where tracers from Masika's machine gun were hitting and whining off. The last helicopter went directly over him; he felt hot brass from the door gun bounce off his helmet and rain down around him. He low crawled away from the NVA toward the opposite edge of the landing zone. Halfway there he got to his feet and ran bent over. Off to his left the machine gun kept up a steady volume of fire and now he could hear rounds going past his head.

He made it inside the line of trees near Masika and Heavy. EB and Holmes lay on the ground, both talking on their radios. A B40 shot across the open field and hit a tree off to his left with its distinct crack and loud boom. AK firing crackled through the trees chest high breaking branches and pulverizing leaves that filtered down over them like slow falling snow.

Sweat rolled down his forehead into his eyes; his jungle fatigues were soaking wet.

"Six!" It was EB holding out the handset to his PRC-77. "Viking."

Glenn took the company net handset from EB and yelled at Holmes, "Tell battalion the LZ is hot and to bounce Max. And tell them to get me a Rash bird up on our company freq – NOW!!... "Viking, this is Odin," Glenn yelled into the handset above the roar of gunfire.

"*This is Viking. We made it to the east wood line, back in the corner. Set up Pineapple's machine gun on our left flank and he's working over that far wood line from south to north. We're tied in to Gamecock's left flank.*"

"Roger. Make sure you have security to your rear. CP is along the same wood line all the way to the north. Keep pressure across the LZ. I'm working my way toward you to check on Riffraff and Gamecock. Break, break... Gamecock, this is Odin, over."

"*Odin, this is Gamecock Sleeper.*"

"Put Gamecock on."

"*He's not here right now. Gotta find him.*"

"Tell him to get back to me soonest with status. Tell him to make sure he's got three-sixty security. Out... Riff Raff, this is Odin. Your status?"

"*Riffraff Sleeper. He's positioning our –*" A ten second burst from an M60 nearby cut through the air. " *I'll get Riffraff.*"

Glenn looked around and spotted his new artillery FO, a first lieutenant named Pete Dannacher. "Dannacher, get me some arty on the other side of the LZ. Do it NOW!"

"Working on it!" A few seconds later a white phosphorous shell exploded a thousand feet in the air well beyond the far woods from which the NVA continued shooting. He heard the FO say into his handset, "Two rounds, on the deck. Will adjust."

Dannacher's crew included a sergeant who struck him as confused and introverted, a Spec-4 radio operator who hadn't said two words since the FO team arrived, and a slightly built, long-haired peacenik from Seattle named Mikey Meade. All of them looked at him now confused and frightened.

Because of Meade's short stature EB had immediately named him 'Mike the Tyke' when Dannacher's team joined Alpha at Sông Bé. Heavy had to step in and break up the fight that followed. "I think that little hippie PFC has a big chip on his shoulder," the five-mike told him before Glenn threatened them both with court martial if the event was ever repeated. Meade was already on probation with his battery and didn't seem to give a healthy damn about much of anything except reading Shakespeare, writing poetry and smoking Kools.

"Dutch one-one, Blue Max one-eight on your push. We're two minutes out. Four snakes with about a half load of ordnance. Where do you want us?"

"Bad guys hold the west side of Sabre. We hold the east side only," Glenn said loudly into the handset. "You're clear in at will. Be advised we have arty out of Evita impacting."

"Roger I have the advisory. Max two-four is lifting off POL at Bù Gia Mập s and will be on station in about ten. He'll contact you on this push when inbound."

Glenn checked on Masika and Heavy, left the ammo box of M60 rounds from his rucksack and went with EB and Holmes in search of first platoon. He found Rankin, had him send a squad to provide security for the CP and its machine gun, then located the second platoon sergeant, Ned Hansen, who was getting an ammo status from his squad leaders. The platoon medic, a chubby kid with a pale complexion, was wrapping a bandage around the arm of a trooper nearby. Lieutenant Cleburne sat behind a tree by himself with his back to the LZ.

"Cleburne!" Glenn yelled to get his attention. "Are you tied in to Viking?"

The lieutenant jumped, and sat bolt upright stammering, "Yes, yes. We're tied in."

"Any wounded?"

Cleburne gave him a wild look and then glanced at his platoon sergeant.

"Yes, sir," Sergeant Hansen said quickly. "Three walking wounded. None of them bad."

"Make sure you're outposted to the rear. No idea how many NVA there are but they might try to flank us and come from behind. Got that?"

"Roger that, Six," Hansen said.

Nolan moved away toward third platoon just as the first Cobra gunship salvoed its ordnance on the far side of the open landing zone. It was an awesome sight from a half of a football field away, and after the last one turned off target and departed, the exchange of small arms fire ceased. Less than two minutes later, he found Thorgier who was talking to one of his squad leaders and pointing out positions behind his platoon.

"Caught a handful of 'em trying to get behind us," the platoon leader said, removing his helmet and wiping his forehead with a faded OD bandana. "Pineapple lit 'em up and they left four bodies. You gonna let me keep him? He's the best 60 gunner I ever had."

"Keep him for now." Glenn replied, looking across the field toward where the artillery had started up again. "I need you to recon the south side of the LZ. I'll send Riffraff with a squad to check the north side. If we can get your platoon from ten to six and Gamecock from two to six, we'll have the LZ secured and they can bring in Echo Recon and Charlie company."

Holmes came over and handed him the handset for the battalion net. "The colonel," he said simply. Glenn removed his helmet, knelt and took the radio call.

"You're holding up the whole invasion. How long before the LZ is secure?"

Anger suddenly welled up in him, and Nolan took a couple of deep breaths to keep himself from replying with something hugely sarcastic that would land him in trouble. *Damn! Been on the ground in a hot LZ for fifteen minutes and he's got a knot in his knickers already.* "We've secured the east side of the LZ and are moving now to secure the south and north ends. Estimate an NVA company holds the western edge of Sabre. Working tube artillery and Max to eliminate the threat... and requested support from RASH." *Don't say another word, or the old man will have your ass, Nolan.*

"Lieutenant No-lann, EB said, nervously lighting a cigarette and then handing over the handset to the company net. "Rash two seven is on station."

"Rash 27, this is Odin. I'm in the eastern tree line of LZ Sabre with an estimated NVA company and probably more across the open area to the west. Where are you and what do you have for us?"

"I'm three minutes south. Flight of four A-37s fifteen minutes out. Pop smoke."

Glenn took a smoke grenade from his pistol belt, pulled the pin and threw it into the open area. "Smoke is out. Break. Break. Viking, Riffraff, Gamecock. Hold your positions. We'll let the Air Force fight the war for a while."

Off to his right, in the direction of the company CP, heavy firing arose; automatic weapons: AKs and NVA .30 cals plus B40s too numerous to count. The crescendo of small arms echoed in the jungle, very near, rising and falling, punctuated with thunderclaps of the RPGs. He was gripped with a sudden fear, imagining the worst. From the corner of his eye he saw the winking of muzzle flashes from the far side of Sabre, across the open expanse.

"Let's go!" he yelled at EB and Holmes, running past them in the direction of the CP.

"Get down, Six!" someone yelled as foliage around him splintered and disintegrated. He ran several steps, tripped and went down hard; a sliver of exquisite pain shot up the length of his arm and he lost his helmet in the dense undergrowth. *Find it later*, he said to himself as he got to his feet and ran bent over toward the CP. When he got there, the artillery FO and his team were flat on the ground and Timmy Horner was working on Lieutenant Dannacher's leg. Several yards away, Masika was firing short, controlled bursts down a path that ran beneath the triple canopy. Two black pajama - clad bodies lay twenty yards away on the narrow trail.

"Rash two seven is rolling hot on the targets to the west," EB told him, gasping for breath when he caught up. "Next pass will be A-37s with five hundred pounders."

"Tell the platoons to keep everyone down... and behind cover. We'll get big chunks this close with nothing between us and the explosions." The aerial display was breathtaking when it happened. He could hear pieces of shrapnel going through the trees around him about six feet over his head as he lay on the jungle floor.

"Don't you wish you had your helmet?" EB asked from behind his rucksack, chain smoking.

"Don't need it," Glenn replied. "If it gets really bad, I'll put my head between my legs."

EB rolled his eyes at him as one of the slow jets dropped his bombs, shaking the earth beneath them. "Why you doin' that?... so you can kiss your ass goodbye?"

*   *   *

"Good work, Nolan. Pass that on to everybody in Alpha," Colonel van Noort told him as they stood at the edge of the jungle on the north side of LZ Sabre. "One of the Ghostrider pilots reported there were hundreds of NVA north and west of here."

"We were lucky. The Air Force and Blue Max did all the work. We found a couple dozen NVA on the west side of the LZ and a bunch of blood trails."

Echo Recon was airlifted in immediately and had already set off toward the south; Charlie company followed them into Sabre and was now moving west. Ammunition resupply had been brought in and Heavy was working with the platoon sergeants to get it distributed. It had been a busy, totally chaotic first hour inside Cambodia.

"There's a lot of gooks around here, sir."

"I suspect so," van Noort agreed. "After the intel reports coming in from division headquarters, I'm more convinced than ever that COSVN isn't far away – somewhere along Highway 7." The colonel pulled out his map and circled an area in grease pencil. "This is where I want you to head and once there, I want you to step on every square meter of it, no matter how long it takes. I'm betting that's where they're located. How soon can you move?"

"In fifteen minutes, sir, when we finish ammo resupply."

"Your troops a little trigger happy?"

"Sure they are. I know I was. But this was good for us – we got rid of the butterflies. Nobody hurt too bad, except my artillery FO. I'm going to need a replacement for Lieutenant Dannacher, right now. Can you speed that up with the lanyard yankers?"

"We'll see. There's a shortage of redleg lieutenants they tell me."

EB caught his attention and pointed to the handset. "Six, the Pink Team is reporting back in. They sound like, well... like real excited. Seems we got ourselves CA'd almost into the middle of one hellacious NVA complex."

"Where?" vanNoort wanted to know.

Glenn took the radio and pulled out his pad. "1st of the 9th reports a complex about three klicks north-northeast of here.– thatch covered hootches, bamboo walkways with street signs, a motor pool and a lumber yard."

"Let's take a look at it on the map." After pinpointing the location, the colonel used Holmes's radio to call back to his headquarters and then turned to Nolan. "Lieutenant, you've got a new mission. Move to and secure the facility the 1/9 located." van Noort rubbed his jaw while looking at the map. "All this intel says we're onto something really big. We just might wipe out Uncle Ho's whole damned command and control in the first couple of days. Game over. How'd you like to be the guy who did that?"

"Sir, I'm takin' it one day at a time."

"Take it however you can. Don't be foolish but don't dawdle either. Get Alpha up and moving. I expect you to be there tonight."

The expectation as it turned out was optimistic. The undergrowth along their route through the jungle was heavy and slowed their movement to a crawl. Alpha company set up their night defensive perimeter a hundred yards from the complex and settled in quietly.

The night was perfectly still, darker than any he could remember; there was simply not a breath of air. The thick, ominous silence and the hot air pressed down on him like a wool blanket as he lay on the wet ground, wrapped in his poncho.

You got through today, he told himself. *One down and... how many to go? It all depends on whether you're talking about the tour or this invasion... We can't say invasion, remember? It's an incursion. Right. Doesn't make any difference to Dannacher. He's out of the fight for the duration. So are Mills and Ludlow. Both with million dollar wounds. They were the two happiest guys in all of Cambodia. You could still see their smiles hovering over the LZ after the medevac bird took them away.*

He closed his eyes, pictured Mary Anne, and immediately drifted off, sleeping fitfully until Heavy woke him at 0400 for his radio shift.

Chapter 22

Some called it *Gotham*, or *Picatinny East*. but within days most called it *Metropolis*.

Glenn Nolan hated all the names and the attention they brought. A public affairs officer giving a briefing to reporters in Saigon, referred to the cache site as a North Vietnamese 'metropolis' and within a day the name stuck with the civilian reporting pool and everybody at MACV. Before long everyone in the 1st Cav was also using the name.

From the time of his initial report from within the site, he was besieged with questions from battalion, through brigade and division all the way up to Saigon and General Abrams' staff. All of the levels of command and the reporters in Saigon had questions without end... and expectations.

By the end of D+1, the 2nd day of the 'incursion', he was able to give only a minimal report of what they had on their hands. Headquarters types, even as close as 2nd Brigade in Sông Bé assumed that since he had reached the complex that he controlled it all. That was Pollyannaish in the extreme.

"This is bigger than anyone in the division ever hoped for," Colonel van Noort told Nolan as they stood in a cleared area beneath the triple canopy of jungle fifteen miles north of the border with South Vietnam. "This will cripple the NVA for years. General Roberts is pleased. Very pleased."

It was the end of D+4, Alpha's fifth day in Cambodia.

Metropolis had already yielded tons of munitions, small arms and crew served weapons, communications equipment and NVA military gear such as uniforms, web gear, pith helmets, canteens and just about anything else an individual soldier needed in the field.

"How big would you say this place is, Nolan?"

"It now looks like the complex is about three kilometers by two kilometers," Glenn replied. "My math says that's almost two square miles – and it's only a day's stroll to Vietnam."

Early on D+3, two squads of field engineers with chain saws rappelled in from a Chinook and began felling trees and clearing underbrush. By mid-afternoon an LZ big enough for a Huey had been gouged out of the dense forest and cases of AK-47s, SKS rifles and ammunition began being loaded on a steady stream of helicopters. One of the Alpha company troops had found a large piece of water-stained plywood from one of the hootches and paint from another to make a sign.

HELP KEEP THIS PARK CLEAN !
Cambodia Parks and Wildlife

- CHUCK

"It must have taken the NVA years to haul this stuff down here from Hanoi. How much have you backhauled so far?" the battalion commander asked, looking around at the long line of soldiers formed along a trail running between a cluster of bunkers and the LZ.

"The last count was five hundred AK-47s, a hundred SKS rifles, forty .30 cal. machine guns still packed in Cosmoline. We found an additional fifteen anti-aircraft machine guns on wheeled carriages but we haven't tried to load them out yet. There's more weapons in other bunkers scattered around and we're still trying to get a complete inventory. I've got Lieutenant Fitzgerald organizing it all and First Sergeant Overton managing the work crews. I told them to concentrate on weapons first, followed by the food stocks. We could use some mechanical transportation for the food. So far we located thirteen bunkers filled with rice, sir, each one holding about twenty tons. I think we should get that out of here early so it can be distributed by the government. A few Mules would make things go a lot faster."

"Did you really run across a swimming pool?"

"Third platoon did. I haven't seen it yet. Lieutenant Thorgier says the far eastern stretch of this place looks like an in-country R&R center. This area we're in is more like a quartermaster depot. If we go another couple hundred meters north, we'll run into their training facilities – rifle ranges and outdoor classroom-type areas. I have a couple of guys from my CP scouring that area for documents. In addition to the Mules, I could use some more manpower to make the work go faster."

"I hear you, Nolan. You keep saying that. But the other companies are running across cache sites, too. This is probably the main hub, but there are other places along the trail system headed southwest." The colonel took a deep breath, and looked thoughtful. "I'll be moving the Recon platoon here, OpCon to Alpha for a while."

"That'll help speed things up, sir."

The colonel pursed his lips and frowned. "What won't help is that I'm taking two of your platoons. I have a mission for you that's even more important than this. We're going to finally take down COSVN. More and more intel points to their location just about where we thought it was all along, and that's only five klicks from here. We're going there and we're putting those bastards out of business once and for all. We move as soon Recon closes on *Metropolis*."

Glenn felt his gut tighten. "You said it's a two platoon operation, sir?"

"It's all we can spare right now. We can't entirely abandon this place, but we can leave one of your platoons to carry on with the backhaul while Echo Recon provides security. It'll slow things down, sure, but it has to be done."

"You want me to attack the whole NVA headquarters by myself, with just two platoons?"

"You'll have first call on all air support in the Division... and you're not going by yourself, Nolan. I'm going with you." van Noort opened his map. "I'll show you the plan."

* * *

"I'm not so sure about this," Mary Anne said to her older brother as they walked together under the muted street lights of 10th Street SE.

Her father had encouraged her to go to Washington with Corey despite her misgivings. In the end, she'd agreed only to keep some semblance of peace in the family. Her history classes in high school had shown her how the Civil War had torn apart not only the country but families as well. It was now happening to her family.

"Come on, sis. Get a life," Corey MacEagan said to his sister. "The forecast calls for unseasonably warm temps for the rest of the week and all the way through the weekend. It's spring here in D.C. Perfect weather for getting out and exercising the 1st Amendment."

She still had second thoughts as they approached a four story building with a large sign out front – **THE HAWKISH DOVE**. From inside came the sound of rock music that grew louder and more insistent as they drew closer. She recognized the tune and some of the lyrics from an anti-war standard by Credence Clearwater Revival as the ballad reverberated out through the main entrance. What was the song? *Favorite Son*. That was it. She wondered if the latest about the band was true – that the Fogerty brothers couldn't get along and the band was splitting up after a couple of years of success. Maybe that was a more accurate metaphor about Vietnam than a song about privileged sons of Washington elite.

"I just wanted you to meet some of the crowd that's working to get 'the general' and his buddies out of the jungle and back home in one piece."

"I wish you wouldn't call him that." She bristled at Corey's patronizing tone and his nickname for Glenn.

"I call him that because he acts that way. Even father has seen the change in him since he went off to that mausoleum on the Hudson."

"Maybe the change is in you."

287

"Don't think so, M.A. I've always hated this war – he's in love with it."

She stopped and looked into his face. "You have no idea – he doesn't love it."

"Then why did he volunteer?"

"I'm not talking about it anymore. Keep this up and I'm going home."

Corey relented, smiling at her. "That would break my heart. I really do want you to meet my friends – especially Tripp. He's something else, and the driving force behind *the Dove*. It's not what you've been used to, but it's typical of what's happening across the whole country."

They joined the line of people squeezing through the front door and at last pushed in.

As she'd expected, it was dark and jammed and rock music pummeled the walls. It seemed like everyone was smoking something making the air close, and she picked up a strange, sweet fragrance inside. While most of the crowd had that disheveled look of the anti-war protester, she was surprised to see some trim young men in power suits and smartly dressed women; she guessed they were political staffers from Capitol Hill or one of the scores of agencies scattered around D.C. Corey led her to the bar and ordered drinks. She had just taken her first sip when they were approached by a tall, long-haired man with an entourage of young and strangely subdued women in tow.

"Corey!" the man said loudly to be heard over the noise, hugging her brother and slapping him on the back. He turned and looked at her with his piercing blue eyes, giving her a warm, inviting smile. "This must be your sister, of course. Certainly not your date. She's far too beautiful for that."

He was tall, very tall. Mary Anne guessed him to be at least six-five because of the way he towered over her brother whose height she'd always thought of as well above average.

"Mary Anne, this is Tripp Karter the driving force behind *Hawkish Dove*, both the Club and the movement. Tripp, my sister Mary Anne, the one I was telling you about."

His eyes seemed to bore into hers as Corey made introductions. In most men, the look would have been intimidating, but not so with this attractive man with the long hair that framed his face like the myriad pictures of Jesus in each classroom at her Catholic high school. He had a captivating look, composed of strangely fused sadness and *joie de vivre*. Something about him was instantly likable.

"I'd love to stay and chat," Karter said, holding her hands in his and looking at her with a peaceful, endearing guise that radiated from him. "But the noise, and the crush… May I invite both of you to the Tower? Phil Ochs is playing tonight. Corey, you know the way."

"Ochs?! Here tonight? Yes, certainly we'll be there," her brother replied, in a way that sounded both honored and subservient.

"Wonderful," Tripp said, still smiling at her. "I look forward to speaking with you, Mary Anne. I want you to rest assured we're doing all in our power to bring home those like your husband who should be here with you rather than in a jungle half way around the world and centuries in the past."

He nodded almost imperceptibly. With a lithe grace born of an inexplicable celebrity he moved away followed by his train of gaunt young girls with their distant, vacant expressions.

"I can't believe it," Corey was saying. "I've been involved here for over a year and this is only the second time I've been invited up. I think it was about you, not me."

The remark frightened her. There was something indefinably sinister about Tripp Karter.

*

"I'm glad you came today, Mary Anne," Tripp Karter said, stroking the dark hair of the girl at his side. The low lighting made for shadows that hid most of the people she'd seen enter, including Corey who'd disappeared with a girl wearing a flowing robe and flowered headband.

"This isn't what I expected," she replied, looking around. She reclined across from Karter on thick, expensive-looking oriental rugs covered with pillows scattered around. "It's like a scene out of Aladdin or Lawrence of Arabia. I expected something more utilitarian."

He chuckled and patted her hand. "It's really not all that opulent. We revolutionaries don't have the money the military industrialists have to throw at such things."

"You consider yourself revolutionary?"

"In the mold of John Hancock or Patrick Henry. George Washington. In his Farewell Address, he warned us away from foreign entanglements… *'a passionate attachment of one nation for another produces a variety of evils…'* I'd say he was rather prescient. Maybe even visionary, like the prophet Daniel, only in our affiliation with Vietnam rather than ancient Israel's relationship with Babylon."

"You've spent a lot of time contemplating," Mary Anne said.

"And studying, and memorizing. We have a great battle going on in America today – it's a battle for the mind… and the soul… *These are the times that try men's souls…* Isn't that familiar? *…The summer soldier and the sunshine patriot will, in this crisis, shrink from the service of their country; but he that stands by it now, deserves the love and thanks of man and woman. Tyranny, like hell, is not easily conquered; yet we have this consolation with us, that the harder the conflict, the more glorious the triumph. What we obtain too cheap, we esteem too lightly: it is dearness only that gives every thing its value…*" Thomas Paine. As true today as it was on December 23, 1776, three days before Washington crossed the Delaware."

"I'm impressed unless that's just for my benefit."

"You think I'm simply trying to impress you?... Perhaps. I've always been wont to impress beautiful women. But let me ask you – have you memorized Scripture or Catechism?"

"You know I have. I'm sure my brother told you I was educated from kindergarten through high school by the nuns."

"He did. So, tell me the truth, aren't there relatively long segments of your Holy book you can recite backwards and forwards? I bet you could quote them right this moment. The Apostles Creed? The Rosary? Why would you think that a red, white and blue patriot like me couldn't do the same with quotes from *his* hero's writings?"

She thought about it briefly and the logic made sense. "So you set yourself up alongside the Founders?"

"Unashamedly. *The Hawkish Dove* is a band of winter soldiers not sunshine patriots."

The young girl next to him rolled and lit a cigarette. She took a drag on it and passed it to Karter who inhaled deeply and exhaled a diaphanous cloud. "Care to mow the grass? Just a short toke maybe?"

"I don't do drugs," she replied, taking in the appley aroma of the smoke.

"How square, and wrong," he answered, and took a second deep drag. "Joy smoke is medicinal. It removes inhibitions and expands the mind to help open the intellect to possibilities, something our politicians and military could benefit from. I think you could, too. Try it and see if I'm lying."

A voice deep within her subconscious told her not to, but another voice – this one new, exciting and dangerous – told her otherwise. Mary Anne debated. She shook her head no. "If you're such a patriot why are you trying to tear the country apart?"

Tripp smiled squeezed her hand. "We're not. Admittedly there are some who are but don't count us among them. We're about righting wrongs and healing the land."

"From what I've seen and from what I've heard from Corey, one of your aims is to overthrow the government."

"Then you've not seen or heard much. And our goals are misrepresented; we want to help bring about change in the way government works, not destruction of it. That said, I have to also add that human government is, at its core, fundamentally flawed. In what way you ask? I'll tell you – because it's made up of humans. Humans are inherently evil – your Catholicism teaches that, does it not? And it's true. There's no clearer testimony to it than this war in Vietnam. Our goal is to first stop the evil, return the country to founding principles and then train the populace in them. Only then can the land be healed and peace be returned."

"That sounds like a monumental task."

"I'm sure it did in 1776 also." Karter closed his eyes and took another drag on the cigarette, holding his breath for what seemed a long while until at last he exhaled. "However great the task, it will be worth it in the end."

Mary Anne sensed her mind was floating and her inhibitions receding, in a pleasant surrender of her will. Was it the drink she had, or the effects of the marijuana smoke? Tripp Karter's aura? Whatever the cause, she was experiencing a mildly satisfying euphoria and her mind told her she wanted more. She thought of Glenn.

"What about the troops?" she asked.

"What about them?"

"Your demonstrations and anti-war rhetoric work against them. It emboldens the North."

Karter smiled paternally. "That's just Nixon administration propaganda. The truth is that the vast majority of the troops over there are against this war, and always have been. Are you aware of VVAW? Vietnam Veterans Against the War?"

"Vaguely. It's a small group of –"

"It started out small in 1967, but now it's huge, and growing larger every day. Enlisted men, officers, former military and current active duty. The unpleasant reality for the administration is that they have lost the hearts and minds of their own military. They are now on my side, not Nixon's. Your husband's a West Pointer isn't he?"

"Yes."

"I'm sure he knows of VVAW; if he's a smart man he's probably already a member."

Not Glenn, she said to herself. *That's not possible… is it?*

"None of the troops over there believes in this war," Karter was saying. "None of them."

"How could you possibly believe that."

"You didn't let me finish my thought. None of them *except* a handful of the careerists, the Lifers who are there to punch their tickets and get their chest-full of medals. Ask your husband if he hasn't crossed paths – and maybe sabers – with them during his time in the Army. The military over there is demoralized, not because of the Peace Movement here but because of the futility of the situation foisted on them."

Mary Anne felt a gnawing guilt for even listening to such things, but also a troubling thought that Tripp might be right. She wanted to leave, but Karter's riveting personality held her there. A solitary man emerged from the shadows off to her left, approached Tripp and bent over to whisper something in his ear.

"Our entertainment is about to begin. Have you ever enjoyed the singing of Phi Ochs?" Karter asked, accepting another joint from the girl next to him. He moved to Mary Anne's side and lit the small cigarette and held it out to her and remained motionless until she took it. "Go ahead. It'll set the right atmosphere for Phil's music. Just try it – once is all I ask."

Mary Anne hesitated and then slowly brought the joint to her lips. The young girl with the long straight hair across from her who had rolled the cigarette watched with an unsteady, vacant glare. *Why does she hate me?* Mary Anne wondered as the sickly sweetness of the smoke rushed into her lungs and her head began to buzz. "Far out, isn't it?" Tripp was saying.

The room whirled, filled with harmony and possibilities – the Age of Aquarius come to life in all its psychedelic delight. She exhaled a lungful of smoke and immediately inhaled another, making her feel lightheaded and radiant. And the haunting melody of the young singer was so in tune with what she was feeling. Peace. Treason. Love. Reason. Oh, Glenn. Forgive me. Please. PLEASE.

She was on her feet, supported by the 'cigarette girl' and someone else, being guided to one of several small couches. She sat among a group of girls and college age boys alongside young professional women and men.

The man standing next to Karter asked him, "So what do you think, Tripp?"

"I think we just found the face of the movement. Young, blond, gorgeous. And a brother and father who can help financially. Three useful idiots and lots of cash. Make sure the press gets plenty of pictures of her standing next to me at the rally tomorrow on the Mall... Is it true about Kent State?" The man nodded. "Good. The timing couldn't have been better. I'll call it *The May 4th Massacre*. People around the country are going to go crazy, especially when we make all the evening news broadcasts tomorrow night. We need to take every opportunity to play it up. This war is the gift that keeps on giving."

"But the angle on the girl... You really want her portrayed as your girlfriend? What about her husband?"

"We can have the press ask the question and leave the answer up to prurient minds and the networks. The husband? – he's in Vietnam and out of the way. It'd be best if he died there leaving behind a beautiful, grieving widow helping us tear down this criminal government and stop an obscene, immoral war …

"What more could we ask for?"

*   *   *

"Four hundred meters through the edge of an old rubber plantation," Two Hatchets whispered, tracing a path on the map for Nolan and colonel van Noort. "The way is mostly clear. We can move quickly to a shallow rise and from there you can see the main house. Very large. Many NVA."

It was midday when Glenn sent his scout team ahead to recon a path through the jungle. They had found a way through what had formerly been a Michelin plantation under French rule in Indo-China decades earlier. He looked at Lone Wolf and TiJean who nodded agreement. All three of his scouts were soaked completely in sweat and looked bushed. He decided to give them a fifteen minute break before moving up.

"That's it, Nolan!" the colonel whispered, but the tension and excitement in his tone was clear. "We found it! The NVA headquarters we've been after for the last five years. Just twenty miles inside Cambodia. This is going to be something to tell your grandkids about! I'm going to get a FAC on station and have him park as many A-37s as he can get the Air Force to give us ten minutes south of here." The colonel made his way to Holmes and put in a call on the secure battalion net.

Glenn turned to his platoon leaders, Rankin and Thorgier.

"You guys heard the colonel. We're going to do this, so let your platoons know what's up ahead and how we're going to get there. Once we get a look at what we're dealing with, we'll work up the tactical plan. We'll probably set up a couple of platoon blocking positions and just bomb the hell out of the place until it's safe to assault and take it."

"Wish we had a couple more M60s," Rankin said.

"I wish we had a dozen more," Glenn replied, and looked past his officers to where Masika and Heavy were breaking out another can of ammo and cleaning the action on their gun. He'd been very pleased with the way the two had become a well-oiled team.

He'd sent Pineapple back to second platoon but kept Masika with him in the CP. The team had pulled them out of more than one tight spot, beginning with the day they were first inserted into Cambodia and during four other firefights in and around *Metropolis* since. But he still wanted additional M60s; and after all the NVA booty they'd found in the complex his goal of making each of his squads a heavy machine gun team looked like it was going to happen.

First Sergeant Overton and the XO had brought half the rear detachment, including the supply sergeant, out to Charo, the new battalion firebase on the border just inside Vietnam. All the good trading material they had was backhauled to the company rear at Sông Bé; Nolan gave Sergeant Kaiser a week to find a half dozen more M60s and radios for the company.

He looked at the battalion commander who was still on the radio, deep in conversation and looking intensely agitated.

"Everything all right, sir?" he asked in a low hushed voice he demanded of everyone in the field. "Anything I can do?"

The colonel glanced quickly at him, then his eyes darted away. " Nothing you can do."

"You sure, sir?"

"Dammit, Nolan! I said no. You having a hard time understanding English anymore?!" Glenn decided that was a question for which silence was the appropriate answer. At last van Noort took a deep breath and exhaled loudly, looking up at the trees. "You've done everything and more I've ever asked of you. Wish I could say the same of the damned chain of command... for your own sake, you never heard me say that. Looks like we're going to have to do this on our own."

"On our own, sir?"

"That's what I said. They said 'no' to my request for air support. We've got COSVN less than three miles away and they won't pull the trigger. To hell with it! I'll do it myself, without airpower. Let's saddle up and go take a look so we can figure out how we're going to do this."

His three man point team led the company through the stand of rubber trees, across a road wide enough for double lane traffic and up a shallow hill overlooking an old plantation house four hundred yards away. It was crawling with NVA – some in black pajamas and others in OD, all of them hurriedly packing crates and boxes onto hand carts. An evacuation was clearly underway and Glenn suddenly felt overwhelmed. What could he do against such a force with only two platoons and without air support? Frontal assault on line? Fire and movement by platoon? Base of fire with a maneuvering platoon? None of that sounded particularly appropriate or sane. But this was a huge deal, a target worth the risk and cost. He gave Mikey Meade coordinates to dial up a fire mission and told him to fire on his command; then he had Holmes call battalion and bounce two sections of Max.

He was bewildered when Meade told him the artillery battery FDC denied his fire mission and was more astonished when Holmes advised him the battalion was not forwarding his requests for gunships and had issued an order to withdraw back to *Metropolis*. Glenn looked at the colonel and asked, "Sir, what the hell's going on?"

The battalion commander grabbed his arm and pulled him off to the side. "They're telling us to stand down," van Noort whispered, looking and sounding angry.

"Stand down? What for?"

"Politics."

"Politics? I don't get it, sir. We can see what looks to be a pretty good size headquarters packing up and bugging out. Even without the Air Force we could bag a lot of them by ourselves with just artillery and ARA."

The colonel breathed deeply. "The president is telling us to back off... to hold up and not go any further. It's a political decision because our short little excursion into the playground and supply depots of our enemy is causing a lot of grief back home. Apparently there are riots in the streets and colleges across America because we're here, taking the fight to the NVA."

"I can't believe that. How do you know, sir?"

"That's the reason they gave me from brigade when I asked for Air Force support. To mollify the dissenters, the president announced our incursion will go no more than seventeen miles into Cambodia. Where we're sitting is almost exactly a mile beyond that line. That's what they told me. Our highers were concerned when we last reported our position because it was so close to their seventeen mile limit. When I gave them my target coordinates they told me to turn around."

Glenn was confused. "So why did we move up?"

Colonel van Noort gave him a piercing look that seemed to penetrate into his very soul. "Because, lieutenant, somebody had to do the right thing. We came here to kill the enemy and take away his ability to fight. We found and relieved him of his supplies and killed some but not enough of his soldiers. We have the opportunity to destroy his command and control – it's sitting down there, less than a half mile away. And we're being told to do nothing. Doing nothing... letting the enemy slip away to fight another day is wrong. It's wrong militarily; it's wrong morally. It makes the sacrifice of some fifty thousand lives a mockery... to them. To their loved ones."

"But it's an order, sir."

"It's a wrong-headed order."

"But that's what a soldier does, sir. He follows his orders."

"That excuse for military malfeasance died at Nuremburg over two decades ago."

Glenn looked back toward the plantation house and suddenly felt exposed. "Sir, we need to move back and get out of here before we draw their attention."

"What if I gave you an order to attack right now, Nolan?"

"I'd be on the horns of a dilemma, sir. I've received an order from battalion to move the company back to *Metropolis*. But you're my commander, so the order you give me is binding. I'd be duty bound to attack, sir. And so I would attack. But I wouldn't order my men to do the same. I guess it would be you and me, colonel. And whether I did the right thing or the wrong thing wouldn't mean a whole hell of a lot of difference to either one of us. Are you ordering me to attack, sir?"

The colonel looked at him with a wry grin.

"No. I'm not ordering you to do anything. You analyzed it perfectly, I'd say, Nolan. But I can't give you any orders." Colonel van Noort shook his head. "I'm no longer your commander. General Roberts relieved me when I told him I was going past the seventeen mile line despite what the president said."

Glenn didn't know how to respond. Finally he said, "I don't understand why you pressed on after being ordered not to."

"Because it was the right thing to do."

"Not sure I agree, sir."

"This isn't the time or place to debate. We need to get your men out of here." van Noort turned away, but stopped after going a few paces. "What I did, I did for a reason. I knew before I started out from Metropolis that I was going to get relieved. I wanted them to relieve me. I wasn't going to just lay down and quit. Officers don't get to do that. Nor do we get to march in the streets, burn down public buildings or stage sit-ins to make a point. But we can still protest. You know how? By doing what's right, especially when we're told to do something wrong."

"Help us to do the harder right instead of the easier wrong..." Glenn whispered.

"The Cadet Prayer. That's right, Nolan. Taking out COSVN is the right thing to do for the troops, for the military, for South Vietnam and for America, despite what politicians in Washington think. Doing the right thing is more important than my personal career... or anybody's career.

"If I don't do it, Nolan, who will?"

Chapter 23

It had been raining three solid days in relentless slashing downpours tempered by brief interludes of partially clearing skies and chill monsoonal squalls.

Everything was soaked through, the troops were miserable and Glenn could feel in his vitals the morale of the company sliding downhill. He wondered what he could do to turn it around amidst the drudgery of moving captured equipment through ankle-deep mud while enduring the stench of rotting jungle and lingering NVA smells reminiscent of dead fish, soured wine and untended urinals.

Metropolis now filled him with revulsion.

Glenn rolled out of his poncho as velvet darkness gave way to subdued dawn; he passed the radio handset to EB who was sitting with his back to a tree while shivering and trying without success to light a cigarette.

"Forgot how dang cold it gets at night during the monsoon," the radio operator said, perched like a scrawny seagull above the soggy soil on exposed tree roots. "Bet ol' Luke the Gook could hear my teeth chatterin' halfway to Hanoi harbor. Worst country in the world."

"Get any sleep?" Glenn asked.

"Hell, no. Who can sleep with his butt in the water and rain peltin' him all night long?"

"Hand me your canteen cup and I'll brew you some coffee."

"I can't be bought off with just a cup of Joe."

"Not trying to buy you off, EB. Tryin' to shut you up. You want to complain or drink hot coffee?" Nolan poured water into the canteen cup and lit a small piece of C-4. A minute later he handed over a steaming canteen cup of instant coffee to his radio operator. "I'm going to walk the perimeter; should be back in a half hour. Call the platoons and have them pick up their trips and claymores. Gamecock should be going out first on 'first light' – remind them."

He went down the bamboo-matted trail to second platoon; he talked with each squad leader and most of the men. Pineapple – all smiles and cheerfulness as usual – asked when the company might be getting more machine guns. He hinted that he'd like to be the company armorer when the slot in the rear came open. Glenn promised he'd keep that in mind.

Lieutenant Cleburne, still distant and aloof, sat under a shelter half he'd tied between four trees in an attempt to keep the rain off while the platoon sergeant and squad leaders were busy getting ready to go out on morning patrol. He was particular about his appearance and seemed able to keep up a natty façade even in the field – hair slicked down from a center part, long sideburns, shrewd little eyes, chin thrust forward, and chest puffed out. *What to do about Cleburne?* He'd talked with Colonel van Noort and expressed some urgency in moving the lieutenant out of the leadership position but they'd not come to any conclusion. Now, with Boomer running the battalion, at least in the interim, things seemed to be on hold. But something had to be done quickly.

The circuit of the small perimeter confirmed his deepening concern about morale.

"Inbound Huey, Six," EB told him when he got back to the CP. "Five minutes out. Don't know who it is. Not our C&C or log bird. Maybe it's the Toonerville trolley or –"

"All right. Give me the handset." He called third platoon and told Thorgier to do a quick recon around the LZ, carved out a week earlier by the engineers, and then outpost it in a couple of places. The workday was beginning a little early. He looked up at the dizzying heights of the triple canopy but couldn't see the sky; the morning had devolved into a light but steady dripping from above. *Weather must not be too awful skosh – at least the chopper pilots don't think so, anyhow... somebody must want to see Metropolis pretty bad, even though we've darn well trashed it,* he thought, rubbing his three week old beard. *Whoever this early bird is, he's gonna be disappointed if he's looking for the Pukka Sahib castle.*

One of the visitors was someone Nolan had met before and he arrived bearing an unanticipated message.

Glenn went to meet the aircraft when it landed and watched two passengers climb out. One was a lieutenant colonel wearing aviator-framed glasses and carrying his steel pot under one arm; his smile was broad and genuine. Seeing Colonel Galvin again was a surprise. The other was an artillery captain with sharp features and sunken cheeks who wore a choker necklace of small wooden beads threaded on a leather shoelace; he sported a long thin waxed mustache and a wild sort of look on his face.

The helicopter rose straight up, did a pedal turn and departed to the west.

"Nolan. It's good to see you again. This is my ALO, Captain Trey Kurtis from the 166th Artillery Battalion. I guess you know I'm commanding the 1st Battalion, 8th Cavalry... You're wondering what I'm doing here," the dark-haired officer said as they walked from the center of the LZ to the tree line. His face became animated and he chuckled to himself. "A good G-2 learns to read faces; a really good G-2 can read minds. And I was better than 'really good'. You believe that don't you?"

"Sir, if you're really that good you already know the answer."

Galvin laughed again. "The Goose said you were pretty quick on your feet. You don't know who I'm speaking of, do you? Guus van Noort. Your former commander and my friend – classmate at West Point. We worked together on the year book – he wrote and I was the cartoonist, illustrator.

"I didn't know that, sir."

"No reason you should." Galvin stopped, looked into his eyes and said, "I'm here to tell you that you're working for me now – at least for a while. You're OpCon to my battalion for the foreseeable future. I took command of the 1st Battalion, 8th Cav a couple of weeks after van Noort became your C.O. I was in Hawaii on R&R when the division went into Cambodia so I'm running to catch up. I came back to learn that your company is straddling the boundary between my battalion and my old buddy's outfit. General Casey thought it best that you report to me considering this boundary situation, and events surrounding The Goose."

"His being relieved," Glenn said evenly.

"Yes. I understand you were with him at the time."

"Yes, sir, I was."

"He thought he was about to capture or overrun COSVN."

"He was certain of it, sir. Certain enough to bet his career on it."

"Goose always did like tilting at windmills, even when we were cadets." Glenn decided the colonel wasn't asking a question or looking for a comment, and remained silent. It had been five days since the incident and Nolan was still unsure about van Noort's motivations and the propriety or wisdom of his actions.

"Someday we'll have to have a long talk about what happened, but not now," Galvin said, looking up at the clouds scudding swiftly overhead. "I came here to inform you of the new command relationship and to ask what I can do for you and your company. This is one of the biggest cache's the division uncovered so far. I'm aware you've been pushed pretty hard operationally. Tell me how the company's holding up."

Glenn had always believed the first responsibility of leadership was to define reality, and the reality was that it had been a hard month for the outfit. "Straight up, sir, morale is not good and it's getting worse. The unit needs a break. I took over Alpha company a month ago and at that time they had been in the field for almost two weeks. Since then, with the exception of two days at Sông Bé, the company has been in the field continuously and we've had a lot of contact. The amount of contact isn't the problem, it's a positive if anything. You can help me by fitting my company into your firebase rotation real soon."

The colonel nodded. "Consider it done. My Bravo company just came on to LZ Mo, but you're next. What else?"

"Get me air mattresses and new ponchos for my soldiers. The monsoon apparently came as a big surprise to the battalion or the brigade S-4, and probably both. We're still sleeping on the ground, in water and mud. If my supply sergeant wasn't roaming around somewhere in II Corps chasing down M60s for me I'd put him on it."

"I can't promise them today, but I'll see you get them as soon as humanly possible."

"And finally, sir. Let me close this damned place down and get the hell out of here."

Galvin frowned and said, "Tell me more."

"Sir, we've been here for over a week. The days are long, which is fine, but we're at the point of diminishing returns. After my experience at Illingworth, I'm not keen on spending long periods of time in the same place when there are lots of gooks around. We've got them confused and back on their heels but that won't last much longer. They'll be back sooner rather than later. We've backhauled all the weapons and food and key supplies they had stockpiled. What's left is odds and ends of lumber and petroleum and ammo. Lots and lots of ammo – stuff we won't ever use. Let me blow up the ammo dumps and torch the place so we can start hunting down their soldiers on our terms rather than waiting here for them to regroup."

"Obviously you've given this a lot of thought," Galvin said. "I'll run some things by the battalion -2 and -3. You won't have to wait long for us. But for now, I want to meet your troops. Wander around to see how they're doing. I want Captain Kurtis to spend some time with your FO and make sure there's no gaps in your artillery coverage."

Glenn looked up at the sky saw rain clouds moving toward them indicating a squall. "Sir, you might want to call in your bird. Looks like we're in for a shower, maybe worse."

He felt something tap the tiny visor of his steel pot and then the back of his neck. Rain. Heavy droplets; then two more became several ushering in a sudden slashing deluge. He was instantly soaked to the skin and shivering. The battalion commander entered the wet jungle through the seething roar of rain and introduced himself to the troops in Alpha company's CP.

What a place, Glenn thought. *Six months of stifling, choking heat and now six months of constant rain. Day after tedious day of hauling out tons of captured booty, or the boredom of slogging through mountain jungle interrupted by moments of sheer terror... What a war.*

*   *   *

Brad yawned and looked out on the jungle hills and fog-shrouded valleys fifteen hundred feet below; here and there steel-colored swirls of monsoon squalls marched across the Cambodian landscape as the Huey circled near the river marking the boundary between Cambodia and South Vietnam. He depressed the floor button while turning toward Norton.

"Can't believe that colonel wanted us to leave him on the ground and go refuel," Brad said. "I told him and that captain they were going to get washed away. You can't tell any of these battalion commanders anything. They're all alike. Man, I hate those guys in Ops for sticking us with C&C today; worst mission in the war. Syzmanski, what's that saying you crew chiefs have about officers?"

"Officers have been making simple shit hard since 1776."

"Of course you're not talking about Warrant Officers."

"Of course not. If I were then I'd have to say: making simple shit hard since 1918."

A radio call came in from the ground unit for them to pick up the two pax they'd delivered an hour earlier. Brad checked the clouds and saw a break they could slip through between squalls and retrieve the two officers. "You got it, Ed. Let's hurry in and get out before we get caught by the next line of storms. Bet this Galvin character and his buddy are plenty ready to come out by now. Your pre-landing check is good."

A few minutes later they were loading the two dripping wet officers aboard.

Brad watched them climb in, all smiles, as if they'd been ushered to the front of the line for entrance into Disneyland. *Grunts. Only gravel agitators would enjoy running around in the rain. Like my stupid brother.*

"Where to, sir?" Brad asked, when the two passengers strapped in and plugged their aviator helmets into the Y-Cord.

"Trey, pass the A/C your map with the three areas we want to recon," the colonel said, pulling a dry kerchief out of a plastic bag and cleaning his glasses. "There's three areas we want to take a close look at just on the other side of the river inside Vietnam. Two to the southwest of Mo and one to the east. I want to get pretty low. And when we get there, we're also looking for LZs big enough for two to four ships."

"We can handle that, sir," Brad replied as Norton brought the Huey to a hover, then ascended straight up eighty feet and turned south. "Which one do you want to recon first?"

"The one east of Mo."

"Roger that." Brad marked his map and switched frequencies. "I got it, Ed."

They flew to the first area and Brad set up a left circling pattern to keep the spot out the left door on the officers' side. He could hear them talking back and forth on intercom and wondered what they found so strategically important about the non-descript piece of jungle that looked just like everything else around it. They located a three ship clearing two hundred yards away. Galvin asked him to drop down for a closer look.

Even at treetop level, Brad could see nothing of military importance. As they left, headed for the areas south and east, he said, "I know a little bit about military history and tactics, and I didn't see a darn thing down there. What's so important about what we just looked at, colonel?" As soon as he'd said it, he knew he'd screwed up. *What have you done now, Nolan? Are you ever going to learn?* The last time he'd flown battalion C&C had been a month earlier, for another lieutenant colonel named Ianetta. He'd asked a casual question – with less sarcasm than this – and Ianetta had reamed him out good. Brad cringed and glanced quickly at Norton who rolled his eyes and gave him that adenoidal stare, his mouth agape.

"That's a very good question, Mr. Nolan," Galvin said, in a calm tone so relaxed, so deftly balanced between irony and casual rejoinder that Brad's jaw dropped. "And it deserves an answer. You'll get one, but not right now. Captain Kurtis and I are a little busy. We'll address your question when we get back to Mo."

"Yes, sir. I didn't mean to interrupt." He managed to keep silent for the rest of the reconnaissance and when they shut down on the VIP pad at Mo, he was glad when the colonel and his artillery liaison officer went up to the TOC without mentioning his outburst. They shut down the aircraft and left the rotor blade untied, then set the switches and throttle for a quick start and sat down on the berm several yards away for a smoke.

""What do you think happens now?" Norton asked, looking over his shoulder toward the top of the small, bald hill where the Tactical Operations Center sat.

"We wait. This is the really boring part of pulling C&C, almost as much fun as flying left hand circles in the sky."

"So we just sit?"

"Yup. We sit. And wait, until the higher ups decide they want to be flown around for a while. This is like practice for the time when you become a corporate pilot, only we're wearing ugly green uniforms, and sitting in the muggy heat or rain instead of an air-conditioned FBO."

Two sergeants and a Spec-4 came down the hill with plates of hot food and cold drinks for the pilots and door gunners. They had just started eating when the colonel came out the TOC and approached them; he was carrying a folded tripod, a large map mounted on thin plywood and an acetate overlay covered in irregular black lines and red marks. The crew began to stand up and he motioned them to sit back down.

"You guys keep eating," Galvin said as set up the tripod and map a few feet in front of where they sat on the berm. "Enjoy it. That's from the artillery mess, courtesy of Captain Kurtis. I'm going to swear you to secrecy on this, but the artillery eats better than the infantry... everywhere. Always choose artillery chow." He finished putting his overlay onto the map and picked up his wooden pointer. "Now to Mr. Nolan's question..."

"Sir, I apologize for speaking out of turn."

"No apology necessary. It was a good question." The colonel gave Nolan a roguish grin. "I'm not going to tell you the old lie about there not being any stupid questions. There are. But yours wasn't one of them. And maybe I'm the one who should apologize. You got here real early this morning and we didn't give you a briefing because I wanted to beat the weather in and out of that company. As it turned out it, we got caught anyhow. So, to your question."

Galvin walked them through a summary of the battalion's operations for the past four weeks including opening LZ Mo and operations along both sides of the river marking the border. It took a half hour. Then he pointed out the grouping of the dark lines on the acetate.

"These lines represent trail systems this battalion and others in 2nd Brigade have discovered over the past six months. Each siting by elements of the brigade is logged and disseminated – that includes reports from aviation assets as well as troops on the ground. You can see the design. This overall pattern where we are here in Phouc Long Province, is called the Jolly Trail System. This is how the NVA move into South Vietnam toward Saigon from Cambodia. We're pretty certain there are three or four major routes they use in this area. You can see that Mo sits on one of these routes and there's one to our east, one to our west. They're not highways, or even dirt roads – they're a series of something more akin to game trails.

"What we looked at this morning are areas where Pink Teams have spotted activity indicating the NVA are moving through our AO while all our forces are in Cambodia. These are places where we may want to insert a platoon from the firebase and hopefully initiate contact. This is not your father's war or your grandfather's war. The old ways of determining key terrain to seize and hold don't apply. We don't have enough troops to completely seal the border, but we can do an effective job interdicting traffic if we're smart about it."

The colonel went silent and took a deep breath, concentrating on the map. And then he looked up at the slate gray sky, rubbing his jaw and finally looking at the younger, firmer faces of the Huey crew. He took a three by five card out of his breast pocket and wrote on it before saying, "So, Nolan, does that answer your question?"

"Completely. Honestly, sir, until now I had no idea what was going on around here. I don't think hardly any of us pilots do. We fly the machines where we're told to, and we know where all the firebases and FARPS are. We're damned good at flying; we can do a CA in our sleep and give you plus or minus a few seconds on the LZ time. We know *how* to do our job, but we don't really know hardly anything about *why* we're doing it. I feel like I got a bunch of the pieces to that puzzle today."

The colonel made another note on his card and placed it back in his pocket. "Now I have a question for you... you have a brother in the division."

It sounded more like a statement than a question. "He's a grunt in the 1st Brigade, somewhere in Tay Ninh."

"He's not there anymore," the colonel said. "He commands A company in the 1/6 Cav and as of last night he reports to me. That's who you took me to see this morning."

"I don't know what to say. We've written back and forth a little since he got in country Last time I got a letter from him he was in 1st Brigade."

"He was there, but no longer. Do you know what he did on LZ Illingworth?"

"No, sir."

"Someday you ought to ask him, or better yet, ask someone who was there. He's an amazing soldier, which he convinced me of again this morning."

Brad looked down and shuffled his feet. *Always in the shadow of big brother Glenn,* he thought. *Here I am exactly half way around the globe and right back into the ringer, eclipsed again. Somebody up there doesn't like me.* He looked up at Colonel Galvin and said, "Actually, my brother's not all that amazing. He was always pretty good at most things... but he still can't hover. And in the Cav, if you can't hover, you ain't shit."

Galvin's face took on the strangest appearance, as if he was trying mightily to keep from bursting. "Mr. Nolan, I can't hover either."

Brad's face and the back of his neck went instantly hot and prickly.

"No problem. I can solve that for you right now. Syzmanski, I need a fireguard. Norton, give the colonel your nomex gloves. Sir, climb into the right seat for your first flying lesson with the world's greatest helicopter pilot and guitar player. Before this afternoon is over you'll be hovering, and a better man than my brother... like me."

Chapter 24

They were hunkered down in an NVA dugout with overhead cover a quarter mile from the huge ammo bunker third platoon had discovered nine days earlier. The position reeked of rotted foliage and wood smoke and human waste he would forever associate with the Far East.

EB Gordon was nervous and more agitated than Glenn had seen since his first day in the company. This was the last and most dangerous event in destroying *Metropolis* – blowing up all the remaining ammunition in the six square kilometer complex. It wasn't as much as EB claimed, but it was no small stockpile either. MACV had issued a statement that it was the third largest ammo cache discovered since American combat troops set foot in Vietnam.

Earlier that morning engineers had spent hours rigging the four demolition sites for destruction with hundreds of pounds of plastic explosives: the headquarters facility, a fuel storage hooch, a small ammo dump and a larger one the troops in Alpha nicknamed *Picatinny East*. After extracting the company to LZ MO, the engineers blew the first three facilities and were extracted, leaving behind a small covering force to finish the last job before they too were picked up.

He ran to the bunker where TiJean, Lone Wolf and Daniel Two Hatchets covered the left flank of their stay behind demo crew. "One minute. Keep your heads down and wait for me to call all clear after the explosion." He gave the same message to the other element in the bunker containing Timmy Horner, along with Masika and Heavy manning the M60.

"Call the Chuck-Chuck and tell him we're going to blow it in sixty seconds," Glenn told his RTO. His pulse quickened as he glanced at his cheap little black faced military watch. Looking at it broke the tension, and he smiled.

The damned six dollar watch.

The property book officer for his old battalion, the 2/8 Cav, had been hounding him for a month with notes about returning the thing so he could balance his books. What a monumental waste of everybody's time! It was at first a nuisance, then devolved into comedy and became finally a shibboleth of the blind adherence to nonsensical rules and regulations that sapped the energy and morale of too many in the Army. He'd left the 2nd Battalion, 8th Cav with no time to clear the unit and still carried the same M16, .45 caliber pistol and field gear he'd drawn four months earlier in a different brigade. But all the property book officer was interested in was the 'disposable' timepiece because it was one of the items he was held accountable for by regulation. The disposable six dollar watch was now a matter of principle. He shook his head.

A long burst from the M60 was quickly joined by rapid fire from the scout team's rifles. He looked out and caught fleeting glimpses of ephemeral figures in black pajamas in frontal assault and flanking them from the north; rounds thudded in front of his bunker, snapped and whined overhead.

Glenn twisted the handle on the detonator...

Nothing.

His mind raced, filled with fear – that their position was untenable against a concerted attack and they'd be overrun, that somehow the NVA had disabled the explosives, and that the helicopters wouldn't be able to get in to a hot LZ. He reset the detonator, and twisted the handle again.

The explosion shook the earth and pummeled the wet, heavy jungle.

He heard EB yelling into the radio that they were under fire and needed immediate extraction. Metal fragments both large and small rained down around them; the NVA attack withered and melted away. Firing stopped and the jungle went silent. He pulled his RTO from their firing position and pointed him down the trail toward the landing zone forty yards away while yelling for his three man scout team to fall back. He ran to the machine gun crew, and ordered Horner to the LZ and watched the medic scamper after EB with the big medical kit banging off his backside. His scout team pulled out, firing as they ran.

"Masika! Heavy! Pull back to the head of the trail! I'll cover you. Go!" He had briefed them on their exit from the complex but they hadn't rehearsed it like he'd been trained in Ranger School. *These guys just don't have the training they need. I should know better! Damn! I should have walked them through this.*

Sporadic firing erupted to their front and Glenn fired a full magazine in short bursts, spraying the heavy undergrowth while his M60 crew dashed toward cover. He inserted another magazine and continued firing. He heard the machine gun over his shoulder and saw rounds chewing up the undergrowth; he was up and running toward the path leading to the LZ.

Glenn dove behind a felled tree, raised up on a knee and fired off a half dozen aimed shots at fleeting shapes, thought he saw their assault line forming and emptied his magazine. Masika sprayed the position they'd vacated with a long burst that seemed to last forever. Glenn looked across the narrow trail and saw Heavy feeding a new belt of ammo into the gun from an OD ammo can.

He heard the chopper behind them, its blades slapping the air with the loud *whop-whop-whop* now so familiar. "Masika! Fall back to the LZ and cover down this trail. Give me a long burst and then I'll cover you."

The M60 blasted away at the movement just thirty yards away; Glenn watched and the gun crew looked at him then made a move to withdraw. He burned through two more magazines and ran stooped over down the trail that had carried tons of weapons and equipment borne by Alpha troops in the last week. As he reached the landing zone a B-40 exploded nearby and he dove into the thick brush just as his M-60 let loose a series of short bursts down the length of the trail. Glenn saw the first Huey lifting off straight up like an express freight elevator loaded with his troops, and then it was gone; the second ship was flaring at the top of the high hover down. He crawled through the vines and plants like octopi toward Masika who continued firing short bursts down the trail.

"Before that bird hits the ground, you two be on it! I'll be right behind you!" When he looked again, the Huey was less than a dozen feet above the ground. "GO! – GO! – GO!...."

Glenn fired off a magazine rapid fire down the trail as the team bolted for the helicopter, and then ran for it only yards behind them. The UH-1 stopped before it hit the ground and instantly started up. His machine gun crew clambered aboard; Glenn leapt for the cargo compartment and got part of the way in with a foot on the skid. The two Alpha troops grabbed his web gear straps and hauled him aboard as the ship rapidly ascended. Masika turned, sat on the floor, pointed the M60 down at the first black-clad NVA reaching the LZ and fired off his remaining belt of ammo.

They skimmed over the tree tops, picking up speed and climbing away from *Metropolis*.

The deck of the Huey was littered with shell casings from the door gunners' and Masika's machine gun; and, even with the ninety knot wind coming in, the faint smell of burnt powder lingered. Heavy was looking at him with wide, frightened eyes, breathing deeply; his gunner was cradling the M60 and leaning back onto his rucksack. He looked at Nolan briefly out of the corner of his eye and nodded once, imperceptibly, with a look of satisfaction and a brief, quiet smile that quickly gave way to his characteristic implacable stare.

Looking back, Glenn saw a large, dark slate gray cloud rising from where *Metropolis* had been. As he watched, artillery rounds began erupting like a rolling barrage all through the complex. It went on and on; now and then there would be a secondary explosion, sudden flashes of reddish black fireballs. He wondered how many of the enemy were down there now. The attack on the stay behind force, he reflected, could have been the NVA finally trying to take back their base camp after a week of getting organized after the surprise of the Cav taking it from them. If it was, they'd picked a bad time to try it. The artillery barrage went on for several minutes, until the Huey crossed the border into Vietnam and began to descend toward the bald knob of a hill. LZ Mo.

First Sergeant Overton and the XO were waiting for him when he got out of the Huey and began walking uphill to the firebase entrance. A half dozen black soldiers approached Masika half way up the hill and each went through the ritual handshake with him – the Dap they called it.

"It sounded like you got out just in time, sir," the first sergeant said. "Me and the XO and L.T. Thorgier were listening to the battalion net while it was going on."

"We had to hurry some, first sergeant," Glenn replied, looking around. "Looks like we've got some work to do on fighting positions while we're here. Where is Thorgier, anyhow? Are the platoons settled yet?"

"Platoon boundaries are marked off," Lieutenant Fitzgerald said. "I walked the perimeter with the platoon leaders and their platoon sergeants. They only got here a half hour ahead of you. They're still sorting themselves out."

"Walk me around then Fitz, so I know where everybody is and what they're doing." *If I was a gook, I'd attack this firebase at a time just like this... when it's in transition and the newcomers are still milling around, getting cleaned up and kicking back after three or four weeks in the bush.* "Where's the company CP on this place?" Fitzgerald pointed up the hill to a small, low bunker made from wooden artillery cases. "Have the platoon leaders meet me there in ten minutes and we'll do the walk together. What else is happening I should know about?"

Fitzgerald smiled at him and said, "Our long lost supply sergeant finally showed up here this morning with six new machine guns. It cost us a dozen pistol belts."

"That's a hell of a deal! We've got what? – six or seven thousand of those things?"

"He's also found a source in the Air Force at Bien Hoa where he can get three cases of T-bone steaks – enough for the whole company – for five belts. He brought along two big barbecue grills the battalion motor pool made for him out of a 55-gallon drum. We're eating steak tonight and tomorrow."

"I may not fire him after all... but I want to inspect those M60s right now."

"Sir, there's one other thing, somebody else you'll want to see," the first sergeant said. "Your brother's here. Someone told me he's your brother, anyhow. He's been flying the colonel's C&C ship for the past few days.... is he your half-brother, maybe?... the name tag on his shirt says: CRAMDEN."

*   *   *

10 May 1970 – LZ Mo
Entry 1 of _____ (who knows how many??)
– 1st full day on the firebase

My temporary boss has convinced me to take up the practice of journaling.

He does it. He tells me all the really great ones did it. Not so sure about me. I don't feel like the next George Marshall or Dwight Eisenhower and I'm not sure I even want to be. Right now I'd settle for being a decent company commander and a Vietnam survivor. One of my favorite quotes – from Winston Churchill – 'the greatest thrill in life is to get shot at and missed'. Been there, done that. A few times. Now I'd like to get through the next 241 days and a wake-up until I DEROS.

Where to start?

After a half hour looking at the blank page in this journal, I'm not encouraged this is going to work for me. I've come up with a dozen reasons why it won't. To begin with I didn't want to, but my new commander isn't one to take "no" for an answer. His name is Galvin. John R. Irish Catholic from somewhere around Boston. He kinda insisted, or suggested strongly, and thata was a-thata. Actually, when I think about it, it was just a passing comment he made. I've only been assigned to his command for a few days but I've noticed he's different from other commanders I've had in my brief and inglorious (so far) career. He has this calm, easy-going sort of 'suggestive' way of telling you to do things rather than barking out orders and wielding the power of rank like most field grades. There's no doubt it's an order but it comes across as both trivial and the gravest obligation a soldier could encounter at the same time. How does he do that?

Maybe that's where to begin – with this Galvin.

What else do I know about him? Not much.

He's a ring-knocker – West Point class in the early fifties, prior service enlisted – a medic, a 'Cav sandwich' (Cav patch on both sleeves – previous tour with the division), infantry branch of course, seems to have a quick sense of humor the limits of which I might have tested already. Note: the first question he asked me was 'how can I help your company?' – that caught me off guard – most high ranking officers want to know what you're doing or what you're planning or most importantly how you can help him. Not only did he ask the question but he actually listened to the answer and did something about it. That surprised me, too. I hear from the sergeant major this guy has apparently been surprising people around his battalion since he got here a week or so ago.

I crossed paths with him a little over a month ago (on April Fools Day) at LZ Illingworth when I was in the 2/8 Cav. (should I be using unit designations and people's names???? and dates? – Galvin says this will help when I retire as Chief of Staff and write my memoirs... sense of humor or mental problem? We'll see.) Also crossed paths with him last night around 2100 in one of my third platoon's positions. He was sitting there talking with some of my troops. The sergeant major warned me he does this. One of the troops was a soldier my RTO calls 'The Cisco Kid' – a Latino with a pronounced Mexican accent. Galvin was talking to him in fluent Spanish – something he learned on his first assignment in Panama and told me he speaks every chance he gets so he can keep current in it. Thorgier told me later his guys talked about it this morning. Everybody likes attention – just haven't seen a colonel until now who had figured that out. Not even Galvin's buddy, Goose van Noort – my former battalion CO. He was relieved for hesitating to follow an order (that's my understanding until I learn more). I was there when that went south. He told me- 'lieutenant, somebody has to do the right thing'. I've thought about that some since he said it. The implications of what he said and why he said it trouble me... but commanding a company in the Cav has enough troubles for me to deal with and there's not much if any time left over for deep thinking, even if I was a deep thinker.

Galvin writes a letter every day to his father, and has all his adult life. And he journals. And he scribbles notes to himself on three by five cards – he carries them around in his pocket. It's a real organized thing – he catalogs them by topic – leadership, tactics, etc. etc. (I don't know what they all are.) He's saving them for when he writes the 'Great American Military Tome on Leadership.' And he just might. He's a published author – wrote and published a book last year called AIR ASSAULT about the history of airborne and airmobile warfare. Strange – the first time I met him he kinda came across as a school teacher type. Obviously he likes to write.

Equally obvious is that Mary Anne doesn't... like to write.

When I got on the firebase yesterday there was a package from her waiting on me. I'd asked her to send me a bunch of condiments as I was developing my repertoire of culinary masterpieces made from C-Rations. Actually, I like C-Rats better than the hot chow I've endured on a long list of firebases. The last good meal I had was in Fort Lewis the night before leaving SeaTac for Cam Rahn Bay. But I'm getting better with cooking C's and would be a lot better with condiments – A-1 Sauce, Heinz 57, Worcestershire, garlic salt, Old Bay, chili powder, cayenne, paprika. She sent it! But there was no letter inside. Disappointing. I've tried to write her at least twice a week. For every half dozen I send, I get one, maybe two back. I get more letters from Benny Barnes than I get from her. I saw him on LZ Evita in early April (the 6th or 7th, I think). He thinks she's still mad at me because I 'volunteered' for Vietnam. I didn't. Not exactly. Sorta. Benbo says she'll get over it – that women are 'all sentiment and fixated on undying devotion and unremitting special treatment – like always thinking about her... and who can think about anything when mortars are in-coming and bullets are flying.' He's not the guy I'm going to for marital advice if I ever need it. I remember thinking one time in Augsburg that maybe we had gotten married too early, or to the wrong people. Got that out of my head in a hurry when I realized I was one of those lucky 'ugly guys who married a beautiful woman'. Still, she seems distant in her letters. Is something going on back home I should know about? I wish she wasn't staying with her family in her parents' house while I'm over here. She's over there and my brother's over here. Wish that was reversed!

He's a pilot in Charlie company 227th Aviation Battalion. The Ghostriders.

I was in the TOC yesterday morning making final coordination for a first light patrol I was taking out to recon the area when I heard the colonel's C&C ship call in. "Good morning, LZ MO! This is Rowwlllfff Cramden and I'll be your Charlie-Charlie all day long..." Over the loud rotor slap in the background I recognized my brother Brad's voice, but the Spec-4 radio operator had to tell me it was the colonel's favorite pilot. I didn't see him until just before noon, in the Operations Center. He was sitting on a folding chair smoking and picking a tune on somebody's guitar. I told him: "You look a lot better sober than you do when you're drunk." He replied, "You don't." Galvin said, "I can see you two really are brothers" which kept the rest of the conversation civil. His co-pilot is a guy named Ed Norton. Didn't believe it at first. I saw Brad really did have a name tag on his nomex that said "Ralph Cramden". We had a good visit and I guess I'll be seeing more of him as long as I'm OPCON to the 2/8.

Best news so far on Mo for me is the arrival of machine guns. All but one brand new.

I got the platoon leaders together yesterday afternoon after I got my first shower in four weeks and my first shave in three. Talked over with them two things: lessons learned since the change of command in Alpha a month ago, and how we were going to employ our M60s. Since the first time I was shot at by an NVA .30 caliber machine gun, I've been obsessed with the M60. I plan to make the company into nine heavy machine gun squads. In a firefight, <u>we will be a battalion</u>. I want every NVA patrol, platoon, company, every battalion (if it comes to that) we encounter to think they've tangled with an American battalion, not one company. Instead of each platoon having one M60, it will have three. Instead of a company going to the field with three machine guns, we will go with ten. Every man in the company – officers and enlisted - except medics and RTOs - will carry a 200 round box of linked M60 ammo. This will add to each soldier's burden, but it will in the end save lives. I wish I'd had three M60s in my platoon on Illingworth rather than just one.

Told the platoon leaders we have to have our best soldiers assigned as machine gunners, and we need to make that known in the company. We'll train them initially, and each time we come on the firebase we'll have at least two mornings of refresher training.

I've detailed Masika, Heavy and Pineapple to be our M60 instructors (Tyrell Hannam, Markeys Johnston, and Kaiholo Ahulani). Training started this morning after a memorial service for the five guys we lost in Cambodia and an awards ceremony Col. Galvin planned.

The memorial service worried me. I didn't know the guys all that well. One of them I'd known only for two weeks. He was a replacement who got to the company after I did. The others were in the company when I got here a month ago, but I'd not gotten to know any of them all that well except Sergeant De Bartola. He was a squad leader in Rankin's RIFFRAFF (1st platoon) and he didn't have to die.

I'm the one responsible for his death.

De Bartola was short when I got here. He had three weeks left in country on his tour when I took over the company. It had been an informal policy of the previous commander that anyone with fifteen or less days left on his tour could serve out his last two weeks in the company rear – duties unassigned. In essence, winding down. I changed that to one week. I figured that was over two hundred weeks (four man years) of duty we were shorting the Army. De Bartola died with eight days left on his tour. He died because I changed a rule.

He also died because his platoon leader let him get sloppy and careless. Since it happened in my company and 'everything that happens or fails to happen is the company commander's responsibility, I bear some (most) of the responsibility. When we first located and occupied Metropolis, Sergeant De Bartola decided he was going to wear a pair of 'Ho Chi Minh racing slicks' he'd found rather than his issue jungle boots. ('racing slicks' are improvised foot gear resembling shower clogs made from worn out rubber tires). I, along with his platoon leader, witnessed this and failed to correct it... or the lackadaisical attitude he began to exhibit. One evening, at the time we were forming a night defensive perimeter, Sergeant De Bartola slipped outside the perimeter to take a crap. He did so without his weapon – a definite no-no. (One of my rules is that one's weapon is NEVER more than an arm's length away.) He encountered (apparently) a lone NVA who shot and killed him. This was a death that need not have happened and it was a leadership failure.

Father Patrick Donahoe (recently promoted to major and now Division's catholic chaplain) officiated at the service. I met Donahoe soon after I arrived in country and he is a friend, though we differ theologically. He did a masterful job at the service and made it easier on all of us, especially me. For my part, it was the most difficult event I've participated in my four plus months here.

The awards ceremony was equally awkward for me, though not as painful.

The worst thing to happen was that I received two decorations, an agonizing turn of events after the memorial service which was to me a stark reminder of my leadership failures. I received an Army Commendation Medal (ARCOM) for my time in Germany (a sort of a pat on the back for surviving one year without a life threatening accident on the Autobahn) and a Silver Star for actions at Firebase Illingworth. Galvin had told me that was coming and I suggested the award be rescinded or at least reviewed and delayed. I felt this was wholly inappropriate for a litany of very good reasons, but Galvin prevailed.

I'm still on probation with the troops in Alpha, a steep incline to gain their confidence.

I'm a good soldier. In Germany, I was the top qualifier in the 24th Division for the EIB – the Expert Infantryman Badge, a much more difficult award to achieve than the Combat Infantryman's Badge. But the issue for Alpha company's troops is whether or not I'm a leader – their leader. That's where I'm on their "wait and see" list.

Having read through this maundering bunkum I've written, I'm still not encouraged about this journaling thing. Maybe I should just get Galvin to lend me his three-by-fives on LEADERSHIP and write 'me too' on them and spend more time working at this company command job.

*   *   *

The Huey landed and stirred a huge red clay dust cloud next to LZ Mo.

Appearing out of the cloud were two soldiers – one a new replacement, a private who looked like a teenager, and an E-5 buck sergeant a few years older who carried his rucksack and rifle with an acquired air of familiarity toward both. He paused, looked around and sniffed the air; a sly, contented grin took over his face.

A stocky black sergeant met them at the gate leading to the log pad. "I'm First Sergeant Overton; Alpha company. You two the replacements they promised me?"

"You're just the man I'm lookin' for, First Sergeant. I'm Sergeant Newman – Case Newman, and I'm hopin' you got a platoon for me to ride herd on, Top."

Overton frowned. *This guy talks a hundred miles an hour. He looks barely old enough to be a PFC much less an E-5... and he's wantin' to be a platoon sergeant?* "Sorry about that, Sergeant Newman, but we're full up on platoon sergeants. We've got a squad open in 2nd platoon, though. I'll talk to the C.O. Tell me about yourself. What class were you in?"

"Class?!" Newman frowned. "Hell, first sergeant, do I look like a Shake 'n' Bake to you? I did my first tour with the 4th ID around Dak To in the Central Highlands two years ago as a Private E-2. Made Squad leader in the 3rd Battalion 8th Infantry recon platoon as Spec-4."

"So you saw some action?"

"Action? Hell yes! first sergeant. One day after our battalion firebase got hit, we counted two hundred sixty-two NVA dead inside our wire. I spent seven months in the Ivy recon *Headhunters*, so yeah, I seen some action, first sergeant. Wanted to get back to the 4th ID but they're all getting' sent home. So, I asked for the next best unit, and here I am. I'll run that squad for you, first sergeant, and I'll make 'em the best damn fighters in the whole company. Probably the whole battalion. That's a promise."

Overton chuckled. He had a good a feeling about this fast talking young sergeant. Maybe Newman was the buzz saw 2nd platoon needed. "Sergeant, the ol' man is gonna want to talk to you. He makes it a point to size up every NCO before we make an assignment. Most likely second platoon. The company CP is half way up the hill to the TOC." He turned and pointed at a small hut made out of dirt-filled artillery shell boxes where three bare-chested soldiers sat. "You wait for him up there with the RTOs. He'll be back in about an hour."

"Been in this Army long enough to get real good at 'hurry up and wait', first sergeant." He trudged up the hill to where two soldiers sat at a makeshift table underneath a poncho

313

spread between four engineer stakes. The third man, a medic, sat at the end of a table repacking his medic's kit. "First sergeant told me to wait here for company commander. Sergeant Case Newman just reporting in. Who might you fellas be?"

"Timmy Horner, company medic."

"Phillip Holmes, RTO. Battalion net.

"EB Gordon. I'm the company RTO for the Six."

"EB?" Newman frowned. "What's that stand for?"

"Ewell Brown."

Newman's eyes lit up. "You one o' them southern crackers named after a passel of Reb generals?" EB gave him a hard, unfriendly stare. "Cool it man. Don't go getting' all bowed up like a Halloween Cat on me. I can dig it. My great, great granddaddy was in the 4th Alabama from the day they were organized in Dalton, Georgia until the sad day they surrendered twenty-one officers and two hundred and two men under Lieutenant Colonel Jeremiah Scruggs at Appomattox. He fought with 'em from Manassas to Cold Harbor and Malvern Hill to Hanover Junction, includin' Gettysburg. My family still lives in Dalton. Where you from, EB?"

"Vicksburg."

"Man, that was an ugly one... damned Yankees. How about you Timmy?"

"Arizona."

"And you? – What did you say your name was again?"

"Holmes. Phillip Holmes. I'm from Maine. A little town called Caribou, not too far from the Canadian border."

"You fellas smoke?" Newman asked, taking the top off a clear plastic holder and offering a Kool to them. "Any idea when the commander's comin' back?"

"Whenever he gets back," EB said, taking one of Newman's cigarettes and lighting it. "He's on a first light patrol with one of *Gamecock's* squads – that's second platoon. He goes on one patrol a day. He'll be back in an hour. Maybe a little sooner. He's still teaching our hippy FO how to shoot artillery without hitting us. They've been working out on the mortars the past half hour. He likes to use 'em for some reason."

Newman looked at his watch. "Think I'll just walk around Mo and get to know the place. I'll be back. Point out second platoon."

After walking the perimeter and stopping in the TOC to talk to the Intel sergeant, he watched the mortars firing and the artillery crews cleaning their howitzers. He spoke to several of the grunts in second platoon and then sat on a bunker near the log pad to watch the goings-on there. The day to day routine was a little different from what he was used to in 4th Division. Most of the troops on the firebase went about their business in a casual way except that it seemed the grunts on the perimeter, while laidback, all had their M16s either within easy reach or slung over their shoulder. It was noticeable enough that he asked a few and heard their bitching about all the "bullshit rules" the C.O. had – like always having your rifle within an arm's length or always covering your beer or soda can with a towel when opening it in the field; no smoking after dark, no shaving in the field, and no nametag or rank on jungle fatigues in the bush, and several others. Newman liked them all.

As he sat smoking and watching the activity on the log pad, he noticed a few of the troops from the firebase approaching the helicopters now and then and engaging some of the door gunners in furtive conversation. He watched closer and realized he was viewing some kind of under the radar business being transacted. And he was pretty sure he knew what it was.

"Case, my man, you gonna hafta find out exactly what's goin' on here, and who's involved." he mumbled to himself.

His interview with Nolan seemed to go alright – he liked that the commander looked him in the eye, talked straight from the shoulder and tasked him to go out on a patrol that afternoon to observe and get a feel for the lay of the land around the firebase. That night before dinner on the firebase, the first sergeant told him he'd be taking charge of third squad in the second platoon and walked him over to meet his platoon leader, Lieutenant Cleburne who told him he was happy to have a fellow Southerner in the platoon.

That evening, as it grew dark, he passed by one of the second platoon bunkers on the berm and smelled that sharp, sweet aroma of incense burning. That could only mean one thing.

"How you fellas doing?" He asked, sliding into the position through a small opening in the back. "I'm Sergeant Newman. Just got assigned to the platoon. Third squad. You're some of my boys," he said, recognizing them from earlier. "Browning. Thorpe. Whittle. Right?"

Cautious glances were shared back and forth between the three young soldiers.

"This is my second tour in the Nam, and seein' as how I didn't just fall off the turnip truck, it's plain as hell what's goin' on here with this incense burning. Let me tell you, boys somethin'. You don't need more 'n one stick of that stuff to hide the smell of what you're smokin'. And you'd be wise not to smoke it when the wind's blowin' in rather than out. You catch what I'm sayin'? And for cryin' out loud, wait 'til it gets dark and the lifers are layin' down for the night."

More surreptitious looks were exchanged between the three soldiers but at last one of them, Thorpe, spoke up. "Not sure I know what you're talkin', sarge."

"If that's true – and it's not – then you boys must be the dumbest grunts in all III Corps."

"Sarge, you want to tell us plain what you're driving at?"

"All right. You boys have some weed and you're about to blast yourselves a roach or two. Is that plain enough? Now my next question is this? – you boys gonna share with your squad leader or you gonna charge me?" Silence, accompanied by more shifty looks between the soldiers. "Go ahead and talk amongst yourselves, but I'm not leavin' til I have an answer."

"We'll share with you... this one time. A show of good faith."

"How am I gonna get my hay after that?" Newman asked.

"One step at a time, sarge. One step at a time," Thorpe replied. He was the apparent leader of the group and was growing a little bolder now.

"What?! You don't think I'm up and up? You think I'm some lifer out for your scalp?"

"Didn't say that. Let's just fire up a roach and share it around, then see where that leads. I'm still trying to wrap my head around the idea you're not a lifer."

"First of all, I'm not much for sloppy seconds. I'll take a solo hit. Y'all can share."

That seemed to quash the conversation, and one of the soldiers reached inside his breast pocket and produced a small plastic bag of marijuana which he deftly rolled into two thin cigarettes; one he passed to Newman and the other he lit for himself. The sergeant lit the marijuana butt and inhaled.

The strange sweetness swept down his throat and rushed into his lungs, and for a moment he felt like his body was fighting a fire within; and then his forehead seemed to expand and his head began to buzz in a muted sound like a faraway chain saw. The inside of the bunker came aglow, as if a light had turned on. He exhaled the lungful of smoke.

"That's some righteous weed you got there, my man," Newman observed. "Is that local?"

"Hawaiian Black. The Air Force brings it in – a crew chief here, a crew chief there. That's what I'm told. Who knows how much of that is true. And really, who cares?"

Newman laughed with them and inhaled again. This time was more pleasant – like the second or third Martini. Marijuana always worked quickly, but this stuff was like jet assisted intoxication. After the third hit, he was almost gone. Almost. He continued to smoke, but stopped inhaling to keep from going completely over the edge. Still, his mind whirled and his vision seemed to dim. *Keep focused, Case. Concentrate. Don't let this get away from you.*

After several minutes his focus sharpened and he noticed the three soldiers had entered an altered state of relaxation, seeming completely and pleasantly at ease.

"So how do I get this stuff on my own?" Newman asked.

"I can get it for you," Thorpe replied.

"And charge me your profit. Don't think I like that idea. Try again."

The soldier shrugged. "You can get it where we do – the helicopter door gunners."

"All of them?"

"There's one on a ship that has a pair of dice painted on the nose, and another that has the numbers 666 inside a wreath. Those are the only ones I know."

"Yeah. Yeah," Newman mumbled, blowing a cloud of smoke into the bunker. "I saw that triple six today on the log pad. But the log birds change every day."

"They usually deliver to a cook in the artillery mess hall. He charges a delivery fee. If you can catch one of the helicopters, like we did today, you can get it direct at a lower price."

"How many people know about this?" Newman asked, leaning against a side wall.

"In the company? The three of us, and two or three in first platoon. Nobody we know of in third platoon. Who knows, there might be some there. Nobody smokes it in the bush, but the firebase... that's a different story."

Newman crushed out the lit end of his cigarette and put it in his pocket, then waited for a few minutes until his head had mostly cleared. He asked Thorpe for the plastic bag so he could take a whiff, which he did and then placed it in one of his breast pockets.

"Whoa, sarge, my weed. I paid good money for it," the soldier said, slurring his words.

"Too bad," Newman replied. "Let me tell you boys something. This shit has no place in the field – in the bush or on the firebase or anywhere else south of the DMZ. I won't have it in my squad and I know the C.O. don't want it in his company. So here's how this is gonna work. No more weed. I'm gonna keep my eye on you guys, and if you ever smoke another joint, it'll be your last, cause I'm gonna shoot you myself. Right between your damn eyes. You hear what I'm sayin'? I ain't gonna die, or let somebody in my company die because some hop head is all doped up. Now that I know who's doin' it and how they're gettin' it, this show is over. Is that plain enough for you? Thorpe? Whittle? Browning? .... Good. Since we all know how to keep score, we can all play the game together. You boys have a good night now, ya hear?"

Newman slipped out of the bunker, looked up at the dark sky, and smiled. "Damn, I do love this Army!"

Chapter 25

Inside the TOC it was dim, damp and hot, with no ventilation and a string of a half dozen bare 100 watt bulbs dangling from the ceiling, powered by a generator near enough to be a constant, intrusive hum. The dugout's interior was a long, narrow trench dug seven feet into the earth, ten feet wide, the width of a D5B Caterpillar standard dozer blade. Halfway back another, shorter trench had been dug at right angles and walled off with wooden pallet slats to make two private sleeping quarters – one for the battalion commander and the other to house the operations officer, S-3, a major named Roberts; both were accessible only from the outside.

Glenn stood near the bottom of the short flight of steps leading outside and observed.

The S-2, a skinny captain wearing black rimmed glasses was marking up the map that sat on a tripod against one wall facing a row of four folding metal chairs. Brad told him Galvin had nicknamed the officer 'Rusksack' and frequently alluded to him as the 'Mad Bomber'. *Got to be a good story behind that*, Glenn thought. There was an easy-going, comfortable atmosphere here that he'd not observed in the other battalions he'd been assigned to. He'd not had enough time in Galvin's battalion to draw any conclusions, but this command was different – good or bad, better or worse, he didn't yet know.

The back end of the dugout housed a couple of field desks and a bank of several FM radios manned by a trio of enlisted men supervised by a sergeant E-7. The roof was composed of logs cut from the surrounding forest, covered in sandbags layered three deep. It was your basic, functional, highly mobile 1st Cav operations center. The staff was shuffling toward the briefing area and Galvin waved at him to sit down on one of the chairs.

"We decided the commander of the base defense should have a seat at the table," the colonel told him as they sat down. "How were your steaks tonight?"

"As good as last night, sir. My troops sure enjoyed them."

"They smelled awfully good." Galvin gave him a mordant look. "I hope you aren't going to make that a habit, lieutenant. I had enough problems and complaints about battalion chow before you started this practice."

"Sir, the grill will be hauled back to Sông Bé first thing tomorrow."

The colonel nodded and looked toward the map. "All right, Rucksack, lead us off."

The captain went through the same litany as the night before, starting with the weather report and detailing the intelligence summaries first from brigade and then the individual reports from the companies in the field, pointing out on the map where each was located currently and the locations of each trail, fighting position and cache site called in that day. He rolled a sketch of the firebase over the map. "Finally, we have this to report from Alpha company, one slash six. Their first and last light patrols yesterday and today reported these six fighting positions around MO, two of them with recent usage, and these three trail sightings, all with recent use in the last twenty-four to forty-eight hours."

Galvin glanced briefly at Nolan and then back at the S-2. "What does that tell us? And why didn't we know about the trails and fighting positions until Alpha came on the firebase?"

"Well, sir, I'd say it confirms for us what we suspected when you chose this location – that we're astride one of the feeders of the Jolly Trail System. As far as why they weren't reported until now..." The captain cleared his throat and looked at Glenn quickly. "Perhaps Lieutenant Nolan has a better idea than I do."

"All right," the colonel said easily, leaning forward, turning and looking expectantly at Nolan. "Why did you find these trails and fighting positions and Bravo company didn't?"

"That's a good question, sir," Glenn responded. *It's because we're hot stuff in the 6th Cav and we're simply better than your companies here, sir... You say that, Nolan, and they'll tan your hide before you die... But it would be a hoot to say it, just to watch their faces.*

"Sir, the previous company opened up the firebase and that's a lot of work. Doesn't leave much or any time to go out and recon. When we got here we could do a lot more patrolling because they'd done all the hard labor on the fighting positions and other stuff on the LZ. That's my guess."

He could tell Galvin liked the answer by the look in his eyes and the quick grin and nod. "Very observant, lieutenant. What would you recommend now that we know we have these trails and positions so close to the firebase."

"Sir, I'd continue the patrolling and I'd also get one or two Pink Teams out here to scour the area, especially between here and the river since we're only two miles from the border. I'd also have them check directly on the other side of the river inside Cambodia for trails leading toward Mo since we don't have troops on the ground over there."

Galvin looked at the S-3. "All right, Nolan, we'll take that under consideration. S-4. What's our supply situation and how did log day go for Charlie company?"

The briefing droned on, much like the few he'd sat in on in Conrad's battalion in Tay Ninh. He guessed they served a purpose, but was glad he wouldn't be dragged through it all that often. It was over in a half hour, the finale being a 'dog and pony show' put on by the artillery liaison officer, the captain with the 'Snidely Whiplash' mustache.

The battalion commander pulled him aside and they went outside to talk.

"You handled that hot potato Rucksack tossed you very well."

"Not a hot potato at all, sir."

"If you say so. I hear you conducted a lot of machine gun training most of the morning."

"Yes, sir. Got in some new guns and trained a lot of gunners and assistants. We need to train on a lot of things." He paused and looked down. "Last night I found out we don't know how to do a 'mad minute'. You probably know that already. It's embarrassing."

The colonel cleared his throat. "I wondered if you were going to do anything about that. You're right. The 'mad minute' last night left a lot to be desired."

"It was pathetic, sir. I'm embarrassed to tears. But we're fixing that." Glenn looked at his watch. "In fact, right now. If you'll wait here for me, sir, I'll be back in one minute." Glenn walked down the hill into darkness and returned shortly. "In just a little while, we're going to practice what we're going to do tomorrow morning at oh-two-fourteen hours."

"Zero-two-one-four?"

"That was the moment the 95C regiment attacked Illingworth, sir," Glenn said, angry all over again; not at the NVA – he knew they were just doing what they were ordered to do. His anger was directed instead at the senior leaders who tied the battalion down with all that extra artillery and piles of ammo. "We're going to show ourselves in Alpha how a company defends a firebase... I hope. If this doesn't come off, we'll do it again, and keep on doing it until we get it right. I'm not going through another night like April 1st."

"You upset, Nolan?"

"No, sir, not –" He stopped himself and pressed his lips tightly together. "I guess maybe I am." They fell silent for long seconds and Glenn was about to say something when a hand-held flare soared upward from company CP in a loud *WHOOOSH* and exploded in a red star cluster.

Immediately, all around the firebase, M16s and machine guns firing tracers in long streams arced into the dark tree lines and an illumination round burst overhead. Countless M79 rounds exploded fifty yards outside the strands of concertina wire. Mortars in rapid succession lit up tree lines with loud double explosions... The noise was deafening. Another flare exploded in a white cluster; the firing stopped as a dozen Claymore mines detonated.

Then everything went dark and silent. Sometime during the exercise the TOC had emptied and a couple dozen people were standing around him. The only thing he could hear was the ringing in his ears; here and there a few whoops and shouts erupting around the berm, then in the artillery pits.

"Damn it," Glenn muttered. "That's unprofessional."

"I don't think a little bit of celebrating is going to harm anything. Noise and light discipline are pretty much shot, don't you think?" Galvin said jovially. "I have to say that was an improvement over last night. That was a Fort Benning quality mad minute."

"Not quite, sir.... If the S-4 could get us some fifty-five gallon drums of *fougasse* – you know that gelatinized napalm stuff – we could come close to Benning."

The colonel shook his head. "Let's not get carried away, Nolan." He laughed again. "Where did all those machine guns come from? How many were there anyway?"

"Ten of them, sir. And they're mine. My supply sergeant traded NVA pistol belts for them – where and to whom, I don't know and don't want to. We'll do this again early in the morning, Only better, after we tighten up some things with the platoon leaders."

Yup, that was better. A lot better...

*   *   *

11 May 1970 – LZ Mo
Entry 2 of ___2___ (so far)
– 2nd full day on firebase Mo

Sitting in the TOC to write. It's late. Big day. Highest highs. Lowest lows.

Today I received my own Kiowa 'Pokey-Pokey Stick', a gift from Daniel Two Hatchets - one of the great presents of all times. It's a few inches shy of a yard, a Cav patch carved into the handle and three narrow painted rings – red, green and yellow. It's to ward off evil spirits and bad luck, and attract pleasant, helpful spirits. Most of all, it's to keep me from poking around in the bushes with my hands and getting bitten by poisonous snakes. I'm told there's a penny inside the handle... so that if I die the NVA will know I didn't die penniless. Cheerful thought!

Two Hatchets is clearly one of my best soldiers. SSG Connie Pratt in third platoon tells me it wasn't always that way. My predecessor in Alpha allowed the troops to drink hard liquor on the firebase and Two Hatchets was a problem drinker who was constantly in trouble – the ol' 'Indian and firewater' problem.... always thought that was something made up for the movies. Apparently not. My rule is beer only – rationed to one a day in the field, two a day on the firebase. Since I got rid of the hard liquor, my Indian has done a complete one-eighty. He's third platoon scout when they're out on patrol, and works with Lone Wolf Edelstein of Brooklyn and TiJean, the Canadian giant as my scout team when we move as a company, or when I've got something I want checked out on the QT by a small, silent team. Two Hatchets can walk into the woods and literally disappear in a matter of a few paces – one might expect that of an Indian, but Lone Wolf and TiJean are darned near as good. In fact, the ability of the average American GI to adapt to the jungle is one of the biggest surprises to me since coming to Vietnam.

I heard all that business about the Japs in WWII being such great jungle fighters and the same thing about the Viet Cong and NVA. Bull! I'll take my guys over theirs any day. After four months here, I've observed that US soldiers get damn good in a big hurry at reading sign and moving in the jungle. It's amazing to watch the transformation of a new guy coming in to the company and seeing him become a really good operator in the field. The NVA are good soldiers – I know that first hand. The Viet Cong?? – don't know. Never fought them. The NVA know their craft, but what makes them most dangerous is that they have no regard for human life, including their own (and because of it they press their attacks – sometimes foolishly.) Americans are just the opposite - we put a high value on life. It seems to me most Orientals are culturally and religiously and educationally bent toward following orders and staying in their place in the pecking order. Again, Americans are pretty much opposite. I think that makes my guys better soldiers. They can think for themselves, they want to know what's going on and WHY... and they can adapt. That's all part of growing up free in a ~~democracy~~ - scratch that... in a representative republic. (Miss Schramm in 8th grade Social Studies would have my butt if I called America a democracy – hard, demanding woman – maybe why she never married.)

I want all my soldiers to be able to think on their own. Not insubordinate, but thinkers. Platoon leaders can't look over every squad leader's shoulder and I can't look over every platoon leader's shoulder every minute. I don't want the soldiers in my company doing stupid things because they're afraid to speak up. I'll let generals and politicians do the stupid stuff.

Like this thing I ran across tonight after the briefing with the S-2, Rucksack.

Last night after the briefing, Rucksack and I talked about something he noticed on the briefing map – a red rectangle straddling the border, about ten or twelve square kilometers on both sides. He'd noticed it on the maps they got the first day of the Cambodia operation and questioned it. Turned out to be an 'off-limits' and no fly area. He guessed the NVA know about it too, and that's where they go to rest up. Said he was looking into what we could do about it through brigade. Restricted zones along the border? For us? Certainly not the enemy! What brainiac in MACV decided that?! What a stupid way to fight a war – setting up safe zones for your enemy. There was one of those near Illingworth, too. At least everywhere I've been has been essentially a free fire zone – if it moves it's not a friendly and that makes it a target. Galvin's philosophy, too because the border areas all the way back to Sông Bé are unpopulated – glad we don't have to worry about civilians in this AO.

Had some guests on the firebase today. One of them was Beaker, Rash 27- the Air Force FAC that I met in Tay Ninh province early on. He was here to "liaison' with us grunts – all clean shaven and smelling of English Leather in his immaculate duck egg blue flight suit and ascot; jaunty little dark blue overseas cap. ('All my men wear English Leather or they wear nothing at all'). Boots shined to high luster and the sparkle in his eye like you see in those movie posters for 'Chitty Chitty Bang Bang' or 'Around the World in 80 Days'. I'm surprised he didn't bring along Mitch Miller and the gang to entertain us with - 'They took the blue from the skies and a pretty girl's eyes and a touch of old Glory, too!'…. Life must be so droll at twenty-five hundred feet, ensconced in air-conditioned sumptuousness looking down on us *mere mortals. So good of you to deign to visit us humans and trod the dusty, dirty terra firma. Didn't say that… But I was thinking it as loud as I could… yup, I'm jealous – and not one bit ashamed. I could have been doing that if it hadn't been for that sorry s.o.b. senator who hates Grandpa Nolan. Beaker entertained the troops in the CP – he told them what he'd heard about me and my rugby days – 'there was an artillery officer there who swore Knocker Nolan was the baddest head-knocker in the East.' EB looked me over, up and down, and asked: 'Is that true, Six, that you played a game tougher than pro football without a helmet?' When I told him I did, he looked at Heavy and Timmy Horner and said: 'Wail, that shore 'nuff explains a lot o' things we seen ol' Odin say and do, don't it?'*

Our other entertainer – actually two of them – George Peppard and Anne B. Davis. She was wonderful, just like I expected from seeing her on TV - and he was a complete jerk. How sad he bothered to come. I was amazed the USO brought Hollywood stars this far out in the bush, especially so close to the border, and I was really looking forward to meeting the guy who not only played in THE BLUE MAX (one of my all-time favorite movies), but also got to do scenes I'll <u>never</u> forget with Ursala Andress. Life is full of disappointments.

It wasn't the only disappointment of the day.

Masika let me down big time – I'm going to have to court martial him. He's not left me much of a choice. I learned of it just this evening.

Tonight, after I talked with Rucksack again about the excluded zones in our AO, First Sergeant Overton told me the bad news. This afternoon, about a half hour after the log bird left, Lieutenant Jeffrees, the assistant S-4 down at the log pad, found Masika and PFC Torres asleep while on outpost duty. Bad news never gets better with age so I talked with Jeffrees, and then Masika's squad leader, platoon sergeant and platoon leader – Lt. Cleburne – to get the facts.

I'm going to sleep on this overnight. At first I thought I'd talk to him this evening, but I'm so damned angry and disappointed that I need to back away for a little while. He's not going anywhere. Neither am I. Neither is this damned problem. Just when I thought I was making a little headway… now this! What the hell was he thinking?!

*   *   *   *

"You know why you're here, Specialist Hannam?" Glenn asked the soldier standing in front of him across the table made from wooden mortar shell crates. It had stopped raining mid-morning; the sun was at its zenith and the firebase was sweltering in the oppressive humidity.

Nolan could see out of the corner of his eye that most of the troops in Alpha company were surreptitiously watching the little drama being played out at the company CP.

"Stand to attention and look straight ahead, soldier, when your commander addresses you and asks you a question!" First Sergeant Overton said sharply. "You hear, soldier?"

Masika pulled himself slowly to his full height and stared straight ahead over the top of Nolan's head. "Yes, first sergeant."

"Do you know why you're here Hannam?" Glenn repeated.

"Because the lieutenant down to the log pad reported me."

"Reported you for what?"

"For sleepin' on OP duty."

"You tack a 'sir' onto that, Specialist Hannam," Overton said. Glenn gave him a hooded sideways look and frowned.

"For sleepin' on OP duty... sir."

"What are we going to do about that?" Glenn asked slowly.

"Don't know, sir. Guess that's up to you."

"Reckon so, Hannam." Glenn took a deep breath and let silence linger until it became painful. "You really screwed the pooch, Specialist. You know what I mean?"

"Yes, sir."

"I don't think you do, Specialist Hannam, so let me tell you," Glenn said evenly, with a hard edge to his voice. "You let down your brothers in the company – I mean all of them... black, white, Latino, Indian, oriental... everyone on the company roster. You let down Sergeant Franklin, your squad leader. You let down your platoon sergeant and platoon leader. You let down First Sergeant Overton who has always, and I mean *always* gone to bat for you since the day he was assigned to Alpha... and you let me down." He let that sink in for interminable seconds. "Because of what you did, everyone in the company is marked and labeled. The word going around Mo is that Alpha is a slacker company. Can't be trusted. Not you. Not me. Not any of us. Do you get what that means?"

"Yes, sir."

"I hope you do. We'll see. People from the battalion commander on down are wondering if that's true. We're not part of their battalion so they've been watching closely, wondering about us. They're wondering if this is the way we normally operate – loose security, slipshod, 'who gives a shit' attitude. You've put the company in a tight bind... and me, too. Is there a good reason why you did this?"

"No, sir."

"Any excuse? Any mitigation?"

Masika hesitated momentarily and finally said, "No, sir."

"We got a mess on our hands, don't we Tyrell?" Hannam's eyes narrowed, smoldering – a flash of defiance – and he glared at Nolan briefly before averting his eyes. *He's got something to say, an excuse, but he's too proud to say it in front of the first sergeant. Come on, man, work with me here.* "Private Torres admitted to sleeping on OP duty and he agreed to accept a company commander's Article 15 instead of a Summary Court Martial. That same offer is on the table for you. You have until tomorrow morning to give me your answer."

"I have a choice?"

"You do. But it's limited to two. Have you ever been given company punishment or court-martialed?" Hannam shook his head no. "All right, let me tell you the difference. A company Article fifteen is non-judicial punishment – that means it's like a slap on the knuckles from your old spinster elementary school teacher's wooden ruler. It stings, maybe breaks the skin, but it's quickly over and done and doesn't leave any lasting marks. By comparison a summary court-martial is official judicial punishment; compared to the slap on the knuckles, a summary court is like taking a half dozen lashes from a cat-o-nine tails... if you're convicted. They'll take meat and leave scars because the conviction will stay on your records. In each case, one officer presides as judge and jury; you can testify on your own behalf or not. You can question any of the witness, and you can consult with a military lawyer before the trial but you're not allowed to be represented by one during trial."

"What would be my punishment?" Hannam asked after some thought.

"Don't know. In each case, the officer makes the call within limits. As the presiding officer of the Article 15, I can put you in confinement for up to seven days, take one stripe from you and take away seven days' pay. Those are the upper limits. A summary court can confine you for a month, sentence you to hard labor for 45 days, take away two-thirds of a month's pay and reduce you three grades to Private E-1. Again, that's the maximum."

The soldier frowned, deep in thought. "Since that's the most I can get, does that mean the court martial officer could also give me no punishment?"

"Theoretically that's possible."

"So, what you goin' to be givin' me, sir, if I choose the Article 15?"

"Not going to say, Hannam. But it's going to be something... I wouldn't be going through this right now if I didn't think you deserved some kind of punishment. Sleeping on OP duty *is not* a small deal in my book. When you're on guard – out in the bush or here on the firebase, people are depending on you for their safety. And I doubt you think it's no big deal either."

"You're goin' to take some money from me, and a stripe." Hannam said it as a statement not a question. "You can put me in jail if you want, but I can't be losin' no money. I know I can't be talkin' you outta dat, but I might could some other officer from somewhere else."

"Or you could end up in Long Binh Jail, fined a month's pay and have your pay reduced for a long time to that of a recruit. Sure you want that? Sure you want to take that chance?"

"Maybe I got to... sir."

"I want you to think about it today and sleep on it overnight. Think hard about it. After breakfast, you come by here and tell me your decision." Glenn looked at the first sergeant who was staring hard at Hannam. "Don't do anything stupid, soldier."

"I'll do what I gotta do, lieutenant."

"And you'll force me to do something I gotta do. I'll see you tomorrow morning at zero eight hundred. Dismissed." He watched Hannam turn and walk slowly away, past the mortar pits on the way to second platoon. "What do you think, first sergeant? What's he going to do?"

"He's gonna take his chances with the Summary Court, sir."

"Why?"

"You heard him, sir. He can't be losin' no money – and he knows you're gonna fine him and he's also pretty sure you're gonna take a stripe. Tell you the truth, sir, I don't think he'd respect you if you did anything else with what you know now."

"What I know now?

Overton took a deep breath. "What you don't know, sir, is that he's the sole support for his grandmother in St. Louis that raised him from a child when his mother died and his daddy ran off. He sends every cent he makes to her and it's hardly enough most months."

"You're right. I didn't know that," Glenn admitted. "But that's not an excuse for falling asleep on guard duty."

"No, sir, it's not. But you gave him time to think this over; you should think it over, too. There's somethin' not right goin' on here."

"What do you know that I don't, first sergeant?"

"Nuthin', sir. But this ain't like Masika. He's too smart to do this, specially after what you done for him." The first sergeant furrowed his brow and stared away, clearing his throat. "He always was looked up to here in Alpha, but what you done makin' him lead gunner and trainer and takin' him into the CP earned him respect from ever-body in the company, white as well as black. And respect is important to a young man without a father comin' from where he did. Just don't think him, of all people, would pay you back this way."

Rain fell in solid, steady sheets as Glenn descended the short flight of makeshift steps and rapped on the entranceway frame of Colonel Galvin's sleeping quarters.

"Who is it?"

"Sir, it's Lieutenant Nolan."

"Come in. Come in. I'm glad you came by. We need to talk," Galvin said immediately from behind the heavy drape of canvas protecting the inner chamber, keeping the rain from coming in and light from shining out. Glenn pulled the canvas aside and quickly entered. "Take off your poncho and sit down. All I've got to offer is the cot. The décor isn't geared for entertaining. How about a beer?"

"Yes, sir, that'd be just fine." He looked around as the battalion commander searched beside the desk, finally producing a bottle of Beck's and handed it over. The colonel was sitting on a camp stool at a small field desk, in the middle of writing a letter; he had his hardback journal open and a small, framed picture of a young blond woman sat on the footlocker against the far wall. Water dripped in a steady cadence near the entrance, puddled, then ran in a small, silvery streak across the middle of the floor and under the wood slat wall.

"What brings you out on a night like this, Alpha Six?" Galvin asked pleasantly, putting away his writing and closing the journal; turning, he struck the footlocker with a muddy boot and the framed picture toppled onto the dirt floor and into a small puddle. He instantly picked it up, wiped it off with an OD handkerchief and looked at Nolan. "Don't tell her I did that."

"Your wife, sir?" Nolan asked and Galvin nodded. "She's very pretty. How did you two meet?" *Idiot!* he instantly said to himself. *What the hell are you thinking? That's not the kind of personal thing you ask your commander. And you just started working for him. Cordial chit-chat isn't why you came here, anyhow. This guy must think you're a complete numbskull.*

The colonel gave him a sideways look, producing a crafty smile. "We met at a tea dance one afternoon at Fort Knox. A tea dance I organized and orchestrated. Why the look Nolan? Didn't they teach you how to do that at the Academy, or during Ranger school?" When Glenn remained silent, Galvin laughed out loud. "Those places didn't teach me either, but necessity is the mother of invention. Are you really interested in the answer to your question?"

Glenn could tell Colonel Galvin was enjoying his discomfort. "Absolutely, sir."

"I'll tell you the short version. I was attending the Armor Officer's Advanced Course at Knox." Galvin found a Beck's for himself, opened it and continued. "I, along with some of my Advanced Course cohorts, was experiencing difficulties meeting girls during my stay at Knox, so one night I got the idea to throw a party to draw girls and repel male competition – a formal affair like a 'Tea Dance' on a football Saturday afternoon when guys would be at the stadium drinking beer with their buddies. I thought it was pure genius, Nolan. And it worked like a charm." Galvin chuckled again and his face lit up. "We had a great female turnout. I saw Ginny right off and made a tactical approach. I learned she was a finalist in the Miss Kentucky pageant. Not long after, we got engaged and then married."

"That's a hell of a story, sir, with a great ending for you."

"And for her, too, lieutenant," Galvin said quickly, with mock seriousness.

"I was just about to say that."

"I'm sure you were. She didn't make it to the Miss Kentucky pageant. She had a choice – continue in the pageant or marry me. She chose wisely." He grinned at Nolan and took a long pull on his beer. "But you didn't come here to talk about how I met Ginny or to tell me you met Mary Anne when you moved to Baltimore and ended up high school sweethearts."

Glenn was surprised. *How did he know that?... Of course – Father Pat.* He'd seen them talking before the memorial service for the guys he'd lost in Cambodia. The Catholic priest had probed him for that background when he was in Conrad's battalion; Galvin was Irish from Boston, and probably Catholic. Mary Anne's father had told him a few years back when he'd asked for her hand how Irish and Scottish Catholics were tight, as if to say that he would never be fully accepted into clan MacEagan until he converted from his Anglicanism.

"No, sir, that wasn't my purpose, but I'm glad I asked. Hope I wasn't out of line."

"Of course not. But what's really on your mind tonight?"

"I've got a problem, sir. A real thorny kind of problem."

"The black soldier caught sleeping on outpost yesterday." Galvin's face grew solemn.

"You've heard." He wasn't surprised. Galvin was the Division intel guru, and had once upon a time figured out a way to meet and marry a girl like the one in the picture. "This is a really sticky situation – for me, and maybe for the battalion, also. The guy is a good trooper. He's a soldier I've elevated in the eyes of the company since I took command four weeks ago – for good reason, I thought. But now I'm not so sure. He's done something inexcusable and it's put me in a real box. I could use some advice, sir."

"Give me the details."

Glenn explained how Hannam and Torres had been detailed as outpost for the log pad for the afternoon two days earlier and were both found sleeping by the assistant S-4, Lieutenant Jeffrees, the assistant S-4 in charge of battalion resupply. He went through the questioning of the soldiers' squad leader, platoon sergeant and platoon leader. "It was all pretty cut and dried, sir. All the stories jived."

"What did Hannam have to say?"

"He manned up and admitted to being asleep."

"Torres?"

"He was scared to death, but owned up to being asleep, too. I told him about the options of either the company Article 15 or the Summary Court. He jumped on the Article 15 – not Hannam. He seems to think maybe he can convince a summary court officer to find him not guilty. He appears pretty sold on taking his chances."

"Does he know what you're intending to give him as punishment?"

"No, sir. He asked but I wouldn't tell him. I'll tell you though – I'm going to give him the max I'm allowed. This is serious business and I don't see any plausible mitigation. I asked but he didn't offer up any."

"I agree it's serious. But I know his reputation; the sergeant major tells me he's a good soldier and your faith in him has seemed warranted... until now. I suggest you sleep on it another night, and let me talk to my Philadelphia lawyer. Rucksack might have some ideas." Galvin looked down, frowning. "When you questioned his chain of command, was it as a group or one by one?"

"All at the same time, sir. Does it matter?"

"Don't know. It may or may not. I'll talk to the Mad Bomber – he's a lawyer, you know – and he'll get back to you." The battalion commander looked at him and said, "He told me the two of you think it's worth looking into that 'Restricted Area' here in our new AO."

"Yes, sir. Rucksack thinks it's odd that there's a no fly-no trespass zone straddling the border. I agree. I think he's on to something. When you look at it on a map, it's like a bridge over the river from Cambodia into Vietnam. The NVA have to know about it, and if I were them, that's exactly where I'd be crossing."

Galvin pulled out his map and spread it on the cot. "I too think he's discovered something. So we're going to mount an op the day after tomorrow. Basically, the concept is to airlift you at first light into this open field on the eastern border of the zone and have you scout along the river for any signs of crossing sites. If there is, then I'll move Bravo company into the box on the Cambodia side and patrol there for logistics bases and movement."

Glenn looked at the map and said, "I like it, sir. I think you're making a smart move."

"I knew you would, Nolan. It's what you and Rucksack suggested to the S-3 this morning. It's wise to subtlety compliment your direct superior; just be *more* subtle in the future." The colonel gave him a crooked, knowing smile. "One other thing. There's a U.S. Senator who arrived in Saigon this afternoon to investigate the situation surrounding your assuming command of Alpha. It seems some of the men wrote their congressmen about the circumstances of your predecessor's being relieved."

A chill went down his back. "Am I in some kind of trouble, sir?" Glenn asked.

"Probably not. I know something of the circumstances myself since Colonel van Noort took over for the officer who relieved your predecessor. This Senator – Reeves is his name – wants to interview the men in your company, including you, according to what we hear. But I don't think this is about you, Nolan."

"Senator Reeves?!" Glenn gasped, incredulous. "Sir, frankly I expect the truth is that this investigation is *totally* about me."

Chapter 26

"Erika, there's a young lady waiting in your office," the middle-aged secretary said to the senior Federal Assistant Prosecutor for Washington.

"This is awfully early for visitors. Her name?"

"Cateline. Wouldn't give me her last name or a business card, but she had a picture of the two of you together with your husband riding horses. I told her she could wait."

Erika Ashby nodded. "Randall and I spent a week with my brother's family at a ranch out west several years ago. I have a whole album of pictures probably just like it. Thanks, Helen." Mitch had picked them up in Denver in a twin engine plane he'd rented and flown them into the little airport at Dubois where he'd reserved rooms for a week at the Triangle C Ranch. She hadn't ridden for years, and Randall was a complete neophyte, but it had been a relaxing time on trails beneath the towering Tetons on the fringes of Yellowstone.

Erika opened her office door and entered. The young girl stood and gave her a quick hug.

"I shan't take long, but I have a rather important request of you," Cateline said.

"What? No chit chat, no girl talk... no 'how are you doing this fine day, Auntie Erika?'"

"Not for the moment. All business, I'm afraid. We need to do something straight away to help my favorite brother."

"Brad?"

"My other favorite."

"Glenn. What's up with him?" Erika asked cheerily.

"I came back from a few days away to find *His Lordship* off to the Orient to muck around in Glenn's business, and I've done something about it. But I need your help."

"His Lordship? You mean –"

"Billy-no-mates. Senator Reeves... The man without friends that I work for, of course," the young English woman said, visibly agitated; her nostrils flared. "He's been talking with another senator about a Congressional Inquiry into something to do with Glenn and his duty assignment. Nothing good, I can assure you. He left for Vietnam Friday of last week and arrived there a day ago. From what I know, I'm certain it's nothing but I'm sure His Lordship means no good thing over it."

"You said you'd done something?"

"I have!" Cateline declared. "I wired him in Saigon with the urgent news that new evidence has surfaced in the investigation into his friends and associates, and that the office of the Federal Prosecutor was again interviewing them."

Erika was surprised, and vaguely troubled. "You know that's not true, Cateline."

"It is now." She pointed at the boxes on the floor. "Copies of documents from the Senator's personal files. You should read them, and then I hope you'll call in some of his friends and chat them up. The Senator was concerned enough to return immediately."

The prosecutor leaned back in her chair and tilted her head as she stared at the young woman. "Cateline, I'm uncomfortable with what you're doing and the way this is heading."

"You fear for my safety? Don't worry about me. But there's something else, isn't there? Do you think perhaps what I'm doing is unethical... do you fear that all this information I give you is inadmissible according to the rules of evidence?"

Erika Ashby nodded. "Elements of both. Yes."

Cateline slowly shook her head from side to side. "I admire your sense of propriety, Auntie. I've always admired that character trait in you and your family – my family – because it's not only admirable but uncommon in the business of government and the legal community. But the facts show clearly it's not a trait shared by Senator Reeves. I admit to a certain personal pleasure in being party to hopefully bringing him to his just rewards. What I'm doing is not unethical, because I'm gathering evidence of crimes committed by my employer. I'm doing this as a private citizen – a citizen with legal training, yes, but not as an officer of the court. Senator Reeves does not deserve special consideration because of his position. You, as a Federal Prosecutor have to follow all the legal prerequisites of evidence gathering; as a private citizen, I don't. I'm perfectly content to have my actions judged by the courts of law and public opinion. There are some who might judge me harshly because of my motives or my taking advantage of the man who hired me. If they judge me harshly, I would like them to hear, in his own words and the words of his chief of staff, their intentions – personal intentions – toward me and others. The tapes are very revealing. I should also point out that you neither requested anything from me nor provided equipment or funding, so the evidence is in no way tainted."

Cateline stood. "I would very much appreciate your calling in at least a few of the men whose names are on the list in one of those boxes. Otherwise, His Lordship may have some rather difficult questions for me when he returns. Time for breakfast or a spot of tea, Auntie?"

*   *   *

Rain fell in a soft, steady drizzle as the four Americans lay on their stomachs in the jungle on the Vietnam side of the border, gazing at the far shore – Cambodia – a hundred yards across the dark, swift river. The short soldier with black frame glasses faced upstream; the largest in the group protected them downstream. It was late – almost twilight.

"This is the main landing place," Daniel Two Hatchets whispered to Glenn, pointing at the marks in the wet earth and the broken foliage. "There is one more downriver two hundred meters, but this one is more recent and shows more usage. It is a wider area. This is where the NVA will land when they come."

Glenn nodded agreement. They had been in 'Rucksack's Box' for three days.

The original combat assault had not been a traditional 1st Cav CA, more like a stealth LRRP insertion, so as not to alert any enemy that might be in or moving through the Restricted Box. He'd sent in his three man scout team reinforced with Pineapple's machine gun team to scout out the LZ area so they could follow on with flights of six without using the normal artillery prep. Everybody from Galvin through the pilots were leery of the idea, but Glenn finally persuaded them. The only thing the battalion commander vetoed was Nolan's plan to be the leader of the scouting team.

The initial element of surprise had worked but within two hours, the company made its first contact with an enemy force, in platoon strength. The firefight was brief but violent until the NVA broke contact and melted away, taking their dead with them. Alpha had continued west until noon, scouting ahead with third platoon paralleling the river a kilometer away. He'd sent Sergeant Newman's squad on a patrol back to the LZ and he'd ambushed three NVA who appeared to be investigating the helicopter activity. Case Newman had only been in the company a little over a week now, but Glenn already recognized he was one of the best soldiers he had in the unit from observing him on patrol around Mo. He was clearly well above the average squad leader.

"We'll move the company down to the river's edge, set up here for the night and see what happens," Glenn told his three scouts. It was barely light enough to see when the last platoon settled into the precarious position on the riverbank, only a hundred yards from Cambodia. To Glenn it felt dangerous; but it also felt right. He would have liked to walk the perimeter but by the time the last elements settled in, there wasn't enough light deep inside the thick jungle where it got dark early. That night, without last light patrols, a final cigarette or hot C-rations, Alpha company bedded down soaking wet, wrapped in their ponchos and on fifty percent alert. Mikey Meade fired in a single night defensive arty target for the company before the jungle went utterly dark and quiet.

The last thing Glenn did was to request a Night Hawk mission, on standby... just in case.

*　　*　　*

"Phouc Vinh Tower, this is Army double-deuce three, five north for landing," Brad announced on the radio.

"Roger double-deuce three. Can you take a look at something near your location for Command Post before landing?"

"Depends what it is, tower."

"We've got incoming mortars originating from near the south side of the 'Woodcutters Box' just about where you are. Can you take a look and see if you spot anything?"

"Roger tower we'll take a quick swing around for you."

"Mr. Nolan, I got something," Syzmanski said over the intercom. "... a somebody at eight o'clock low running along the top of a dike toward the north tree line."

"Roger, got him. Let's go down and take a look. Coming left. Keep an eye on our passenger to make sure he doesn't fall out."

Brad made a hard left turn and dropped out of the sky toward a lone figure running toward the trees, and passed twenty yards in front of him just a few feet above the ground. The runner turned and headed the other way so Nolan made another and closer pass which caused the man to again turn around and run along the dike. He did a quick pedal turn and pointed the nose of the Huey at the man – an old man, Brad could now tell – who stopped, breathing heavily. Brad turned the helicopter ninety degrees.

"What do you think, Syz? Does he look like one of the bad guys," Brad asked.

"They all look like bad guys to me, Mr. Nolan, especially when they're running. He could easily be the guy firing that mortar at the base."

"He sure could." Brad hovered the Huey closer as he looked out the side window. The rotor wash pummeled the old man who stood hunched over in the dust cloud with his loose clothing flapping in the wind. The man stood erect and held Nolan's gaze defiantly.

"You want me to light him up with the M60, Mr. Nolan?"

At last Brad said, "No, Syz, let him go. This doesn't feel right, and I'm not going to live with this on my conscience the rest of my life... leave him alone. Let's head for the barn. How's our passenger doing back there?"

Syzmanski laughed as the Huey nosed over, and shuddered trough translational lift. "He's still doing an overspeed going around those Rosary beads of his."

They had picked up the middle aged major – a chaplain – on the road between Phouc Vinh and Sông Bé on the way back from their mission with the 1/8 Cav. Norton had noticed a solitary figure on the road which he swore was a lone American giving them a friendly wave.

'Couldn't be,' Brad had told him. 'How could a lone G.I. get that far away from friendlies by himself?' Norton had insisted it was an American and that they take a closer look. As they passed overhead, the G.I. waved merrily up at them, and the crew decided to land and pick him up. It turned out to be an American – a Catholic chaplain, new in country, who'd needed to get to Sông Bé. He'd been told by somebody in Phouc Vinh that Sông Bé was only 'just down the road' and since it was a nice day, he decided to walk. Brad had Syzmanski give him a headset and then took him up to three thousand feet and showed him his destination twenty miles away. The chaplain had gone pale and pulled out his Rosary.

"He'll be all right once he gets back on the ground. We'll get the C.O. to put him up for the night and give him a ride up there on the way out tomorrow."

"If we hurry," Norton said, "we just might make it back before the mess hall closes."

"A hot meal in the mess hall and maybe a nice hot shower," Brad replied, casting a sideways glance at his co-pilot. "Wouldn't that be great for a change?"

"Yeah, wouldn't it?" Norton looked back at him. "Good call, Brad,... on that old gook back there. You did the decent thing... the right thing."

"Guess, nobody will ever never know for sure, will they?"

"The world may not. But the crew that flies with you does. And that's what matters."

*   *   *   *

The early morning sun cast long shadows across the MacEagan back yard. It was the time of day she loved most; the time when she felt most at peace with herself and the world.

Mary Anne sat by herself at poolside sipping coffee and listening to the transistor radio; WCAO was doing a countdown of number one hits for the year 1970 and had gotten as far as *Bridge Over Troubled Water*, the haunting Simon and Garfunkel tune that *troubled her* for the six weeks it had stayed on the top of the list. It had been after Glenn arrived in Vietnam.

The last two weeks, since the Hawkish Dove rally in Washington that turned into a weeklong orgy of civil disobedience, had left her hollow and self-loathing. The only positive to come from it was that she'd found the courage to stand up to her brother and her father. *What was I thinking?* she asked herself again.

Despite outward appearances – her academic and athletic accomplishments in high school – she had always been a 'daddy's girl' and like her mother, very docile. No longer. Step one was to leave his house. Deanna had been right about that. *Why didn't I listen to her when she visited that time?*

She looked around the back yard, remembering all the memories she'd be leaving behind – cuddling on the second floor porch swing with Glenn, that first kiss in the gardener's shed. She wished he were here now. *We just haven't had time to get to know one another.* She heard the mail truck pull up to the corner; her spirits brightened.

"There's one in there from your soldier, missy."

"You always make my day, Mr. Grayson."

He had been their letter carrier for as long as their family had lived in the house – since 1955. She'd been in the third grade then and had written a story about him for an Armistice Day school assignment. She had learned – she couldn't remember how any more – that he had served in World War Two and gotten him to tell her about it. They had been friends since; and he had been one of the small crowd she invited to her wedding.

"Mother, why do you subscribe to *so many* magazines that you never even open?" she said out loud, dropping the mass of mail onto the large island in the middle of the kitchen. Two periodicals slipped off onto the floor and when she stooped to pick them up she gasped.

Her face was on the cover of *LIFE* magazine under a banner *Faces of Protest.*

It was a picture of her standing between Corey and Tripp Karter; Corey was in his priest's collar and Karter was mugging for the camera with his arm around her shoulder.

She quickly opened the magazine to the contents page, found the article about the May 4 rally of Hawkish Dove and nervously sat down at the kitchen table. She read with growing despair and anger about herself, about her *and* the charismatic protest leader as if they were somehow joined at the hip, and his movement, now in ascendancy. The article was filled with more pictures, half-truths and partial quotes from her and Karter and others.

My marriage and my life are over when Glenn sees this. It'll kill him. He'll never forgive me. Think, Mary Anne! Think!

She picked up the phone and dialed the one person she knew she had to talk to about this before anyone else.

"*Hallo.*"

"Aynslee, this is Mary Anne. Something awful has happened. It's not about Glenn," she added quickly. "It's not about him yet, but it will be soon. It's about me and it's in a major magazine, and I need your advice. Do you have some time?"

"*Mary Anne, you know I do. I always have time for you.*"

"You'd better sit down. I'm afraid this is going to take a while."

*　　*　　*　　*

"Sông Bé tower, this is Army two-two-one-two, five south for landing POL to refuel and reposition to the tower. We're a Nighthawk bird on standby."

"Roger twenty-two-twelve, cleared into POL. Call for reposition when ready."

"There you go," Brad said to the crew over the intercom. "Nothing to it. You guys are gonna thank me for this. Think of tonight as part of your R&R."

"I hope you're right, Mr. Nolan," Syzmanski replied. "You're sure the C.O. promised three full days? Is that written down anywhere?"

"If the major says it, I believe it."

"Three days and three nights in Vung Tau, right?"

"And the use of your bird the whole time, chief," Nolan added. "What makes that so good is that the best beaches along the South China Sea are only thirty miles north. White sand. Cobalt blue water. We'll take a case of grenades and do some fishing offshore."

They had gotten back to the company a few hours earlier just in time to catch the mess hall open for supper for a change and the chow still somewhat hot. Afterward, the Ops officer had approached them about a last minute mission for that evening. He sweetened the deal with a three day pass to the in-country R&R facility at Vung Tau. That sealed it. After an hour nap, they pre-flighted and set off for Sông Bé, arriving shortly before nine at night. Butler and Syzmanski slept in the helicopter while, inside the tower shack, the pilots took turns sleeping and monitoring the radio.

The weather was bad and getting worse; neither pilot expected a call that night.

*   *

Glenn shivered once, twice, three times... each more violent than the last.

Normally he could fall asleep quickly and remain utterly motionless until awakened for his nightly shift on the radios. This wasn't one of those normal times. He'd grown accustomed to the air mattress and sleeping beneath his poncho tied to surrounding trees like a low tent. He'd found that wearing an issue OD sweater under his soaked jungle fatigue shirt not only kept him warm in the wet mountain jungle monsoon but also dry – a fleeting, three or four hour victory. For the other twenty he was soaked; tonight the cold, wet jungle was winning.

The silence, and the darkness, were menacing, ill-omened – like the calm before a storm, the serenity before disaster.

He slowly raised his head, moving his eyes through the brutal, cheerless gloom thinking he could make out the river several yards away, darker even than the murky rainforest. The rain had slackened but large droplets continued to fall. His shoulder was sore and a stabbing pain came and went in his right elbow. He pushed his hand down between his legs, stretching the arm and kneading the aching joint with his opposite hand until he got some relief then looked at the luminous dial of his disposable six dollar military watch.

I wonder if they're going to court-martial me or just take the six bucks out of my next pay check. Yeah, why don't they take the money out of my check?! I'll never know it... Just like I never see it when they take whatever they take out for my three meals a day. How damn ludicrous!... making officers pay taxes and pay for their meals in Vietnam... it's like making Brooks Robinson buy a ticket to get into an Orioles game... why am I thinking about that?... oh, yeah... what time is it?... look at the watch again. Zero-two-one-seven. Only forty-three minutes until my next watch... and four hours until the sun comes up... idiot!... the sun doesn't come up in the bush during monsoon season...

There was a silent, stealthy movement in front of him – a man, an earthen gray form against the darkness. Glenn's mouth went dry and his throat grew swollen as it had that night on Illingworth when the three NVA appeared out of the dust cloud and crested the pitifully low berm. Where had this man come from? How did he get through the perimeter?

"*Tó Neinilii*," the form whispered. It was Daniel Two Hatchets, calling him the Navajo equivalent to the Norse rain god, Odin, a practice he'd adopted after they found the NVA hospital beneath the waterfall weeks earlier. He should have known – only Two Hatchets could suddenly materialize out of nothing without a sound. But could he see in the dark, too? "There is movement on the river. Come."

He followed the ethereal form of the Indian down to the river bank, to a thick, towering tree looming up like some huge black mass holding up the darkness and the harsh wall of the jungle at the water's edge. He could make out the form of an M60 but couldn't guess at the gunner or assistant a foot away; the silence pressed down on him, but eventually he could make out the deep, rhythmic breathing of the two-man crew. And then the muffled, far off sound of wood against wood and an irregular, muffled *thchink* of metal against metal.

Two Hatchets spoke in the softest of whispers. "Rafts. Weapons... from upstream. They come here or the landing downstream."

Glenn's pulse rose and the breath caught in his throat. "How soon do you think?"

"A half hour. No more."

"Stay here with the gun. You initiate the fight with a long burst from this M60. Counting on you, Two Hatchets."

"I will not disappoint you, *Tó Neinilii*."

Glenn made his way slowly and quietly back to the CP and whispered to EB. "Call the platoons and tell them to go to one hundred percent alert. Do it quietly. Emphasis on quietly. There's movement on the far side of the river. Get that started and then get the platoon leaders on the horn for me – I need to talk to them, most *ricky tick...* Give me the battalion handset." His hand was shaking as he depressed the rubber 'push-to-talk' switch and whispered, "Pillar three-five, this is Surge two-six on Secure, over."

"*Surge two-six, this is Pillar three-five, go ahead, over!*" the battalion radio operator said in a booming voice that made Nolan cringe. It sounded thunderously loud in his ear, loud enough to be heard for miles in the deathly silence, although he knew that wasn't happening.

"Surge two-six, we have movement on the river and expect contact imminent. Bounce the Night Hawk now and give me ETA and callsign ASAP. I say again, ASAP. Have him contact me on my company internal push – callsign Dancer three-two. Read it back to me."

"*Roger, Surge two-six. Bounce Night Hawk and have him contact you on your company internal frequency – 38.6 – and advise you of ETA and callsign.*"

"Roger all that. You might want to wake the colonel or the S-3 or both."

"*Will do.*"

He thought for a few seconds, trying to remember where Meade and his team were located when he last saw them before the night descended. He crawled through the wet undergrowth, came across a body and shook it. It was his artillery spotter.

"Mikey," he whispered. "Movement on the river. Everybody up. Super quiet. Remember, we have a Night Hawk to work. Get your battery laid in on pre-registered target *Alpha one-six-alpha* but don't fire until I give you the word. Stay close to me."

"Are they close?"

"Other side of the river. Half hour or less. Super quiet." He felt his way slowly back to EB thinking he should have thought through this earlier and had Alpha better prepared.

EB handed him the company radio handset and whispered. "Platoon leaders on."

"Viking, Gamecock, Riffraff, this is Odin. Contact from across the river in less than a half hour. Make sure we're on one hundred percent alert. Do it super quietly. Do you copy?"

"*Riffraff, roger.*"

"*Gamecock, roger.*"

"*Viking, roger.*"

"We have a Night Hawk inbound. Make sure everyone holds their fire on the river until the first long burst from the M60 in the middle of Viking – Two Hatchets is working with them and will initiate the firefight. Gamecock and Riffraff hold your fire until and if you have contact from the flanks or rear. There might be somebody coming to meet the river rafts. Be smart. Be violent. You copy?"

"*Riffraff, roger.*"

"*Gamecock, roger.*"

"*Viking, roger.*"

"Odin, out."

He gave the handset back to EB and exhaled a deep, nervous breath.

"You okay, Six? Sounded like you done let all the air outta your air mattress."

"Shut the hell up," Glenn whispered. "I said quiet and I damn well meant it."

*   *

"Dancer three-two, this is the Ghostrider Night Hawk on your push about twenty minutes out," Brad said airily over the radio. "Understand you've got some movement and might need some help."

"*Roger that, Night Hawk.*"

The response was so soft it was almost unintelligible and Brad cranked up the volume on the radio. "The 'Night Whisperers' are whispering really quiet aren't they Ed."

"You know where we are, Nolan?" Norton asked nervously. They were five hundred feet above the ground, it was pitch black outside, and he could tell they were in and out of wispy clouds. All that made the co-pilot nervous. Inside the cockpit the faint red glow of instrument lights cast them in a macabre glow. "This is beginning to feel like the night we were lost and trying to find Tân Sơn Nhứt airport... and that was no fun."

"We're not going to do anything stupid. Plus it's not raining; not even drizzling."

"If scud running at night below five hundred feet isn't stupid, what is?"

"Good question, Mr. Norton," Syzmanski said over the intercom.

"Better question, chief – are these guns and the spotlight working?" Brad asked. "Don't want to repeat last time we flew this bird. Not a good idea to show up at a gun fight without working guns. Give me a three second test fire on the mini-gun first, and then on the .50 cal., Butler." Both guns worked and then Syzmanski flicked the searchlight on and off. "Ready to rock and roll. We should be six or eight minutes south of Mo. When we hit Mo, we need to be at just under fifty-five knots – that's sixty miles per hour or one mile per minute. Makes

Brian Utermahlen

navigation easier. It's two miles – or two minutes – from LZ Mo to the river, and then we turn left ninety degrees and go six minutes down the river to where the grunts are."

"Then what?" Norton asked.

"We do what we do. Then we go back to Sông Bé, refuel, head home and pack our bags for a three day vacation in beautiful Vung Tau by the South China Sea."

"You sure we can find Mo in this weather?"

"Let me show you how." Brad switched the FM radio the battalion frequency. "Pillar three-five this is *RRoowwwwlllfff* Cramden."

"*Ralph, what are you doing up here? I thought we sent you home hours ago.*" Colonel Galvin's Boston accent, softened and polished smooth from years of service in the southern U.S. and Central America was unmistakable over the radio.

"We're your Night Hawk. Request you pop a mortar illum round over Mo and then advise when we pass overhead. We're about three minutes out." Shortly, an illumination round exploded directly in front of them and soon after they received a call that they were passing directly over the blacked out firebase. "Norton, I've got the controls. Punch the clock and give me a ten second countdown to two minutes... switch me over to FM 38.6. Dancer three-two, this is Night Hawk on your frequency. Seven minutes out."

The 'night whisperer' acknowledged. A minute later Brad turned.

"Everybody keep a close eye out. Gonna try to get a little lower so we don't blind ourselves with the searchlight in this scud... Dancer three-two, Night Hawk six minutes out."

"*We have multiple NVA rafts in the river,*" came the whispered reply.

"Three-two, can you mark your position?"

"*Are you shittin' me?!*"

"Guess that pretty much answers that, Mr. Nolan." Syzmanski said nervously.

"Eyes peeled everybody."

"This is crazy, Brad," Norton said anxiously.

*   *

Mark my position?! I ask for help and the damn rotorheads send me a moron like that?! Glenn was incredulous, and so nervous he could hardly breathe.

The muffled sounds from out on the river grew marginally louder until a dense, opaque form took shape maybe fifty yards in front of him moving swiftly from right to left, driven by the deep, swift current. *They're going to pass us by.* Another earthen-colored shape formed upriver with a low silhouette and heavy rod shapes sticking up ten or fifteen feet, off to his right and closer to the shore. His pulse raced and his breathing quickened as though he was running up a steep hill. Blood pounded in his temples.

He could hear the distant slapping sound of rotor blades now, thumping and echoing through the narrow river valley. Voices now out on the river; strident, high pitched shouting.

*　　*

"One minute," Norton said over the intercom. "River's six hundred feet below – I hope."

"All kinds of room," Brad replied easily, but his stomach was churning and he forced himself consciously to relax his death grip on the controls. The rotor blades beat loudly in the narrow course of the river.

"*Night Hawk, this is Dancer two-three, you're two hundred meters east of us. We're on the south side of the river. At least two and maybe more rafts in the middle of the river.*"

"Let's light up the river down there and see what we have, Syzmanski. Butler, you can fire at anything on your side. Syz, let's not hit the friendlies on the shoreline."

The crew chief turned on the bright searchlight.

"Holy shit, Mr. Nolan!... look at all those damn rafts!"

*　　*

Glenn was astonished at the noisy, brightly lit apparition appearing high to their right like a ghostly Grim Reaper when the bright search light from the helicopter came on and lit up the area in front of third platoon.

Instantly the machine gun next to him stitched a thin line of red tracers a few feet above the water into a large raft filled with NVA soldiers and equipment. Two more M60s upstream came to life and seconds later, another off to his left opened up on a target he couldn't see from his position. Rounds from the mini-gun on the helicopter made a continuous string of red, snaking down on the river; the heavy, full-throated .50 caliber chewed up the far shoreline. A large raft filled with mounds of equipment upended flinging bodies into the murky river. Third platoon was pumping out volumes of M16 and volleys of 'chunker' rounds from their M79s.

The helicopter moved past them in what seemed like slow motion, firing non-stop on the river and finally disappearing around a bend in the river off to their left.

*   *

Brad came to a hover eighty feet over the river while Syzmanski continued firing point blank into two rafts lashed together. Bodies by the dozens were floating in the river now and the thick poles lashed together had mostly come apart, floating away with the current.

"We'll make a run back upstream and see what's left to clean up," Brad said as he did a slow pedal turn and headed upstream. Green tracers laced the night from the Cambodian river bank from four locations; Syzmanski knocked out the sources one by one with the mini-gun.

"I'm out!" the crew chief hollered over intercom.

"Already?!"

"I've been firing steady the whole time! These barrels are glowing, Mr. Nolan."

"Butler?!"

"Almost out, too," the right side gunner said and then began firing again, straight down into a masses of floating debris until he too ran out of ammunition. "Okay, now I'm out."

"All right, guys, I think that's all we can do for tonight. Back to the barn before the weather goes zero-zero... Dancer two-three this is your Night Hawk. We are end of mission – out of ammo and heading for the barn before the weather goes completely to hell."

"*Any chance you can rearm, refuel and come back?*" came the whispered request.

"Not going to lie to you. Even if the weather allowed, you're looking at a couple hours assuming we can find the right ammo at this hour. Sorry. We'll relay the request to our OPS and see if they can do anything."

"*Thanks for the help. Be advised we're going to be firing artillery out of Mo for now.*"

"We'll be clear in a minute. We counted nine rafts – all destroyed. Been our pleasure. Night Hawk out... Norton, put me up on Galvin's frequency. We'll give a quick report on the way back." He was suddenly drained but forced himself alert; he looked at the needle pointed toward the Sông Bé non-directional beacon and started a gradual turning climb away from the river allowing himself the indulgence of a brief thought about Vung Tau.

Chapter 27

Galvin entered LZ Mo's operations center with his helmet under an arm, stopped briefly to look at the Situation Map and then waved his battalion intelligence officer over.

"Welcome back, sir. How'd the briefing at brigade go?"

"I should have taken you along, Rucksack. Most of the talk was about last night on the river. Any updates in the past couple hours?"

"A few sir," the skinny captain replied, adjusting his glasses and making a grease pencil mark on the acetate covering the map. "Third platoon Alpha 1/6 reported five more NVA washed up on the shore three hundred meters southwest of Alpha's night location. Alpha reported another secondary explosion from artillery a few hundred yards inside Cambodia just after you left this morning and then another twenty minutes after that. Lieutenant Nolan requested a Pink Team for damage assessment and they reported a suspected ammo bunker exploded and possibly two more close by. They sighted three NVA on foot, engaged with the gunship and claimed all as KIA. They also did a recon of the river downstream of Alpha and reported four rafts in various stages of destruction littering the shore line. Nolan said he's saving a pristine SKS rifle for you, sir."

The battalion commander stroked his jaw, frowning at the map. "Nolan's pretty well covered his side of that 'Box' with platoon and squad patrols, right?"

"Yes, sir."

"I think it's time then to move him across the river and let him recon what's left of the 'Box' and have Williams hold fast where he is. I'll have Major Roberts work that up for us. We'll move Nolan tomorrow or the next day." The colonel pulled a folding chair close to the map and sat down. "How are you doing on that investigation for Alpha?"

"I've put together a brief of preliminary findings. Would you like to see it?"

"For now, just give me the highlights. What have you learned?"

"Quite a bit, colonel." The captain pulled up a chair and looked around before speaking in a low, quiet tone. "I talked to Lieutenant Jeffrees, who caught these two soldiers sleeping and then I talked individually to the soldiers' squad leader – Sergeant Dunne, the platoon sergeant – Staff Sergeant Hansen, and Lieutenant Cleburne. I also talked to Specialist Hannam, PFC Torres and the other members of Hannam's squad, plus the platoon medic. I then talked to four other soldiers in the company, and that led me to interview a couple of our radio operators here in the TOC. I talked to all of them one on one, and I've summarized all the interviews."

"Give me your conclusions. I'll read the details for myself."

"First major conclusion is that Lieutenant Nolan has a real problem in his second platoon. A leadership problem in the person of the platoon leader, Lieutenant Cleburne."

Galvin nodded. He was aware of the situation. Goose van Noort had discussed it with him over a beer a day before the Cambodian operation. A casual, passing conversation about how he was dealing with Nolan's request to move Cleburne out of the company. There had been something about hard liquor at Bù Gia Mập airstrip.

"What's the nature of the problem?" Galvin asked

"Confidence, sir. Or really a lack of confidence in Lieutenant Cleburne among the platoon. I don't think most of his soldiers trust or even like him."

"That's no excuse for sleeping on duty. Did you get that from Torres and Hannam?"

"No, sir, neither. I heard it before I talked with them. They didn't say 'yea' or 'nay' when I brought it up. Torres got all wide-eyed and said he respected all officers. Hannam never said a word in response. Just gave me that smoldering look that I hope never to see again."

"You're first finding is that Cleburne's men don't like or trust him. That's not unique in the annals of our military. Soldiers have been disliking, even killing their officers from time to time since the days of Valley Forge."

"But it does have a bearing on this case, sir. Cleburne had the platoon sergeant assign Hannam extra shifts of guard duty on the firebase out of spite for all the attention he was getting for being the company expert and trainer on the M60. I got that from the medic and confirmed it with the platoon sergeant who was very uncomfortable verifying my information. Cleburne has them scared... except maybe Sergeant Dunne, Hannam's squad leader. He pitched a fit about it. To no avail."

"Did he tell the company commander?"

"No, sir."

"Any reason why not?"

Rucksack shrugged. "None I could find. There might be lingering anger in some minds over the change of command situation in the company back when, but I didn't delve into that."

"What else?"

"I found that Hannam was doing double duty, maybe triple duty when they came on the firebase. Lieutenant Nolan was using him and another soldier as his M60 instructors which took up his mornings; his platoon was giving him work details in the afternoons and sending him out on last light patrols each evening; and, Hannam was working on the guns under the lights inside the TOC late into the night the day before he was caught sleeping by Lieutenant

Jeffrees. People were burning his candle at both ends for him – nobody was getting pulled in so many directions by so many people. It seems Lieutenant Cleburne had it in for him and did what he could to make his life miserable. But here's the kicker, sir. According to PFC Torres, he – Torres – is the one who's responsible for the whole situation."

Galvin squinted over the top of his glasses. "How so?"

"Sir, you know how soldiers are..."

"I would hope so, or else the American taxpayer wasted eighty thousand dollars on my West Point education."

Rucksack ran his fingers nervously through his short dark hair. "Sir, I didn't mean –"

"Continue, captain. I'll try to forget that before your next OER."

"Yes, sir... well, what I meant to say was that we all know the saying among us grunts about grabbing some sleep every chance you get. Torres said they were both really fagged out, and put themselves on fifty percent alert – one sleeping and the other awake on guard duty. I've checked it out with both companies on LZ Mo since then and they all do it like that. I'm not surprised or offended over the practice. I don't think you are either, colonel. Torres told me he was the one who was supposed to be awake on duty when Jeffrees caught them."

"So why didn't they own up to it when Lieutenant Nolan confronted them?"

"That, sir is a very good question. Torres didn't speak up because he was scared to death. I think Hannam didn't speak up because he wasn't going to 'rat out' a fellow soldier. It's the only thing that makes any sense."

Galvin intertwined the fingers of both hands and placed them behind his head, leaning back on the metal folding chair. "Go out and talk this over with Nolan."

"What should I tell him to do about Specialist Hannam, sir?"

"Nothing. Tell him what you told me. He'll figure out on his own the right thing to do..."

*　　*　　*

25 May 1970 - Cambodia
Entry 14 of ___14___ (so far)
– inside 'The 'Box'

A lot more signs of NVA activity here than on the Vietnam side of the border continues to be the norm. Yesterday even ran across some stock animals – a cow and half a dozen pigs in a small fenced-in area next to a sleeping dugout with overhead thatch roof. Still no signs of fighting positions or overhead cover. My impression is the NVA in this area don't fear detection or the consequences – or didn't at least before we showed up. They say we're leaving Cambodia by the end of June. WHAT THE HELL FOR??? This is where the enemy is and they're back on their heels!

Stupid way to fight a war.

PFC Mikey Meade is working out well as my artillery forward observer. He's gaining the confidence of the troops and confidence in himself. So much so that he's now swaggering a bit more than I like. That night along the river was the real turning point, I think. He fired missions for a couple hours after the Nighthawk left and got a couple of spectacular secondary explosions. That's luck of course, but it really boosted his self-esteem (not that he ever had a lack of ego). I sent him out on a platoon patrol with Lt. Rankin that got into a half hour firefight – Rankin did a good job working with the gunships and Meade handled the artillery well. Only had two troops with minor wounds – neither evacuated. Couldn't report any enemy KIA – they took all their dead with them.

Have been really liking this temporary assignment to the 1/8th. I'm learning a lot from this Galvin – he's calm, cool, collected... all the time. When we were back on LZ Mo I asked him how he was able to keep his keel so even. He said: 'I give ulcers, I don't get 'em.' Good retort but I don't necessarily believe that's all of it. People want to work for him – I know Brad does and he says all the pilots would drop whatever they're doing to help if he said he needed it.

Even those cocky s.o.b.'s in the Air Force. On Mo, I learned Galvin has standing instructions that we always have free fire boxes in our battalion operations area for the Forward Air Controllers (the 'RASH' callsign pilots) if they're bored and looking for some action. He has Rucksack and the S-3 pick out good targets and pass them along. What that means is that we always have a FAC within a couple of minutes of the company if we make contact. One of them (Rash 27) now calls me each morning on my company frequency when he lifts off Phouc Vinh to ask if I have anything going. I think that's all on account of how Galvin treats the air assets that support us.

Sent 'Pineapple' off today to his hometown – Honolulu – for R&R. He richly earned it in my short time in the company. I have never seen anyone as happy. Everyone likes to get out of the bush, but to go back home – that would be heaven. He's engaged to some local girl he grew up with and there was a rumor he might come back married. Good for him! Just as long as he doesn't come back smelling like Old Spice and stinking up my jungle.

Got a strange package from Mary Anne this morning during resupply (Log Day) – and it was hand-delivered by my old roommate, Benny Barnes. I'm still wondering how he wangled that.

It was a box containing A-1 Sauce, Heinz-57 Sauce, black pepper, McCormick chili powder, onion salt, garlic salt and Old Bay. A month ago, I'd sent her my recipes for grilled ham slices and 'Nolan's Own Chicken Noodle Casserole from C-ration chicken and noodles, plus cheese and crackers'. I told her I could do a lot more – and better – if only I had some *decent spices. I guess she got the hint. It was a pleasant surprise. The other item wasn't — not at first, but I've pretty much gotten over it.*

Also in the box was a letter from her and a copy of Life magazine with her picture on the cover standing next to her brother and a tall, stork-looking guy badly in need of a shave, a haircut and a decent set of clothes. I told Benny as much about the guy and he remarked that I could be talking about myself. Good ol' Benny the BSer — it took the sting off what I was feeling as I looked at the picture of her smirking brother and some hippie guy with his arm around my wife. He stuck around while I read the letter, and then he wanted to talk. I didn't want to but he insisted. After I read her letter, it was pretty clear she'd been pressured into going to a protest rally by her father and brother. She promised she wasn't going to be doing that again — and swore that the story was filled with half-truths and fabrications on just about everything. I believe her and that settles it.

It's getting dark and starting to rain again. This monsoon crap is getting old.

*   *   *

She came out of the surf, her bikini dripping wet, reminding him of Ursula Andress in *Dr. No* only she was much more captivating — and she was his. He watched her approach, seduced as he always was by her sensuous smile, her lithe athletic grace and the voluptuous soft curves of her body, barely hidden by the swim suit. Strange, he thought, how they were alone now on the beach.

Mary Anne stood over him, blocking out the harsh sun, cold water cascading from her onto his face and down his chest. She held out something; two somethings — a box of salt water taffy and a large bucket: Thrasher's French Fries from the boardwalk at Ocean City — food of the gods, deep-fried and drenched in malt vinegar. He loved them, almost more than life itself... *Really?*

"*For you,*" she said quietly, whispering. She reached toward him, touched his shoulder, softly at first. "*This is for you... for you...six... yes, six more higher... six... a higher calling...*" He smiled at her, more content than he'd ever been. She shook him again, more urgently. "*...six... six... call...*"

"Six, wake up man. Higher's calling."

He awoke with a start. EB was shaking him hard, and whispering urgently; a steady drizzle dripped from the triple canopy onto his poncho tent. "What?"

"Battalion, on the secure radio. S-3 wants to talk to you. Orders."

Glenn looked at his watch. It was a few minutes before midnight. *What in the world?* He'd been asleep for almost four hours and his radio watch didn't start until 0400. "This is Lieutenant Nolan," he whispered, ignoring radio procedure on the secure set. "Who's this?"

"Lindy Egan here, Glenn - duty officer tonight. Wait one for the S-3." In a few seconds, Butch Roberts came on the radio. *"Lieutenant, this is Major Roberts, I have an order for you that came down as a mission from 2ⁿᵈ Brigade. Are you in a position to copy, over?"*

"In a position to copy? What in the world?" Nolan whispered urgently. "Can't this wait until first light, major?"

"Negative. This is an order from brigade. You're expected to comply immediately."

"Give me the mission – I've got a good enough memory."

"There are coordinates you need to read back to me after checking them on your map."

"Is this some kind of goofy operational readiness test or something?"

"Negative. I assure you it's not. I've been back and forth with Brigade Ops for the last half hour on this and they're dead serious. This comes from the brigade commander himself... and it has to be done now."

Glenn was suddenly wide awake, and worried. *From the Brigade commander? What does Daughtry want now?* he asked himself.

Glenn knew little about Colonel Eugene Daughtry, except what he'd read in the brigade commander's autobiography, a copy of which Boomer Cameron had given him; apparently it was required reading for newly arriving 2ⁿᵈ Brigade officers. Daughtry went to Europe in 1944 to lead a platoon and then a company in the 90ᵗʰ Infantry division at age 22. He commanded that company during the D-Day invasion and before the end of the first three weeks had been given command of a battalion and promoted to lieutenant colonel, the youngest officer to reach that rank in any branch of service during the war. Glenn had met the colonel only once, but the man made it clear he considered himself more knowledgeable about platoon, company and battalion operations than any soldier of any rank serving in Vietnam. Glenn searched for his red penlight. In the back of his mind was the question why an officer who had achieved the rank of lieutenant colonel in 1944 had advanced only one rung up the ladder in the succeeding twenty-six years. He found his poncho liner, spread it out and slipped beneath it with his map; he opened the map and took a small green notebook from a waterproof container in one of his breast pockets.

"All right, major, I'm ready to copy," Glenn whispered into the handset.

"Here's the coordinates." Butch Roberts slowly recited the eight digits and had Glenn repeat them back. *"Your mission is to move your night location to that position."*

Glenn was utterly shocked. "Say again! I'm sure I didn't hear that right."

"I say again, reposition your company's night location to the coordinates I gave you."

Nolan was outraged. His breathing came in short, rapid gasps. Finally, he depressed the 'push to talk' switch, heard the characteristic hum of the secure connection and asked, "Am I on the squawk box in the TOC? If I am, you turn that damned thing off."

He lay there on the wet ground and shivered. His fatigues were soaked through and he was cold. Most of all, he was furious. *What are those people smoking back there?! That's the dumbest damned thing I've ever been told to do in my entire life – bar none. Has everybody in my chain of command gone stark raving nuts?!*

Major Roberts said over the radio. *"Lieutenant, the speaker in the TOC is off. Look Nolan, I know you're upset. Just stay calm."*

"Calm?! It's almost midnight; it's raining; it's cold; it's as dark as the bottom of a well on the back side of the moon... and you're telling me to get my company up in the dead of night while it's raining, and move. You realize what you're telling me to do, don't you? Pick up a dozen trip flares with invisible trip wires... in the dark, and a dozen and a half Claymores... without making noise and giving away our position... and then go find two automatic ambushes... and move a hundred soldiers a kilometer to set up a new night location because some damned full bird colonel thinks he needs to prove how much he knows about company operations. Frankly none of that makes any sense at all."

"It's an order, Nolan. And that order comes directly from Colonel Daughtry."

"Did anyone think to ask WHY?"

"The colonel says you're in a less defensible position than the one he's ordering you to."

"And he knows this how?"

"Come on, Nolan. You know what's going on. I tried."

"Try harder, Major."

"I hear what you're saying, but an order is an order. Just follow it."

Glenn remained silent for a while, seething at the monumental idiocy. Failure to follow orders in combat had major implications – career ruined, maybe incarceration. What they were telling him to do was stupid, really stupid, and he would quite likely get people killed doing it.

Finally Nolan said, "Does Colonel Galvin know about this?

"The Boss isn't here on the firebase right now. He's back in Sông Bé for the night."

"I'll wait for him to get back."

"Nolan, that's not going to work. This comes from the brigade commander himself."

"Major, you can't give me that order... or any other. Officially, you're not in my chain of command. I only take orders from my direct superior in the chain. Wake up the old man wherever he is in Sông Bé and tell *him* to give me the order. Then we'll go from there. At least he's in my chain of command. Wake him up. I'm not taking orders from staff officers who don't have the authority or responsibilities of commanders." There was a long silence and he imagined Roberts was probably stomping around the inside of the TOC, furious at him. Finally Glenn transmitted. "I'm giving you an out. All you have to do is tell brigade you have a company commander in the field who doesn't understand the order and needs guidance from the originator in his chain of command... that's not unreasonable, major."

"They won't buy it, Nolan."

"Just tell them to call me on the battalion frequency."

"You're not going to get the brigade commander. It'll be the S-3. He's the one I've been talking to for the last half hour."

"I'll talk to him and tell him the same thing I told you. Until I receive an order from Colonel Galvin or Colonel Daughtry himself, I'm staying put."

"He's going to be beaucoup unhappy."

"Life is tough... Out here." Nolan turned off the small pen light and threw back the poncho liner. It was raining harder now and he was wide awake; crawling through the wet brush, he found EB and gave him the handset. He whispered, "Brigade may be calling me. If they don't, just wake me for my radio watch at the normal hour."

"Sông Bé's a good forty miles away," his RTO replied. "It's hard enough getting battalion to come through clear on a night like this, even with the long whip antenna, and they're a lot closer."

Glenn reached over to the radio, unscrewed the antenna and laid it on the ground. "EB, we'll keep what just happened between you and me. All right? Wake me at zero four hundred."

"What the hell they tell you to do, Six?"

"Sounded like something really stupid... but I could be mistaken. Reception on this end was really lousy. You probably ought to get Heavy to order up a new antenna next log day."

*   *

A line of Alpha company soldiers queued up to the Huey sitting in the middle of the small landing zone hacked out of the jungle by a squad of engineers that had rappelled in early that morning. They formed an unbroken line from a small, thatch-roofed hooch holding three and a half dozen 122mm rockets in wooden crates with Chinese markings to the spot where they were being loaded eight at a time into the helicopters. Each ship came in loaded with supplies for the company and departed with rockets originally destined for firing points around Saigon, and major American bases nearby.

Heavy was off to the side along with one man from each platoon, stacking boxes of C-rations, LRRP rations, water canisters, assorted cases of sodas, beer, and various munitions and explosives along with duffle bags of clean fatigues. It was the same routine every fourth day except that their resupply of ammo and smoke grenades and C-4 plastic explosive had skyrocketed in the thirty-five days they had been in Cambodia.

Glenn sat inside the wood line on the edge of the one ship hover down LZ, watching the activity and mentally reviewing the last four days' activities.

They had cleared the Cambodia side of 'The Box' in a week and a half – discovering and backhauling tons of ammunition and weapons and additional tons of rice. It got to the point they were uncovering so much rice they couldn't send it out fast enough and were burning it in place or scattering it.

The Huey was finally loaded and departed with NVA rockets and their canvas carriers.

He glanced at Heavy and his crew sorting through supplies, distributing the myriad stuff and things to work parties from the platoons. Masika had been detailed to company supply operations and was passing out boxes and crates and metal water canisters to a work party sent by second platoon. Glenn caught his attention and waved him over.

"Masika. Have a seat. You've probably been wondering about the progress of the court martial against you from the incident on Mo a couple of weeks back. I've finally decided." The muscular black man looked back impassively at Nolan and remained silent. "I've decided to drop the Summary Court Martial charges."

"Why, lieutenant?"

"Because, all things considered, you're not guilty of the offense," Glenn said. "If you'd given me all the facts in the beginning when I asked, you could have saved me, you and a bunch of other people a lot of trouble. Once all the facts were gathered, it was clear you were innocent. You're not guilty, but I am disappointed. You didn't give me all the facts when I asked you and because of that I almost made a mistake."

"I never lied to you, sir."

Glenn pursed his lips and looked up at the wisps of clouds drifting low overhead. "I asked you what happened, and you didn't tell me the whole truth. My grandfather has a saying about that – a half truth is a whole lie. You think about that. I understand you didn't want to rat out Torres. You two were taking turns grabbing some winks. I get that. Outpost duty in the middle of the day at a firebase doesn't require one hundred percent alert of all hands. But it does require more than zero percent. Am I making any sense here?"

Hannam nodded.

"I'm really disappointed you didn't trust me. I like to think I'm trustworthy, but you didn't trust me with the whole truth." Glenn was silent for a few seconds and at last said, "Anyway the incident is behind us. The innocent are exonerated and the guilty are being punished appropriately, or soon will be. Case closed. You've got a lot of work to do on the log pad and I have things I've got to do. That's all, Masika."

The soldier rose slowly and took a couple of steps back toward the mound of supplies, but stopped and turned to look at Nolan. "You're wrong about one thing, sir... about me trustin' you. I did trust you. I trusted you would dig and get all the facts. You're right I didn't want to rat on no soldier in the company, but I did trust you to dig 'til you find out the whole truth."

Glenn watched Hannam walk back to the piles of supplies, and then EB was demanding his attention as he pointed up at the chopper on short final. "Six, that's the C.O. comin' in."

"Who?" Glenn asked over the loud slapping of rotor blades echoing through the jungle.

"The commander!" the RTO shouted at him. "Fella named Galvin – wears aviator specs and talks funny, like a Boston yankee. We been workin' for him nigh onto a month now."

*One of these days, EB. T*he ship dropped off the battalion commander and departed. Galvin took his arm, guiding him to a felled tree where they could talk privately.

"Another feather in the cap of Alpha company," Galvin said, casting a glance over the stacked crates of the big rockets, looking amused. "Except... the brigade commander came by Mo to survey the haul. He appreciated the rockets but didn't like the absence of the launchers that go with them. He told me you owe him forty-two launchers, and he's serious about it."

"Sir, I corrected that report when we figured out the carriers weren't launchers."

"Too bad, Nolan. That water is already over the spillway, and Colonel Daughtry isn't letting you off the hook. He's not a man to make casual utterances, and believe me he's dead serious. The rockets had gotten you back in his good graces, but missing launchers cancelled out that 'attaboy'. I suggest you find them before your Efficiency Report comes due."

"If they're around here, sir, we'll find 'em," Glenn said, thinking idly that Galvin must be pulling his leg. "You yanking my chain, sir? I thought you reserved that for Rucksack."

EB came up to him and interrupted. "Six, we got us a VIP on short final. Might want to get you a shave and a clean set of fatigues."

"Who?"

"Callsign says it's the Division commander."

Glenn glanced at Galvin. "Any idea why he's coming here, colonel? I'm not sure this is such a good idea. One of my clearing patrols made contact not far from here this morning."

"General Casey goes where he wants to."

"That's all well and good, sir. But I don't want to be the ground commander responsible if he gets hurt." He remembered the general well from that hot early morning at Illingworth after the nightlong attack. It seemed now like a different geological age. He gave Galvin a somber look. "If I'd known, I'd have taken more precautions."

"The general doesn't want special treatment. I know. I traveled with him a lot when I was on staff. He wants the hard, ugly truth, not some façade. He's a soldier. Do what you always do – that's what he really wants to see. Generals get too used to having doors opened for them, spit shine and fresh paint applied to everything because of them. Be yourself."

The Huey, with a prominent red placard adorned with two white stars fixed to the bulkhead behind the right seat, descended haltingly into the hole. Once on the ground, General Casey climbed over the right side controls, left his helmet on the seat and strode across the open area with his perfectly starched and shaven aide and a photographer in tow. *So much for ugly truths and façades, or spit shine,* Glenn thought. Looking at the aide dutifully two steps behind and to the left of the general, he remembered the day on the rifle range in Hohenfels Germany. The brigade commander, a crusty old colonel arrived to view the proceedings and he'd made the mistake of falling in on the colonel's right side during their tour of the range – 'the general's slot' Colonel Wadsworth pointed out. He'd not committed *that* crime since.

"Colonel Galvin, glad you're here," General Casey said, smiling easily as his helicopter lifted off. He extended his hand first to Galvin and then to Glenn. "And it's good to see you again, Captain Nolan." Glenn was unsure whether or not to correct the general and decided on silence. The general turned to his aide who placed something in his hand. "Nolan, you're wondering what in blue blazes is happening out here in the middle of Cambodia to get the division commander out of his headquarters. Do you know what day this is?"

The question caught him off guard, and the truth was he had no idea. Every rainy day ran in to the ones before and after with such epic monotony he had to concentrate and search his memory. "It's Friday, sir. June 5th."

"That makes it exactly two years since your graduation from the academy. And that earns you these." Casey opened his fist and showed him two sets of silver captain's bars – railroad tracks. "We have seven from the class of '68 spread throughout the division and I thought it appropriate to search out and promote each of you personally. You're my fourth. Colonel Galvin, would you assist me? Remember to smile – this is supposed to be a happy occasion."

They stood on either side of him and pinned the shiny insignia to the collars of his torn and dirty jungle fatigues. The photographer took a dozen shots, from various angles.

"I just came from the First Battalion Sixth Cav and had a similar ceremony on LZ Charo with your classmate, Benjamin Barnes," General Casey said while smiling at the camera. "He asked me to pass along to you that he was promoted a good half hour ahead of you."

Glenn smiled indulgently. "I can only guess he wanted me to know that so I'd be sure to address him as 'sir' from now on."

Casey belly laughed and shook his head. "That is *precisely* what he said. You two know one another pretty well I take it."

"Same cadet company for four years, sir, and roommates more than once. We played sports together and our wives are best friends. He's the little brother I'm glad I never had."

The general seemed to find this richly amusing and asked several questions about his cadet years, seeming not to be in much of a hurry. Finally he said, "I'd like a private word with Colonel Galvin and then a walk around your company, captain, to meet some of your men. Would you excuse us for just a minute."

The general and Galvin walked a few feet away. "Jack, you're going to have to release Nolan's company back to his battalion. Mike Blair buttonholed me on Charo and reminded me about our agreement. He took over his battalion while you had his Alpha company engaged in that 'Box' operation. But now that's over, he wants his company back. Daughtry agrees."

"Hate to lose him, sir. He's been a real asset."

"Of course! Your Jumping Mustangs are the top battalion in the division for number of enemy killed and equipment captured since we entered Cambodia. It didn't hurt you had an extra company."

"No, sir, and it didn't hurt it was Nolan's company. They had a pretty good record."

"You always did understate everything when you were Division G-2."

"You're right, sir. Can you give me a week? I've got one more thing I need him to do, and I'd also like to get his company back on Mo for a few day's rest." Casey gave him a quick, piercing glance that held the faintest glint of – of what? the colonel wondered. Challenge? Amusement? And then the general smiled, a swift little upturn at the corners of his mouth. "They've been out for nineteen hard days. I'd like to give them a break. When I last talked to Mike, he seemed inclined to put them right to work in the bush."

Casey nodded, while taking a quick look at Nolan who was on the radio with a small notebook out. "You've got five days, not a week. I'm holding you to it, Jack. Did you hear we sent Sergeant Lockhart back to the States to receive 'The Medal' at a White House ceremony."

"Yes, sir. I did hear. I passed that along to Nolan because he got to know the sergeant pretty well that night on Illingworth."

"And? How did he react?"

"He was thrilled for Lockhart. His words were – and this is a direct quote; he said, 'My knowledge of Medal of Honor history isn't what it should be, but I doubt that anyone ever deserved it more than Sergeant Lockhart.' Sir, that tells me a lot about both men."

General Casey grunted and looked back at the colonel. "Does he know how close a call it was between him and the sergeant."

"No, sir, and I didn't tell him... not that I think he would have been disappointed in not getting it, but because he'd think it was outrageous that *anybody else* was even considered."

The general looked casually around the landing zone as shirtless, unshaven troopers broke into C-ration cases and loaded ammunition into M16 magazines or poured water from plastic sleeves into canteens. "I'd like your thoughts on something. I'm going to be needing an Aide before the end of the month, and I'm considering two candidates – one of them is Nolan. How does that strike you?"

Galvin knew this question was coming. He'd gotten a 'heads up' from Mike Conrad who had been Nolan's battalion commander and was now on division staff. "A bad idea, sir."

"Care to elaborate?"

"A bad idea... not because he wouldn't do an outstanding job for you – and the division – and learn a lot in the process. Sir, the timing isn't good, for several reasons. He's only had the company for two months, so if you remove him now, that means the unit will have had three commanders in less than three months. There are lots of problems in the company and he's working through them with reasonable success. Pulling him out now would harm the unit."

"Specifics, colonel."

"Sir, Captain Nolan is effectively addressing some ingrained problems in the company. Tactically, he's brought in extra machine guns and trained the teams, instituted aggressive patrolling. In fact, in my battalion we've established many of his practices as standard operating procedure over the past month. It's largely a matter of personal leadership – and he's providing most of it because he has to. There's the issue of near term leadership turnover. His most experienced platoon lieutenant will be promoted out of the company before the end of June. His next most experienced platoon leader will rotate home two weeks later. His other platoon leader is under performing and should be replaced."

"Every company faces turnover, Jack. It's never a good time to lose proven leadership."

"True, but taking Nolan away would have the effect of removing *all* the proven officer leadership in a matter of just a few weeks. He's one of the most experienced company grade officers we have in the division right now... and he's only had his company for two months. Taking Nolan out would result in the company having no experienced officer leadership."

Casey's eyes narrowed and he furrowed his brow, thinking.

"There's also Nolan's personal and career development to consider," the colonel continued. "He just made captain and he's only a couple of months into his first and likely only chance at commanding a company in combat. He should be given the opportunity to finish.

He's a fighter, sir, and he's tactically savvy. We shouldn't take officers like that out of the field when they want to be there, and we desperately need field commanders now."

Casey nodded and looked at the colonel out of the corner of his eye. "You know, I miss our nightly chats at division. All right, Galvin. You've done what I asked – given me a lot to think about. Are you done now?"

"Yes, sir... except to say I think Captain Nolan would benefit greatly at some point in his career from working closely with you the way an Aide would, only not at this moment in his career. Maybe after he finishes his company grade assignments and completes his branch Advanced Course. I think he's someone you should keep your eye on, and perhaps consider mentoring. Someday he's going to be a general officer."

*   *   *

6 June 1970 – Cambodia. Promoted to Captain yesterday – along with every other guy in my graduating class. One year to first lieutenant; one more year to captain. With the war declared over by the president and the historical precedents of our military, we probably won't see our next promotion until we get ready to retire.

Benny now has a company in the 1/6 Cav. He expects me to call him sir since he got his automatic promotion to captain only minutes before me. He can pound sand and kiss my...

Rained constantly all day. Journaling a challenge.

9 June – Vietnam side of the river. Returned to LZ Mo around noon. Pretty constant drizzle for the past three days. Learned from Colonel Galvin we are returning to our parent battalion the day after tomorrow. Don't know how I feel about that – as if my feelings made any difference.

Realized I really don't like being on the firebase. I feel safer in the jungle where I have more control over my circumstances and reactions to events. The unit is really beginning to operate like a big Ranger patrol and that makes me feel a lot more secure than sitting on the firebase. (paranoia because of Illingworth? Maybe.) Plus: (1) firebases are muddy as hell in the raining season – much more so than it is in the jungle. (2) the food is better – I <u>hate</u> the chow served by the battalion mess hall – apparently so does the Recon Platoon. They tear-gassed the mess sergeant tonight after wiring his sleeping bunker shut. It would have been funny except that my company got blamed for it. I would eat C's or LRRP rations any day of the week versus the mess hall slop.

A problem with Pineapple – he took a week of leave on top of his R&R to Hawaii. I was contacted via radio in the field and approved it. When he got back he was a <u>total mess</u>. His *girl – the one he'd been dating since fifth grade and he was engaged to – dumped him the last day of his R&R/leave after he'd dropped a lot of money on her. Plus he got a lot of crap from his lifelong friends about the war. Maybe going home wasn't such a great thing after all. His first night back in the field he refused to go out on patrol. (This from a guy who was always one of my top two or three enlisted in the company???) We talked. I told him if he didn't go, he was forcing me to take action I'd prefer not to. He said: "I should give a shit. Put me in Long Bin Jail and throw away the key." Sergeant Newman, his squad leader, begged me to give him a couple of days to straighten him out. I did. A couple of days later, Pineapple was his old self, minus a lot of money, a fiancée and friends back home. What a war.*

LTC Galvin is my military savior. He took Lt. Cleburne off my hands with some hocus-pocus with buddies of his on division staff. The lieutenant is now the assistant S-4 on LZ Mo responsible for resupply days to the companies in Galvin's battalion. He has only two people reporting to him. The colonel tells me Cleburne is happy to be out of Alpha and away from me. The feeling is mutual. The colonel did say I'm still on the hook for writing the Officer Efficiency Report for him, which I'm happy to do. In fact, I've been working on it almost since I took over the company a couple of months ago. Galvin gave me a replacement – a tall black OCS lieutenant named Web duBois. I think he's going to work out fine.

General Casey stopped by Mo and we talked. For some reason, he thinks I'd make a good Aide-de-Camp and he asked me to seriously consider the position. There's nothing I'd be less qualified for or less interested in. Command – that's why I chose infantry and why being the C.O. of Alpha Company is probably the best job I'll ever have.

Crossing paths with the Division commander twice in the same week – and not for the purpose of getting my ass chewed! Feels like getting shot at and missed.

<u>*12 June 1970 - somewhere in Cambodia*</u>. *Second day back in the 1/6 Battalion. Feel like a stranger, sorta. Boomer Cameron is now the S-3, Operations officer. The S-2 is new. Benny is no longer on the firebase – LZ Charo. Of course Colonel van Noort isn't the battalion commander – Lieutenant Colonel Mike Blair is. The whole episode of van Noort's brief and explosive tenure as commander is baffling and worrisome to me.*

I'd love to have a beer with 'The Goose' and talk about it.

Blair seems decent – a little tentative when we talked on the firebase. Not at all like van Noort's looming presence, or Galvin's calm, quiet professionalism punctuated with flashes of humor. Blair is new - finding his way. Wonder what my guys thought of me on day one?

<u>*14 June – Cambodia*</u>. *First contact in a week – first time with Blair and Boomer. What a nightmare.*

Managing Blair in the battalion C&C at fifteen hundred feet altitude and the brigade commander at three thousand feet – a chore. Blair and I have to have a long talk about who is running the fight on the ground. He's new and feels he has to do something.

I'm reconsidering General Casey's offer to be his aide.

17 June – Cambodia – somewhere. The rain is still incessant and no contact. It only took three days for signs of indifference and laxity to start showing up.

We're still locating some little caches but not like it was only a couple of weeks ago. The NVA seem to have melted and moved away, out beyond the seventeen mile limit and are waiting for us to go back to Vietnam in a couple of weeks.

18 June – Cambodia - Around noon, came across a dirt road under the canopy – a HIGHWAY - wide enough to drive a tank down with room to spare; or, march a column of men eight abreast. Scared me. I could feel the tension in the troops too. Set up and patrolled a kilometer north and south before crossing. Caught two NVA in khaki strolling along the road toward us. Got one and the other got away. Shoddy marksmanship. Need to work on that next LZ duty. This will keep my guys alert for a while – a day or two.

26 June – One week, two log days, no contact with the enemy, relentless rain grinding us down. I'm hoping for a little firefight to snap us out of it.

27 June 1970 – Cambodia. Three days until all US forces must be out of Cambodia by order of the President of the United States of America.

It seems that every single, solitary unit in the 1st Cav is getting flown out of beautiful idyllic Cambodia over the next two days to be clear a full twenty-four hours before the Commander-in-Chief has declared we will be out. BUT... somebody didn't bother to figure out that my company isn't within five days walking distance from an open area big enough to land even one lone Huey. 'Another fine mess you've gotten me into, Ollie said to Stan.' We've got a three day walk to the border even if we bust our humps and throw away all tactical security. And even if we get there in time, there's the river – sixty, seventy yards across; deep, swift. I've got a baker's dozen people who can't swim, and only four of us who have ever made a tactical river crossing. I hated river crossings in Ranger School.

We're not going to make it out on time, and that's probably career limiting.

*　　*　　*

The Huey made its approach and then descended slowly to a fifteen foot hover over the river. The pilot turned its nose toward the small open area on the Cambodian shore and eased toward the ground guide holding his M16 over his head. The helicopter stopped with its tail boom hanging over the water.

"Ain't it just amazin' what those pilots can do with them Hueys, sir?"

"It is, Sergeant Newman," Glenn agreed, looking sixty yards across the dark river at the dense foliage growing to the waters' edge. The elevation rose steeply on the Vietnam side of the river and the jungle appeared extremely dense. Two rubber bundles, several coiled climbing ropes and a large duffle bag were tossed out of the cargo compartment onto the ground.

They had averaged better than five kilometers a day to arrive at the river with six hours of daylight left to make a river crossing and return to Vietnam under the president's deadline. It had felt like a reckless, chancy dash through the woods compared to his normally measured and secured pace when moving through an area. He couldn't afford the time to patrol ahead of the company to avoid ambush, and had tasked Sergeant Newman and his squad to work with his two remaining scouts to lead the way. Newman was down to six men in his squad and with the addition of Two Hatchets and Lone Wolf called his point team 'the Crazy Eights.'

In the end, Newman pulled it off.

Soon after arriving at the river, he'd talked through the plan with his platoon leaders, Newman, and the three men in the company other than himself who'd been through Ranger School – Rollie Thorgier, Staff Sergeant Nelson who was Rankin's platoon sergeant in first platoon and his new second platoon leader, Web duBois.

He waved Mikey Meade over as Newman's squad was unpacking the equipment.

"I want artillery targets fired downriver, upriver and behind our landing point directly over there," he said to his forward observer as he pointed directions. "All of them five hundred yards from here. You work that up and when you're ready to start firing let me know."

"Ready to go right now, Six. Worked that up last night and got the targets plotted with the FDC on Charo. We're ready to start adjusting."

"Get to it." He turned to EB and told him to advise the platoons they were going to be firing artillery around their crossing site.

Meade had done well since their first day in Cambodia when they his lost his officer. Glenn was more than satisfied with how his 'Seattle Shakespeare' artillery forward observer had performed after a shaky start on his first operation. His hair was too long, he chain-smoked Kools, wore a damned peace symbol around his neck and had a tendency to smart off now and then... but the kid really could adjust artillery. It wasn't a surprise he'd already figured out what was needed and was ready to go. When Alpha was reassigned to their original battalion, the artillery battery commander had sent out a first lieutenant to replace Meade. Glenn sent him back on the next helicopter and told the battalion he wasn't in need of a new FO. The scenario had been played out before and he hoped he wouldn't have to do it again.

In short order, the crossing began.

Four men at a time sat in two small black rubber rafts with their rucksacks and weapons between them pulled themselves across the swollen river hand over hand linked to a rope tied at each end to a stout tree using a knot called the 'transfer tightening system' – a trick learned during the jungle phase of Ranger School along the Yellow River in the Florida panhandle. At the far shore they were helped out, grabbed their gear and moved into the jungle to provide security for the rest of the incoming company.

The boats were then linked together and pulled back to Cambodia empty and the process repeated. For the next hour, while artillery fired on the far shore and an observation helicopter scoured the jungle for signs of the enemy, company troops pulled themselves across the river; with each trip the security perimeter expanded in Vietnam and decreased in Cambodia until all were across.

Alpha company, the first American unit into Cambodia, was the last one out; it was a day later than the rest of their division but five hours before President Nixon's deadline.

Chapter 28

Brad thought the three South Vietnamese officers and their enlisted interpreter looked decidedly unhappy when he turned and looked at them.

He and Norton had picked them up in Sông Bé on the way to FSB Charo where they were scheduled to spend a week in the field with one of the companies in the 1/6 Cav. They had also taken on board two soldiers – a reporter and a photographer from the *CAVALAIR,* the bi-weekly little newspaper of the division.

The Vietnamese – a colonel, a captain and a lieutenant – wore light blue berets, rakish Tiger stripe camouflage fatigues adorned with myriad badges, and spit-shined jungle boots. *Headquarters Commandos*, Brad thought as he looked at them again. He had no idea of the motivation behind the ARVN officers' stay and didn't much care. Maybe this was another step in *Vietnamization* of the war, a phrase the politicians back home were fond of bandying about.

"Three days and a wakeup until R&R. You boys gonna miss me while I'm in Australia?" Silence answered. He tapped a finger on his helmet mic. "Hello! Hello! This thing working?"

"Yeah, sure, Mr. Nolan," Syzmanski finally said. "We're missing you already."

"That's better, chief. And you, Ed?"

"I've hired a professional mourner and a Jewish wailing woman to help remind us of our dire state of affairs without you being here to inspire and guide us. Australia's gain is our loss."

"Guys who go there always return with the disease," Syzmanski said over the intercom.

"Propaganda from the chaplain to keep us from enjoying ourselves," Brad replied. "You guys are just jealous. Tex Haskell and I have been looking forward to this forever. Man, the stories we've heard from the guys who've been there. It's more than the mind of mortal man can comprehend."

"You and Tex are going together?" Norton asked, turning his head and looking at him. "There goes another ally."

Brad laughed. "Eat your heart out, Norton." He looked five miles in front of them and saw barren earth poking through the jungle. LZ Charo. Like Mo, it had been positioned to cover the withdrawal of Americans from Cambodia; both sat only a couple of miles from Cambodia, and both were likely to stay active for a while.

"Charo at twelve o'clock, five miles," Brad announced. "Ed, why don't you fly the bird today and let me gather my strength for the demanding week of chasing women that lies ahead in Sydney?"

"You're so full of it. You're planning to take today off?"

"And tomorrow. Not much for me to do. We've got a single company to log today, and C&C tomorrow. Weather's not going to hold us up – hasn't rained in four days and its forecast to stay severe clear for a while. The war's over, haven't you heard?

"We might as well go home..."

"Many NVA close by, *Tó Neinilii*," Daniel Two Hatchets whispered to Glenn as they knelt at the head of the lead platoon in the company. "Fresh signs all around the complex."

"How many would you guess?"

"Dozens... times dozens. The trail leads east and then south."

I can't believe this, Nolan thought. He was in a quandary.

It was their resupply day and they hadn't found a suitable landing zone yet. Here they were less than a thousand yards from the river, having been back inside Vietnam little more than a day and they had run across another large NVA supply site. He now had a company a third smaller than the size of the one he'd taken into Cambodia – fifty-nine men, and he wasn't sure that was enough to secure the entire site if what Lone Wolf and Two Hatchets were telling him was accurate. And he assumed it was.

Second platoon had come across a single small hut on their first light patrol. When they had called it in, Glenn moved the company to link up with them, sent his two scouts and Case Newman's squad to recon the area, and called in an initial report to the battalion. The recon team found five small huts, along with two pits containing ammunition, each pit about eight feet wide, thirty feet long, and five feet deep lined with black plastic and covered with plastic and cut foliage. The huts contained mortar tubes, a number of machine guns – both .30 caliber and .51 caliber – along with AK47s and recoilless rifles; There were mounds of ammo for each. Even more intriguing were the hand-crank and gasoline powered generators, and the switchboards plus phones and large spools of field wire. It was all extremely well camouflaged, and the camouflage was very, very fresh.

Glenn had EB get the platoon leaders up to the CP to work out a plan for securing the site, and had Holmes call battalion to get a Pink Team out to scout the nearby area for him. He had Meade fire and register two artillery targets five hundred meters to the north and to the east of the cache site just in case.

The Pink Team arrived a half hour later, found a spot close to Alpha company's location that would do for a single ship landing zone without too much work. It was a small opening covered in waist high grass with a few small trees and some low, scattered undergrowth they cut down with machetes. By mid-morning they were ready to start receiving supplies and back hauling weapons, ammunition, and an assortment of other pieces of NVA equipment.

The log bird called departing Charo and EB handed the handset to Glenn.

"Able Wonder one-zero, this is Rowwlllllff Cramden. Got you a letter from Jennnyyyy."

Glenn replied, "This is Wonder one-zero. You have time to play mailman?"

"Always looking out for you. Mom insisted... This letter smells oh so fine."

"You don't really have a letter from the Polock."

"I do. She's a romantic – a soft touch for wayward children and lost causes. Go figger."

Colonel Blair and Boomer Cameron flew in at noon with three ARVN officers, a reporter and a photographer to walk around the complex.

An exact accounting of all the various calibers of ammo was left for others to do later but Glenn knew it was a sizeable amount. They found a dozen .30 caliber machine guns with over twenty thousand rounds and four of the big .51 caliber machine guns; forty-six AK47s, four 82mm mortars with 100 rounds, nine 60mm mortars with over 300 rounds, and three 57mm recoilless rifles with twenty rounds. There were fifty vests filled with Chinese Communist fragmentation grenades and dozens of Rocket Propelled grenades, the dreaded RPG. They loaded it all out before nightfall.

What dogged him most was the communications and electrical equipment: Four generators and three Chicom telephone switchboards. What size unit would need that?

And what was he supposed to do with three ARVN officers left on his doorstep?

*   *

The morning routine of first light patrols went quickly and soon they were saddled up, moving toward their first company patrol base. They had gone two hundred meters by his pace count, when the foliage grew less dense and the terrain ahead began to fall off.

This didn't feel right; he had EB call Gamecock and tell him to stop.

Glenn dropped his rucksack and went forward.

"You guys should have stopped us sooner," Glenn told his second platoon leader. He walked several paces out in front of the company, looked around and then down into the yawning crevasse running from higher ground on the right toward the river a half mile away.

No way we're going through that. We'd be like fish in a barrel if there's anybody over there." He started to turn toward the company when someone yelled, "Get DOWN!!"

Glenn heard the shout but it was immediately drowned out by the sudden roar of gunfire crackling around him; he turned and stared at dense green vegetation twenty-five yards away on the other side of the ravine. The jungle came alive now with the blinking of muzzle flashes that seemed close enough to reach out and touch. *Dozens times dozens* Two Hatchets had said, but he was way wrong. The world around him turned to slow motion as he raised his M16.

A B40 rocket exploded in the trees nearby with a sharp, loud *karump* like lightning striking at arm's length, and then two more exploded even closer. Newman was yelling at him to get down and tugging on his jungle fatigues trying to pull him to the ground. Beyond him, Two Hatchets and Lone Wolf were firing rapidly. He could see two of his M60 gunners – Pineapple and Stevens – firing short bursts that sent red tracers slicing through the winking lights across the ravine. A third string of red from somewhere in second platoon seemed to be dueling with a line of green NVA tracers off to his right; two M79 grenades exploded almost simultaneously and the green tracers ceased.

He was on a knee, surveying the firefight, watching the far side undergrowth moving, coming to life like an angry, flopping beast and hearing Newman continuing to yell, "Six! Get down!!" The smell of burnt powder assaulted his nose. *Got to get to the radios*, he told himself.

He was up and running, dodging through a gauntlet of trees and brush and his own soldiers on the ground, while bullets slapped at branches around him. A root tripped him and he grabbed at a tree to keep from falling. Another B40 exploded, this time on their right flank near Rankin's platoon. An M60 fired off a long burst that seemed to go on and on and on. Muffled explosions of 40mm grenades from his M79s steadily erupted and M16s from second platoon – some on automatic, most not – kept up a high volume of fire.

Glenn got to the CP and jumped over EB who hugged the ground next to his rucksack. He landed hard next to Holmes; behind him, Timmy Horner and Heavy had found some cover; Mikey Meade was on his radio, talking feverishly while lying flat on his stomach.

"You call battalion yet?!" he yelled.

Holmes nodded. "Already told 'em to bounce Max and get us a FAC on station. Colonel Blair wants a situation report."

"Tell him we're in a firefight with a bunch of gooks with B40s and machine guns. Don't know how many." He turned to EB. "Any reports from the platoons about casualties?" When his RTO shook his head, Glenn turned back to Holmes and said, "No casualties to report so far, but he should get a standby medevac out to Charo. Tell him we're going to need at least one kick-out resupply of ammo – all kinds – when the first chance comes. Probably one or two more after that. When we call we're going to need it quick. Emphasis quick."

EB tugged on his shirt and handed over the handset. "Rash two-seven."

"Rash two-seven this is Wonder One-Zero," Glenn said to the Air Force Controller. "We're in contact with at least a company of NVA two north of Charo, less than a klick inside the border. Where are you?"

"*Rash two-seven... Halfway between you and LZ Mo. Got a flight of four A-37s with five hundred pounders twenty minutes out.*"

"Can they get here sooner?!" he yelled over the cacophony of gunfire and explosions.

"*Rash two-seven. We'll see what we can do. I'm fully loaded and can be there in five or less. Pop smoke – I should see it from here.*"

"Gamecock, this is Odin, Pop smoke for Rash," Glenn said over the radio. Several seconds later, a column of purple smoke began filtering upward through the trees.

"*This is Rash two-seven identifying the Goofy Grape smoke. Where's the target?*"

"From the smoke, heading zero-one-five degrees. Distance less than fifty meters. Make your runs east to west. Be advised the border is really close and we've got artillery firing from LZ Charo on the same target. "

"*I can make my runs without crossing their gun-target line, but when the A-37s get here you're going to need to shut it down until they're clear.*"

"Roger that."

The exchange of gunfire fell off to a trickle for a couple of minutes and then again came to life. The ebb and flow of weapons firing. It was always that way in a firefight Why? He had no idea. Looking toward the enemy location, he saw for the first time his CP had a direct line of sight to the NVA positions, and that meant they had a direct line of sight to him. *I've got to move these guys!* He glanced around quickly for better cover; suddenly Case Newman was kneeling beside him.

"Sir, I need your climbing rope." They had punctured and sunk the life rafts after their river crossing but they were still carrying one of the long ropes – his fault since he'd forgotten to put it on the helicopter when they were backhauling all that NVA equipment the day before. "Palmer in my squad slipped down the side of the ravine and he's yelling he's hit. Me and one of my guys are goin' down to get him."

"I'll bring the rope and give you a hand."

"No, sir. We need you here doin' all that gunship and aircraft and artillery stuff you do... and runnin' the company." Newman gave him a quick, devilish smile. "Sir, we got those bastards right where we want 'em... We're kickin' their ass good and we need you to finish 'em off. Ain't this just the best damn thing in the world, sir?!"

The young sergeant grabbed the rope from his hand and slithered away on his stomach. Immediately the Air Force forward air controller was back on the radio. He could see the American artillery impacting and creeping toward the smoke. Over the next ten minutes Rash two-seven fired a dozen high explosive rockets and made two passes with his machine guns and then held off to await the arrival of his jets. Mikey Meade continued firing artillery missions; the rumbling explosions crept closer and closer until they could hear the shrapnel whistling through the trees and snapping branches just a dozen feet above their heads.

The firing dwindled and finally stopped... for less than two minutes.

When it roared back, all the incoming fire seemed centered on the exposed company command post. Dust and dirt was being sporadically kicked up around them; rifle and machine gun fire pulverized the trees a few feet over their heads, covering him with tree limbs and bits of bark. *How long has this been going on?* he wondered.

He was talking to Colonel Blair explaining he had two wounded and was in need of immediate medevac as soon as they got a lull in the fighting. No, he wasn't going to maneuver one of his platoons to try to outflank the enemy. It was obvious the enemy significantly outnumbered him and he was not going to split the company into small elements easily defeated in detail. Fragmenting the company would negate their advantage in supporting artillery and air. He was about to tell the colonel this when the firing from across the ravine increased exponentially, roaring over and crushing them like a rogue wave.

Bullets snapped all around him, dirt flew and foliage splintered, floating down on them.

EB turned toward him – a small, perfectly round hole an inch below his left eye oozed blood. "Six, I'm hit," he said weakly. The RTO's face registered surprise, disbelief. He coughed and blood gushed from his mouth.

Glenn threw himself in front of his RTO and stacked his and his RTO's rucksacks in front of him as a shield. He knelt and took the five quart canteen from his rucksack and placed it under EB's head. "You're going to be all right! Stay with me. You're going to be all right!"

"Six, get down!" Holmes shouted, grabbing his arm.

Glenn pulled away and yelled, "Get that damned medevac out here now, Holmes!... MEDIC! Horner, get up here!" He turned to face the ravine and picked up his rifle.

A sudden bright flash blinded him and a savage blow to his chest knocked him over backwards; his head hit the ground hard. Fighting for breath and skirting along the edge of consciousness, he tried to open his eyes but couldn't. He could still hear the gunfire, but soon that faded to silence and he was plummeting down a long dark spiral like the Biblical 'bottomless', bordered in red.

The vortex closed around him.

So this is what it's like? he thought and then... nothing.

*   *

Brad heard the call for help from Ghostrider two-three on the company UHF frequency.

"This is Ghostrider one-four," Brad replied as he and Norton sat on the VIP pad at firebase Lois waiting on Colonel Ianetta, "What do you need?"

"*Got a unit in contact north of Charo. Call sign Able Wonder. Pig Farmer Wallace tried to kick out ammo but took fire. He's headed for Sông Bé with mechanical problems and a wounded door gunner. I've got coordinates and freqs if you can help.*"

Brad told Syzmanski to unload the colonel's portable radios and flight helmets. He was lifting off as he replied, "We'll be there in fifteen. Already have the location and frequencies. We logged the unit yesterday. Big fight?"

"*Looks like it. An NVA company or more. There's a medevac, a couple sections of guns and a flight of A-37s inbound. Artillery and mortars firing from Charo. The grunts are going to need a kick out of ammo on short notice. Position on the log pad and be ready for a quick launch. Call when you're on short final and I'll update you.*"

"Will do."

"What is it with your brother?" Norton asked.

"The boy has been unlucky his entire, sorry life. Except with this one woman. I'll tell you about it someday."

Off in the distance he saw the Air Force forward air controller diving and firing rockets.

*   *

Water from a canteen streamed across his eyes, into his ears and nose and mouth, then down the back of his neck.

Glenn was gagging and trying to push the water away. He tried to blink but found it difficult, as if someone had poured a truck load of sand into his eyes. He seemed to be inside the pain in his chest, a description he'd heard used by victims of heart attacks... but that wasn't the problem. Long seconds later, he was finally able to blink, and then to see a little bit through the distortion. He recognized Timmy Horner's face.

"What happened, Doc?"

"Dirt in your eyes," Horner yelled to be heard above the harsh, dissonant sound of gunfire. "You're all right. Machine gun rounds hit the ground right in front of you kicking up dirt and gravel that blinded you. One of the bullets hit your M16 driving it into your chest. It's a really bad bruise, and you're going to hurt for a long time. You'll live, but the gun's ruined."

"EB?!"

"Not good. Nothing I can do for him. He needs a real doctor and a hospital. Now!"

Glenn closed his eyes and took several deep, painful breaths. "Where's the medevac?"

"Not too far away. But he can't come in while we're still in contact."

"The bastard!" Glenn said angrily. "Get him in here! Where's my radio?"

Horner held him down when he tried to get up. "Medevac doesn't do any of us any good if he gets shot down, Six. The NVA are too close and he'd be a really easy target. Do you remember a log bird trying to get ammo in and being run off?"

"Today?"

"Ten minutes ago."

Nolan shook his head and looked at EB who was motionless on his side, face down. Incoming rounds were still hitting around him and thudding into the two rucksacks. Glenn lifted himself up on an elbow and said to Holmes. "Get me Rash two-seven."

After a painful coughing session he reached for the handset Holmes held out. "Rash, this is Wonder one-zero. Where are the A-37s?"

"Two minutes out, one-zero. Where do you want their ordnance?"

"Same place you put those HE rockets."

There was a noticeable pause. *"Sure you want five hundred pound bombs that close?"*

"Roger that. Or closer. Got to get them off our backs in a hurry. We need medevac bad. "

"Keep your head down... You're sure about this?"

When they came, the lumbering A-37s – a tandem seat twin engine jet trainer for years in the U.S. – flew over at what seemed like treetop level. The explosions of the five hundred pound bombs lifted him off the ground, and chunks of metal whistled over their heads feet above the ground. Glenn adjusted them closer on the second pass. NVA firing fell off to almost nothing after the first sortie of bombs, and stopped after the second.

The jungle went eerily silent.

"Holmes, give me the radio," Glenn demanded, coughing and holding his chest. "This is Able Wonder one-zero. Send in that medevac bird. NOW!" he said over the battalion frequency. "We have four critical WIA to get out of here... And get a bird out here with some damn ammo. We're just about out." He picked up the handset to EB's company net radio and heard a call from the medevac ship followed by Blue Max.

He stole a look at EB again; Horner was tending to him with Heavy's help. The RTO looked at him and tried to smile. Glenn nodded in his direction and felt hollow, impotent. *Keep it together, Nolan*, he told himself. *People are depending on you. You've done this before.*

Soldiers were helping the walking wounded to the place several yards away where a yellow smoke grenade had been thrown. While Glenn talked the medevac ship in, Heavy lifted EB in his arms and carried him to the smoke. The sound of rotor blades grew louder; a Huey moved over them, stopped, and a jungle penetrator lowered through the jungle canopy.

Glenn watched as the wounded were lifted through the triple canopy. Watching EB hoisted up and pulled inside the Huey was the worst moment of his tour.

As the medevac departed another radio call came in, from the log bird who approached dragging his skids through the tops of trees and stopped directly overead.

Looking down on him from the left pilot's seat sixty feet above was a kid with a gaudily painted flying helmet – a yellow and black 1st Cav patch above the left ear, a light green circle pierced with a yellow lightning bolt on the visor cover and – he knew without seeing it – a smartass warning label on the back.

No pilot in the Cav decorated his helmet like that except his little brother.

The assistant supply officer – a shirtless, freckled first lieutenant named Jaeger who had commanded the battalion Recon platoon until recently – was leaning out to spot the drop point. He waved the troops away and then started pushing wooden boxes of ammo out of the Huey's cargo compartment as fast as he could. Firing from across the ravine began before half the ammo was out, but the ship stayed over them until all cases were out, then it pulled up and disappeared from sight.

The firefight had been going on at high intensity for well over an hour and despite all the air support – gunships and Air Force – and all the artillery and mortar rounds fired, the enemy showed no signs of disengaging. *These guys came prepared to stay and fight*, Glenn thought, as he talked to a second section of gunships and adjusted their firing runs.

Over the next two hours, Meade adjusted artillery fire from his own battery on Charo and another from LZ Mo. Rash two-seven called leaving the area to refuel and was replaced by Rash two-five who brought with him another flight of four A-37s. A little after two in the afternoon, firing on both sides ceased and Brad was able to get a second resupply of ammunition. Twenty minutes after, first platoon was engaged by a sizeable force of NVA and fifteen minutes after that, third platoon was similarly attacked from a distance of less than twenty-five yards. The NVA across the ravine increased their rate of fire and second platoon's machine guns and M79s responded.

They were now surrounded.

Thorgier's platoon had been unpressured and out of the fight the whole time until attacked. Their part of the fight lasted less than a quarter of an hour and the enemy in front of them melted away under the withering fire of his M60s. Rankin's Riffraff came under increased pressure and Glenn moved two of third platoon's machine guns to support him. By three o'clock, the enemy's flanking attacks on first platoon withered and Glenn directed a series of rocket attacks on them by Cobra gunships that caused them to break off completely.

A third kick out resupply came at four o'clock. By then the firefight had been going on for six hours with a few sporadic respites and Glenn hoped the NVA were by now running low on ammunition and troops. *How can they take this kind of pounding and keep coming back?* he wondered. A half hour after their last resupply, during one of those strangely quiet pauses, the firefight exploded again in an intensity that exceeded anything they had endured so far. It went on for ten minutes; then as suddenly as it began, it ceased and the jungle was again soundless.

Is this fight over? Glenn wondered. He went forward and watched the far side of the ravine for any movement. Minutes later, he warned the company that second platoon was going to recon by fire and had Masika fire several bursts into the far bank. There was no response.

The NVA had melted away, leaving him with four more wounded on top of the five he'd medevac'd earlier, and five dead Americans they would have to carry out – three from second platoon, one from first and Meade's RTO, the quiet Specialist 4 named Herrara. Glenn couldn't remember exchanging more than a sentence or two with the radio operator. He called the battalion on the secure radio to report in.

"*Your intentions?*" Colonel Blair asked.

"We're going to move back a couple of hundred meters to the LZ we used yesterday so we can get out our dead and wounded. I'll need three body bags."

"*And after you get your casualties out?*"

"By then it'll be dark. We'll have artillery from Mo and Charo fire through the night to keep pressure on them as they withdraw."

There was a pause on the radio and then the battalion commander came on. "*Have you considered pursuit?*"

"Tonight?! In the dark?! After seven hours in contact? With less than fifty guys..."

"*Higher is pressing us to keep the pressure on. I want you to look at the possibility and we'll talk about it.*"

"Sir, we *are* keeping the pressure on the enemy. By shelling his likely avenues of withdrawal." *What in the world is Daughtry thinking? Pursuit? – running around in the jungle at night after a whole day of fighting with a worn out half-strength company chasing down a numerically superior enemy force? I've wounded and bodies to get out...*

He was about to say something hugely sarcastic about sending out one of the Garrison Cowboys from 2nd Brigade staff to rappel in and lead the effort, but thought better of it.

"We'll go back through the contact area first thing tomorrow and do a thorough sweep of the enemy position. I'll need a Pink Team at first light."

Lieutenant Rankin broke through the tangled jungle. "We've got two NVA out in front of my platoon trying to surrender."

"*Chu Hoi*? Sounds like a trap. Let me take a look." He handed the handset to Holmes and followed Rankin. When he got there, first platoon had two wounded North Vietnamese in tattered black pajama uniforms, spread eagle on the ground.

"I say we kill 'em," one of the soldiers said and the others nearby nodded agreement.

"We don't kill prisoners," Nolan replied immediately. "And they might have something on them that's valuable. I'll take them back to the CP. Riffraff, I need an RTO. Give me one of yours. He can help me with these guys." Back at the CP, he took the handset and was about to call battalion.

Holmes stopped him.

"Six, we need one more body bag," the pale, skinny radio operator said softly.

"For...?"

"Doc."

"Horner?...Timmy?! No!" He shook his head and turned away, gripped by that same mute despair, the debilitating anguish that overwhelmed him when he first saw EB wounded, and again later when he watched him being hoisted up on the jungle penetrator. At last he whispered, "Can't be. I don't believe it."

"Third platoon just brought him in. He's dead, Six... Timmy's dead."

Chapter 29

The bar in Kings Cross was called the *Texas Tavern* and Happy Hour started at five.

It was a long narrow room, loud, populated by American troops on R&R and Aussie girls – all looking for a good time. Drinks were free if they weren't Chivas Regal or Crowne Royal but rather local beer and bottom tier whiskey or scotch. This was nirvana for Warrant Officer aviators with an unsophisticated palate and an eye for pretty women, which Brad Nolan had never been bashful about claiming as his two most salient traits. It was half past five and Brad was working on his third double bourbon on the rocks, already feeling lightheaded.

He glanced again at the door of the crowded American bar looking for Tex Haskell who had flown down to Sydney with him and gone on to their hotel with their luggage. Tex had wanted to get a shower and change clothes after the long flight from Tan Son Nhut; Brad was more eager to get started on his R&R.

Australia was legendary among the American soldiers and airmen in Vietnam. Every guy Brad knew who'd gone there had come back with a smile on his face and stories too wild and too good to be true. According to all reports, Sydney was a beautiful city with stunning, loose women who spoke an intriguing version of the King's English and a male population totally focused on drinking beer, swimming and playing Australian football to the exclusion of female companionship. Into that void stepped U.S. military men, including Brad Nolan.

Haskell came through the door, wearing his white Stetson, making him look even taller than his six foot three. He navigated his way through the crowd to Nolan.

"I'm surprised you're still here," Haskell said, looking around. "This must be what it's like backstage at the Miss Universe contest. Holy smokes, Nolan. Gunship jocks would call this a 'target rich environment'. Where does a guy begin?"

"I'm starting with that dark-haired girl at the table near the end of the bar – the one who looks like Miss March. And then I'll come back for Miss May, the blond sitting with the twins by the back wall near the juke box. Did you get me a room and drop off my bag?"

"I signed you in with the military assistance people in the main lobby. Gruff old sergeant, but nice hotel. Your bag's with the bell captain. They wouldn't give me a room key. You have to sign for that in person."

"No big deal." Brad finished the remainder of his drink in one big gulp and stared briefly at the dark-haired girl. "She's gorgeous, isn't she, Tex? I hope she's got the stamina to stay up with the world's greatest helicopter pilot."

Haskell looked at him sideways. "I thought you were going to ask her out, not me."

"You wish. But that girl she's with..."

Haskell cast a wary eye at the two girls and said, "Not on your life, friend."

"I'm serious, Tex. I need you to be my co-pilot tonight on this."

"I'll *never* be your co-pilot, Nolan. I've already forgotten more about flying than you'll ever know; more about women, too. I heard from Norton what it's like to be your right-seater."

"I only ask three things from my co-pilot... All you gotta do is say: 'Nice landing, sir – lunch is on me, and – Sir, I'll take the ugly one'. And you owe me one... or two or three."

He stood up, and felt just a little unsteady. He had no idea what he'd been drinking except it had been free bourbon, which had at first tasted like some kind of petroleum distillate, but had gotten better the more he drank. Now he had the beginnings of a good buzz, and felt irresistible. *Poor girl, she doesn't have a chance. Be gentle with her, Nolan.* Brad walked with Tex toward the table where she sat talking with another girl – a plump redhead with the palest complexion he'd ever seen. He stopped directly across from the girls and waited. When they finally looked up at him it was with inexpressible amusement. The dark-haired girl smiled and nodded coyly.

"Hello. I'm Brad Nolan, an American pilot. I'd like the pleasure of buying you a drink."

She smiled even more broadly and glanced quickly at her friend. "Very nice of you, Yank, but that won't be possible. I'm sorry."

Shot down? Right out of the chute. This doesn't happen to me.

He cleared his throat and said, "All things are possible to those who believe."

"How quaint," the girl said, her eyes still amused. "And what is it that you believe?"

"I believe it's destiny that I buy you a drink, and that we strike up a conversation that leads to an interesting evening for the both of us, and who knows what after that."

"Destiny, eh?" the dark-haired girl said. Her friend giggled and covered her mouth with a hand. "I still think that's not possible, because you see, to begin with this is Happy Hour and drinks are free which I believe you already know having consumed three of them yourself."

"And you know this how?"

"We've been watching you, my friend and I. We have a rather significant bet as to how long you could stay seated on that barstool before falling off." She stroked her chin with a forefinger. "Now it looks like we'll never know, will we? So, you've gone and spoiled our fun, it seems."

He stood looking down at her perplexed, wondering how he was going to convince her. "The fact is, I'd not planned on buying you a drink here, but a drink with dinner at the restaurant of your choice. You didn't come here just for free drinks and to people-watch, did you, Miss... I don't believe I caught your name."

"Zara."

"Glad to meet you. My name is –"

"Brad Nolan. I know. I caught that the first time."

"There you go! I *believe* that we've struck up a conversation that's prelude to an interesting dinner and perhaps more. See, all things are possible to him, and to her, who believes. I guarantee you won't get a better offer from anyone else here, even if they had the wisdom and the courage to invite you to share this evening." He placed both hands over his heart and took a deep breath. "Take me, take a soldier; take a soldier and mayhaps find a king. What sayest thou, then to my humble entreaty?" She looked momentarily stunned. "Well, what say you, my pretty?"

"Oh, go ahead, Zare!" the redhead girl said, laughing. "He's a bloody poet, not some hooligan. He's not askin' ya to marry him, after all." She looked at Haskell and smiled prettily. "Aren't you just a Boomer, mate? Would you like to get out of all this noise and have a drink at my place and leave these two to their business?"

"I reckon I could be persuaded, ma-am," Tex replied, removing his hat.

"And look, he's got manners. I'm partial to you Yank cowboys... and those fellas that call themselves Cajuns, too. What's your name?"

"Folks call me Hopalong Beaudreaux," he drawled in his best East Texas twang, giving her a shy smile that made him look like a young, slim imitation of Gary Cooper.

The girl looked inexpressibly entertained. "All right, 'whatever your real name is', hang on to your hat, and that big belt buckle. You're a fair dinkum cowboy, Mr. Hopalong."

"I guess I am, all roped and branded."

"I don't use ropes, but I can tell you sure you're not going to forget tonight. Zare, darlin', sorry but you're on your own. You take the car and we'll catch a cab." Nolan watched his buddy stroll out the door with the plump redhead, then looked back at the dark-haired girl.

"I guess I will let you buy me a dinner and a drink after all," the girl said. Her dark brown eyes rested on him for a moment, "I should warn you, I'm not a cheap date."

"And I should warn you I'm not easily put off."

"So, I've seen." She looked into his eyes with an impish expression. "I hope you like seafood, Mr. Brad Nolan."

During the drive to the restaurant, he learned she was the daughter of a cattle rancher and winemaker who lived a hundred miles west of Sydney near an old gold mining town called

Bathurst. Her family had lived on the land since before the great Hill End Gold Rush in the mid to late 1800s, she told him, breeding cattle and sheep; in the early twentieth century a great grandfather had also begun cultivating cool weather grapes which later gave birth to a small winery. She loved the area and the land, but the farm was struggling and she'd decided to get a degree from the Wollongong University's Business School in Sydney.

"So you're going to save the family inheritance?" he asked, his voice sounding distant to him. Good luck to you."

"Whatever may come, I don't see a long term future for me in the cattle business," she told him over a dinner of King George whiting and what she called 'mudddies' – crustaceans that looked like Chesapeake Bay Bluefin crabs that had been boiled rather than steamed in Old Bay. "My father's not much the business man and my brother is off in the Army for the next few years. I hope we can keep the place afloat until he comes back, although he's not much better at the business end than father. But you're not interested in all that, are you?"

"I'm interested in everything about you," he replied, taking another sip of the wine she'd ordered for them. *Is that the second bottle?* She was right about not being a cheap date.

"I know exactly what all you Yanks are all interested in. My mother told me about it. She met one of your Marines when they were here in the Big War, and while she didn't let on much it was clear she was warning me about how you Diggers are only interested in having a naughty with every Sheila you can. That's why you were trolling the Texas pub, wasn't it?"

"I have no idea how to answer that."

"Because it's true?" She gave him a quick smile as she cracked open a crab claw.

"No, because I didn't understand a word of what you said." He finished off his wine and poured another glass.

She looked at him with abrupt understanding. "Oh, I see. Well... a Digger is a soldier, and a Sheila is a girl, any girl. And 'having a naughty'... come now, surely I don't have to explain that to a strapping young Yank who's been away from women for a while." He felt his face grow warm and saw the amused look on her face. "Ah, I see you didn't need that explained after all."

"This is not turning out like I imagined." He wasn't sure what he'd expected and realized he was having a terrible time focusing and trouble remembering her name.

They were sitting by a window in a very nice, and expensive, restaurant that looked out over Sydney Harbour where the lights of buildings were now coming on as the sun set. He'd seen pictures of the harbor before, but being there was wholly different; an experience made even better by this Aussie girl's company. Don Shirk had told him about his R&R two weeks earlier. He'd met a girl in the same bar and she'd taken him back to her apartment and kept him a virtual prisoner for a week; Shirk's only comment was that it was *totally amazing*, but one day he wanted to go back to see what Sydney actually looked like. The dinner continued in a haze; he was trying to act and sound sober, knowing he wasn't.

"I want to go see the beach," he declared when the check came and he finished off his second after dinner drink. *How much have I had?* he wondered, realizing he was slurring his words and closed his eyes to keep the room from spinning while trying to remember just how many drinks he'd had in the last two hours. Zara helped him across the dining room, out to the parking lot and into her car; it was dark when she parked next to a boardwalk.

"This isn't a good idea," she told him when he insisted he wanted to go for a walk. "It's bloody cold out here, and the water's frigid."

The next thing he realized was that he was walking knee deep in the surf and suddenly thinking that he was making a mess of a perfectly good opportunity with this girl – *a looker!* he told himself. The horizon was tilting and he felt himself stumble. *Oh, man, am I drunk or what?... and this girl – she's not gonna be happy... what's her name?*

*   *

"You won't believe it when I tell you who they were, Nolan," Lieutenant Colonel Conrad said as they sat in the 2nd Brigade briefing room at Sông Bé. Mike Conrad had been the 1st Cav Division G-2, Intelligence Officer, since mid-April when he replaced Galvin.

"The two Chu Hoi, sir?"

"I'll start with them. One was a simple line soldier in a rifle squad, but the other was a real lucky find – a staff planning officer for the 95C NVA regiment. Our old nemesis from when you were one of my platoon leaders in Tay Ninh."

"You mean, we were up against a company from the 95C?"

"Not a just a company, Nolan. A reinforced battalion. Somewhere between nine hundred and a thousand. Just about what they hit us with at Illingworth. One of the guys you captured was a planner for that attack, and he was still part of the planning team. 95C was staging for an attack on LZ Charo. According to the planner, they were no more than two days away from launching it when you stumbled into them. Sobering, isn't it?"

Glenn gave a low whistle, thinking back over the last week since making the river crossing, wondering why the NVA hadn't attacked the day before while the company was distracted with backhauling all that ammo.

The night of the firefight he'd moved the company back near the complex they'd found the day before. They loaded their dead and wounded onto Brad's helicopter while it was still light enough to see; a second sortie took out the two NVA. Darkness was quickly falling when Glenn heard Vietnamese voices, and a radio playing music. Driven by frazzled nerves, he found the source and confronted the three South Vietnamese officers who were acting like they were alone in the jungle. He'd smashed the small radio, pulled his .45 pistol and pointed it at the ARVN colonel's forehead. He told the interpreter to inform the officers that if he heard another sound, they would be bound, gagged and probably shot. The next morning, he put them on the C&C ship headed to Charo before moving the company back to the contact site.

"Tell me what you encountered when you returned to the scene of the firefight," Conrad was saying.

"We arrived at the contact site and I left first platoon there. I took second and third platoon across the ravine to the other side, crossing about a hundred meters to the south where the ditch was shallower. We found a lot of trash – personal equipment, ammo crates and boxes, several rifles and other weapons... but not nearly as much as I'd expected. We found a few limbs – arms, legs – but no bodies. You know how the gooks are about policing up their dead." It was the grisliest sight he'd seen in the six months he'd been in the Cav and he doubted he'd ever erase it from memory." There were lots of bloody drag marks, numerous craters from five hundred pound bombs and 105mm artillery. A lot of the trees – an awful lot of the trees – showed extensive damage. After a half hour recon, we set off northeast toward the river because there were trails and drag marks leading that way."

Conrad stopped him. "That half hour recon... be more specific about the NVA positions and facilities encountered."

"Hasty fighting positions and operating tables." The colonel nodded. "There were two sandbagged and very well camouflaged pits. One was probably ten feet wide by thirty feet long and contained three rudimentary tables. Operating tables I'm sure, because they were covered in blood. The other was less than half that big with only two short tables. The larger one had taken an almost direct hit from a five hundred pounder. We found body parts nearby and there were crude surgical instruments in both. There was obviously a lot of surgery performed there." For a brief instant he thought of Timmy Horner. He averted his glance so that Conrad wouldn't see his eyes. "The Air Force dropped a lot of bombs that day, sir."

Conrad nodded. "The amount of ordnance you expended was prodigious."

"I would have used ten times that much if I could have, sir... if it would have saved the lives of the soldiers I lost." Glenn had also been advised by Colonel Blair there were some questions about the abnormally high number of Pink Teams he'd been requesting since taking over the company. "What puzzles me, sir – and puzzles me more now that I know the enemy's strength, is that they were so close to us the day before and didn't attack while we were busy loading out their stockpile of weapons and ammunition."

Colonel Conrad smiled ruefully. "That was one of my questions, too. The prisoners said they didn't know your exact size and the activity of your scout team kept them from finding out. I think if they had known, they would have attacked you either the first or second night. They supposed you were headed for Charo, according to the officer you captured. When you found the cache, they thought they couldn't contest it because of the aerial reconnaissance of the Pink Teams; they opted to stay concealed and hoped to still take Charo."

"What's so crucial now about that firebase, sir? Cambodia's over."

"Tactically, not so important. But strategically... Overrunning that LZ would have been a huge propaganda victory. After all the pronouncements from Washington about clobbering the NVA in Cambodia and setting them back years... think what the reaction would have been if one of the firebases of the division that had supposedly accomplished that was overrun."

"Tet '68 all over again,.." Glenn mused. "The press would have labeled all we did in Cambodia a huge failure and ramped up the call to pull all of us out immediately."

"Possibly." Conrad made some notes and turned to a clean sheet in his folder, scribbled a heading and looked up. "Tell me what happened on the river after you did your reconnaissance of the contact site the morning after."

Glenn's pulse jumped. "Nothing much to tell, sir. We got shot at and my scout team returned fire. None of my people got hit. It was over in ten or fifteen seconds."

"That's it?"

"Yes, sir. I wasn't there when it happened, but that was the report I got."

"You weren't there?" The colonel frowned at him. "How's that possible?"

"I was with the second platoon and we stopped fifty meters from the riverbank. I sent a squad under Sergeant Newman along with my two man scout team to scope out the river. They were detected by a raft headed toward the far shore which fired at them and they returned fire."

"That's it?"

"That's all I got when I asked.... that's all I need to know."

Conrad didn't look happy with the answer. "Did your men fire into Cambodia from the riverbank on the South Vietnam side?"

"If they did it was because they were fired upon and defended themselves. We have that right, still. If the rules of engagement have changed, we don't know a thing about it. We're still dropping bombs from B-52s over there, aren't we?"

"We are." The corners of Conrad's mouth ticked upward in a quick smile. "I just wanted to see if you and the others all had the same story. You do." He put his pad into a black issue briefcase. "You boys just about finished off what was left of the 95C regiment, according to that one prisoner you sent us."

"Sir, I'd say the American taxpayer did. They're the ones who paid for all that artillery and air power. We just put it where it did the most good. Honestly, sir, I just wish they'd have let us stay in Cambodia another month to complete the job... and that they had let us go beyond seventeen miles. Can I ask you a question about that, colonel?"

His question was interrupted by the division sergeant major who came in and whispered in Conrad's ear. The colonel's face went pale and he looked at Glenn in disbelief. "General Casey's helicopter went down this morning...

"And they just confirmed there are no survivors."

*   *

Brad pried open his eyes and the sun was shining full on his face.

What time is it? He shivered and looked at his left wrist. His watch was gone – the Breitling Aviator chronometer his parents had given him for his high school graduation. Also missing were his wallet and the vintage leather A-2 flight jacket he'd inherited when he graduated from flight school – an irreplaceable heirloom his father had worn during the Second World War. She had even taken his belt! It wasn't his, but belonged to Haskell – handmade western leather with a large silver buckle his friend had won at the county rodeo his junior year in high school. Tex had loaned it to him before they left Phouc Vinh when Brad realized he didn't have a belt. The only thing of any value she hadn't taken was a few crumpled Australian dollars he'd had in one of his trouser pockets.

"Damn her!" he said aloud, and struggled to his feet. His clothes were wet and sand covered; he had no idea where he was or even the name of the hotel where he was registered. He was cold, confused, embarrassed... and really angry – at her; at himself.

He found a taxi driver who knew the three main hotels where the American soldiers on R&R stayed; inside an hour he was dropped off at one of them.

"You're an American?... an officer?" the starched and spit-shined staff sergeant at the lobby desk asked, incredulous and disapproving when he looked up at Brad. He scanned printouts in a three ring binder and told him, "Your lucky day. You're registered here, Mr. Nolan." He didn't feel lucky, nor did he feel very well, even an hour later after a long hot shower and a shave. It was late morning before he was ready to try the hotel restaurant.

He was on his third cup of coffee, still wondering how to come up with the money to pay for everything, from room to food to transportation back to the airport. He debated going to the police but wasn't sure anything would come of it – he didn't have the girl's name or address and couldn't remember much if anything that she'd told him about herself. He realized he'd be hard pressed to provide even a vague description. Tall, short, color of eyes? He couldn't remember. About all that came to mind was that she had dark hair, an Australian accent and a pretty smile. *Good luck finding her with that description*, he thought. *I'll never hear the end of this from the guys in the platoon.*

"Enjoying breakfast, Yank?" He turned and looked as the girl slid into the seat facing him in the booth and put her large handbag down. "I came by to return some things you left on the beach last night. I wasn't sure that I'd dragged you far enough so you weren't below the high tide line, and decided to keep them so the water didn't destroy 'em or you lost the lot of it to hooligans or treasure hunters. I was surprised you had so much money on yourself, and wearin' a watch what looks like it would fetch a hefty price on the Sydney black market. So, here it all is. Didn't want you to think I was havin' a lend of you."

Brad was speechless as he listened to her rambling, matter-of-fact explanation. She laid all his belongings on the table and passed the leather jacket to him. "I don't know what to say."

"A 'thank you very much' would seem in order, don't ya think?"

"Of course. Thank you." He took a deep breath. *Her eyes are deep brown. Remember that.* "I... I do have a question." He hesitated, and finally asked, "Am I still a virgin?"

She looked at him and shrugged innocently. "No idea. I left two minutes after you passed out because I was sure you were there for the night. Sleepin' on a beach beside a drunk isn't my bowl of rice. If something naughty happened, I can't vouch for it, because I wasn't party to it. Tellin' the truth, I doubt it. You can't remember this morning, and when I left you last night you couldn't walk much less do anything else."

"I feel I should do more than simply say 'thank you' for bringing back my stuff – some of it very precious and important. I've made a bad first impression. Let me make it up to you."

She smiled, and chuckled. "A bad impression?! That you have – at the pub, at dinner, and on the beach. I do like to help lost pups and stray cats; it's why I volunteer at the animal shelter, but even I know a lost cause when I see one. We'll just leave well enough alone and go our separate ways. What is it you Yanks say? – no harm, no foul."

"We also say 'forgive and forget'. I like that better."

"All right, Mr. Nolan –"

"Brad."

"All right, Brad. I forgive you, but it's going to take me more than a little while to forget. You were off your face when we first met and completely drunk by the end of the evenin'. You're still quite the sight hung over, frankly. No, I'm not likely to forget ya."

"Without forgetting, one never truly forgives."

"Perhaps you're right," Zara said, grasping her bag and beginning to slide out of the booth. "I'll give it some thought."

"Please don't go." He reached out to touch her hand. "I want to make it up to you."

"Afraid I must. There's much for me to do at the station. Father called and said we've lost a half dozen jackaroos and I have to get home immediately."

"Anything I can do? Some way I can help that might get me back in your good graces?"

She stopped and looked pensive, squinting an eye while deep in thought. Looking him over as if she was a 4H judge at a county fair, Zara finally asked, "Can you sit a horse?"

"My dad is the real horseman in the family, but I've ridden some over the years."

"Ever spent a whole day in the saddle?"

"Sure, lots of times." It was a lie – maybe more an exaggeration – but he figured that if he was going to makes amends and get to know her, he'd have to go outside his comfort zone to do it. "So, you need help rounding up these jackaroos your father lost? I'm your guy." He thought she was really pretty when she smiled at him.

She grinned, then laughed aloud. "You have no idea what you volunteered for, do you?"

"As long as I'm doing it with you, it doesn't matter."

She laughed again– a merry sound, and her face lit up. "We'll see how much you think it does or doesn't matter by sundown, Yank."

*   *

"He's a really smart dog, isn't he?" Brad asked her as they sat side by side in rocking chairs on the broad front porch of the big ranch house on her father's cattle farm – *Suzanne's Fancy Station.* The short-haired animal with a speckled reddish coat was about a foot and a half tall at the shoulder and weighed about twenty-five pounds. He had been sitting completely still, staring alertly at Brad for twenty minutes. "What kind of dog is it?"

"He's an Australian Cattle Dog. We call them ACDs, or Queensland Heelers," Zara replied, putting her feet up on a small stool. "Father just calls them Heelers. Max is a red

Heeler. We've had blue Heelers, too, and all of them have been very smart, but he's the smartest one I can remember."

The sun was going down behind the big house casting everything on the mostly barren shallow slope in front of them in amber. They had arrived mid-afternoon and immediately her father had put them to work with the dog rounding up sheep and goats from nearby fields and herding them into pens outside the massive barn near the large main house. It had taken them almost two hours and by the time it was over, Brad felt like he'd worked all day.

They had driven west out of Sydney on the Great Western Highway for over an hour until reaching Bathurst, the small mining town now transforming itself into a tourist destination. From there, they had turned northwest and followed alongside a river, the Macquarie, that at places formed the boundary of her family's cattle ranch. Once through the high, wide entrance gate, macadam gave way to a dirt road that in three miles brought them to a large, rambling house. It looked like it had stood for a hundred years and inside appeared to have been last decorated before World War One.

"That dog is the smartest animal and hardest worker I've ever seen."

Brad had watched Max nipping at the heels of the sheep and goats, separating and herding them into two different outside pens. Zara's father had wanted them moved inside the barn, so Brad stepped into the goat pen to push and prod them through the small door. After fifteen minutes of trying, he had moved only three inside. Zara and her father had watched quietly until the old man suggested he might have another way. He shouted a command and in less than two minutes the dog herded all three dozen goats inside the barn.

"Your dad had a good laugh on me this afternoon, didn't he?"

"We both did. It's part of the hiring on process. It shows who has experience as a Jackaroo and who doesn't. A smart station hand doesn't try to do a cattle dog's job."

"I guess I'm not a smart hand, am I?"

"You've got potential. Not much, but we're desperate," she said, fighting back a grin.

"Is that what your dog is trying to tell me now?"

"Actually, I think he's still taking your measure. You have him a little confused. He was always my brother Jocko's dog. Now here you are, wearing his clothes and going in and out of the house like he did. You even have some of his mannerisms. Max knows you're not my brother, but he hasn't quite figured out where you fit in, so he's sizing you up and deciding whether or not you belong." She pushed the felt drover's hat back on her head. "By tomorrow sundown, we'll all know where you stand around here."

"Where do you think I stand?"

"Don't know yet. I'm waiting for Jocko's dog to tell me. It's a good sign he hasn't bitten your leg or herded you into the barn with the goats. Tomorrow, bright and early we'll see if you outrank the cattle." She was enjoying herself at his expense and that felt like progress.

"So what are we doing tomorrow?" he asked.

"Moving cattle from two different pastures at the north end of the station to pastures closer to the house. About two hundred head all told. Max will do most of the work. Our job is to keep them headed in the right general direction and chasing down the rare wanderer. We have to move each herd about forty or forty-five kilometers, so it'll be two long days."

"Twenty-five miles? That's a long trip. Just how big is this place?"

"Three hundred thousand acres. Three twenty-one actually."

"My grandfather has a hundred acre place in Pennsylvania that's average for the area. That always felt big when I was growing up. But this is huge."

"Not among the old stations. Anna Creek Station in South Australia is over six million acres – larger than Israel, and more than seven times your King Ranch in Texas." Zara looked around at the rolling vista – meager lawn and dusty escarpments ran west, downhill toward a long ridge beyond which the river flowed toward Bathurst thirty-five miles away. "It doesn't look like much, but it's ours; been in the family since my great great grandfather staked the claim before the time of your Civil War in America. It was a struggle to keep it afloat until the Great War in Europe when Australia was the breadbasket of the Empire. My grandfather remembers driving cattle and sheep to Sydney and down the main street to the ships. It's hard to imagine that today."

"Things change."

"Some do. But we still do things around here pretty much like he did back then, except that we raise and breed more cattle than sheep. That changed after the First War when the dingoes grew more numerous and daring, and started taking a toll on the sheep herds. The family made some major changes in the late twenties – reducing the number of sheep and breeding heartier cattle. Some stations breed Santa Gertrudis like your King Ranch does. In New South Wales we breed mostly the Australian Braford. While you're here maybe I'll show you how to inseminate a cow."

"That's not exactly what I had planned for R&R." He turned his head and smiled at her. "When I first saw you at the Texas Tavern I had you pegged for a Playboy Playmate rather than a farm girl." She looked sideways at him. "There's nothing wrong with farm girls."

"Being out here in the country, learning to be a Jackaroo isn't what you had in mind coming to Sydney, was it?" When he hesitated, she added, "Tex told me all about your plans."

Brad frowned and gave her a withering glance. "When did you talk with him?"

"This morning. He was in my apartment when I got up and made myself a cup of coffee. He came out of Sophie's bedroom wrapped in a towel and got gobsmacked when he saw me in the kitchen in my nightie." She smirked at the look Brad gave her. "Sophie and I, we share a two bedroom flat. Your friend spent the night. He assumed you were there. I disabused him of *that*; he told me where you were staying and that's how I found you. I assume he and Sophie are now familiar... with each other."

Brad didn't know what to say. "Is it possible that you –"

"No, it's not," she quickly cut him off.

"I was going to ask if it was possible you might have a cold beer around. I'm parched." When she hesitated he said, "Look, I'm not going to repeat last night. I'm not a drunk. Sure I like to drink, like a lot of guys – it's a part of being in the Army, especially as a pilot." He thought about the partying at Delaware, the drinking binges during flight school and at the Red Hawk; the fiasco of his first night in Sydney. "Maybe a cold glass of water."

"I apologize. Had no right to go off cranky on you like that."

"I earned it after last night." *You can't un-ring the bell, Nolan*, he thought, wondering if coming out here had been a good idea after all. Max got up slowly, walked over to him and sat down, placing his muzzle on Brad's thigh, looking up at him.

"I think someone's made a decision about you, Yank."

*   *

It had been the longest, toughest day of his life, and it was only half done.

Fortunately, it was the last day of the little roundup and there was light at the end of the tunnel. Sitting all day in the saddle atop the thickset Australian stock horse would have been hard enough, but it was the frequent up and down, dismounting and mounting that wore him out both days. He hadn't expected the calves to need so much attention; they had a knack for finding and falling into holes, getting stuck in the small ravines and erosion ditches or entangled in the thick brush. The Brafords may have been hearty and well-bred for the harsh conditions of the cattle station, but their offspring were stupid, Brad thought.

At the end of the first day, he'd eaten dinner and immediately fallen asleep in Jocko Morton's bed with Max on the pile of blankets next to the nightstand.

It seemed like only minutes later Zara awakened him, leaving him a cup of hot coffee while he got dressed and went to the front porch where she sat sipping from a steaming mug. He ate the sandwich she'd made for him and then they saddled their horses.

"We're going to move a herd to one of the west pastures, near the river. The Jackaroos reported many signs of dingoes and feral hogs in the area where we're going," she told him simply, and handed him a .30-30 Winchester carbine to put into the rifle scabbard lashed to his saddle. "Better safe than sorry."

It was late morning when they arrived at their destination and Max started rounding up the herd. Brad was covered in dust and had already gone through most of his canteen of water. He and Zara sat beneath a tree while they each ate half of a sandwich.

"I see why your family works so hard to hold on to this place," he told her. "It's hard country and its tough work, but there's something special about the land. I hear you talking about uncles and grandparents and great grandparents who lived and died around here over a couple of centuries. Your family has real deep roots. I envy you that."

"It's a responsibility," she replied, a shadow of sadness crossing her pretty face. "My brother and I are the last ones left to run the operation. None of the rest of the family seems much interested. Most of 'em have moved to the city and gone soft. It's a sad tale. Father's still well and able, thank goodness. And so is Mum."

"And you?"

"A regular Jillaroo, and have been all my life. I'm getting my degree so I can use it to keep the finances of the place right side up without havin' to pay some accountant a king's ransom to balance the books... and to help my Da' make good business decisions. We run on a tighter margin these days than in the past. There's not a lot of money to be made most years. A couple years of drought and we're in trouble; otherwise it's a living."

"But it's your land."

"We don't owe any on that, for sure. But we're year to year in debt – for seed and equipment mainly. We lost those Jackaroos here lately because we didn't pay 'em what they thought they were worth. Jobs in the cities and towns pay more and being a stockman isn't everyone's cup of tea."

She told him about the winery and how that had come about – her father had been convinced by their banker in Bathurst it would be a good addition. She hadn't been persuaded, but it wasn't her decision to make. It turned out to be marginally profitable, but in the past couple of years the wild boars and feral hogs encroached on the vineyards and caused serious damage. It was one of her biggest concerns.

All the while she was telling him about their wine-making, she was casting more frequent glances toward the western sky which was growing noticeably darker.

"We're going to have to get moving, Brad. There's a storm coming and this time of year they can move pretty quickly. Looks like we'll be heading right into it." She whistled loudly and got the dog's attention, gave a command and he immediately started concentrating the herd of about six dozen cows and twenty calves. Brad and Zara mounted up and began moving the small herd due west at a slow trot.

A half hour later the wind picked up and minutes after that he felt the first fleeting drops of rain. When it increased, he stopped to put on the long waxed cotton duster tied to his saddle. He was fastening the leg straps when he saw her veer away from the herd and head into some thick brush in pursuit of a stray calf; she dismounted and disappeared into the thicket. He mounted and headed back toward the left flank of the drove when he saw Max dash away from the herd and disappear into the thicket Zara had entered.

Something was wrong.

He didn't know much about driving cattle or handling cattle dogs, but the red Heeler hadn't left the herd once the whole previous day. *Why now?* he wondered. Loud squealing came from the stand of thick brush and the dog began barking furiously. Instantly, he jumped from his horse, grabbed the carbine from the scabbard and dashed into the woods.

Twenty yards in he came across a clearing; near the middle of it Zara faced a large wild hog. The dog kept the animal at bay by darting at it, circling, biting at its hind legs. On one of its rushes, the hog caught Max and tossed him into the air and then turned on Zara.

Brad threw the carbine to his shoulder and fired. The dark brownish hog went down; he worked the lever, aimed at the animal's head and pulled the trigger again.

"Ugly thing," she said. "Thank goodness she didn't catch Max with a tusk. I should know better than this." She looked at him and said, "I found the calf but there were two little pigs in here foraging around. All of a sudden I was between them and their mother. These things – these damned 'Captain Cookers' – are becoming a nuisance, and they're dangerous. They ruin fences, dig up our vineyards, and even kill off ground nesting birds. I think there's more feral hogs and wild boars than humans in Australia these days." She took the carbine from him, went over to the two little pigs and shot them both. Handing the gun back to him, she said, "We have to get going. Max! – Herd!"

The final two hours of their drive was done in a steady downpour.

He was cold, soaked and wondering how much further they had to go when they crested a small rise beyond which he saw a barn surrounded by a large pen. Just beyond that was a small, square house with a large front porch that wrapped around the front and one side.

Roo herded the cows into the pen and Brad locked it. After unsaddling and feeding the horses inside the barn, he shook the water off his duster and followed Zara into the house.

"This is one of our homestead houses," she said, lighting a kerosene lamp, and holding it up to view the open shelves stacked with cans of food. An old flat topped wood burning stove squatted near the back of the room. There were two small piles of hay, each covered by a wool blanket. A rectangular table and four chairs were the only pieces of furniture. "It's not much but its shelter. You get some wood from the side porch and I'll get a fire started to make coffee. Then we'll see what you'd like for dinner."

"How long will it take to get back to the house?"

"We won't make it back tonight. It'll be pitch dark in an hour, and there are two creeks between here and the station house that will be over their banks with this rain. That's not something we want to try in the dark. But we've got food, water, dry shelter and fire." She pointed to one of the straw piles. "That's your bed. The other is mine. Max sleeps with you."

"I'm going to sleep on a pile of straw, with a wet dog, in a shack with a tin roof that makes so much noise we have to shout at each other? ...and eat cold food out of a can? My life in Vietnam is more civilized."

"You were warned," Zara said, raising her eyebrows as she wrapped her arms around his neck and gave him a kiss. "That was for being a good sport. I know you had something very different in mind when you decided on Sydney for your Rest and Relaxation."

"I don't know. Things are looking up, aren't they?"

"Perhaps." She nibbled his ear then kissed him again, longer this time. When she finally released him, she was out of breath. "That was for what you did this afternoon to save my life."

"All I did was –"

"You shot a large angry sow about to rip me and the dog into pieces," Zara interrupted. "I once saw an uncle badly gored. I know what you did." He was about to say something but she silenced him with a quiet kiss. "And this..."

Brad closed his eyes and leaned toward her.

The slap to his face jolted him.

"And this is for thinking that I was one of those girls who showed up at the Texas Tavern with only one idea on her mind plus a pair of panties and a toothbrush in her purse."

Before he could react she pulled him close and kissed him, whispering in his ear. "And this is for me, because I finally allowed myself to find out just how good a kisser you really are, Brad Nolan."

Chapter 30

The Huey landed outside the main gate of the firebase amid a cloud of reddish-brown dust and Glenn Nolan jumped out onto the hard clay of LZ Mo once again.

He walked through the barbed wire entrance, glancing around at the familiar clutter of an operating base on the point of the 1st Cav spear. Other than seeing Colonel Galvin again, he wasn't looking forward to his day. The battalion commander awaited him at the top of the hill near the entrance to the operations center standing beside his sergeant major. He was a barrel chested old soldier with a square jaw and an unfriendly scowl reserved for junior officers and NCOs who didn't live up to his standards. Galvin approached, smiling, and grabbed his hand.

"Good to see you again. I won't delay you now, but I hope when you're done we'll have time to visit. I'd like your take on something Rucksack uncovered a few days ago."

"I'd like to visit some, sir."

"As would I. Sergeant Major, would you have one of our soldiers on commo duty call down to the log pad and have Lieutenant Cleburne come see Captain Nolan." He turned to Glenn and said in a low voice, "I expect you're not looking forward to this conversation."

"Sir, My grandfather is fond of saying that life would be a lot more pleasant and a whole bunch easier if we got to choose our duties and responsibilities." He remembered the first time he'd heard grandpa Nolan voice the sentiment and recalled how much it impacted his outlook on life from that day on. "I didn't choose to have the responsibility for this officer, but it's my duty to honestly rate his performance."

"Where would you like to do this, Nolan?"

"The table outside the CP used by the company on the firebase, sir, if that's possible. There's as much privacy there as anywhere."

"I'll inform Captain Parry. He's a classmate of yours, isn't he?"

"Yes he is, sir. I'd like to visit with him also, time permitting."

"We'll make sure it does."

Glenn sat at the table and watched the lieutenant talking to the crew at the logistics pad, elaborately gesturing and lecturing first one, then the other. He knew the radio call had gone out minutes earlier but Cleburne was delaying intentionally; he was certain of it. The lieutenant slowly donned his jungle fatigue jacket and took his time getting to the small, shaded table outside the command post bunker reserved for the firebase security company. Nolan sat quietly, calmly lit a cigarette and watched as Cleburne slowly sauntered up the hill. He approached the table swaggering; a jaunty smile creased his face.

"Good to see you again, Glenn," Cleburne said, self-assuredly. "Hope the boys in my platoon are still doin' you a good job. You look like you're off your feed, son. How much weight have you lost since I last laid eyes on you?"

"Have a seat, lieutenant," Nolan said evenly, in a flat, unemotional tone. Cleburne seemed more full of himself than ever, Glenn thought as he laid the folder on the table between them. "We're here to go through the formal process of your Officer Efficiency Report. First of all, I want you to know – "

"Yeah, yeah. I know," Cleburne interrupted. "Change of duty and all that. Damned Army formalities... let's get it over with so's I can get back to real work. Got Charlie company to resupply today, and those boys *do not* like to be kept waitin', you know what I mean? I can read it for myself," he said, abruptly picking up the folder.

"All right, lieutenant. Go ahead. We'll discuss the report after you've read it, if that's your preference."

Glenn watched Cleburne closely as he read the narrative and then the numerical score. He saw the color quickly rise in his throat and observed his jaw muscles clenching; he thrust his chin out but kept his gaze glued to the form. Finally, he put the sheet down and raised his eyes, glaring hatred.

"You son of a bitch," he said disgustedly. "This is a piece of shit. Do you realize what you've done?"

"I'm a very self-aware man, lieutenant."

"Think so?" the officer scoffed, leaning forward and giving him a false, glittering smile. "You think you're special, God's gift to the damned Army... but you're not. You're an asshole, Nolan. Always have been. And you've always been a worthless company commander, too. Best damned day of my life was when I left Alpha."

Glenn remained silent, staring back, meeting the lieutenant's scowl. Conversing with the southerner was like trying to defend oneself against a dirty fighter in a boxing ring, never knowing when the next head butt or low blow or elbow would come. He'd known this wasn't going to be pleasant, and not just because of the words and score on the O.E.R form. He'd expected rancor from the former platoon leader and had decided to let the man's bile run its course. They could talk respectfully about it, or drop it, or do whatever else Cleburne wanted, but it was going to get done.

"You son of a bitch," Cleburne said again. "You did this on purpose."

"Believe me, I gave a great deal of thought to what's on that report. I've been fair... and honest." He wanted to add that the Reviewer – Colonel Galvin – had not disputed anything contained in the report and had signed off with a few generally sanguine comments. "My intent wasn't to antagonize or intentionally demean you. I didn't say anything that isn't supported by fact and I didn't demean you. It's balanced, it's fair, and it's true. You were counseled more than once about every point concerning areas needing improvement."

Cleburne would not look at him but glowered at the form, breathing loudly through his nose. "I wish you'd just gone ahead and ripped me a new one. You intentionally made this bland with just enough... a whiff of condemnation not blatant enough that somebody on a promotion or a retention board would see it for what it really is – a hatchet job. And the numerical rating... low enough to torpedo my career, but just high enough to pass muster because it doesn't look like you're intentionally screwing me, which you are." He raised his head and looked daggers at Glenn. "I'll have you know my family has been serving in uniform all the way back to the War of 1812, and because you probably come from a long of cowards, that makes you feel threatened. Admit it – you're afraid I'll show you up; make you look bad. You just don't like me."

"This isn't about personal animus."

"Sure it is, and the dimwits in my chain of command will pass this through and it'll land in my permanent personnel file in D.C. And you're the worst of the lot."

"You don't have much respect for the officer corps, do you?"

"I sure as hell don't have any respect for you." Cleburne stood up abruptly, and Glenn looked at him with hooded eyes but remained seated. "I'm not signing that damned thing, Nolan – I don't agree with it and I refuse to put my signature on it. Deal with that."

"I don't have to. Actually you don't sign this Efficiency Report, as it turns out. There's not even a place on the form for your signature, only the rater and endorser. And the truth, lieutenant, is that I'm not required to show it to you."

Cleburne continued to glower at him. "Yeah, I see. So you just wanted to rub my face in this damned lousy report, didn't you?"

"Honestly? I thought about just sending it forward, and you'd never be the wiser. But that's wrong. It would have been gutless and dishonest on my part. You were a lousy platoon leader, Cleburne, and I counseled you on it more than once, but like every soldier over here you deserve to be treated with respect and honesty. I have a copy for you, and I –"

"You can go to hell, Nolan. You haven't heard the last of this. "

"I believe I have. I think you're too savvy to take this any further. You should consider your standing, not only up your chain of command, but down the chain as well... You think about what I just said, lieutenant." Glenn watched his former platoon leader stomp down the hill. One thing Glenn had to admit, Cleburne was right about what he'd done to the lieutenant's career. He thought about his first sergeant's admonition months earlier.

Colonel Galvin was waiting for him inside the TOC.

"How'd it go, Glenn?"

"Exactly as I expected, sir." Glenn sat down and took a deep breath. "I'm pretty sure I'm not on his Christmas card list anymore."

"Occupational hazard of the trade we've chosen. It's easy to be a commander when things are tranquil and going well. Anybody can do it then. It's more challenging when things aren't falling nicely into place. You may have done him a favor by giving him the wakeup call he needed early in his career. Some day he might just appreciate it."

"I doubt it, sir."

He hadn't done what he'd done to reform the lieutenant. He'd tried that by counseling several times without success. The war was winding down and there would be a reduction of force not too many years down the road. The lieutenant was an OCS grad with a Reserved rather than a Regular commission and he'd be on the bubble for retention, even without a mediocre Efficiency Report in his file. Cleburne would never survive the cut now – and he didn't deserve to.

He'd wrestled with the responsibility of having such an impact on someone's career; in the end, he realized it was his duty as an officer, and always would be, not only to help those who had earned the right to advancement, but to do something about those who failed to pass muster. He hadn't taken any pleasure in what he'd done, but was convinced it was the right thing to do – for the good of the Service.

"I never was and doubt I ever will be on Lieutenant Cleburne's good side."

The colonel shrugged. "Maybe. Maybe not. But one man I know for sure was on your side. General Casey. He thought a lot of you. If he'd lived, I'm convinced you would have gotten to know him well in coming years."

"I was really sorry to hear about our loss. Got the news when Colonel Conrad was debriefing me about our little set-to after we crossed the river. It's still hard to believe he's gone. I wish I'd gotten to know him. He was quite a guy."

"More than most people will ever know," Galvin said, nodding agreement. For a long moment he grew silent and reflective. "I was privileged to work closely with him. He was a future Army Chief of Staff for sure. Maybe Chairman of the Joint Chiefs. He was Lyman

Lemnitzer's aide in the early fifties a decade before he became Chairman of the JCS, so Casey had experienced the positive effects of proximity to a young general on his way up. I think it's possible he may have been offering that to you at some point. He didn't say, but..."

Glenn pondered that for a moment. It was possible but unlikely, he thought. He still didn't see himself as a general's aide, or a person that a rising star like Casey would be interested in mentoring. "We'll never know, sir. Got too much on my plate to give it any more than a passing thought."

"Well, Nolan here's something I would like you to give some thought to. I'm going home in about four months and I've already started lobbying for another command. I think I've told you already the path to success in this Army is paved with command assignments. That's what the Army is all about. Always command. Fight for command. You should remember that."

"Understood, and I agree, sir."

"Nolan, when I leave here, I'm going to request another battalion command. In Germany this time. If I get it, I want you to seriously consider being one of my company commanders."

Glenn was pleasantly surprised. He watched the colonel's expectant face; was he serious? "Sir, I'd be honored."

"I can put you down, then?"

"I'll have to talk it over with my wife, and I have some questions."

The colonel's face creased in a smile. "You're negotiating with me already for perks, aren't you, captain?"

"No, sir. It's just that Mary Anne wasn't happy with my assignment before – I was gone from home three quarters of the time. And we're talking about an infantry company, aren't we? I'm not signing on as headquarters commandant in a Supplies and Services battalion, right?"

"You don't want to run a bakery or a laundry-bath-graves registration operation?" Galvin asked and laughed heartily. "Don't worry, we'll work out the details over time, Nolan. Your job is to stay healthy and make it home. All things become possible after that."

He returned to Charo after lunch, hitching a ride on Galvin's C&C ship while the colonel conferenced with the brigade commander on LZ Mo.

The Ghostrider pilots knew him as Brad's brother and let him fly in the right seat. It was the most fun he'd had since graduation. He couldn't hover, but since he'd been taught to fly single engine airplanes by his father, he could keep it straight and level and make an approach almost to the ground before having to give up and call for help from the pilot in the other seat to save it from crashing. They let him do some treetop flying – hedge hopping in his father's vernacular – and an approach into the field at Bù Gia Mập airstrip when they took a detour to refuel. He couldn't believe how much he enjoyed himself, *Brad gets to do this every day? Little brother always was the lucky one.*

By the time he climbed out of the Huey at Charo he was unaffectedly happy for the first time in a long, long while. The ordeal with Cleburne was behind him; the offer from Galvin was a rare bright spot and had given him some hope. And tonight they would have steaks on the big grill built for him by the engineers at Sông Bé – *for a paltry five pistol belts*. He dropped his rifle and pack by the CP and reached into the company headquarters cooler for a beer, popped the tab top and took a large gulp of cold Budweiser. Holmes was eyeing him with a strange, faraway look as was Heavy, whose arm was wrapped and held in a sling from the bullet wound to his shoulder.

"Sir, word just come in from Japan," First Sergeant Overton said quietly, not wanting to look him in the eye. EB and two others had made it to the American hospital there. "We got good reports about Heller and Mitchell bein' well enough to go to Walter Reed."

"And EB? How long before he goes stateside?"

"Sir, for all the world I wish I didn't have to tell you this... but EB... he ain't goin' home like that. He didn't make it, sir. There weren't nothin' the docs could do for him."

Glenn was torn with rage and grabbed Overton's jungle fatigue shirt with both hands and shook him. "He's fine, dammit. I *know* he is. Go find me the truth this time!"

"Sir, wishin' him alive won't make it so."

"He looked around fiercely at the soldiers in his CP.

None of them would look at him.

*   *

Dear Mary Anne –

I'm worn out. I'm ready for this to be over. I think about you all the time. Nine months since I've last seen you seems like eternity.

I can't put in words how much I long to be away from here and with you in Hawaii - the anticipation is more that I can bear.

Every once in a great while I get to see Benny since we're in the same battalion. There is safety and solace in numbers. Benny is still Benny.

Surprised? Me neither.

It's even nice for me to have my little brother around. We didn't spend a lot of time doing things together growing up. We ran with different crowds and had different interests, but he's now become more interesting. I've flown with him and my opinion is that every one of his landings is basically a controlled crash.

He met a girl in Australia when he was on R&R. I have no idea if that's heading anywhere. Probably not –

One thing I'll never be able to explain is the American press. Within days of our exiting Cambodia, a reporter from U.S. News & World Report showed up wanting to do a story. My company was on the firebase and my commander pointed me out. It was eye opening. The guy said he wanted to do a story on how enemy booby traps affected morale. The problem was that we had never encountered booby traps, nor had anyone in the Cav as far as I knew. He insisted we had. I insisted we hadn't and tried to educate him. No luck. A month later a story came out by this guy describing how the morale in our battalion suffered because of NVA booby traps. Gotta love journalism.

Another reporter showed up from TIME magazine wanting to do a story. This one was sent by division headquarters. He was a Frenchman who'd served in one of their Army units in the past for a year or two. He prided himself on being an expert on Southeast Asia, a modern liberal thinker about war, drugs, sex, rock and roll and the U.S. military. His questions were more like statements with a little inflection on the end and I got a bad feeling about what was going on and began to back off. He picked up on it and claimed that he and his photographer weren't the "hit squad." A sure sign they were. The two of them spent a total of a week with the company, four days in the field and then a couple of days on the firebase. Something tells me this isn't going to end well. I guess we'll see.

They say that the first casualty of war is Truth. That's TRUE! Amazing the lack of integrity in the press about this war and who knows what else.

What most interests me right now is seeing you again. The pictures you sent of you at the beach were great – I loved them, but it's just wasn't enough. Even though we're going to Hawaii with Benny and Deanna, and I'm looking forward to 'pal-ing around' the way we used to in Germany, I honestly want to spend all my time with you in the Royal Hawaiian rather than with them. I told that to Benny a week ago and he wasn't insulted.

I'll see you at the Reception Center in Honolulu three weeks from now.

I love you more than ever and I think about you every free moment.

All my love,
Glenn

While First Air Cavalry Division military activity from January through June of 1970 was at a high level, the months following the division's departure from Cambodia were some of the most peaceful for the Skytroopers in the history of the Vietnam Conflict.

For the 1st Battalion 6th Cavalry, the four month period beginning in March found the unit at or near the top of the division in terms of the number of enemy killed and amount of enemy materiel captured. For a six week period after the first week of July 1970, their contact with the NVA inside South Vietnam fell to practically zero. This development brought with it a new set of problems, euphemistically called opportunities and challenges.

There is a generally accepted truism, shared by American ground combat soldiers, that seems to have grown up through the conflicts of twentieth century generally stating: *Combat is days and weeks of boredom interrupted by moments of sheer terror.* This was especially true in the mountain jungles along the border with Cambodia in the weeks after the "Incursion".

The North Vietnamese in III and IV Corps, if not wholly eradicated, were dealt a serious setback by America's brief, surprise foray into their untouchable sanctuaries inside Cambodia north of Saigon. The amount of supplies captured and enemy troops killed all but ended their ability to conduct operations against American forces or the Army of South Vietnam in the provinces in and around Saigon from the Cambodian border to the South China Sea.

This situation did not last terribly long.

*   *   *

It was the middle of the afternoon and from LZ Evita, Glenn could see ten miles west, across a broad, heavily jungled valley dotted with open areas perfect for helicopter operations.

The monsoon had played itself out and they were back again into the dry season; as chill, wet and miserable as the monsoon had been, the dry season was even more unpleasant. The jungle remained damp beneath the triple canopy, and the smell of rotted vegetation still overpowered. The heat soared during the day and where before their fatigues were soaked by the constant rain, they were now soaked by their own sweat.

The previous afternoon Alpha company had come onto the firebase, recently reopened by the battalion. It was the time to unwind and finally get a shower under a dripping five gallon bucket, a haircut, a shave and a clean set of jungle fatigues. He would give them a day to relax before running them through a training regimen overseen by the platoon leaders.

He was nine months into his tour, six months of that commanding Alpha. His soldiers now were younger, newer, and less experienced. Over half had come to the unit since the time of the river crossing and they were draftees who made little pretense of desiring to seek out and engage the NVA – their problem was that he did and while some of his soldiers wanted to play 'search and avoid', Glenn's sole focus was on finding the NVA and eliminating them.

Only Rankin remained of the officers who'd been there when he came aboard.

He was watching a familiar scene playing out less than five miles away in the valley - out there. Amid pillars of smoke from artillery explosions and rockets from Cobra gunships, his buddy Benny and his Bravo company were fighting off a determined NVA attack.

The NVA had initiated the contact with a heavy mortar attack, and that meant it was a force of some size and sophistication. The artillery on Evita had been firing for an hour and already a second team of gunships were on station ready to join the battle. Glenn had been in the TOC when the fight started and heard Benny's voice on the radio, shrill and insistent, reporting details and initial casualties. It didn't sound good – *it never does*, he told himself.

But he sensed this firefight was different.

Most of their engagements with the NVA in the past two months had been minor and short-lived, lasting only brief minutes before the NVA broke contact. The enemy no longer seemed to have the power or the will. He'd been called to 1st Cav Division (Rear) on his company's last stay on LZ Evita to debrief a recent operation and one of the field grade planners commented that it seemed the war was over since the end of the Cambodian incursion, as if that was disappointing. *Rear area commando*, Glenn had thought to himself. His most consistent, nagging problem was keeping the company constantly vigilant. Comments like that made his job that much harder.

An edict had come down through the chain of command that artillery rounds were being 'allocated' – limited to 'essential missions', whatever that meant. It was ludicrous.

What a way to fight a war.

As he sat at the company command post bunker, twenty yards from the TOC, he saw Boomer Cameron come outside, look at the distant smoke of battle and head down the hill in his direction.

Don't do this to us, Boomer. We just got here. Bravo company can handle this.

"Saddle up your company, Nolan. The lift birds will be here in a half hour. Your mission is to link up with Bravo and provide them support. They're getting eaten up by those mortars."

Glenn couldn't believe it. "It'll be dark in a couple of hours."

"Then you'll have to be careful."

"You want us to link up at night with a company that's been in a serious firefight most of an afternoon? That's crazy."

"No, that's your mission, and you'll do it, captain. Get your company ready to go and come up to the TOC for a briefing. We're putting you into the 'football field'. You've been in there before – it's no more than five hundred meters from B company's position. You don't have much time," the operations officer said and went back up the hill.

Glenn gazed after him and looked at his RTO who had replaced EB. *Almost three months*, he thought. The radio operator was already on the horn telling the platoon leaders about the change of plans. Schlosser was now one of the old hands; he'd been assigned to Alpha the day after Nolan had taken command and after working with Glenn for only a week, knew without being told what to communicate, to whom and how.

"Well, 'Shy', hell of a development, eh?" Glenn asked, and saw the soldier shrug. Schlosser's quiet, retiring diffidence, which had earned him the nickname, was starkly distinct from EB's brash cockiness and presumptuousness. "Back in the frickin' war to bail out Bravo. We won't even get our damned steak dinner now."

Shy shrugged again. "Don't mean nuthin'." It was the Vietnam grunt's answer to every rotten deal and disappointment.

"You got that right. Round up Holmes, Doc, Masika and Mikey Meade's crew for me."

At the briefing, he learned from Boomer that Benny's situation was worse than he'd suspected. Bravo company was surrounded; he reported three dead and several more wounded and was running low on ammunition. By the time the flight of five helicopters arrived, forty minutes had passed and Benny's situation had gone from bad to worse. Glenn's anxiety continued to grow. It would take four turnarounds to move his whole company and once on the ground they might have a half hour of light, no more. Moving through an NVA force willing to stay and slug it out with a U.S. company and attempting to link up in darkness would leave him open to walking into an NVA ambush and the real prospect of Americans firing on Americans. He hoped the enemy would be scared off by the show of force from reinforcements and that they'd break contact. Realistically, wasn't counting on it.

When they finally took off, daylight was fading fast and so was Nolan's optimism.

Once all of Alpha was on the ground, Colonel Blair in the C&C was barely able to see the smoke from each company and give Nolan a distance and heading to Bravo company before having to depart. Glenn had insisted Boomer get him some kind of night capable Air Force support to provide him cover for the move. To his surprise a C-130 gunship arrived on station shortly after his last sortie of troops were on the ground. He remembered they'd had a similar aircraft at Illingworth the night of the attack – it had lingered on station for a long time and was surprisingly effective.

Alpha company assembled and moved a hundred meters in the dark before Glenn called a halt and formed the company into a night perimeter. He called Benny on the secure radio.

"Ben-bo, this linking up in the dark is really a bad idea. My guys are super edgy and I'm sure your guys are too. What's going on with you? I don't hear any firing from your direction."

"*The gooks pulled back when you guys came in*," Benny replied, sounding prickly and worn out. "*Don't know which direction they went. Last contact was a half hour ago.*"

"No probes? Nothing?"

"*Nothing.*"

Nolan debated, and finally said, "I don't care what battalion said. I'm staying put about four hundred meters from you – a heading of two-six-five degrees from your location. I've got C-130 gunship on station and I'm going to have him make a few runs halfway between us with his mini-gun. Can you mark your position with any kind of light – a strobe light... anything?"

"*Negative on that. I wouldn't even if I could!*"

"Okay, I can."

"*You sure this is a good idea?*"

Over the next half hour the Air Force gunship fired his mini-gun on several passes between the companies; the ship lingered another hour, made two more runs and departed.

Early the next morning the two cautious, skittish infantry companies finally linked up. He found his old roommate sitting on his helmet, talking on the radio. Benny gazed up at him with bloodshot eyes, looking completely exhausted.

"You and your boys get prettied up for us, or you going somewhere special?" Glenn asked when he saw Benny's troops wore a thick, fresh layer of camouflage paint on their faces. Barnes always made a big show of using the black, green and brown camo sticks when he was either going to or leaving the firebase, and was the only company in the battalion that did. He wondered if they really used them much for the three to four week stretches in the field.

"Got to look good for the boss," Benny replied. "He's pulling us back to Evita."

"Pulling *you* back? I didn't hear about that. What's this? This is our rotation on the LZ."

"He told me yesterday when you guys started inbound. I've got a pickup time of high noon. You're supposed to clear the route back to the 'football field' and cover our extraction."

"I was tasked to get the NVA off your back. Mission accomplished. I got things to do." Glenn was surprised, borderline angry, and wondered if Benny was making it up. He'd planned to turn the company over to the XO for a few days and go back to Phouc Vinh to spend a day flying with Brad. He'd done it before and had gotten thirty hours of stick time flying the Huey under his belt. He told himself it was business – liaison with the aviators – but it was really about having fun. "I heard nothing about switching places with you."

Benny produced an impatient, furtive smile. "You're the one always sayin' how you'd rather be in the bush than on the damned firebase. If you're unhappy, take it up with Blair."

"Navigate your own way to the LZ. We'll find which direction the gooks went and head that way. We'll keep them occupied while you guys get extracted. Give me a half hour."

Thirty minutes later, after Two Hatchets and Case Newman's squad found signs of the North Vietnamese withdrawal, Alpha company headed south in pursuit of the enemy while Bravo headed west toward the landing zone.

Shortly before noon, Second platoon engaged a small enemy element southeast of their location; Newman's squad found a spot where a mortar base had been laid and a few minutes later fired on four men carrying mortar rounds strapped to their backs.

Three times that afternoon they moved the company patrol base further south; an hour before sunset third platoon encountered a large force a hundred meters south of the company and started a firefight that lasted almost until dark.

It had been a long, hot and tiring day of running gun battles and pressuring the enemy so they couldn't rest long enough to mount a coordinated attack; they had counted six enemy dead. The NVA used the darkness to slip away, but Glenn worried that the last contact had given them a good fix on Alpha company's position. He pointed due East two hundred meters to set up for the night. "No complaints, no argument, just do it," he told his platoon leaders... and be quiet about it. Real quiet."

By the time Alpha stopped to set up for the night, it was barely light enough to see across the perimeter as his tired troops quietly formed their night defensive position. Mikey Meade was making a radio call when the first ominous hollow *THUNK* of a mortar round leaving its tube echoed through the jungle; it was followed by three more. Everyone froze. Glenn's heart jumped, and the company waited. Nothing in the jungle struck terror like the sound of enemy mortar fire – there was no way of knowing where it was going to land or when, and the silent waiting between the sound of a round firing and the explosion seemed to linger forever.

The explosions erupted two hundred meters away – in the location where they had been twenty minutes earlier, before crabbing off to the flank. Meade began adjusting artillery toward where they'd heard the hollow echo of enemy mortars firing; Holmes whispered urgently on the battalion radio frequency and finally handed the handset to Nolan.

American artillery fell dangerously close to them now; Glenn could tell it should be on top of the North Vietnamese. Meade kept it going for a quarter hour, and then the jungle went silent. Still nervous, Alpha silently went about setting out trip flares and Claymores, finally settling into fifty percent security. An hour after the first mortar rounds were fired, he heard the sound of wood being chopped. *Stretchers,* he thought. In less than a minute, 105mm artillery from Evita again fell on the enemy mortar platoon.

For the rest of the night, there was no more NVA activity.

Chapter 31

A brilliant, perfectly formed rainbow arched above the sundrenched mountains of Oahu.

Glenn Nolan stepped from the bus onto the wet parking lot of the Fort DeRussey Reception Center in the Waikiki area of Honolulu, looked around and said, "Finally!"

The flight was a day late arriving because of a maintenance problem and unplanned stopover in Manila, making it an unbearably long journey from Saigon. He tried unsuccessfully to convince himself that maybe it was all for the best. His – and Benny's – original plan was that both of them would fly out of Saigon on the same plane to meet their wives in Honolulu and go from there without a rigid schedule. But Benny had been late getting his request in and he'd been assigned a flight out of Cam Ranh Bay that left a day after Glenn's. Now, it looked like he would land only a few hours after Nolan's mechanically delayed arrival.

Glenn entered the large, chaotic throng in DeRussey's huge reception hall. The place was filled with noise – dozens upon dozens of couples embracing and kissing, people shouting and women breaking past the hopelessly outmatched uniformed guards to run to their husbands or boyfriends. He looked around the crowd of women still behind the rope barrier and finally located Deanna and Mary Anne at the same instant they spotted him. Even in the noise of the crowd, he could hear her call his name and saw her duck lithely beneath the rope and run toward him.

From a yard away she leapt at him, knocked off his overseas cap and wrapped her arms around his neck as he swung her around, kissing her and then whispering urgently in his ear. The whole episode seemed to happen in adrenaline-induced slow motion. Her words bubbled out tripping over one another as she laughed and cried, said over and over she loved him while chastising him for being late. He kissed her again – a long, lingering kiss – and she whispered in his ear: "Take me to the hotel room now or lose me forever, soldier."

"I'm not ever going to lose you, sweet thing."

"What are you waiting for? It's just a short walk."

"I hate to interrupt, but have either of you seen my Benny?"

Glenn and Mary Anne turned their heads to look at Deanna.

"He probably didn't have time to tell you," Glenn said, "but typical of my old buddy, he messed up. He got himself booked on a different flight that left a day later than what we'd planned. The good news, is that should put him here a little later this afternoon. A couple hours at the most. If you want, I can check on the flight ETA for you."

"He didn't mean that," Mary Anne said quickly. "I've got him booked for the rest of the day... and tonight. I'm afraid you're on your own for the next few hours... Sorry."

"No, you're not," Deanna replied. "I wouldn't be if the roles were reversed. Let's plan to meet for breakfast in the morning around nine."

"If we're not there call the room at noon or leave a message at the front desk," Mary Anne said and winked at her friend. Glenn picked up his small bag and took Mary Anne's arm, leading her outside where the midday sun was shining and the fronds of tall coconut palms surrounding the DeRussey reception hall swayed in the gentle breeze.

"The *Royal Hawaiian* was good enough to give us a room with a balcony and of a view of both the ocean *and* Diamond Head," Mary Anne told him as they walked across the park holding on to his arm and resting her head on his shoulder.

"Why did you choose that old place? It's been around for a hundred years, hasn't it?" He remembered as a kid returning to the States from his father's assignment in Japan. They stopped in Hawaii and his mother had wanted to stay there. It was fully booked, but he and Brad had wandered through the hotel's first floor halls and outside gardens one day at the beach. His recollection was that it was a large pink castle that looked like an ancient Spanish mission in Texas or Southern California.

"Less than fifty years as a hotel. Hold your water, Glenn, until you've seen it. I promise you'll like it."

And he did.

He let out a low whistle when she opened the door. It wasn't just a room with a great view – it was a two bedroom suite with a giant four-poster bed in the master bedroom, a large sitting room and doors opening not to a balcony but a huge, covered lanai with an unrivaled view of Waikiki's beach. A basket of flowers sat on a sideboard in the sitting room and another of fruit had been placed on a dining table outside.

"I'm sure I can't afford this," he said looking around. "I expected we'd have a decent room, but what I had in mind was like roughing it compared to this."

"You want to rough it? We can do that. I'll tell them to give us slow room service." She grabbed him by the arm, pulled him inside and pushed him backward onto the bed. Jumping on top of him, she began kissing his face, his neck and his mouth while unbuttoning his khaki uniform shirt. Her breath came in quick, short gasps as she unbuckled his belt. "Oh, I missed you. I missed this! We're not leaving this room, Glenn Nolan, until you make up for staying away all these months."

"And if we get hungry?"

"We've got room service... slow room service."

She stood, pulled the brightly colored sundress over her head, and let him look at her momentarily; then she pushed him to his back again and slid next to him.

Late afternoon shadows were lengthening across the lanai and a cool ocean breeze wafted through their room.

They lay on the bed together naked, propped against pillows and covered with a single sheet; her head rested on his shoulder and they sipped from fine crystal wine glasses. He turned his head and looked out toward the deep blue of the Pacific. All his life he'd been a vivid dreamer with visons so intense and memorable they often seemed more real than life itself.

I hope this isn't one of those dreams.

"What did you say?" Mary Anne asked softy.

"Nothing."

"It was something. Something about a dream."

"I was just thinking that I hope this isn't a dream."

"I guarantee it's not." She reached beneath the cover and ran her hand down his thigh while nibbling on his ear. "That doesn't happen in your dreams."

"It does when I dream of you." He again looked outside at the ocean and then back at her. She was the most gorgeous woman ever, and she was his. He wrapped an arm around her. "Nothing and nobody compares to you. I'm the luckiest man in the world. There may be a million guys who think that, but I'm the only one who's right."

She smiled up at him. "Why don't I order Chateaubriand for two and a bottle of that Riesling we liked so much in Augsburg? We can eat outside on the lanai by candlelight as the sun goes down and then you can make love to me again."

"I don't think I care to wait that long."

"I hoped you'd say that." She kissed him, purred seductively and pressed her body against him.

"You were such a sweet, innocent little private school girl..."

"I *was*. But that was before I met you." She stroked his face and ran a finger down the length of his nose. Her mind drifted back to their first date after he'd gotten his driver's license.

By then it was clear to her she'd found her life's love, her mate. She remembered thinking at the time how lucky she was – he was a handsome catch. All her friends said so. Tall. Dark. An exceptional athlete who also knew how to dance and kiss. And he was... substantial – that was the word her best friend Kalista used in describing him. He was accomplished at everything he tried – sports, academics... he was taking flying lessons and had lived in foreign countries much of his life. Mr. Substantial. He had taken her to the drive-in north of the city, in Timonium, on that first 'car date'; all she remembered of the movie was the title – *Charade,* and that Audrey Hepburn was the female lead. It wasn't all that she recalled. She remembered being pleasantly shocked he'd known how to undo her bra.

"It was hard at times, but I'm glad we waited this long for R&R," Mary Anne whispered in his ear. "Less than eight weeks until you come home for good."

He pressed a finger against her lips. "No talk of that. Not this week. I don't want to be reminded of anything about 'over there' while we're together. There's nothing that exists outside you and me. Us. If we never leave this room over the next six days, I'll be the happiest guy in history. All I want to do is be with you."

She rolled on top of him and smothered him with kisses. "Oh, Glenn...

There was a knock on the door – three hard raps. Before either could speak, the knock was repeated. This time it was more urgent. Mary Anne put a finger to his lips.

"I don't care who that is," she whispered, "we're not letting anybody intrude on this."

"Mary Anne! Mary Anne!... Glenn! Are you in there. I've got to talk to you!"

Mary Anne cupped her hand over his mouth. "Benny's flight is delayed, like yours was," she whispered. "She doesn't know what to do with herself and wants some company, that's all. We're not going to let that –"

"It's something important," he said.

"Mary Anne! Glenn!... I really need to talk to you guys! Please!! Please let me in!"

"Listen to her. She's frantic," Glenn said. "That's not like Deanna."

"But you said..."

"Maybe she's been injured or... I don't know. She needs help." He pulled the cover back and put on the heavy terry cloth robe with its embroidered hotel coat of arms on the breast pocket. "Give us a minute," he called out.

When he opened the door, she burst out crying and clung to him.

"It's just... He's dead, Glenn. Benny's dead!"

"No. That's not possible," he said, shaken. "I just saw him three days ago. He's fine. This is some kind of mix up."

"No, Glenn. They told me he didn't make it."

"Trust me. It's just another one of the Army's failures of communication." He was furious. *Damn the Army for doing this to her... to him.* It was impossible.

Benny had been on LZ Evita – he'd seen him there when he left headed for Saigon. Benny's company was in the field getting resupplied and he'd come in on the log bird. He planned to spend that day on the firebase before catching a ride to Phouc Vinh and then an Air Force Caribou to Cam Ranh. Evita hadn't been mortared since they reopened it over two months ago and action in the area had been all but non-existent for a couple of weeks. This was some monumental screw up; he was certain.

"Give me a few minutes to get clothes on and I'll go back to the Reception Center with you. We'll wait together for the plane he's on. This is just some typical Army screw-up."

"The plane landed an hour ago! He wasn't on it!" she wailed. "I was standing there with all the other wives before the busses pulled up and I saw the soldiers in their summer greens walking around calling out names. One by one as they stepped forward the soldiers whispered something to each and I could see those women melt before my eyes. I realized what was happening – they were being told their husbands weren't coming! That they didn't make it out." Deanna rambled wildly, her eyes wide and bloodshot, tears streaming down her face. She sobbed and pressed her head against his chest. "And then... and then they called out my name and I thought – oh, no! oh no! Not Benny! But it was! What am I going to do, Glenn? What am I going to do now?!"

"Right now, you're going to sit down here with us and stay calm. We'll get you a large glass of ice water, and you have to drink it. You hear me?" He helped her out to the lanai to an overstuffed wicker chair with an ottoman. "Have you had anything to eat this afternoon? All right, we'll get you some fruit. I want you to drink the water and eat some fruit, and then we'll get you something more solid. That's what you do now, before we do anything else. I'm going over to DeRussey to check out this story. Your job is to stay here until I get back. All right? Are we clear on that, Deanna?"

She nodded, sighed and gave him the most forlorn look he'd ever seen.

"Good. I'll be back as soon as I can." He went inside the suite and looked for the suitcase of his clothes Mary Anne had brought. "Keep her occupied until I get back," he told her. "Give her water, coffee, some fruit. No booze. That'll make things worse. Order some dinner and get her to eat. More than anything, she needs a friend to talk with – someone to listen. We're her friends. We have to get her through this."

Mary Anne's heart sank. *Why this? Why now?!*

"How long do you think this is going to take?" she asked.

"No idea," he replied, his mind whirling. "I'm not even sure DeRussey has the communications necessary to check this out. Probably not. I'll have to find a place where I can communicate back to Vietnam. Somewhere that has an HF hookup. Hawaii has all kinds of commo throughout the Pacific. I'll find something."

"Oh, Glenn!"

He heard the distress, the utter disappointment, in her voice.

"This happens in the military, Mary Anne. We're our own community – a family, more or less. A sad, sometimes dysfunctional family that has to look out for its own."

He remembered the time at Edwards when his father was test flying the F-4 and there had been a terrible accident. People came and went all night through their house. It was frightening and utterly confusing to him at the time. He remembered his father taking charge and helping a woman he remembered only as 'Rebel's wife'. Her wailing was much like that of his best friend's widow. *Not his widow, damn it Nolan. Not his widow... not yet!*

*   *

The boarding call for Deanna's Los Angeles flight was announced.

"You two have been the greatest. Really. I couldn't have gotten through this week without you. I'm still not over it, but I'm better, thanks to you guys." She tried to smile gamely, took a few deep breaths and then gave Mary Anne a hug.

It had been a difficult four days for all of them.

Glenn had spent the first forty-eight hours trying to reach First Cavalry Division headquarters after Deanna's arrival at their room. He'd gone to Fort DeRussey, Joint Base Pearl Harbor-Hickam, and Fort Shafter. Nobody was able to put him in communication with his division and few were even interested in trying. Frustrated with the Army and Air Force, he tried the Navy and stumbled across a facility commanded by a senior Navy Captain responsible for all the military communications throughout the Pacific for the Department of Defense. Finally, he was able to convince a section chief in charge of HF communications to help. By the end of the second day he was patched through a series of commo links all the way to Sông Bé and was able to talk to the battalion personnel officer who confirmed Benny's death. The story he was told about the circumstances was not only plausible, it was understandable... and reasonable knowing Benny.

Benny's company was attacked near the completion of its resupply day after Glenn had departed for Saigon. Bravo company was temporarily commanded by one of the platoon leaders while Barnes was on R&R, but when the firefight broke out Benny convinced the log bird pilot to take him back out to the company. Five minutes after landing, a B-40 rocket exploded inches from him. He was the only American killed that day.

"I'm sorry," Glenn said to Mary Anne as they waved goodbye to Deanna when she went down the jet-way. "I've paid hardly any attention to you since I got here."

"I have to admit I wasn't happy about it the first couple of days." She gave him a brave, sad smile. "You're a good person, Glenn. You always have been. You're generous with people. It's one of the things I admire most about you. I don't know anybody who would or could have done what you did for her – all the phone calls from friends, arranging the flight home and someone to meet her at the airport; the stories about you and Benny... you even got her to laugh a few times. "

"Ben-bo was a character. But I was doing it for me, too. As long as I was busy, I didn't have to think about it too much. The stories were..." He looked down and shook his head. "He was like a brother – I was closer to him than to Brad. I'm going to miss Benny a lot."

"We all will." She slipped her arm under his and rested her head on his shoulder, watching down the long jet-way until Deanna was out of sight. "But Glenn Nolan, we're not going to let anything else get in the way of this R&R now. We have two days to pack in a week's worth of sights and sounds... and other things. You and I can grieve more later, but today and tomorrow we're putting everything out of our minds except each other and this island. No military talk, no visiting the Arizona memorial, nothing but you and me. First stop is for authentic Hawaii shave ice – and then out to the north shore to watch the surfers. A dash through the pineapple plantations and some snorkeling in *Hanauma Bay*. There's a five-star luau on the beach right in front of the hotel tonight."

"We're going to do all that in what's left of today? You're going to wear me out, girl."

"It's a short walk from the luau to the bedroom. You'd better not be worn out." Mary Anne took his arm and guided him away from the crowded passenger gate and down the long passageway leading outside. She was relieved the ordeal was over, but felt guilty. Benny had been her friend, too, and she'd spent most of her adult life very close to Deanna.

Put that out of your mind! she said to herself. *For now.* What was that phrase Sister Deline at school was always saying? A Bible verse, wasn't it? – *'tomorrow will be anxious for itself... sufficient for the day is its own trouble.'* No more trouble for today. We've had plenty enough already.

As they passed a large newsstand, a display of the latest *TIME* magazine caught her eye. On the cover was the scruffy face of a bareheaded soldier – his beard was dark and long, like his hair. He was frowning and pointing at something. *What in the world is Glenn's picture doing on the front of a national magazine?* she wondered. *This can't be good, and we've had all the bad news we can handle for a while.* She tried to divert his attention.

"What the hell?!" he said. He stopped and glared at the magazine cover, then picked up a copy and started thumbing through it.

"Glenn, please don't."

"Don't what?" he replied.

"Don't get all wrapped around that picture."

"It's not just the picture!" he said in a loud voice that gained the attention of the middle aged Hawaiian behind the counter.

"You want to buy copy of magazine?"

Nolan pulled a dollar out his wallet and handed it over. His face grew severe and he muttered, "Look at this! *Not The Army It Once Was*. What the hell kind of title is that?! Damn that guy!" Several people near the stand turned at the loud sound of his voice and looked disapprovingly down their noses at him.

"Glenn, don't spoil what little is left of our time in Hawaii. Don't read that magazine now. Do it on the plane going back. Please wait 'til later, all right?"

"Later? I'm not going to ruin these next couple of days. But it's not every day that my picture gets plastered on the front of a national magazine, and under a title like that. That son-of-a-bitch told me that if and when the article came out he'd deliver me the very first copy before it hit the streets. So much for honesty in the media. What a damned fool I am! Look at these pictures and the captions and the tag line quotes. This article makes it sound like we're a bunch of dopers and shirkers."

It had happened; she could see him building into an angry frenzy as he looked through the pages and knew from experience he'd be a long, long time getting over it – probably days or weeks. *So much for an idyllic day on Oahu followed by a luau and a romantic evening on the lanai afterward*, she thought.

I hate this war and this Army... I hate everything about them both.

Chapter 32

The loud slapping of the Huey's main rotor blades beat down on the tiny jungle opening as the helicopter descended and came to rest. It was swarmed by a half dozen troops in dirty jungle fatigues throwing boxes and duffle bags from the cargo compartment.

Glenn Nolan climbed down wearing a rucksack and carrying his rifle easily in hand.

"What you doin' here, Six?" Masika yelled in his ear over the turbine engine noise.

"Finishing out my tour. Where's the CP?" the soldier pointed with a finger and he headed in that direction. Holmes and gawked at him when he threw down his rucksack and steel pot next to the radio. "Get the platoon leaders up here," he ordered.

He was angry. And he had been for a solid week, since putting Deanna on the plane home at the Honolulu Airport.

The last three days of R&R with Mary Anne had been an utter catastrophe – and it was his fault. Everything and everybody who crossed his path had managed to set him off; Benny's death, the damned article by the Frenchman in *TIME*, the traffic on Oahu; even Mary Anne telling him to cool down or pleading with him to relax and enjoy the few days left in Hawaii had irritated him. He couldn't stop himself. The return to Vietnam and his first night back was just as disastrous.

He'd spent that initial night at the 1st Cav headquarters in Bien Hoa, a couple dozen miles from Saigon. During dinner at the Officer's Mess a major had recognized him and asked if he was the one in the recent article on the cover of the magazine. Then he'd made some disparaging remarks about the lack of discipline and leadership in line companies. Glenn had stood abruptly and offered to educate the officer outside. Glenn called him a coward, a fool for believing anything in the press, and a satire upon soldiership and honor. Dinner ended hurriedly and the other officers left Nolan to finish his meal alone.

His return to the battalion was less problematic.

He'd convinced the colonel to let him resume command of Alpha since he'd only been gone a week and the battalion was now suddenly two company commanders short. He'd gone straight back to the field with only a quick thirty minute Ops and Intel briefing.

Looking around now he was struck by the realization that only Holmes remained from his original CP and he was due to rotate home in a few weeks. First Sergeant Overton was gone. He was starting all over again.

That was fine with him. There was a small core of the old hands he knew and could count on. Case Newman was still around and he could build what he wanted around the young buck sergeant. The NVA were either still recovering from the body blows they'd been dealt in May and June, or they were concentrating on replacing supplies rather than engaging in combat. Either way, he'd find and deal with them – for EB, and Timmy Horner; and for Benny. The war was winding down in the 1st Cav area and so they would have to take more risks, be more audacious with their patrolling. He didn't have much time left on his tour; but he planned to remedy that.

"Surprised you're back. How much longer before you DEROS?" Meade asked.

He turned and looked at the artillery spotter who was running his fingers through his long, dark hair. "Two months on this tour, Mikey. I'm thinking about extending for six and getting an ARVN advisor slot with MACV."

"You're not serious," Meade said, screwing his face into a frown. You don't really want to be out in the bush with them, do you?"

"Somebody's got to."

"If you're really goin', sir, then I want to go with you," Newman said from behind him. Glenn turned and saw the sergeant looking at him with his sly, devilish smile.

"You still got time left on this tour, Case. The Cav isn't going to let you go."

"My old platoon sergeant from back in the 4th Division is in the personnel section at MACV and he can make it happen. For both of us. But sir, if you're goin', then I want to be there with you."

"We'll see. For now, we've got to get out of this log site and disappear back into the woods. The company's been here all day and I want to get a move on as soon as I can talk to the platoon leaders. How's second platoon doing?"

"Well, sir, it's like this – we got us two cherry machine gunners. Last two log days, we picked up a half dozen replacements and they're all dumb as a stump, sir. Looks like Basic Training is doin' a decent job sucking all that civilian nonsense out of their heads, but a piss poor job of replacin' it with military smarts."

"Situation normal. That's why the good Lord created platoon sergeants like you, and why you need to stay here to train up our troops."

Minutes later he was briefing the platoon leaders on his return to the company and future operations. Forrest had been leading 2nd platoon for five months and would be rotating out in another three or four weeks for a rear area job. The other two platoon leaders were new and green. Sewall was an Academy grad, the younger brother of a classmate from the school, who had arrived three weeks earlier and had immediately worried Nolan because of his odd behavior and aloofness from the troops. Krulack was fresh out of OCS and had the look of a yearling deer caught in headlights. Glenn realized he'd be spending all his time on patrol watching and training both, a prospect he welcomed.

A few minutes later, he'd given the order to move out when a single shot rang out from the 2nd platoon area causing everyone to hit the ground. Glenn dropped his rucksack and ran toward the sound. When he got to the platoon, Lieutenant Forrest and Case Newman were standing over a young trooper who was writhing on the ground, attended by the platoon medic.

"Asshole shot himself in the foot," the platoon sergeant said. "New guy."

"Accident?" Glenn asked.

Newman shook his head negatively. "His squad leader and one other guy saw him do it on purpose. I seen it before, sir. Had a guy in my squad on the first tour who did it, and heard of it happenin' twice in another company. Nicked himself between the big toe and the next one. That's painful as hell but it ain't fatal."

"What's your name, soldier?" Glenn asked, kneeling next to him.

"Guthrie. Rob Guthrie."

"Does it hurt?"

"Hurts like crazy, sir. You got to get me out of here. I need a doctor."

"First of all, Guthrie, I'm the company commander. I give orders to you, not the other way around. You're not going back to the rear until your court martial comes up. Probably a couple of months from now. Until then, I'm declaring you fit for duty."

"Sir, you can't do that," the medic said. "However it happened, he's wounded and we've got to medevac him out. Walking on that foot will be really, really painful."

Glenn slowly turned his head, staring malevolently at the medic, a Spec-4 who had come into the company two weeks before Cambodia. "Walters, I'm not risking the lives of my soldiers by waiting around here after announcing our location to the entire world for the past six hours with helicopters and now a gunshot. We're moving out. You patch him up and get him ready to move. If it takes longer than thirty seconds, you'll have to catch up to us. And you, Private Guthrie... if and when I let you out of the field, you're going straight to Long Binh Jail, where you'll have all the time in the world to sit and moan about the pain from your self-inflicted wound." Glenn stood and walked through the jungle toward the company CP.

*　　*　　*

He awoke from a nightmare in which he'd been tied spread-eagle to four stakes on top of a mound of fire ants and termites.

He couldn't see it in the impenetrable darkness of the jungle, but Glenn knew his body was covered with pale red, itchy bumps; he could feel a terrible burning sensation. He'd had the same reaction to something twice in the past week and the CP medic, 'Doc' Haworth who took over for Timmy Horner in July, had on both occasions slathered him from head to toe with something like Calamine lotion. The itching this time was far worse. He looked at the glowing hands of his watch; it was a few minutes after three a.m.

I can gut this out 'til sunup, he told himself, scratching his arms and chest.

He willed himself to stop scratching for as long as he could but finally gave in. Looking back at his watch, only two minutes had gone by. *This is going to be one long night, Nolan.*

There was no amount of will power that could keep him from scratching the rash, and he worried that whatever was causing his whole body to break out in hives seemed to be worse this time than the previous two combined. Doc had told him not to scratch the itch because even with the zinc and ferric oxide lotion he'd run the risk of infection scraping the skin with his filthy hands. The itching sensation grew exponentially and time all but stopped.

He was light-headed, disoriented and his breathing devolved into short gasps like a dog panting after long exercise in summer heat. He started shivering followed by bouts of sweating. Glenn felt he was about to pass out and remembered a trooper in the company a month earlier coming to him as they pulled into a night location. *What was his name? Dickerson.* He'd said: *'I was just* stung by a *bee and you gotta get me a medevac – in five minutes I'm going to swell up and you're going to think I'm about to die. I'm allergic to bee stings and I got to get to a hospital right away.'*

The strength oozed from his body; Glenn tried to stand and couldn't, but managed to crawl to where he thought Haworth was. "Doc," he whispered shaking Haworth's shoulder. "Doc... I can't breathe. I can't breathe..."

And then he slumped over, unconscious.

*   *

Jenny sat up quickly in bed when the Charge of Quarters shook her. "Sorry to have to wake you, captain," the CQ said, "but your name was on top of the 'on-call' list. We've got an inbound. Twenty minutes out. One patient."

"Details?"

"Everything they told me is on the message sheet here, ma'am."

"Who's the doc on call?"

"Major Ramey. I'm going to wake him next."

She sat up, ran her fingers through her hair and dressed quickly. She finally looked at the summary sheet and was relieved to see she wouldn't have to prep the operating room for this one. A quarter hour later she and Virgil Ramey stood outside by the lighted helipad waiting on their patient. When the medevac bird sat down two hospital orderlies helped the patient out and supported him as he tried unsuccessfully to walk on his own. Jenny ran toward them, took the IV bottle from the helicopter medic, held it high and followed along behind.

"Anaphylactic Shock," Ramey said inside the operating room after reading the medics' notes stuffed inside the patient's pocket and unbuttoned the soldier's jungle fatigue shirt. "Take his pulse and blood pressure again and give him a shot of epinephrine, then sponge him down." She hesitated, looking at the patient's face. "C'mon Jen, get it together. Something wrong?"

"I know this soldier."

"All the more reason for you to hop to it. Get a move on."

Several minutes after receiving the shot Glenn opened his eyes, blinking and grimacing. He gave Jenny a ragged, anxious smile.

"Hello, soldier," she said.

"Hello yourself."

"What? No smart comeback? No witty repartee."

"My repartee-er seems to be having problems... or maybe it's disabled," he replied, looking troubled. "Where am I? Phouc Vinh?"

"You are," the doctor said. "Do you know how you got here?

"Something bit me and the next thing I know I'm on a jungle penetrator with the wind whipping through the trees and a bright spotlight on me."

"Why do you say something bit you?"

"I don't know. I saw several large centipedes the past couple of days – ugly bastards bigger around than my thumb; about a foot long and sporting big pincers. I assumed they were poisonous and that one of them got me."

"I haven't found anything anywhere on your body that would indicate that. Not a single mark. "You allergic to anything?"

"Hard work. Lead."

"I'm talking about foods – shellfish, peanuts, milk, eggs. Medications you might be on."

"Doc, I've been eating C-rations and LRRPs for almost a year, and the only meds I'm on is those damned malaria pills they force us to take."

"I hear you," Dr. Ramey replied. "We'll run some tests and see if anything pops out. How are you feeling now?"

"Embarrassed. Anxious to get back to the company. How soon can you release me?"

"It all depends. For now, you need to get some rest. Nurse, let's get him into one of the recovery room beds and keep an eye on him. Plenty of fluids, blood work every six hours."

"How soon can I get back to my company? Doc, I'm feeling great. Really."

Ramey nodded. "Sure you are. But for now we'll keep you under observation for a few days and then we'll let you know. Listen soldier, you could have died out there. In the last war you would have with something like this. Don't push your luck."

One of the orderlies, a tall blond kid, helped Glenn down the hallway, into the recovery bay and onto an Army bunk. He fell into the bed and immediately drifted off to sleep. When he awoke, early morning light was coming through the windows and Jenny was sitting on a chair next to him, asleep. He turned over and she sat up, touching his arm.

"You do this for all your patients?" he said softly.

"Only the VIPs," she whispered back, curling her fingers around his wrist to check his pulse. "How are you feeling?"

"I feel great. Honest. I'm ready to check out of here and get back to the company."

"Checking out isn't going to happen for a while." She looked at her watch. "I've got to draw some blood and take it down to the lab. After that, we'll get breakfast. And then it's bed rest for you – doctor's orders."

A half hour later they were at a small table in the corner of the mess hall.

"I feel like my old self again," he lied to her when they'd finished breakfast. "You need to tell the doctor to release me back to the unit."

"You're not your old self, Glenn," she said quietly. "You almost dropped your tray going through the line. You're still weak and your walk is unsteady. As soon as we're done here, back to bed. Let me take care of you. "

"Listen, Jen. I'm perfectly fine. Are we going to have a problem, you and I?"

"Only if you don't follow orders," she said airily. "By your own admission, this is your third episode with this allergic reaction. To what we don't know yet. Until we do, it's not safe to let you go back, even to the firebase. And certainly not to the field with your company. The next time this happens it probably will kill you. Do you have a death wish?"

"I have a mission."

"And what's that?"

"It's personal."

"Well. whatever you think it is, are you willing to chance dying for it?"

"You can give me some of that medicine you gave me last night to take with me. If by some weird chance this happens again, I can give myself a shot."

"We're not going to do that," she said softly. There was something different about him now. "Let me... let us take care of you the way you need. Sending you back to the field with a few milligrams of epinephrine and a needle won't do. That's reckless. It'd be totally harebrained for me to do that."

He became visibly agitated, drumming his fingers on the table; his eyes darted quickly around the mess hall. "I can't stay here. I've got a job – a mission and keeping guys alive. I can't keep them alive sitting here goofing off."

"You're not goofing off." She looked away. When she looked back at him, her face was troubled. "I have to ask you something. Please don't think I'm some silly school girl... Why haven't you stopped by the hospital – to visit one of your troops, to say hello, how are you doing? Thanks for patching up my guys. Not a visit, not a word from you... and I asked each one of your guys we sent back to give you my regards and pass along a note. Nothing but silence. Are you angry with me?"

"No, I'm not angry," he said, turning away. When he looked back his eyes were filled with turmoil. "I got your messages."

She was perplexed. "But you didn't respond to any of them. Why? What have I done?"

He didn't want to tell her the truth. He worried about his feelings for her because of that evening at Fort Lewis, and the two encounters at Tay Ninh. And it was his fault. He knew he was way out of line at Lewis for coming on to her the way he did. He was a married man intensely, passionately in love with his wife, as his R&R had reminded him. His thoughts about her embarrassed him, filled him with shame; talking with her now, overwhelmed him and seared his conscience. The truth was he felt guilty about her, and that scared him...

"You haven't done anything, Jenny. You're a good, sweet person. Unfortunately, I'm world's worst letter writer and an abject failure at keeping up with people. My social skills are non-existent; maybe that's why I have no friends. It's all my own fault. People tell me I'm compulsive. I guess I am. That's why I have to get out of here and get back to my troops."

She stared at him in confused amazement. "You made it completely clear from the beginning you were married and we both agreed on boundaries – that the relationship went no further than casual conversation over dinner. Since then, I saw you twice – once to give you a shot and the other time to stitch up a cut on your arm. That's hardly cause for a guilt trip."

"Yeah, you're right," he admitted at last. "I'm a little distracted now. There's so much to do. I have to get back to my troops."

She produced a relieved smile and said, "I'm glad I haven't offended you. But, honestly, Glenn, what do you really think you can accomplish in the next seven or eight weeks that you haven't already? You've spent your whole tour in the field. Most officers spend six months in the bush and six months in a reasonably comfortable staff job, call it a tour and go home."

"That's not me."

She sighed heavily and looked away. "You're not going to win this war by yourself."

"Not trying to. Just want to do my part."

"You have."

"No, there's still a lot I need to set right."

It was clear she wasn't going to help him get released any time soon. But did he really need her help? He wasn't under armed guard and the Ghostriders were pretty close by. He had a plan, and it would work.

He returned to recovery bay and fell asleep to the sound of Vietnamese conversation between two hooch maids cleaning the room. It was a musical, enchanting language he'd always thought, though he rarely heard it and understood none of it when he did. *There's a metaphor in that somewhere, Nolan*, he thought.

He slept most of the day; after dark, he dressed and walked to the *Red Hawk* where he found Brad and Ed Norton and arranged for a ride back to the battalion the following morning. By sunup he was back on LZ Evita, pleased with himself for executing his escape from the hospital. The plan had worked. But he'd planned without allowing for Jenny.

*   *

"The C.O. went back to Sông Bé last night for a briefing this morning at brigade," Boomer told him as they stood outside the TOC drinking coffee a half hour after sunrise. "He radioed out here and told me you're not going back out to Alpha. The hospital commander at Phouc Vinh went through command channels about your leaving without being officially released."

"Am I in trouble, Boomer?"

The major laughed heartily. "Nobody's planning an awards ceremony for you."

Glenn took a deep, frustrated breath. "I just want to get back to the company. I promised those guys I'd be back as they were hauling me up on that jungle penetrator."

"Not going to happen. Our commander is in no mood to do anything on your behalf just now. He's getting bombarded with questions from Washington about that damned magazine article and now this. General Abrams wants you to visit with him in Saigon. And before that, General Putnam wants to see you at Division Forward headquarters in Phouc Vinh. You're a very popular guy all of a sudden." The major shook his head and laughed again. "Maybe popular isn't the right word. The Pentagon has a lot of angst going on over the article."

"Most of that was B.S. Half quotes, or out of context. That Frenchman totally misrepresented the incident with Pineapple and –"

"You know what the real heartburn in Washington is?" Boomer interrupted. "Uniform violations, Nolan. That cover photo. You didn't have a name tag on, or insignia of branch and rank on your collars."

"That's their big beef?"

"And the fact you were unshaven."

"That's crazy."

"Obviously you've never worked in the Pentagon." Cameron poured out the last of his coffee on the ground. "The first thing you have to do is get a clean uniform and report back to the hospital and straighten out your release. Then go see General Putnam and after that, General Abrams. There's a three star down in Saigon you have to contact to set it up – sooner rather than later. You'll be gone awhile. When you get back, I'll have a plan in place to set you up on a small jump firebase with a platoon of infantry – two tubes of 105 arty, a couple of mortars, a radio and a couple of cooks."

"Am I being banished?"

"Actually not. We got IR readings a few nights ago from a Mohawk that shows some pretty heavy traffic about twelve or thirteen miles from here. The colonel tentatively agreed to put a small firebase right in the middle of those readings to see if we can scare up some action. I think I can convince him to put you in charge of it. I'll tell him we're dangling your butt out there as bait. It sounded to me like something you'd like to do."

Glenn nodded. "It sounds better than sitting on my ass in the TOC each night listening to radio silence."

"Yeah. My thought exactly. For now, you get yourself cleaned up and back to Phouc Vinh and sort out that mess you left. You're to see the head nurse at the hospital. Apparently she was the one who put out the 'All Points Bulletin' on you."

*   *

He found Jenny in an examining room of the hospital.

She was restocking a tall cabinet with medical supplies when he entered; she immediately turned her back leaving him standing in awkward silence. At last she closed the cabinet doors and turned slowly to face him; she held his gaze and detected a seething anger behind his eyes.

"You caused me a lot of trouble," Glenn said crossly.

"Not nearly as much as you caused me... *and* this hospital staff."

He took a deep breath and exhaled loudly through his nose. "I've been ordered to see you about getting officially released from here. DD form *something or another*. I'm in a hurry."

"Sorry, Captain, but that's not the way things are done in this or any other hospital," she said with deliberate calm. "There are procedures to –"

"To hell with your procedures. Just give me the damned form. I've got a lot to do."

Jenny raised her eyebrows, looking indignant but remaining calm. "The procedure for releasing patients from medical channels who were received by medevac requires an exit examination and signature of the attending physician. Dr. Ramey is on rounds with a new surgeon, so it'll be a while. Maybe an hour. You'll have to wait."

"I don't have an hour."

"I'm sorry, but that's too bad."

"No it's not! It's not too bad, and you're not sorry in the least. This is your petulant little way of getting back at me and ruining my day!"

"If I had intended to ruin your day, captain," she began deliberately, "I'd have given you what you wanted – a free pass back to your company and a *final* episode of anaphylaxis. If we had released you back to the field, the next time you came here it would be in a body bag."

"You don't know what you're talking about, damn it!"

She stared at him, fighting back an angry response and finally answered in a low, calm tone. "Of course I don't know what I'm talking about. You're so much better informed than I am, so much smarter – on everything. What would I know about anything having to do with medical conditions? And you don't have to raise your voice."

"I'm not the one who's yelling."

"Yes you are. You're also the one who's not getting his release until I can work it into my crowded schedule so all the 'I's' get dotted and 'T's' get crossed."

"Don't –" Glenn suddenly pounded a fist on the examining table and swept the instruments on a small table next to it onto the floor. "Don't do this, Jenny!" He roared. "Don't mess with me damn it! I – don't – have – the time – or patience – to put up with this crap! Get me the damned form!" he said through clenched teeth.

"Yell all you want, but no form until the doctor gives you a final checkup and reviews your blood work."

"I'm fine, my blood is fine!" He glared at her fiercely. "I've got an appointment with the division commander in fifteen minutes and I *will not* be delayed by the likes of you!"

"By the likes of me?! What's that supposed to mean?"

"You know what I mean." He had no idea why he'd said it, or even what he'd intended. Everything and everybody – even Jenny – was so damned frustrating. *What the hell is wrong with people any more*, he thought.

"I'm not so sure I do know what you meant. If you wanted to insult me, well... good for you! Mission accomplished. So now I guess I'm less important than hooch maids, latrine burners, and all the stray dogs in South Vietnam? You have some gall talking to me like that."

"What's all this noise that's going on in here?" the middle aged nurse said, sticking her head in and looking from Jenny to Glenn and back again. "What's all this yelling? You're disturbing patients in recovery."

"We were having a little discussion about release forms," Jenny said. "I let it get out of hand. Apologize to the patients for me."

"What's all this stuff on the floor?"

"Just a little accident. The table got bumped."

"Uh, huh," the nurse said warily as she looked at Glenn's name tag. "Nolan. You're that wayward patient she was trying to find for hours last evening." Glenn stared back at her without replying. "Jen, the colonel was looking for you. Why don't you see what he wants while I clean up this... accident."

"I'll clean it up, Shirley. It was my fault."

"Tell you what, if I'm not done when you get back you can help me finish the cleanup. Now, listen to mama Shirley." When Jenny left, the older nurse turned to Glenn.

"Captain," she said, drawing down her brows and scowling, "first of all, I'm going to do all the talking and you're going to do all the listening. You need to understand something. I know who you are and what you did. That girl, my head nurse, and the best head nurse I ever worked for in almost twenty years in this Army... that girl was frantic to find you last night, because she's responsible for everything that goes on in this hospital. The commander signs reports and gives speeches, but the head nurse really does all the work. And she's good at it.

"So when you went missing, that was a big deal. You need to know that because you don't have the foggiest idea what she's been through. None of you grunts do. You might see two or three wounded or killed in a given week, but since we opened this hospital back in April we've received more casualties on any given day than you've seen in total during that whole time. Grunts, artillerymen, pilots, door gunners, mechanics... Whoever. We get 'em all. You take it easy on her, you hear me. She's earned it."

"I have to have a release form."

"You heard what she said. Come back later." Nan looked at the instruments strewn on the floor. "I should make you clean this up. And I will if you're not out of here in two seconds."

Glenn stared back silently but finally turned and left. Minutes later, Jenny returned as Shirley was putting the last of the instruments in the sterilizer. "Want to talk about it, Jen?"

"He's changed since I first met him," Jenny replied softly. Her eyes were red and she looked shaken. "He was different today than I've ever seen."

"War does that to some. To a lot of them. He didn't hurt you, did he?"

"No. But he scared me," Jenny replied softly.

"Threatened you? We need to talk to the C.O. and take care of that if he did. You can't let someone get away with it. I know you know that. I've seen and heard you put most of these doctors in their place when they needed it. I didn't think much of anything scared you. But that look in your eyes tells me there's more to this story. There is, isn't there?"

"I was reminded of my Psych rotation in nursing school. I remember the doctor saying we're all on the edge of a very thin line, millimeters away from going crazy, that it's a quick jump from one side of the line to the other. I saw that in him today. The look in his eye was frightening. He's been under a lot of stress and I think he stepped across that line."

"Maybe you both did."

"No, I'm fine."

"You're sure?"

Jenny shook her head slowly up and down. "I'm sure. A little tired, maybe. Didn't get much sleep last night."

Shirley reached out and patted Jenny's hand. "It's a good thing you're going home next week, Jen. We'll miss you, but we're happy for you. Go home, unwind. Forget about this as best you can."

"I will. Believe me I will."

It was nearly impossible to believe it would be over in a few days. The end of her tour in less than a week. She would miss the girls who had gotten her through these past many months – Jill Conly, Ellen Garvey, Judy Burns, Peg Tomlinson, and more. Many more who had helped her survive this in ways large and small. As she thought of the names she saw the faces and knew they would always reside in a special place in her memory. "I'll remember these special people in all three hospitals. But I'm going try my best to forget what we had to do.

"When I get on the big bird home, I'm going to shout '*Good Riddance*' and shake off every single memory about Vietnam."

Chapter 33

Glenn turned the corner beside the Artillery Mess on the sprawling Division Forward base at Phouc Vinh. He went down the row of well-kept hooches that housed the division staff and transient officers until he reached the last of the low, sandbagged structures – a smaller building with a screened in porch. He rapped once on the door and entered. Inside, Colonel Galvin sat behind a small table scratching out notes on cards and writing in his journal; he looked up and greeted Glenn with a broad smile, leaning back in his chair.

"Thanks for coming," he said pleasantly. "I was afraid you might not be able to get away from your duties to spend time with me my last night in Vietnam. Your brother's picking me up at sunrise to shuttle me off to Saigon."

"I'm not all that busy. That small firebase we set up hasn't attracted any NVA interest. We've been trying, but no luck starting a fight." The biggest challenge he'd had there so far was figuring out how to make an antenna out of bamboo and WD-1 field wire so they could hook up a small black and white TV to watch The Bob Hope Show in Saigon on AFVN.

Galvin chuckled. "Glad I'm not taking you away from anything important."

"Didn't say it wasn't important, just that it was my biggest challenge so far."

Galvin nodded. "You've been on my mind these past few days. How did the meeting go with General Abrams?"

"Never saw him as it turned out. He was busy, I guess. I spent an evening and a morning with his deputy, a three star named Dempsey." The visit to MACV headquarters had been an anti-climax, interesting but in his mind a two day boondoggle. Creighton Abrams was on an inspection of American units in II Corps implementing his 'Clear and Hold' strategy that paired small U.S. units with ARVN regulars, a departure from Westmoreland's 'Search and Destroy' approach. Dempsey had met him at MACV headquarters, entertained him with drinks and an evening meal in his new air-conditioned double-wide trailer, and tried to make a generally meaningless visit seem consequential. "Nothing was accomplished. I guess the commanding general had pretty much already come to his conclusions about me and the company and that damned article."

"You're probably right. But not in the way you think. I've had exit interviews with Generals Putnam and Abrams and, by correspondence, General Westmoreland. I have an appointment with him as soon as I get back."

"Because of me?"

"Because of you, and that Frenchman from *TIME*. And the article he wrote." Galvin reached into a small cooler beside the field desk and handed over a cold, dripping bottle of Beck's. "That's part of the reason I asked you to come here. I'll tell you about it. But before I do, we need to talk. I've learned you're about to do something extremely unwise. The division personnel officer is an old friend, and he told me you put in for a six month extension of your tour and requested a MACV advisor's slot."

"Yes, sir, I have."

The colonel grew serious and said, "You're making a big mistake. I told your brother the same thing when I learned he requested an extension to fly Cobras for *Blue Max*."

"Brad's doing that for fun, and the thrill. I'm extending because it's important."

"Important to whom?"

"To the Vietnamese Army. We're pulling out and they're soon going to be doing all the heavy lifting. I'm not sure they're ready."

"You could be right. In fact, you probably are. But correcting that isn't your job."

"If not me, then who, colonel?"

"I admire the sentiment and your sense of duty, but in this case, it's misplaced. You've done everything you were asked to do – and more," Galvin said evenly. "I witnessed that when you were a platoon leader in Mike Conrad's battalion and a company commander OPCON to me during Cambodia. The first question General Abrams asked me was whether or not you were a good soldier. I told him you were exceptional, a fighter, and the best infantry company commander in the 1st Cav during 1970. From my position on division staff and later as a battalion commander I'm certain of it. I told him you possessed all the requisite qualities and capabilities to someday be a general officer."

"Sir, I don't know what to say."

"I didn't tell you that to make you feel good about yourself and what you accomplished here. I related that brief snippet of our conversation to give you a sense of your potential. Don't throw that away. In the coming years and decades, the Army is going to need you and many like you. This war is ending badly, and that's not a terribly big surprise. Many saw this coming from the beginning." The colonel's face became serious and intent. "A lot of really smart people advised against going to war on the side of a corrupt government, but we did it anyway. People will be debating the strategy and tactics for a long time but there won't need to be a debate about the corruption of our South Vietnamese allies. You, Nolan, are not going to correct that situation by extending for six months. Nor is Brad."

"But, sir... after all the blood and treasure, we can't just walk away."

"Our part in this conflict has been handled badly from the beginning. Not the military side of it so much as the political. And you won't change the politics. You can't. And if the politics remain as they are, the outcome of the conflict is a foregone conclusion."

Glenn observed the colonel's face, the swift perceptive look in his eyes, the high intellect, the purposeful level-headedness that so clearly saw the world and the Army as they really were. He knew Galvin was right.

"Doing a risk-benefit analysis of your staying on for another six months indicates to me that the benefit you might provide some ARVN commander is miniscule compared to the benefit you can provide the U.S. Army in years to come. Why should the Army risk losing that? Why should you? Go home to your wife. Start a family. Prepare for higher levels of command and don't ever forget the hard earned lessons of this conflict. Then make sure we don't repeat the mistakes."

There was a brief silence between them. A cute little Vietnamese girl in a dark blue mini-skirt and see-through white blouse came down the road, swaying her hips and waving at GIs she passed. He'd seen her before on one of his rare trips to Phouc Vinh. Brad had told him the word going around was that she was a spotter for the NVA mortars. Who knew? It made him think how glad he was to have spent his entire time in the field in areas where anything that moved was an enemy, and he'd not had to make the hard, split-second decisions about who was friendly and who was not.

"Sir, I'm in a quandary. I'm not so sure I want a career in the Army," Glenn finally said.

"At times, I'm not so sure I do, either.."

Glenn was surprised. "But you were talking about years and decades from now, and not letting the same things that went wrong happen again in the Army."

"I'm not always totally happy with my career choice. Sometimes I don't like the Army... or some of the people in it I have to work with. But my default position is to do everything with an eye on a long term military career. Did you know that I was relieved during my first tour?"

"No, sir, I didn't."

"Well, I was. I happened to be the S-3 in a brigade and the brigade commander fired me. We disagreed about tactics and whether or not we were fighting a strategic defense or strategic offense. He had his way of doing things, and he thought my way of running operations was incompatible with his thinking. So, he moved me out. Was he right? Time will tell. It was one of those things."

"But you didn't resign."

"No, I finished my tour and went home and wrote a book about airmobile warfare where I proved historically and logically that I was right. General Westmoreland gave it a glowing review and I came back for my second tour as a battalion commander and proved my point."

Glenn smiled at him. "So, the pen really is mightier than the sword."

"It all depends. I wouldn't go out with a Parker T-ball Jotter and take on a Ninja warrior who was armed with a Samurai sword. But that's not my point. My point is that no career, the Army included, is always going to be a totally happy affair. Sometimes, you can get into a position where the right answer is to leave. That's a personal decision, and one you can't take lightly. But the people who aren't prepared to make that move harm themselves and the institution. Here's what I would tell you.

"If you do continue to make the Army your career – and I hope you do – always plan to leave it on short notice. Always have somewhere to go, have something you can do. Don't put yourself in a position where you have no options but to stay on and muddle through. That doesn't benefit you or the Army. I'd give that same advice to someone working for IBM or General Motors."

"That's well and good. But, how? Do you have something you can jump to right now?"

"If I left the Army tomorrow, I have a teaching job waiting on me in a nice, up-scale private school in Massachusetts. I love teaching, and as an author of few books, they'd love to have me."

"I see," Glenn said. He was amazed at the colonel for talking 'sedition' about leaving the Army, a prospect that West Point would never have countenanced. The idea was so remote from his thinking over the last half dozen years he felt almost traitorous now even listening to the notion. But it made absolute sense.

"You're not the first to hear this from me. I told your brother the same thing. I don't talk this way to everyone, only those I think will understand and benefit. If you're that good, the Army will work at retaining you if they perceive you have other options."

"But the Army is so big and faceless, so inanimate," Glenn countered. "They don't seem to have the time or will to get to know everyone individually."

"You're right," Galvin agreed. "Remember that rainy night on Mo when I told you about meeting Ginny? Remember what I told you about why I was at the Armor school for the Officers Advanced Course?"

"You did it to stand out, to separate yourself from the crowd."

"You were listening. Good!" The colonel looked pleased, like a teacher whose student has finally grasped the teaching point. "Stand out in the crowd. You've done that by your performance as a combat leader, and while it may not seem like it now, that article in *TIME* magazine which looks like a negative, may turn out to be a positive. I know that General Putnam thinks it is and that General Abrams does, too. General Westmoreland? In time he will as well, after I meet with him."

Glenn was surprised. Had Galvin sought out the upper echelons of the chain of command to do this for him? It dawned on him it was possible. But why?

"I have a proposition for you," the colonel said, opening his own bottle of beer. "I'm going to Germany after some leave; I'd like you to go with me. It seems pretty certain that DA will honor my request to command an infantry battalion in Europe and I'm putting together a team to go with me. Two of my commanders from the 1/8 have signed on. How would you like to be one of my company commanders again?"

"You mentioned this in passing once before. I wasn't sure if you were serious or just feeling me out. But... I'd be honored, sir."

"Do I note some apprehension?"

"I'm not so sure about my wife." As much as Glenn was delighted in the prospect of returning to Europe, surely for an extended tour lasting more that twelve months this time, he was equally sure Mary Anne wouldn't be. "She didn't like the separation. I spent better than half my time away at Hohenfels and Graf and on move out alerts."

"That's part of the cost of being on the front line of the Cold War. I can't promise it would be much different over there this time, but I can promise you challenge and reward."

Glenn thought for a moment. He sensed this was one of those consequential moments when the course of his life would change significantly. An offer was on the table. Galvin was surely somebody destined for significant achievement either in the Army or civilian world, or maybe both. He'd heard both his father and grandfather talk about being mentored and mentoring others in the military. *How does that happen?* he wondered. Maybe this was it for him in his career.

"Colonel, I'm going to say yes. Conditionally. If you actually do get that battalion command, I'll go with you... if, and it's a big if... if I can do it without destroying my marriage. I think I can. I'm going to work real hard on making it all come together."

Galvin smiled and shook his hand. "Can't ask for more than that. When you get back home, come by and see me. I'll be in Washington for a little while. We'd love to have you and Mary Anne spend a few days with us. Ginny's an Army brat and I know she'd be helpful in explaining things to your wife. Now let's figure out how to convince your brother to get out of this place and go back to college while he can."

*　　*　　*　　*

Jenny, still dressed in the same fatigues she'd been wearing since leaving Phouc Vinh four days earlier, walked down the long empty corridor at the Oakland air terminal. Her flight had been cancelled and another wouldn't leave until the next afternoon, so she'd decided on an earlier flight out of San Francisco. Oakland was just beginning to wake up, and she saw the first signs of vendors opening their kiosks and little shops, custodial staff finishing their cleanup from the night before. In the back of her mind was that still nagging question about what really awaited her. Lines had already formed at ticket counters in the main lobby and she was aware of the looks of veiled of hostility – more than she had expected.

You didn't anticipate a big brass band did you now, Kolarik? – No, and I didn't expect a hostile mob, either. – Well, get over it, because that's the way it is. – And it don't mean nuthin', remember that. – YUP. It don't mean nuthin'.

But it did mean something. When her father had come home from World War II, he'd had brass bands, ticker tape parades and people who were thankful for his time spent in uniform. Even those who'd never heard a shot fired anger or seen a single drop of blood were treated with respect. It was a time when duty, and honor, and service were in vogue.

Vietnam changed all that. Not at first, but over time.

It seemed now that most of the population back home saw the war in Vietnam as wrongheaded and the soldiers who fought in it as the face of the evil that had become what the press was calling a quagmire. She had read the articles and seen the reporting turn on the soldiers who were no longer viewed as heroes like their fathers' generation but baby killers and misfits, or at best, fools.

Jenny didn't ask or need or even want the band or the parade, just transportation to San Francisco International across the bay some twenty miles. She checked on commercial buses and taxis, but none were running at that early hour, and there was a transit strike going on so public transportation was non-existent. She decided to get some breakfast.

A restaurant on the concourse was open and beginning to fill with business travelers in suits and ties along with a few families herding bleary-eyed kids. She hung her small suitcase on her right shoulder, hefted the duffel bag over her left shoulder and grabbed her overnight case with one hand, the purse with the other and struggled into the restaurant. Dropping her heavy load on the floor, she slid onto a stool between two men who looked at her with thinly veiled scorn. One of them turned his back to her and the other got up and moved.

Surprised at first, her reaction turned to disappointment, then despair and soon to anger. People she didn't know had treated her with contempt simply because she was in uniform. After all she'd put up with, sacrificed and done all those months in Vietnam, these people didn't even want to sit next to her at a breakfast bar. The injustice of it seemed monumental. The waiter behind the counter took his time getting around to her, taking her order last and even bypassing her for a couple of late arrivals who came in after her. When she tried to catch his attention he turned away until she walked behind the counter and poured her own coffee.

A call to Oakland Army terminal requesting transportation proved fruitless, so she did what she had always done since high school – improvised. She decided to hitchhike. Burdened with suitcase, duffle bag, overnighter and purse, she struggled outside under the weight and stuck her thumb out once she came to the highway.

Jenny was no stranger to hitchhiking; for most of her time in Vietnam it was the only way she got around. She would stand out on the runway at Tay Ninh or Phouc Vinh dressed in fatigues, boonie hat, pony tail and a smile for the pilots. Getting a ride was a cinch. But after an hour on the side of the road in Oakland, she realized that wasn't the case back home in 'the world', especially if you were wearing a military uniform.

Rush hour was in full swing and cars whizzed by her; most drivers simply ignored her but some went out of their way to show their displeasure. Several slowed and yelled obscenities; one threw a bag of trash and another almost hit her with a half full can of soda. Several gave her the finger. She tried to ignore them all. Her patient wait for a Good Samaritan lasted well into a second hour until at last two guys about her age driving a hand-painted red, yellow, blue and orange Volkswagen bus pulled to a stop twenty feet past her. Hot, tired and dirty, she ran toward the van, dragging her luggage awkwardly behind her.

"Thank you so much for stopping," Jenny wheezed, out of breath and sweating. A stray lock of hair fell across her face and she swept it back in place. "Are you guys going by the San Francisco International?"

"We sure are," the young man said with an easy, relaxed smile as he opened the passenger side door and got out. His hair was long and curly, bleached by the sun; his eyes were pale blue and framed by thin wire-rimmed granny glasses. His jeans were ragged and dirty with holes in the knees and fraying around the cuffs. A large, multi-hued peace sign adorned his worn denim vest.

Jenny gave him a tired smile, thanked him and picked up her duffle bag to put it into the van. "I'm so glad to find someone going by the airport."

"Yeah, we're going there, sucker," he said sarcastically, "but we're not taking any of you Army pigs with us. Wouldn't be caught dead with some baby killer in our bus, bitch."

The man laughed out loud, a haunting and derisive cackle, and slammed the door in her face. And then he spit on her – a large glob of brownish colored saliva that clung to her fatigues above the right breast pocket..

She was stunned as he laughed in her face again and jumped back into the van. The driver floored the accelerator as he hooted and cackled uncontrollably with his buddy. The VW's wheels spun, throwing gravel and dirt back on her as they sped away. Several drivers of other cars that passed by laughed at her and shouted incomprehensible insults.

"I'm not some pig!" she yelled after the VW bus. "And I'm not a baby killer, I'm a nurse, damn you – I save lives, I don't take them!" She looked down at her chest where the lump of spittle oozed down over her name tag like some large, malignant slug. The site turned her stomach; she was too tired and shaken to wipe it off.

Why did he spit on me? I never did anything to him, or any of these other people. All I ever did was what the Army told me was my job. Don't you people get it? People like me who saw that damned war firsthand are more anti-war, anti-killing than the most vocal peace marcher. Insensitive, uninformed creeps!

She sat down on her duffle bag, covered her face with her hands, and cried.

After a while, she dried her eyes and held out her thumb. Those who didn't scream at her, she realized, all had the same hardened look on their faces – a combination of surprise at seeing a young woman in uniform and hatred for what she represented. They were looking right through her it seemed, not bothering to even try concealing it. She tried not to let it bother her, but it did.

She'd never felt so alone or unloved. Another hour passed. She almost wished she was back in Vietnam where she expected there would be some who hated her because she was numbered with the enemy but there were some – many, actually – who cared for her and appreciated what she did. Jenny thought about the argument with Glenn and regretted it, wishing she hadn't reacted the way she did. He was one of the good guys and she lamented the angry shouting match in the operating room, wishing now she'd handled his fury differently. But she'd never get the chance to set things straight – their paths would never cross again. He was a careerist, and she'd decided long before leaving Phouc Vinh that when her obligation was up in a few months that would end her sad, desolate time in the Army. She'd had enough of the fighting and hatred and bitterness, the long, lonely stretches away from family and friends. *For what?* she asked herself. *For what?*

It was almost eleven a.m. and she had been sitting beside the road for three hours, having given up on ever getting a ride in time to make the flight leaving from San Francisco. Her dream of returning to the tranquility she'd left a year earlier had been shattered; the hope that everything would be wonderful once back in the States had been dashed at a California roadside. She resigned herself to spending the night in the Oakland terminal; she picked up her heavy load of luggage and turned away from the traffic just as a battered '57 Ford pulled to the curb and stopped next to her.

"Hey, missy," the old black man behind the wheel said, "I give you a ride."

Jenny turned and looked at him as he got out and shuffled over to give her a hand. He limped badly and was bent over stooped shouldered; his face was rough and dry and deeply lined, but his eyes were soft. His clothes were frayed around the cuffs.

"I'm going to the airport in San Francisco," she said, afraid this was another disappointment in the making.

"Well, I be going to the other side of Oakland, but I'll take you. I been by here five times and seen you sittin' here tryin' to hitchhike and you ain't got no ride yet. Had to come back. Didn't want you to spend the rest of your life sittin' here by the side o' the road." He smiled at her and labored to pick up the duffle bag. "Got you some kinda heavy load in here, young lady. That look on your face tell me you got a big load in your heart, too. I seen how people been doin' you."

"It wasn't the kind of welcome I expected," Jenny said.

"You coming back from the Nam?"

She nodded. "I was an operating room nurse."

"I guess you done seen a lot, little lady."

"More than I ever wanted to."

"And then you comes back to this kind o' rough manners." He ran his bony fingers over his short-cropped hair. "Not everybody is like what you seen this mornin'. People ain't all bad. It's just that some folks is crazy mixed up about that war over there and just don't think right."

"War – and this one in particular – really messes up people's minds," Jenny said. "Before I went to Vietnam, I was kind of bubbly, excited about life."

"Don't you go losin' that, little girl."

That advice is a little late, she thought. *I lost it and I won't ever be the same. Not ever.*

CONSULO

Chapter 34

"Please state your full name, rank, and branch of service."

"Glenn Alan Nolan. Captain. United States Army."

He looked around the small, austere hearing room, wishing he was elsewhere – Germany, Benning, in grad school. *Hell, even back with Alpha in Vietnam*, he thought. *Anywhere but at Fort Belvoir testifying in my former commander's court martial..*

His return home from Southeast Asia had been disappointing.

He'd returned to the States three weeks earlier and had spent half that time on leave, unfortunately with his in-laws who were less happy about his being there than he was. He was about to book a vacation to the Bahamas to get away with Mary Anne before reporting to Fort Benning when the summons to the court-martial was delivered. They had been able to spend a couple of days and a night just outside Washington with Colonel Galvin where Glenn learned the plans for the colonel's taking a battalion in Germany had been scuttled because the Army needed him for some kind of high level planning position.

"*Command*," Galvin had told him when he broke the news. "*Always seek to command. That's where the heart and soul of the soldier and the future of the Army lies in those who...*"

"Please take your seat on the witness stand, captain." The military lawyer looked briefly at the notes spread out at the prosecutor's table and at last looked up. "Captain Nolan, please state for the record how it is that you know the defendant, Lieutenant Colonel McInnes."

"He was my battalion commander in the first battalion, sixth Calvary in the 1st Cavalry Division for approximately two weeks in the Republic of Vietnam."

"That would be the dates of 6 April until 18 April 1970."

"Yes, sir that's correct." Glenn stole a good glance at Colonel McInnes who was staring at him with that same angry gaze Glenn remembered from the night on Firebase Evita, and from both instances where they crossed paths in the following weeks.

"You were on LZ Evita the evening of 7 April when the incident concerning the mortar attack in the indictment occurred."

"Objection!" the defense counsel said, rising to his feet. "The *alleged* incident and surrounding circumstances are not yet established."

"Sustained," the presiding officer said. He was a Brigadier General Glenn had never seen or heard of before; his hair was mostly gray though he appeared young, and the look on his face indicated he too would have been glad to be elsewhere. "The Prosecution will address the incident as 'alleged' in his statements. Continue."

"You were there on LZ Evita the evening of 7 April at the time of the alleged incident described in the charges preferred by the 1/6 Battalion Surgeon, Captain Norman Hadorn?"

"Yes, sir, I was."

"And why were you there?"

"I'd been assigned as commander of Alpha Company effective 6 April while in the first brigade and arrived on the firebase the afternoon of 7 April for Ops and Intel briefings and to meet for the first time with Colonel McInnes, the battalion commander."

The prosecutor walked him through an excruciatingly detailed recounting of his first twenty-four hours in the 1st Battalion 6th Cavalry – events, times, locations, people. It took an hour and a half. He amazed himself with how much he remembered. He thought back to the times he'd listened to his father and pilots who had flown with him in Korea and the big war tell their tales and wondered how they could remember all the little details of missions flown in the distant past. He understood that now.

"Was the colonel wounded by enemy fire?" the prosecutor asked near the end of his testimony.

Out of the corner of his eye, Glenn could see McInnes glaring at him in the same way he had that resupply day when Glenn had been certain his military career had ended. The look was meant to intimidate. *He's a petty little tyrant, petty and vindictive and a fraud, just like Cleburne in 2nd platoon. People like him have to be stopped. If you don't do this, Nolan, who will?* "The colonel was outside his bunker for less than a minute, and that was a good three or four minutes after the last NVA mortar landed. There was no possible way for him to be wounded or to coordinate counter battery fire."

After a brief recess, the questioning continued, this time from the defense counsel. An hour later, the court adjourned after the presiding officer announced the court-martial would re-convene the following afternoon at fourteen hundred hours.

On the way back to the Visiting Officers' Quarters, wrung out by the long day and withering cross-examination by McInnes' defense counsel, Glenn decided that since the next day was open he'd visit someone in Washington he hadn't seen in years.

His sister, Cateline.

*   *

The sign outside the tall, open doors of the Senate Office Building's hearing room announced the purpose of the Foreign Relations Committee's morning deliberations.

Glenn entered and found a seat halfway down the crowded room, across the aisle from a sizeable contingent of bearded, disheveled men his age or slightly older, all wearing assorted odds and ends of military regalia. Most wore issue jungle fatigue jackets in plain olive drab or tiger stripe camo with assorted unit patches sewn in odd places, haphazard rows of military ribbons and soiled boonie hats with braided strips of various bright cloth for hatbands. They looked grubby and utterly bedraggled with their long unkempt hair and scruffy beards; they stared with contempt across the broad aisle at him as he sat there in his dress greens.

Several rows in front of him sat John Kerry the sole occupant of the long table reserved for witnesses testifying before the Senate Committee for Foreign Relations. Kerry, wearing rumpled, unpressed fatigues, was half turned in his chair, chatting with a man in a light tan suit who was talking to him earnestly. Glenn was close enough to hear the former Navy boat captain say, "No, I'm going to read it pretty much exactly as it is…" Kerry's thick, dark hair completely covered his ears and the collar of his fatigues.

The members of the committee entered the hearing room from a side door and made their way slowly to the slightly raised dais and took their seats behind microphones and wooden nameplates. Before Senator Fulbright sat down, Kerry rose and went forward, extending his hand and engaging the smiling committee chairman in conversation. The other Senators – Democrats Symington, Pell, and Reeves along with Republicans Aiken, Case, and Javits – all looked on cordially as the tall, stoop-shouldered witness shared a brief, amiable moment with the Arkansas legislator who'd served in Congress since just a few months before the end of World War Two.

As Glenn watched, he caught a glimpse of Cateline standing behind Senator Reeves.

Their eyes met briefly; he smiled at her and winked, and was surprised when she gave him a stern looked and averted her glance. *What was that about?* he wondered, but had little time to dwell on it as Kerry took his seat and Senator Fulbright called the meeting to order amid flashing bulbs.

"The committee is continuing this morning its hearings on proposals relating to the ending of the war in Southeast Asia," Fulbright began. "This morning the committee will hear testimony from Mr. John Kerry and, if he has any associates, we will be glad to hear from them. These are men who have fought in this unfortunate war in Vietnam. I believe they deserve to be heard and listened to by the Congress and by the officials in the executive, branch and by the public generally. You have a perspective that those in the Government who make our Nation's policy do not always have and I am sure that your testimony today will be helpful to the committee in its consideration of the proposals before us."

As the committee chairman spoke, Kerry busied himself looking through his notes, setting them in place; after a moment, he swept his long hair from his eyes and looked up.

"I would like to add simply on my own account," Fulbright was saying, "that I regret very much the action of the Supreme Court in denying the veterans the right to use the Mall."

This was met with a smattering of applause from the contingent of veterans who had requested the privilege of camping in the National Mall, and had gone ahead and pitched their tents anyway in defiance of the Court's decision.

"...I want also to congratulate Mr. Kerry, you and your associates, for the restraint that you have shown, certainly in the hearing the other day when there were a great many of your people here. I think you conducted yourselves in a most commendable manner throughout this week. Whenever people gather there is always a tendency for some of the more emotional ones to do things which, are even against their own interests. I think you deserve much of the credit because I understand you are one of the leaders of this group. I have joined with some of my colleagues, specifically Senator Hart, in an effort to try to change the attitude of our Government toward your efforts in bringing to this committee and to the country your views about the war. I personally don't know of any group which would have a greater justification for doing it and also a more accurate view of the effect of the war."

Glenn searched the dais again and saw Cateline positioned well in the background away from the other senators; once again she glared at him briefly, seemed to shake her head from side to side, and looked away quickly. *What's up, sis*? Glenn asked himself and kept staring at her but she refused to look at him. Finally, he glanced at Senator Reeves who was frowning at him – an unfriendly look, clearly disdain, flickered in the man's eyes momentarily. Senator Javits said something supporting his Democrat colleague's statement, and then the chairman was saying,

"You may proceed, Mr. Kerry."

"Thank you very much, Senator Fulbright, Senator Javits, Senator Symington, Senator Reeves, Senator Pell. I would like say for the record, and also for the men behind me who are also wearing the uniforms and their medals, that my sitting here is really symbolic," Kerry said, sounding grave as if giving an inaugural. "I am not here as John Kerry. I am here as one member of the group of one thousand, which is a small representation of a very much larger group of veterans in this country, and were it possible for all of them to sit at this table they would be here and have the same kind of testimony.

"I would simply like to speak in very general terms. I apologize if my statement is general because I received notification yesterday that you would hear me and I am afraid because of the injunction, I was up most of the night and haven't had a great deal of chance to prepare my remarks."

Glenn noticed that Kerry mostly read from notes in front of him as he spoke, and his words were both eloquently phrased and expertly delivered with precise meter and articulation.

"I would like to talk, representing all those veterans, and say that several months ago in Detroit, we had an investigation at which over one hundred fifty honorably discharged and many very highly decorated veterans testified to war crimes committed in Southeast Asia, not isolated incidents but crimes committed on a day-to-day basis with the full awareness of officers at all levels of command.

"It is impossible to describe to you exactly what did happen in Detroit, the emotions in the room, the feelings of the men who were reliving their experiences in Vietnam, but they did. They relived the absolute horror of what this country, in a sense, made them do."

Something doesn't make sense, Glenn told himself. *Either this guy is the greatest orator since Demosthenes – or MacArthur... or he's damned well- rehearsed.* What had he said to that man just before the committee members entered the room? *"...I'm going to read it pretty much exactly as it is..."* Could that have been a speechwriter? He wondered.

"They told the stories," Kerry was saying in his somber, measured tone, "… at times they had personally raped, cut off ears, cut off heads, taped wires from portable telephones to human genitals and turned up the power, cut off limbs, blown up bodies, randomly shot at civilians, razed villages in fashion reminiscent of Genghis Khan, shot cattle and dogs for fun, poisoned food stocks, and generally ravaged the countryside of South Vietnam in addition to the normal ravage of war, and the normal and very particular ravaging which is done by the applied bombing power of this country."

Glenn felt the hair stand up on the back of his neck and his face went hot even before the witness badly mispronounced the name of one of the most feared warriors in history. *Are you one of these supposed war criminals?!* He wanted to shout, and get up from his seat and drag this long-haired ignoramus out of the room.

"We call this investigation the "Winter Soldier Investigation." The term "Winter Soldier" is a play on words of Thomas Paine in 1776 when he spoke of the Sunshine Patriot and summertime soldiers who deserted at Valley Forge because the going was rough. We who have come here to Washington have come here because we feel we have to be winter soldiers now. We could come back to this country; we could be quiet; we could hold our silence; we could not tell what went on in Vietnam, but we feel because of what threatens this country, the fact that the crimes threaten it, not reds, and not redcoats but the crimes which we are committing that threaten it, that we have to speak out. I would like to talk to you a little bit about what the result is of the feelings these men carry with them after coming back from Vietnam.

"The country doesn't know it yet, but it has created a monster, a monster in the form of millions of men who have been taught to deal and to trade in violence…"

How dare you condemn every one of us who ever wore the uniform over there! How dare you! Glenn felt like every eye in the room was on him as he sat there. Except for the back of Kerry's head, everything went out of focus and the sounds of the man's voice, and the murmur of myriad staffers and the clicking of cameras all fused into a dull indecipherable roar. *So now we're all monsters – war criminals knowing nothing except dealing and trading in violence, ready to explode.*

"… and who are given the chance to die for the biggest nothing in history; men who have returned with a sense of anger and a sense of betrayal which no one has yet grasped."

Benny, and EB, and Timmy Horner and all the rest didn't die for nothing –

"As a veteran and one who feels this anger, I would like to talk about it. We are angry because we have been used in the worst fashion by the administration of this country. In 1970 at West Point, Vice President Agnew said 'some glamorize the criminal misfits of society while our best men die in Asian rice paddies to preserve the freedom which most of those misfits abuse,' and this was used as a rallying point for our effort in Vietnam…"

He couldn't listen to any more of this – his senses seemed to shut down and he retreated inward where the rant of this out-of-uniform buffoon with his prep school manner and air of superiority no longer existed or mattered. How could this panel of supposed national leaders sit there with silly smirks and looks of approval on their faces and condone to this? He heard little of the rest of the droning monologue of Kerry's remarks, nor much of the question and answer session that followed, paying no attention except to marvel at the way all of them addressed this self-important talebearer as if he were a high ranking diplomat or an expert in foreign affairs. The occasional applause got his attention, but only served to increase his anger.

When the chairman called the session to an end fifty minutes later it was well past noon.

Noisy conversation erupted, bouncing off the high ceiling, and people around him started to rise, pushing him to the center aisle. Once again he caught a fleeting glimpse of Cateline and he pushed forward toward where the senators were talking to one another and staffers. Reporters with a microphones and cameramen standing next to them were asking questions of Senator Reeves who looked like royalty holding court. The crowd moved and pulsated as if alive while people jostled one another, some in an effort to leave and some to get closer to the elected officials to hear what they were saying. Glenn was pushed from behind and lost his balance as he bumped roughly into someone in front of him.

Suddenly, he was face to face with John Kerry.

"Excuse me," Glenn said, briefly surprised.

Kerry's prominent jaw thrust forward and he peered back looking irritated and indignant. He looked at Glenn's uniform, noticed his rank and the crossed rifles of the infantry officer on his lapels. For a brief moment, everything seemed to go silent and people watched the two of them as if this was that moment in the ring when a referee gives instructions to two boxers before round one.

"You were lying through your teeth, Kerry," a voice nearby said loud enough that several people turned.

Abruptly, several flashbulbs went off, causing Glenn to see spots.

In an instant, Kerry was hustled out a side door and Glenn turned toward the direction where he'd last seen Cateline. He thought he saw her exit through a door to his left. Glenn quickly pushed through the crowd into a small side corridor where he saw her glance over her shoulder at him and then slip through an entryway. Half running, he followed and went through the door after her; as soon as he was inside, he realized he must have made a mistake – he was in a small men's room. The door closed behind him, and he heard it being locked.

He turned and looked at his English sister.

"Cateline, what –"

She put her hand over his mouth, and placed her finger to her lips, then checked each of the three stalls before turning to him and whispering, "What are you doing here, Glenn?"

"That's a fine welcome."

"Don't be so barmy. Tell me. Quickly!"

"I've been called here to Washington as a witness in a court martial. I'm not saying any more until you give me a hug. Mom always said a body's not healthy unless he gets ten hugs a day. You're not hugging that arsehole Reeves, I hope."

She scowled at him and replied, "That's disgusting."

"I think the British word is manky."

"It's that, too. I don't have time to explain. But… I can't have people around here knowing you and I are related. I shall tell you why later. Does Erika know you're in town?"

"She knew I was coming to D.C. but I haven't seen her yet. I got in yesterday morning."

"Leave your hotel and phone number with her and I'll get back with you some time in the next few days. Quite likely the day after tomorrow, in the evening. But as far as anyone around here knows, we aren't related. That's all I can say. Now, into a stall with you, and don't emerge from hiding for three or four minutes after I leave."

"Am I on *Candid Camera*?"

She pushed him into the stall. "Three minutes, no less." With that she unlocked the Men's Room door, looked quickly outside, and left.

*   *   *   *

Harrison Reeves smiled to himself as he put his feet up on the desk and leaned back in his large leather swivel chair with a single malt scotch in one hand and silver gray cigar smoke curling from a *Belicosos Finos*, 52 Ring in the other.

The television in his Senate office was tuned to CBS Evening News because the senator liked Cronkite – and liked him a great deal. He was part Walt Disney, part Edward R. Murrow and thoroughly Progressive, though few people inside or outside CBS News knew or even suspected. The network anchorman was convinced world conflicts could only be avoided by strengthening the United Nations as a first step toward a world government patterned after America with a legislature, executive and judiciary, plus police to enforce its international laws and keep the peace. To do that, of course, Americans would have to yield some of their sovereignty – a bitter pill perhaps, but necessary to bring in a New World Order. Walter Cronkite was, according to the Gallup Poll, the '*Most Trusted Man in America*' and his endorsement was worth somewhere between three and seven points in any survey or political race. Lyndon Johnson had learned that when Uncle Walt declared in early 1968 the Vietnam War was un-winnable.

"Senator, you need to see this," Brandon Oakes said, after letting himself into Reeves' inner office. "A front page picture in the Post above the fold. And a very interesting article beneath. I think there's an opportunity for you here."

Reeves looked back, annoyed at the interruption, but his face changed when he saw the photograph of Kerry and Glenn Nolan apparently confronting each other. The caption and the header of the accompanying article cast the incident as a clash of wills over Vietnam. "What kind of opportunity?"

"Hold your own hearing into the Army's role in trying to disrupt the Senate Foreign Relations Committee deliberations. According to the article, this captain defamed your witness this morning in the presence of quite a few witnesses, and he physically assaulted him. Kerry had to be whisked out of the committee room before things got ugly."

Reeves looked at the picture closely. "I know this officer. It's that damned Nolan."

"Yes, sir, I thought you'd appreciate that."

"Why should I?"

"Because you've been looking for a way to deal with him since he entered West Point."

"And even if I wanted to 'deal with him' how would I do it."

"You can discredit the captain, put the Army on the defensive vis-à-vis their rogue officer *and* raise your own profile all at the same time. Sir, this group of Kerry's can really be helpful. But we have to strike while the iron is hot. I'll get the print media and TV to keep the story alive for a few days, and you can call a special meeting to bring in the captain to testify. And here's where it really gets good. These Vietnam veterans that follow Kerry... they can testify against him as rebuttal character witnesses." Oakes produced a tight-lipped smile. "I've already talked with two who will swear this Nolan committed some of those acts Kerry testified to this morning. If we need more, they can be produced. We've got to stop this war at any cost, sir. You've said that many times. Here's a chance to do that, or at least put more pressure on the Administration. I can set up another hearing for early next week and get some air time for it on the Sunday talk shows. Yes or no, Senator?"

*   *   *

Glenn lit a cigarette and leaned on the balcony railing outside the Potomac Room of the Fort Belvoir Officer's Club, gazing at the river below.

Chip Harkins' wedding reception had been held here less than a week after graduation and he remembered most of it, up to the point where he and Benny had gotten too drunk to catch the garter Chip tossed out after taking it off the leg of the girl their buddy had married. None of the other four brand new second lieutenants from the class of '68 had been sober enough either – 'Chi Chi' Maldonado, Eddie Garner, Bud Parsons, and 'Dusty' Rhodes. They had all had a great time in their brand new Dress Blues trying to impress the bridesmaids; Benny had even taken one of them back to their motel room afterward which forced Glenn to sleep overnight in his car. Thinking about that day, so filled with promise and the beginning of not only a marriage but a glorious career stretching out in front of all of them seemed so long ago. And now, so sad.

Chip had been killed at LZ Ripcord the last week of May in 1970, a week before they all got promoted to Captain. Parsons had been killed at LZ Jay just days before Illingworth had been hit by the 95C NVA regiment. And he'd lost Benny a few months after that... Benbo, the guy with all the luck in the world riding with him – three out of eight from that one wedding party. He blew a cloud of smoke upward into the breeze. *For what?*

"Those things are going to kill you, Nolan."

Glenn turned and looked over his shoulder in the direction of the voice, which came from a short, stocky, black-haired man dressed in civvies who appeared a little older. His beak of a nose and dark, lively eyes reminded him of Hod Mirsky from the rugby team at the academy. "A lot of things have tried to kill me in the last year or so."

"But the coffin nails actually will, given time."

Glenn recognized the man from the court martial proceedings and noticed a cigarette cupped in his hand. "Then why do you smoke?"

"For the same reason I run with scissors in my hand – makes me feel dangerous. Since I left the Nam, I crave excitement. Especially now." The man extended his hand. "Rueben Favreaux. I'm with the Veterans Administration, sitting in on the trial to see if there are any implications for the VA. At least that's what I told my supervisor. Think of me as the man who's gonna save your ass, Nolan. You can call me Pooch. And if nobody has said it to you yet – Welcome home, baby killer."

"I'm not on trial. And I don't need anyone watching out for me."

"And you, my friend, are appallingly wrong," Favreaux replied. He glanced inside and said, "They serve a decent chicken teriyaki and a passable spaghetti with meat sauce. I'll buy you lunch and maybe even a drink on the VA's dime and tell you why I, and your sister, say you're off beam."

Favreaux called Baton Rouge home, Glenn learned over lunch, though he'd spent less than a year there after his birth. His father, an Acadian, had been born and raised a hundred miles west in Lake Charles and worked for the Calcasieu gas company. Favreaux himself had served in early '66 with the Big Red One in Vietnam as an infantry platoon leader and later on the Division staff in the G-1 section. Returning home, he'd finished college on the GI Bill and graduated from Ole Miss.

"My family spent a lot of time banging around the oil patch in Louisiana, Oklahoma and Texas while I was growing up," Favreaux said over a cup of coffee as they waited for their lunch order. "Being a Catholic in mostly Southern Baptist towns wasn't much fun. But it made me tough… and smart. I can spot a phony or a lie at a hundred miles."

"So, you're called 'pooch' – that must have made things interesting when you showed up in a new school. Nearly as bad as being a boy named Sue."

Favreaux smiled crookedly. "Love that song, but it wasn't like that. The name came from my dad's best friend growing up in Acadiana. His name was Poocho, and from the time my dad got married, everybody in my family knew the first boy was going to be called 'Pooch'. It was pre-destined. All my friends call me by that name. You can, too. "

"All right, Pooch… what are you and my sister trying to save me from?"

"Not a what, but a who. Senator Harrison Reeves."

Glenn was skeptical. "I know he's had it in for my family since he and my grandfather crossed paths a long, long time ago, but I don't even know the man."

"Well, I can't tell you his motivations, but I can tell you that he laid a booby trap for you two days ago. Within a week to ten days you're going to be called to testify before the Senate Foreign Relations Committee supposedly to refute the testimony of that guy John Kerry."

Glenn was wary. "How do you know this?"

"Cateline told me. She works for Reeves and somehow overheard him directing his chief of staff to get in touch with some of those guys from the VVAW to be on hand to refute anything you say… *and*, to do it in a way that makes you a potential perjury target. Perjuring yourself under oath before Congress is serious stuff, Nolan. Think about what it would do to your career. Hell, to your whole damned life. Even an allegation of impropriety from a Senator would deep six you." Favreaux took a deep breath and exhaled loudly through his nose. "I know that probably sounds far-fetched."

"As a matter of fact –"

"I suspect that Reeves and Teddy Kennedy were the driving force behind having Kerry testify in the first place. Both are rich Progressives who made a U-turn on Vietnam when Nixon got elected. I have it on pretty good authority that Kennedy had his own speechwriter work with Kerry on his statement before Foreign Relations. Wouldn't be surprised to find Reeves' fingerprints all over those notes he was reading from."

Glenn thought back to his initial impression of the ex-Navy Swiftboat captain – the testimony had seemed too polished and the presentation too well rehearsed.

"All right, Pooch," Glenn said after a while, "just for the sake of argument, and since you're paying for lunch, how and why are you involved?"

"You want the long or short version?"

"I have some time. I don't have to be back in court for two hours."

"The short version then." Favreaux lit another cigarette and continued, leaning forward and speaking earnestly. "I'm a man on a mission, Nolan. Actually, I'm a man that a mission plucked up and forced itself on. I'm a crusader against deceit and dishonesty."

Glenn smiled in spite of himself at the Cajun's intensity. "A crusader… against deceit and dishonesty. Does this mission come with a superhero mask and cape?"

Favreaux's mouth twitched and he worked his tongue around the inside of his cheek while staring hard into Nolan's eyes as if searching for a rejoinder. "You know, I'm going to let that slide, Nolan. Not because it was clever, but because you just might be unique, an oddity – a West Pointer who maybe has a sense of humor. But don't push your luck."

"All right, fair enough. So who sent you off on this crusade?"

"The Veterans Administration. Inadvertently. I was working summers for the VA office in Jackson and that first summer a request came from Washington to check the background of a Vietnam vet from Mississippi who had put in for some kind of benefit. All the required forms and documents were attached and I was assigned to do a quick review and add a couple of documents, then send it back to Washington. On the surface it all looked legit, but I love researching so I dug deeper in our files and found the guy's background was bogus. I sent back a recommendation to deny the benefit and went about my business."

"So, from that one case you started this crusade?" Glenn asked.

"Not just the one case," Favreaux replied, sounding testy. "Before the summer was up, I'd found a half dozen similar attempts at fraud. In every instance, headquarters in Washington had already approved giving the benefit and was just looking for some paperwork justifying their decision. The next summer the same thing happened – only I got handed a bunch more cases. Close to three dozen in ten weeks. All but two were fraudulent. Think about that, Nolan. Three dozen cases of fraud from one little field office in Mississippi. Multiply that by maybe fifty field offices around the country plus headquarters in D.C."

"So you're saying there's a problem with Vietnam era veterans submitting phony documents to get benefits they don't deserve? That's great," Nolan said caustically. "Now there's another thing to prove all of us are not only ticking time bombs ready to explode but crooks as well."

The Cajun shook his head from side to side. "It's not Vietnam vets, it's vets *and* pretenders – mostly pretenders as far as I've been able to tell from all wartime eras. I'm amazed that career civil servants haven't been all over this for years. Decades… . That a summer intern like me ferreted this out in just a few weeks of part time work strains credulity. But that's based on just my three years of summer employment. The VA came to me just before I graduated college and offered me a job here in D.C. to do full time what I'd done in the summers in Jackson. I'm working for them now, going to law school at night and giving expert testimony in court."

"You've got a gift, I guess."

Favreaux searched Glenn's eyes. "I'm going to take that as a compliment, captain. But, yeah, I do. I admit to being a little anal about the research; for some reason, I just dig it. Always loved following clues and solving mysteries. The time I spent in division G-1 in Nam gave me an understanding of how the Army keeps personnel records – it's actually logical and straightforward."

"You sound surprised."

"Aren't you? The tone of your voice says you are. The fact that the records are there and fairly easily researched isn't what should surprise you, though. The reality that it's real easy to fool our government, and the public in general about military service. That should make you sit up and take notice. The government doesn't know how to mine its own data in its files."

"So your crusade, so to speak, is really to reform a government bureaucracy."

"Of course not! That's a fool's errand and too small a fish to fry. No, the Fabulous Favreaux is about righting the wrongs done by pretenders," Pooch said, running his fingers through his hair and casting a baleful glance at Glenn. "Don't you see? There are people out there pretending to be like us – like you and me and others we stood shoulder to shoulder with in some serious shit – and they're giving all of us a bad name. They dishonor those who fell and ruin the perception of those of us who somehow made it back. That pisses me off, Nolan, and I'm going to put a stop to it."

"Sounds like a pretty big job for one man."

"I don't know what I can't do until I do it, and I'm not Don Quixote tilting at windmills. Actually, I have some help – from two guys at the National Archives, a handful of journalists, a few academics both inside and outside the VA, a growing list of law enforcement officers and private investigators. It's not a lot of people… yet. Recently I added two people from your family: your aunt Erika Ashby – my first federal prosecutor – and your stepsister, Cateline. And now you."

"Me? How can I help you?"

Favreaux's eyes took on a bright gleam. "By letting me save your sorry carcass."

"That's the second time you've said that."

"You want to know how it happens? All right, here's how all that stuff I just laid out works. Like I said, you'll be subpoenaed to testify – under oath mind you – before the Committee on Foreign Relations supposedly to provide balance to the Kerry testimony. But it's a sham. You're a sacrificial goat. To Reeves, you're perfect for the role. You're an active duty Vietnam vet who looks good in the uniform, and one with a certain level of public exposure – maybe fame – shall we say, because of that article in *TIME*."

"Notoriety or infamy would be more accurate."

Favreaux's face took on an amused glow and he laughed, a flat taunting cackle. "You didn't much care for the hit piece that Frog writer laid on you, eh? Don't blame you. But that's your concern not mine. My issue is to shine a high intensity spotlight on the people who dishonor our time in uniform by claiming things they don't deserve while tarnishing our service. If I had the time, I could show you how big a problem this is. It goes way beyond just defrauding the government. But the pressing action right now is you and this public lynching you're walking into."

"Honestly, this sounds off the wall."

"Then let me give you some information." Favreaux reached into his briefcase and pulled out a large brown expandable envelope four inches thick. "This is what I've got so far on the guys who attended that 'Winter Soldier' get together in Detroit Kerry talked about. Most of them were phonies. Either they were people who had never been in the service before, or people who embellished – no, that's too kind – people who wholly falsified and glamorized their actual service."

"For example?"

Favreaux laughed again. "Aha, you don't believe me. Well, sir, look at this." He pulled a manila envelope out of the pile on the table and opened it. "Remember Kerry during the hearing talking about 'taping wires from portable telephones to human genitals and turning up the power'. You know who that came from? This guy. Michael Schneider. How do I know? Because I was there. I heard that discussed myself. Didn't believe it. Checked it out, and sure enough, this guy was never even in Vietnam even though he claims to have been a squad leader and then a platoon leader in the 101st where he won a silver star, bronze star and a purple heart. The truth is, he deserted from Germany, was picked up in New York, escaped and was picked up in Oklahoma on murder charges and he's now in the Eastern State mental hospital in Vinta, Oklahoma. Not what anybody would call a credible witness. Yet his assertions found their way into Kerry's speech. In fact, none of those crimes Kerry mentioned are backed up by any evidence. So that's what you're up against. You saw what those Senators allowed into testimony and how they praised that guy for telling the 'real story' about American soldiers in Vietnam. You saw the looks on their faces."

The Cajun leaned back in his chair and let the silence linger.

"From what I was told, the plan is this. Senator Reeves will call you as a rebuttal witness to Mr. Kerry's remarks because you confronted him and called him a liar in the Hearing room."

"I never did that. It wasn't me."

"The Washington Post said it was. And that's therefore what it is. Once you're on the witness chair and say anything at all, they'll have two or three or four VVAW witnesses to impeach you. And suddenly you've perjured yourself before Congress. But fear not, The Fabulous Favreaux, Guardian of Truth, is here. You're in good hands, pal."

Chapter 35

"I've arranged a meeting for you with the Archbishop," Dr. MacEagan told his daughter, looking up from the morning paper when she entered the kitchen and poured a cup of coffee.

Mary Anne shook her head from side to side and turned away. "I never asked you to do that, and I have no desire to see him. I told you that before."

"You need spiritual guidance in this, my dear. He's a longtime friend and counselor to our family, and he's eager to provide any help he can. He simply wants to get to know you a little better so he can more effectively marshal the archdiocese's resources."

"I'm not talking to an old celibate about my personal matters," she said, raising her voice. "And I don't need help from any resources of the Baltimore Archdiocese!"

"You're distraught. You'll understand why you have to do this when you've seen him."

Her father had been pressing her since she'd come to stay with them while Glenn was in Southeast Asia. He'd become more insistent since her return from Hawaii; it was clear to him she was upset over whatever transpired there. What it was he could only guess, but his oldest daughter was clearly distressed and he reminded himself of the old aphorism: 'a son is a son 'til he takes a wife, but a daughter's a daughter all of her life.' Her despondency over the last year troubled him, and he knew the source of the problem.

She'd married the wrong young man, confirmed when he returned from Vietnam.

Glenn had refused to convert or agree to the children being baptized and raised Catholic. Now with the deteriorating happiness of his daughter and the obstinance of his son-in-law on several fronts he was convinced he had to take action for Mary Anne's sake. The situation seemed to him to have grown critical and so he sought the advice of a wise old friend in the church about what his daughter could and should do. Divorce, of course, was out of the question – he and the archbishop agreed totally on that. But there were other avenues to reconciling the situation. He'd broached the subject with his daughter and her resistance disappointed him.

His son-in-law had deepened the disappointment when he made himself a public spectacle in Washington the week before by confronting that Kerry fellow in front of reporters and calling him a liar after the Bostonian testified before the Senate committee investigating

American military atrocities. The incident had made the local evening news in Baltimore and the front page of the *Washington Post* the day it happened. He'd gotten some ribbing from some of the hospital staff the following day, and it irked him.

"I'll pick you up here at eleven and we can have lunch at Hausner's before visiting the Archbishop. You always liked it there," he said, smiling at her, pleased when she didn't object.

*   *   *

Glenn looked worriedly around the rapidly filling dark-paneled committee room. It was fifteen minutes until the hearing started and he'd not seen or heard from Favreaux even once in the last three days.

There was a loud current of chatter in the Senate Hearing Room as orderlies placed water pitchers and glasses at several places on the raised dais, photographers adjusted equipment and sound technicians made final checks on audio equipment. Wooden name plates on the dais indicted five senators would attend: Stallings, Meyer, Burney, Alexander and Reeves. Glenn's name was on a printed card in a stand in front of a table mic. There were three other cards with names: James Murray; Dirk Krykowski; Alan Phipps. Behind the microphones sat three men dressed much like John Kerry had been a week earlier in the same room – long unkempt hair, soiled jungle fatigue shirts, and a ribbon or two over their left breast pocket. One of them had a full beard and wore a boonie hat, while the other two looked like they hadn't shaved in over a week and were bareheaded. He looked at them and nodded; they gazed at him briefly, looked scornfully at his Dress Green uniform and turned away to talk among themselves.

Glenn sat down, and wiped his brow with a handkerchief. When he looked up, he saw Cateline at Senator Reeves' spot on the dais, placing a leather-bound writing tablet next to the large gavel. She looked back at him with no hint of recognition, but held his gaze for several seconds before moving off toward the side door and departing. Seeing her strangely buoyed his spirits. Favreaux suddenly sat down next to him.

"The Fabulous Favreaux, reporting as promised," he said with a broad smile, looking and sounding exhilarated. "This is going to be something!"

"Where the hell have you been?"

The Cajun grinned, and his face took on a kind of manic elation. "At Department of the Army, day and night working on this for you. I said the Army's record keeping system made sense, I didn't say that made it easy. But knowing the names of the three stooges over there made it a lot simpler than it would have been. And I got the right ones. It's them all right," he said, reaching into the large canvas messenger bag and pulling out a stack of files. "This one is Krykowski. Here's the one on Phipps. Here's Murray. The other files are my bonus. These are guys I've been researching and ran across while doing your job," he said, excitedly.

"What's in these packets?"

"Three folders – one for you, one for the committee and one for anybody in the news media that wants one. The folder on each of those guys contains their DA Form 2-1, the Military History Record of each man. Everybody in the Army has one. It lists everything the soldier has ever done while in the Army and when he did it. Every assignment, every award, every qualification, everything. Only one of these guys actually served in Vietnam – Phipps. He was a wheeled vehicle mechanic in Bien Hoa with the 263rd Truck Battalion. He was court-martialed for dealing drugs in September 1968 and shipped to Leavenworth where he served two years. Neither Krykowski or Murray ever got to Vietnam, but they're all going to claim they were there. Another thing," Favreaux said, handing him an envelope with a half dozen black and white photos, "you'll find these interesting. Pictures of you and the Kerry fella from last week. Senator Reeves got them blown up poster size for today."

"So, what good does all this do me?"

Favreaux's eyes lit up in nervous excitement. "Here's how all this is going to work." He explained to Nolan the process the hearing would most likely follow. "Pretty simple, but the fun begins when you challenge the Kerry statement. You wrote that out, didn't you?"

"I did, and the opening statement. I was really hoping you'd take a look at them before this morning."

"Sorry, no time now. You're not nervous are you? You're only testifying before five senators and a half dozen cameras and..." Favreaux looked around. "... maybe a dozen reporters. No big deal. Did you talk to anybody in the Army about this hearing?"

"No. I've been tied up with that court-martial. Should I have?"

"Probably. Oh well, too late now. Don't worry about it. Just look over these summary sheets on each of those three guys. This is going to go fine. At some point – after one of them makes a statement about their service in Vietnam, introduce me and I'll run through their actual military record as a rebuttal to whatever they say. I've done this dozens of times in court cases. Don't worry."

The hearing began ten minutes late due to a roll call vote in the well of the Senate. It was ten-thirty by the time all the witnesses had been duly sworn in and the photographers seated in front of the witness table had taken several pictures of them. Glenn was the only one with an opening statement and he was allowed to read it.

"My name is Glenn A. Nolan, Captain, United States Army. I served one tour in the Republic of Vietnam from January 13, 1970 through January 13, 1971 with the 1st Air Cavalry Division. Four months of my tour was as a platoon leader, seven months as a rifle company commander, and three weeks as a commander of a small fire support base in Phouc Long province a few miles from the Cambodian border. I am currently assigned to Fort Benning, Georgia as an instructor at the Infantry School. I'm here today, I've been told, as a rebuttal witness to the statement made by Mr. John Kerry to the Senate Foreign Relations Committee one week ago on April twenty-second..."

He paused, took a deep breath to calm himself and looked at each of the senators. Out of the corner of his eye he saw Cateline enter and sit down at the side of the room just off the dais. She looked at him and he thought he saw her nod and wink.

"I didn't ask to be here and I can neither support nor deny any of the allegations made by Mr. Kerry. I was in the hearing room the day he testified, but I had never heard any of these allegations before and I never witnessed anything like what he described during my tour in Southeast Asia. I am aware of the charges against Lieutenant William Calley and his court martial conviction a month ago. I firmly believe the actions of the lieutenant are the rare exception rather than the norm for American soldiers, so in that sense I disagree with the thrust of the Kerry testimony I heard. What I heard was a list of allegations. I did not hear supporting evidence other than vague allusions to unnamed people at a conference called Winter Soldier. I can't rebut or comment on Mr. Kerry's allegations because there are no facts or evidence to rebut. I'm not an expert witness about atrocities. I'm just a soldier who served in Vietnam who never saw or committed or even heard of such acts as were alleged by John Kerry."

There was a flurry of flashbulbs in front of him that was unsettling and he felt Favreaux grab his elbow and whisper something he couldn't understand into his ear.

"Thank you, captain," Senator Reeves said, looking displeased. "You say you can't rebut Mr. Kerry's sworn testimony, yet it's widely reported you confronted him immediately afterward and called him a liar. How did you know he was lying if what you say in your opening statement is true?"

"Senator, I did *not* confront Mr. Kerry, nor did I call him a liar. The reporting of that was unfortunately –"

"In error perhaps?" Reeves interrupted. "Apparently not." He pointed a finger at someone near the south door of the room and four easels with poster size black and white photos were brought in and set up along the side of the room. One of the pictures was the one used by the Washington Post. The others showed the same instant captured from different angles. "These are photographs taken that day by various news agencies. These show very clearly that you and

Mr. Kerry are obviously in some kind of confrontation. See the look on his face... and yours? How can you say you didn't confront him? Remember you're under oath, captain."

"Senator, the room was very crowded that day and when the hearing ended there was a lot of jostling and the crowd pushed forward. I was shoved from behind and bumped into Mr. Kerry. It was an accident."

"Really? Why did you call him a liar?"

"I never called him that, sir. Somebody in the crowd nearby said it. I don't know who but it wasn't me."

"You're telling this committee that you never called him a liar? Once again, remember you're under oath."

So this is it, Glenn thought. *This is a threat, and Reeves went right to it. Damn! Favreaux was wrong about how this was going to go.*

"Yes, sir. I realize I'm under oath. I swear I never called him that."

Reeves leaned back in his chair and crossed his arms over his chest. *I can't believe how easy this was. That pathetic opening statement – he set himself up, right off the bat.* He turned and looked at the other three witnesses. "Were any of you present that day?"

All three nodded, leaned forward and acknowledged into the microphones they were. Each said they were sure that Nolan had called Kerry a liar.

"We seem to have a difference of opinion here," Reeves said, smirking and slowly shaking his head. "What do you have to say about that, captain? The Bible says that in the testimony of two or three witnesses a thing is established."

Glenn felt his face go warm like prickly heat. This was way out of his league, and he'd not been prepared for it. His gut tightened and he felt a sudden fear cut through him like a hot saber. He looked at the three witnesses who wouldn't return his gaze. *They're the liars. Scraggly bastards.* Glenn took a deep breath and looked at the pictures on the easels again.

"Well, captain?" Reeves asked. "How do you respond to three men who claim you said what you now deny saying?"

Glenn looked at the senator, then back to pictures. "Senator, it was extremely noisy in here in the first minutes after the hearing. If someone heard Mr. Kerry called a liar, he would have had to be real close to the person who said it in all that noise. What you have in those four photos is a panorama of the moment that slur was uttered. If – and I emphasize 'if' – I had been the one to say it, anyone who heard it would have to be in one of those photographs. My point senator, is that none of these three at the witness table with me today are in any of the photographs. If they are, I'd ask them to point themselves out in those pictures."

An undercurrent of murmurs swept across the hearing room and Senator Reeves angrily gaveled the crowd quiet. He looked at the three VVAW witnesses and then back at Nolan. "I'll take that under advisement."

"Senator, if it pleases the committee, I would very much like to challenge the credibility of these witnesses who made this false accusation about me."

"It's not been determined that it's false. Let me say for the record we have the word of three highly respected veterans."

"Sir, I've been publicly accused by these three men of slander. I'd like the opportunity to challenge that characterization and the credibility of these men," Glenn replied.

"This is a senate inquiry, captain, not a trial court."

"Understood, sir. However, I'd like to enter into the hearing's record the military service history of each of these three men."

Reeves's face grew stern and a prominent blood vessel appeared on his forehead. "You are out of order, captain. Where did you obtain these records?" he demanded.

"From the Veterans Administration, senator. Specifically a Mr. Favreaux."

"And who is this person?!"

"A government employee of the VA. He's right here behind me, sir."

Reeves again gaveled for quiet as murmurs began in the audience.

"Reuben Favreaux," the Cajun said, quickly sitting beside Nolan and taking the microphone. "I'm employed by the Veterans Administration and my responsibility is investigating fraudulent claims against the VA made by veterans and by some who attempt to pass themselves off as having served when they have not."

Reeves looked around quickly, caught the attention of Brandon Oakes and waved over his senior advisor. "Do you know this Favreaux?" he asked in a sharp whisper, covering the microphone with his hand.

"No, but I can find out real quick," Oakes replied and hurried off.

Reeves turned back toward the room and said, "I'm sorry but I'm going to have to rule you're out of order, Mr. Favreaux. You have no standing in this hearing. We can't have just anyone providing testimony before the Senate. I'm accountable to the committee in particular and to the whole of the Senate to ensure all those who testify here have been properly vetted and you sir have not been so examined. So I'm going to have to require that you step back and refrain from further outburst or you *will* be escorted out by the sergeant at arms."

Favreaux nodded and whispered in Glenn's ear, "Reeves is losing control of the narrative. Keep pressing to get those records accepted into the official minutes of the meeting."

Glenn glanced toward Cateline but she'd moved or left the room. Favreaux gave him a quick smile and a thumbs up.

Reeves conferred with his four senatorial colleagues out of range of the microphones. After a few minutes, Brandon Oakes returned and whispered into Reeves' ear away from the others, "This Favreaux is a worker bee at the VA, doing what he claimed to do. Nolan probably does have the copies of the official records and that's not good news for us."

"How did this happen?" the senator asked angrily. "What do you suggest now?"

"Senator, keep the ball up in the air. Don't accept the files into the official record of the hearing... Say you need to have staff examine the documents for authenticity before allowing them on the record. Adjourn the meeting until a date uncertain in the future. Your excuse is an emergency meeting called by the State Department. I just set it up. If anybody checks, that'll stand the test."

"When we're finished here," Reeves said anxiously, "you and I need to talk."

The Senator returned to his chair, gaveled for quiet and said, "Captain Nolan. Please provide the military records you mentioned to my staff assistant after we adjourn so that the committee staff can authenticate them. I regret to inform you, though, that I am forced to adjourn far sooner that I'd like because of an emergency meeting called by the State Department that I must attend. This hearing will be adjourned now and reconvened at a date sometime in the near future determined by our committee clerk who will contact all of the participants and witnesses as soon as a suitable time on the Senate calendar can be determined. You will be contacted as soon as it is. I thank the witnesses and ask that you accept my apology for this unexpected and unwelcome delay. We are now adjourned."

Harrison Reeves banged down the gavel and stormed from the room by a side door.

Favreaux grabbed Nolan's hand and shook it. "Nice job, rookie. You did good for your first time out of the chute."

"I feel like I got rolled. What do you think happens now?"

"For you, I don't know. Maybe that girl behind you does."

Glenn turned around and looked at Cateline who quickly said, "Captain Nolan, I'm the staff assistant for Senator Reeves. I was told to collect some documentation from you before you left. May I have it, please?" Her eyes darted left and right as she leaned forward and said, "Erika is outside in the hallway. She'd like to see you. By the way, you were very impressive under fire... good show."

*　　*　　*

"Thank you, Father," Dr. MacEagan said to the Archbishop and shook his hand as they stood at the door inside the priest's large office.

"No need to thank me. I think it's an obvious and appropriate action. If the young man entered into the marriage on the fraudulent grounds you say, then an annulment would clearly be in order."

"I assure you, he did. When he indicated he'd be willing to listen to reason about raising the children in The Faith, it seemed apparent he was sincere. Unfortunately, time has proven our hope to be in vain."

"I don't doubt what you say, doctor. But your daughter seems very reluctant to consider the step."

MacEagan nodded. "At the moment, she is. She's young and not very wise in either the ways of the world or the church. I realize now I should never have allowed the marriage to go forward in the first place. But I was weak. She's our eldest daughter and it's been too easy to accede to her wishes, but the time has come to do the right thing. Over time, with the family's help and your guidance, she will. I'm sure of it."

Chapter 36

"Not Fort Campbell! When did this happen?" Mary Anne moaned. "Please, Glenn tell me that's not true. After all I've heard... Jeannie and Barb say they looked into it and there's not so much as a one bedroom apartment to live in for a hundred miles around that place."

"I know. I've heard about the housing shortages," he said quietly as he fixed them drinks before dinner. "It's what you'd expect with the 101st just getting back from Vietnam a little while ago. Bart and Jack and I are going up to Clarksville this weekend to scope things out. Ollie Meyer got orders there too and he has some contacts in the real estate business he gave us that could help. I'll look into it."

"You decided to take off this weekend without talking to me?! I won't stay in this awful place by myself without a car, Glenn. I won't! Isn't there something you can do about this? Anything?!" She sighed deeply and said, "I don't know how much more of this I can take."

He took a deep breath and looked at her. *Man she's beautiful – even when she's mad at me*, he thought. *She has a right to be upset after all I've dragged her through since I got back from Nam. Benning, Wolters, Rucker, back to Benning. And now to Campbell. Five moves in less than two years, and each with a whole houseful of furniture. She's had a different life, living in that big house for as long as she can remember. That's a far cry from what we had during flight school – a trailer in Mineral Wells that winter with water pipes freezing solid, or the dumpy little rancher in Enterprise Alabama after that.*

"Look at this place," she said, swinging her arm in a wide circle, all at once wild with rage. She promised herself she wouldn't blow up at him again, but the dismal quarters with its low ceilings and ridiculous plumbing and unsafe electrical circuitry gripped her like an iron fist. And now this news about moving again! "They don't call Custer Terrace the 'Captain's Ghetto' for nothing. And we've lived here twice now. You know, the unit across the street was without electricity again for the whole day. Can you imagine how it would be in here if we couldn't run that little window unit you bought? With all the wiring problems, it's a wonder the whole place doesn't catch fire!"

"We'll find something nice at Campbell. I'm sure. Ollie says the communities outside the gates are a beehive of building. All kinds of new housing is going up."

"A new house? How long does it take to build one from scratch? Six months? A year? It means another long separation, doesn't it?" she said, looking away and flopping wearily into the overstuffed chair near the small front window. He made no reply which upset her more than if he'd given some pitiable denial. "You told me the next assignment was going to be different. More permanent. Less Army hassle. Better housing. And I bought it all. But nothing's going to change is it? Promise me when your commitment is up a year from now, we'll talk seriously about a future. They're letting junior officers go like there's no tomorrow; with the draw down Army-wide what kind of future is the military with that going on?"

He hesitated, and wouldn't look at her. "It's... it's going to be more than a year."

"But your five years is up next June?"

"I owe an additional three years' service on top of the five from my original West Point service commitment."

She eyed him ferociously. "Tell me you're not serious!"

"An officer has to pay back two for one on the time spent in schools. That's what I was told by my branch in Washington.."

"Three more years?! We'll be stuck in Clarksville or Hopkinsville for four long years?! Oh, but no, that won't happen will it? The Army in all its blessed ingenuity will find a reason to move you after nine months or a year to some other god-forsaken hole in the wall post – probably just as soon as this new house of yours gets finished. That *would be* the Army way, wouldn't it? They don't care about you – about us."

"Tours will stabilize now that we're out of Vietnam. Things will settle down and normalize," he said guiltily.

"Really?! What does that mean? You're sure that there's not another contingency somewhere in world that's calling for an Airborne Ranger helicopter pilot with combat experience?" She clenched her hands and watched him gazing at her. He was frowning, troubled. *What is wrong with him that he doesn't see military life for what it really is? How could he be so calm, about it all, so stupidly, insanely unfaltering.* To her surprise she realized she was quietly weeping. "I don't know how much more of this I can take. We've moved eight times in the four years we've been married. You've been absent almost half that time, and we've not had one decent place to live. For all your diligence, and your selection as one of the first dozen in your class to attend the Advanced course, we're still treated like second class citizens – by civilians and even by the blessed Army."

He gave her a somber smile. "It's bound to get better. The history of the Army is one of ups and downs. Feast or famine."

"Uncertainty, followed by uncertainty. You can live like that, Glenn. I can't." She wiped her eyes with a tissue and sighed. "I know that's how your whole life has been. Moving around, never in one place for all that long – that's something you thrive on. When we were dating in Baltimore you told me so, more than once. I remember you saying how you always looked forward to the next set of orders your father got so you could explore what was over the next hill. I need more stability. Look at us. Look at this place." She flung an arm at the dingy walls and ceiling in a gesture she knew was overly dramatic, maybe hysterical, but she didn't care. "Just look at where we are. This is disgusting. It's degrading... it's indecent!"

He crossed the room, knelt on a knee beside her and touched her arm. "I know it's not all that either one of us wished it would be here..."

"Or anywhere else we've lived since we were married."

He wanted to remind her of how much she had enjoyed the little apartment in Augsburg. *But we were just married then and the thrill of just being together in the first months of marriage had let her overlook a lot of things... in the housing and in my first real assignment.* He kissed her gently. "There are worse places and duty. I think we'll find Campbell will be a turning point. I really do."

"Oh, Glenn. Always the eternal optimist." But even as the thought formed, his look contradicted her. His face looked older and sadder than she'd ever seen. His eyes seemed dark, with indomitable, angry sadness. She guessed he'd suffered something or some things while in Southeast Asia more terrible than she could imagine, but he kept it bottled tightly. It was Benny's loss, and probably others. Only once had he shown any symptoms of what they were now calling *post-traumatic stress.*

"I'll make all this up to you," he was whispering as he kissed her again. "I promise I will. I'm not totally committed to or sold on a twenty or thirty year career in the Army."

"Don't say that if you don't mean it."

"But I do. Nothing is more important to me than you. I swear it. We'll find a way."

She smiled at him thinking: *Don't make it worse for him. You can't let down this good, decent man.* "I know we'll find a way. Love always does. Disregard my hysterical ramblings. It's the legacy of a spoiled upbringing and private school education. We're going to be all right Glenn. We will."

But even as she said it, a wave of apprehension swept over her. He wouldn't find a place for them near Fort Campbell, ready to move in, and another long separation was in their future. Where would she go? Her family's home in Baltimore? Her parents would insist but she dreaded the idea, thought it dangerous for their marriage, but where else was there for her to live? When she spoke, her voice was faint, a little tremulous and she felt light-headed.

"Promise me everything is going to be all right."

*   *   *

Erika Ashby took a deep, nervous breath, opened the door to the large conference room and entered.

"This is all very dramatic, Erika," Harrison Reeves said, leaning back in his chair with the fingers of his hands intertwined and resting on the polished mahogany table. His facial expression was perfectly impassive, aloof and unrevealing except that his pale blue eyes glinted annoyance. When the assistant prosecutor sat down across from him without responding, he made a show of opening a silver cigarette holder engraved *H.G.R* and offering it to her. When she declined, he lit a Benson & Hedges, turned his profile to her and closed his eyes as if dismissing her.

"Senator, I had hoped you would take my advice and have your lawyer present."

"I thought it unnecessary and likely to impose an unwarranted and adversarial tenor to our little tête à tête. I have nothing to hide from you or anyone else. Besides, we're old friends are we not?" He turned his head toward her and smiled. "I remember you as a young teen in Manila when your family was stationed there. You used to visit our quarters often and ride with Michelle and your mother. How are they, my dear?"

Erika ignored his question, opened her briefcase, removed a stack of files and looked across the table at him. "I'm here today to advise you that you're being indicted on three separate counts of subornation of perjury, and –"

"Subornation of perjury?! That's insane!"

"You remember those three supposed Vietnam veterans at the hearing you called to trap my brother?" She slid a file folder toward him. "This is the transcript of your conversation with them and your chief of staff. You knew they were giving false testimony and you clearly coached them."

"You're making this up, counselor," Reeves said tightly. His glance fell on her stack of folders as she pushed them across the table one by one.

"Multiple counts of falsification of official records, and several violations of the Tillman Act, the Taft-Hartley Act, the Federal Corrupt Practices Act, and the 1971 Federal Election Campaign Act. Violation of Congressional franking privileges. Seventeen counts total. Allowing you to come to this building and to hear the indictment in private is a courtesy to the office you hold. I have no desire to create a spectacle of a sitting Congressman – even you. Although some had wished to confront you in the Capitol Building to apply the handcuffs and force you to do the 'perp walk' for the benefit of the evening news, cooler heads prevailed."

"Surely you don't –"

"Surely *I do think* this is going to stick, Senator," Erika interrupted. "I know it will. This case has been in the works for several years and I assure you that it's most solid. I'm sending over two dozen evidence archive boxes of files as disclosure to your personal lawyer as soon as we're done here. And with my former boss, Rupert Whitcomb, now two years retired and living in Boca Raton, you're without the cover you once enjoyed in the D.C. Prosecutor's office. We've also brought back the original lawyer working this case and he eagerly picked up where he left off before your friend Whitcomb shipped him out to the hinterland. "

For the first time Harrison Reeves looked uncertain. He turned toward Erika and said, "I've beaten a whole hell of a lot of better lawyers than you'll ever be. You don't scare me."

"I'm sure I don't." Erika watched the Senator's eyes. *He thinks he has a chance... like he's one of the gods, loose again in the midst of us mortals. Don't do this,* she told herself. *Don't let him trick you into doing something that scuttles all these years of work, that keeps you from setting all his wrongs right. Why is it that evil always wins?! Back away. Don't tip all your hand!* But the temptation was too great, the decades of patiently doing the right thing in the right way too agonizing. "You can't beat the evidence you're about to face."

"The hell you say. Surely you've had some scintillating successes in the past few years, albeit against lessor opposition than you'll encounter with me. I've bought and paid for the best lawyers this country ever produced, sweetheart. Despite your record, you'll come up a day late and a dollar short like everyone else in your family – your father, your brothers... that worthless little nephew of yours. The best lawyer I ever faced left the courtroom with his tail between his legs and his reputation in tatters. There isn't a man alive that can beat my legal team."

"That might be true, Senator. But the lawyer you're up against isn't male."

Reeves' face evidenced an angry, defiant amusement. Or perhaps it was his habitual contempt for everyone around him. Ericka found the look intimidating despite knowing the evidence she held, the witnesses already deposed and the growing number lining up to testify. "By the time I'm done with you, Erika, there won't be a law firm or a prosecutor in the country who'll even return your phone calls. You'll just be the latest in your family to rue the day he or she dared cross me. Nothing you could possibly have worries me in the least."

"Talk to your legal team," Erika said, gazing hard at him across the table and leaning forward. "Review the photographs of yourself with lobbyists aboard yachts and on various beaches across the Caribbean. You should also listen to the tapes. They contain virtually all of the conversations you've had in the last few years in which you violated laws and the confidence of many who trusted you."

"You're bluffing, counselor. There's nothing illegal about vacationing," Reeves responded dismissively, but his eyes and the prominent, throbbing blood vessel on his forehead told her he was growing agitated. "And there's no possible way you could have recorded any conversation I had. That would require evidence and a court order to obtain, neither of which you have."

Erika smiled prettily at him. "We'll see."

"We most certainly will," Reeves replied with intense irritation. He rose suddenly, glared at her and leaned menacingly across the table, placing both hands on the polished wood. "We're done here. You have no idea with whom you're dealing."

"Actually, Senator, I have an excellent idea who and what you are. I've known for most of my life, even as a young girl riding with your ex-wife. Michelle is, by the way, on the list of witnesses for the prosecution and her story is a compelling one. And it's not that of an angry woman looking for revenge against a former husband."

"Of course it's not. It's the tale of an unrepentant adulteress, and you should know your own father is central to that scandalous narrative. Are you sure you want to drag him and your mother into this? It won't be pretty, my dear. I can assure you."

"In the end, truth will win out. Truth and the facts."

Reeves chuckled mirthlessly. "Truth? The facts? In this town?! You're even more naïve than I suspected, young lady. I imagined you were more worldly-wise than that. Truth and facts mean less than nothing in this town. You should have figured that out by now. Washington runs on power and money, my dear. To hell with facts... and this silly idea of truth?! You're really more unsophisticated and simple than I suspected."

He's really worried, she thought. *Nobody has ever talked to him like this and he doesn't know how to handle it.* She was surprised to find she was shaking with relief, and rage and disgust. "My side will stick with the facts, senator, and they're compelling. Your team of all-star litigators ought to look closely at the witness list and the facts bearing on the case. I'm willing to offer a plea bargain, modest though it may be. You should consider it when proffered."

"You can go to hell, little girl." He stood upright, towering over her.

They stared at one another for a long minute until Erika said, "And you, senator, can go to the Jessup, Maryland Correctional Facility for the next few decades. I understand there's a dress code there that requires you wear a coat and tie when you entertain visitors, but you and I both know you won't be bothered by visitors, except perhaps your attorneys. For now, the officers waiting outside will place you under arrest and you'll be arraigned downtown first thing tomorrow morning."

"I'll be out on bail an hour from now."

"Maybe. Maybe not. When and if you're eventually freed on bail, know that all the airports have been alerted. Don't even think of leaving the U.S. You should have brought your lawyer with you, as I recommended since its past five o'clock. You won't reach him tonight, so I hope you enjoy your evening in the city lockup."

The senator stuck his chin out defiantly. "You just signed your own career death warrant, counselor. You have no idea of what I can bring down on your head."

"Actually, I do," Erika replied, looking him in the eye. "I know the power of a sitting senator. I worked for Senator Payne from before Pearl Harbor until his death. He commanded the respect of everyone in government because he had the integrity you lack. We both know you have no real friends on the Hill or anywhere else in this town. You'll be surprised at how little power you really have."

"I used to like you, Erika, when you were a teenager visiting our quarters in Manila. But you've grown into someone I hate."

"Hatred is a coward's revenge for being intimidated. Thank you for the compliment." She went to the conference room door and opened it. Two somber looking plain clothes detectives entered and handcuffed Reeves while reciting the Miranda Rights. As they led him out, Erika saw Cateline standing in the outer office watching the brief episode and caught a brief glimpse of the shock on the senator's face when they passed one another.

"What are you doing here?" Reeves asked harshly.

"I came to see your prosecutor, and just happened on this cheery sight," the Brit said. "I wish I had a camera, but then, I can always clip the pictures from tomorrow morning's newspaper, can't I?"

"Cateline, I've always been fond of you," the senator said, amending his tone to one more considerate and fatherly. He smiled and nodded in the false, overly courteous formality that was his trademark. "I hope you'll remember how well I've taken care of you these past few years."

"I remember quite a bit, Senator Reeves," she responded flatly and turned away from him. She found Erika sitting in a chair, leaning back with her eyes closed. "He's quite the intimidating old bastard, isn't he, auntie? But by the looks of him, you've taken away much of his starch."

"He's worried."

"As well he should be."

"He'll be a tough adversary, despite what we have. They'll challenge the tape recordings you took of the conversations in his office."

"Let them," Cateline said. "Even if some judge throws them out, which I doubt, Reeves is finished in your Senate. I've sent copies to every Democrat in your Congress who's mentioned anywhere on the tapes."

"That's not the way I do things, Cateline," the prosecutor said, walking to the window and looking outside at the sizeable crowd of reporters and photographers milling around the entrance to the building.

"I suspected as much, Auntie Erika. That's why I didn't tell you."

"I suppose you also alerted the press that's outside."

Cateline shrugged and gave her aunt an impish, innocent smile.

*   *   *   *

Glenn stood on the gravel of the unpaved street looking at the wooded lot; a car drove up and a middle aged man in jeans and work boots got out, walked over to him and said, "Nicest lot in the whole development, Glenn. That split level is going to be perfect for it, sitting just on that little rise halfway back."

"Honestly, Mr. Hatch, I'm having a hard time imagining it anymore."

"I know we're a little behind getting started, but –"

"Seven weeks this Friday, sir."

"There's been just a lot of unforeseen circumstances crop up, Glenn. I've kept you informed. You know I have."

""Yes, you have. Every time I asked. But it's wearing thin, sir. You told me two weeks ago the lot would be cleared by today." He turned and looked at the thick undergrowth and dense stand of mostly mature trees. "There's no indication anyone has even walked the property much less marked the trees to be left standing. Almost two months and not a single lick of work. That's unacceptable."

"We've had some weather delays on other projects and –"

"That's not my problem, sir, it's yours. You promised me a start date and a completion date. This project doesn't seem to be anywhere on your priority list and winter's coming on. I've heard about the heavy rains and ice storms. If anything, the reasons for delays will increase."

"I'll have a crew out here the day after tomorrow."

"I have no confidence that's going to happen. You told me exactly the same thing a week ago, and two weeks before that. As much as I like the location and the house plan, I don't think it's going to come about in the foreseeable future. I asked you out here because I want out of the contract."

The contractor frowned and cleared his throat. "I can't do that."

"Can't do what?"

"I can't let you out of the contract. There isn't a firm date for beginning construction so legally as long as I'm making a good faith effort... I have documentation showing I have."

Glenn gave him an angry look. "Mr. Hatch, that's dishonest and we both know it."

"Maybe, but I'm within state law and regulatory requirements. You're going to have to go along with me about this. These construction delays I've been experiencing are customary and acceptable."

"Not to me, sir. I've got a wife living with her parents a ten hour drive away, a twenty-four hour a day assignment on post, and a sizeable down payment of my money sitting in your bank account accruing interest for you. And I've got nothing to show for it."

"Sometimes you just have to bite the bullet, Captain."

Glenn looked down briefly, then took a deep breath and looked up. "Well, Mr. Hatch, I don't think this is one of those times."

"I'm telling you it is."

"It's possible that I can't legally force you to release me from this contract," Glenn said easily, squinting at the bright sky. "I forwarded a copy of the contract to my sister who specializes in real estate law for a prestigious New York firm, and another copy to my aunt who's a federal prosecutor in Washington, D.C. They're good and they'll find any flaws there are in the contract. I also have a meeting with the commanding general and several other officers petitioning him to put your construction firm off-limits to all soldiers on Ft. Campbell. I'm taking that same group of officers to speak with the Attorney General of Tennessee concerning your business practices."

Glenn could tell he had the construction man's attention. He locked his eyes on the older man until Hatch looked away.

"But if none of that works out," Glenn continued, "I guess we're stuck with each other. That may be the worst thing of all for you. You see, I've been visiting other of your homes around here under construction. Two of them have the same floor plan as the one I chose. I noticed that you're shorting those houses on construction materials."

"I don't need to listen to this."

"But you should. You see, Mr. Hatch, when you get started on my house, I'm going to be on site every day making sure I get two-by-four studded walls like the drawings call for – that's part of the contract, too. I notice that neither of the other two houses meet standard in that, or the depth of the footers for the foundation, or the size of moldings, the quality of carpet or appliances. You're probably making an extra seven to eight percent profit by doing that. It's clear you're cutting some serious corners. You won't do it on my house. If you try, I'll have the Clarksville building inspector out here in a heartbeat, and you'll rip everything out and re-do it right. That's a promise."

"It sounds like a threat, captain."

"I guess it does. Well, you think about it."

He drove back to the house owned by a bachelor lieutenant where he rented a room and shared costs for meals and utilities. It was an hour after supper when Hatch called to advise him they could mutually agree to declare the contract null and void, and Glenn would receive a full refund of his earnest money. Though he'd lost two months on his search for a place for them to live, it was the most positive development of his brief stay at Campbell,

Two letters and a phone call awaited him when he arrived home the next day – the phone call and one of the letters was from Cateline.

"Wonderful! The letter arrived this day – I was certain it would. What do you think of the headline?" she asked when he returned the call.

It was on the front page of the Wall Street Journal – the two right side columns topped by a picture of Senator Reeves and a short two line title in bold: **Reeves Accepts Plea Bargain**. "Looks like you two girls finally nailed him. Congratulations."

"I wish I could have been in on the plea discussions. I know it was a terribly difficult month of negotiations but I remain convinced Erika was far too easy and let him off with twenty-five years in a minimum security facility."

"At his age, that's a life sentence."

"Believe me when I say he deserved far worse, Glenn. If you only knew... he was and is a most loathsome creature."

"Tell you the truth, I couldn't be less interested in him. I've got bigger fish to fry than Harrison Reeves – I'm living out of a suitcase in a basically unfurnished house and I just wasted two months in my efforts to get a house built. Mary Anne is a day and a half drive away and I haven't heard a word from her in a month and can't get her on the phone. My assignment is awful, the new Modern Volunteer Army is a disaster and –" He stopped abruptly, lowering his voice. "And as you can probably tell I've turned into whining malcontent."

"You do sound at wit's end. It's not the Glenn Nolan I know and love."

"It's not the Glenn Nolan I know and love either."

"Have you given any thought perhaps to leaving the Army for another career?"

He chuckled into the phone. "Not since supper tonight. But I still owe almost three years due to schooling. I'm kinda stuck here for the time being."

"Something will come up, I'm sure of it. You're a resourceful chap and remain one of my two favorite brothers."

"One of your only two brothers, Cateline."

"That also is true," she said and broke into laughter. "I should very much like to come visit you sometime soon. I gather Tennessee is on the American frontier. Are there many Indians about?"

"Only had one attack on the fort since I've been here, and just two white women carried off by raiding parties. That's pretty civilized I'd say."

"Yes, I'd say also. It's good to hear the laughter in your voice. I daresay it's important to keep one's sense of humor in your situation."

He had always enjoyed Cateline – the big sister with the odd take on life, the dry British sense of humor and funny accent. He'd finally gotten to know her one summer while in high school when they all spent a couple of weeks at his grandfather's summer place on Long Island. He thought her aloof and stuffy at first, but that had passed quickly and he'd been sorry the vacation was over so soon, just as he was really getting to know her. They had stayed in touch long distance, and she'd come to his graduation from the academy.

"Glenn, I'll call again soon. Promise. The firm is throwing a bash tonight and it's all hands on deck for the party and those who miss it are given the black spot when it comes to partnerships. But I wanted to chat you up over the good news about Reeves. I'll call again tomorrow night."

He hung up and felt restored after the brief conversation. Things were going better, he was sure of it. He'd gotten out from under the contract with Hatch, the episode with Senator Reeves was now finally closed. He'd decided to spend more time flying in spite of Major Howell's directive that he limit himself solely to the administrative duties delegated to the executive officer of a combat assault helicopter company. And, tomorrow or this week – sometime soon – he'd find something suitable for Mary Anne to call home. He missed her so much he ached for wanting to be with her.

The other letter caught his eye when he placed the telephone receiver on its cradle.

It was in a larger than normal envelope with a 'Registered Letter' sticker and a return address of: *THE CATHOLIC CENTER, 320 Cathedral Street, Baltimore, Maryland.* One of his roommates must have signed for it when delivered. He felt a sudden chill as if a cold breeze had invaded the room, and he shivered for an instant. All at once he felt a clutch in his gut, that same instant of fear and uncertainty he'd experienced more than once in Vietnam when the hollow *'thunk'* of an NVA mortar tube wafted through the silent jungle. Worst case scenarios rushed through his thoughts. *Her priest was writing to inform him she was terribly ill... or in a bad accident? – that explained why he hadn't heard from her.* Or did it?

He slit the envelope open and extracted the contents – five pages – and unfolded them. It was a form letter from the Archdiocese of Baltimore, and not an original but a copy. He gasped at the title, centered at the top of the first page.

Annulment of Marriage

His breathing grew rapid as he glanced at the lines typed in on the form. His name. Hers – not her married name but *Mary Anne MacEagan.* In stilted, overly formal language it announced the final dissolution of their marriage, and the reason given was his entering the marriage under the false pretenses of converting to the Catholic religion and failing to agree to raise all children resulting from the marriage in the Catholic faith.

"What?!" he yelled loudly so that it echoed through the house. He was stunned and the remainder of the form was a blur to him as he searched its contents. "This was her damned father's doing!" he said aloud, and reached for the phone. He dialed the long distance number and waited.

"*MacEagan residence,*" the young female voice said.

"Is this Hailey?"

"*Yes, this is she.*"

"Hailey, this is Glenn. I'm calling from Tennessee and I need to speak with Mary Anne. Is she there? Please, I've got to talk to her."

"*I'm... I'm not sure I can let you do that,*" the girl said nervously.

"Hailey! Hailey, listen. This is an emergency. A crisis. Do hear me? It's very urgent and I must speak to your sister right away. Is she there?"

"*Yes, but Glenn –*"

"You've got to go get her for me."

"*But father said not to allow –*"

"Your father would not want to keep your sister from hearing about this emergency," Glenn said, certain that the doctor was behind the letter he held in his hand. "Hailey, just get your sister to the phone. Please. I know she wants to hear about this situation."

There was a brief silence.

"*Mr. Nolan, she is already aware of the situation, and has been for some time,*" Dr. MacEagan said on the line. "*I assume you received the letter from the church and it's the reason for your call. Hear me when I tell you – she's no longer your wife and she has no interest in seeing or speaking to you ever again.*"

"I don't believe that. And I won't until she tells me that herself... face to face."

"That's not going to happen. You're no longer a part of her life, Glenn. Accept that and move on."

"You don't dictate her life any more. When we got married –"

"That marriage was illegitimate from the start. The church and the state of Maryland are in agreement about that. You will not see her again, nor will you attempt to contact her."

"Dr. MacEagan, you can't stop me from doing either. She's my wife and I will see her."

"That would be unwise. There is a legal restraining order against you that prohibits your approaching closer than a hundred feet to her presence and closer than a hundred yards to our house. You're a violent young man who volunteered for the most brutal assignments in Vietnam, and like many others of your ilk, you committed some of the most sadistic acts in the history of warfare. You're a danger – to my daughter, my family and even to yourself. I highly recommend you seek counseling and treatment."

"None of that is true, and you know it."

"I profoundly disagree. Know this – she is no longer your wife and she no longer wishes to see or communicate with you in any way. Let me be very clear, young man. If you try to see her, you will be arrested and prosecuted."

"This is wrong, doctor. What you're telling me about her is flat wrong, and I *will* see her again. Soon. I don't believe she had any part in this charade you're pulling. I think she's a prisoner in your house, and I'm going to rescue her from that. You can take that to the bank, sir. Do you understand?"

There was no reply – the line had gone dead.

Chapter 37

The note tucked into the corner of the blotter on his desk was scrawled in Spec-4 Durant's all but indecipherable script.

1427 hrs. – Call received from West Point Military Academy
Superintendent MG Sidney B. Berry – call back soonest.

What in the world does this mean? Glenn wondered looking at the name and the phone number. *Nothing good, that's for sure. The last time I ran into General Berry was one of the worst days in my military life... maybe in my entire life, period.*

He toyed with the idea of letting the call go until the next day when he might be a little more in the mood – the morning's mission in support of the 506th had been awful, just plain awful, and he was still irritated and out of sorts. The infantry company hadn't been at the briefed coordinates and a front had blown in halfway through the mission. *The damned grunts in this VOLAR Army can't tie their own boots without screwing up. Man, I've had it with the 101st. This is the most screwed up damned division...and it's getting worse.* He looked at the note again and took a deep breath. "Bad news doesn't get better with age, Nolan. Call the general back and get it over with."

He checked to see how long it was until Happy Hour at the O-Club as he dialed.

"General Berry," came the immediate response over the line in the familiar, crisp inflection that even the hollow echo of the phone line couldn't mask.

Glenn was briefly surprised. *Why no secretary or aide answering?* he wondered. "Sir, this is Captain Glenn Nolan, commander of Delta Company 101st Aviation Battalion at Fort Campbell, Kentucky. I have a message to call you."

"You have a new job, captain," the general said in his flat, characteristically direct tone, forgoing any pleasantries. "You're transferred to West Point, reporting directly to me."

"Sir?" Glenn was instantly uncomfortable. Generals didn't go on recruiting forays down through the company grade ranks. "Shouldn't I be hearing this from my chain of command?"

"Your chain of command will be properly briefed. This comes directly from General Rogers, the Deputy Chief of Staff for Personnel. Vocal orders will be called down in the next hour, if they aren't there already, so you can start clearing post; written orders to follow."

"Excuse me, sir?"

Glenn swore under his breath. *What in the world?* The last thing he wanted was to be the general's aide. He had taken command of the company only three months earlier and needed at least another six months to a year to turn it around and make it combat effective. Wearing greens every day, running to the cleaners for the general and his wife instead of showing up at the flight line was not his idea of being a soldier. One of his principles since pinning on pilot's wings was that an aviation commander did three things, in order: Fly; Lead; Train. He'd worked hard to get command of this aviation company, a truly plum assignment, and there was no place in his plan for becoming a 'go-fer' for the Superintendent of West Point.

"Sir, I just took over this aviation company a few months ago. There's a lot I have to do."

"I'm well aware of your situation and your preferences, captain. At the moment, your personal desires take a back seat to the needs of the service."

So he trots out the universal bromide, Glenn thought. *For the good of the damn service.*

"Look, captain, I don't care about your desires. I happen to agree that you're sadly lacking in the requisite qualities I demand of my aide-de-camp. That's not the job I have for you. I've created a temporary position of Special Assistant to the Superintendent."

"I don't understand what that means, sir."

"The responsibilities aren't yet finalized. That's your first assignment – to figure out what the job entails and write the position description."

"Sir, I respectfully request that I be allowed to remain in –"

"Request denied."

"– that I be allowed to remain in my current command position until I complete the necessary work to return D Company to a satisfactory readiness condition."

"I say again, captain, request denied."

"Sir, for the good of the service –"

"For the good of the service, Captain Nolan, you *will* proceed to the United States Military Academy without delay arriving on post ready for duty not later than 0900 this coming Monday, 13 October," the general said, sounding testy now and wholly out of patience.

"Sir, I appreciate your confidence in me. But as important as I'm sure the assignment is, it sounds like the last thing in the world I want to do."

"Throughout your Army career, captain, there will be many things you don't *want* to do. I have my marching orders… and now so do you. End of conversation. I'll see you in six days. Come prepared to work harder than you ever have before."

The loud click and the silence that followed signaled the conversation was over.

"Damn!" Nolan said loudly, tempted to throw his coffee mug at the far wall of the office. "I really should have gone to see that corporate head-hunter in Nashville when I had the chance. You're an absolute idiot, Nolan!"

He sat down and swung the big swivel chair to look outside. *I finally get a command slot in aviation, my first command in almost five years, and this happens... whatever this is. I'll never get another shot at an aviation command. After all that time as Major Howell's XO – all the extra duties and none of the flying.* "This is the last straw! You hear that, Nolan?!"

Out of the corner of his eye he caught sight of the framed picture of Mary Anne with him on a balcony of the Neuschwanstein Castle in Bavaria their first and only spring in Germany. He felt a tug behind his heart and his eyes became moist. He'd heard nothing from her since that night of the phone call with her father two years earlier. Despite Dr. MacEagan's warnings he took leave and went directly to her home in Guilford, only to be picked up by pair of city cops in front of their house for violating the restraining order. Fortunately one of them was a veteran, having served in the Cav in '67 and let him off with a warning. It now seemed like an age since he'd last seen her. He pushed the conference button on his phone and gave Durant a number to call then sat for a long while, silently looking at the picture.

Two hours later the company clerk stuck his head in after knocking once. "Sir, there's a call for you on line two. He said to tell you the fish are biting down on Cottonwood Creek."

Glenn swung his chair around and picked up the phone. "No interruptions, Durant – no matter who it is." When the clerk had closed the door, he punched the illuminated button and said, "Is there ever a time the fish aren't biting on that creek? How are you doing, grandpa?"

"The real question is how you're doing... after your little talk with the Supe."

"You know about that?"

"I still have some friends in the Army – the son of a classmate is a two-star working for General Bernie Rogers. He gave me a 'heads up' yesterday about your new assignment. I don't want to barge in and interfere. If I am, tell me. The last thing you probably want or need is some gray beard like me messing in your business with General Berry."

"I'm glad you called me back. You got time to listen to me bellyache again?"

"Always... Do you know what this is about?"

"Not really. All I know is that he's getting me taken out of a good command slot and a flying assignment and ordering me to West Point for an admin job as his so-called special assistant. Sounds to me like a lot of spit shine and brass polish."

"I'm just reading between the lines, and I've been out of the loop for a long, long time, so keep that in mind. But, one thing I know is this – he's got a lot of dangerous water to navigate and he's in need of a good team of people to help him do it. He thinks you're one of them."

"What do you mean by dangerous water?"

"I'll tell you when you get here. You clear post as fast as you can and stop by the farm for a couple of days on your way to the academy. We'll do a little bird hunting, some fishing… shoot a few rabbits. Maybe I can get your grandmother to have a fresh apple pie waiting for you. And we'll talk, you and me."

*　　*　　*　　*　　*

The ring-necked pheasant flushed with a loud cackle and noisy flurry of beating wings. It was a sound that had always surprised and in its own way frightened him the first time it happened each hunting season.

Glenn watched his grandfather shoulder the double barrel shotgun, smoothly swing on the surprisingly swift bird and drop it forty yards from where they stood. The yellow lab ambled over, retrieved the upland game and brought it back, then dropped it at their feet. Dave Nolan reached down and stroked the dog's head.

"Just a couple of years ago, he'd have taken off hunting again, but he's getting a little long in the tooth any more. We both are. How many you got, Glenn?"

"Three birds, and a rabbit."

"That makes enough for your grandmother to make us a dinner of her cheesy fried pheasant breasts. Let's go sit under the tree by the pond and rest awhile."

Dave Nolan removed his hunting jacket, leaned back against a tree and retrieved a small thermos of coffee, pouring some steaming liquid into the top and passing it to his grandson. The older Nolan lazily scratched the dog behind its ears while looking across the field to the small farmhouse, with its dormers and broad covered porch, nestled beneath two tall oaks. "There's something special about old dogs," he said wistfully, then turned his faced toward his grandson. "Remember we talked down by the river a few years back when you were trying to decide about going to West Point?"

"Like it was yesterday."

"A lot I told you back then applies to what the current Supe is asking you to do now. The past few days I had time to contact friends and find out what's going on in the Army these days and how our old school is faring. Most people don't know it but there are big changes happening in both. General Berry has been handed a tough assignment. Tell me what you know about him."

"Not much. Some from the normal post scuttlebutt at Fort Campbell and a little from that *LIFE* magazine article that came out in September of '70. I had one run in with him shortly after I got to Campbell in late '73, and I did my best to steer clear of him after that."

"What did you think of that article?"

"Not much. I guess it was probably a hit piece like the one *TIME* did on me. Honestly, any more I don't trust the press any farther than I can throw your tractor. When I got back from Vietnam, I watched CBS News every night and recorded what I was hearing and compared it to what I knew were the facts. I lost all the faith I ever had in Cronkite."

"You may have gone a little overboard, but I understand. A healthy dose of skepticism about the press always served me well when I was in uniform." The older man thought back to the time when a young reporter named Eamon Kilroy had shown up in North Africa and at Eisenhower's direction attached himself to the infantry division he commanded. He'd been leery of the press too. "All that said, how do you read your new boss? Just as important as knowing the troops under you is knowing the guy over you."

"He's hard to get to know; his self-confidence borders on egotism. He's blunt, demanding, and has no qualms about relieving officers, but my guess is that he's as demanding of himself as he is of subordinates. He's intimidating and I think he knows and uses that – he sure scared hell out of me that one time a couple years back."

Glenn had classmates who had personal experience with the current Supe – some were positive, some negative. All had strong opinions.

"He's a Southerner; a religious man. They say he's not someone in whose presence you want to tell a ribald joke. He has principles and stands up for them. He's the kind of person some people really like and some really dislike – there's probably no middle ground among people who know him. He's a warrior, not a politician, and while some would question his methods, no one would question his physical courage or patriotism."

Dave Nolan pursed his lips and nodded. "You sound like an admirer."

"Can't say yes or no because I don't know him personally. Those are just my observations. I could be wrong on some or all of it. I'll be able to tell you in a week whether or not I like him. What I can tell you right now is that I'm not looking forward to this job or reporting directly to him."

"I still have some contacts in the press and the Army, and from what I've learned in the past few days, you've got a fairly good read on your new boss."

"We'll see. What I don't understand is why he called you."

"I think it's because he might be a student of history. He found some of my notes in the archives of the Cadet Library dating back to the years just after the Great War." Glenn gave him a questioning look. "It's a long story, but what it boils down to is that Douglas MacArthur recruited me back in 1919 much like General Berry called on you, and for a similar job. It was a time when the academy was facing a crisis comparable, but not identical, to what it faces today. It's something called Public Law 94-106, signed by President Ford three days ago. You know what that is?"

"Not a clue."

"It's a law passed in Congress mandating that on 7 July next summer women will enter each of the military academies with the graduating class of 1980. Our school, along with Navy and Air Force, is going co-educational."

Glenn was shocked. "I didn't know. There was some background noise about it – but I didn't pay much attention." He shook his head in disbelief. "Congress really did that? Is this because of the feminists? They helped ruin my marriage and now my school? Since when did the military academies become a test bed for social experiments? I don't think I want to be a part of this."

"That's the first thing that crossed my mind the time MacArthur approached me when I returned from Europe after the First War. I was pretty well fed up with the Army at the time and had an offer from my war time commander who was going back into private law practice."

"But you did it anyway."

The old man shook his head. "MacArthur was persuasive, and let's say he swayed me. I'm glad he did. You should approach this assignment with an open mind. Years down the road you won't regret the experience."

Glenn sipped at the coffee and let his gaze travel across the rolling hills of the farm. "I don't know that I want to stay in the Army. What it's evolved into is not what I signed on for. And it's not just that I've got the 'seven year itch' either. In the back of my mind I have this worry that I've got to make a move one way or the other pretty soon now. I don't think anybody in the civilian world hires guys like me after age thirty."

Dave chuckled and his eyes lit up. "Now where did you hear that?"

"Figured it out on my own. I started putting out some feelers soon after I got to Campbell, and I've been on a couple of job interviews just to see how that works. Nothing serious. And while in both instances, the companies appreciated my experience in managing people, I detected a tentative hint that I was approaching some hurdle because of my age. It was like people were saying, 'We appreciate your service, but it's time to grow up and find something meaningful to do with your life.' Do you know what I'm saying, grandpa?"

"I do. I ran into that about the same place in my career as you."

It was the trip back East in the early 20's, right after he and Denise had met that old Texas Ranger at the Lawry place near Beeville. They were stationed at Whalen then, a dusty hole in the wall at the edge of nowhere in south Texas. They'd gone back to spend time with his father-in-law who had offered him a job in his metals company. *How things in this world have a way of repeating themselves*, he thought. They spent a few days in Duncannon to see his family briefly on the way to New York, and one day he'd had stopped for a beer in the Hotel Doyle. Big Mike Ryan was still tending bar, and he remembered the old man had asked him: '… *you still playin' soldier?*' It had sounded like a rebuke, or a lingering disappointment in him; as the next few days passed he sensed it was a general feeling around town.

"Glenn, you've still got a couple of years before reaching the ripe old age of thirty."

"Time passes quickly the older you get."

Dave Nolan chuckled. "Tell me about it. Still, I think you should approach this with an open mind. While they've done some work at West Point in anticipation this would pass Congress, there's still a lot to do in the next eight months, and the first few years afterward. Your performance at the academy, in Vietnam, the Infantry Advanced course and in his old division impressed the Supe, and the Commandant. Being personally selected by the Superintendent and the work you do on this will be a highlight of your résumé."

"I hope that highlight is bright enough to be worth it," Glenn replied dolefully. "He said my first assignment was to find out what the job really entailed and then write the position description. Sounds like he doesn't really know what he wants."

Dave Nolan smiled, his eyes lighting up merrily. "Don't worry, he knows what he wants. Almost completely. You fit a profile he wants to fill – that's how MacArthur chose me all those years ago. Otherwise he probably wouldn't have picked you. Before you go see him, take stock of yourself. What have you done since graduation well enough for a general to take note of? What talents do you have that he's lacking? Everybody, even two star generals have shortcomings. Find somebody who has spent a lot of time close to him and pick their brain. And when you work for him, above all be brutally honest."

Glenn finished the coffee and looked toward the wood line a couple hundred yards away to the south where a doe and her fawn grazed warily, raising their heads often and looking around. The hunting had been good that morning and he commented on it.

"I used to hunt this farm when I was kid. It belonged to ol' man Köhler back then, and he'd let me hunt if I shared my birds and my rabbits with him. He even let me and Dewey Martin fish this pond. I shot my first pheasant when I was eight, I think it was, at the bottom of this hill near the fence line. Got it with that gun you're using – it belonged to my dad and he let me try it out that day. It was one of the first hammerless side-by-side shotguns in all of Perry

County. He called it 'the little gun' because it was a set of sixteen gauge barrels on a twenty gauge frame in a time when everybody shot twelve or ten gauge guns. On my next birthday, he gave me that gun and a dog. I remember it as a major turning point in my life. Glenn, I want you to have my 'little gun'. I think you're about to experience a turning point yourself, regardless of which path you choose – civilian or military. That little sixteen will be a reminder for you." Dave Nolan stood up slowly and stretched. "Let's get back and clean these birds for your grandmother."

As they walked across the field through the corn stubble left after the recent harvest, a name came to Glenn's mind – someone who could help him get to know his new boss better before meeting him.

*   *   *

"Captain Nolan, the Superintendent will see you now," the secretary said.

Glenn looked at his watch and noted it was 0934. He'd been kept waiting for well over a half hour and it angered him. *I guess he didn't say he'd see me at 0900, only that I should report then. I'm going to have to listen real close to exactly what he says.* He knocked once, loudly, and entered the general's office. He quickly looked around, taking in the bookshelves, rich appurtenances, the family pictures on the credenza and a second general officer seated on a leather chair across the desk from the superintendent..

"Sir, Captain Nolan reporting as ordered," Glenn said, standing at attention and saluting. *This feels just like being a damned plebe again.* General Berry looked as trim as he had the last time he'd seen him at Campbell; the superintendent visually inspected his uniform and returned the salute.

"Fatigues, Nolan?" the general said, frowning, and glancing at the other officer in the room – a completely bald man who looked vaguely amused; a single star adorned each epaulet of his dress greens. "Is this some kind of *statement*, captain?"

"No, sir. You said to come prepared to work harder than I ever have before. Fatigues seemed appropriate." He could tell Berry wasn't satisfied with the answer.

"General Ulmer, Captain Nolan, my Special Assistant."

The general offered his hand and said, "Glad to have you aboard, captain. My aide tells me good things about you. He's a classmate of yours – Jim Vaught."

"Appreciate that, sir," Glenn replied to the Commandant of Cadets. "Jim and I played rugby and baseball on the same teams. We also went through Jump School together during the summer before our first class year."

"Jim tells me you were quite the rugby fullback. You and another of your classmates who played scrum half – Barnes – supposedly made an effective pairing."

"We had our moments, sir. Are you a fan of the game?"

"I've seen a few matches but I'm still having a hard time following the rules – the same with lacrosse. But I do enjoy the hitting in both. Perhaps someday you can enlighten me from the sidelines about the rules and strategies."

"It'd be my privilege, sir." *I wonder how both games will be impacted by Public Law 94-106*, Glenn thought and decided this wasn't the time, place or audience to ask.

"I'll hold you to it, captain." The Com stood and turned to General Berry. "I'll see you at the mess hall for lunch with the First Captain." With that, he turned and left, closing the door quietly as Glenn's eyes followed him; when he looked back, the Supe was filling a pipe bowl with tobacco while staring at him across the broad wooden desk.

"I expect you've gotten over your initial reluctance." Berry said, lighting a wooden match and dragging on the pipe stem.

"Not exactly, sir. I'd rather be back with my company, and I still have a lot of questions."

"So do I," the general replied, opening his top right desk drawer. "After reading this, I watched you closely for the first few months after you arrived at Campbell. I wanted to see if you were worth keeping." He pulled out a magazine and tossed it on the top of his desk. "Someday soon you're going to have to explain this to me in detail."

Glenn looked at his picture on the front of the now familiar and notorious TIME Magazine – the unshaven face, the torn jungle fatigue jacket without a nametag above the slanted right pocket; no rank on the collar. He was bare-headed and in need of a haircut. Staring back at the general, he said, "I'd be happy to explain, sir. I'd like to discuss both our articles – yours and mine."

The general's jaw jutted forward and he leaned back in his big chair, deliberately crossing his arms over his chest, head tilted to one side, eyes narrowed to skeptical slits that seemed to bore straight through him; it was a most daunting stare. Berry lit the tobacco in his pipe. "Have you figured out yet what your assignment entails?"

"Not really, sir. I've got a start, but not much of one." Glenn produced a lone, single-spaced sheet neatly typed and placed it on the general's desk. "These are a few points, questions rather than answers – most of it from my grandfather's recollection of his time here with General MacArthur in the early '20's."

The general looked at the ceiling, contemplating. "Your grandfather was a heck of a soldier in his day. The War College still studies his campaigns as commander of the 12th Division in North Africa and Sicily, and his year commanding XXX Corps under Patton in Europe. When I was the Assistant Commandant of the Infantry School at Benning, I was pleased to learn they still studied his night attack on the French town of Cirey when he was a company commander in the Rainbow Division. Joyce Kilmer did a superb job of recording the details in his report to William Donovan."

"They had stopped teaching it by the time I went through the Advanced Course, sir."

"A shame. But I suppose you know the story better than anyone."

"Actually, sir, my grandfather never talked about it."

Berry frowned at this as if he didn't believe it. He went back to reading the paper Glenn had given him and looked up when done. "Not much of a start and most of your assumptions are off. Fundamentally your job is one of Project Manager, responsible for monitoring and keeping me and General Ulmer abreast of the myriad parts in the overall effort – costs, deadlines, potential bottlenecks and any obstacles needing command attention. One element to add to your job description immediately – you are to be my combat curmudgeon, Nolan."

Glenn had no idea what this meant and gave the Superintendent a puzzled look.

"I pride myself in being able to accurately read soldiers and so far as I can tell, you're a perfect fit for the job I have in mind. You, Nolan, are going to have the privilege and responsibility of finding all the flaws in our plans and bring them to my attention; in essence to be a burr under our collective saddle blanket. From what little contact we've had so far I think you're perfect for that."

"You want me to play 'devil's advocate' and tell you where you're off base."

"Both me and General Ulmer. But being a Christian man, I'd never want anyone to advocate for the Deceiver, the Adversary. I think of it more as your putting a stone in our shoe now and then."

"Does this come with hazardous duty pay, sir? I've never known a general officer – except one – who liked to be told when he was screwing up."

Berry produced a tight-lipped smile. "Your grandfather. That's where I got the idea. Apparently, he kept a corporate killjoy on his board of directors at Barrett Enterprises when he was their CEO and found it very useful. The difference in your case is that I expect you, within the bounds of military decorum, to not only identify defects but make recommendations on how to fix them. I don't want just problems, I want solutions also."

Glenn weighed what he'd just heard and decided this assignment had suddenly become wholly different, and more demanding than he'd originally thought. But it was still a staff job, something for a bean counter or a project engineer and someone with well-developed social and political skills. This wasn't him and he was more sure than before he was the wrong man for the job.

As if reading his mind, the Superintendent looked at him with a piercing gaze and said, "I'm not a man known for failing, nor is General Ulmer. From what little I know of you from the officers under whom you served in Germany and Vietnam, you're also one unaccustomed to failure. I expect you to excel and I'm certain you'll do well in this assignment."

Glenn wasn't as confident in the outcome of his working closely with not just one but two generals. The problem was a knotty one, and he was still hoping Berry would see he was not a good fit for this position.

"Sir, I'd still like you to reconsider my assignment here. I'm not a staff officer, I'm a troop commander, and I wish to stay in command of my aviation company. It's an operational rather than staff position, and I wish to concentrate on leading troops in my career."

The general clearly didn't like the comment. "The Army's promotional system requires alternate periods of action and reflection. You've commanded three companies – two infantry and one aviation. You're due a period of deliberation, shall we say, to increase the breadth of your military experience. This will actually enhance your career and potential for promotion."

"Sir, I respectfully disagree. Commanding an Assault Helicopter Company is a major's billet, so my being selected for that command places me, I would think, in position for early promotion consideration. I'll likely never again get an opportunity to command such a unit. Leaving that assignment now will hinder my promotion opportunities… unless this position as the Supe's special assistant is a field grade rather than a company grade slot."

Berry gave him a stern look. "I hope you're not lobbying me for a promotion, captain."

"I'm trying to be up front by giving you every reason I can think of to pick somebody else for this 'opportunity'," Glenn said. "I *am* asking that I not be penalized. I don't want to lose a chance for promotion at a time when the force is being drawn down, and I don't want to lose my only chance at commanding an aviation company."

The general squeezed his lips into a tight, thin line as he stared at Nolan and finally said, "You, captain, are beginning to sound like a whiner and complainer. I never have, and don't now, abide grousers in my command."

Another reason to send me back to Campbell, Glenn thought. "I'm just pointing out, sir, that my experience and training… and preference, always has been and always will be in the area of command rather than staff work."

"I've studied you since I ran across the TIME article, shortly before we first met at Fort Campbell when I commanded the division. You're something of an enigma, and I like the challenge of unraveling mysteries."

"You think I'm a mystery, sir?" Glenn asked, incredulous at the thought. "General, every person who's ever known me would say I'm an open book. What you see is what you get."

The general's face became very still and somber; he reached for the lone file on his desk and opened it. "Your records indicate otherwise. From the time you entered USMA in '64 until now, your performance is a study in contradiction. You were an excellent student in high school, scored very high on the SAT and the civil service exam; you did exceptionally well on the Graduate Record Exam your senior year at the academy. Yet your academic achievement during your four years here was mediocre; your final academic standing was below the middle of your class."

"High school was a lot easier than college, sir. Most of us found that to be true."

"But you were in 96th percentile of the GRE First Class year."

"Something about those standardized tests was easy. Some can take them, some not."

"There's more to it than that and we both know it. You were a good, actually an exceptional athlete, yet your peers and your tactical officers all said you were a cadet who happened to be an athlete rather than the other way around. But, you only rose to the rank of Cadet Lieutenant instead of Cadet Captain. You lobbied to get out of a Regimental staff position – just like you're trying to lobby me to reconsider your assignment now."

"In my senior year, sir, I found myself overloaded with athletics and clubs in addition to the academic load."

"All things you volunteered for and enjoyed."

"Yes, sir, but people were depending on me in the extra-curricular activities. I couldn't let them down. And I couldn't let the extra work of cadet rank interfere with my grades."

"That's a convenient excuse, not a legitimate reason."

"I wasn't lying, sir."

"You put yourself in a position to avoid responsibility from what I see."

"If you really think I did that then, sir, and that I'm doing something similar now with you, that should be reason enough to replace me as your special assistant. Like I said, sir, I'd really be lousy at it."

General Berry looked at him without smiling. "I appreciate candor, but I don't welcome your trying the same stratagem on me now that you did with your tactical officer back then. I'm surprised you would. Everything about your Army career shows you pursuing rather than avoiding responsibility; seeking the difficult assignments rather than the easy route. Perhaps that's why two different raters on your OERs said that you possessed the qualities that would someday make you a general."

This came as a complete surprise to Glenn. He knew Colonel Galvin had put that into his OER narrative for the interim efficiency report he'd written when his company was OpCon to the 1/8 Cav in Cambodia. It dawned on him that the general might be offering in an oblique way some mentoring. He knew that it was a common practice for senior officers because someone likely had done it for them. Was that what the general was doing – taking an interest in him and offering a hand up into a higher saddle? Maybe... but probably not.

"One of the things which positively influenced my selection of you was your qualifications as an aviator," the Superintendent was saying. "I enjoy flying and the technical challenges of it. I plan to keep current and fly routinely while here. At my rank, I'm required... not required, but it's highly recommended, and expected, that I fly with an instructor pilot in the other seat. Since you're both an IP and an instrument examiner, your assignment here fulfills multiple needs I have. And since you're already reporting to me..." General Berry again went slowly through the ritual of tamping down the tobacco in his pipe bowl and relighting it. "I've come to the end of my patience for listening to your excuses, captain. It's time for you to get to work. Your title will be: Project Manager – Incorporating Female Cadets into USMA. Here's your first assignment.

"General Ulmer and I agree that our basic approach toward female cadets is that the women will do everything that male cadets do except where physiological differences indicate it makes sense for there to be some modification of expectations. Our problem is that neither of us is experienced in the field of physiology. That's where you come in. Add to your job description a requirement to become an expert in male and female physiology." The general relaxed back into his chair, looking vaguely pleased with himself. "You will be the primary resource on the subject to both me and the Commandant of Cadets. I expect you to make both of us experts in our own right so we can handle questions and complaints from Washington... and there will be. And from the disgruntled grads – and there'll be plenty of them, too. Before you can think of another complaint to field, let me tell you that I'm providing someone with medical expertise to assist you."

The Supe looked at his watch, picked up the phone and punched one of the buttons. "Good. Thank you, Mrs. Compton," he said, "Send the major in." He turned toward Nolan after placing the phone on its cradle. "Our medical expertise is here. She's the head nurse at the hospital and has an excellent reputation."

The door opened and General Berry stood, smiling paternally as the young woman in dress greens entered. She gasped and her jaw dropped when Glenn turned to look at her. Their eyes locked. Instantly, he felt his face flash hot and the hair on the back of his neck quickly stood on end.

Awkward silence descended.

"Major Kolarik, I gather you two have already met," the general said uncomfortably, looking back and forth between them.

"Yes, sir," Jenny replied without taking her eyes off Glenn.

"She was the most headstrong nurse in all of III Corps during my time in Vietnam, sir," Glenn said quickly, continuing to stare into her eyes.

"The captain had the well-deserved reputation as the most difficult patient any of my nurses had ever encountered."

The Superintendent cleared his throat and looked slowly from one to the other. At last he said, "Whatever history the two of you have will not interfere with your working together. Both of you *will* comport yourselves professionally; that's an order."

Chapter 38

"I love crisp fall days," Jenny said.

They sat side by side on a bench near Battle Monument taking in the sights of autumn and the view north up the Hudson toward Newburgh. "The hills along the river are just gorgeous, aren't they? I always liked fall while growing up in Jersey, but the leaves in the city never compared to this. I think this has to be one of the most beautiful places on the planet."

"We'll see how you feel about that in January when the temps hover around zero, the wind blasts downriver, and everything here turns gray – it's called gloom period."

They had been dismissed from the Supe's office after a brief and uneasy few minutes of instruction from him concerning their working relationship and his expectations of what they would deliver in the coming months.

"I think you've got our new boss worried, Kolarik. Army majors don't go around during duty hours hugging officers of the opposite sex, especially in front of a general."

"What can I say, Glenn? I've always been a hugger. I think it's a Polock thing."

Glenn gave her a doleful smile. "What was that all about when you called me obstreperous? I thought that was restricted to describing teenagers."

"You're obstinate, too," Jenny said, looking charmingly rueful. "I guess we're stuck working together. I didn't want to do this when the general first buttonholed me, but honestly I'm looking forward to it now... if we can put aside old baggage. I hope we can. I have to know – are you still angry at me for getting you pulled out of the field before I left the Cav?"

"I wasn't ready to leave my company."

She gave him withering sideways look of disapproval. "You'd spent over ten months in the field, your immune system was weak and you'd just been medevac'd out in the middle of the night with anaphylactic shock. Something over there had your number. But you didn't answer my question – are you still upset with me?"

"No," he said quietly. "I acted like an idiot. My whole world was coming apart at the seams; at least it felt that way. My best friend was killed, my company was taken away. I was angry at everything and everybody, and couldn't control it. I said and did some really stupid things. You weren't the only target of my wrath. I got over it in a couple of weeks but you were gone by then and I didn't have a chance to apologize... until now. That's a long way around to saying 'I'm sorry' – will you forgive me?"

"I will, and I do." She leaned close and bumped his arm with her shoulder. "And I'll even get rescinded the outstanding warrant that's out on you for a psyche eval."

"I'm not the Nolan who needed psychiatric testing. That was my little brother."

Jenny smiled broadly. "I always liked Brad, even when he gave our nurse's hooch at Papa Vic that awful nickname. You know what he called the nurse's quarters there at the hospital, don't you? Really?! You don't? That's hard to believe. I thought everybody in the Cav had heard about that. He called the nurse's hooch *The H&L Motel*, and damned if it didn't catch on. I can't believe you didn't hear about the 'Hookers & Lookers No-Tell Motel'. I loved Brad to death, but some of the girls would have shot him on sight given half a chance."

Glenn chuckled. "That's my little brother. Always in some kind of trouble."

"I can't believe it's been five years since I last saw him. Whatever happened with Brad?"

"Long story short – he went to Australia, married a girl he met on R&R. Now he's a cattle and sheep rancher. And a wine maker – not just a drinker anymore."

"Just like that?!"

"There's a few more details. He started back to college, hated it and dropped out again. Got in touch with this girl down under and went there to help her run the family farm. Somehow he convinced this girl to marry him. He loves the whole deal about being a rancher and he's done well for himself. You should have latched on to him when you had the chance. He always was head over heels in love with you."

Jenny shook her head slowly. "Too young. But I'm happy for him."

"Yeah, me too. He's a good guy. Wild, but good. I think this Aussie girl is just like him. I can't wait to see how my nieces and nephews turn out."

"And you? Any children yet?"

"Not going to be any..." Glenn replied and looked away, gazing steadily north up the Hudson. "Mary Anne divorced me two years ago, when we were transferred to Fort Campbell. She had the marriage annulled. Her father paid off some church official or tribunal to make it as if we were never really married... after five years as husband and wife."

She patted his arm when he looked back at her. "I'm sorry."

"So am I," he said sadly. "So... am... I... Another casualty of that damned war. Happened to a lot of us. A classmate of mine down at Campbell had it happen to him, too. He says – and I don't know how he comes by his figures – but he says about half our class that got married right after graduation is now divorced. We suffered more casualties in Vietnam than any other class except '66, but we had even more casualties after we got back."

"I'm sorry," she said again, more softly.

"It is what it is – don't mean nuthin'…"

They were quiet for a long while until she broke the uncomfortable silence.

"Let's drive up to Newburgh. I know a quaint little inn at the foot of a mountain, with a view of the river. They've got good food and great Old Fashioneds… You still like them, don't you? I remember you were drinking one – actually several more than that – the night we met at the Lewis O-Club."

"A bit of serendipity, that was. You were on the way back to the war after escorting the body of one of your Dustoff pilots home." He took a deep breath and again looked upriver toward Newburgh. "Did you ever find Mr. Right?"

"I did, but he died on me," she said quietly, and looked into his eyes when he turned toward her. *Then I did again,* she thought. *I met a guy I fell for – but he was happily married. He almost died on me, too. Now here he is, suddenly back in my life.*

*　　*　　*

"*Signorina,*" the old man said in an Italian accent, taking her hand and slowly caressing it. "You are wasting your time with this *sciotta,* this Army *idiota.* You are too good for him, and he will make you *molto disgraziato.*"

Jenny smiled sweetly at him, and glanced at Glenn.

"I on the other hand –" the old man continued, wiping his mouth with a folded napkin.

"Vincenzo!" a rotund, older woman standing at the door of the kitchen called out toward their table. "Come! The steak is ready and you are busy making eyes at the pretty *bambolina.* Back to work old man or I will leave you and take all your money with me when I go!"

"Promises, promises, old woman," the old man yelled back, then he turned back to Jenny, caressing her hand again. "You have no engagement ring or wedding band. This is good. I will be back soon. Do not marry him before I return," he whispered, and then hurried to the kitchen.

"I think he's in love with you," Glenn said, sipping his wine. "My guess is he falls in love several times each night, so don't let it go to your head, Nurse Kolarik. You're not the first and you won't be the last. Trust me."

"Be serious," she replied, smirking at him. "This is the strangest place, Glenn. How in the world did you find it?"

"My Aunt Erika and Uncle Randall brought me here one night during my June Week. They heard about it from somebody at the Thayer Hotel and thought it sounded interesting. The food was really good and the old man and the old woman were entertaining. Back then they had a dog that walked around the place looking for handouts – an old German Shepherd who loved steak, and loved spaghetti even more."

"Not much variety in the menu."

"Probably why it's so good. That, and they taste test every batch that comes out of the kitchen, I guess to get immediate feedback from customers."

"I noticed that they sat at almost every table and had a bite to eat – like they did with us." She looked at him over the rim of her glass as she took a sip of wine. "And they used to let their dog roam around?! This is a *really* quirky place."

"Old World hospitality – great food." Glenn poured some wine and looked at her over the candle in the middle of the table. "It works for me. I wish this job assignment worked as well."

Jenny again sipped her wine and gave him a questioning glance. "Maybe you don't like your coworker?"

"You? Your being here is the only thing that makes this bearable. I don't get anything at all about this assignment. I'm a square peg in a round hole if there ever was one."

"How so?"

"If you could've sat in on my first day interrogation by the Supe you wouldn't have to ask. He made a better case for my not being here than I did. But he still wants me for some reason that's way beyond *my* comprehension."

"For one thing, you're teaching him to fly."

"Helping him work out the kinks after a long layoff. He could find anybody to do that."

"You flew with him today, right? How'd it go?"

"I've had better flights," he said satirically.

"That didn't sound good."

"We both survived it."

"Oooo – that sounded even worse."

"The crew chief is probably burning up the telephone lines back to his unit looking for another assignment. A couple of Berry's approaches to the parade field at Camp Buckner were a little dicey. He's not as good a pilot as he fancies himself. That's understandable. Generals commanding airmobile divisions get a quick forty hour orientation and then their wings. None of them can fly. But in truth, he was better than I expected. While in Vietnam he spent about a year in the cockpit with a guy named John Fox who obviously taught him an awful lot. But the general's not the guy I'd volunteer to fly with if I had a choice. After today I'm even more confused about why he chose me."

"But you're such a nice guy, Glenn. Maybe he just likes you."

He frowned at her and said, "And you told me once that *I* needed a psyche eval. No, his liking me can't be it. He said I was an enigma, and then went on to lay out what sounded like an Article 32 investigation of my record since day one at the academy in '64 until now. A pretty damning case about my indifference, lack of motivation and sub-par performance while a cadet – no, he doesn't like me." Glenn again drank from his wineglass and contorted his mouth while shaking his head. "I'm not real wild about him either after our run-in at Campbell a couple of months after I got there."

"That was years ago, wasn't it?"

"I still have nightmares about it."

"Oh, please!" Jenny replied sarcastically, a pained look on her face. "Don't be so theatrical. It couldn't have been all that bad."

"It was mid to late January, and at the time I was taking every weird mission possible just to get some flying time. I had a standby mission for an Air Force nuclear weapons flight that was going to pass through our area one Sunday afternoon. Well, I took the mission just to get a little flying in."

"The general didn't chew you out for that."

"Not exactly. We got hit with hellacious freezing rain storms in the winter time, and the night before the mission, we got blanketed by one. Our aircraft was parked outside and got covered with about two inches, so I got our maintenance officer to move the Huey inside a hangar to melt the ice. That didn't work because the inside of the hangar never got all that warm. I got to the flight line just after the general but in time to see him walk into the hangar and catch our lieutenant standing on top of the helicopter beating the ice on the main rotor blades with a big wooden baton."

"The general bawled you out for that?"

"Oh, yeah. Our lieutenant was really, really thumping the crap out of those blades up to the moment the general got across the hangar floor and stopped him. If he hadn't stopped him when he did, our maintenance officer would have pureed those blades. It was quite a sight."

Jenny saw a picture in her mind, and tried to hide a grin. "How bad was it?"

"The top skin looked like a golf ball with hundreds of extra dimples." Glenn took another sip of his wine. "Do you know how much two UH-1H main rotor blades cost?"

Jenny shook her head.

"I didn't either at the time, but I was certain it was more than my take-home pay for the next several months. When Berry found out I was the pilot in command, he walked me across the hangar and stood me at attention and chewed me out with... let's say with great gusto. I have *never* been chewed out like that before or since."

Jenny laughed loudly, then sheepishly put her hand over her mouth when diners from tables nearby looked at them. "I'm sure you're exaggerating."

"You'd be *surely* wrong, Nurse Kolarik. I was really glad when his assignment as Division Commander of the 101st ended five months later. I felt like I could breathe and go to the Officers Club again. "His liking me isn't part of the reason I'm here. Maybe he's just looking for the right moment to finish what he started at Campbell Army Airfield hangar #2."

"So you think he brought you here because he doesn't like you? That makes no sense at all, and it doesn't square with what I hear from your friend, Jim Vaught," Jenny told him and gave him a perplexed look. "He says General Berry appreciates candor. And we all know how candid you are – always in the extreme."

"He's told me that more than once. I think it's because he wants an extra go-fer who's an instructor pilot that can taxi him around wherever he wants to go."

"There are lots of better pilots than you."

"Really? You think so?"

"Certainly pilots with more experience." She leaned forward and held his gaze. "I think he brought you here because he sees something in you he likes and thinks he needs. It may be your age, your proximity to your own graduation, or some other perspective. Or maybe he just wants to mold a future general. Or maybe all of that."

Glenn wondered. General Berry had called him an enigma at their first meeting in his office. *That goes both ways, general,* he thought. There were times the man was as inscrutable as the Chinese.

"Let me tell you about something that happened last week on the second flight I took with him. Like I said, the general isn't the Army's greatest pilot. That's understandable to a point, and I think he wants to be treated like every other pilot… again, to a point. I'm pretty tough on him in the cockpit, like I am with all my students. So, I gave him one warning about his preoccupation with his sightseeing instead of paying attention to the task of flying. Not long after that, he was sight-seeing again so I chopped the throttle on him."

"You what?"

"I quickly rolled off the throttle. It's like the engine suddenly quits and it's an immediate emergency. It's a standard check ride tactic. I wasn't giving a check ride – he's a long way away from being ready for that – I did it primarily to get his attention."

"Did you?"

"Oh, yeah. You bet I did. The first time, and both times afterward. He didn't appreciate it the first time, and gradually grew even less enamored. I told him I was going to do it every time he started daydreaming instead of flying the ship. At the end of the flight when I dropped him off in front of his quarters before taking the ship back to Stewart field, I reviewed the points on which he needed work before being ready for a check ride. I could tell by his silence and that stare… you know the one – the sideways look that could peel paint and melt girders –"

"I think he reserves that one for you," Jenny said impishly, looking pleased.

"Could be. Anyhow, he finally says in a very flat, monotonic voice that I am to 'visit' him in his office at 1730 sharp. And then he got out and went into Quarters 100. I thought I'd really stepped over the line this time, and wasn't looking forward to reporting to him that afternoon. But strangely, when I got there, he was still in his flight suit, only he'd removed the nomex top, and had two glasses plus a bottle of Kilbeggan on his desk."

"Kilbeggan?"

"An expensive single malt Irish whiskey. And he acted as if this was a daily routine. I don't know if he drinks Irish whiskey, but somehow he knew that I did. And then we talked – about flying, about how much he appreciated my holding him to high standards in the cockpit. He told me about his perspective on the three types of officers – the warriors, the dancers and prancers, and the princes who sit on thrones. He said that he viewed me as a warrior like himself, and that he'd chosen me because of it."

Jenny listened with raised eyebrows. "See! You're making progress, Glenn. It sounds like you two are best buds now. And you say you don't know him?"

"One conversation does not a confidant make. Remember the relationship between familiarity and contempt? Besides, he did most of the talking and I did most of the listening and drinking, which was fine by me. Killbeggan is a damned fine whiskey."

"You said he'd removed his nomex shirt. Maybe he was sending you a message that rank didn't matter… at least at that moment."

Glenn pondered this briefly and finally said, "Maybe. Maybe not. I still don't feel comfortable around him. I can't get a grip on exactly who he is. What about you? You've worked with him longer than I have. What's your take on our boss?"

"I'm still trying to figure him out, too. I'll tell you one incident I had," she replied, resting her chin on clasped hands. "He and his wife love to dance, so they often hold formal parties. She's a Quaker by the way and he's a Southern Baptist – I don't think either faith is high on dancing. Another interesting side note: when they talk to each other it's always '*Thee*' and '*Thou*'. Anyhow, I was at one of those affairs, dancing with him, nervous as I could be and trying to make small talk. I said something about how I enjoyed working for Dr. Corcoran at the hospital. He gave me a disapproving look and said, 'Everybody on this post works for me. That includes you.' I was shocked, and embarrassed. But next morning there was a very nice handwritten note on my door that said, '*I apologize for my conduct last evening. Please pray for me that I'll be more considerate.*' It was signed – Sid Berry."

"That doesn't much help me figure him out."

"You asked. Honestly, I can't figure him out either."

They ate in silence for a while as he pondered what she'd said.

"Jenny, you always challenge me. You make me think, and I need that," he said at last. "I'm really glad you came here with me tonight."

"So am I." She put her teeth on her lower lip, and took a deep breath. "But – is it me, or a fond memory of being here with someone else? Did you bring Mary Anne to this place?"

"Yes, we came here that once, with my aunt and uncle. But I wasn't thinking of that until you mentioned it."

Jenny looked into his eyes, and then abruptly glanced away. "That was an unfair question, wasn't it? But I'm getting too old to play games, Glenn. I'm getting up there in years. I'll soon be thirty and lying about my age on official documents. The hands of my biological clock seem to be picking up speed."

"I'm not playing games with you, Jenny." He reached across the table and placed his hand on hers. "Being thrown together with you at this place – at this time – seemed really awkward and uncomfortable at first. But not now. It's like this is somehow all predestined, like it's one of those episodes, an event in life, either monumental or not, that alters your course."

"I'd like to believe that, Glenn," she said softly, looking away.

"What's stopping you?" When she didn't reply, he said, "It's me, isn't it?"

"It's not you. It's everything about us. This is a mistake, isn't it? You and me working together for General Berry. I told you that night at Lewis I wouldn't play 'the other woman' and yet I still feel like I'm doing it... This is so awkward."

"Only if we make it so. And you're not playing the other woman. I'm not married any more… and I'm not on the rebound or any of that psychobabble nonsense." He reached across the table and took her hand gently, looking into her eyes. "I want you to go away with me."

"Go away with you?" she asked, looking at him, puzzled.

"For a few days. General Berry is going to Washington for the weekend this Friday and then staying over for three or four days of meetings. Have you ever been to Nantucket?"

"No. Have you?"

He nodded and smiled at her. "A couple of times, when I was in high school. My dad flew us all out there in a twin engine Cessna they had at the Aberdeen Proving Ground flying club. This time of year, the water will be almost too cold to swim – high fifties – but there's still lots to do. It'll be fun."

"High fifties? Are you kidding?! No way I'm going swimming in late October. It'll be blustery and cold, and –"

"Low sixties in the daytime and low forties to low fifties at night. That's not so bad, really. Not swimming weather, I'll grant you, but good for bike riding and long walks and shopping... and stuff. We can take our work with us and do it on the beach or in a local pub. It'll be a nice getaway. Come on, Jen, don't be a dog in a manger."

"You're a real sweet talker you are, Glenn Nolan."

He kissed her lightly. "Is that a yes?"

"I don't know..." She broke off, sounding distressed, but he was sure he saw a softening in her eyes, a swift little shadow of wonder and perhaps a hint of delight. "How does one get to Nantucket from here? Drive and take a ferry?"

"You could. But I'd rather fly. It'd be a lot easier and more scenic. I was thinking of taking the Supe's Huey. I could fly it – you could stewardess and co-pilot. We could sleep on the deck or on the ground under the bird at night and avoid the cost of a room."

"Not only does that sound perfectly awful, it also sounds utterly illegal. Grand theft helicopter... misappropriation of government property. We would both grow old in Leavenworth. Give me the keys to your car. I'm driving us home and no more wine for you."

"What if I told you I reserved a Cessna 172 from the West Point flying club?"

"I'd want to see your pilot's license." She smiled at him, tilted her head and rested her chin on the back of her hand.

"Is that the only thing keeping you from saying yes? If it is –" He pulled out his wallet and after a few seconds produced a card which he slid across the table toward her. "I expect you can ride a bike. The island's only ten miles across. I'll pick you up Friday morning at eight o'clock, and no, you won't have to bring along a sleeping bag. I have two rooms reserved at the Brass Lantern Inn."

"You're too sure of yourself," she said guardedly, but the way she was looking at him told him he'd sealed the deal.

"I thought that was one of the things you liked about me, my self-confidence. That's what you meant by obstreperous, isn't it?"

Jenny shrugged happily, watching his eyes. "I'll let you go on thinking that."

Chapter 39

"Nolan, your idea of a meeting with the First Captain and the cadet Regimental Commanders and their staffs turned out all right," General Berry said, grabbing his hat from the coat tree beside his office door. "Made this session with all the under classes at Ike Hall a little easier, knowing what to expect. What did you say the cadets are calling this assembly or confab or whatever you named it?"

"They're calling it *Stump the Stars*, sir. Except for the third classmen – they're calling it 'Stump the Chumps', but you know how Yearlings are."

Glenn had spent most of the past month talking to cadets in the Mess Hall at meal time, at small get-togethers in the First Class Club, and various other places. But the most profitable gatherings tended to be at his own quarters over drinks and dinner. By the time it was over, he'd talked with a couple hundred cadets and thought he had a pretty good idea of their concerns and gripes. He'd briefed Berry and Ulmer on his findings, set up a meeting with the cadet leadership and the first of a series of Q&A meetings with the assembled Corps of Cadets.

As they together walked around the Plain, the general seemed distant, pre-occupied. When he lingered at the base of Battle Monument, gazing upriver toward Target Field and Storm King Mountain, Glenn intruded on his thoughts.

"Everything all right, sir?"

Berry's jaw jutted forward, a pugnacious gesture Glenn had learned presaged some determinate decision or unalterable action. "This is a heck of a mess, isn't it, captain?"

"You mean the Honor situation, sir?"

"I mean all of it – moving our academy to co-education and the circumstances surrounding the cheating on that Electrical Engineering exam assailing us at the same time. General Ulmer tells me the cheating problem may well spread to a hundred cadets by the time it's done. I talked with the Secretary of the Army this morning before you came over. We may be getting some more 'help' from Washington whether we want it, or need it or not." Berry clasped his hands together behind his back and his jaw seemed to jut out even further. "Fortunately, I had a study commissioned about the Honor Code and System soon after I took over. I had about a three or four-hour conversation with General Knowlton, my predecessor, the night before he left. Hopefully the work on this recent study will get us through."

Glenn had heard the rumblings of an honor scandal – that's what the newspapers and the academy detractors would call it. The news had shocked him. "Sir, I've always thought the Honor System was one of the distinguishing marks of all the academies, especially here. It's one of the things that makes this place unique; special. You're not saying there's something wrong with that?"

"There's a difference between the Honor Code and the System that implements it. The system is where the problems lie according to the Buckley Study."

"There's also a problem with the Code, sir. It's stated in the negative instead of the positive. A cadet *will not* lie, cheat or steal… It should be: a cadet *will always* be honest and above reproach."

Berry turned and looked at him. "You're right, of course. I've often thought the same myself. Positive instead of negative. I want you to pursue that further, Nolan. Get a copy of the Buckley Study and evaluate it from that perspective. Then you and I and the Com can discuss it before all the assistance from Washington overwhelms us. Time is of the essence."

"Sir, right now I don't have the time. I'm still consolidating all of our findings on physiology from the studies at Benning, Knox, Jackson and Sill and comparing and contrasting with the Navy, Air Force and Marine boot camps. Major Kolarik and I are developing training modules for this summer's Beast Barracks cadres and tactical officers in each cadet company."

"Major Kolarik can finish that for us."

"I'm not sure she can, sir. We each bring different but complimentary skills to the work."

"And you also like spending time with her."

Glenn shrugged. "She's reasonably good company and easy to work with, yes."

The general frowned and drew his mouth down, giving Glenn a sideways look of disapproval. "Am I to assume that when you two spent the Christmas holidays together, or weekends at your family's retreat on Long Island that you're busying yourselves on West Point business using your so-called complimentary skill sets?"

"Yes, sir, you could say that." Glenn looked quickly at his watch. "Sir, we need to get moving or we'll be late, and that wouldn't set a good standard for the Corps."

"We'll talk more about this later, Nolan. For now, you get a copy of that report and immerse yourself in it."

"I will, sir," Glenn replied, tapping the face of his watch. "We shouldn't leave the Com alone with that crowd."

The theatre in Eisenhower Hall was filled when Berry and Nolan entered. They stopped outside the door and talked briefly with General Ulmer; as soon as they entered the massive room, the large audience of cadets stood to attention and General Berry called out, "At Ease!"

The "Stump the Stars" duo plus Glenn took their seats on stage. The superintendent began the proceedings instantly.

"We're here today to inform you that we, the United States Military Academy, are going to accomplish this tough mission we've been tasked with, and do coed education better than any institution in America, civilian or military. All of you know that one of the hallmarks of this great country is that the military is submissive to the civilian leadership, specifically the U.S. Congress. The founders made it so in order that this nation would not descend into the catastrophic political chaos that attends to other systems in which the military only follows orders and leadership it happens to like.

"It's moot whether or not you or I like the idea of co-education at West Point. The nation has spoken through its elected Congress and issued us an order which by law and by military protocol we are obliged… or perhaps I should say, *required* to follow. We will. All of us.

"What does this mean? It means we have to adapt our entire culture, the way we communicate and interact to a set of circumstances wholly different than anything encountered in the last one hundred and seventy-four years. We, the leadership of West Point still have questions for which we don't yet have answers, but fewer than we had just six months ago. We know, General Ulmer and I, that you have questions too. And we've spent time listening – through the tactical officers and others, like Captain Nolan to my right who many of you have spent time with. He is the overall project manager for this effort. If we don't have answers to your questions today, he will, or he'll find out and get back to you.

"Before I open up the floor to questions, I'd like to make one obvious but important point about the reality we face after July 7, 1976, and it's this: everything – and I mean every single solitary thing in our interactions with the newly arrived female cadets can be misinterpreted and grossly taken out of context. I'm talking about common things we say and do – all can easily be misinterpreted and viewed as harassment, or persecution or just plain bad manners. Keep that in mind as we take our first steps in a few months as a co-educational institution. Now, what are your questions?"

A long, uneasy silence ensued and Glenn looked around at the young faces in the auditorium, some attentive, some bored; others smirking and still others looking confused. *Was I ever that young?* The silence lingered, and with it a certain tension in the air; he wondered if he'd made a mistake in suggesting the audience be so large. It had seemed such a good idea at the time.

As he pondered how the Supe was going to deal with him if this all fell flat, the ominous first question from the audience arose. A slightly built second classman made his way to one of the many microphones scattered about the large auditorium.

"Sir," the cadet began slowly, almost apologetically, "given the facility limitations... common latrines and showers in the barracks and the close proximity of rooms... and, the historic tendency of cadets to amble about the hallways in less than full uniforms..."

"You mean going around in your underwear," Glenn interrupted into the microphone.

"Yes, sir, that's what I meant."

Glenn stole a glance at Jenny who was standing just inside the doorway. He caught her eye and winked; she winked back and gave him a sly smile.

"Well, sir, my question is: will the female cadets be consolidated into one barracks area or one company or what?"

"A very reasonable question, one we've given a lot of thought to," General Berry said. He nodded to the Commandant to answer this vexing query.

Without hesitation, General Ulmer charged into his answer. "The only way to properly integrate and achieve the intent of Congress was this – the female cadets will be spread throughout the Corps."

The raucous, excited response of four thousand cadets was immediate, unmistakable, and predictable. General Berry looked at Glenn and slowly shook his head.

As Ulmer turned to Berry to try and understand the reason behind all the enthusiasm, the Superintendent buried his head in his hands, then looked up at the audience and said,

"See what I mean."

*   *   *

"So tell me, Nolan, how do you think it went?"

"Before or after the first question, sir?"

General Berry's eyes narrowed into cynical slits as he leaned back in his large brown leather swivel chair and crossed his arms. "So you don't think it went well."

"Actually, sir, once it got going, I think it went fairly well. You and the Com got your message out and heard feedback. Some feedback, but not a whole lot. The troops want to be heard, to be talked with, not down to. Mission accomplished... somewhat."

"What would you do differently?" Berry asked tapping his fingertips together.

"I'd have a similar session with all the Tactical officers. Pretty much the same subject, but maybe expand it to include the Honor issue." He saw the general frown and quickly added, "I heard from the cadets in the small groups at my quarters that tactical officers are a part of the problem with the honor system. It wasn't my topic, but one of the second classmen brought up on his own."

"Details?"

"No sir, only the vague feeling I got that the system has changed and is being used by the Tac officers to enforce regulations. The cadets really didn't like that, and it seems to me if that's happening, it would undermine the foundation of the Code."

Berry sat forward and put a fist into his palm and rocked slowly, contemplating. "Something like that is in the report I told you to review. Back to 'Stumping the Stars' – other thoughts ?"

"I'd do it with the cadets again in a month, and then again just before Graduation, and I'd concentrate on the lower classes. The graduating class really doesn't much care right now; they're too busy thinking about their cars, and graduation week, and getting married. It's the lower classes that have the most skin in the game and that's where there's opposition." The general looked like he wanted to hear more, so Glenn continued. "They hear all the arguments from the standpoint of equal rights, equal opportunity, egalitarianism, and all of that, but they're not buying it. Most of the alumni aren't either. Disgruntled grads – that's where you'll get most of your problems."

"You don't have to tell me, Nolan. I've gotten several letters already accusing me of dereliction and cowardice. I've lost friends already over this."

"Only wet babies like a change, sir. "

Berry gave him a half-hearted grin and said, "But, we're making progress."

Glenn took a deep breath, contemplating, and finally said, "Is that a question, sir?"

"No. An observation. You agree or disagree?"

"The 'curmudgeon' disagrees. The other me is…" Nolan sat back and asked, "Are we into Kilbeggan time, sir? This will sound better after one or two Irish whiskies."

"We are."

"All right, then – I'm ambivalent. Sometimes I'm with the program, and sometimes I'm not. As you well know, sir, I have a lot of faults, but indecision isn't one of them. I want to be with the program but I can't, not all the time. Not after all the research and reports and analysis that Major Kolarik and I have put together. The physiology by itself says this is a bad idea – for West Point and for the Army. Your comments to me the first day I arrived here tilts me further in that direction. I want to follow what the Congress says to do, but the hurdles are… well, considerable."

"Continue, captain."

"Sir, you asked me how I thought it went today. I think we hit a looping single over the infield when we needed a home run. The cadets didn't ask the really tough questions that are on their minds. I've heard some of them in my quarters, but they didn't get asked today. And I don't see where we're addressing the concerns of the alumni."

"The Association of Graduates is handling that."

"From a distance, and with canned responses. Who's dealing specifically with the grads here on post? From what I hear – admittedly a small sample – they think they're being ignored.

They have many of the same questions and concerns as the cadets but no avenue to raise them. An approach similar to 'Stump the Stars' would probably work. But the format has to be set so that the really tough questions get to the floor and get dealt with."

"What are these questions of theirs?"

"The concerns seems to center around the fear of setting up double standards."

The general's face became animated with displeasure. "I've said from the beginning there will not be double standards."

"I've heard you say that, and so have the cadets and the grads."

"Because it's true. We will train women in leadership and academics to the standards of West Point so that they may enjoy the same military education the academy has traditionally provided male cadets. They will then assume roles in the Army in suitable positions. Women have been in our military organizations for a long, long time."

"The question no one hears an answer to is – will females be required to select their branch from only the combat arms, as do the males?"

"That's a ridiculous question, Nolan. Of course women won't be commissioned in the combat arms. American women in the late 20th century, are not as effective in combat as men are, and never will be. And I don't think America is the kind of country that wants to send its women into the ugliness of ground combat you and I have witnessed. I know it's not just physiology; more importantly, it's the psychology. By nature, women are not warriors. That's not condemnation, it's really a commendation. Most men can be trained into it, but women cannot, except in very rare and very isolated cases. All of that is documented."

"To the detractors, that's one of the examples of a double standard, sir." Glenn wondered if he had again stepped over the line. This problem of double standards was the most emotion laden change issue for the classmates who had button-holed him since his arrival. "Sir, I've gotten more than an earful over this since my arrival. Perhaps it would be best if I laid out a memo with the questions most frequently asked and provide that so you and General Ulmer don't get blindsided in the future."

"That would be most helpful, of course. But in the end, you can rest assured that our goal will not change."

"The curmudgeon says that Congress set the goal posts in the wrong place on the wrong field. That's what you're hearing from those who oppose this move."

Chapter 40

Glenn pulled the bicycle to a stop in front of his quarters, hit the timer button on his watch and dismounted after wiping the terrycloth wrist band across his forehead. Although it was still early, the day was already hot and muggy.

"How far this time, Nolan?" The tall, rangy captain in summer dress greens stood and uncoiled from his sitting position on the front steps of Glenn's Stoney Lonesome quarters.

Harv Clayton had been in the same platoon as Benny and Glenn during that first two months at the academy in the summer of '64. At the end of Beast Barracks, he'd been assigned to F-2, 'The Zoo', a name the company wore proudly and routinely reinforced. The Texan from El Paso hadn't lost his drawl, his love of horses or his propensity to tell people exactly what was on his mind. He'd been called back to the Academy as a company tactical officer fifteen months earlier and was one of about two dozen in the first wave of returning '68 grads populating the academic and tactical departments.

"Twenty miles plus a couple of tenths," Glenn replied, taking a drink from his water bottle. "An hour and nine minutes."

"Good time."

"It's pretty flat almost the whole way once I get through Washington Gate. Didn't feel like tackling Storm King Highway or 9W this morning. Too dark and too steep this early in the day." He took another drink. "What are you doing here, Harv? I would've thought you'd be real busy this week."

"I am... But I had to stop by and apologize for last Saturday."

"You got the wrong place and wrong person, my friend. You need to square that with Jenny, not me."

Clayton nervously fiddled with his uniform hat. "Thought I'd sort things out with you first. Sorry I made such an ass of myself at your girlfriend's shindig Saturday."

"Like I said, talk to her."

"I will. Maybe I'll take her to lunch at the O-Club. You wouldn't mind, would you?"

"She's free and over twenty-one," Glenn replied, smirking at his friend. "I learned a hard lesson a half dozen years ago about trying to tell Major Kolarik anything... especially what to do with her social life. Come on in for coffee."

They sat at the table in the small kitchen waiting for the percolator to finish.

"I let my mouth get ahead of my brain last Saturday, and I'm sorry for putting you and her in an awkward place. Shoulda kept my trap shut, I guess. But after this summer..." The captain sighed and looked worried. "This isn't gonna work, Glenn. I don't know how our guys in the academic departments view things, but nobody I know in the Tactical Department is for this plan to integrate women into the Corps. We all thought it was a bad idea when it first came up and nothing about this summer changes our minds."

"You made your position real clear on Saturday."

Clayton rubbed his jaw. "I know. I called Ricky Saylor and told him I was sorry for exploding all over him like I did. But that doesn't change my mind or the facts. You probably know the details better than any of us. Am I wrong in saying this is bad idea?"

"Time will tell, Harv."

"That's not an answer. You were never one to beat around the bush, Glenn, or to call a spade a damned shovel. From where I sit, the summer proved this is a bad idea we should put a stop to before we get too far down the road to change things back to the way they should be."

"You can't unring a bell, Harv."

"Is that your way of saying our school, our Army, can't change something we tried and found to be a mistake, a bad decision?"

"It's being a bad decision is your opinion, not a statement of fact."

"It's the truth!" Glenn's classmate took a deep breath and looked away. "You've seen the same things I've seen this summer – you observed the training, witnessed bayonet drill, watched the Plebes on the obstacle course, went on the Plebe Hike. Hell, you and Jenny – Major Kolarik – did physiological studies and observed Basic Training at Benning and Knox. You know better than anyone what the results show. The damned politicians declare men and women are interchangeable parts without any difference and the Army salutes it as if it's true."

"That's not exactly the case."

"Damn, Nolan! Now you're hedging on me, too."

"No, I'm not. I heard what you said to Rick on Saturday."

"You might have heard, but you didn't *really* hear. Let me tell you some things. Until this recent idea of integrating women into everything men in the Army do –"

"Right now, it's just Basic training," Glenn interrupted.

"And all the military academies. Like us. Ten, twelve years from now, it'll be everything. We both had infantry companies in Nam. You ready to have a girl right out of high school as one of your machine gunners, or put somebody's teenage daughter into a body bag? When you get your battalion, you want to be told that half your commanding officers have to be female?"

"That's not going to happen, Harv. You're exaggerating."

"Says you. A decade ago, it was beyond the realm of possibility that boys and girls would be bunking together in Basic or in the barracks of our old alma mater. Tell me that's not true. Look, until just a couple of years ago, women in the Army were separate from men; they were WACs or nurses with their own chain of command."

"You really think women should be segregated from men in the military?"

"If it ain't broke, don't fix it. No need to. It's worked fine so far as I can tell. Women were separated from men except for clerical or administrative type jobs. It worked, but it's all changing right before our eyes – right here. Now. And I'm telling you, we've only begun to see the ramifications and problems. What happens when young ladies and testosterone-laden young men get together in close proximity? Yeah, that's right. It's called sex. Promiscuity. That's a real good thing to throw into the mix of combat units in training or on the battlefield."

"American women will not be in combat units. That'll never happen."

"Then why the hell are they taking up slots in this place where *everybody* has to go into a combat arms branch except those physically disqualified by injuries? If they don't go into Infantry, Artillery, Engineers, Signal or Armor, isn't that a double standard? And this place is all about everybody being equal and starting from day one having to earn everything he – and now she – gets or possesses. Aren't we fundamentally changing West Point's mission – to provide the Army senior combat leaders – the very reason for this place to exist?"

Glenn didn't have a good answer. He looked at his classmate and thought about the times over the past several months he'd asked himself the same nagging questions. "I still think you're wrong about women in combat. I don't think women are now or ever will be clambering to go to Ranger School, or get into infantry combat. I don't think they really want that, nor do I think it's the right thing for the nation to do. We have a higher opinion of women that to put them into something like that. But even if that should happen, it's been done successfully before. What about the Israeli success of placing women in combat units of their Army?"

"Nolan, that's a really dumb question. And I know you know it. We both know that's a bald faced lie. Women in Israel are trained in self-defense and they carry weapons. But they aren't integrated into combat units. That's a myth. And I got that from General Berry. Everybody in the Tactical Department knows it, and so do you."

"Just checking to see if you'd done your homework."

"I have. I may have a hard time now and then keeping my temper under control but I have my facts straight... and my logic, too. And listen, I'm not against expanding opportunities for women beyond the old WAC and nurse specialties. My issue is the combat roles.If the Army has to provide equal Leadership training for female officers, why not set up a similar academy for women with all the same instruction and opportunities for leadership within the female chain of command that has served us so well up to this point? I'm tellin' you that co-ed chains of command will create a mountain of problems we haven't begun to think through yet. Is West Point ready to deal with promiscuity between cadets, sexual harassment between members of the Corps?...Sexual favors traded for good ratings. Rape?"

"That's not going to happen," Glenn replied angrily.

"Think not? I'm going to do you the favor of assuming you really don't believe that."

"You don't have to do me a favor. We attract a student body with high levels of integrity. And we raise everyone to an even higher level through the Honor Code."

Clayton nodded agreement. "No argument with that. But we're looking at mixing groups with physical, biological differences at an age when they are most sexually active and looking for a place to vent that. What we're doing is like throwing gasoline on a fire or giving teenagers the keys to the car and the liquor locker."

"Poor choice of metaphors, Harv."

"I don't think so. You weren't like that as a cadet? Everybody in the Zoo was. Me too."

"Well, you're from Texas."

"Compliments won't get you anywhere, Nolan." Harv flashed a crooked grin and pulled out a pack of Marlboros; he offered the pack to Glenn and lit his own. "But listen. Co-ed dorms may work in civilian colleges. I won't argue that. But they won't work here, or anywhere else in the military. And the reason is that girls – young women – are really vulnerable to predation from male superiors, or upperclassmen. Much more so than in any college. In a civilian university, if a young female is being pressured to do something demeaning or she feels trapped, she has an out. She can move to another dorm or off-campus and continue on with her education. That's not the case here or in Annapolis or at Air Force. Women are stuck in a hierarchical military organization in which a superior has tremendous control over subordinates with no alternatives except to quit and go home. We're not doing them a favor."

Glenn lit the cigarette and poured them each a cup of coffee. He knew that if his old friend laid out the same argument to Jenny, he'd find an ally.

"Take Jenny out to lunch and apologize. Don't rile her up like you tried to do me. She'll stick you for an expensive bottle of wine."

"I'll take my chances. Glenn, deep down you know everything I told you is true. The question, Nolan, is what are we going to do about it?"

"What are *you* going to do about it?"

*   *   *

TO: MG SB Berry, Superintendent
            BG WF Ulmer, Commandant of Cadets

FROM: Cpt GA Nolan, Project Manager
            Special Assistant to the Superintendent, USMA

Date: 31 August 1976

SUBJECT: **AFTER ACTION REPORT – Beast Barracks – Class of 1980**

This report summarizes the planning for, reception and initial training of the USMA Class of 1980.

The purpose of the report is to chronicle the planning, actions, results and costs for your study and evaluation, as well as historical recording and as a basis for the future development of further necessary changes to administering the academy as a co-educational institution.

<u>Executive Summary</u>

The class of 1980 entered West Point on 7 July 1976.
It was the first class in the history of West Point to include females.

Glenn sat back from the typewriter and took a deep breath. He'd been procrastinating over the report the entire weekend and most of Monday after his conversation with Harv – reading and re-reading his journal notes, re-organizing his twelve months of interim reports into a half-dozen major headings, setting it all aside and then picking it up again and starting over. Jenny had been an easy distraction to help him drag his feet Sunday afternoon. *I should have learned to type a long time ago. Had this same problem at the Advanced Course when I waited until the last minute and almost boloed that major Staff Study ... how do writers do it – thinking and typing at the same time?*

"Nolan. Got a minute to talk?"

Glenn turned and looked at General Berry standing in the doorway; it was the first time the Supe had ever come to his office. Something was up. What was Harry Reasoner's comment about helicopters? – *if something bad hasn't happened, it was about to.* The same could be said of General Berry when he was on the prowl.

"Yes, sir. I'm having a hard time getting started on the report. I could use a break."

"This won't take long, and then you can get back to it." The general closed the door and sat down on the only other chair in the small office. "I want you to know I appreciated how you worked us into the cadet aviation orientation. Some of those cadets will one day be telling their grandchildren how the Superintendent of West Point gave them their first helicopter ride."

Glenn smiled to himself remembering the look on the Supe's face when they settled into the middle of the formation of eight Huey's down at Target Field that morning a week earlier. "I could tell you weren't all that happy at first about formation flying, sir."

"I have to admit the idea of flying with a National Guard unit worried me a little."

"Most of them are Vietnam vets with thousands of hours and much more experience than the average pilot now on active duty." Glenn watched the general in silence, and detected his boss was ill at ease, clearly uncomfortable. "Sir, you didn't stop by to talk about formation flying, did you?"

"No... no, I didn't. Last week while you were out at Camp Buckner, I got a call from a friend in the Department of the Army. He said you'd been making some inquiries about separation from the service. Tell me about it."

The back of Glenn's neck tingled and he felt his face go instantly hot. "I asked a few questions of Infantry branch. Some were about the possibility of a future command assignment in aviation, some were about career planning and promotions. I did ask about my situation if I were to voluntarily or involuntarily separate from active duty."

Berry looked at him stoically. "With your background and record, you're not going to be let go. You have to know that."

"We all know the old saw about assuming. I'm just being prudent, sir."

The now familiar shadow of disapproval washed over Berry's features. "I disagree."

Glenn held the general's stare for a few seconds and then nonchalantly shrugged.

"There's nothing prudent about a talented soldier walking away from a promising career, Nolan. I'd personally hate to see you do that. Those of us fortunate to serve in the Army are privileged and blessed in our opportunities. And you have a family tradition of service to fall back on as well."

"Fall back on or live up to, sir?"

"Both I would imagine," Berry replied, in an even, thoughtful voice. "The whole focus of your family throughout this century has been on serving the nation. Growing up in such a family is a privilege. You carry on a proud legacy in an honored national institution, like your father and his father before him. It would be wrong to throw that away."

Glenn hesitated. "But what if that national institution is changing in ways that make it impossible to stay?"

"That's not the case. Certainly, the Army has to change to meet future challenges. I imagine your father and grandfather faced far more change in their careers than you will."

Glenn pondered this, and thought it was probably true. "You could be right, sir. The amount of change may well have been greater, but the change direction was always the same."

"How do you mean?"

"I think the history of the military in the twentieth century, in general, has always been toward making the service better, more capable. The armed forces were hamstrung during the Depression by the civilian leadership's indifference toward preparedness and consequent lack of funding. The Army expanded and contracted, but always the *real* military, including West Point, kept their eye on the ball – training and taking care of the troops. They stuck to their guns on those, as far as I can tell."

"And you think that's no longer the case? I challenge you on that. Look at the establishment of the Training and Doctrine Command three years ago. It will transform the military."

"I hope it lives up to that billing, sir. I can't say, but even if it does, that's only half the equation. Where is a similar effort on the personnel side. I don't see it. In fact, what I see happening is clearly detrimental. Even if TRADOC is wildly successful, it'll be for naught if the personnel situation continues down the path it's on now."

"In your opinion."

"No, sir, in reality. VOLAR is an utter catastrophe. Race and drug problems are rampant Army-wide; the numbers of seasoned officers and NCOs exiting the service are huge. I saw at Campbell that recruiters sent us people that should never have been signed up, and wouldn't have been in prior decades."

He thought of an episode that distilled his worries in one fleeting episode. It happened in the motor pool of his own company when one day he observed a recently recruited mechanic stenciling a number on one of the compressors – CP-5. The five was backwards and when he asked the soldier what was wrong with the stencil, the answer was: *'What? Ain't that CP-5?'*

The motor pool was one thing, but he found similar problems among his helicopter crew chiefs. The aircraft engine decks were filthy and the log books showed a deteriorating fleet. His trip to the New York Guard unit, on the other hand showed their aircraft immaculate and well-maintained by comparison.

"Now we have to accept significantly lowered enlistment standards to meet published goals," he declared. "Why? - because we're politically committed to this idea of suddenly turning the military into an all-volunteer force. Numerical goals are met but readiness suffers."

"Not even the best change is without attendant problems," the general replied. "There are always growing pains, but we'll come out the other side better than before. We professionals have to soldier through. As long as you've got good health and the energy and the hankering to move on and do new things, there are many, many opportunities. That's what is so exciting about spending a lifetime in the Army."

"I don't know, sir. I don't see much in the way of opportunity." Glenn took a deep breath and remembered the general alluding to him as complainer during their first meeting. "I see obstacles on the rise and my opportunities dwindling. That damned article in TIME magazine..."

"LIFE did their best to hurt me too, but in the end I don't think they damaged my career, and your episode won't hurt you either." The general's eyes narrowed and he looked genuinely angry. "I know for a fact that General Abrams, in 1970 after your article came out, commented to both his deputy commander and his chief of staff at Military Assistance Command – Vietnam that you looked to be a damned fine company commander. That's high praise from the man who not long after became Chief of Staff of the Army."

"I didn't know that, sir. I wish he was still around."

He remembered the first uncomfortable days when the article went public and neither the reporter nor the photographer had showed at the firebase with the first copies. He knew he'd been played. And then the avalanche of questions from DA in Washington. Silly things that officers who had experienced combat should have known. And that major at Bien Hoa, with his silly, sophomoric comments. *I should have dragged him outside*, Glenn thought in a brief flash of anger. "My biggest critics weren't those who knew me or the Cav or even senior officers in DA. It was the majors and lieutenant colonels at the time who are now moving into the senior ranks of the Army as colonels and Brigadier Generals."

"Some of whom are or will be your supporters, some of which are likely mentors. I know that General Westmoreland didn't like what he saw of your performance in the TIME article, but as my case, people who knew you well went to bat for you. Two battalion commanders and one of the division commanders during your service in Vietnam wrote letters to him about you."

"I really appreciate that."

"You should. I've read them and frankly, they were the deciding factors in my choosing you for this assignment. When reading your article through the lens of experienced officers who knew you, it was obvious that you had been treated unfairly by the press. Many in your branch realize that also. I know I do. In the long run, your abilities came to the attention of superiors in a way that would have been impossible without the publication of the article. It's akin to the story of Joseph in the Bible... his brothers meant their action for evil, but God meant it for good. You're making it out to be a lot worse than it is, Nolan."

"The press is no longer an ally… or even an impartial observer of the facts."

"Our relationship is at best strained, which makes it all the more imperative that the next generation of leaders have the perspective and appreciation of that reality as you and I do. Future leaders will have to be more adept at dealing with a hostile press corps. That seems a help rather than a hindrance to your career, captain."

The general leaned back in the chair and crossed his arms over his chest. "That article in LIFE portrayed to me a man who was ambitious in a selfish way, an officer who was single mindedly focused solely on getting ahead – a man who had no feeling for his family nor for his soldiers. That isn't me. That article in TIME wasn't you, in the same way. We'll both survive."

"I hope you're right, sir. Honestly, you're more confident about it than I am."

"Confidence, Nolan. Be confident in yourself," the general said enthusiastically, like a preacher at a Baptist tent revival coming to his sermon's final point. " – in your actions and your motives. I think frankly and modestly that I'm the right man for this institution at this time. Confidence in self is like morale in a combat unit – it's essential to success."

The general's eyes never left Nolan as if waiting for an *Amen*.

"Insofar as the admission of women is concerned, I'm taking the soldierly approach and, by God, I expect those women to act like soldiers since they're in a school for soldiers."

General Berry looked hard at him. "Nolan, you cannot even consider leaving the service now. The Army is an essential part of your being. The blood of soldiers runs in your veins. You have proven your mettle in combat and peacetime. You have exhibited compassion and a love for soldiers without sacrificing professionalism. You are destined for great things. I didn't have the privilege of serving with you in battle, but even in peacetime I can see why others said you'll one day be a general officer. You cannot honorably walk away from such a duty."

Glenn debated telling Berry other facts about his career outlook he'd been made aware of on his last trip to Washington, and quickly decided to keep them to himself. The list was long and laying it out to the general would sound like bellyaching to a lifelong soldier. Besides, he was tired and wanted to at least get a start on the report. "I'll take that under advisement, sir. And I thank you for taking the time."

The general stopped abruptly, appearing uncomfortable. Glenn felt self-conscious and at a loss for words. The Superintendent quickly regained his composure and said, "Now, moving on, the Secretary of the Army has decided –"

There was a crisp single rap on the office door, and then it was flung open. "Move it, Nolan! Those steaks won't –" Jenny Kolarik stopped in mid-sentence, startled; her eyes clouded over and she murmured something indecipherable under her breath. "Excuse me, sir, for interrupting."

The general stood and was immediately the proper Southern gentleman: erect, shoulders back and nodding in a courtly way toward her. "That's quite all right, major," General Berry said, in a diffident, almost apologetic tone. He glanced at his watch and looked directly at Glenn. "It sounds like you two have dinner plans and my presence is impeding your evening. What is it those steaks won't do, Major?"

Jenny cleared her throat and quickly regained her poise. "I was about to say those steaks won't grill themselves. Captain Nolan fancies himself something of a master with a grill, and I was going to remind him he didn't have much time to marinate our filets."

"I *am* hindering you two." Looking at Glenn again, he said, "We were about done anyway. Perhaps, if you want, we can continue our discussions later, Nolan. In the meantime, I suggest you give your notes and journal to my secretary. She's just obtained one of those new IBM Mag Card typewriters and needs to learn how to use it. She can transcribe the notes and you can get to work on your report in a day or two. Until then, I have something else I need you to do. But that can wait until tomorrow."

General Berry inclined his head toward Jenny, excused himself and left them alone.

"Bad timing, Glenn. Sorry."

"No, not really. Just a little career counseling session and we were about done."

"Does he know about your interviews with Bechtel and Hercules Chemical?"

Glenn shook his head. "No, not yet. I haven't gotten an offer back from either, so we were talking in generalities – it was more like a pep talk about the Army than a counseling session."

"So, you still haven't made up your mind."

"About what?"

She frowned at him, and looked disgusted. "Oh, I don't know. ... about whether you want to use A-1 or Worcestershire on your steaks... go blind or run rabbits... about you and me."

"I hate to tell you but actually, we didn't talk about you," he said lightheartedly and immediately regretted it when he saw the look of deep disappointment in her eyes. "I'm sorry. That was thoughtless. I can be a real jerk at times, can't I? How can I make that up to you?"

"I'll let you off easy, captain. Bring an expensive bottle of wine by the house for dinner tonight. A *very* expensive bottle."

"You and the wine."

She looked down the hallway, then gave him a quick kiss on the lips.

"I suggest you bring your shaving kit, too... for in the morning." She cocked her head and looked at him seductively.

The phone rang and he signaled for her to stay as he picked up the receiver.

"Captain Nolan speaking."

"Glenn, this is your old grandpa."

"What can I do for you, general?" he asked, expecting to be told the first thing he could do was to stop calling the old man by 'that damned title.'

"I'd like you to meet me down at the old shore house at noon the day after tomorrow. I'll be taking your grandmother there and I could use your help getting her into the upstairs bedroom and moving some furniture around. Hate to bother you with this..."

"No, no, that's all right. Glad to do it. I can be there in two hours if you need me. Is there anything I can do before you get there?" Glenn asked, sure he heard some worry in his grandfather's voice. "Is everything all right? Is Grammy okay?"

There was a long pause on the other end of the line. *"We got some bad news from the hospital today. They recommended I move her into hospice. She has no intention of going there, but she agreed to go to the old place on Long Island. I'll be getting hold of the rest of the family tonight and tomorrow to let them know."*

"I can make those calls for you."

"No, I think its best coming from me."

"I'll go down and open up tonight and get everything ship-shape before you two get there."

"I hate to impose..."

"It's not imposing... it's my privilege. Call me at the main house if you need anything at all." He hung up and looked toward Jenny. "I'm sure you didn't get any of that. My grandmother got some bad news from the doctor today and grandpa is taking her to their Long Island house. The doctors told him she should be in a hospice, but she isn't going for that."

"People don't come out of hospice care. This is serious, Glenn."

"Sounded like it. I guess people who go in those places never come out. My grandfather is calling all of the family." He ran his fingers through his hair. "I'm going to have to back out of dinner tonight and go there to get the place ready."

"I'll go with you."

He took a deep breath and looked up at the ceiling. "No need for that, Jenny."

"I'm going anyway. This is what I do, Nolan. She might be glad to have a nurse around." Jenny looked quickly at her watch. "I'll run home and pack – you pick me up in an hour." We'll have that place inspection ready when she gets there."

"You're a good kid, Kolarik."

"I have my moments. Now stop stalling and get moving."

Chapter 41

"So there I was.... a-trompin' through the piney wood near to ol' Lake Popolopen – which is up the river in New Yawk close by that Yankee-infested rock pile they call West Point even though it's in the East... so my band of merry shave head Kaydets was just a-hangin' on mah ever word because they know'd ah was the fount of all knowledge, guardian of all truth, the dream of women-folk and the envy of all red-blooded American military men. Now this was just after the big War where ah was called upon to save the life of one Davey Nolan more than once as it was his habit to get lost 'cause he couldn't read a map or use a compass... and since as how he couldn't hit the inside wall of a broom closet with an 'ought-three' Springfield when he was locked inside one..."

"You know, Andy, this tale just keeps getting longer and more filled with what Bess Truman tried for years to get Harry to call *fertilizer*," Dave Nolan said. "How long is it going to take for you to move this story along to that bridge over the chasm and the swift and deep water? We've only got about five hours of daylight left."

"Hold your water, general. Ah'm gittin' to it."

Glenn looked at the family and friends around a fire pit on the lawn near Long Island Sound. Fauser's arrival the previous day with Michelle Payne had changed the atmosphere of the family gathering. The old Arkansas razorback had story after story about their years at the West Point as cadets, their time at the academy with MacArthur, years during the Depression at Fort Benning and the Philippines, serving together in North Africa and Europe during World War II. Glenn was learning things about his grandparents he'd never known.

"Do you think any of this is true?" Jenny asked, whispering in Glenn's ear. She'd flown down with him three days earlier in the Cessna belonging to the academy's flying club.

"Some. Maybe even most of it though my grandfather says to believe none of what the old guy says and only half of what you see him do. I think Fauser's aim is to take everybody's mind off the reason the family's here,... and to empty my grandpa's liquor locker."

"I shouldn't have insisted on coming here with you. I'm out of place and it's awkward."

"No it's not. The family loves you – and you needed to meet my parents at some point. You already knew Brad. I'm glad he and Zara were able to get here so fast."

His Aunt Erika had taken control of organizing the family gathering – assigning sleeping arrangements and parceling out responsibilities for preparing meals. Andy had commented a couple times that she was the best soldier in the whole Nolan clan and now called her 'First Sergeant'. She came out of the main house and interrupted his story telling.

"Sorry to butt in, general, but my mom would like to speak to you and Michelle."

"I always do what 'the boss' says," Fauser replied and stood slowly, balancing himself with a cane. Sticking his elbow out, he said, "Miz Payne, would you allow me?"

When Michelle and Andy Fauser entered the bedroom, Denise was sitting up in the large leather recliner looking out the window toward the gathering around the fire pit and beyond to the old wooden pier jutting into the Sound. She turned her head slowly and waved a hand toward the chair next to the window.

"Please have a seat, Michelle. Andy you can stand because you won't be staying long."

"I walked all the way up those stairs on this bum leg just to be sent packin' so soon?" Andy complained. "You're a hard woman, Denise Nolan."

"Actually I'm in a forgiving mood today, Andy. I just wanted you to know I've decided to forgive you for all the trouble you got Dave into over the years."

"Beggin' your pardon, but that scorecard is about all even. I remember the times when –"

"I was thinking about that day you talked him into parachute jumping from a plane when we were all stationed at West Point. Mitch was three, Erika was an infant and Elise was pregnant with Zack. What you two did was absolutely crazy. You didn't give a moment's thought to what would have happened to us if that crazy stunt had killed you. I know it was your idea – you and that Navy pilot."

"Pug Johnston. Truth be told it was his idea from muzzle to butt plate."

"I don't believe that for a second, but I forgive you both. You can leave now and make up more tall tales for my children and grandkids." She gave him a quick peck on the cheek and whispered in his ear, "Thank you for coming. You take care of my husband when I'm gone."

"Aw hell, woman. Don't go talkin' like that," he replied, flummoxed and lost for words.

He left and she turned to Michelle. "Thank you for coming and bringing Andy along. I love him to tears but I learned a long time ago you have to stay one step ahead of him. It's been a long time since we've seen one another, hasn't it?"

"A dozen years." Andy and Michelle had attended a football game at the school Glenn's plebe year. It was a month after Elise passed away and Denise asked them to come up for a long weekend to take his mind off it. Michelle and Andy's wife had been best friends since college. "I think that weekend was the time Andy and I finally buried the hatchet. Thank you for making that possible for us."

Denise shied a hand at her. "That wasn't my doing."

"I'm going to have to disagree with you. Denise, when I think back, you were always the one doing things like that for me, from the day we first met at the Founders Day Ball in, I believe, 1921. My goodness, that's over a half century ago. You invited us to join you at your table of friends. That was such a kind gesture. You'll never know how much I appreciated it. And later, at other posts when our paths crossed." Michelle paused for a moment, thinking back over the years. "Remember that dinner we girls had at your quarters in the Philippines after a day of shopping in the market? An old woman tried to convince us to buy that awful smelling fruit. I can't remember now what it was called."

"Durian fruit," Denise offered. "She said it would make all of us stay beautiful forever; but you said it smelled like asphalt marinated in turpentine and we'd all be better off growing old gracefully."

Michelle laughed. "That was such a wonderful day. I had many good days like it when we were all stationed there. Our tour in Manila was my favorite time and place of all. You were the one who made that happen, too. I learned to play bridge in the islands because you included us in your group."

"You taught Erika to ride."

"Yes. And you got back in the saddle."

"I loved those rides the three of us took along the beaches south of the city."

"It was special. We all had fun riding, and Mitch cared for my horses at the post stable."

"You spoiled him by paying him too much."

Michelle tilted her head and wrinkled her brow. "No I didn't. Denise, we've had this argument before. Whoever's right, Mitch overcame it. You should be very proud. I just read an article about him in the Wall Street Journal saying his development of that new fighter plane for McDonnell Douglas is going to make them a solid profit and put the Air Force years ahead of the Russians. I couldn't be happier for him if he were my own son."

Denise nodded slowly. "Maybe because he could have been your son."

"Whatever do you mean?" Michelle asked, looking perplexed.

"You know. And so do I. You and Dave were an item before I met him. And afterward. You two spent a week together before he went off to Europe in the First War. You were engaged and planned to marry before he left, but the War intervened and he was shipped overseas early so the wedding never happened."

"Denise, please don't think –"

"I've known about it for a long while. Honestly, it never bothered me, but I'm curious about some things now and I'm running out of time."

*

Fauser came slowly down the front porch steps with the aid of his cane and walked over to where his old roommate was sitting by himself gazing at a sailboat a mile offshore. Jenny and Glenn were wading ankle deep digging for clams and Mitch was lowering the Boston Whaler inside the boathouse for a spin around the Sound. Brad and Zara sat on the dock talking, with their bare feet dangling over the water.

"Your wife sure knows how to carry a grudge, pard," Fauser said, sitting heavily in the chair and lighting a cigarette. "Six damn decades that's woman's been mad at me. But your wife finally forgave me for that time we jumped outta Pug's aeroplane up at Stewart Field as if I had any part in coming up with that crazy idea."

"We both know who's idea that was."

"Yes we do. But I refused to tell her it was actually you."

"Denise knows better than that."

"She's up there now with Michelle, cookin' up somethin'." Fauser blew a cloud of smoke that dissipated quickly in the onshore breeze. "Dangerous pair o' females when unsupervised. Michelle especially. I was talkin' with Erika about the trial that sent your buddy Reeves to jail. It was his wife – I should say his ex-wife – that kept pushing the prosecutor's office these past years to do something. Her and that sassy little granddaughter of yours. Ol' Harry Reeves never knew what hit him. Sorry bastard. Guess you're happy."

"Hate to disappoint you, Butternuts, but I didn't get any pleasure out of his conviction. It didn't bring my boy back. Didn't change anything, really. To tell you the truth, I wish none of it had ever happened."

They were silent for a few minutes and then a burst of laugher came through Denise's open bedroom window. Dave recognized Michelle's distinctively rich, musical laugh; for a brief moment it brought back a memory of the first time he's heard it – at the gate outside her house in Harrisburg when he went to see her father about the Senator's appointment to West Point. And there was that time before the war at Camp Mills, not far down the road...

"They're laughin' at you, son," Andy said, tossing his head toward the house. "Told you those two were cookin' up somethin'."

Dave shrugged. In another few seconds, the sound of their laughter reached him again.

"You'd best look into that before you got yourself a full-fledged conflagration happenin' here, right under your nose."

"I'm not worried – neither of them is armed."

"A body could still be hurt being this close the burstin' radius of them two. Think I'll sashay down to see how young Glenn and that nurse are doing with their clam diggin'. I like that girl. She's a cutie an' she don't let that grandson of yours get away with nothin'. Reminds me of Denise."

Dave nodded slowly. "Me too. I told that boy years ago that every soldier should be lucky enough to marry a nurse like mine."

"Reckon he listened. But he ought to close the deal with her before some other fella steals a march on him and snatches her up." Andy rose deliberately from the chair and walked slowly down to the shoreline.

Dave watched him talk for a while with Glenn and Jenny, then leisurely walk out to the end of the dock and sit down on the wooden bench next to his other grandson and Zara. A hand lightly touched his shoulder and he looked up to see Michelle gazing down at him.

"She wants to see you, Dave. She thinks it's time."

"No!" he said abruptly, getting up from the chair. "Not now! I'm not ready for this."

"You have to be – for her sake." She took both his hands in hers and looked into his eyes. "There's something I have to tell you."

"Michelle don't."

"I have to. Dave Nolan, I've loved you all of my life. Every time our paths crossed I was convinced it was because we were meant to be together. I realize now how terribly wrong I was. Everything that happened between us all these years wasn't about me or you, and surely not about the two of us. It was about her. You made the right choice when you married Denise." She blinked rapidly. "Go. She needs you to be there for her right now."

Denise was staring outside when he entered their bedroom. "I'm glad Glenn brought his girlfriend. We had a nice chat yesterday. I like her. She reminds me of myself at that age."

"You were more volatile."

"I had to be. You were less pliant than our grandson."

"I'm not going to argue with you."

"You'd be a fool to." She reached out and patted his hand. "Remember I told you once when you were still in the service that it was clear to me you were in love with two women?"

"I thought those two women we were talking about was you and the Army. I think I said something about the Army being a jealous lover."

"You did," Denise replied and took a deep, labored breath.

"I didn't satisfy your curiosity, did I?"

"No you didn't. I thought it really strange how you were always so nervous around Michelle – at first I thought it was Harrison making you uncomfortable, but over time that didn't make sense. It finally came together for me one night in Washington. It was in '42, at one of Ethel Terry's 'War Widow' parties, after you and Andy went to Benning to form that division you took to North Africa." Denise coughed and reached for the glass of water on the small table. "Elise Fauser had a little too much wine and let something slip. I pressed her on it, and she ended up telling me the whole story about you and Michelle – about how you dated her at the academy before we met and also about the two of you two getting back together for a week or so here on Long Island before you went overseas. She also told me you two were engaged before you shipped out for Europe with the AEF."

"I should have told you," he admitted, embarrassed.

Denise shrugged. "Honestly, that didn't bother me. By then, we'd been married a long, long time. We had a son in the Air Corps, a daughter working in Washington and a second son about to go to college. In all the time we've been married, you never gave me a single reason to doubt your fidelity to our marriage vows. I wasn't worried in the least about your straying with her or anyone else. I was angry with you that night, but it was about your going back in the Army, not about dating someone more than twenty years earlier. I'd grown to like Michelle very much by then. Still do."

"We were never actually engaged. She and I talked about it, but the Army moved up our sailing date. You know how I feel about things happening by chance."

"I'm just as glad you didn't tell me. If you had, I'd have felt guilty for not telling you about Malcolm Andrews."

"Who?"

"The son of one of my father's acquaintances. He proposed to me the summer you graduated from the academy, and I almost went through with it. I was still angry at you for not asking me to marry you when you graduated, especially after all the time I spent helping you rehabilitate your knee that winter. Of course you know about my other engagement."

"You weren't engaged to Phillip. I got home from the war in time to talk you out of it."

"Not exactly, Dave. We were pretty far along. He'd already asked, and I'd already accepted the ring. The party was just the official announcement. You were very persuasive." She smiled at him. "And you did it right out there by our dock. I know we've had some pretty good fights over the years, but how could I possibly be angry at you over an old girlfriend? She didn't get you, I did."

He felt his heart melt toward her. "I'm one very lucky guy."

She coughed again and tried to catch her breath. "You're not the only one who's lucky."

They sat silently for several minutes, holding hands.

"It's been a good life," Dave said at last. "I've always thought of you as that young girl I dated at West Point, and the nurse at Allery who challenged me."

"And you were always the cadet and the young major in the AEF I couldn't quite tame."

"What happened to us?"

"We got old, Dave. But I loved every minute of it. Every single minute – even when I complained about you and the Army and...." Denise turned her face away. When she finally spoke, her voice was barely audible. "There's a card for you under my pillow. I want you to read it after I'm gone."

His eyes grew moist and he placed his hand on her arm. "Don't say that! You're going to get better. I know it."

"Dave, I'm not. And that's okay. I've lived a good life. Most of it with you. Our children, except for one, have grown to be successful adults. Our grandchildren have also and one of them is a fine picture of what our Glenn would have been had he lived. I have no regrets." She closed her eyes and her body seemed to go limp.

"Denise! No!" He took her hand in both of his. "Look at me!"

She opened her eyes and gave him a gentle, peaceful smile. "I love you, Dave."

Then her eyes closed slowly and she was gone.

In two wars he'd seen death many times, often up close and in all its worst, soul-searing expressions. But no experience in his life had left him feeling so utterly empty as this. The sounds of female laughter from far away drifted through the window – Erika, Cateline and Brad's wife Zara reacting to one of Andy's stories down at the dock. Seagulls called out to one another, their screeching clear and close. The sound of his own breathing and his pulse pounded loudly in his ears. He was numb as he gazed at her face. *She looks so peaceful now...*

"I wish I'd been a better husband to you," he whispered. It was a long time before he released her hand. He thought of the card she'd mentioned and went to the bed. Tucked under the pillow was a small envelope with his name written on it in her flowing script. He remembered the times as a cadet when his heart leapt at the site of her handwriting on letters to him. He pulled out the simple card with the words **Thank You** printed on the front and below it a handwritten inscription: *for giving me the exciting life you promised years ago.*

He opened the notecard and read the dozen last words she'd written him, and for the first time in his life he wept.

Chapter 42

Erika hung up the phone and sat down at the kitchen table.

"It's all arranged now, Dad – funeral home, the service late afternoon the day after tomorrow and burial here in the Barrett family plot next to her parents. It's going to be just family – the way she wanted. I contacted her brother and my cousins on her side. I also asked Andy and Michelle to stay over since Mom always counted them as family. The obituary will be in the local paper and the *New York Times*. Mitch is contacting them and doing the writing. Anything else you can think of?"

He shook his head.

"No... Thanks Erika for taking care of this. I don't think I could have done it. Never wanted to think about it even when we both realized it was close." He stared out the window toward the Sound, remembering the first time he'd seen the place. He was a cadet just finishing his second year and she had invited him to spend the summer with her family. "Her great grandfather bought this place during the Civil War when the whole island was nothing but grassland and a handful of farms. He bought it because it was one of the few areas that had freshwater springs. There's a lot of history and memories here. Your mother and I had great times together at this place. It'll will be yours when I'm gone. Yours and Mitch's. She'd want it kept in the family."

"I know she did." Erika also knew that neither she nor Mitch had much interest in using the place or keeping it up. After retiring from Barrett, Inc., her father had hired two Amish – a carpenter and a stone mason – to help him build four small cottages for the use of family and friends. She'd rarely taken advantage of them and neither had her brother, but Andy and Michelle and other of their friends had from time to time.

"Michelle volunteered to take care of catering for the funeral," Erika told her father. "She has a lot of contacts in the city. And another thing – did you know she's talked to Brad and Zara about becoming a partner in their ranch? Brad says she offered to pay off their debt."

*   *

"Glenn, here's the deal," Brad said to his brother as they sat together on the pier. "She offered to give me a personal loan of two hundred thousand at zero percent interest for ten years. At the end of that, the interest goes to five percent over a thirty year term."

"That's not a loan, it's a gift," Glenn said. "She won't live to collect a fraction of it."

"I told her that. She said she knows. It's something she wants to do for us. You and me."

"What do you mean you and me?"

"I told her about you looking around and thinking about maybe leaving the Army. She sweetened the deal so I could buy that twenty thousand acres to our north where the vineyard is so we can expand the cattle operation *and* the winery. You could move down under and we'd be partners. I'll run the cattle operation and you run the wine business."

"I don't know anything about making wine."

"Honestly, I don't know much more. But we're making a little bit of cash on it anyway. There's a good chance of making some real money from winemaking, but it's going to take more attention than I can give it. Got some other ideas to increase profits, but not a chance of following up on them with just Zara and me. When Michelle gives me the loan, I can pay off our debt, expand the cattle business to where it's profitable consistently, and hopefully have enough left over to make real money off the winery. But I need a partner I can trust to make it all happen."

"I don't know. Let me think on it, Brad."

"What's stopping you?"

"A number of things.

"You told me you're past your service commitments, and you don't like the way the Army's heading. They won't let you fly and Infantry branch doesn't like their officers to have a secondary career path in aviation – for you that it's a career killer."

Glenn nodded agreement. "Colonel Galvin got hold of me a few weeks back. He's asked me to work for him in his new assignment."

Brad's face lit up. "You're still in touch with him?! Okay, working with him again would be cool. But that won't last forever."

"He's going to be one of the military's senior leaders someday and I think he's offering to mentor me. I could ride his coat tails to an interesting career."

"Maybe. But is that what you really want? If you do that, you're still not your own boss. And you like being in control of your own destiny. Right? Didn't you just tell me the best job you ever had was commanding that infantry company in the Cav? You liked it because you were pretty much on your own, calling your own shots. You're never going to have that situation again in the Army. I think Dad got out of the Air Force for the same reason. He was at a point where he couldn't run his own show as a Group commander and the service was telling him he'd come to the end of his flying days. Sound familiar?"

Glenn took a deep breath. *If I quit the Army now, would I always regret leaving my calling and wondering if Galvin was right that one day I'd be a general?* But it wasn't the rank, though he viewed attaining stars was as exulted as any position in the civilian world – he'd always thought his grandfather's success at the head of Barrett Enterprises paled by comparison to his Corps and Division commands in the Second War. Leaving the military now, at a time when it was clearly on the ropes following Vietnam, felt like running away from responsibility, an act of cowardice in the face of a challenge when all the best hands were needed to fight the battle.

He thought about the chat he'd had with his grandfather and Uncle Rand the evening before while sitting at an outside table drinking coffee laced with homemade Irish cream. The conversation turned to Vietnam and the war's genesis. His grandfather and Randall Ashby had provided facts unknown to him about false reports, policy statements, and ill-conceived strategies that led to the Gulf of Tonkin Resolution...

*

"The war in Southeast Asia has been going on for seven or eight centuries," Dave Nolan told his grandson. "The Vietnamese have been fighting people like the Chinese and a host of others in the region for a long, long time. We were just the latest. And probably not the last."

"I've never heard that before," Glenn said. "How do you know that?"

"From several sources. I first read one of Ho Chi Minh's speeches about his country in his early radical period. I was reading everything I could lay my hands on about the Orient during the boat ride over to the Philippines in the mid 30s when I was sent there. By then, Ho had lived in America, the U.K., France, Russia, India, China and was a committed communist. Apparently that happened while he was in France. I read some of his prison diary poems in the fifties. Can't remember why now."

"He became a communist in France?"

Dave shrugged. "They may be our oldest ally, but they have some strange tendencies. I've always been a little leery of them since the first war. There was another source that came out in '68, around the time you graduated from West Point – a small bluebook pamphlet, about eighty pages, published by the Republican Party explaining why they split with Johnson on Vietnam. It had a lot of ancient history of the country, and more recent revelations."

"What kind of revelations?" Glenn asked.

"Inside information from the Kennedy and early Johnson years; accurate reports about the beginning of the path toward our involvement in Vietnam that was known to few."

"Your grandfather ran it by me, and I could vouch for the accuracy of many allegations concerning the Johnson administration," Ashby said. "The second Gulf of Tonkin incident that our Navy had with the North Vietnamese gunboats never really happened. One of our naval vessel commanders initially reported being attacked but rescinded that report after a few hours. He was ordered by Defense to stand by his original report. Bundy and McNamara altered the facts. Johnson wanted to be lied to. Everybody else went along. The resolution passed unanimously in the House and received only two 'nay' votes in the Senate."

"That's really how it happened?!" Glenn was incredulous, and instantly angry.

"Our involvement didn't start with Johnson. It actually went back as far as Eisenhower who sent a handful of advisors in the late 50s to help the Diem regime combat the communist Viet Minh. Kennedy upped the ante soon after taking office. Not long after the Bay of Pigs fiasco, Kennedy had a summit meeting with Khruschev and came home chastened and feeling humiliated. The Republican bluebook indicated that Kennedy sent the Special Forces to Vietnam mainly to prove his manhood to Khrushchev."

"How could they know that?" Glenn wanted to know. "I don't believe it."

Dave Nolan took a deep breath and said, "You should... because it's true. I met with him and his brother Bobby along with McNamara and Bundy a few days after he returned from the Vienna meeting with the Soviet premier. He was clearly shaken. I witnessed his actions over a six week period while I worked with General Taylor to finalize a report on the Bay of Pigs."

"You're saying Kennedy got us involved in Vietnam because his manhood had been ridiculed? That's incredible!" Glenn turned and looked at his uncle. "And you're telling me the whole Gulf of Tonkin incident was a fraud?!"

"It was manipulated for Johnson's political purposes. 1964 was an election year and he needed something to prove to the electorate he was harder on Communist expansionism than Goldwater. The incident wasn't what it was portrayed to be. A few investigative reporters did good work unearthing the facts. You ought to read Halberstam's *The Best and the Brightest*. He gets it right."

"And you knew what Johnson and McNamara were doing was false, didn't you Uncle Rand? What we were told about the reasons for going to Vietnam was a lie, then. Why didn't you do something?"

"There were many others in State and the Pentagon. I couldn't stop it by myself."

"But you knew it was wrong. You could have tried to stop it."

"I was one of three assistant Secretaries of State. The junior one."

"But you were on the inside. You could have... should have tried. Somebody should have stopped it, put a bright spotlight on it. If not you, then who?"

"Don't be so hard on your uncle. He tried. And he's making up for not trying harder by making the changes in the State Department now."

Glenn looked down at his hands folded in front of him, resting on the table. He thought about the guys in his platoon in Vietnam and the ones in Alpha who had died. EB and Timmy Horner and all the rest. He shook his head slowly and then looked back at his grandfather. "You know what this all means. It means we killed fifty-eight thousand of our guys for a lie. McNamara and Johnson's lie."

"I'm afraid the first victim of war is always the truth. I know what you're feeling."

Glenn looked out toward the Sound and stared at nothing for long minutes. *Maybe I was too hard on Randall. But damn it, he should have done something.* His thoughts shifted to his conversation a few days earlier with Harv Clayton... *What are you going to do about it?* his friend had asked about the changes at West Point.

Glenn wondered if years down the road some junior officer might ask him a similar question about his role in changing the academy, or deserting the military in its hour of need.

What about Jenny? Glenn asked himself, realizing things between them were becoming more complicated. He had to begin factoring her into the equation. *What would she want to do?*

He was still asking himself that question an hour later as he and Brad sat on the dock.

"I have an offer from an engineering firm in Pittsburgh, and a couple other irons in the fire," he told Brad. "There's something else – another complication."

"You're talking about Jenny. For pete's sake, Glenn. Marry her and get it out of the way. She'd follow you anywhere."

"She has a good career in the Army doing something she's called to do and I'm not sure she'd be willing to give that up. It's a big part of her personality and who she is."

"Ask her. Come on, man, what's your hangup? You've never been this indecisive. Something I don't see here?"

Erika came out on the porch and yelled across the lawn to him. "Glenn, there's a call for you. Long distance. I can tell them to call back or get the phone number, but I think you need to take this."

"All right, I'll take it," he replied and jogged across the lawn to the house. When he picked up the phone and heard the voice he was startled beyond words.

"Glenn, I have to see you."

"Mary Anne? How...?"

"It took me a week to track you down. Please don't hang up on me," she replied, sounding perilously close to tears. *I made a terrible, terrible mistake. Forgive me... I was such a fool. Leaving you wasn't my idea, but he's my father."*

"Mary Anne, I've wanted to talk to you about this for a long time, and I still do. But this is really a bad time for me right now."

"I know. You're aunt told me about your grandmother. I'm so sorry for you and your family. If I had known, I would never have intruded."

"The funeral's the day after tomorrow. Maybe I can call you back at the end of the week.

"I've got to see you now!" Mary Anne begged, distraught. She made a swift little sound of distress – part moan, part gasp.

"See me now?! That's just not going to be possible. It's been almost four years. Another three days isn't going to make a difference. We can talk, but not now."

"I have to know. I have to see it in your eyes. I really want us to be together again – as man and wife," she said. *"I left my parent's house and I'm staying with a friend in Silver Spring until I can sort this out. I need you. I want us to start over."*

"Mary Anne, I forgive you. I really do. But I've moved on. I thought we both had." But even as he said it a still, small voice in the back of his mind was telling him that maybe a reconciliation with her was possible.

"I don't want to live knowing you hate me and –" She stopped and began to sob.

"I don't hate you. I couldn't possibly do that," he said softly.

"But you don't love me any more... and you won't see me?"

His breath caught in his throat, and then he took a deep breath. "I never stopped loving you, Mary Anne. That's something I can't do."

She continued to ramble; one minute pleading, the next demanding, sounding as if she was filled with raging mortification over what she'd done. He was worried she might endanger herself. Was this just an act, a ruse? He couldn't be sure, but he felt compelled to do something to help her. "All right. I'll see you. Tomorrow. I've only got one day. There's a small airport just east of Silver Spring near the University of Maryland. It's called College Park Airport. I'll fly down and meet you there at noon, and we'll talk. But no promises."

He hung up the phone and was instantly sorry he hadn't gotten her phone number. The more he thought of it, the worse the idea of seeing her again became. From the day she'd kissed him in the small potting shed behind her family's house, he'd never been able to resist her. Now she was talking about getting back together, manipulating him with pleas and tears.

Really, Nolan – what are you thinking? He wondered.

*   *

"You're not responsible for her anymore," Jenny said.

"She sounded desperate."

"She manipulated you. You said it yourself, and you're allowing her to get away with it."

Jenny crossed her arms over her chest. *You're sounding like a jealous shrew*, she told herself. *This is conduct unbecoming and a sure-fire way to drive him away. But you knew this was going to happen eventually, didn't you? – it always does. Each guy you fall for has a fatal flaw – Chip Pelland ran around on you in high school, Shortstop got himself killed in Vietnam, that resident at Walter Reed just wanted you to provide free room and board. And now you find out Glenn is being dragged around by a ring in his nose put there by his ex-wife.* She felt miserable, and sorry for herself. *Better to find out now than later.*

"She's not going to manipulate me, Jen."

"She already has. But that's all right." Jenny said bitingly. "You made your decision to go see her and talk through whatever you have to talk through. Do what you have to do."

He looked at her self-consciously. "I'm sorry I've upset you. That's the last thing I wanted to do. Please, don't give up on us."

"Glenn, really. There's really no 'us' to give up on. We're friends, co-workers on a project for the Supe," she replied off-handedly.

"Neither one of us believes that... It's not what you said that evening in Nantucket."

"We both had too much Chateau Ste. Michelle. Honestly, I can't recall any of our conversation after the first bottle," she lied. They were silent for an awkward moment until she said, "I was right when I said I was intruding here. This is a time for family. I should be getting back to the school and the hospital. I've left too many loose ends there."

"Please don't leave."

"I really should. We're behind schedule on the after-action report for General Berry. I'll finish it up and do a first pass edit and you can review and finalize it when you get back." She walked to her cottage and went inside, leaving him to stare after her.

Brad came across the lawn toward him. "You look like you just lost your best friend."

"She's not real happy with me. I told her I was going to see Mary Anne tomorrow."

"I can't imagine why in the world that would upset her," he offered sarcastically.

"Don't you go giving me a lot of crap, too. I'm going to see her because she sounded desperate over the phone; maybe suicidal. Stranger things have happened."

"She's not your responsibility."

"Jenny said the same thing."

"I think she might be onto something. It's been four years since Mary Anne left you, right? Not a peep out of her since. All of a sudden she needs help from you?"

"I still need to talk to her. She's got issues – so do I. Her father ramrodded the whole thing and I still don't know how and why it went down. I want to know what really happened. Then I can put it behind me. But I don't want to lose Jenny in the process." He realized he *was* angry with his ex-wife for putting him in this position. And angry with himself for letting her do it. "I need a favor, Brad. I'm going to Maryland tomorrow morning after sunrise and I'll be back before sunset. It's an easy flight down and back to College Station – a couple hours each way in the Cessna. I need you to make sure Jenny's still here when I get back."

As it turned out, the short flights to and from the small airport inside the Washington beltway were more problematic than he'd expected.

*　　*　　*

It was noon and the September sky over Long Island Sound was clear and cloudless. *Bomber's sky*, Brad thought, thinking of a phrase his father often used. He was sitting on the side porch of the main house where he had a view of both the north and south approaches to the runway his father had carved out years earlier to make the old cottage more accessible.

"The wind's out of the south so he'll be approaching from over the water."

"If he comes back," Jenny said.

"He'll be back soon," he replied. Glenn was almost twenty-four hours overdue, and if he didn't show up soon he'd miss the funeral service. He wondered what Jenny was thinking now – probably the worst: that Glenn had extended his stay with Mary Anne for a day, maybe more. That wasn't good. He remembered as a kid growing up across the street from the MacEagans that Mary Anne was always able to get Glenn to do whatever she wanted. Did she still hold that kind of sway over his older brother? Brad hoped not.

Jenny glanced at him quickly and looked away, stroking her jaw absently. She studied the toes of her shoes and then gripped her arms together as if she were chilled.

She doesn't know what to think or what to do with herself, Brad thought. *Where the hell are you, big brother?* Michelle and Andy Fauser greeted them, walked up the short flight of steps and sat down in the matching Adirondack chairs next to them. Fauser lit a cigarette and Brad wondered how the old man could chain smoke and drink the way he did and still survive so long. As he looked around, he saw a dot on the southern horizon that quickly became the shape of a high-wing plane. He pointed and said: "Looks like my brother found his way home."

Jenny's face grew fretful; she got up without a word, went down to the pier by herself and sat alone on the bench looking toward the broad expanse of Long Island Sound.

The Cessna made a tight descending turn, aligned itself for landing and finally touched down on the grass strip. It slowed and made a U-turn headed back toward the small pad near the boathouse. Brad got to the plane as his brother climbed out, stretched and looked around; the two brothers talked briefly and then Glenn walked toward Jenny.

She turned around and watched him until he was halfway down the pier, anxiety written across her face; then she stood and took a tentative step toward him.

"I wasn't sure you'd be back," she said, looking into his eyes and placing her hands on his chest when he tried to kiss her. "I waited all day yesterday without so much as a phone call. Why didn't you come back when you said... or at least call?"

"It's a long story. Nothing worked out the way I expected."

"That's not an answer, Glenn. And I think I deserve one." She searched his eyes for a sign. "Yesterday was the worst day of my life."

"Yesterday wasn't a very good day for me either. You want everything?"

"Horns and all."

"I'm still sorting a lot of it out for myself."

"Darned if I don't feel like I'm eavesdroppin' on somethin' private between that young man and his girl," Fauser said to Michelle.

"You never minded doing that to me before."

"I don't get into your personal affairs."

"You most certainly did," she said, leaning back and turning her head to look at him. "Do you remember the night at the West Point Officers' Club when we had the going away party for Dave and Denise?"

"That's fifty-some years ago, woman. Go to war, Miss Agnes. There's a statute of limitations on ever-thing after that damned long!"

Brad bounded up the steps headed for the door and Andy stopped him.

"What's goin' on with your brother?"

"If you're asking what's going down there on the dock right now, I don't have the foggiest. But if you want to know why he's a day late getting back..." Brad held up a short piece of black rubber hose. "Fuel line broke on the plane. He had to put it down on some farmer's place in New Jersey. It was late afternoon when he left that girl he went to see, and the fuel line gave way just before dark. He was lucky to find a field where he could put it down that late in the day. He slept on the ground and it took him until mid-morning to find a farmhouse. They had this tubing and he jury-rigged a repair, then nursed it back here." Brad glanced over his shoulder. "Looks like airplane problems are the least of his worries."

"Mary Anne and I talked for more than three hours," Glenn said as they sat side by side on the bench. "I recognized that we didn't talk enough before or during our marriage – certainly not about critical things – the things that eventually let us drift apart and made her susceptible to being led down the path by her father and her brother. The Army didn't help us either. We both realize now what a huge influence the military was on our relationship. We came to the conclusion that we didn't know each other or the military life all that well before we were married."

"That amazes me. Frankly, I find it hard to believe," Jenny said, deciding this was something Mary Anne had convinced him of. "Didn't know one another?! You two dated for three years in high school and four years at West Point."

"That's right – she went to an all-girls Catholic high school; I went to an all-male high school and an all-male college... reform school... whatever you want to call it. That's not necessarily bad, unless you hitch that to two people who don't communicate well on crucial things like their faith and relational needs. To me, jumping out of airplanes was cool – a thrill, a notch on my career six-gun while to her it was yet another separation. That happened over and over; Ranger School, maneuvers in Germany, Vietnam, flight school, Fort Campbell. She suffered, I enjoyed. Neither of us really talked about it or dealt with it. At a crucial point – my assignment to Campbell where another separation was forced on us because of housing shortages – her father stepped in and it was easy for her to go along. She never had a chance, nor did our marriage. And dating at West Point while I was there? Ha! Not much."

Jenny gazed at him for a moment with terrible intensity, and then she gave him the saddest look he'd ever seen on a woman's face. "You sound like you feel sorry for her."

"I *am* sorry for her. She's been treated badly. By her family – her father, her older brother. By some guy named Tripp Karter who's big in the anti-America, anti-war movement. In a real sense by me. I asked her to forgive me for my part in breaking up our marriage."

"And did she?"

"We forgave each other. It took a while to get it out in the open and for us to deal with it, but we eventually did."

"So... you two spent last night making up?"

He gave her an odd, puzzled look for a brief instant, and then his eyes brightened as if the light had just gone on. "Oh!... No, I took off from the airport down there yesterday afternoon!

Later than expected for sure. I spent last night in a field somewhere east of Woodstown, New Jersey. Fuel line broke on me and I had to set it down. I wasn't going to go roaming around some farmer's place in the dark. Those people own guns. I finally fixed the bird well enough to get back here. Brad's trying to find a part for it now. Between him and my father, they'll get it fixed before noon tomorrow."

He paused. *I don't talk enough with Jenny, either. Maybe it's a good thing this crazy wing-ding with Mary Anne happened when it did, the way it did. Nothing by chance, right?* Glenn looked at his watch and put his arm around her shoulders.

"I'm a good soldier, and a good troop commander. But the last forty-eight hours have shown me I'm a pretty poor communicator most of the time – especially on a personal level. I have a way of assuming folks understand what I'm thinking even though I don't articulate my thoughts very well." He paused, cleared his throat nervously and continued. "I'm not a very good listener either."

He paused again, trying to think of the perfect way of phrasing his next thought.

"When we talked a couple of evenings ago your comments, your reaction told me I hadn't been as clear as I should have been about how I view our relationship."

"Is this conversation headed somewhere?" Jenny asked.

He smiled at her. "It is. Hang in there."

She shrugged. "I'll try."

"My crystal ball doesn't give me a real clear picture of the future. I don't know if I'm going to stay in the Army or get out. If I get out, I don't know which of several options I want to pursue. The only thing I know is that whatever path I follow, I want you at my side."

She gasped and covered her mouth with a hand. Her next move startled him – she stood and turned her back to him.

"Are you proposing to me, Glenn Nolan? Nobody ever proposed to me before so I have no idea what it sounds like. Well?! Are you?"

He came to her and placed his hands on her shoulders and whispered in her ear. "I am. I don't have a ring for you but we can shop for one together."

She didn't know what to think; it was all coming so fast. She'd spent the whole last day angry at him for leaving to go back to his wife, and her normally reliable intuition said he was still in love with Mary Anne. But now he was saying something entirely different. *What should I believe?*

"Glenn, we don't really know one another all that well. Are you sure you're not making the same mistake all over again?"

"I think we do know each other. We're much more than just casual acquaintances, friends, co-workers on a project for the Superintendent at West Point."

She turned around, placed the palm of her hand against his chest and looked up into his face. "Oh, Glenn. I want to believe you. I'm not sure I can. My heart tells me you're still in love with her."

"Jenny, I'm saying I want to spend my life making you happy. I have a ton of other things I want to tell you, but right now saying 'I love you' is at the top of the list. I love you Jennifer Kolarik, more than life. You and only you. I'm asking you to marry me. Will you?"

Her eyes grew moist and she wiped away the tears.

"What do you think's goin' on down there?" Andy asked, lighting another cigarette.

Michelle shrugged and said, "I think it's likely that we're seeing the genesis of great grandchildren for your old roommate."

"Nope. I think she's givin' him 'what-for' over goin' to see his former wife. See how she got up and moved away from him. Turned her back and left him sittin' by hisself. Then when he tried to make it up to her, she pushed him away and cried because he hurt her feelings."

"Andy Fauser you are such a romantic."

"Which puts me to mind of them two questions I asked you at that goin' away party for Dave and Denise at West Point years ago. You said a little while back I was prying into your private life. Maybe I am, maybe I'm not. But you never did answer me that night."

"I didn't like you very much back then. And I recall the feeling was mutual."

"Well, that's all water under bridge. So tell me – just what did you and Davey do that week you spent together here on this island before we went off to fight Kaiser Bill?"

"Andy, I'll tell you the same thing I did back then – you don't get to ask that question."

He frowned and squinted at her. "I'm a man not easily put off. Are you still in love with my old Pennsylvany Quaker buddy?"

She took a long, deep breath, and her eyes grew moist. "Yes I am, Andy. I have been all my life... but you knew that without asking. And I also loved Glenn and Brad and Mitch and Denise's Glenn all their lives, too. There's something about those Nolan men." She squeezed his hand and whispered. "Let's give those two out there some privacy."

She took one last look across the lawn toward the pier and followed Andy inside.

Brian Utermahlen

EPILOGUE

Erika Nolan was promoted to Chief Prosecutor in Washington, D.C. and later ran for the office of Senator as a Democrat representing the state of Maryland on a populist platform promising to clean up the U.S. Congress. The Democratic party machine in the state effectively blocked her candidacy.

Mitch Nolan continued to lead the project team at McDonnell Douglas to a successful launch and unveiling of the F-15 Eagle, a next generation multi-role fighter with unparalleled range, weapons load and all weather capability. It was instantly the world's premier fighter and would remain so into the twenty-first century. For his efforts he was made an executive vice president in the corporation. His only regret about the project was that neither of his sons would get to fly the plane he developed.

Randall Ashby returned to government service as a senior advisor working directly for the Secretary of Defense. His major contribution was in helping guide the military to correct politically imposed practices that had diminished both the stature and capability of the Army in the Vietnam era. In the years following the end of the Vietnam War, he was a key resource to writers who exposed the poor decision making, high level duplicity, and conduct of senior Johnson administration appointees and other politicians.

Cateline Glendenbrook left Washington and returned to law practice in New York City. Two years later she was made a partner with Blaine, Johnson, Armistad and Meyer.

Harrison Reeves was incarcerated in the Jessup Maryland Detention Center in August 1976 following his plea arrangement with the D.C. Prosecutor's office. It was the first time in sixty-six years that Maryland was without a Senator named Reeves representing them in Washington. At his first parole hearing five years later, his request was denied. Detention Center records indicate he had only two visitors in the seven years before his death. His home in Silver Spring Maryland, including the property, was sold at auction to a development company whose majority partner was Michelle Payne; the house was demolished and the grounds donated to the state. Reeves was buried in a public cemetery in downtown Baltimore.

Mikey Meade went home to Seattle after his Vietnam tour was over and immediately drifted back into the drug culture for two years. He realized that an early death as befell Janis Joplin and Jimmi Hendrix was likely to be his fate too if he didn't change. But he'd never been successful in anything he'd tried and no one had ever helped him overcome circumstances.

Except one time – in Vietnam, when his company commander had trusted him enough to give him a job and the support he needed to succeed. He moved to North Platte, Nebraska, married and became an electrician. He purchased an abandoned school house in the middle of the prairie and started a pheasant hunting lodge which catered to doctors, oil men and other clients.

Years later he would tell his friends and family that Vietnam saved his life, and although he couldn't quit chain smoking, he never again touched any illegal substance.

Tyrell Hannam stayed in the Army and completed a twenty year career. Nearing retirement, he was assigned to quality control for the Army at Frankfort Arsenal in Philadelphia and became one of the military's primary experts in the development of a light machine gun that came to be called the Squad Automatic Weapon. After retiring from the Army, he was hired by the Frankford Arsenal in Research and Development at the Pitman-Dunn Laboratories working on a wide range of armaments such as laser guided ballistics and caseless ammunition. He lived to see most of the weapons systems he'd worked on become standard military issue.

Lieutenant Braxton Bragg Cleburne was involuntarily separated from the Army in 1974. He became half owner of a truck stop on U.S. Highway 82 near Sylvester, Georgia.

Case Newman remained in the Army almost all of his adult life; he was up and down the sergeant's ladder more times than he could remember. Along the way, he rubbed shoulders with almost everybody who was anybody in the officer and enlisted ranks. He was a technical consultant to Tom Hanks and Stephen Spielberg for their movies about the military and had small parts in each. He became a member of the Screen Actors Guild and wrote a book about his life but couldn't sell it to any of the studios.

Lee Haskell returned to Texas and bought a ranch west of Austin in the hill country near the James River where he raised cattle and goats. He leased the land for deer hunting and eventually built a large log cabin hunting lodge which developed into one of the prime hunting destinations and shotgun sports complexes in the Lone Star State.

Ewell Brown 'EB' Gordon was buried at the Vicksburg National Military Cemetery with full military honors. His home town began celebrating the 4th of July once again in 1976.

Brad Nolan did receive the loan Michelle promised at the time of Denise's funeral. He and Zara paid off the family debt, and with what remained they increased the cattle herd and upgraded the main Station house and outbuildings. Within six months he began paying back the loan with interest; when questioned by Michelle, he revealed it was at the 'strong urging' of his grandfather who insisted he not take advantage of a close family friend.

While the Station's cattle operation showed signs of recovery, Brad and Zara's winery continued to struggle. They finally gave in to economic realities and reluctantly realized they would likely have to sell off the vineyards, the winery itself and much of the surrounding land.

*   *   *

Zara was frustrated. She changed her assumptions again and reworked the numbers. This time it came out even worse. Finances were tight. They had stopped the bleeding, but the patient was going to be a long time in recovery. *Even with a sweetheart deal on the loan, we're going to be poor as Job's turkey for a long while*, she told herself. *Maybe we should have taken the offer from that corporation last year for the whole kit and caboodle. I hate to say it, but we have to sell the winery.*

Selling the entire Station was something she didn't want to think about but there had been a time when it looked like it was their only alternative. It was happening everywhere – big corporations were buying up individual family operations and turning a profit on mechanization and volume. But it seemed sacrilegious to even consider selling a place that had been in the family for longer than anyone remembered, but the realities were what they were.

It's a shame we can't turn the winery around. They had tried.

They had talked to other local winemakers but got little helpful information. Brad had met with a German, a Frenchman, and an American from near Seattle, Washington. Some of the information was useful; most wasn't. It was a full time job and Brad couldn't do it himself.

Zara left the stack of paperwork in the office to saddle her horse and go for a ride to clear her head. As she walked across the front porch headed toward the stables, she saw in the distance a car pulling an ocher cloud of dust coming down the long road toward the house. She watched until it came to stop, and a man about her own age emerged from the driver's side.

"Is that you, Glenn?!" she asked as he stretched his back. She peered at the dust-streaked windshield while descending the steps but the dust and slant rays of afternoon sun obscured her view. "Who's with you?"

"C'mon Zare – You should know who it is."

A woman with her blond hair pulled back into a pony tail, wearing sunglasses and a dark felt drover's hat got out of the car and walked toward her.

"Good gracious, what in the world are you two doing here?!" she said, gave them each a hug, and then asked, "Is it possible we're sisters-in-law?"

Jenny held out her hand to display the ring. "It happened two weeks ago. Spur of the moment. A small, private ceremony with a few friends. It was a shotgun wedding."

Zara's mouth opened, caught in alarm. "You're not –"

"No, I'm not pregnant. But Glenn did hold a gun to my head. He waved two tickets for a round-the-world trip in my face and told me the plane was leaving in eighteen days and he was going to be on it with his wife – either me or some other woman."

Zara eyeballed Glenn who raised his hands in a futile gesture of surrender. "You didn't!"

"She kept putting me off on setting a date. What was I supposed to do? I figured she's a nurse so she works best under pressure. I just supplied some, that's all."

"What if she'd said, *No*?"

"I had names of a few debutants I'd gotten from the Society pages of the New York Times." Jenny slapped his arm and shoved him. "Actually, I knew I didn't need a Plan B."

Zara took Jenny's arm and guided her toward the house. "I want to hear all about it. Where you've been, where you're going. Pictures of the wedding? Most important, how long you can stay?" She stopped and turned to Glenn. "You bring the luggage – second floor, up the stairway, third door on the right. Yank soldiers know how to follow instructions I'm told."

"I'm not in the military anymore," Glenn said. "Neither of us is."

Zara gave both of them a surprised look. "I definitely need to hear about *that*."

Brad came out onto the broad front porch, his sleeves rolled up and wiping his hands on a rag. When he saw Glenn his face broke out in a wide smile. "You're a long way from home, big brother. What in the world are you doing here?"

"I'm your damn wine-making partner, remember?"

"You don't know anything about making wine."

"I might surprise you."

Brad came down the steps and grabbed his brother's hand, then threw his arm around Glenn's neck. Man it's good to see you. How's the family? – especially our old grandpa. He looked like a lost soul last time I saw him."

"Still does. He misses grandma a lot. I helped him move to the shore cottage before we left so he could be closer to her. Offer me a beer and I'll tell you about it."

They walked up the steps and into the Station house.

*   *

528

Dave Nolan died late in the fall one year following the passing of his wife.

He'd sold the farm outside the small Pennsylvania town of his birth and was in the process of opening up the shore cottage on Long Island. When asked if he might be better off in a retirement village, he told family and friends he wanted to be close to his wife in the place where the most important events of their life together had occurred.

He went to bed one evening at the family retreat, and true to his lifelong habits his clothes for the following day were precisely laid out and the book he was currently reading sat on the nightstand by his bed. It was bookmarked with a *Thank You* card.

He failed to awaken the following morning.

The Pentagon contacted the family to make arrangements for a military funeral at either West Point or Arlington – their choice. The instructions he'd left behind made clear his desire to be buried next to his wife in a private ceremony restricted to immediate family. His obituary in the New York Times was two short paragraphs.

In the years that followed, local residents reported seeing a woman in black and an old man using a cane visiting the graves on the anniversaries of the deaths of Dave and Denise Nolan. Each time they left flowers until one year the woman visited the graves alone and left a small, hand-carved wood lantern on a chain at the base of Dave Nolan's headstone.

She was never seen again.

HISTORICAL NOTES AND FOOTNOTES

The West Point class of 1968 graduated 706 cadets as 2nd Lieutenants. It knows itself as the class that began in peace and graduated in war. The ***Gulf of Tonkin Resolution*** which opened the Vietnam conflict to wide-ranging American combat involvement was passed by Congress on August 10, 1964, one month and ten days after the class entered West Point. The class of '68 had the second highest number of casualties in Vietnam of all West Point classes.

The 1st Cavalry Division was originally established in 1921 and has fought in every major U.S engagement since. It was the first truly airmobile division and was re-created as such for the purpose of developing and conducting helicopter-borne operations in Vietnam. It was the primary U.S. combat force conducting the incursion into Cambodia on May 1, 1970.

LZ Illingworth, LZ Jay, LZ Ike, LZ Flashner, LZ Mo were actual firebases. LZ Evita and LZ Charo are fictional. The attack on LZ Illingworth happened basically as described. Spec-4 Peter C. Lemon was awarded the Congressional Medal of Honor for his actions that night.

LTC Mike Conrad is an historical figure. He commanded the 2/8 Cav at the time shown in the book, went on to become the division intelligence officer and years later commanded the 1st Cav Division as a Major General (two star).

LTC John R. Galvin is an historical figure. He commanded the 1/8 Cav at the time shown in the book. Galvin began his 45 year military career as an enlisted man in the Massachusetts National Guard, graduated from West Point in 1954 and eventually attained the rank of General (4-star). He served as Supreme Allied Commander, Europe June '87 – June '92. In 1997, he was awarded the U.S. Military Academy Distinguished Graduate Award.

LTC Guus van Noort is a purely fictional character.

The 1/6 Cav Battalion is fictional. There was no 6th Cav in the 1st Cav Division in Vietnam.

Jenny Kolarik is a fictional character. She is representative of a group of women who served with great distinction and courage but with no fanfare and very little recognition.

The 25th Surgical Hospital in Tay Ninh was a real life facility. The 5th Surgical Hospital in Phouc Vinh where Jenny was head nurse is purely fictional. The vast majority of U.S. infantrymen and helicopter pilots never saw an American woman in Vietnam.

C Company 227th Aviation Battalion (the Ghostriders) was an actual Assault Helicopter Company in the 1st Cavalry Division (Airmobile). Many of the aviation incidents in the book are based on recollections from a large number of aviators who served in this unit.

HISTORICAL NOTES AND FOOTNOTES
(continued)

Most Vietnam infantry and aviation sequences are loosely based on actual events relayed to the author by veterans, authors, or from personal experience. I am particularly grateful to classmates, John Hedley and Scott Vickers for permission to use some of their personal experiences as they lived and recorded them, and Dave Gerard for his chart of '68 stats.

President Lyndon Johnson is quoted accurately from historical accounts written by noted authors during and shortly after his presidency. His conversations with Harrison Reeves are fictional, as is Reeves himself.

The Gulf of Tonkin incident is accurately portrayed, based on the recollections of a Navy sonar operator aboard a sister ship of the USS Maddox.

The actions and ultimate conviction of Senator Harrison Reeves is based loosely on a U.S. Senator of that era who was convicted of illegal activities somewhat similar to those of the fictional character, and sentenced to prison.

General Sidney Bryan Berry (Feb. 10, 1926 – July 1, 2013) is an historical character. Berry's philosophies, perspectives, actions in **COUNTRY** are in accordance with his own words, and are drawn from his oral autobiography on file at the Army War College, Carlisle, PA. General Berry was a rated Army aviator, but did not fly while Superintendent.

He was 50th Superintendent of the U.S. Military Academy (West Point) from 1974-1977. His tenure was noted by two major events – (1) a cheating incident in the Spring of 1976 in which approximately 100 cadets were initially separated from the Academy; (2) the admission of the first females to West Point in July 1976. Neither event is dealt with in detail as the author's primary purpose was to tell the story of Glenn Nolan at a point in his career when he is considering his future, not to re-fight past battles already decided.

General Berry opposed the admission of women to West Point until the law was passed by Congress and signed by Gerald Ford. He followed orders and implemented the directive as if it was his own. Later, while recording his autobiography for the Army War College, he stated: "...my gut feeling, and perhaps an expression of my bias, is that West Point is weaker rather than stronger because of the presence of women cadets, and in the long run, the Army is likely to be weaker because of the watering down of the male population who should be going out, most of them, into the combat arms of the Army."

The events portrayed in the episode concerning *'Stump the Stars'* actually happened.

USMA Class of 1968 Statistics Summary

I.	Total number cadets entered, July 1964:	1000
II.	Total number graduated, 1968:	706
III.	Years served on active duty	9,688
IV.	Number of Combat Duty Tours	591
V.	Deceased, as of 31 December 2013:	60
VI.	Combat Related Deaths	20
VII.	First Class to Get Christmas Leave as Plebes	
VIII.	First Class to Witness an Army Football Victory over Navy in 6 years	
IX.	First Class to incur a five year service obligation after graduation	
X.	Cadet Regimental Commanders	4
XI.	Corps Squad Team Captains	19
XII.	First Asst Sec Def for Special Opns & Low Intensity Conflict	1
XIII.	Deputy Assistant Secretary of Defense for Reserve Affairs	1
XIV.	Deputy Assistant Secretary of the Army for Strategic Infrastructure	1
XV.	USMAPS Commandants	1
XVI.	*Number of General Officers:*	13
	Generals:	0
	Lieutenant Generals:	4
	Major Generals:	6
	Brigadier Generals:	3
XVI.	*Number of Valor Awards & Purple Hearts:*	359
	Distinguished Service Crosses:	2
	Silver Stars:	63
	Distinguished Flying Crosses:	18
	Soldier's Medals:	11
	Bronze Star w/V	128
	Air Medal w/V	35
	Army Commendation Medal w/V	38
	Purple Hearts:	115
	Number of reported CIBs (Combat Infantryman's Badge)	87

XVII.	Number of Distinguished Service Medals:	18
XVIII.	Number of Legions of Merit:	110
IXX.	Number of Doctors & Dentists:	50
XX.	Number of PhDs	15
XXI.	Number of Lawyers:	50
XXII.	Number of Ministers/Priests:	5
XXIII.	Number of Judges	2
XXIV.	Number of USMA Deans of the Academic Board	1
XXV.	Number of USMA Academic Department Heads:	1
XXVI.	Number of College Presidents	2

Branch Selected upon Graduation:	
Armor	91
Corps of Engineers	68
Artillery	183
Infantry	189
Signal Corps	68
Military Intelligence	27
Tech and Admin Services	48
U.S. Air Force	22
U.S. Marine Corps	1
U.S. Navy	0
No Commission	7
Allied Cadets	2

Athletic Honors:	
Major Army "A"	90
College All-American	1
Olympic Athletes	1
Olympic Gold Medal	0

Brian Utermahlen

ABOUT THE AUTHOR

Brian Utermahlen is a graduate of the U.S. Military Academy at West Point, NY – Class of 1968, where he was a three year letterman on the Army Lacrosse team.

On active duty as an infantryman, he was an Army Ranger, a parachutist, and a helicopter pilot, serving in Germany, Viet Nam and the U.S.

He is an infantry combat veteran with the 1st Air Cavalry Division in Viet Nam. Following six years on active duty, he returned to civilian life as a manager for the DuPont corporation, Conoco, Inc. and BMC Software. He flew helicopters for 12 years in the Delaware National Guard.

He is retired in south Texas where he enjoys shooting sports, hunting and fishing. Along with his wife, Dianne, he spoils three granddaughters – Kaitlyn, Abigail and Megan.

His first novel – *THE HOFFMAN FILE* - was published by DELL.

The first book in the Pass in Review series – **DUTY** – received the Bronze Award from the Military Writers Society of America (MWSA) in the category - 'Best Historical Fiction – 2012'

The second book in the Pass in Review series – **HONOR** – received the Silver Award from the Military Writers Society of America (MWSA) in the category – 'Best Historical Fiction – 2013'

Made in the USA
San Bernardino, CA
13 April 2015